OF LOVE AND LIFE

Three novels selected and condensed
by Reader's Digest

OF
LOVE
AND
LIFE

The Reader's Digest Association Limited
LONDON

*

The Reader's Digest Association Limited
11 Westferry Circus, Canary Wharf, London E14 4HE

www.readersdigest.co.uk

Printed in France

CONTENTS

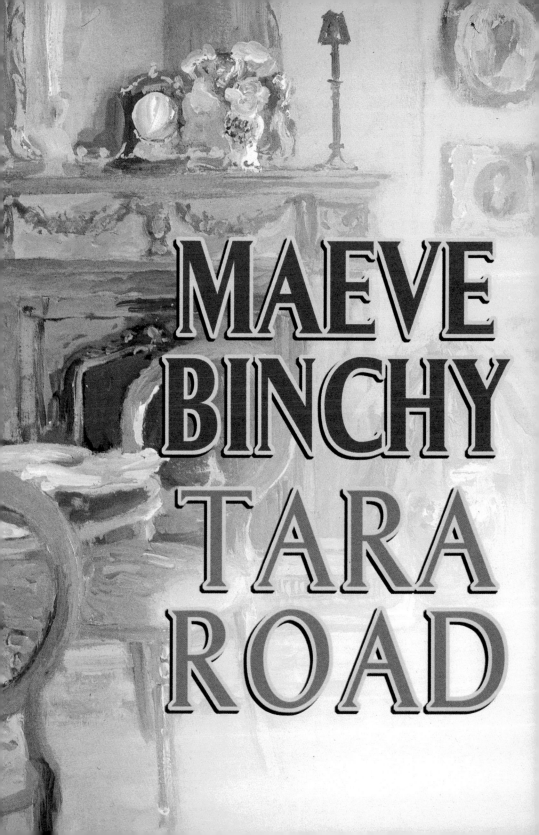

MAEVE BINCHY
TARA ROAD

ℓᴐ

From the moment Danny Lynch sets eyes

on 16 Tara Road in Dublin, he knows it is

the house for him. It may well be falling

down, damp and shabby, but he can make

it perfect. Ria, his bride, is less certain, but

as she and Danny build their lives together,

they pour all their love and attention into

making 16 Tara Road a very special home

for their two children. Life for Ria is

complete, but Danny has always been

a wanderer and a dreamer . . .

ℓᴐ

RIA'S MOTHER had always been very fond of film stars. It was a matter of sadness to her that Clark Gable had died on the day Ria was born. Tyrone Power had died on the day Hilary was born just two years earlier. But somehow that wasn't as bad. Hilary hadn't seen off the great king of cinema as Ria had. Ria could never see *Gone with the Wind* without feeling somehow guilty. She told this to Ken Murray, the first boy who kissed her. She told him in the cinema. Just as he was kissing her.

'You're very boring,' he said, trying to open her blouse.

'I'm not boring,' Ria cried with some spirit. 'Clark Gable is there on the screen and I've told you something interesting. A coincidence. It's not boring.'

Ken Murray was embarrassed as people were shushing them and others were laughing. He moved away and huddled down in his seat.

Ria could have kicked herself. She was almost sixteen. Everyone at school liked kissing, or said they did. Now she was starting to do it and she had made such a mess of it. She reached out her hand for him.

'I thought you wanted to look at the film,' he muttered.

'I thought you wanted to put your arm round me,' Ria said hopefully.

He took out a bag of toffees and ate one. Without even passing her the bag. The romantic bit was over.

'Should you not talk when people kiss you?' Ria asked her sister.

'Jesus, Mary and Holy St Joseph,' said Hilary, who was getting dressed to go out.

9

ar experience with fellows.'
yone had heard. 'Will you
he hissed. 'Mam will hear
g anywhere ever again.'
vas not going to stand for
ow woman left with two
ninking that her girls were
would die happy if Hilary
of their own. Nice homes,
rden even. Nora Johnson
to move somewhere nicer
ney lived now.
rway she didn't hear, she's

. She was tired, she said,
vhere she worked at the
down and get transported

to help her tonight. Mam
was to leave her handbag
up to go to the bathroom
metimes it was Ria's job to
owing Hilary to creep in
pocket.
Ria wondered.
bbing on to fellows when
nt to stay out late because

confident as she sounded.
friends at school said she
and blue eyes. But people
of sparkle like other girls.
u're fine, you've got natu-
you're small, fellows like
uld be very nice indeed.
left on the landing.
etter. Ria left school and
of fellows, it turned out.
n any rush. Possibly she
n to marry.
ed.

Nora Johnson thought that men might regard travel as fast. Men preferred to marry safer, calmer women. It was only sensible to have advance information about men, Nora Johnson told her daughters. This way you could go armed into the struggle. There was a hint that she may not have been adequately informed herself. The late Mr Johnson, though he had a bright smile and wore his hat at a rakish angle, was not a good provider. He had not been a believer in nor a subscriber to life insurance policies. Nora Johnson did not want the same thing for her daughters when the time came.

'When do you think the time will come?' Ria asked Hilary.

'For what?' Hilary was frowning a lot at her reflection in the mirror.

'I mean, when do you think either of us will get married? You know the way Mam's always talking about when the time comes.'

'Well, I hope it comes to me first, I'm the eldest. You're not even to consider doing it ahead of me.'

'No, I have nobody in mind. It's just I'd love to be able to look into the future and see where we'll be in two years' time. Wouldn't it be great if we could have a peep?'

'Well, go to a fortuneteller then if you're that anxious.'

'They don't know anything.' Ria was scornful.

'It depends. A lot of the girls at work found this great one. It would make you shiver the way she knows things.'

'You've never been to her?' Ria was astounded.

'Yes I have actually, just for fun.'

'What did she tell you?' Ria's eyes were dancing.

'She said I would marry within two years, and that his name began with an M, and that we'd both have good health all our lives.'

'How many children?'

'She said no children,' Hilary said.

'You don't believe her, do you?'

'Of course I do, what's the point giving up a week's wages if I don't believe her?'

'You *never* paid that!'

'She's good. You know, she has the gift.'

'And where did she see all this good health and the fellow called M and no children? In tea leaves?'

'No, on my hand. Look at the little lines under your little finger round the side of your hand. You've got two, I've got none.'

'And everyone who is going to have children has those little lines and those who aren't haven't?'

'You have to know how to look.' Hilary was defensive.

'You have to know how to charge, it seems.' Ria was distressed to see the normally levelheaded Hilary so easily taken in.

'So it looks like I can do what I like without getting pregnant.' Hilary sounded very confident.

'It might be dangerous to throw out the pill,' said Ria. 'I wouldn't rely totally on Madame Fifi or whatever she's called.'

'Mrs Connor. Wait until you need to know something, you'll be along to her like a flash.'

It was very hard to know what a job was going to be like until you were in it and then it was too late.

Hilary had office jobs in a bakery, a laundry and then settled in a school. There wasn't much chance of meeting a husband there, she said, but the pay was a bit better and she got her lunch free, which meant she could save a bit more. She was determined to have something to put towards a house when the time came.

Ria was saving too, but to travel the world. She worked first in the office of a hardware shop, then in a company that made hairdressing supplies, and then settled in a big, busy estate agency. Ria was on the reception desk and answered the phone. It was a world she knew nothing of when she went in, but it was obviously a business with a huge buzz. Prosperity had come to Ireland in the early eighties and the property market was the first to reflect this. There was huge competition between the various estate agents and Ria found they worked closely as a team.

On the first day Ria had met Rosemary. Slim, blonde and gorgeous, Rosemary also lived at home with her mother and sister, so there was an immediate bond. She was confident and well up in everything that was happening. Ria assumed that she must be a graduate or someone with huge knowledge of the property market. But no, Rosemary had only worked there for six months. It was her second job.

'There's no point in working anywhere unless you know what it's all about,' Rosemary said confidently. 'It makes it twice as interesting.'

It also made Rosemary twice as interesting to all the fellows who worked at the agency. There was a sweepstake being run secretly on who would be the first to score.

'It's only a game,' Rosemary said, laughing. 'They don't really want me at all.' Ria was not sure that she was right; almost any man in the office would have been proud to escort Rosemary Ryan. But she was adamant, a career first, fellows later. Ria listened with interest. It was such a different message from the one she got at home.

Ria's mother said that 1982 was a terrible year for film stars dying. Ingrid Bergman died, and Romy Schneider and Henry Fonda, then there was the terrible accident when Princess Grace was killed.

It was also the year that Hilary Johnson got engaged to Martin Moran, a teacher at the school where she worked in the office.

Martin was pale and anxious and originally from the west of Ireland. He always said his father was a small farmer, not just a farmer but a *small* one. Since Martin was six foot one it was hard to imagine this. He was courteous and obviously very fond of Hilary, yet there was something about him that lacked enthusiasm and fire. He looked slightly worried about things and spoke pessimistically when he came to the house for Sunday lunch.

There was a problem connected with everything. The war in the Falklands would have repercussions for Ireland, mark his word. And the trouble in the Middle East was going to get worse, and the IRA bombs in London were only the tip of the iceberg. Teachers' salaries were too low; house prices were too high.

Ria looked at the man her sister was going to marry with wonder.

Hilary, who had once been able to throw away a week's salary on a fortuneteller, was now talking about the cost of having shoes repaired and the folly of making a telephone call outside the cheap times.

Eventually a selection was made and a deposit was paid on a very small house. It was impossible to imagine what the area might look like in the future. At present it was full of mud, cement mixers, diggers, unfinished roads and unmade footpaths. And yet it seemed exactly what her elder sister wanted out of life. Never had Ria seen her so happy. For Hilary the time had come. It would be a winter wedding and as a wedding feast they would have a small lunch in a Dublin hotel, just family.

Ria wore a bright scarlet coat to the wedding, and a red velvet hairband and bow in her black curly hair. She must have been one of the most colourful bridesmaids at the drabbest wedding in Europe, she thought. It was so obviously what Hilary wanted, but Ria knew it was nothing at all like what she wanted herself.

When Monday came she decided to wear her scarlet bridesmaid's coat to the office. Rosemary was amazed. 'Hey, you look *terrific*. I've never seen you dressed up before, Ria. Seriously, you should get interested in clothes, you know. What a pity we have nowhere to go to lunch and show you off, we mustn't waste this.'

'Come on, Rosemary, it's only clothes.' Ria was embarrassed.

'No, I'm not joking. You must always wear those knock-them-dead colours. I bet you were the hit of the wedding!'

'I'd like to think so, but maybe I was a bit too loud. Anyway, now I'll just have to get a whole new wardrobe!' Ria twirled round before taking off her scarlet coat and caught the eye of the new man in the office.

She had heard there was a Mr Lynch coming from the Cork branch. He had obviously arrived. He wasn't tall, about her own height. He was handsome, and he had blue eyes and straight fair hair that fell into his eyes. He had a smile that lit up the room. 'Hello, I'm Danny Lynch,' he said. Ria looked at him, embarrassed to have been caught pirouetting around in her new coat. 'Aren't you just *gorgeous*?' he said. She felt a very odd sensation in her throat, as if she had been running up a hill and couldn't catch her breath.

Rosemary spoke, which was just as well because Ria would not have been able to answer at all.

'Well, *hello* there, Danny Lynch,' she said with a smile. 'And you are very welcome. You know, we *were* told that there was a Mr Lynch arriving, but why did we think it was going to be some old guy?'

Ria felt a pang of jealousy as she had never before felt about her friend. Why did Rosemary always know exactly what to say, how to be funny and flattering and warm at the same time?

'I'm Rosemary, this is Ria, and we are the work force that keeps this place going, so you have to be very nice to us.'

'Oh, I will,' Danny promised.

Oddly he seemed to be talking to Ria when he spoke, but maybe she was just imagining it. Rosemary went on, 'We were just thinking of going out at lunchtime to celebrate Ria's new coat.'

'Great! Well, we have the excuse, all we need is the place and to know how long a lunch break so that I don't make a bad impression on my first day.' His extraordinary smile went from one to the other; they were the only three people in the world.

Ria couldn't say anything; her mouth was too dry.

'If we're out and back in under an hour then I think we'll do well,' said Rosemary.

'So now it's only where?' Danny Lynch said, looking straight at Ria. This time there were only two of them in the world.

'There's an Italian place across the road,' Rosemary said.

'Let's go there,' said Danny Lynch, without taking his eyes away from Ria Johnson.

Danny was twenty-three. His uncle had been an auctioneer and that's where Danny had gone to work when he left school. They had sold grain and fertiliser and hay as well as cattle and small farms, but as

Ireland changed, property became important. And then he had gone to Cork City, and now he had just got this job in Dublin.

And where was he staying? Rosemary had never seemed so interested in anyone before. Ria watched glumly. 'Tell us now that you don't live miles and miles away, do you?' Rosemary had her head on one side. No man on earth could resist giving Rosemary his address and finding out where *she* lived too. But Danny didn't seem to regard it as a personal exchange; it was part of the general conversation. He spoke looking from one to the other as he told them how he had had the most amazing bit of luck. There was this old man he had met, called Sean O'Brien. A real recluse. And he had inherited a great big house in Tara Road, and he wasn't capable of doing it up, so what he really wanted was a few fellows to go in and live there. So that's where Danny and two other lads lived. They had a bedsitter each, and kept an eye on the place.

What kind of a house was it? the girls wanted to know.

Tara Road was very higgledy-piggledy. Big houses with gardens full of trees, small houses facing right onto the street. Number 16 was shabby now, Danny said, but it must have been a great house once.

Ria sat with her chin in her hands listening to Danny and looking at him and looking at him. He was so enthusiastic. The place had a big overrun garden at the back. It was one of those houses that just put out its arms and hugged you.

Rosemary must have kept the conversation going and called for the bill. They walked across the road back to work and Ria sat down at her desk. *Things don't happen like this in real life. It's only a crush. He's a perfectly ordinary small guy with a line of chatter. He is exactly like this to everyone else.* So why on earth did she feel that he was so special?

Before the office closed Ria went over to Danny Lynch's desk. 'I'm going to be twenty-two tomorrow,' she said. 'I wondered . . .' Then she got stuck.

He helped her out. 'Are you having a party?'

'Not really, no.'

'Then can we celebrate it together? Today the coat, tomorrow being twenty-two. Who knows what we'll have to celebrate by Wednesday?'

And then Ria knew that it wasn't a crush, it was love. The kind of thing she had only read about, heard about, sung about or seen at the cinema. And it had come to find her in her own office.

At first Ria tried to keep Danny to herself, not wanting to tell anyone about him or to share him with other people. She clung to him when they said goodbye as if she never wanted him to leave her arms.

15

want to be with me and yet you don't. Or am I just a thick man who can't understand?' His head was on one side, looking at her quizzically.

'That's exactly the way I feel,' she said simply. 'Very confused.'

'Well we can simplify it all, can't we?'

'Not really. You see for me it would be a very big step. I don't want to make a production out of it all, but you see I haven't with anyone else. Yet I mean . . .' She bit her lip. She didn't dare tell him that she wouldn't sleep with him until she knew that he loved her. It would be putting words in his mouth.

Danny Lynch held her face in his hands. 'I love you, Ria, you are utterly adorable.'

'*Do* you love me?'

'You know I do.'

The next time he asked her to go back to the big rambling house she would go. But, oddly, he didn't ask her at all in the days and nights that followed. He told her about himself, his time at school where he was picked on because he was small and how his elder brothers taught him to fight. His brothers were in London, both of them. His parents lived in the same house as they had always done. They were very self-contained, went for long walks with their red setter. She felt that he didn't get on well with his father, but Ria didn't probe. Men hated that kind of intimate chat. She and Rosemary knew this from reading magazine articles. Fellows didn't like being questioned about feelings. So she did not ask him more about his childhood and why he rarely went to see his parents.

Danny didn't ask questions about her family, so Ria forced herself not to prattle about how her father had died when she was eight, and how her mother was still bitter and disappointed by the memory of him. There was no shortage of things to talk about in those heady days. Danny showed her books about houses and pointed out things that she would never have noticed. He would love to own the old house, Number 16 Tara Road, he told her. He would do it up and take such care of it. He would put so much love into the house that the house would return his love.

It was wonderful having Rosemary to talk to. Ria told her everything: where they went, what Danny was interested in, about his parents in the country.

Rosemary listened with interest. 'You've got it very bad,' she said eventually.

'Do you think it's foolish, just a crush or something? You know a lot about these things.'

'He seems to have it just as bad,' Rosemary pronounced.

'He *says* he loves me, certainly,' Ria said. She was answering Rosemary's question but she didn't want to sound too confident.

'Of course he loves you, that was obvious the very first day,' Rosemary said, twirling her long blonde hair round her finger. 'It's the most romantic thing I've ever seen. I can't tell you how envious we all are. Total love at first sight and the whole office knows. What nobody knows is are you sleeping with him?'

'No,' said Ria firmly. And then, in a much smaller voice, 'Not yet.'

Ria's mother wondered was she ever going to meet him.

'Soon, Mam. Don't rush things, please.'

'I'm not rushing anything, Ria. I'm just pointing out that you have been going out with this fellow every single night, week after week, and common courtesy would suggest that you might invite him home.'

'I will, Mam. Honestly.'

'Are you going home for Christmas?' Ria asked Danny.

'I don't know yet.'

'Won't they expect you to go back?'

'They'll leave it to me.'

She wanted to ask about his brothers over in England and what kind of a family *was* it if they didn't all gather round a table for a turkey on Christmas Day. But she knew she must not sound too inquisitive. 'Sure,' she said unconvincingly.

Danny took her hands in his. 'Listen to me, Ria. It will be different when you and I have a home. It will be a real home, one that people will want to come running back to. That's what I see ahead for us. Don't you?'

'Oh, yes, Danny,' she said, with her face glowing. She did understand. The real Danny was a loving person like herself. She was the luckiest woman in the world.

Someone always behaved badly at the office party.

This year it was Orla King, a girl who had drunk half a bottle of vodka before the festivities started.

'Get her out before the top guys see her,' Danny hissed.

It was easier said than done. Ria tried to urge Orla to come with her to the ladies' room.

'Piss off!' was the response.

Danny was there. 'Hey, sweetheart, you and I have never danced,' he said. 'Why don't we go out and dance a bit where there's more room?'

'Yesh,' said the girl, surprised and pleased.

In seconds Danny had her out on the street. Ria brought her coat. The cold air made Orla feel sick. They directed her to a quiet corner.

'I want to go home,' she cried afterwards.

'Come on, we'll walk you,' Danny said.

When they let her in the door of her flat she looked at them in surprise. 'How did I get home?' she asked with interest. 'Will you come in with me?' Orla ignored Ria entirely.

'No, honey, see you tomorrow,' Danny said, and they were gone.

'You saved her job, getting her out of there,' Ria said as they walked back to the office party. 'She's such a clown . . . I hope she knows how much she owes you.'

'She's not a clown, she's just young and lonely,' he said.

Ria got a stab of jealousy as sharp as a real pain. Orla was eighteen and pretty; even drunk and with a tear-stained face she looked well. Suppose Danny was attracted to her? No, don't suppose that.

Back at the party they hadn't been missed. 'That was very smart of you, Danny,' Rosemary said with approval. She looked magnificent, with her blonde hair swept up in a jewelled comb, a white satin blouse, tight black skirt and long slim legs. For the second time that evening Ria felt a pang of envy. She was dumpy and fuzzy-looking. How could she keep a man as gorgeous as Danny Lynch?

He whispered in her ear, 'Let's circulate, talk to the suits for a bit and then get away.'

She watched him joke easily with the senior staff, listen courteously to their wives. Danny had only been there a matter of weeks. Already they liked him and thought he would do well.

'I'm getting the Christmas Eve bus tomorrow,' he said later. 'I'll miss you.'

'Me too.'

'I'll hitchhike back the day after Christmas. I wonder, could I come and see you at home and, you know, meet your mother maybe?'

He was asking, she hadn't forced him.

'That would be great. Come and have lunch with us on the Tuesday.' All she had to do now was force herself not to be ashamed of her mother and her sister and her dreary brother-in-law.

It wasn't a military inspection on Tuesday. It was only lunch. Ria wondered whether Danny would bring a bottle of wine or a box of chocolates or a plant. Or maybe nothing at all. Three times she changed her dress. That was too smart, this was too dowdy. She was struggling into the third outfit when she heard the doorbell ring.

He had arrived.

'Hello, Nora, I'm Danny,' she heard him say. Oh God, he was calling her mother by her first name. Mam would just hate this.

But she heard in her mother's voice the kind of pleased response that Danny always got. 'You're very, very welcome,' she said, in a tone that hadn't been used in that house for as long as Ria could remember.

And the magic worked with Hilary and Martin too. Eager to hear about their wedding, interested in the school where they worked, relaxed and easy-going. Ria watched the whole thing with amazement.

And he had brought no wine, chocolates or flowers. Instead he gave them a game of Trivial Pursuit. Ria's heart sank when she saw it. This was not a family where games were played. But she had reckoned without Danny. Their heads were bent over the questions. Nora knew all the ones about film stars and Martin shone in general knowledge.

'What hope have I against a teacher?' Danny groaned in despair.

He said he was leaving long before they wanted him to go. 'Ria promised to come and see the place where I live,' he said apologetically. 'I want us to go while there's still light.'

'He's gorgeous,' Hilary whispered.

'Very nice manners,' her mother hissed.

And then they were free.

'That was a lovely lunch,' Danny said as they waited for the bus to Tara Road. And that was all he would say. There would be no analysis, no defining. Men like Danny were straightforward and not complicated.

And then they were there. And they stood together in the overgrown front garden and looked up at the house in Tara Road.

'Look at the shape of the house,' Danny begged her. 'See how perfect the proportions are. It was built in 1870, a gentleman's residence.' The steps up to the hall door were huge blocks of granite. 'Look how even they were, they were perfectly matched.' The bow windows had all the original woodwork. 'Those shutters are over a hundred years old. The leaded glass over the door has no cracks in it. This house was a jewel,' Danny Lynch said.

There he was living in it, well, more or less camping in a room in it.

'Let's remember today, the first day that we walked together into this house,' he said. His eyes were bright. He was just as sentimental and romantic as she was in so many ways. He was about to open the peeling front door with his key, and he paused to kiss her. 'This will be our home, Ria, won't it? Tell me you love it too.' He meant it. A boy of twenty-three with no assets. Only rich people could buy houses like this, even one in such poor repair.

Ria didn't want to pour cold water on his dreams, but this was fantasy. 'It's not possible to own a place like this, surely?' she said.

'When you come in and see it you'll know this is where we are going to live. And we'll find a way to buy it.' He talked her through the hallway with its high ceiling. He pointed out the original mouldings on the ceiling to take her eyes off the bicycles clogging the hallway. He showed her the gentle curve of the stairs, and made no mention of the rotting floorboards. They passed the big room with its folding doors. They couldn't go into it because the landlord was using it as a storeroom for giant-size containers.

They went down the steps to the huge kitchen with its old black range. There was a side door here out to the garden, and numerous storage rooms, pantries and sculleries. The magnitude of it all was too great for Ria to take in. This boy with the laughing eyes really thought that he and she could find the money and skills to do up a house of this size.

If it were on their books back at the office it would have the customary warnings printed all over it. In need of extensive renovation, suitable for structural remodelling, ready for inventive redesign. Only a builder or developer would buy a property like this.

The kitchen had an uneven tiled floor. A small cheap tabletop cooker had been laid on the old black range.

'I'll make us some coffee,' Danny said. 'And in years to come we'll remember the first time we had coffee here together in Tara Road . . .' At that moment, as if on some kind of cue, the kitchen was suddenly lit up with one of those rays of watery winter sunshine. It came slanting in at the window through all the briars and brambles. It was like a sign.

'Yes, I will remember my first coffee with you in Tara Road,' Ria said.

'We'll be able to tell people it was a lovely sunny day, December the 28th, 1982,' said Danny.

As it happened it also turned out to be the date of the first time Ria Johnson ever made love. And as she lay beside Danny in the narrow bed she wished she could see into the future. Would they live here together for years and have children and make it the home of their dreams?

She wondered if Hilary's fortuneteller, Mrs Connor, would know. She smiled at the thought of going to consult her. Danny stirred from his sleep and saw her smiling.

'Are you happy?' he asked.

'Never more so.'

'I love you, Ria. I'll never let you down,' he promised.

She was the luckiest woman in the country. No, she told herself, who was luckier anywhere? Make that the world.

2

THE NEXT WEEKS went by in a blur.

They knew that Sean O'Brien would be glad to get rid of the place. They knew that he would prefer to deal with them, young people who wouldn't make a fuss over the damp and decay. But they still had to give him what the house was worth. So how could they get it together?

There were sheets of paper building up into piles as they did their sums. Four bedsitters upstairs would bring in enough to pay the mortgage. Ria had £1,000 saved; Danny had £2,500. They had both seen couples with less than they had get their hands on property.

They invested in the price of a bottle of whiskey when inviting the landlord to discuss the future. Sean O'Brien proved to be no trouble. He didn't want to live in the house, but in a small cottage by a lake in Wicklow where he fished and drank with congenial people. He thought that the going rate for the house would be in the neighbourhood of £70,000. However he would take £60,000 for a quick sale.

It would have been a bargain for anyone with the money to restore it. For Danny and Ria it was impossible. They would need 15 per cent of the price as a deposit. And £9,000 was like £9 million to them.

Ria was prepared to change the dream, not Danny. He just wouldn't let go of the idea. It was too good a house, too beautiful a place to let slip from their hands into the possession of some builder. Now that Sean O'Brien had faced the notion of selling, he would want to sell.

It was hard to keep their minds on the sales they had to handle in the office. Doubly hard because every day they were dealing with people who could buy Tara Road without any trouble at all.

People like Barney McCarthy, for example. The big bluff businessman who had made his money in England as a builder and who bought and sold houses almost on a whim. He was in the process of selling a large mansion that had been a rare mistake. The house was elegant but it had turned out to be too remote, too far from Dublin. Quite simply Barney had spent too much on it. Senior partners in the estate agency, smooth-talking men, pointed out to Barney that the upkeep of such a house was enormous and that they could count on the fingers of one hand the likely buyers in Ireland. They had looked outside the country too, but with no success.

There was a conference in the agency about it. Danny and Ria sat with the others listening to the worrying news that Barney might be taking his business elsewhere. Danny opened his mouth to say something and then changed his mind. Ria knew that he had thought of something. She knew from the way his eyes danced.

After the meeting he whispered that he had to get out of the office. 'I've got an idea how Barney can sell his house.'

'Why didn't you tell them?'

'I'm telling *him*. That's how we'll get our money. If I tell them we'll only get a pat on the back.'

'Oh God, Danny. Be careful, they could sack you.'

'If I'm right it won't matter,' he said. And he was gone.

Rosemary called Ria. 'Come into the ladies' room. I want to tell you something.'

'I can't. I'm waiting for a call.' Ria couldn't leave her post in case Danny rang. 'Tell me here, there's no one around.'

'Well, it's very hush-hush.'

'Speak in a whisper, then.'

'I'm leaving, I've got a new job.' Rosemary pulled back, waiting to see the amazement and shock on Ria's face. She saw very little reaction at all. Perhaps she hadn't explained it properly.

She explained it all again. She had been offered a better job in a printing company. It had just been agreed. It was very exciting. She would tell them here in the agency this evening. Ria barely listened, she was so sick with worry.

Rosemary was not unnaturally offended. 'Well, if you can't be bothered to listen,' she said.

Ria was stricken. 'Look, I can't tell you how sorry I am. It's just that I have something on my mind. Please forgive me. Please tell me about your new job, please.'

'Ria, will you *shut up*,' Rosemary hissed. 'I haven't told them yet and there you go bleating about my new job. I think you're unhinged.'

Ria saw Danny come in the door, walking quickly, lightly, as he always did. He slid into his desk and gave her a thumbs-up sign. Immediately she dialled his phone extension.

'What happens now, Danny?'

'We sit tight for a week. Then all systems go.'

Ria hung up. She thought the day would never end, the hands of the clock were crawling past. Rosemary went in to the managing director and came out having given her notice. Across the room Danny seemed to be perfectly normal, chatting to people, laughing, working on the phone. Only Ria, who knew his every heartbeat, could see the suppressed excitement.

They went to the pub across the road and without asking her what she wanted he bought them both a large brandy.

'I told Barney McCarthy he should put in a soundproofed recording studio. Cost him another twenty thousand.'

'Why on earth . . .?'

'He could sell it to pop stars. It's the kind of a place they'd want, carve out a helicopter pad as well. And, Ria, wait for this, I looked him in the eye and I said, "And another thing, Mr McCarthy, I thought if I came to you directly with this idea that maybe I could sell it for you myself."' Danny sipped his brandy. 'He asked me was I trying to take his business away from my employers. I said yes, I was, and he said he'd give me a week.'

'Oh God, Danny.'

'I know. Isn't it wonderful? Well, I can't do it from our office, so I'll develop flu tomorrow, after I've taken all the addresses and contacts I need home. If I sell Barney's house by next week we'll have the deposit on Tara Road and more. *Then* we can go to the bank, honeybun.'

'But they'll sack you, you won't have a job.'

'If I have Barney McCarthy's business, any estate agents in Ireland will take me. Just a week of iron-hard nerve, Ria, and we're there.'

'Iron nerve,' she agreed.

'And remember this day, sweetheart. March the 25th, 1983, the day our luck changed.'

'Will Danny be back for my going-away drinks?' Rosemary asked Ria.

'Yes, I think his flu will be better by then,' Ria said loudly.

An hour previously Danny had rung to say that Barney's forces had soundproofed a wine cellar already and the equipment was being installed. Tomorrow the manager of a legendary pop group was flying over to inspect it; Danny would be travelling with him. It was looking very good.

And it was very good. Barney McCarthy got his price. And Danny Lynch got his commission. And Sean O'Brien got his £60,000. And Danny told his employers what he had done, and that he would leave as soon as they wanted him to. They invited him to stay and keep Barney's business with them, but Danny said it would be awkward.

They parted on good terms, as Danny Lynch did with everyone and everything in life.

They were like excited children as they wandered about the house planning this and that.

'This front room could be something *really* special,' Danny said. Now that Sean O'Brien's containers had been moved out, anyone could see what perfect proportions it had: the high ceiling, the tall windows, the big fireplace.

'We'll get a gorgeous soft wool Indian carpet,' Danny said. 'And look here, beside the fireplace do you know what we'll have—one of those big Japanese Imari vases. Perfect for a room like this.'

Ria looked at him with stunned admiration.

'How on earth do you know all this, Danny? You sound as if you'd done a course in fine arts.'

'I look at places, sweetheart. I'm in and out of houses like this all day. I see what people with taste and style have done. We'll have such a good time doing it up.' His eyes were shining.

Ria nodded, not trusting herself to speak.

The pregnancy test was positive. The timing could not be worse. As she lay awake at night, she rehearsed how she would tell him that she was pregnant.

When she did tell him it was completely by accident. Danny said that the hall was bigger than he had thought and maybe they should have a painting party at the weekend, get everyone to do a bit of wall each.

'What do you think, sweetheart? I know the smell of paint will make us all sick for a day or two but it will be worth it.'

'I'm going to have a baby,' she said suddenly.

'What?'

'Yes, I mean it. Oh, Danny, I'm so sorry.' And she burst into tears.

He laid down his coffee cup and came over to hold her tight. 'Ria, Ria. Stop, stop. Don't cry.'

But she went on sobbing and shaking in his arms. He stroked her hair and soothed her as you would a child. 'Shush, shush, Ria. I'm here, it's all right. We wanted children. We were going to get married. So it happened sooner rather than later. That's all.'

She looked at him in wonder. He was smiling his big wide smile. Inasmuch as she could understand anything, he really did seem to be overjoyed.

'Danny . . .'

'What were all the tears about?'

'I thought, I thought . . .'

'Shush.'

'Rosemary? Can we have lunch? I've got some marvellous news.'

'What makes me think it has to do with lover boy?' Rosemary laughed.

They went to the Italian restaurant where they had gone that day with Danny last November.

'Well, tell me,' Rosemary said. 'Stop pretending to look at the menu.'

'Danny and I are getting married. We want you to be the bridesmaid.'

'Married?' Rosemary said. 'Well, aren't you the dark horse. All I can say is well done, Ria. Well done!'

Ria felt that she would have preferred Rosemary to say that this was great; 'well done' sort of implied that she had won by trickery. 'Yes. Aren't you happy for us?'

'Of course I am.' Rosemary hugged her. 'Stunned but very happy for you. You got the man of your dreams *and* a beautiful house as well.'

'Nobody's seen the house yet but you. I'm almost afraid of what the families will say when they do.'

'Nonsense, they'll be dead impressed. What are they like, Danny's parents?'

'I haven't met them yet, but I gather not at all like Danny,' Ria said.

Rosemary made a face. 'Never mind. Now, down to serious things. What will we wear?'

'You know I'm pregnant?'

'I thought you might be. But that's good, isn't it? It's what you want?'

'Yes, it is.'

'So?'

'So, we shouldn't really be thinking of big white weddings and veils and all that stuff.'

'What would Danny like? Isn't that all that matters? Would he like the whole works or a few sandwiches in the pub?'

Ria didn't even pause to think. 'He'd like the full works,' she said.

'Then that is exactly what we'll have,' said Rosemary.

Nora Johnson was amazed at the news. 'You do surprise me,' she said.

Ria was irritated by this response. 'Why do I surprise you, Mam? You know I love him, you know he loves me. What else would we do but get married?'

'Oh certainly, certainly.'

'What have you against him, Mam? You said you liked him, you admired the fact that he bought a big house and is planning to do it up. He's got good prospects, we won't be penniless. What objection do you have to him?'

'He's too good-looking,' her mother said.

Hilary was no more enthusiastic. 'You'd want to be careful of him, Ria. Danny's a high-flier. He's not going to be content with earning a living like normal people do; he'll want the moon.'

She met Barney McCarthy before she met Danny's parents. She was invited to lunch. In fact it was a little like a royal command.

Danny was excited. 'You'll like him, Ria, he's marvellous. And he'll love you, I know he will.'

'I'm nervous of going to that restaurant, it will all be in French and we won't know what all the things are.'

'Nonsense, just be yourself. And never apologise or write yourself down. We are as good as anyone else. Barney knows that, that's how he got on, by knowing it about himself.'

Barney was a large square man of about forty-five. He wore a well-cut suit and an expensive watch and he carried himself confidently. He had an easy manner, but still, despite the pleasant, inconsequential conversation, Ria couldn't avoid the feeling that she was being given an interview. And with a sense of satisfaction after the coffee she realised that she had done very well.

Orla King was the one who told Ria that people in the office didn't really like her working there any more. Not now that she was engaged to marry Danny Lynch. People said that she would be telling him everything, giving him leads.

'I had no idea.' Ria was shocked.

Danny told Barney McCarthy that Ria had decided to leave the company, to go before they asked her to.

Barney was unexpectedly sympathetic. 'That's very hard on her. She was in that firm long before you went in and rocked the boat. Maybe I'd have a job for her.'

One of his business interests was a new dress-hire agency. A very classy outfit called Polly's. They took Ria immediately.

'Should I not have a week's trial or something?' Ria asked Gertie, the tall pale manageress with her long dark hair tied in a simple ribbon behind her neck.

'No need,' said Gertie with a grin. 'Instructions from Mr McCarthy to hire you, so you're hired.'

'I'm sorry. That's an awful way to come in anywhere,' Ria apologised.

'Listen, it's fine, and you're fine and we'll get along great,' said Gertie. 'I'm only telling it to you the way it is.'

They went to see Danny's parents. It was a three-hour journey by bus. Ria felt very sick but forced herself to be in good spirits. Danny's father waited in the square where the bus came in. He drove an old van with a trailer attached to it.

'This is my Ria, Dad.' Danny was proud and pleased to show her off.

'You're very welcome.' The man looked old, stooped and shabby. He was about the same age as Barney McCarthy but he looked a different generation.

His mother seemed old too, much older than Ria had expected. They lunched on ham and tomatoes, bread and a packet of chocolate biscuits. Danny's parents said they were not really sure if they could come to Dublin for the wedding, it was a long way and there might be work here that would be hard to get away from.

It was obvious that this was not so. Ria protested, 'It would be wonderful to have you there. We're going to have the reception in Tara Road and you'll see the new house.'

'We're not great people for parties,' Danny's mother said.

'But this is family,' Ria begged. She looked at Danny. Surely he wanted them there? Didn't he? She waited for him to speak.

'Ah, go on. Come on. It's only once in a lifetime.' They looked at each other doubtfully.

'We'll come up and see the house another time,' Danny's father said.

There was no more to be said. 'Of course you will,' Ria said soothingly.

'Did you not want them to come?' she asked on the bus journey home.

'Sweetheart, you could see yourself they didn't want to come,' Danny said.

She felt disappointed in him. He should have persuaded them. But then men were different, everyone knew this.

It was a very mixed gathering at the wedding. They had invited Orla from the old office and Gertie from Polly's. One of Danny's brothers, Larry, came over from London and was best man. He looked like Danny, same fair hair and lopsided smile, only taller, and spoke now with a London accent.

'Will you be going home to see your parents?' Ria asked.

'Not this time,' Larry said. He hadn't been to see his father and mother for four years.

Barney McCarthy was there. He apologised that his wife Mona had not been able to come. She had gone to Lourdes with three friends, it had been long arranged. Barney had sent two cases of champagne in advance and he stood chatting easily among the forty people who toasted handsome Danny Lynch and his beautiful bride.

Ria had never thought she could look as well as this with her dark curls swept up into a headdress and a long veil trailing behind her. Barney McCarthy had insisted that the wedding party should be kitted out for free at Polly's. The dress Ria had chosen had never been worn before, thick embroidery and lace from head to toe, the richest fabric she had ever seen.

Rosemary had been there to advise and suggest throughout. 'Stand very straight, Ria. Hold your shoulders right back. Don't scuttle up the church; when you get in there walk slowly. You look gorgeous. You're a dream, go for it, Ria.' The bridesmaid's enthusiasm was infectious. Ria walked almost regally into the church on the arm of her brother-in-law who was giving her away.

Danny had actually gasped when she came up the aisle.

'I love you so much,' he said as they posed by the wedding cake for pictures. And Ria suddenly felt sorry for whoever else was going to wear this dress when it was cleaned and back out in the agency.

No other bride could ever look as well or be so happy.

They had no honeymoon. Danny went back to looking for work and Ria went back to her job at Polly's. She enjoyed working there and meeting the extraordinarily varied streams of customers.

Gertie was kind to the brides and didn't fuss them. She helped them choose but didn't steer them towards the most expensive outfits.

'Why is it called Polly's?' a bride-to-be asked Ria one day.

'I think it's something to do with Pretty Polly,' Ria explained.

'That was very diplomatic,' Gertie said admiringly afterwards.

'What do you mean? I hadn't a clue why he called it Polly's. Do you know?'

'After his fancy woman. It's hers; he bought it for her. You knew that.'

'I didn't, actually. I hardly know him. But I thought he was a pillar of the Church and all that?'

'Oh yes, he is when he's with the wife. But with Polly Callaghan . . . that's something else.'

'Oh, that's why the cheques are all to P. Callaghan. I see.'

'What did you think it was?'

'I thought it might be a tax thing.'

'But I thought you were great pals with him.'

'No, Danny sold his house for him, that's all.'

'Well, he told me to give you the job and to organise all the gear for your wedding, so he must think very highly of your Danny.'

'He's not the only one. Danny's out at lunch today with two fellows who are thinking of setting up their own firm. They want him to join them.'

'And will he?'

'I hope not, Gertie, it would be too risky. He has no capital; he'd have to put the house up with a second mortgage as a security or something. I'd love him to go somewhere where he'd be paid.'

'Do you tell him this?' Gertie asked.

'Not really. He's such a dreamer, and he thinks big, and he's been right so often. I stay out of it a lot of the time. I don't want to be the one who is holding him back.'

'You have it all worked out,' Gertie said with admiration. Gertie had a boyfriend, Jack, who drank too much. She had tried to finish with him many times, but she always went back.

'No, I don't really have it worked out,' Ria said. 'I *look* placid, you see, that's why people think I'm fine. Inside I worry a lot.'

'Did you say yes to them?' Ria hoped that Danny couldn't hear the anxiety in her voice.

'No, I didn't. Actually, I didn't say anything. I listened instead.'

'And what did you hear?'

'How much they wanted Barney's business and how seriously they thought I could deliver it. They know all about him. They told me about companies and businesses he has that I never knew about.'

'And what are you going to do?'

'I've done it,' Danny said.

'What on earth did you do?'

'I went to Barney. I told him that anything I had was thanks to him and that I had this offer from fellows who knew a bit too much about him for his comfort.'

'And what did he say?'

'He thanked me and said he'd come back to me.'

Barney McCarthy called that night. He had been thinking of setting up a small estate agency business himself. All he had really needed was to be prompted to do it. Now he had. Would Danny Lynch manage it for him? On a salary, of course, but part of the profits as well.

Not long after this they were invited to a party at the McCarthys' home. Ria recognised a lot of faces there. Politicians, a man who read the news on television, a well-known golfer.

Barney's wife, Mona, was a large comfortable-looking woman. She moved with ease and confidence among the guests. She wore a navy wool dress and had what must have been real pearls round her plump neck. She was probably in her mid-forties, like her husband. Could Barney *really* have a fancy woman called Polly Callaghan? Ria wondered. A settled married man with this comfortable home and grown-up children? It seemed unlikely. Yet Gertie had been very definite about it. Ria tried to imagine what Polly Callaghan looked like, what age she was.

Just at that moment Mona McCarthy came up to her. 'I understand you work at Polly's,' she said pleasantly. 'Will you continue working after you've had the baby?'

'Oh, yes, we need the money and we thought we'd give a foreign student a bedsitter in the house and she could look after the baby.'

'When Barney was starting out I went out to work. It was to make money to keep Barney's builder's van on the road. I always regret it. The children grew up without me. You can't have that time back again.'

'I'm sure you're right, we'll certainly talk about it. Maybe the moment I see the baby I won't want to go out to work ever again.'

'I didn't certainly, but I went out after six weeks.'

'Was Mr McCarthy grateful? Did he know how hard it was for you?'

'Grateful? No, I don't think so. Things were different then. We were so anxious to make a go of it, we just did what had to be done.'

She was nice, this woman. No airs and graces, and they must have been a little like herself and Danny years ago. How sad that now when they were old he fancied someone else.

Ria looked across the room. Danny was at the centre of a little circle telling them some funny story.

Danny's parents could never have been guests in a house like this. Barney McCarthy when he was growing up would not have been in a place of this grandeur. Perhaps he saw in Danny some of the same push and drive that he had had in his youth and that was why he was encouraging him. In years to come they might be entertaining at Tara Road and everyone would know that Danny had another lady somewhere.

She gave a little shiver. Nobody knew what the future had in store.

Barney McCarthy was looking at some land in Galway and he needed Danny with him. Barney drove fast and they crossed the country quickly.

A table had been booked in advance and waiting for them was an attractive red-haired woman in her mid-thirties, wearing a cream-coloured suit.

'This is Polly Callaghan.' Barney gave her a kiss on the cheek and introduced her to Danny.

Danny swallowed. He had heard about her from Ria. He hadn't expected her to be so glamorous.

'How do you do,' he said.

'The boy wonder, I'm told,' she smiled at him.

'No, just born lucky.'

'You weren't born lucky,' Polly Callaghan said. 'You were born sharp, that's much better.'

'And did they have the same room?' Ria asked.

'I don't know, I didn't check.'

'But, you know, were they lovey-dovey?' She was eager to know.

'Not so you'd notice. They were more like a married couple really. They acted as if they knew each other very well.'

'Poor Mona, I wonder does she know?' Ria said.

'Poor Mona, as you call her, probably doesn't give a damn. Hasn't she a palace of a house and everything she wants?'

'She may want not to share him with a mistress.'

'I liked Polly Callaghan, actually. She was nice.'

'I'm sure,' said Ria, a little sourly.

Polly came into the shop next day and introduced herself. 'I met your husband in Galway, did he tell you?'

'No, Mrs Callaghan, he didn't.' For some reason Ria lied.

Polly nodded approvingly. 'He's a bright lad.'

'He is indeed.' Ria smiled proudly.

Polly looked at Gertie carefully. 'What happened to your face, Gertie? That's a terrible bruise.'

'I know, Mrs Callaghan. Didn't I have a fall off my bicycle. I hoped it wasn't too noticeable.'

'Did you have to have a stitch?'

'Two, but it's nothing. Will I get you a cup of coffee?'

'Please.' Polly looked after Gertie as she left to make some coffee. 'Are you two friends, Ria?'

'Yes, yes indeed.'

'Then talk her out of that lout she's involved with. He did that to her, you know.'

'Oh, he couldn't have . . .' Ria was shocked.

'Well, he did it before. He'll kill her in the end. But she won't be told, not by me anyway. She might listen to you.'

'Where's *Mister* Callaghan?' Ria asked Gertie when Polly had left.

'There never was one, it's only a courtesy title. Did she tell you that Jack did this to me?'

'Yes. Did he just come in and punch you in the face?'

'No, it wasn't like that. It was an argument, he lost his temper. He said he didn't remember picking up the chair. He didn't mean it. He's so sorry, you have no idea.'

'He hit you with a chair? You can't take him back.'

'Look, everyone in the world's given up on Jack, I'm not going to.'

'But you can see why everyone in the world's given up.'

'Don't start, Ria. Please don't start. I've had my mother and Polly Callaghan. Not you as well.'

The baby was due in the first week of October.

'That will be Libra, that's a good star sign. It's got to do with being balanced,' Gertie said.

'You don't believe all of that, do you?'

'Of course I do.'

Ria laughed. 'You're as bad as my sister Hilary. She and her friends spent a fortune on some woman in a caravan, they believed every word.'

'Oh, where is she? Let's go to her. She might tell you if it's going to be a girl or a boy.'

'I don't want to know that badly.'

'Ah, come on. And we'll get Rosemary to come too. *Please*,' Gertie said. 'It'll be a laugh.'

Mrs Connor had a thin, haunted face. She did not look like someone who was being handed fistfuls of fivers and tenners by foolish women in exchange for a bit of news about the future. She looked like someone who had seen too much. Maybe that was all part of the mystique, Ria thought, as she sat down and stretched out her hand.

The baby would be a girl, a healthy girl, followed some years later by a boy.

'Aren't there going to be three? I have three little lines here,' Ria asked.

'No, one of them isn't a real child-line. It could be a miscarriage, I don't know.'

'And my husband's business, is it going to do well?'

'I'd have to see his hand for that. Your own business will do well, I can see there's a lot of travel, across the sea.'

Ria giggled to herself. It was twenty pounds wasted, and the baby would probably be a boy. She wondered how Gertie and Rosemary had got on.

'Well, Gertie, what did she tell you?'

'Not much. She was no good really.'

Rosemary and Ria looked at each other. Rosemary was aware of Jack and his lifestyle.

'I expect she told you to walk out on your current dark stranger,' Rosemary said.

'Don't be so cruel, Rosemary, she did *not* say that.' Gertie's voice sounded shaky.

There was a silence.

'And what about you, Rosemary?' Ria wanted to break the tension.

'A load of old nonsense, nothing I wanted to know.'

'No husband?'

'No, but a whole rake of other problems. You don't want to be bothered with it.' She fell silent again and concentrated on driving the car. As an outing it had not been a success.

Barney McCarthy said that Danny and Ria needed a car. They began to look at the ads for secondhand motors. 'I meant a company car,' he said. And they got a new one.

Danny had to go to London with Barney, so Ria drove him to the airport. Just as she kissed him goodbye she saw the smart figure of Polly Callaghan getting out of a taxi. Ria looked the other way.

But Polly had no such niceties; she came straight over. 'So this is the new car. Very nice too.'

'Oh, hello, Mrs Callaghan. Danny, I'm not meant to park here, I should move off. Anyway I should be at work.'

'I'll keep an eye on him for you in London. I won't let him get distracted by any little glamour-puss.'

'Thanks,' Ria gulped.

Ria gave up work a week before the baby was due. They were all very supportive, these people she had not even known a year ago. Barney McCarthy said that Danny must stay around Dublin, so that he would be nearby for the birth. Mona said that they shouldn't waste money buying cots and prams. She had kept plenty for grandchildren; it was just that their two daughters hadn't provided them with any yet.

Rosemary, who had been promoted to run a bigger branch of the printing company, came to see her.

'I'm just no good at all this deep breathing and waters breaking and everything,' Rosemary apologised. 'I've no experience of it.'

'Nor I,' Ria said ruefully. 'I've never had anything to do with it either, and I'm the one who's going to have to go through with it.'

'Ah well. Does Danny go to these prenatal classes with you? I can't imagine him . . .'

'Yes, he loves it in a way.'

'Of course he does, and he'll love you too again when you get your figure back.' Rosemary was wearing her very slim-fitting trouser-suit and looked like a tall elegant reed. She meant it to be reassuring, Ria thought, but because she felt like a tank herself it was unsettling.

Ria's mother came too, full of advice and warnings.

The only one who didn't come was Hilary. She was so envious of Tara Road that it pained her to come inside the door and see the renovations. Ria had tried to involve her in the business of looking for bargains at auctions, but that hadn't worked. Hilary became so discontented at the size and scope of her own house compared to Ria's that the outings would end in disaster.

Ria decided to drive to see Hilary. She didn't care what snide remarks would be made by her sister about the smart car. She wanted to see her and talk to her the way they used to before all this money and style got in the way.

Martin was out; he was at a residents' meeting where they were organising a protest. Hilary looked tired and discontented.

'Oh, it's you,' she said when she saw Ria. Her eye was drawn to the car at the gate. 'Hope that will still have tyres on it when you leave.'

'Hilary, can I come in?'

'Sure.'

'You and I didn't have a fight about anything, did we?'

'What are you going on about?'

'Well, it's just that you never come and see me. I ask you so often it's embarrassing. We used to be pals. What happened?'

Hilary's face was mutinous. 'You don't need pals any more.'

Ria was not going to let this go. 'Like hell I don't need a pal. I'm scared stiff of having the baby in the first place. People say it's terrifying and that no one admits it. I'm worried that I mightn't be able to look after it properly and I'm afraid that Danny's taken on too much and that we'll lose everything. At times I'm afraid he'll stop loving me if I start whingeing about things, and you *dare* to tell me I don't need a pal.'

Things changed then. Hilary's frown had gone. 'I'll put on the kettle,' she said.

As they sat drinking their tea Hilary said, 'I didn't mean to be stand-offish. It's just that you have everything, Ria, really everything . . . a fellow like a film star . . . and you've got that house and the flash car outside the door here and you go to places and meet celebrities. How was I to know that you might want someone like me around . . . ?'

As she was about to answer that, Ria got the dart of pain that she knew was waiting for her. The baby was on the way.

Orla called round to Tara Road. One of the Lynches' bedsitter tenants explained that both Ria and Danny were out. Danny was probably at his office. Ria had taken the car somewhere. Orla thought she would call on Danny at his office. She had been drinking since she left work; she didn't feel like going home yet. And Danny might like to go for a pint. And he was extraordinarily attractive.

Rosemary smiled at the man across the table. He was a big customer at the print shop. He had asked her out many times. Tonight was the first time she had said yes and they were having dinner in a very expensive restaurant. They were doing a colour brochure for him. It was for a charity heavily supported by businessmen.

'And do you have the full list of your sponsors so that we can set them out for you with some suitable artwork?'

'I have them back at my hotel,' he said.

'But you don't have a hotel room,' Rosemary said. 'You *live* in Dublin.'

'That's right.' He had an easy, confident smile. 'But tonight I have a hotel room.' He raised his glass at her.

Rosemary raised her glass back. 'What an extravagant gesture not to have checked first whether the room would be called on.'

He laughed at what he thought was her grudging admiration. 'You know, I had this premonition that you would come to dinner with me and end the evening with a drink back at the hotel.'

'And your premonition was exactly half right. Thank you for a delightful dinner.' She stood up.

He was genuinely amazed. 'What makes you come on like this all promises and teasing and then a bucket of cold water?'

Rosemary spoke clearly. She could be heard at the nearby tables. 'There were no promises and no teasings. There was an invitation to dinner to discuss business, which was accepted. There was no question of going to your hotel room. We don't need business that badly.'

She walked head held high from the restaurant, with all the confidence that being twenty-three, blonde and beautiful brings with it.

Danny had been about to leave his office when Orla King arrived. Pretty as a picture but definitely slurring her words.

'Would you like to go to the pub for the one?' Orla asked.

'No, sweetheart. I'm bushed,' he said.

'A pub livens you up. Come on, please.'

'You'll have to forgive me tonight, Orla.'

'What night then?' she asked. She ran her tongue over her lips as she smiled at him.

He could either go at once, risking a scene and possibly leaving unfinished business, or he could offer her a drink from the bottle of brandy he kept for Barney. 'A small brandy, then, Orla.'

She had won, she thought. She sat on his desk with her legs crossed as Danny went and found the bottle. Just then the phone rang.

'Oh, leave it, Danny. It's only work,' Orla pleaded.

'Not this time of night,' he said, picking it up.

'Danny. This is Polly Callaghan. It's urgent. Barney's here. He has chest pains. I can't call the cardiac ambulance to come here, I want you to call it to your house.'

'Yes, of course.'

'But it's a question of my getting him there.'

'I'll get a taxi to you. I'll make the other call first.'

At this stage the petulant voice of Orla could be heard. '*Dan-ny*, come off the phone, come over here.'

'And you'll get rid of whatever companion you have with you?'

'Yes.' He was clipped.

And even more clipped dealing with Orla. 'I'm sorry, Orla, sweetheart. Brandy's over . . . I have an emergency.'

'You don't call me sweetheart and then ask me to leave,' she began.

She found herself propelled towards the door, while Danny grabbed his jacket and phoned an ambulance all at the same time.

She heard him give the Tara Road address. 'Who's sick? Is it the baby arriving?' she asked, frightened by his intensity.

'Goodbye, Orla,' he said, and she saw him running down the street to hail a taxi.

Barney was a very grey shade of white. He lay in a chair beside the bed. Polly had made unsuccessful attempts to dress him.

'Don't worry about the tie,' Danny barked. 'Go down and tell the taxi man to come up and help me get him down the stairs.'

Polly hesitated for a second. 'You know the way Barney hates anyone knowing his business.'

'This is a taxi man, Polly. Not MI5. Barney'd want to get there quicker.'

Barney spoke with his hand firmly holding his chest. 'Don't talk about me as if I'm not here. Get the taxi man, Polly, quick as you can.' To Danny he spoke gently. 'Thank you for getting here.'

'You're going to be fine.'

'You'll look after everything for me?'

'You'll be doing it yourself in forty-eight hours,' Danny said.

'But just in case . . .'

'Just in case, then. Yes, I will.' Danny spoke briskly.

At that moment the taxi man arrived. If he recognised the face of Barney McCarthy he gave no sign. Instead he got down to the job of easing a heavy man with heart pains down the narrow stairs of an expensive apartment block to take him to another address from which the ambulance would collect him.

They couldn't find Danny. He wasn't at Tara Road. He wasn't at the office. Ria gave Barney McCarthy's telephone number to Hilary in case Danny might be there, but his wife Mona said that Barney wasn't at home and she hadn't seen Danny at all.

Ria wanted him beside her. He had said so often that this was *their* baby, he would be there for the birth. Where in God's name was he?

'*Danny!*' That was the scream before the baby's head appeared. The sister was speaking and she could hardly hear. 'All right, Ria. It's over, you have a beautiful little baby girl. She's perfect.'

Ria felt more tired than she had ever been. Danny had not been here to see Annie, his daughter, born.

Orla King felt that she was now losing her mind because of drink. Not only did the guilt of trying to seduce a man on the night that his wife was having their first baby hang heavily on her, but the subsequent confusion in her brain worried her. She knew that Ria must have been at home because she heard Danny call the ambulance to Tara Road. But then she heard from everyone else that Ria was at her sister's house and they had to get a neighbour to drive Ria's car to the hospital as Hilary couldn't drive. Orla knew now that she was hallucinating and having memory failure. She went to her first Alcoholics Anonymous meeting.

And on the first night she met a man called Colm Barry. He was single, handsome, and worked in the bank. Colm had dark curly hair and dark sad eyes.

'You don't look like a banker,' Orla said to him.

'I don't feel like a bank clerk, I'd rather be a chef.'

'I don't feel like being a typist in an estate agency, I'd like to be a model or a singer,' Orla said.

'There's no reason why we shouldn't be these things, is there?' Colm asked with a smile.

Orla didn't know whether he was making fun of her or being nice, but she didn't mind. He was going to make these meetings bearable.

For a very long time Gertie refused to see Jack, and then, to everyone's disappointment, she agreed to meet him just once. Jack had been put off the road for drunken driving and consequently sacked from his job. Gertie found a chastened and sober man. They talked and she remembered why she loved him. They asked two strangers to be their witnesses and they were married in a cold church at eight o'clock one morning.

Gertie decided to leave Polly's for a job in a launderette with a flat upstairs, just round the corner from Tara Road. It was a bare living.

Polly Callaghan remembered the night that Annie Lynch was born because it was the night she thought she was going to lose Barney for ever. She had loved him without pausing to count the cost for twelve years, since she was twenty-five years old. Now at last he had got the warning that he needed to make him change his lifestyle, give up the cigarettes and brandy. Polly had been urging this for years, while his wife had provided comfort food. Barney McCarthy was only in his forties; he had years of living ahead of him.

Polly had been grateful to Danny Lynch for his speedy response. Grateful yet disappointed in him. He obviously had a girl with him in his office when she had called that night. Polly had heard her giggling. Polly was not one to sit in judgment on a man having an affair outside marriage. But she thought that Danny was fairly young to have started. *And* it was, after all, a night when you might have expected him to be with his wife who was having their first baby.

Rosemary remembered very well the time that Annie Lynch was born. It had been something of a turning-point in her life. First there was that loutish man who had booked a hotel bedroom and had assumed that she was going to share it. And this was the time she felt unexpectedly attracted to a man called Colm Barry who worked in the bank near where she worked. He was genuinely helpful and seemed admiring of Rosemary's skills in expanding the business. He must be about thirty, a tall man with black curly hair which he wore a little long on his collar.

The bank didn't approve, he said with some satisfaction.

'Does it bother you what the bank thinks?' Rosemary asked.

'Not a bit. does it bother *you* what other people think?' he asked in return.

'It has to a bit at work, because if they see a youngish woman they're inclined to ask to speak to a man. Still! In this day and age I have to try to give off some kind of vibes of confidence, I suppose. So in *that* way it bothers me. Not about other things though.'

He was easy to talk to. Some men had that way of listening to you. She really liked him. Why should women always wait to be asked out? She invited Colm Barry to have dinner with her.

'I'd love to,' he said. 'But sadly I'm going to a meeting tonight.'

'Come on, Colm. The bank can survive without you being at one meeting,' she said.

'No, it's AA,' he said.

'Really, what kind of car do you have?' she asked.

'No, the other lot, Alcoholics,' he said simply.

'Oops.'

'No, don't worry. Think me lucky that I get the support that's there. Now that you know the score you might be a little less interested in having dinner with me.' He was wry but not apologetic, just preparing himself for a change in attitude. Rosemary paused long enough for Colm to feel that he could speak again and end things before they had begun. 'We both know that you must find someone who is . . . let's say substantial. Don't waste time on a loser like a drinky bank clerk.'

'You're very cynical,' Rosemary said.

'And very realistic. I'll watch you with interest.'

'I'll watch you with interest too,' she said.

Mona McCarthy always remembered where she was when she heard that Barney had been taken into intensive care. She was in the attic rooting out a children's cot for young Ria Lynch.

Danny had rung to say that Barney was fine but they had thought it wise to err on the side of caution and had arranged an ECG. Danny was sending a car for her straight away.

'Where did it happen? Is it bad?' Mona asked.

Danny was calm and soothing. 'He was at home with me, in Tara Road, we were working all evening. He's fine, Mona. You'll see for yourself when you come in.'

She felt better already. He was an amazing boy, Danny, so well able to calm her while he should be in high panic himself over his wife's labour.

'And, Danny, I'm delighted to hear the baby's on the way, how is Ria?'
'What?'
'Ria's sister phoned me, she . . .'
'Oh shit, I don't believe it.' He had hung up.
'Danny?' Mona McCarthy was confused. Hilary had said she couldn't find Danny at Tara Road. Now he had said he had been there all evening. It was a mystery.

Danny Lynch never forgot the frantic rush from one hospital to the other. He cried into Ria's dark hair and took the baby gingerly into his arms. 'I'll never be able to make it up to you, but there is a reason.' And of course she understood. He hadn't known her time had come.

He had not known it was possible to love a little human being as he loved Annie. He was going to make his little princess a home that was like a palace. He had a truly beautiful daughter, a house that someone of his education and chances could only have dreamed about. He had a loving wife. Life had been very good to Danny Lynch.

All Ria's fears and worries that she had blurted out to her sister Hilary seemed to have been groundless. She was able to manage her baby, and Danny loved her more and more as time went on.

Annie grew up a sunny child in a happy home, her blonde straight hair like her father's, falling into her eyes.

And Ria took photographs of Annie and the house. So that Annie would not grow up thinking things had always been luxurious. Ria wanted her to see how she and the house had in a way grown together.

The day before the carpet arrived, and then the day it was in place; the day they finally got the Japanese vase Danny had always known would be right; the huge velvet curtains which Danny had spotted at the windows of a house which was being sold at an executor's sale.

Most of their life was lived in the big warm kitchen downstairs, but Danny and Ria spent some time every day in the drawing room, the room they had created from their dreams. They delighted in finding further little treasures for it. The old candlesticks that were transformed into lamps, more glass, a French clock.

Ria did not go back to work. There were so many reasons why it made more sense to be at home.

Danny's office wasn't far away. Sometimes he liked to come home to lunch, or even to have a cup of coffee and relax. Barney McCarthy came to see him there too. Ria would leave the men to talk.

Barney McCarthy often said admiringly, 'You were very lucky in the wife you got, Danny. I hope you appreciate her.'

Danny always said he did, and Ria Lynch knew this was true. Not only did her handsome Danny love her; as the years went by he loved her more than ever.

MRS RYAN HAD GREAT HOPES for her two elegant daughters, Eileen and Rosemary, and believed that they would marry well and restore her to some kind of position in Dublin society. Mr Ryan was a salesman who spent more and more time away from a home where he never felt welcome. His daughters grew up hardly knowing him except through the severe thin-lipped disappointment of their mother who managed to make sure they realised that he had let them all down. Mrs Ryan was bitterly disappointed when Eileen announced that she was going to live with a woman from work called Stephanie, and that they were lovers. And Rosemary was showing no sign at all of landing the kind of husband who might change everyone's fortunes. She had moved into a small flat as soon as she could afford to. Life at home was no fun at all but Rosemary visited her mother every week for a lecture and a harangue about her failure to deliver the goods.

'I saw that Ria coming out of the Shelbourne Hotel as if she owned it the other day,' Mrs Ryan said.

'Why don't you like her, Mother?'

'I didn't say I didn't like her, I'm just saying she played her cards right.'

'I think she played them accidentally,' Rosemary said thoughtfully. 'Ria had no idea it was all going to turn out for her as well as it did.'

'That kind always know they don't take a step without seeing where it leads. I suppose she was pregnant when she married him?'

'I don't know, Mother,' Rosemary said wearily.

'Of course you know. Still, she was lucky, he could easily have left her.'

'Would you like to come out and have lunch in Quentin's one day next week, Mother?'

'What for?'

'To cheer you up. We could get dressed up, look at all the famous people there.'

'There's no point, Rosemary. Who would know what we came from or anything about us? We'd just be two women sitting there. It's all jumped-up people these days, we'd only be on the outside looking in.'

'I have lunch there about once a week. I like it.'

'You have lunch there every week and you haven't found a husband?'

Rosemary laughed. 'I'm not going there looking for a husband. But you do see a different world there. Come on. Say yes, you'd enjoy it.'

Her mother agreed. They would go on Wednesday. It would be something to look forward to in a world that held few other pleasures.

In Quentin's Rosemary pointed out to her mother the tucked-away booth where people went when they were being discreet. A government minister and his lady friend often dined there.

'I wonder who's in there today,' her mother said.

'I'll have a peep when I go to the loo,' Rosemary promised.

At a window table she saw Barney McCarthy and Polly Callaghan. They never bothered with the private booth. Their relationship was known to everyone in the business world.

Eventually Rosemary went to the ladies' room, deliberately taking a roundabout route so that she could pass the secluded booth. With a shock that was like a physical blow Rosemary saw Danny Lynch and Orla King inside.

'Who was there?' her mother asked when Rosemary returned.

'Nobody at all, two old bankers or something.'

'Jumped-up people,' her mother said.

'Exactly,' said Rosemary.

Ria was anxious to show off the new cappuccino machine to Rosemary.

'It's magic, but I'll still have mine black,' Rosemary said, patting her slim hips.

'You have a will of iron,' Ria said, looking at her friend with admiration. Rosemary, so tall and blonde and groomed, even at the end of a day when everyone else would be flaked out. 'Barney McCarthy brought it round, he's so generous you wouldn't believe it.'

'He must think very highly of you.' Rosemary managed to lay a tea towel across her lap just in time to avoid Annie's sticky fingers getting onto her pale skirt.

'Well, of course Danny nearly kills himself working all hours. He's so tired when he gets home he often falls asleep in the chair before I can put his supper on the table for him.'

'Imagine.' Rosemary was grim.

'Still, it's well worth it, and he loves the work, and you're just the same; you don't mind how many hours you put in to be successful.'

'Ah yes, but I take time off too. I reward myself, go out to smart places as a treat.'

Ria smiled fondly at the armchair where Danny often slept after all the tiring things he had been doing. 'I think after a busy day Danny regards getting back to Number 16 Tara Road as a treat. He has everything he wants here.'

'Yes, of course he has,' said Rosemary.

Nora Johnson pushed her granddaughter up and down Tara Road in a pram, getting to know the neighbours and everyone's business. Now retired, she had settled into a compact mews at Number 48A Tara Road. Small, dark, almost birdlike, she was an authority on nearly everything. Ria was amazed how much her mother discovered about people.

'You just need to be interested, that's all,' Nora said.

In fact, as Ria knew very well, you just needed to be outrageously inquisitive and direct in your approach. Her mother told her about the Sullivan family in Number 26; he was a dentist, she ran a thrift shop. They had a daughter called Kitty just a year older than Annie, who might be a nice playmate in time.

Nora brought her clothes to Gertie's launderette for the sociability of it, she said. She knew she could use Ria's washing machine but there was a great buzz in a place like that. She said that Jack Brennan should be strung up from a lamppost and Gertie was that extraordinary mixture of half-eejit half-saint for putting up with him. Gertie's little boy John spent most of his time with his grandmother.

She reported that the big house, Number 2 on the corner, was for sale, and people said it might be a restaurant. Imagine having their own restaurant in Tara Road! Nora hoped it would be one they could all afford, not something fancy, but she doubted it.

The girls in the bank admired Rosemary Ryan. She always dressed immaculately, and she was so much on top of her business. The man who owned the print shop left her to run everything. She was only the same age as they were and look at all the power and responsibility she had managed to get for herself. They thought she sort of mildly fancied one of the clerks, Colm Barry, but then that couldn't be possible. Rosemary Ryan would want a much higher achiever than Colm Barry.

Rosemary had all her documentation done before she came to the bank each Friday. As she stood in line that Friday, to her amazement she saw Orla King in animated conversation with Colm Barry. Orla had what Rosemary considered cheap and obvious good looks. Too tight a top, too short a skirt, the heels on her shoes too high. Still, men didn't see anything too flashy in it; they appeared to like it. As Orla was leaving she called, 'Cheers, Colm, see you Tuesday night.'

'I gather that you and the lovely Ms King are going out socially,' Rosemary said to Colm, when she reached the window.

'Yes, well, that's right, sort of . . .' He was vague.

Rosemary realised that it must be at an AA meeting. People would tell you of their own involvement but they never told you who else went to the meetings. 'Anyway, it's a very small forest, Dublin, isn't it? We all find out about everyone else sooner or later.'

'What do you mean?' he asked, suddenly wary.

'I only meant if we were in London or New York we'd never know half the queue in the bank, that's all.'

'Sure. By the way, I'm leaving here at the end of the month.'

'Are you, Colm? Where are they sending you?'

'I'm brave as a lion. I'm leaving the bank altogether. I'm going to open a restaurant at Number 2 Tara Road. And as soon as I get started I'll send you an invitation to the launch.'

'Now that *is* brave. I'll tell you what I'll do, I'll print the invites for you as a present,' she said.

'It's a done deal,' he said.

Danny and Barney McCarthy were going to look at property very near Danny's old home.

'Will we all go together and take Annie to see her grandparents?' Ria suggested.

'No, love. It's not a good idea this time. I'm going to be flat out look-ing at places, and there's going to be nothing but meetings and more meetings in the hotel.'

'Well, you will go and see them?'

'I might, I might not. You know the way it's more hurtful to go in somewhere for five minutes than not to go at all.'

Ria didn't know. 'You could drive down a couple of hours earlier.'

'I have to go when Barney goes, sweetheart.'

Ria knew not to push it. 'Fine. When the weather gets better I'll drive her down to see them.'

'Would you like to drive down to the country with me to see Danny's parents?' Ria asked her mother.

'Well, maybe. Would Annie be carsick?'

'Not at all, doesn't she love going in the car? Will you make them an apple tart?'

Nora was pleased to make one, and did a lot of fancy latticework with the pastry.

Ria had written well in advance and the Lynches were expecting them. They were pleased to see little Annie, and Ria took a picture of them with her to add to the ones she had already given to them.

They had cold ham, tomatoes and shop bread for lunch, which was all they ever served. 'Will I warm up the apple tart, do you think?' Mrs Lynch asked fearfully, as if faced with an insuperable problem.

How had these timid people begotten Danny Lynch who travelled the country with Barney McCarthy, confident and authoritative, talking to businessmen and county families?

'And you were down here a few weeks ago and never told us,' Danny's father said.

'No, indeed I was not. I think Danny may have been nearby, but of course he would have to stay with Barney McCarthy all the time.' Ria was annoyed. She had known that somehow Danny's stay would get back to them. Why couldn't he have come over for an hour?

'Well, now, when I was in the creamery there, Marty was saying that his daughter works in the hotel and that the pair of you were there.'

'No, it was Barney who was with him,' Ria said patiently. 'She got it wrong.'

Ria knew what had confused the girl; Barney McCarthy must have brought Polly with him on the trip. So that's where the mistake lay.

In September 1987, shortly before Annie's fourth birthday, they were planning a party for the grown-ups in Tara Road. Danny and Ria were making the list, and Rosemary was there as she so often was.

'Remember a few millionaires for me, I'm getting to my sell-by date,' Rosemary said.

'Oh, that will be the day,' Ria laughed.

'Who is on the list?' asked Rosemary.

'Gertie,' said Ria.

'No,' protested Danny. 'That mad eejit Jack Brennan will turn up looking for a fight or a bottle of brandy or both.'

'Let him, we've coped before,' Ria said. There were the bedsitter tenants, they'd be in the house anyway, and they were nice lads. They would ask Martin and Hilary who would not come but would need the invitation. Ria's mother would come just for half an hour and stay all night. 'Barney and Mona obviously,' Ria said.

'Barney and Polly actually,' Danny said.

There was a two-second pause and then Ria wrote down Barney and Polly.

'Jimmy Sullivan, the dentist, and his wife,' Ria suggested. 'And let's ask Orla King.'

Both Danny and Rosemary frowned. 'Too drinky,' Rosemary said. 'Unreliable.'

'No, she's in AA now. But still too unpredictable,' Danny agreed.

'Well, I like her. She's fun.' Ria wrote her name down.

'We could ask Colm Barry, the fellow who's going to open a restaurant in the house on the corner,' Rosemary suggested.

'In his dreams he is,' Danny said.

'He *is*, you know, I'm doing the invitations to the first night.'

'Which may easily be his last night,' Danny said.

Rosemary was annoyed at the way he dismissed Colm. She decided to say something to irritate him. 'Let's ask Colm anyway, Ria. He has the hots for Orla King, like all those fellows who see no further than the sticky-out bosom and bum.'

Ria giggled. 'We're all turning into matchmakers, aren't we?' she said happily.

Rosemary felt a great wish to smack Ria. Very hard. There she stood, cosy and smug in her married state. She was totally confident and sure of her husband and it never occurred to her that a man like Danny would have many people attracted to him. Orla King might not be the only player on the stage. But did Ria do anything about it? Make any attempt at all to keep his interest and attention?

Of course not. She filled this big kitchen with people and casseroles and trays of fattening cakes. She polished the furniture they bought at auctions for their front room upstairs, but the beautiful round table was covered with catalogues and papers. Ria wouldn't think in a million years of lighting two candles and putting on a good dress to cook dinner for Danny and serve it there.

No, it was this big noisy kitchen with half the road passing through and Danny's armchair for him to fall asleep in when he came home from whatever the day had brought. She looked at Danny and admired his handsome smiling face. He stood there in the kitchen of his big house holding his beautiful daughter in his arms while his wife planned a party for him. A man so confident that he could take a girlfriend to within a few short miles of where his own mother and father lived. And in front of Barney McCarthy too. Rosemary had heard the laughing tale of how Ria's father-in-law had got the wrong end of the stick as usual. Why was it that some men led such lucky lives that nobody would blow a whistle on them? Things were very, very unfair.

'We must have plenty of soft drinks,' Ria said to Danny on the morning of the party.

'Sure, with people like Orla and Colm off the sauce,' he agreed.

'How did you know she was in AA?' Ria asked.

'I don't know, didn't you or Rosemary say? Someone did.'

'I didn't know; I won't say anything,' Ria said.

'Neither will I,' Danny promised her.

As it happened it was a night when Orla lapsed from her rule. She had arrived early, the first guest in fact, to find Danny Lynch and the wife that he had said meant nothing to him in a deep embrace in their kitchen. The home where Danny Lynch claimed he felt stifled was decorated, warm and welcoming. The little girl toddled around. She would be four shortly, she told everyone, and she thought that this was her party. She was constantly trying to hold her daddy's hand. This was not the scene that Orla had expected. She thought she might have one whiskey.

When Colm arrived she was already very drunk. 'Let me take you home,' he begged.

'No, I don't want anyone to preach at me,' Orla said, tears running down her face.

'I won't preach, I'll just stay with you. You'd do that for me,' he said.

'No, I wouldn't, I'd support you if your fellow was behaving like a shit. If your fellow was here and behaving like a hypocritical rat I'd have a whiskey with you, that's what I'd do.'

'I don't have a fellow.' He made a weak joke.

'You don't have anything, Colm, that's your problem.'

Colm was aware that Rosemary was beside them. He looked at her for help. 'Should we try and find whoever this fellow is that she thinks she loves?'

'No, that would be singularly inappropriate,' Rosemary said.

'Why?'

'It's the host,' she said succinctly.

'I see.' He gave a grin. 'What do you suggest?'

Rosemary wasted no time. 'A couple more drinks until she passes out.'

'I couldn't go along with that, I really couldn't.'

'OK, look the other way. I'll do it.'

'No.'

'Go, Colm. You're not helping.'

'You think I'm very weak,' he said.

'No, I don't. If you're in AA you're not meant to get a fellow member to pass out. I'll do it.' He stood aside and watched Rosemary pour a large whiskey. 'Go on, drink it, it's only tonight, Orla. One day at a time, isn't that what they say? Tomorrow you need have none. But tonight you need one.'

'I love him,' wept Orla.

'I know you do, but he's a liar, Orla. He takes you to Quentin's; he takes you down the country to hotels with Barney McCarthy and then he plays housey-housey with his wife in front of you. It's not fair.'

'How do you know all this?' Orla was round-mouthed.

'You *told* me, remember?'

'I never told you. You're Ria's friend.'

'Of course you told me, Orla. How else would I know?'

'When did I tell—?'

'A while back. Listen, come up here and sit in this alcove, it's very quiet and you and I'll have a drink.'

'I hate talking to women at parties.'

'I know, Orla, so do I. But not for long. I'll send one of those nice boys who live in this house to talk to you. They were all asking who you were.'

'Were they?'

'Yes. You don't want to waste your time on Danny Lynch.'

'You're right, Rosemary.'

Rosemary went to find the boys who rented the rooms in Danny and Ria's house.

Nora Johnson said afterwards it was amazing how much drink they put away, young fresh-faced people. And wasn't it extraordinary that young, very drunk, girl shouting at everyone. And she had gone into one of the boys' bedsitters. And what a funny chance that someone had opened the door and they had been seen in bed. Danny had said he hadn't thought that any of it was funny. Orla was obviously unused to drink and had reacted badly. She hadn't meant to go to bed with one of those kids. It was out of character for her.

'Oh, come on, Danny. She's anybody's, we all knew that back when we worked in the agency,' Rosemary said in her cool voice.

'I didn't know.' He was clipped.

'Oh, she was.' Rosemary listed half a dozen names.

Danny glowered about it all.

'Didn't you enjoy last night?' Ria looked anxiously at him.

'Yes, yes, of course I did.' But he was absent, distracted. He had been startled, frightened even, by Orla's behaviour. Barney had been unexpectedly cold and asked him to get her out quickly and quietly.

Barney never again mentioned the behaviour of Orla King at the party in Tara Road. He assumed that the relationship would now be at an end. And he assumed correctly. Danny called at Orla's flat to tell her so. He spoke very directly and left no area for doubt.

'You don't think you're going to get rid of me like that,' Orla cried. She had managed to stay sober after the upsetting events of the night in Tara Road, but this news was not helping her resolution. 'You've not done with me, Danny Lynch. I can make trouble for you.'

Gertie's sister, Sheila Maine, came home from the USA for Christmas. She and her husband Max had not been in Ireland for six years. Not since their wedding day. They now had a son, Sean, the same age as Annie. Sheila seemed astounded at how prosperous the people were, and how successful the small businesses. When she had left to go to America to seek her fortune at the age of eighteen, Ireland had been a much poorer country. 'Look what has happened in less than ten years!'

Sheila was thrilled with it all. Anything was possible in the Ireland of today. Look at all Gertie's smart friends, with their good jobs and their beautiful houses. Gertie herself was not particularly well off; her launderette was at the less smart end of Tara Road. And her husband Jack, though charming and handsome, seemed vague about his prospects. But they had a business, and a two-year-old baby boy.

Sheila wanted to know was there a good fortuneteller around. A lot of her neighbours in America went to psychics, some of them very powerful, but they wouldn't know you like an Irish woman would.

'Let's all go to Mrs Connor,' Gertie suggested.

'She didn't get things right for me years back, but I hear she's red-hot at the moment. Why not, it's an adventure, isn't it?' Rosemary agreed.

'Well, she did tell me my baby would be a girl. I know it was a fifty-fifty chance but she was right. Let's go to her,' Ria said. She had stopped taking the contraceptive pill back in September. But as yet the time had not been ripe to tell Danny.

Mrs Connor told Sheila, having heard her accent, that she lived across the sea, possibly in the United States, that she was married reasonably happily, but that she would like to live back in Ireland.

'And will I live back in Ireland?' Sheila asked beseechingly.

'Your future is in your own hands,' Mrs Connor said gravely, and somehow this cheered Sheila a lot. She considered the money well spent.

To Gertie, with her anxious eyes, Mrs Connor said that there was an element of sadness and danger in her life and she should be watchful for those she loved. Since Gertie was never anything but watchful for Jack, this seemed a good summing-up of affairs.

Rosemary sat and held out her hand. 'You were here before,' the woman said to her.

'That's right, some years back.'

'And did what I saw happen for you?'

'No, you saw me in deep trouble; unsuccessful and a bad friend. It couldn't have been more wrong. I'm in no trouble, I have lots of friends and my business is thriving. But you can't win them all.' Rosemary smiled at her, one professional woman to another.

Mrs Connor raised her eyes from the palm. 'I didn't see that, I saw you had no real friends, and that there was something you wanted which you couldn't get. That's what I still see.' Her voice was sad.

Rosemary was a little shaken. 'Well, do you see me getting married?' she asked, forcing a lightness into her voice.

'No,' Mrs Connor said.

Ria was the last to go in.

'Can you show me your palm, please, lady. We're here for you to know are you pregnant again?'

Ria's jaw fell open in amazement. 'And am I?' she said in a whisper.

'Yes, you are, lady. A little boy this time.' Ria felt a stinging behind her eyes. Mrs Connor had been right about Annie, remember, and right about Hilary having no children at all. Possibly there were ways outside the normal channels of knowing these things. She stood up as if to go. 'Don't you want to hear about your business and the travel overseas?'

'No, that's not on. That's somebody else's life creeping in on my palm,' Ria said kindly.

Mrs Connor shrugged. 'I see it, you know. A successful business, where you are very good at it and happy too.'

Ria laughed. 'Well, my husband will be pleased, I'll tell him. He's working very hard these days, he'll be glad I'm going to be a tycoon.'

'And tell him about the baby that's coming, lady. He doesn't know that yet,' said Mrs Connor, drawing her cardigan round her.

Danny was not really pleased when he heard the news. 'This was something we said we would discuss together, sweetheart.'

'I know, but there never is time to discuss anything, Danny, you work so hard.'

'Well, isn't that all the more reason we *should* discuss things? Barney's so stretched these days, money is tight, and some of the projects have huge risk attached to them. We might not be able to *afford* another baby.'

'Be reasonable. How much is a baby going to cost? We have all the baby things for him. We don't have to get a cot, a pram or any of the things that cost money.' She was stung with disappointment.

'Ria, it's not that I don't want another child—it's just that this isn't the best time. In three or four years we could afford it better.'

'We won't have to pay anything for him, I tell you, until he is three or four.'

'Stop calling it him, Ria. We can't know at this stage.'

'I know already.'

'Because of some fortuneteller! Sweetheart, will you give me a break?'

'She was right about my being pregnant. I went to the doctor next day.'

'So much for joint decisions.'

'Danny, that's not fair. That's the most unfair thing I ever heard. Do I ask to be part of all the decisions you make for this house? I do bloody not. I don't know when you're going to be in or out, when Barney McCarthy will come and closet himself with you for hours. I don't know if we are to see his wife or his mistress with him each time he turns up. I don't ask to discuss if I can go out to work again, and let Mam look after Annie for us, because you like the house comfortable for you whatever time you come home. And I don't take the pill for a bit and suddenly it's a matter of joint decisions. Where are the other joint decisions, I ask you? Where are they?' The tears were running down her face. The delight in the new life that was starting inside her seemed wiped out.

Danny looked at her in amazement. His own face crumpled as he realised the extent of her loneliness and how much she had felt excluded. 'I can't tell you how sorry I am. I truly can't tell you how cheap and selfish I feel listening to you.' He buried his face in her and she stroked his head with sounds of reassurance. 'And I'm delighted we're having a little boy. And suppose the little boy's a little girl like Annie, I'll be delighted with that too.'

Brian was born on June 15 and this time Danny was beside Ria and holding her hand.

Annie said to everyone that she was quite pleased with her new brother, but not *very* pleased. This made people laugh so she said it over and over. Brian was all right, she said, but he couldn't talk and he took up a lot of Mum and Dad's time. Still, Dad had assured her again and again that she was his little princess, the only princess he would ever have or want. And Mam had said that Annie was the very best girl not only in Ireland, or Europe, but on Earth and quite possibly the planets as well. So Annie Lynch didn't have anything to worry about.

Gertie's baby Katy was born just after Brian, and Sheila Maine's daughter Kelly around the same time. Gertie didn't bring her two children to Tara Road. The atmosphere in Ria's home was so different from their own. A big kitchen where everyone gathered, something always cooking in the big stove, the smell of newly baked cinnamon cakes or fresh herb bread.

Not like Gertie's flat where nothing was ever left out on the gas cooker. Just in case it might coincide with one of the times that Jack was upset. Because if Jack was upset it could be thrown at anyone. But Gertie came on her own to Number 16 from time to time and did a little housework for Ria. Anything that would give her the few pounds that Jack didn't know about. Just something that might tide them over if there was trouble.

Rosemary's business was now very high profile. She was often photographed at the races, gallery openings or at theatre first nights. She dressed very well and she kept her clothes immaculately. Whenever she visited Ria's house, Ria had taken to offering her a housecoat to wear in case the children smeared her with whatever they had their hands in.

'Come on, that's going a bit far,' Rosemary laughed the first time.

'No, it isn't. I'm the one who'd have to spend years apologising if they got ice cream or puréed carrots all over that gorgeous cream wool. Put it on, Rosemary, and give me some peace.'

Rosemary thought they could have more peace if they went upstairs to that magnificent front room and drank their wine there rather than being in what was like a giant playpen with children's toys and things all over the floor and Ria leaping up to stir things and lift more and more trays of baking out of the oven. But it was useless to try and change her ways. Ria believed that the world revolved around her family and her kitchen.

Danny saw her in the pink nylon coat and was annoyed. 'Rosemary, you don't need to dress up to play with the children.'

'Your wife's idea,' Rosemary shrugged.

'I didn't want them messing up her lovely clothes.'

'Wait till she has kids of her own,' Danny said darkly. 'Then we'll see some messed-up clothes.'

'I wouldn't bet on it, Danny,' Rosemary said. Her smile was bright, but she felt that she was being put under a lot of pressure from all sides. It wasn't enough to look well, dress well, and run a successful business. Apparently there was no such thing as a private life in this city.

Rosemary resented the excessive interest people had in marrying others off. Why was she not allowed to have a lover that no one knew of, or indeed a series of them? She was successful and glamorous but so what? You had to find a mate and breed children as well, otherwise it counted for nothing in people's eyes.

'Why don't you sign up with a marriage agency?' Ria said now, unexpectedly.

'You have to be joking me! Now you've joined them all.'

'No, I mean it. At least you'd meet the right kind of person, someone who wants to settle down.'

Rosemary met Polly Callaghan at several gatherings. Their paths would cross at press receptions and the openings of art galleries or even at the theatre. 'Did you ever think of a marriage agency? No, I'm not joking, someone suggested it to me as a reasonable option.'

'Depends on what you want, I suppose.' Polly took the suggestion seriously. 'You don't look like the kind of woman who wants to be dependent on a man.'

'No, I don't think I am,' Rosemary said thoughtfully.

Rosemary invited as many influential people as she could rustle up to come to the opening of Colm Barry's restaurant.

Ria was disappointed that Danny would not try to do the same. 'You know an awful lot of people through Barney,' she said pleadingly.

'Sweetheart, let's wait until it's a success, then we'll invite lots of people there.'

'But it's now he needs them otherwise how else will it *be* a success?'

'I don't suppose for a moment that Colm is expecting the charity of his friends. In fact he'd probably find that just a little patronising.'

Ria didn't agree and she said as much to Rosemary.

'Now don't be so quick to attack him. He may be right in a way. Much more useful to take business people there for meals when it's up and running.' Rosemary spoke soothingly, but in reality she knew very well why Danny Lynch didn't want to go to the opening. Danny knew that Orla King was going to sit at a piano in the background and sing well-established favourites. She had proved herself once to be a loose cannon on the deck, and unpredictability was the last thing Danny Lynch wanted around him. Especially since Barney McCarthy's finances had taken such a battering recently and there were rumours of much speculative building to try and recoup the losses.

Rosemary went to the opening night and reported that it had been very successful. Colm devised the menus and did most of the cooking himself; he had a *sous-chef*, a waiter, a washer-up and his sister Caroline to help him. A lot of the customers had been neighbours; it boded well for the future.

'This really is a great area, you two were very lucky to come in here when you did,' Rosemary said approvingly. 'Isn't it a pity that there aren't any proper apartments or mews flats around here? I could become your neighbour! What I need is a little house just like the one your mother has, Ria, or a penthouse with a nice view. I'd like a roof garden if possible. Keep an eye out for me, Danny; it doesn't have to be Tara Road, somewhere nearby.'

'I'll get it for you,' Danny promised.

In three weeks he came back with news of two properties. Neither owner was willing to build. It would be a question of Barney McCarthy buying the building, his men doing the renovation and, subject to planning permission, getting a penthouse-style apartment custom-built for Rosemary. They could start drawing up plans as soon as she liked.

Danny expected Rosemary to be very pleased, but she was cool. 'We are talking about an outright buy not just renting? And I could see the titles for all the other flats in the house?'

'Well, yes,' Danny said.

'And my architect and surveyor could look at the plans?'

'Yes, of course.'

'And inspect the building specifications and work throughout?'

'I don't see why not.'

'What's the word on a roof garden?'

'If there's not too much heavy earth brought up there the structural engineers say that both houses could take the load.'

Rosemary smiled one of her all-embracing smiles that lit up the room. 'Well, Danny, that's great, lead me to the properties,' she said.

'So Lady Ryan is going to grace us with her presence in the road,' Nora Johnson said. She had come to introduce the new element in her life, a puppy of indeterminate breed. It seemed to have too many legs yet there were only four; its head looked as if it were bigger than its body but that could not possibly be so.

'Does it have a name, Mam?' Ria asked.

'Oh it's just 32, no fancy name.'

'You're going to call the dog Thirty-Two?' Ria was astounded.

'No, I mean where Lady Ryan's penthouse is being built. The dog is called Pliers, I told you that.' She hadn't but it didn't matter. 'They all know she's coming to Tara Road, everyone's heard of her.'

Rosemary Ryan was featuring now in the financial press. The printing company was going from strength to strength and had taken on several foreign contracts. They printed picture postcards for some of the major tourist resorts in the Mediterranean, they had successfully tendered for sporting events as far afield as the West Coast of America. Rosemary had bought shares in the firm and it was only a matter of time before she would take it over entirely. The man who had employed her as a young girl to help in a very small print shop looked in amazement at the confident poised woman who had transformed his business.

When Gertie had another 'accident' her mother took the children back to live with her. 'You think I'm doing this for you, but I'm not, I'm doing it for those two defenceless children that you and that drunken sot managed to produce.'

'You're not helping me, Mam.'

'I am helping. I'm taking two children out of a possible death-house. If you were a normal woman instead of half crazed yourself you'd be able to realise that what I'm doing is helping you. Indeed I don't understand, two terrified little children who jump at the slightest sound, and you won't get a barring order and throw that lout out of their lives.'

'You're the religious one, you believe in a vow, for better for worse. We'd all stay when it's for better, it's when it's for worse it's harder.'

'It's harder on a lot of people all right.' Her mother's mouth was a thin hard line as she packed John and Katy's things for yet another trip to their granny's in their disturbed young lives.

'**I**t's all taking longer than we thought,' Rosemary said.

'Look at the contract, you'll see there are contingency clauses,' Danny laughed.

'*You* covered your back, didn't you?' She was admiring.

'No more than you did.'

'I just insured against shoddy workmanship.'

'And I just insured against wet weather, which indeed we had,' he said.

Ria was cutting out pastry shapes at the kitchen table with the children. Brian just wanted them round, Annie liked to shape hers.

'What are they talking about?' Brian asked.

'Daddy and Rosemary are talking business,' Annie explained.

'Why are they talking it in the kitchen? The kitchen's for playing in,' Brian said loudly.

'He's right,' said Rosemary. 'Let's take all these papers up to the beautiful room upstairs. If I had a room like that I wouldn't let it grow cold and musty like an old-fashioned parlour, I tell you that for nothing.'

Good-naturedly Danny carried the papers upstairs.

Ria stood with her hands floury and her eyes stinging. How *dare* Rosemary make her feel like that? Tomorrow she would make sure that that room was never again allowed to lie idle.

'Are you OK, Mam?' Annie asked.

'Sure I am, of course.'

'Would you like to be in business too?'

For no reason Ria remembered the fortuneteller, Mrs Connor, prophesying that she would run a successful company or something. 'Not really, darling,' Ria said. 'But thanks all the same for asking.'

The next day Gertie came. She looked very tired and had huge black circles under her eyes.

'Don't start on at me. *Please*, Ria.'

'I hadn't a notion of it, we all lead our own lives.'

'Well, that's a change in the way the wind blows, I'm very glad to say.'

'Gertie, I want us both to tidy the front room, air it and polish it up properly.'

'Is anyone coming?' Gertie asked innocently.

'No,' Ria answered crisply. Gertie paused and looked at her. 'Sorry,' said Ria.

'OK, you're kind enough not to ask me my business, I won't ask you yours.'

They worked in silence, Gertie doing the brass on the fender, Ria rubbing beeswax into the chairs. Ria put down her cloth. 'It's just I feel so useless, so wet and stupid.'

'*You* do?' Gertie was amazed.

'I do. We have this gorgeous room and we never sit in it.' Gertie looked at her thoughtfully. Someone had upset Ria. It wasn't her mother; Nora Johnson's stream of consciousness just washed over her all the time. Hilary talked about nothing except the cost of this and the price of that; Ria wasn't going to get put down by her own sister. It had to be Rosemary. Gertie opened her mouth and closed it again. Ria would never hear a word against her friend; there was nothing Gertie could say that would be helpful.

'Well, don't you agree it's idiotic?' Ria asked.

Gertie spoke slowly. 'You know, compared to what I have this whole house is a palace, and everyone respects it. That would be enough for me. But on top of all that you and Danny went out and found all this beautiful furniture. And maybe you're right . . . you *should* use this room more. Why not start tonight?'

'I'd be afraid the children would pull it to bits.'

'No, they won't. Make it into a sort of a treat for them to come up here. Like a halfway house to bed or something. If they're beautifully behaved here they can stay up a bit longer. Do you think that might work?' Gertie's eyes were enormous in her dark haunted face.

Ria wanted to cry. 'That's a great idea,' she said.

'Barney's coming round for a drink before dinner this evening, we'll go to my study,' Danny said.

'Why don't you go to the front room instead? Gertie and I cleaned it up today and it looks terrific.'

Together they went up to the room. The six o'clock sunshine was slanting in through the window. There were flowers on the mantelpiece.

'It's almost as if you were psychic. This won't be an easy discussion so it'll be good to have it in a nice place.'

'Nothing wrong?' She was anxious.

'Not really, just the perpetual Barney McCarthy cash-flow problem.'

'Is it best if I just keep the kids downstairs out of the way?'

'That would be terrific, sweetheart.' He looked tired and strained.

Barney came at seven and left at eight.

Ria had the children tidy and ready for bed. When they heard the hall door close they came up the stairs together, all three of them, the children slightly tentative. This room wasn't part of their territory. They sat and played a game of snakes and ladders. They played it carefully as if it were a very important game. When the children were going to bed, for once without protest, Danny hugged them both very tight.

'You make everything worth while, all of you,' he said in a slightly choked voice.

Ria said she would be up to see that they had brushed their teeth. 'Was it bad?'

'No, not bad at all. Typical Barney, must have everything this minute. Overextended himself yet again. He's desperate to make Number 32 a real show house, you know. It's going to be his flagship, people will take him seriously with this one. It's just that it's costing a packet.'

'So?'

'So he needed a personal guarantee, you know, putting this house up as collateral.'

'*This* house?'

'Yes, his own are all in the frame already.'

'And what did you say?' Ria was frightened. Barney was a gambler; they could lose everything if he went down.

'I told him we owned it jointly, that I'd ask you.'

'Well, you'd better ring him straight away and say that I said it's fine,' she said.

'Do you mean that?'

'Listen, we wouldn't have had this place without him. You should have told me earlier. Ring him on his mobile.'

That night after they had made love Ria couldn't sleep. Suppose the cash-flow problem was serious this time. Suppose they lost their beautiful home. Danny lay beside her in an untroubled sleep. Several times she looked at his face and by the time dawn came she knew that even if they did lose the house it wouldn't matter, just as long as she didn't lose him.

Danny spent a lot of time on Number 32. Sometimes, Ria felt, too much time. The property had been gutted and the long top-floor apartment had a wraparound roof garden with a view stretching out towards the Dublin mountains. At night it would look magnificent with all the city lights in between. The interior was cool and spare, a lot of empty wall space, pale wooden floors, kitchen fittings that were uncluttered and minimalist.

It was about as unlike Ria's house as anyone could imagine. Ria fought to like the clean lines seen in the artist's impressions, and as the project proceeded she visited the site often and forced out words of praise for a place that seemed to her like a modern art gallery.

'If we get the right kind of tenants in here Barney's home and dry,' Danny told Ria. 'He's into the prestige end of things not the mickey mouse conversion. We need a good write-up in the property pages, and Rosemary can organise that. We need a politician, a showbiz person or a sports star to buy the other flats. We want the word to get about. I asked Colm to tell the nobs who come into his restaurant, but sadly his brother-in-law Monto Mackey is the only one who came enquiring.'

'Monto and Caroline want to live in a flat in Tara Road?'

'I didn't think he'd have the cash but he does. And cash is what he offered, suitcases of it.'

'No!' Ria was astounded. Colm's beautiful but withdrawn sister was married to an unattractive car dealer, a large, florid man interested more in going to race meetings than in his wife.

'Barney was delighted, of course, always a man for the suitcase of money, but I convinced him that it was quality we wanted here, not dross like Monto Mackey.'

'I wonder could I clean for Rosemary, do you think?' Gertie asked Ria.

'Gertie, you run a business, you haven't time to go out cleaning for people. You don't *have* to either.'

'I do.' Gertie was short.

'But who's looking after the launderette?'

'It looks after itself. I have kids in there doing it for me. I make much more per hour cleaning than I pay them.'

'That's ludicrous.'

'Has she got anyone already to clean?'

'Ask her, Gertie.'

'No, Ria, you ask her for me, will you? As a friend?' said Gertie.

'Of course I won't have Gertie cleaning for me. She should be managing that run-down washeteria and minding her children.'

'Rosemary, go on, you need someone you can trust.'

'I'll have a firm, contract cleaners twice a week.'

And that was it as far as Rosemary was concerned. She was now much more interested in creating her garden. The trellis arrived and was erected immediately. Days later the instant climbers in containers were carried upstairs.

'Lots of roses, of course,' Rosemary explained to Ria. '"Blush Rambler", that's a nice pink here on this side and "Muscosa" and "Madame Pierre Oger", all on this side. I thought I'd go for blocks of colour, more dramatic to look out at.'

She gave a housewarming party. Ria knew hardly anybody there; Danny and Barney knew a few. Polly was in attendance that night, so Ria had to be sure not to mention the party to Mona. Colm had hoped that he might tender to do the catering but Rosemary had chosen some other firm. 'Clients, you know,' she said lightly, as if that covered everything.

There were photographers there and Rosemary was photographed with a politician. Barney and Danny were taken with an actress, out on the roof garden with a bank of flowers and a panoramic view in the background. Rosemary was on the financial pages, the others on the property pages. Enquiries about Number 32 Tara Road came flooding in. Everyone was happy.

Ria didn't often take Brian up to Rosemary's apartment. He was three now; he upset the calm of the place with his endless noise and perpetual toddling and constant sticky hugs and demands for attention. Annie wouldn't have wanted to come. There was nothing to entertain her at Rosemary's and too many areas that seemed off limits.

'You *must* bring the children with you,' Rosemary would insist. But Ria knew that it was easier not to, so she left the children with her mother on one of the many Saturday afternoons that Danny was working, and walked up to see Rosemary on her own. It was so peaceful and elegant, as if she hadn't unmade a bed, cooked a meal, or done any washing since the day it had been shown off at the housewarming. Even the roof garden looked as if every flower had been painted into place.

They would sit on the terrace with their feet up, and the heavy scent of the flowers all around them. Maybe if their place was less untamed and wild, she and Danny could sit like this on a Saturday afternoon and watch the children play. Maybe they could just talk to each other, read the papers together sometimes.

'Is there a lot of work keeping all this the way it is?'

'No, I hired a man from a garden centre. He comes once a week for a few hours. When I bought this flat I bought up part of the garden at the back of the house as well. There's a summerhouse near the back entrance where he stores a few tools. He's cultivated a herbaceous border down there, but up here the whole trick was to make the garden labour-saving. Just nice easycare shrubs which sort of bring themselves up.' It always seemed so effortless when Rosemary described things.

As she walked down Tara Road she thought what a lovely road it was just as the summer was starting. The cherry trees were in bloom everywhere, their petals starting to make a pink carpet. Ria never stopped marvelling at the variety of life you could find in the Road—houses where students lived in great numbers in small flats and bedsitters, their bicycles up against the railings just as they had been outside their own house until this year when Danny and Ria had been able to reclaim all the rented rooms for themselves. If she turned right outside Rosemary's house the road would go past equally mixed housing, high houses like their own, lower ones half hidden by trees, then on past the small lock-up workshop where the road changed again into big houses in their own grounds until it came to the corner with a busy street. And round the corner to where Gertie lived and worked, where the handy launderette had plenty of clientele among the bedsitterland around.

Her mind full of gardens, Ria noticed that almost every house had made more effort than they had. But it was so hard to know where to start. Some of that undergrowth needed to be cut down, but then what?

Colm Barry called when Ria and Hilary were having lunch. 'Well, you two don't stint yourselves, I'm glad to see.' He seemed happy to accept their invitation to join them.

'Oh, Ria can afford to buy the best cuts of meat,' Hilary said, reverting to type.

'It's what she does with them that's so delicious.' Colm appreciated the cooking. 'And the way they're served.'

'It's hard to get good fresh vegetables round here,' Ria said.

'Why don't you grow your own?' Colm suggested.

'Oh Lord, no. It would be such hard work digging it all out back there. Neither Danny nor I have the souls of gardeners, I'm afraid.'

'I'd do it for you at the back if you like,' Colm offered.

'Oh, you can't do that,' Ria protested.

'I have an ulterior motive. Suppose I was to make a proper kitchen garden out there and grow all the things I want for the restaurant in it, then you could have some too.'

'Great, then we'll do it,' Ria said with pleasure.

And from that time on Colm became part of the background in their house in Tara Road. He let himself in silently through the wooden door that opened onto the back lane; he kept his gardening tools in a small makeshift hut at the back. He dug an area half the width of the house and the whole length of the garden. This left plenty of space for the children to play in.

'It really looks rather nice you know,' Danny said thoughtfully one day. 'And the whole notion of mature kitchen garden at rear is a good selling point.'

'If we were to sell, which we're not going to do. I wish you wouldn't frighten me saying things like that, Danny,' Ria complained.

'Listen, sweetheart, if you worked in a world where hardly anything else is discussed then you'd talk in auctioneer-speak too.' He was right, and what's more he was good-tempered and happy. He was very loving to Ria sometimes, dashing home from work saying he thought of her so much that he couldn't concentrate on anything else. They would go upstairs and draw the curtains. Once or twice Ria wondered what Colm working in the garden might think.

The anxiety over the McCarthy finances seemed to have subsided. Danny didn't work so late at night. He took his little princess, Annie, out on walks and visits to the sea. He held the hand of his chubby son Brian as the child changed from stumbling to waddling and eventually to running away ahead of them.

The back garden changed slowly and laboriously. Ria tried to sympathise when all Colm's sprouts failed, when his great bamboo bean supports blew down in the wind and when the peas that he had tried to grow in hanging baskets produced hardly anything at all.

On the other side there was a swing, a garden seat and a homemade barbecue pit.

Brian was seven in June 1995. Danny and Ria were going to have a barbecue for his friends. They only wanted sausages, Brian said.

'Not lovely lamb chops?' Danny asked.

'Ugh,' Brian said.

'Or those lovely green peppers Colm grew, we could thread them all on a skewer and make kebabs.'

'My friends don't like kebabs,' Brian said.

'Your friends have never had kebabs,' Annie said. She was close to being twelve, only four months away. It was really hard having to deal with someone as infantile as Brian.

The arrangements for his party were very tedious. Annie had suggested giving Brian two pounds of cooked sausages and letting all his friends heat them up on the barbecue. They'd never know the difference and all they cared about was lots of tomato ketchup.

'No, it must be right. We had a great party for your seventh birthday, don't you remember?' her mother said.

Annie didn't remember, all the birthdays had merged into one. But she knew that they must have made a fuss over it like over all celebrations. 'That's right, it was terrific,' she said grudgingly.

'You are beautiful, Annie Lynch, you're an adorable girl.' Her mother hugged her until it hurt.

'I'm awful, look at my desperate straight hair.'

'And I spend my life saying look at my frizzy hair,' Ria said. 'It's a very annoying part of being a woman, we're never really satisfied with the way we look.'

'Some people are.'

'Oh, all the film stars your gran goes on about, all these beauties, I expect they're happy with themselves, but nobody we know.'

'I'd say that Rosemary is OK with the way she looks. She sort of smiles at herself, Mam. Not only in mirrors, but in pictures, anywhere there's glass. It's true, isn't it, Dad?'

'Totally true, Princess,' said Danny.

'You didn't hear what was said,' they both accused him.

'Yes, I did. Annie said Rosemary smiles at her reflection in mirrors and indeed she does, always has.'

Annie looked pleased, Ria felt put out. It was such a criticism of her friend and she had never been aware of it. 'Well, she's so good-looking she's entitled to admire herself,' she said eventually.

'Good-looking? I think she's like a bird of prey,' Annie said.

'A handsome bird of prey, though,' Danny corrected her.

'Mam looks much better,' Annie said.

'That goes without saying,' Danny said, kissing each of them on the tops of their heads.

Nora Johnson came into the kitchen from the front garden. 'I've been tying the balloons to the front gate so that they'll know where the party is and I see Lady Ryan coming down the road wearing a designer outfit.'

Ria went out to greet Rosemary who had bought a great amount of individually wrapped chocolate ice creams which were at home in her freezer. 'I'll come back in an hour so you don't have to bother putting them into your freezer. Will Annie help to entertain the boys when they get here?'

'No, I don't think entertaining a dozen seven-year-old boys is Annie's idea of a good summer afternoon. She'll keep her distance. Danny has a whole lot of games planned for them.'

Rosemary laughed admiringly and went back to Number 32 to change into something more suitable for a children's party.

The party guests had begun to arrive. Very soon they were punching each other good-naturedly. There didn't seem to be any reason for this, no real aggression, that was the way boys behaved. Annie's friends were much gentler, Ria said to her mother as they separated one pair of warring boys before they crashed into Colm's vegetable garden.

'Where *is* Annie, by the way?'

'In her room, I think.'

Annie was not in her room as it happened, she had gone out of the back gate and was walking up the lane that ran parallel to Tara Road. She had seen a small thin ginger kitten there the other day. It had looked frightened, not as if it was used to being petted. Perhaps it was abandoned and she might keep it. Annie tried to remember which was the back gate where she had seen the little kitten. It wasn't as far up the road as Rosemary's.

She stood in the lane in her blue check summer dress squinting into the afternoon sun, pushing her straight blonde hair out of her eyes. Perhaps she could peep through the keyholes of these wooden doors. Some of them were quite rickety and it was easy to see through the cracks anyway. One of the back gates was a smart painted wooden door you couldn't see through at all. Annie stood back a little. This must be Number 32 where Rosemary Ryan lived.

She had a garden upstairs on the roof and a summerhouse in the back garden, which faced away from the house and towards the back wall. This might well be where the kitten had wandered.

Annie knelt down and looked in the keyhole. No sign of a cat. But there were people in the summerhouse. They seemed to be fighting over something. She looked more carefully. It was Rosemary Ryan struggling with a man. Annie's heart leapt into her throat. Was she being attacked? Rosemary had her skirt right up round her waist, and the man was pushing at her. With an even greater shock than the first one Annie realised what they were doing. But this wasn't the way it was done. Not what people almost did at the cinema and on television. That was different. They kissed each other and lay down, it was all gentle. It wasn't like this, all this shoving and grunting.

Annie pulled back from the keyhole, her heart racing. She hadn't seen who the man was; he had had his back to her. All she had seen was Rosemary's face. All screwed up and angry, upset. Not dreamy like it was in the movies. Maybe she had got it totally wrong, this mightn't be what they were doing at all. Annie looked once more.

Rosemary's arms were round the man's neck, her eyes were closed, she wasn't pushing him away, she was pulling him towards her.

Annie straightened up in horror. She couldn't believe what she had seen. She started to run down the lane. When passing Number 16 she could hear the noise coming from Brian's party. But she didn't stop. On she ran, tears blinding her eyes until, just as she was getting to the main road and back to normality, she fell. One of those unexpected falls where the earth just jumped up to meet you with a thud.

It winded her totally and she had trouble in getting her breath. When she struggled to stand she saw she had grazed both knees as well as an arm. She leaned against the wall of the end house and sobbed.

Colm heard the noise and came out. 'Annie, what happened?' No reply, just heaving shoulders. 'Annie, I'll run and get your mother.'

'No. Please don't. *Please*, Colm. Brian's having a party, I don't want to go home.'

Colm took this on board. 'You could come into my house, into the bathroom and wash your poor knees. Then I'll give you a nice lemonade or whatever you like in my restaurant.' He smiled at her.

It worked. 'Yes, I'd like that, Colm.'

Together they went in and he showed her the bathroom. 'There are facecloths there, and if I put a little Dettol in the water . . .' She seemed helpless, unsure of how to start. 'If you like I could dab them for you, take any grit out?'

'I don't know . . .'

'Would I stay here while you do it, and tell you if I see more bits that need to be done?'

He got the first smile. 'That would be great.' He watched while the child touched her knees tentatively with the diluted disinfectant, and wiped away all the grit and earth. 'I can't reach my elbow, will you do that, Colm?'

Gently he cleaned her arm and handed her a big fluffy towel. 'Now, pat it all dry.'

'There might be spots of blood on the towel.' She looked anxious.

'All the more work for Gertie's launderette then.' He smiled.

They went into the cool dark bar of his restaurant. At the bar there were four high stools. He gestured her to one of them. 'Now, Miss Lynch, what's your pleasure?' he said.

'What do you think is nice, Colm?'

'What I always have is a St Clement's. It's a mixture of orange and lemon. How does that sound?'

'Great. I'd like that,' said Annie. 'Do you not drink real drinks then?'

'No, they don't suit me.'

'Do you miss not being able to drink real drinks?'

'Well, I suppose I wish I was the way other people are—you know, having a nice glass of wine or two of an evening. But I'm not able to stop after that so I can't start.' Annie looked sympathetic. 'However, there are lots of things I can do that others can't,' Colm said cheerfully. 'I can make wonderful sauces and great desserts.'

'Brian's awful friends want ice creams in silver-paper wrappers! Imagine!' Annie's laugh had a slightly hysterical tinge in it.

'Nothing happened out in the lane to make you fall, did it?' Colm asked.

The child's expression was guarded. 'No. Why?'

'No reason. Listen, will I walk home with you now?'

'I'm all right, really, Colm.'

'Of course you are, don't we know that? But I have to go for a walk every day, all chefs must, it's a kind of rule, stops them getting big stomachs that keep falling into their saucepans.'

Annie laughed. It wasn't possible to think of Colm Barry having a tummy like that. He was nearly as slim as Dad. They set off together. Just as they came to the front of the house they saw Rosemary Ryan unloading the ice creams in a cool-bag from the back of her car. Annie stiffened. Colm noticed but said nothing.

'Heavens, Annie, what terrible cuts! Did you fall?'

'Yes. On the road in front of Colm's restaurant,' Annie said quickly.

Colm was surprised.

'You were lucky you didn't fall in front of the traffic.' Rosemary had lost interest in it, now she was hauling out the boxes of ice creams. They could hear the shouting and screaming of Brian's friends from the back garden. 'My public is waiting for me and the ice cream,' Rosemary laughed. 'I think we know which they are waiting for more.' She moved ahead of them through the basement and out to the back.

'Thanks, Colm,' Annie said.

'Don't mention it.'

'It's just that it's . . . well, it's nobody's business really where I fell, is it?'

'Absolutely not.'

'So thanks for the St Clement's and everything.'

'I'll see you around, Annie.'

Ria's mother was in the kitchen. She had kept sausages for Annie. 'I couldn't find you so I put them in the oven to keep warm.'

'You're great.'

'The boys are about to have the cake. Lady Ryan arranged sparklers.'

'Mam hates it when you call her that.' Annie giggled and then she winced at the pain in her elbow.

Her grandmother was full of concern. 'Let me wash that for you.'

'It's OK, Gran, it's done, Dettol and all.' She moved to the window. 'Look at Auntie Hilary with all those awful boys.'

'She loves them, she's brought a big dartboard where you throw rings on. There's fierce competition.'

'Why didn't Auntie Hilary have any children, Gran?'

'The Lord didn't send her any, that's all.'

'Maybe she didn't like mating,' Annie said thoughtfully.

'What?' Nora Johnson was at a loss for words.

'There must be some people who just don't like the thought of it. I bet that's it. You could ask her.'

'It's not the thing you ask people, Annie, believe me.'

'I do, Gran. There are some things you don't talk about at all, you just put away at the back of your mind. Isn't that right?'

'Absolutely right,' her grandmother said.

Later on the parents of Brian's friends came to collect their sons, and they stood in the warm summer evening in the back garden of Tara Road. Annie watched her mother and father stand there in the centre of the group, passing round a tray of wine and little smoked salmon sandwiches. Dad's arm was round Mam's shoulder a lot of the time. Annie knew from the girls at school that parents still want to make love and all that, even when they didn't want children. It seemed horrible.

4

ANNIE HAD THIS GIFT TOKEN from her grandmother. It was for more money than she had ever spent before on clothes. Up to now Annie had only bought shoes, jeans and T-shirts on her own. But this was different, it was for something to wear for all the parties this summer. It had seemed normal for Ria to go with her and help her choose. It had even seemed like fun. That was some hours ago. Now it seemed like the most foolish thing either of them had ever done in their lives.

When Annie had looked at something with leather and chains, Ria had gasped aloud. 'I knew you were going to be like that,' Annie cried.

'No, I mean, it's just . . . I thought . . .' Ria was wordless.

'*What* did you think? Go on, Mam, say what you thought, don't just stand there gulping.' Annie's face was red and angry.

'Why don't you try it on?' Ria said weakly.

'If you think I'm going to put it on now that I've seen your face, and let you make fun of me . . .'

'Annie, I'm not making fun of you. We don't know what it looks like until you put it on, and it's your token.'

'I know it is. Gran gave it to me to buy something I liked, not some awful revolting thing you want me to wear.'

'No, no. Be reasonable, Annie. I haven't steered you towards anything at all, have I?'

'But you never look. You never look at anything or anyone, otherwise you wouldn't wear the kind of clothes you do.'

'Look, I know you don't want the same clothes as I do.'

'*Nobody* wants the same clothes as you do, Mam. I mean, have you thought about it for one minute?'

Ria looked in one of the many mirrors around. She saw reflected a flushed angry teenager, slim with straight blonde hair, holding what appeared to be a bondage garment. Beside her was a tired-looking woman with a great head of frizzy hair tumbling onto her shoulders, wearing a black V-neck sweater over a flowing, black and white skirt. She had put on comfortable flat shoes for shopping. It had all looked fine in the hall mirror at home. It didn't look great here.

'I mean, it's not even as if you are really old,' Annie said. 'Lots of people your age haven't given up.'

With great difficulty Ria forced herself not to take her daughter by the hair and drag her from the shop. When had it happened, whatever it was that made Annie hate her, scorn her? They used to get on so well.

Ria made one more superhuman effort. 'Listen, it's *your* treat, your gran wants you to get something nice and suitable.'

'No, she doesn't, Mam. Do you never listen? She said I was to get whatever I wanted, she never said one word about it being suitable.' Annie turned away with tears in her eyes.

Nearby a woman and her daughter were looking through a rail of shirts. 'They must have a pink one,' the girl was saying excitedly. 'Come on, we'll ask the assistant. You look terrific in pink.'

Ria turned away so that nobody could see the tears of envy in her eyes. Would Annie think she was sulking if she left her now? Would she be relieved? 'Annie, you know your father arranged that a sanding machine be delivered today?' she began tentatively. Danny had had the peculiar idea to take up their carpets and bring out the beauty of the wooden floors. They didn't look a bit beautiful to her, but Danny knew about these things.

'Mam, I'm *not* spending the weekend doing that, it's not fair.'

'No, no, I wasn't going to suggest it. I was going to say I should go home and be there when they arrive, but I don't want to abandon you.' Annie stared at her wordlessly. 'Not that I'm much help, really. I'm inclined to get confused when I see a lot of clothes together,' Ria said.

Annie's face changed. Suddenly she reached out and gave her mother an unexpected hug. 'You're not the worst, Mam,' she said grudgingly. From Annie this was high, high praise these days.

Ria went home with a lighter heart. She had just got in the door of her house in Tara Road when she heard the gate rattle and the familiar cry: 'Ree-ya, Ree-ya'. It was her mother and the dog, the misshapen Pliers. Nora Johnson bustled in, sure as always of her welcome. Hadn't she called out from the gate to say she was on her way?

Ria Lynch's kitchen was a place with a welcome. So unlike the way things had been when Ria was young herself and nobody was allowed out to their kitchen, a dark murky place with its torn linoleum on the floor. Visitors weren't encouraged to come to her mother's house at all.

It had been the same in Danny's family. To this day his parents didn't mix with neighbours or friends, they held no family gatherings. Ria looked around with pride at her big cheerful kitchen where there was always life and company, and where she presided over everything.

Danny seemed delighted to see his mother-in-law when he came into the kitchen and gave her a big hug. He wore a blue sports shirt that he had bought for himself when he was in London. It was the kind of thing that Ria would never have chosen for him in a million years, yet she had to admit it made him look impossibly young. Perhaps she *was* the worst in the world at choosing clothes.

'Nora, I know why you're here, you came to help with the sanding,' Danny said. 'Not only do you give our daughter a small fortune for clothes but now you're coming to help us do the floors.'

'I did not, Danny. I came to leave poor Pliers with you for an hour while I go and visit the old folks down at St Rita's.'

'You must drive the old fellows mad down there, a young spring chicken like yourself coming in to dazzle them,' Danny said.

'Go on with your flattery, Danny.' But Nora Johnson loved it. Pleased, she patted her hair and bustled out again, smart and trim in her suit. 'Your mother's wearing well,' Danny said. 'We'll be lucky to look as spry at her age.'

'I'm sure we will. And aren't you like a boy rather than a man free-wheeling down to forty,' Ria laughed. But Danny didn't laugh back. That had been the wrong thing to say. Foolish Ria, to have made a joke that annoyed him. She pretended not to have noticed her mistake. 'And look at me, you said that when you met me first you took a good look at my mother before you let yourself fancy me—women always turn into their mothers, you said.' Ria was babbling but she wanted to take that strained look off his face.

'Did I say that?' He sounded surprised.

'Yes, you did. You must remember?'

'No.'

Ria wished she hadn't begun this, he seemed confused and not at all flattered by her total recall. 'I must ring Rosemary,' she said suddenly.

'Why?'

The real reason was so that she didn't have to stand alone with him in the kitchen with a feeling of dread that she was boring him, irritating him. 'To see is she coming round,' Ria said brightly.

'She's always coming round,' said Danny. 'Like half the world.' He seemed to say that in mock impatience but Ria knew he loved it all, the busy, warm, laughing life of their kitchen in Tara Road. Danny was as happy here as she was: it was the life of their dreams. It was a pity they were so tired and rushed that they had not been making love as often as they used to, but things would be back to normal soon enough.

Rosemary wanted to know all about the shopping expedition when she arrived. 'It's wonderful seeing them coming into their own,' she said. 'Knowing what they want and defining their style.'

She wore smart well-cut jeans and a white silk shirt, what she called weekend clothes. Her hair was freshly done; she was the salon's first client every Saturday morning week in week out.

Rosemary now owned the printing company. She had won a Small Business Award. If she were not her longest-standing best friend Ria could have choked her.

'Well, go on, Ria, tell me, what did she buy?' Rosemary thought it had been fun and that Annie and Ria had bought something.

'I'm no good at knowing what to look for, where to point her,' Ria said, biting her lip.

She thought she saw a flash of impatience in Rosemary's face. 'Of course you are. Haven't you all the time in the world to look round shops?'

Before Ria could reply, the van containing the sander arrived and the men who delivered it were offered coffee, and Brian, looking as if he had been sent out as child labourer digging in a builder's site instead of having just got out of bed, came in with two even scruffier friends, scooping up cans of Coke and some shortbread to take back upstairs.

Ria saw Danny standing at the kitchen door watching everything. He was so boyish and handsome, why had she made that silly remark about him approaching forty?

Still he had got over it, it had passed. His face didn't look troubled now, he just stood there watching almost as if he were an outsider, someone viewing it all for the first time.

Ria found her hand going to her throat and wondered was she getting flu? This was a marvellous Saturday morning in Tara Road. Why was everything upsetting her? She wondered what would happen if she were to write to a problem page. Would the advice be that she should go out and get a job? Yes, that would be a reasonable response. Outside people would think that a job took your mind off things, might make you feel a bit more independent, important. But she *had* a job. No, the solution could be as old as time. It was simply that she was broody. It was time to have another baby.

They were going to have dinner with Rosemary, just the three of them. Ria knew what would be served: a chilled soup, grilled fish and salad. Fruit and cheese afterwards, served by the big picture window that looked out onto the large well-lit roof garden.

Rosemary could always put an elegant meal on the table without any apparent effort. And it was always arranged so well. Grapes and figs tumbling around on some cool modernistic tray, a huge tall blue glass jug of iced water, white tulips in a black vase. Stylish beyond anyone's dreams. Modern jazz at a low volume on the player, and Rosemary dressed as if she were going out to a premiere.

Ria walked with Danny along Tara Road. Rosemary's apartment was worth a small fortune now, Danny said. Sometimes she wished he didn't speculate so much about what the retail value of each house was. But then that was his business.

Ria looked around her as Rosemary went to get them their drinks. Everything looked as pristine as the day she had moved in. The paintwork was not scuffed, the furniture had not known the wear and tear of the young. Ria noticed that there were art books and magazines arranged on a low table. They wouldn't remain like that for long in their house, they would be covered with someone's homework or jacket or tennis shoes. Rosemary's house didn't really feel like a home. More like something you would photograph for a magazine.

She was about to say that to Danny as they walked home along Tara Road, but Danny spoke first. 'I love going to that house,' he said unexpectedly. 'It's so calm and peaceful, there are no demands on you.'

Ria looked at him walking with his jacket half over his shoulder in the warm spring evening, his hair falling into his eyes. Why did he like the feel of Rosemary's apartment? It wasn't Danny's taste at all. Much too spare. Deep down Danny wanted a house with warm colours and full of people.

If they had been having Rosemary to dinner tonight it would have been seven or eight people round the kitchen table. The children would have come in and out with their friends. There would have been music in the background, large bottles of wine already open at each end of the table, a big fish chowder filled with mussels to start, and large prawns, and thick chunky bread. A roast as main course and at least two desserts. That was the kind of evening they all enjoyed.

But it was a silly thing to argue about, so Ria, as she did so often, took the point of view she thought would please him. She tucked her arm into Danny's and said he was right. It had been nice to be able to sit and talk in such a relaxed way.

'We're lucky we have such good friends and neighbours,' she said with a sigh of pleasure. That much she meant. As they turned in to their own garden they saw that the light was on in the sitting room.

'They're still up.' Danny sounded pleased.

'I hope they are nothing of the sort, it's nearly one o'clock.'

Ria was annoyed. She had hoped that tonight she and Danny could have a drink together in the kitchen and they might talk about the possibility of another baby. Another little head cradled at her breast, two trusting eyes looking up at her, Danny at her side. It was exactly what they needed. She had her arguments ready in case there was resistance. Why did the children have to be up tonight of all nights?

It was Annie, of course, and her friend, Kitty. There had been no mention of Kitty coming round, no request that they might take Ria's bottles of nail varnish to paint each other's toenails or borrow her fitness video which was now blaring from the machine. They looked up as if mildly annoyed to see the adults returning to their own home.

'Hi, Mr Lynch,' said Kitty, who rarely acknowledged other women but smiled at any man she saw. Kitty looked like something in a documentary television programme about the dangers of life in a big city. She was waif-thin and had dark circles under her eyes. These were a result of late nights at the disco. Ria knew just how many because Annie had railed at the unfairness of not being able to get similar freedom.

Danny thought she was a funny little thing, a real character. 'Hi, Kitty, hi, Annie. Why, look, you've painted each toenail a different colour. How marvellous!'

The girls smiled at him, pleased. 'Of course there isn't a great range,' Annie said apologetically. 'No blues and black or anything. Just pink and reds.'

'Oh, I *am* sorry,' Ria said sarcastically, but somehow it came out all sharp and bitter. It was *her* make-up drawer they had ransacked without permission, and she was meant to be flattered but also to feel inadequate at not having a technicolour choice for them.

'Was it a nice night?' Annie asked her father. Not because she wanted to know but because she wanted to punish her mother.

'Lovely. No fussing, no rushing around.'

'Um.' Even in her present mood of doing anything to annoy her mother Annie couldn't appear to see much to enthuse about there.

Ria decided not to notice the angry resentment that Annie felt about everything these days. Like so many things, she let it pass. 'Well, I suppose you'll both want to go to bed now. Is Kitty staying the night?'

'It's Saturday, Mam. You do realise there's no school tomorrow.'

'We still have some sit-ups to do.' Kitty's voice was whining, wheedling as if she feared that Mrs Lynch might strike her a blow.

'You girls don't need sit-ups.' Danny's smile was flattering but yet couldn't be accepted. He was after all a doting and elderly father.

'Oh, Dad, but we do.'

'Come here, let's see what does she tell us to do.'

Ria stood with a small hard smile and watched her husband doing a ridiculous exercise to flatten his already flat stomach with two teenagers. They all laughed at each other's attempts as they fell over. She would not join them, nor would she leave them. It was probably only ten minutes yet it felt like two hours. And then there was no warm chat in the kitchen, and no chance of loving when they went upstairs. Danny said he needed a shower. He was so unfit, so out of training these days, a few minutes' mild exercise nearly knocked him out. 'I'm turning into a real middle-aged tub of lard,' he said.

'No, you're not, you're beautiful,' she said to him truthfully, as he took off his clothes and she yearned for him to come straight to bed. But instead he went to shower and came back in pyjamas; there would be no loving tonight. Just before she went to sleep Ria remembered how long it had been since there had been any loving. But she wasn't going to start worrying about that now on top of everything else.

On Sunday Danny was gone all day. There were clients looking at some new apartments. He had to go and supervise the whole sales approach. No, he wouldn't be back for lunch.

The phone rang and Ria answered it hopefully.

'Ria? Barney McCarthy.'

'Oh, he's already gone to meet you there, Barney.'

'He has?'

'Yes, up at the new development, the posh flats.'

'Oh, of course, yes.'

'Are you not there?'

'No, I was delayed. If he calls back, tell him that I'll catch him up.'

'Sure.'

'And you're fine, Ria?'

'Fine,' she lied.

Danny had been tired when he came back last night. Too tired to respond when she had reached out for him. It had been a long day, he said. For Ria, too, it had been a long day, pushing a heavy sanding machine around the floor, but she hadn't complained. Now they were back in familiar territory, a big noisy breakfast, a real family starting the week together in the big bright kitchen.

Danny had his head stuck in brochures about the new apartments. 'You couldn't *give* away anything with carpet wall to wall nowadays,' he said. 'Everything has to have sprung oak floors or they won't consider it. Where did all the money come from in this society? Tell me that and I'll die happy.'

'Not for decades yet, I have great plans for you first,' Ria laughed.

'Yes, well, none for tonight, I hope,' he said. 'There's a dinner, investors, I have to be there.'

'Oh, not again!'

'Oh, yes, again. And many times again before we're through with this. If the estate agents don't go to the promotions then what confidence will they think we have in it all?'

She made a face. 'I know, I know. And after all it won't be for long.'

'What do you mean?'

'Well, eventually they'll all be sold, won't they? Isn't that what it's about?'

'Yes, this phase. But this is only phase one. I was talking about it on Saturday with Barney.'

'Did Barney get you yesterday?'

'No, why?'

'He got delayed, I told him he'd find you at the development.'

'I was with people all day. I expect someone took a message. I'll get it when I get into the office and ring him then.'

'You work too hard, Danny.'

'So do you.' His smile was sympathetic. 'Look, I organised that sander and you had to do most of it as it turned out.'

'Still, if you think it looks nice?' Ria was doubtful.

'Sweetheart, no question. It adds thousands to.the resale value. Wait till we do the upstairs as well. This place will be worth a fortune.'

'But we don't want to sell it,' Ria said, alarmed.

'I know, I know. But one day when we're old and grey and we want a nice apartment by the sea or on the planet Mars, or something . . .' He ruffled her hair and left.

Ria smiled to herself. Things were normal again.

'Sweetheart?'

'Yes, Danny?'

'Was anyone looking for me at home, any peculiar sort of person?'

'No. Nobody at all, why?'

'Oh, there's some crazy ringing up about the apartments, she says she's being refused as a client. She's ringing everyone at home.'

'A woman did ring, but she didn't leave any message. Just kept checking who I was.'

'And who did you say you were?'

Suddenly Ria snapped. It had been a stressful weekend, filled with silly unrelated things that just didn't make sense. 'I told her that I was an axe murderer passing through. God, Danny, who do you think I told her I was? She asked was I Mrs Lynch and I said I was.'

'I'm telling the Guards about it, it's nuisance calls.'

'And did you say that in the office . . . you know who she is?'

'Listen, honey, I'll be late tonight, you know I told you.'

'A dinner, yes I know.'

'I have to run, sweetheart.'

He called everyone sweetheart. There was nothing particularly special about it. It was ludicrous but she would have to make an appointment with her husband to discuss having a baby, and a further one to do something about it if he agreed that it *was* a good idea.

Ria had a mug of soup and a slice of toast for her supper at seven o'clock. She sat alone in her enormous kitchen. The blustery April wind blew the washing on the line, but she left it there. Brian had gone to a friend's house to do his homework and Annie was going to have a pizza with her gran. Her friend Rosemary was at home no doubt cooking something minimalist. Her other friend, Gertie, had been avoiding a drunken husband by walking that ridiculous dog, Pliers, all day, or so Ria's mother said. How had it happened . . . the empty nest? Why was there nobody at home any more?

They all came back together when she least expected it. Annie and her grandmother, laughing as if they were the same age. Brian came in. He seemed pleased but not surprised to see his grandmother. 'I saw Pliers tied to the gate, I knew you were here.'

'Pliers? Tied to the gate?' Ria's mother was out of the house like a shot. 'Poor dog, darling Pliers. Did she abandon you?'

They heard the sound of a car. Danny was home. Early, unexpected.

'That friend of yours is even more scattered than you are, Ria.' Nora Johnson was still smarting over the dog. 'Imagine, Gertie left poor Pliers tied to the gate. He could have been there for hours.'

'He wasn't there when we came in a few minutes ago, Gran,' Annie reassured her.

'No, I saw Gertie running up Tara Road. It could only be a couple of minutes at the most.' Danny was reassuring too. 'Hey, where's supper?'

'No one came home.' Ria's voice sounded small and tired. 'You said you had a business dinner.'

'I cancelled it.' He was eager, like a child.

Ria had an idea. 'Why don't we go to Colm's restaurant, the two of us?'

'Oh, well, I don't know, anything will do . . .'

'It wouldn't do you at all. No, *you* deserve a treat. I'll phone Colm and book a table.' Ria was on her feet.

'I eat out too much, being at home's a treat for me,' he begged.

But she had the phone to her ear and made the booking. Then she ran lightly upstairs and changed into her black dress and put on her gold chain. This was the best chance she would have to talk to her husband about future plans.

They walked companionably down Tara Road to the corner. The lights of Colm's restaurant were welcoming. Ria admired the way that it was done. You couldn't really see who was inside but you got the impression of people sitting down together.

'Very few cars outside,' said Danny, cutting across her thoughts. 'I wonder how he makes any kind of living.'

'He loves cooking,' Ria said.

'Well, just as well that he does because there can't be much profit in tonight's takings from the look of the place.' She hated it when Danny reduced everything to money. It seemed to be his only way of measuring things nowadays.

Colm's sister Caroline took their coats. She was dressed in a smart black dress with long sleeves and she wore a black turban covering her hair. Only someone with beautiful bone structure could get away with something as severe, Ria thought to herself. 'You look so elegant tonight, the turban's a new touch.' Was she imagining it or did Caroline's hand fly to her face defensively?

'Yes, well I thought that perhaps . . .' She didn't finish her sentence. Despite the serene way she smiled and seemed to glide across to show them to their table, there was something tense there. They were a strange pair, the brother and sister: Caroline with her overweight husband Monto Mackey, always in a smart suit and an even smarter car; Colm with his discreet relationship. He was involved with the wife of a well-known businessman, but it was something that was never spoken of. Colm and Caroline seemed to look out for each other, as if the world was somehow preparing to do one of them down.

She glanced at Danny, handsome, tired-looking, boyish still, puzzling over the menu. Wondering if he would go for the crispy duck or be sensible about his health and have the grilled sole. She could read the decisions all over his face.

Colm came to the table to greet them. He made a point of spending only forty seconds and putting a huge amount of warmth and information into that time. 'There's some very nice Wicklow lamb, and I got fish straight off the boat down in the harbour this morning. The vegetables as you know come from the finest garden in the land, and if you're not sick of eating them yourselves, I suggest courgettes.'

Ria chose the lamb and Danny said that because he really was as fat as a fool these days he must have plain grilled fish with lemon juice and no creamy sauce. 'You're not fat, Danny, you're beautiful.' She reached out and touched his hand. Danny looked embarrassed. 'It's all right, we're allowed to hold hands, we're married. Now that couple over there, they're the ones who shouldn't be caught.' She nodded over at a couple where the older man was being playful with his young companion.

'Ria?' Danny said.

'Listen, let me speak first. I'm delighted your dinner was cancelled tonight. We don't have time to talk these days, no time to do anything, not even make love.'

'Ria!'

'I'm not blaming either of us, it just happens, but what I wanted to tell you was this . . .' She stopped suddenly, unsure how to go on. Danny was looking at her, confused. 'You know how I said you look young? I meant it. You're just like you looked when Annie was a baby, with your hair falling into your eyes, unable to believe that you could be a father.'

'What are you saying? What in God's name are you saying?'

'I'm saying that honestly, Danny, I can see these things. It's time for another baby. Another start of a life. You're more sure and comfortable now, you want to see another son or daughter grow up.' A waiter approached them with plates of figs and Parma ham, but something about the way Ria and Danny sat facing each other made him veer away. 'It's *time* for you to have another child, to be a father again. I'm not thinking of myself only but of you, that's all I'm saying,' Ria said, smiling at the strange shocked look on Danny's face.

'Why are you saying it like this?' His voice was barely above a whisper. His face was snow-white. 'Why? Why this way?'

'I'm just saying that it's the right time. That's all. I'm thinking of you and your future, your life.'

'But you're so calm . . . this isn't happening.' He shook his head.

'Well, of course, I want it too, you know that, but I swear I'm thinking of you. A baby is what you need just now. It will put things into perspective, you won't be rushing and fussing about developments and market share and everything, not with a new baby.'

'How long have you known?' he asked.

It was an odd question. 'Well, I suppose I've always known that with

77

the other two grown-up almost the day would come.'

'They'll always be special, nothing would change that.' His voice was choked.

'Well don't I *know* that, for heaven's sake, this would be different, not better.' Ria sat back from her position hunched up and leaning over the table. The waiter seized the opportunity and slid in their plates without any comment. Ria picked up her fork but Danny didn't move.

'I can't understand why you're so calm, so bloody calm,' he said. His voice trembled, he could hardly speak.

Ria looked at her husband in astonishment. 'I'm not very calm, Danny, my darling, I'm telling you I think it's time we had another baby and you seem to agree . . . so I'm very excited.'

'You're telling me *what*?'

'Danny, keep your voice down. We don't want the whole restaurant to know.' She was a little alarmed by his face.

'Oh my God,' he said. 'Oh God, I don't believe it.'

'What is it?' Now her alarm was very real. He had his head in his hands. 'Danny, what is it? Please?'

'You said you understood. You said you'd been thinking about my future and my life. And now you say that *you* want another baby! That *you* do, that's what *you* were talking about.' He looked anguished.

Ria was going to say that the way it normally happened was that the woman had the baby but something stopped her. In a voice that came from very far away she heard herself ask the question that she knew was going to change her life. 'What exactly were *you* talking about, Danny?'

'I thought you had found out and for a mad moment I thought you were going along with it.'

'What?' Her voice, impossibly, was steady.

'You know, Ria, you must know that I'm seeing someone, and well, we've just discovered she's pregnant. I am going to be a father again. She's going to have a baby and we are very happy about it. I was going to tell you next weekend. I thought suddenly that you must have known.'

The noise in the restaurant changed. People's cutlery started to clatter more and bang loudly off people's plates. Glasses tinkled and seemed about to smash. Voices came and went in a type of roar. The sound of laughter from the tables was very raucous. She could hear his voice from a long way off. 'Ria. Listen to me, I wouldn't have had this happen for the world, it wasn't part of any plan. I wanted us to be . . .'

This was too much to cope with. It wasn't fair that she should have to cope with something like this. 'Tell me it's not true,' she said.

'You know that it's true, Ria sweetheart. You know we haven't been getting on, you know there's nothing there any more.'

'I don't believe it. I *won't* believe it.'

'I didn't think it would happen either, I thought we'd grow old together, like people did.'

'And indeed like people do,' she said.

'Yes, some do. But we're different people, we're not the same people who married all those years ago. We have different needs.'

'How old is she?'

'Ria, this has nothing to do with—'

'How old?'

'Twenty-two, not that it matters . . .'

'Of course not,' she said dully.

'I was going to tell you, maybe it's better that it's out now.' There was a silence. 'We have to talk about it, Ria.' Still she said nothing. 'Aren't you going to say anything, anything at all?' he begged.

'Seven years older than your daughter.'

'Sweetheart, can I tell you this has nothing to do with age.'

'No?'

'I don't want to hurt you.' Silence. 'Any more than I already have hurt you and honestly I was wondering could we be the only two people in the whole world who'd do it right? Could we manage to be the couple who actually *don't* tear each other to pieces . . . ?'

'What?'

'We love Annie and we love Brian. This is going to be hell for them. We won't make it a worse hell, tell me we won't. Sweetheart?'

Ria stood up. She was trembling and had to hold the table to keep upright. She spoke in a very low, carrying voice. 'If you ever . . . if *ever* in your life you call me sweetheart again I will take a fork in my hand, just like this one, and I will stick it into your eye.' She walked unsteadily towards the door of the restaurant while Danny stood helplessly at the table watching her go. But her legs felt weak, and she began to sway. She wasn't going to make the door after all. Colm Barry put down two plates hastily and moved towards her. He caught her just as she fell and moving swiftly he pulled her into the kitchen.

Danny had followed them in and watched, standing uncertainly as Ria's face and wrists were sponged with cold water by Caroline.

'Are you part of the problem, Danny? Is this about you?' Colm asked.

'Yes, in a way.'

'Then perhaps you should leave.' Colm was courteous but firm.

'What do you mean . . . ?'

'I'll take her home. When she's ready and if she wants to go, that is.'

'Where else would she go?'

'Please, Danny.' Colm's voice was firm. This was his territory.

Danny left. He let himself into the house with his front-door key. In the kitchen Danny's mother-in-law, her dog and the two children were watching television. He paused in the hall for a minute considering what explanation to make. But this was Ria's choice, not his, how to tell and what to tell. Quietly he moved up the stairs. He stood in the bedroom, uncertain again. After all, she might not want him here when she returned. But suppose he went elsewhere? Might not this be another blow? He wrote a letter and left it on her pillow.

Ria, I am ready to talk whenever you are. I didn't think you'd want me here so I've taken a duvet to the study. Wake me any time. Believe me I'm more sorry about all this than you'll ever know. You will always be very, very dear to me and I want the best for you. Danny

In the kitchen of Colm's restaurant the business of preparing and serving food went on around them. Colm Barry gave Ria a small brandy. She sipped it slowly, her face blank. He asked her nothing about what had happened.

'I should go,' she said from time to time.

'No hurry,' Colm said.

Eventually she said it with more determination. 'The children will worry,' she said.

'I'll get your coat.' They walked from the restaurant in silence. At the gate of the house she stopped and looked at him. 'It's like as if it's happening to other people,' Ria said. 'Not to me at all.'

'I know.'

'Do you, Colm?'

'Yes, it's to cushion the shock or something. We think first that it's all happening to someone else.'

'And then?'

'I suppose then we realise it's not,' he said.

'That's what I thought,' Ria said.

They could have been talking about the vegetables or when to spray the fruit trees. There was no hug of solidarity or even a word of goodbye. Colm went back to his restaurant and Ria went into her home.

She sat down in the kitchen. The table had crumbs and some apple cores in a dish. A carton of milk had been left out of the fridge. There were newspapers and magazines on the chairs. Ria saw everything very clearly, but not from where she was sitting. It was as if she were way up in the sky and looking down. She saw herself, a tiny figure sitting down there in this untidy kitchen in the dark house while everyone else slept. She watched as the old clock chimed hour after hour.

'Mam, it's the drill display today,' Annie said.

'Is it?'

'Where's breakfast, Mam?'

'I don't know.'

'Oh, Mam, not today. I need a white shirt, there isn't one ironed.'

'No?'

'Where were you, were you at the shops?'

'Why?'

'You're in your coat. I could iron it myself, I suppose.'

'Yes.'

'Has Dad gone yet?'

'I don't know, is his car there?'

'Hey, Mam, why isn't there any breakfast?' Brian wanted to know.

Annie turned on him. 'Don't be such a pig, Brian. Put on the kettle, you big useless lump.'

'You're just sucking up to Mam because you want her to do something, make you sandwiches, drive you somewhere, iron something. You're never nice to Mam.'

'I am nice to her. Aren't I nice to you, Mam?'

'What?' Ria asked.

'Aw here, where's the iron?' Annie said in desperation.

'Why have you your coat on, Mam?' Brian asked.

'Get the cornflakes and shut up, Brian,' Annie said. Ria didn't have any tea or coffee. 'She had some before she went out,' Annie explained.

'Where did she go?' Brian, struggling with cutting the bread, seemed puzzled.

'She doesn't have to account to you for her movements,' Annie said.

'Bye, Mam.'

'What?'

'I said, goodbye, Mam.' Brian looked at Annie for reassurance.

'Oh, goodbye, love, 'bye, Annie.'

They went round to get their bicycles.

'What is it, do you think?' Brian asked.

Annie was nonchalant. 'They could be drunk, they went out to Colm's restaurant, maybe the pair of them got pissed. Dad's not up yet, you'll note.'

'That's probably it all right,' said Brian sagely.

Danny came into the kitchen. 'I waited until the children left,' he said. His hair was tousled and his face pale and unshaven. He had slept in his clothes. She still felt the strange sense of not being here, of watching it all happen. She said nothing but looked at him expectantly.

'Ria, are you all right? Why have you your coat on?'

'I don't think I took it off,' she said.

'What? Not even to go to bed?'

'I didn't go to bed.'

Suddenly her head began to clear. They were no longer little matchstick figures down below. She was here in this messy kitchen wearing her coat over her good black party dress. Danny, her husband, the only man she had ever loved, had got some twenty-two-year-old pregnant and was going to leave home and set up a new family. A very great coldness came over her.

'Go now, Danny, please.'

'You can't order me out, Ria. We have to talk. We have to plan what to do, what to say.'

'I will take whatever attitude I like to take, and I would like you not to be here any more until I am ready to talk to you.' Her voice sounded very normal.

He nodded, relieved. 'When will that be?'

'I don't know, I'll let you know. Go now.' He was undecided. 'Now,' she said again.

He went upstairs and she stood listening to the sound of his opening drawers to get clean clothes. He came back downstairs, looking hangdog and at a loss. 'Will you be all right?' he asked. She looked at him witheringly. 'I know it sounds stupid, but I do care and you won't let me talk. You don't want to know what happened, or anything.'

She spoke slowly. 'Just her name.'

'Bernadette,' he said.

'Bernadette,' she repeated slowly. There was a silence then Ria looked at the door and Danny walked out, got into his car and drove away.

When he had gone Ria realised that she was very hungry. The figs and the Parma ham had not been touched last night. She cut two slices of wholemeal bread and sliced up a banana, then she made some coffee.

She had just begun to eat when she heard a tap at the back door. Rosemary came in carrying a yellow dress she had brought to lend to Ria. It was one she had hardly ever worn.

'It looks nothing in the hand but try it on, it's absolutely right for the opening of the flats.' Ria looked at her wordlessly. 'No, don't give me that look, you think it's too wishy-washy but honestly with your dark hair and say a black scarf—' Rosemary stopped suddenly and looked at Ria properly. She was sitting white-faced, wearing a black dress and gold chain and eating a huge banana sandwich at eight thirty in the morning. 'What is it?' Rosemary's voice was a whisper. 'Ria, what's happened? What are you doing?'

'I'm having my breakfast, what do you think I'm doing?' Then it was all too much. 'Oh God, Rosemary, he has a girlfriend, a girlfriend who's pregnant. She's twenty-two, she's going to have his baby.'

'No!' Rosemary had dropped the dress on the floor and come over to embrace her.

'*Yes*. It's true. She's called Bernadette.' Ria's voice was high now and hysterical. 'He's left me, he's going to live with her. It's all over. Danny's gone. Oh Jesus, Rosemary, what am I going to do? I love him so much.'

Rosemary held her friend in her arms and muttered into the dark curly hair, 'Shush, shush, it can't be over, it's all right, it's all right.'

Ria pulled away. 'It's not going to be all right. He's leaving me.'

'And would you have him back?' Rosemary was always very practical.

'Of course I would. You know that,' Ria wept.

'Then we must *get* him back,' said Rosemary.

'Gertie, can I come in?'

'Oh, Rosemary, it's not such a good time. It's just . . .' Rosemary walked past her. Gertie's home was a mess. A lamp was at a rakish angle and a small table now in three pieces stood in the corner. Broken china and glass seemed to have been swept to one side.

'I'm sorry, you see . . .' Gertie began.

'Gertie, I haven't come here at nine o'clock in the morning to give your home marks out of ten. I've come for your help.'

'What is it?' Gertie was justifiably alarmed.

'You're needed up in Ria's house now. You have to come, I'll drive you. Come on, get your coat.'

'I can't, I can't today.'

'You have to, Gertie. It's as simple as this, Ria needs you. Look at all she does for you when you need her.'

'Not today, tell her I'm sorry. She'll understand. Ria knows what the problems are in this house, she'll forgive me for not coming this once.'

'She might, I won't. Ever.'

'But friends forgive and understand. Ria's my friend.'

'Well, I'll tell you what *you* are, Gertie. You are a weak, selfish, whingeing victim and you deserve to get beaten up as much as you do.'

Rosemary had never been so angry. She walked to the door without even looking back to see how Gertie was taking it. Before she got to her car she heard steps behind her. Out in the daylight she saw the marks on Gertie's face, bruises that had not been visible indoors. The women looked at each other for a moment.

'He's left her. The bastard.'

'Danny? Never! He wouldn't.'

'He has,' said Rosemary, starting up the car.

Ria was still sitting in her party dress. 'I haven't told Gertie anything except that Danny *says* he's moving out. All we want is to help you get through today.' Rosemary was completely in charge.

'You're very good to come, Gertie.' Ria's voice was small.

'Why wouldn't I? Look at all you do for me.' Gertie looked at the floor as she spoke, hating to catch Rosemary's eye. 'So where do we start?'

'I don't know.' The normally confident Ria was at a loss.

'I'll pick up Annie and Brian from school and take them back to my place, to have supper and watch a video.' Rosemary saw the look of doubt on Ria's face about this and added, 'I'll make it such a good video that they won't be able to refuse. Oh, and I'll invite the awful Kitty as well. I'll also book you a hair appointment with my hairdresser.'

'It's too late for hairdos and makeovers, Rosemary. We're way beyond all that. I couldn't do it, it would be meaningless to me.'

'How else are you going to fill in the hours until he comes home?' she asked. There was no answer. Rosemary made a brisk phone call to the hairdressing salon, where she booked Mrs Lynch in for a style cut and shampoo and also a manicure.

'I'm not usually so feeble, but I don't think I have the energy to explain all this to my mother and Hilary,' Ria began.

'You don't have to, I will,' Rosemary said.

'The house is a mess.'

'It won't be when you get back,' promised Gertie.

'I don't believe any of this,' Ria said slowly.

'That's what happens, it's nature's way of coping. It's so you can get on with other things,' said Gertie who knew what she was talking about.

'It's like an anaesthetic, you have to go on autopilot for a while,' said Rosemary, who had an explanation for everything but would have had no idea what it felt like to see a huge pit of despair open in front of you.

Ria didn't really remember the visit to the hairdressing salon. She told them she was very tired and hadn't slept all night, they would have to excuse her if she was a little distracted. She let them get on with it, and when it came to paying they said that it was on Rosemary's account.

Back in Tara Road, Ria looked at her watch. There were hours before Danny came home. Ria had never known time pass so slowly. She walked aimlessly round the house touching things: the table in the hall where Danny left his keys. She ran her hand over the back of the chair where he sat at night and often fell asleep with papers from work on his lap. She picked up the glass jug he had given her for her birthday. It had the word Ria engraved on it. He had loved her enough last November to have her name put on a jug and yet in April another woman was pregnant with his child. It was too much to take in.

Ria looked at the cushion she had embroidered for him. The two words 'Danny Boy'. She could remember his face when she gave it to him. 'You must love me nearly as much as I love you to do something like that for me,' he had said. Nearly as much!

Danny didn't call out as he usually did. He didn't leave his keys on the hall table. He looked pale and anxious. If things were normal she would have worried. But things were not normal so she just looked at him and waited for him to speak.

'It's very quiet here,' he said eventually.

'Yes, isn't it?'

They could have been strangers who had just met. He sat down and put his head in his hands. Ria said nothing. 'How do you want to do this?' he said.

'You said we must talk, Danny, so talk.'

'You're making it very hard for me.'

'I'm sorry, did you say that *I* am making it hard?'

'Please, I'm going to try to be as honest as I can, there will be no more lies or hiding things. I'm not proud of any of this but don't try to trip me up with words and phrases. It's only going to make it worse.' She looked at him and said nothing. 'Ria, I beg you. We know each other too well, we know what every word means, every silence even.'

She spoke slowly and carefully. 'No, I don't know you at all. You say there'll be no more lies, no more hiding things. You see, I didn't know there had been any lies or any hiding things, I thought we were fine.'

'You thought that this was all there was? And you didn't think it had all changed? You thought we were just the same as when we got married?' He seemed astounded.

'Yes, the same. Older, busier. More tired, but mainly the same.'

'But . . .' He couldn't go on.

'But what?'

'But we have nothing to say to each other any more, Ria. We make household arrangements, we rent a sander, we make lists. That's not living. That's not a real life.'

'You rented the sander,' she said. 'I never wanted it.'

'That's about the level of our conversation nowadays, sweetheart. You know it's not the same any more, like it was.'

'I don't, I don't know that. It's not totally perfect, you work too hard. Well, you're out too much. Maybe it's not work after all. I thought everything was fine, and I had no idea that you weren't happy here with us.'

'It's not that.'

She leaned over and looked him right in the eyes. 'But *what* is it, Danny? Please? Look, you wanted to talk, we're talking. You wanted me to be calm, I'm being calm. What is it? If you say you weren't unhappy then why are you going? Tell me so that I'll understand. Tell me.'

'There's nothing left, Ria. It's nobody's fault, it happens to people.'

'It hasn't happened to me,' she said simply.

'Yes, it has but you won't face it. You just want to go on playing Happy Families.'

'But we *are* a happy family, Danny. Don't we have the most marvellous children and a lovely home? Tell me, what more do you want?'

'Oh, Ria, Ria, Ria. There's more for both of us. We're not old people. I want to be somebody, to have a future and a dream and to start over.'

'And a new baby?'

'That's part of it, yes, a new beginning.'

'Will you tell me about her, about Bernadette? About what you and she have that we don't have. I don't mean glorious sex of course. Calm I may be, but not quite calm enough to hear about that.'

'I beg you, don't bring bitter accusing words into it.'

'I beg *you* to think about what you say. Is there anything bitter and accusing about asking you why you are suddenly ending a life that I thought was perfectly satisfactory? I just asked you to tell me what you are going to that's so much better. You can't feel that it's all over. You got involved with somebody much younger, you were flattered. Of course I'm furious and upset, but it doesn't have to be the end.'

'You think it's just a fling. It's not, Ria. I love Bernadette, I want to spend the rest of my life with her, and she with me.'

Ria nodded as if this was a reasonable thing for the man she loved to be saying about somebody else. She spoke carefully. 'What did you think would be the best end to this discussion?'

'I suppose I hoped you'd agree that what we had was very good at the time but it was over and that . . . that then we would talk about what to do that would hurt Annie and Brian least.'

'And you didn't think there was anything that you and I could talk about which would get us back together the way it used to be—well, used to be for you?'

'No, love, that's over, that's gone.'

'So when you said talk, it wasn't talk about us, it was talk about what I am to do when you go, is that it?'

'About what we both do. It's not their fault, Annie and Brian don't deserve any hardship.'

'No, they don't. Do I, though?'

'That's different, Ria. You and I fell out of love.'

'That's not true. I love you. I love the way you look and the way you smile, I love your face and I want to have your arms round me and hear you telling me that this is all a nightmare.'

'This isn't the way it is, Ria, it's the way it was.'

'You don't love me any more?'

'I'll always admire you.'

'I don't want your admiration, I want you to love me.'

'We can't have everything we want,' he began.

'You're having a pretty good stab at it, though.'

'I want us to be civilised, to decide where we'll all live . . .'

'What do you mean?'

'Before we tell the children we should be able to give them an idea what the future is going to be like.'

'I'm not telling the children anything. You tell them what you want to.'

'But the whole point is not to upset them . . .'

'Then stay at home and live with them. Give up this other thing. That's the way not to upset them.'

'I can't do that, Ria,' Danny said. 'My mind's made up.'

That was the moment she believed that all this was actually happening. Up to then it had all been words, and nightmares. Now she knew and she felt very, very weary. 'Right,' she said. 'Your mind's made up.'

He seemed relieved at the change in her. He could see that somehow she had accepted it was going to happen. Their conversation would now be on a different level: discussion of details, who would live where. 'There won't be any hurry to move immediately, disrupting their school term, but maybe by the end of the summer?'

'Maybe *what* by the end of the summer?' Ria asked.

'Well, we'll have to sell the house. It would be much too big for—'

'Sell Tara Road?' She was astounded. 'But, Danny, this is our home. This is where we live. We can't sell it.'

'We're going to have to. How else can everybody be provided for?'

'I'm not moving from here so that you can provide for a twenty-two-year-old girl.'

'Please, Ria, we must think what we tell Annie and Brian.'

'No, *you* must think. I've told you I'm telling them nothing, and I am not moving out of my home.'

There was a silence.

'Is this how you're going to play it?' he said eventually. 'Daddy, wicked monster Daddy, is going away and abandoning you, and good saintly poor Mummy is staying . . .'

'Well, that's more or less the way it *is*, Danny.'

He was angry now. 'No, it's not. We're meant to be trying to be constructive and make things more bearable for them.'

'OK, let's wait here until they come home and let's watch you making it bearable for them.'

'Where are they?'

'At Rosemary's, watching a video.'

'Does Rosemary know?'

'Yes.'

'And what time will they be back?'

Ria shrugged. 'Nine or ten, I imagine.'

'Can you ring and get them back sooner?'

'You mean you can't even wait a couple of hours in your own home for them?'

'I don't mean that, it's just if you're going to be so hostile . . .'

'I won't be hostile. I'll sit and read or something.'

He looked around wonderingly. 'You know I've never known this house so peaceful. The place is always like a shopping centre in the city with doors opening and closing, with your mother and the dog and Gertie and Rosemary and all the children's friends coming in and out, and food and cups of coffee.'

'I thought you liked the place being full of people?'

'There was never any calm here, Ria, too much rushing round playing house.'

'I don't believe this, you're just rewriting history.' She got up from the table and went over to the big armchair. She suddenly felt this huge tiredness. She sat in the chair and closed her eyes and knew that she could sleep there and then in the middle of this conversation that was about to end her marriage.

'I'm so sorry, Ria,' he said. She said nothing. 'Will I go and pack some things, do you think?'

'I don't know, Danny. Do whatever you think.'

'I'm happy to sit and talk to you.'

Her eyes were still closed. 'Well, do then.'

'But there's nothing more to say,' he said sadly. 'I can't keep on saying that I'm sorry things turned out like this.'

'No, you can't,' she agreed.

'So maybe it *would* be better if I were to go up and pack a few things.'

'Maybe it would.'

For a while she could hear him upstairs moving from his study to the bedroom. And then she fell asleep.

She woke to the sound of voices in the kitchen.

'Usually it's Dad fast asleep,' said Brian.

'Did you have a nice time?' Ria asked.

'It's not even in the cinemas for another three weeks.' Brian's eyes were shining.

'And you, Annie?'

'It was OK. Can Kitty stay the night?' Annie asked.

'No, not tonight.'

'But, Mam, *why*? We told Kitty's mother that she'd be staying.'

'Not tonight, Annie. Your father and I want to talk to you and Brian.'

There was something about her voice. Something different. Grudgingly Annie escorted her friend to the door.

Danny had come downstairs. He looked pale and anxious. 'We want to talk to you, your mother and I,' he began. 'But I'll do most of the talking because this is about . . . well, it's up to me to explain it all really.' He looked from one to the other as they stood alarmed by the table. Ria still sat in the armchair. 'It's very hard to know where to start, so if you don't think it's very sentimental and slushy I'll start by saying that we love you very, very much, you're a smashing daughter and son—'

'You're not sick or anything, Daddy?' Annie interrupted.

'No, no, nothing like that.'

'Or going to jail? You have that kind of voice.'

'No, sweetheart. But there are going to be some changes, and I wanted to tell—'

'I know what it is.' Brian's face was contorted with horror. 'Are we going to have a baby? Is that it?'

Annie looked revolted. 'Don't be disgusting, Brian.'

But they both looked at Ria for confirmation that this wasn't the problem. She gave a funny little laugh. '*We're* not, but Daddy is,' she said.

'Ria!' He looked as if she had hit him. His face was ashen. 'Ria, how could you?'

'What is it, Daddy? What are you saying?' Annie looked from one to the other.

'I'm saying that for some of the time I won't be living here any more, well, for most of the time really. And that in the future, well, we'll all probably move house, but you will have a place with me and also with Mummy for as long as you like, always, for ever and ever. So nothing about us will change as far as you're concerned.'

'Are you getting divorced?' Brian asked.

'Eventually yes. But that's a long way down the line. The main thing to establish is that everyone knows everything and there are no secrets.'

'That's what your father wants to establish,' Ria said.

'Ria, please . . .' He looked annoyed.

'And is Mam making it up about you having a baby? That's not true, is it, Dad?'

Danny looked at Ria in exasperation. 'That's not the point at the moment. The point is that you are my daughter and my son and nothing can change that.'

'So it is true!' Annie said in horror.

'Not a baby!' Brian said.

'Shut up, Brian, the baby's not coming here. Dad's going away to it. Isn't that what's happening?' Danny said nothing, just looked miserably at the two stricken young faces. 'Well, is it, Dad? You're leaving home and going to live with someone who's pregnant?'

'Your mother and I have agreed that we are not the same people we once were . . . we have different needs . . .'

Ria gave a little strangled laugh from the armchair.

'Who is she, Daddy? Do we know her?'

'No, Annie, not yet.'

'Mam? Won't you stop him? Won't you tell him you don't want him to go?' Annie was blazing with rage.

Ria wanted to leap up and hold her hurt angry daughter to her and tell her just how bad it all was, how unreal. 'No, Annie. Your father knows that already, but he has made up his mind.'

'Oh, Mam, everything's ending, Mam.' Brian's face was white.

'Brian, it's all right, that's what I'm trying to say to you. Nothing's changing. I'm still Dad, still the same Dad I was all the time.'

'You can't leave Mam, Dad. You can't go off with some other one, and leave Mam and us here.' Brian was very near tears.

Annie spoke. 'She doesn't care, Mam doesn't give a damn. She's just letting him walk out. She's not even trying to stop him.'

'Thank you very much, Ria, that was terrific.' Danny was near to tears.

She found her voice. 'I will not tell the children that I don't mind and that it's all fine. It is not all fine, Danny.'

'You promised . . .' he began.

'I promised nothing.'

'We said we didn't want to hurt the children.'

'*I'm* not walking out on them, *I'm* not talking about selling this house over their heads. Where am I hurting them? I only heard about your plans last night and suddenly I'm meant to be saying this is all for the best; we're different people with different needs. I'm the *same* person, I have the same needs. I need you to stay here with us.'

'Ria, have some dignity, *please*,' he shouted at her.

They seemed to realise that the children hadn't spoken. They looked at the faces of their son and daughter, white and disbelieving and both of them with tears falling unchecked. They were beginning to realise that their life in Tara Road was over. Nothing would ever be the same. An eerie stillness settled on the kitchen. They watched each other fearfully.

Danny spoke eventually. 'I wanted it told differently but maybe there's no good way of telling it,' he said helplessly. They said nothing. 'What would you like me to do? Will I stay here in the study tonight so things will be sort of normal, or will I leave and come back tomorrow?'

It was obvious that Ria was going to say nothing.

He looked at the children.

'Go,' said Brian.

'Stay,' said Annie.

'Not if you're going to leave anyway, go now,' Brian said.

They all looked at Annie. She shrugged. 'Why not?' she said in a small hurt voice. 'What's the point of hanging about?'

'It's not goodbye, sweetheart . . .' Danny began. 'Can you understand that?'

'No, I can't, Daddy, to be honest,' she said, and she picked up her school bag and without a backward glance went out of the kitchen door and up the stairs.

Brian watched her go. 'What's going to happen to us all?' he asked.

'We'll all survive,' Danny said. 'People do.'

'Mam?' Her son looked at her.

'As your dad says . . . people do, we will too.' The look that Danny gave her was grateful. She didn't want his gratitude. 'The children have said they'd like you to go, Danny. Will you, please?'

He went quietly and the three of them heard him starting his car and driving down Tara Road.

Ria had a little speech ready for them at breakfast.

'I wasn't much help last night,' she said.

'Is it all really going to happen, Mam? Isn't there anything we can do to stop it?' Brian's face was hopeful.

'Apparently it *is* going to happen, but I wanted to tell you it's not quite as sad and awful as it seemed last night.'

'What *do* you mean?' Annie was scornful.

'I mean that what your father said was quite true. We do both love you very much and we'll be here, or around if not here, whenever you need us until you get bored with us and want lives of your own. And if you want to be with him, at a weekend say, then that's where you'll be, and if you want to be with me, then I'll be here or wherever and delighted for you to be with me. That's a promise.' They didn't rate it much. 'And what I suggest is that you ring your dad at the office today and ask him when and where he'd like to meet you to talk to you and tell you about everything.'

'Can't you tell us, Mam?' Brian begged.

'I can't really, Brian. I don't know it all and I'd tell it wrong.'

'And does everyone know about it?' Annie asked.

'No, I don't think many people do.'

'Well, do they or don't they?' Annie was abrupt and rude. 'I mean does Gran know, Auntie Hilary, Mr McCarthy—people like that?'

'Gran and Hilary don't know, but I expect Mr McCarthy does.' Her face was like stone.

'Do you get custody of us, Mam, or does Dad?'

'I would think you would probably live with me during the week in term-time.'

'Because she wouldn't want us, is that it?' Annie was suspicious.

'No, no. She knows your father has two children, she must want to welcome them.'

'What's her name?' Annie wanted to know.

'I don't know,' Ria lied.

'You *must* know, of course you know,' Annie persisted.

'I don't. Ask your father.'

'Why won't you tell us?' Annie wouldn't let go.

'Leave Mam alone. Why do you think she knows?'

'Because it's the first thing I'd have asked,' said Annie.

Danny used to laugh at the way Ria made a list of things to do. She always headed it *List*. Old habits die hard. She headed it *List* and sat at the table when the children had gone. Their hugs had been awkward but some pretence at normality had been restored. The tears and silences of last night were over. The list covered many phone calls.

She must ring her mother first and prevent her coming anywhere near the house, then ring Hilary. She would ring Rosemary at the printing company and Gertie at the launderette.

And lastly she would ring Danny. Beside Danny's name she wrote firmly: *Do not apologise*.

'Danny?'

'It was awful,' he said. 'I'm so sorry.'

Ria looked at her list: *Do not apologise*, it ordered her. She had wanted to cry and say she was sorry, that they were not the kind of people who snarled at each other like that. She wanted him to come home and wrap her in his arms. *Do not apologise*, she read, and she knew she had been right to write it down. Danny was not coming home to her. Ever.

'There was hardly any way it couldn't have been awful,' she said in matter-of-fact tones. 'Now, let's see what we can salvage. I've told the children to call you today and that maybe you could meet them one evening to tell them what it's going to be like. Let them know some actual plans.'

'Plans?'

'Well, you do have a place to live, I imagine?'

'Yes, yes.'

'And would it have enough room for them to stay?'

'Stay? It's just a small flat.'

'And is it nearby?' She kept her voice interested, without emotion.

'It's in Bantry Court, the block that Barney developed a few years back. It's not mine, it's Bernadette's. She got it from her father when she was eighteen. It was an investment.'

'It certainly was,' Ria said grimly.

'He's dead now,' Danny said.

'Oh, I see.'

'And her mother's sort of worried about the whole situation.'

'She knows you are married, I presume?'

'Yes.' There was a silence. He spoke again. 'You know it will take time to get everything sorted out.'

'Children are easily distracted, be sure to emphasise holidays to them, tell them about the weeks you can take them away in the summer. Remember you once talked of renting a boat on the Shannon?'

'Do you think they'd like that? I mean, you know, without you?'

'But they're going to have to learn that it will be without me from now on when it's with you. We *all* have to learn that.'

'But what would you do? If we all went away?'

'I'd go on a holiday myself maybe.'

'But, sweetheart . . . where would you . . . ?'

'Danny, can I ask you not to call me that?'

'I'm so sorry. Yes, you did ask me, but you know it means nothing.'

'I know *now* it means nothing. I didn't always.'

'Please, Ria.'

'OK, Danny. We'll say goodbye now.'

Ria hung up.

It had been less upsetting than she had thought.

5

RIA LOST ALL SENSE OF TIME. Sometimes when she went to bed she woke thinking it was morning and then realised that she had only been asleep for half an hour. The empty side of the bed seemed an enormous vast space. Ria would get up and walk to the window, hugging herself as if to try to ease the pain. Just after midnight and he was asleep in some apartment block wrapped round this child. It was too much to bear. As she sat long hours staring out of the window while stars disappeared and dawn came, Ria thought that perhaps her mind had broken down without her noticing it. Yet she appeared to function during daylight hours. The house was cleaned, the meals were cooked, people came and went.

Sometimes during the day Ria would stop whatever she was doing with a physical sense of shock as she remembered something else that had been a lie. That coloured shirt that he had bought in London. The girl had chosen it for him, hadn't she? Bernadette must have been in London with him. Ria had to sit down when she realised that. The bill for the mobile phone. Almost every call was to her number, the number that was his now in case of emergencies. What a fool, what a trusting fool she had been. Then she would argue that view. If you loved someone you trusted him. Surely it was as simple as that.

Annie's mood-swings went the whole way from blaming her mother to blaming herself. 'If you'd only been a bit more normal, Mam, you know, if you'd stopped yacking and cooking he wouldn't have gone away.' The next day it might be, 'It's all my fault . . . he called me his princess but I didn't spend any time with him, I was always in Kitty's house. He knew I didn't love him enough, that's why he went and found someone else not much older than me.'

Once or twice she asked Ria if they might write a letter to Dad saying how lonely they were without him. 'I don't think he knows,' Annie wept.

'He knows.' Ria was stony.

Brian had his views as well. 'It was probably all my fault, Mam. I didn't really wash enough, I know.'

'I don't think that was it, Brian.'

'No, it could have been, you know the way Dad was always washing himself and wearing a clean shirt every day and everything?'

'People do that, you know.'

'Well, could we tell him that I wash more now. And I will, I promise.'

'If Dad left just because you were filthy he'd have left ages ago, you've been filthy for years,' Annie said gloomily.

Then Brian decided that his father had left on account of sex. 'Maybe he went off to her because she's interested in having sex night and day.'

'I don't think that's right,' Ria said.

'No, but it might be part of it. Could you telephone him and say you'd be interested in having it night and day too?' He looked a bit embarrassed and awkward to be talking to his mother about such things, but he obviously felt that they had to be said.

'Not really, Brian.' Ria was glad that Annie wasn't in the room.

Annie was in the room however when Brian came up with his trump card. 'Mam, I know how to get Dad back,' he said.

'This should be interesting,' Annie said.

'You and he should have a baby.' The silence was deafening. 'You could,' Brian went on. 'And I could baby-sit. It would be a great way of getting pocket money.' He looked at his mother's stricken face. 'Or listen, Mam, if Dad came back, I'd do it for nothing,' he said.

Wouldn't it be wonderful, Ria thought, if she could be miles away from here, not to have to reassure people that she was fine, and that everything was fine, when in fact the whole world was as far from fine as it would ever be. She put off going out because of the people she would meet, yet she knew it was dangerous to hole up in Tara Road and be the reclusive, betrayed wife.

She heard a sound at the front door and her heart lifted for a moment.

How could the sound of a leaflet being pushed through a hall door still make her think that Danny had come back? She must make an effort today to live in the real world. Like knowing what she was doing and what time it was. She looked at the clock automatically when she heard the Angelus bell ringing midday. At the same time the telephone rang.

It was a woman with an American accent. 'I do hope you'll forgive me calling a private home, but this was the only listing I could get for a Mr Danny Lynch, estate agent. Enquiries didn't have a commercial listing.'

'Yes?' Ria was lacklustre.

'Briefly, my name is Marilyn Vine and we were in Ireland fifteen years ago. We met Mr Lynch and he tried to interest us in some property—'

'Yes, well do you mind if I give you his office number? He's not here.'

'Of course, but if I could take one more minute of your time to ask you is this something he might do. I wondered did he know anyone who might like to do a house exchange this summer. I can offer a comfortable and I think pleasant home with a swimming pool in Westville— it's a college town in Connecticut—and I was looking for somewhere within walking distance of the city but with a garden . . .'

'This summer?' Ria asked.

'Yes. July and August. I know it's not much notice.'

'And why did you think of Danny?' Ria asked in a measured voice.

'He was so knowledgeable and he was my only contact. I felt sure he might put me on to someone else if it wasn't his particular scene.'

'And would it be a big house or a small house you'd want?' Ria asked.

'I don't really mind, I wouldn't be lonely in a large place and anyone coming here to Westville would have a house with plenty of room for four or five people. They could have the car too, of course, and there are very attractive places to go.'

'Well, aren't there agencies and things?'

'Yes, of course, and I can go through the Internet. But just at the moment I don't feel like talking to strangers much, negotiating with them. I guess it does sound a little odd.'

'No, I know exactly how you feel.'

'Am I talking to Mrs Lynch?'

'I don't know.'

'I beg your pardon?'

'We are going to get divorced.'

'This was not a good time to ring. I can't tell you how sorry I am.'

'No, it was a great time. We'll do it.'

'Do what?'

'I'll go to your house, you come to mine, July and August. It's a deal.'

'Well, I suppose we should exchange details . . .'

'Of course we should, I'll send you a photo of it. It's Victorian; you'll love it. It's in Tara Road, it's got all kinds of trees in the garden and lovely polished wooden floors and some old stained-glass windows, and . . . and . . . and . . . the original mouldings on the ceilings and . . . and . . .' She was crying now. There was a silence at the other end of the line. Ria pulled herself together. 'Please forgive me, Marion is it?'

'Marilyn. Marilyn Vine.'

'I'm Ria Lynch and I can't think of anything I'd like to do more than get away from here and go to a quiet place with a swimming pool and nice drives. I could take my children for one month and the other month I could spend on my own, thinking out my future. That's why I got a bit carried away.'

'Your house sounds just what I want, Ria. Let's do it.'

Marilyn Vine put down the telephone on her kitchen counter and went out into her garden with her cup of coffee. She sat by the pool where she had swum earlier. It was ten minutes past seven in the morning. She had just agreed to exchange houses with an agitated woman going through some kind of life crisis. A woman she had never met. A woman who might well not have the right to exchange houses, whose property could be under some kind of legal review pending divorce.

All Marilyn knew was that it was very foolish to make early-morning, spur-of-the-moment decisions. She would never do anything like this again. The only question now was whether she should call back and unpick the arrangement before it had begun to take root, or write a letter?

She could call and say the home exchange was no longer possible from her end, that she had family duties which she could not ignore. She smiled wryly at the thought of her being someone with family responsibilities. But Ria in Ireland wouldn't know this.

Marilyn would not allow herself to brood. Very soon now she would need to go to work. She would drive up to the college campus and take her place in the car park. Then, greeting this person and that, she would walk to the Alumni Office where she worked.

They would look at her with interest. How strange she hadn't gone to Hawaii with her husband. Greg Vine's visiting lectureship had seemed exactly what the couple needed. But Marilyn had been adamant she would not go, and had been equally resolute in giving no explanation to her colleagues and friends. Their interest was genuine but so was their mystification that she would not go to a sunny island with the urging of a loving husband and the support of a caring department in the college that would hold her job open for her. What would they say if they knew what an extraordinary alternative she had been contemplating?

Marilyn finished her coffee, straightened her shoulders and squared up to what she had done. She was an adult woman. She would have her fortieth birthday this summer, on August 1. She would make whatever decisions she felt like making. She nodded towards the telephone as if affirming the conversation she had made on it earlier. She looked at her reflection in the hall mirror. Short auburn hair, green anxious eyes, tense shoulders, but otherwise perfectly normal. Not at all the kind of person who would have decided something so unbalanced.

Marilyn picked up her keys and drove to work.

Ria sat down and held on to the table very tightly. Not since she was a teenager had she been abroad alone. Well, at least she had a passport and a few weeks to get everything organised at this end. From force of habit, Ria got a piece of paper, wrote the word *List* and underlined it. As she began to write down what she had to do, her chest tightened. Was she completely mad? Why did it seem such a good idea? Why do I want it so much? Ria asked herself. When I got up this morning I hadn't a notion of going to a house in Connecticut for the summer. Is it so that I'll be able to offer the children something the equivalent of their father's trip on the Shannon? Is it that I want to be somewhere where Danny Lynch isn't the centre of the world?

I might half forget him out there, Ria told herself. I might not see his face everywhere I look. America might cure that. And the awful belief that the man doesn't leave on the first affair. There could have been other women who had slept with her husband. How great to go to a place where nobody had met Danny and certainly not slept with him.

But still it was a very sudden decision to have made. She knew nothing about Marilyn Vine. Promising a total stranger that she could live here in Tara Road. In normal times she would not have done anything so wildly lacking in caution. But these were not normal times.

Ria firmed up her shoulders. She *was* a strong person despite a lot of evidence to the contrary. She liked the sound of Marilyn. She was someone who had appeared just when she was needed.

With bleak determination Ria applied herself to the list.

Danny had taken Annie and Brian to Quentin's, which he thought would be a treat for them, but it was turning out to be a mistake.

'Right, now do we see anything we like?' Danny looked from one of them to the other hopefully.

'I might have a hamburger but I don't see it on the menu,' Brian said.

Danny hid his annoyance. 'Look, here, they say ground beef served with a tomato and basil salsa, that's more or less it,' he pointed it out.

'Why don't they *call* it a burger, like normal places?' Brian grumbled.

'They expect people to be able to read and understand things,' Annie said dismissively. 'Do they have vegetarian things, Dad?'

Eventually the choice was made and Brenda Brennan, the suave manageress, came and took their order personally.

'Is that her?' Brian whispered when she had gone.

'Who?' Danny was genuinely bewildered.

'The one, the one who's going to have the baby, the one that you're going to live with?'

'Don't be *ridiculous*, Brian.' Annie's patience was now exhausted. 'She's as old as Mam, for God's sake. Of course she's not the one.'

Danny felt the time had come to reclaim the purpose of the evening. 'Your mother and I have had a very good conversation today, very good.'

'Well, that makes a change,' Annie grumbled.

'Are you coming back?' Brian asked hopefully.

'Brian, this is what your mother and I were talking about. It's a question of what words we use. I've not gone away, I haven't left you two, of course I haven't. I'm going to be living in a different place, that's all.'

'What kind of place?' Annie asked.

'Well it's only a flat at the moment, but Mr McCarthy has found us a house and very soon we'll move in and you'll come to stay there as often as you like. It's got a lovely garden, and it will be your home too.'

'We've got a lovely garden in Tara Road,' Annie said.

'Yes, well now you'll have two.' He beamed with pleasure at the thought of it.

They looked at him doubtfully.

'Will we each have our own room?' Annie asked.

'Yes, of course. Not the day we move in, because there'll be alterations to be done. Mr McCarthy's people will divide a room for you. In the meantime when you come to stay one of you can sleep on the sofa in the sitting room.'

'Doesn't sound much like a second home to me, sleeping on the sofa,' Annie said.

'No, well it's only temporary.' He kept his smile bright.

'And how many days will we stay there?' Brian asked.

'As many as you like. Your mother and I talked about that very thing today. You'll be delighted when you go home and discuss it with her, we both agree that you are the important people in all this—'

Annie cut across his speech. 'And will she be like Mam and say keep your room tidy and you can't come in at this hour?'

'Bernadette will make you very welcome. She's so looking forward to meeting you. When will we arrange that, do you think?'

'You didn't say if she'd be making rules,' Annie persisted.

'You'll be as courteous and helpful in this new house as you are in Tara Road.'

'But we're *not* helpful in Tara Road,' Brian said, as if this was something his father had misunderstood.

Danny sighed. 'Suppose we decide a time and place to meet Bernadette?'

'Do we have to meet her?' Annie asked. 'Wouldn't it be better to wait until the baby's born and everything, get all that out of the way?'

'Of course you'll meet her,' Danny cried. 'We're all going away on a boat on the Shannon for a holiday, all of us. We want to meet together long before that.'

They looked at him dumbfounded.

'The Shannon?' Annie said.

'I don't honestly think Mam would like a holiday with . . . you know, *her* coming too,' Brian said slowly.

Annie and her father exchanged glances. They both began to explain to the boy who was, after all, only ten years of age, that his mother would not be coming with them on this long-planned holiday.

In Marilyn's office there was much talk of the annual alumni picnic in August. Many past students looked forward to this weekend as the high spot of the year. It was a highly successful fund-raiser for the college and maintained close contacts between present and past. Marilyn and Greg had hosted many a family in 1024 Tudor Drive. They had always been delighted with the pool in the hot August weather and many had kept in touch over the years.

A meeting for the plans for the picnic was in progress. Marilyn knew she must speak before work would be apportioned. She cleared her throat and addressed the professor of education. 'Chair, I must explain that I will not be here during the months of July and August. I have accepted the leave of absence so kindly offered to me by the college. I leave at the end of June and will be back after Labor Day, so may I ask you to give me maximum input to the early preparation work in the knowledge that I will not be here for the event itself?'

A group of faces looked up, smiling. Greg would be so pleased. He had been distraught when Marilyn wouldn't accompany him to Hawaii.

He had moved heaven and earth to get the position and the professorial exchange; once it had been achieved he couldn't go back on it. Now Marilyn was going to join him at last.

Ria didn't want to spring her plans on everyone without being able to show them something to back up that this was a good idea. It would take a week at least before she got the documents from Marilyn. She had prepared a little dossier of her own, which she would send off today or tomorrow. She had photographs of the house both inside and out and cuttings from the *Irish Times* newspaper's property section showing the kind of place that Tara Road was. She put in a map of Dublin, an up-to-date tourist guide to the city, a restaurant guide, a list of books Marilyn might like to read before she came. She gave the address of her bank, the name, telephone number and fax of their bank manager. Also a terse and unemotional note to say that the house was owned jointly between her and Danny; its ownership was not in dispute. He would look after the children for the month of July. She enclosed a list of friends and contacts that would be of help to Marilyn when she arrived.

Perhaps a week was too optimistic; she might have to keep her secret for a little longer than she had hoped. But a Fedex van turned up the very next day at her house with all Marilyn's details. Hardly daring to breathe she looked at the pictures of the swimming pool, the low white house with the flowers in the porch, the map of the area, the local newspaper, and the details of the car, shopping facilities and membership of a leisure centre and club which could be transferred to Ria while she was in residence. There were golf, tennis and bowling nearby, and Marilyn also said she would give her a list of emergency contacts.

In a note as terse and unemotional as Ria's own letter, Marilyn explained that she needed some space to think out her future. She had not joined her husband on a short sabbatical in Hawaii, because there were still matters she had to think through. With her bank details she also added that she had not yet told her husband about the exchange, but that there would be no problem and she would confirm this within twenty-four hours.

Ria still had to tell Danny. Did they all know about them in his office, she wondered as she rang and asked to be put through to him?

'Can you come round and collect your things soon, Danny? I want to try and organise the place a bit.'

'There's no huge hurry, is there?'

'We have to do it some time. Come today if you can, with the car. And there are a few other things I want to talk to you about anyway. Come before the children get back, won't you?'

'But I'd like to see them.'

'Sure, and you can any time, but it's not a good idea to see them here.'

'Ria, don't start laying down rules.'

'But we agreed not to confuse them; they're to be equally welcome in each home. I'm not going to be over in your place when they visit you, and it makes sense for you not to be in my place.'

There was a silence.

'I'll come over,' Danny said.

Heidi Franks picked up the telephone on Marilyn's desk.

'Good afternoon, Marilyn Vine's phone, Heidi Franks speaking . . . Oh, Greg, nice to talk with you . . . no you've just missed her. She'll be back in ten minutes. Can I take a message? Sure, sure. I'll tell her. Oh, and Greg, we're all thrilled she's going out to you. It's a great decision . . . Today. At the meeting. Yes, for July and August. No? You don't? Could it be a surprise? Oh, I'm really so sorry I spoke. Listen, better let her talk to you about it, Greg.' Heidi replaced the receiver slowly and turned round.

At the door stood Marilyn with a white face. *Why* had she told the faculty before she had told Greg? Now things would be worse than ever.

Danny looked at Ria, astounded.

'This is *not* going to happen. Believe me, this is so mad that I can't even take it in.'

Ria was calm. 'It's only going to cost our fares, and I've been onto the travel agency. They're not crippling.'

'And what exactly would you call crippling, might I ask?'

'The price of a meal in Quentin's for two children who only wanted a burger and a pizza,' she said. 'You're going to be able to hire a lovely cruiser on the Shannon for them; I don't have the money for that. In fact I don't know *what* money I'll have, so I've arranged a grand holiday for them in a place with a lovely pool. *Look* at it, Danny, at no cost except the fare. We'll just go out to the grocery and I'll cook there instead of here. I thought you'd be pleased.'

'*Pleased?* It's not on, Ria.'

'We've arranged it.'

'Then unarrange it.'

'Will you explain to the children that there'll be no holiday for them with me, no chance to see the States? Will you look after them for two months instead of one? Well, *will* you, Danny? That's what this is about.'

'No, it's not about this, it's about you putting a gun to my head, that's what it's about.'

'I'm going on July the 1st, Marilyn Vine's coming here that day. The children can come out to me on August the 1st. I've checked the flights, there are seats available, but we need to book soon.' Her voice was very steady and she seemed very sure of what she was saying.

Danny reached out and unwillingly dragged Marilyn Vine's envelope to him to look at the contents. That was the moment when Ria knew she had won and that the trip was on.

Marilyn sent a very short email to Greg at the University in Hawaii:

Very much regret not getting in touch about my summer plans. Please call me at home tonight at any time that suits you and I will explain everything. Again many sincere regrets,
Marilyn

He called at 8.00pm. She was waiting and answered immediately.

'It must be about three o'clock in the afternoon there,' Marilyn said.

'Marilyn, I didn't call to discuss the different time zones. What's happening?'

'I'm truly very sorry and Heidi is distraught, as you can imagine. Another hour and I would have emailed you asking you to call.'

'Well, I'm calling now.'

'I want to get away from here. I find it stifling.'

'I know, so did I. That's why I arranged for us to come here. What are your summer plans as you call them? Where are you going, Marilyn?' His voice was cold now.

'I'm going to Ireland on July the 1st.'

'*Ireland?*'

She could see his face, lined and suntanned, and his glasses pushed up on his forehead, his hair beginning to thin a little in the front.

'We were there years ago together. Do you remember?'

'Of course I remember. We were on a conference for three days and then three days touring the west, where it rained all the time.'

'I'm not going for the weather, I'm going for some peace.'

'Marilyn, it's very dangerous in your state of mind to go and bury yourself in some cabin on the side of a mountain there.'

'No, I'm not doing that. It's a big suburban house actually, in a classy part of Dublin. It's an old Victorian building. It looks lovely, four storeys altogether and there's a big garden.'

'You can't be serious.'

'But I am. I've arranged an exchange with the woman that owns it, she's coming here to Tudor Drive.'

'You're giving our house to a total stranger?'

'I've told her that you may possibly come back, that it's not likely but that work may bring you back.'

'And will her husband be coming back from time to time to visit you?'

'No, they're separated.'

'Like us, I suppose,' he said. 'For all the phrases we wrap it up in, we are separated, aren't we, Marilyn?' He sounded very bleak.

'Not in my mind, we're not. We are just having time apart this year. Do you want to hear about Ria?'

'Who?'

'Ria Lynch, the woman who's coming.'

'No, I don't.' Greg hung up.

'I'm not going,' Annie said.

'Fine,' her mother replied.

This startled Annie. She had expected that she would be persuaded and coaxed. She reached for the picture again. But her face was still mutinous. 'It's ridiculous us going out there,' she said.

Ria said nothing in reply, she just continued to set the table for breakfast. She had moved the big chair with the carved arms where Danny used to sit. Not a big public statement, she had just put it in a corner with a pile of magazines and newspapers on it.

It was surprising how she still expected him to come in the door saying: 'Sweetheart, it's good to be home.' Had he said that on the days when he had been making love to Bernadette? The thought made her shiver. All those nights when he fell asleep exhausted in the big chair, perhaps it was exhaustion from making love to a young girl.

Ria knew that it was having to put on a face for the children that kept some hold of her sanity. She looked at them as they sat at the table, and a wave of pity came over her. These were children who were having to face an entirely different summer than the one they had a right to expect. Ria would be very gentle with them.

She answered Annie thoughtfully. 'Yes, I know it sounds ridiculous to go there, but it would be a new experience for us all to see America and no hotel bills to pay. And then of course there would be someone who would come here and mind this house for us all, that's important.'

'But who is she?' Annie groused.

'It's all there in the letter, love. I left it for you to read.'

'It doesn't *tell* us anything,' Annie said.

And in a way she was right. It didn't speak of any friends or relations in Westville, nothing about a circle of people she knew. Ria's letter had been much more people-orientated. But nothing would please Annie anyway so this wasn't relevant.

'Has Dad fixed up the date of the Shannon trip?' Ria asked them.

They looked at each other guiltily as if there was something to hide.

'He says the boats are all booked,' Brian said. 'But he may be making it up.'

'No, Brian, of course he wouldn't make it up, he's dying for a trip on the Shannon.'

'Yeah, but *she* wasn't,' Annie said.

'Did she tell you to your faces?'

'No, we haven't met her yet,' Brian said.

'Well, then . . .'

'We're meeting her today,' Annie said. 'After school.'

'That's good,' Ria said emptily.

'Why is it good?' Annie would fight with her shadow today.

'It's good because if you'll be spending July with Bernadette, the sooner you meet her the better. Then you'll get to know her.'

'I don't want to get to know her,' Annie said.

'Neither do I.' Brian was in rare agreement with his sister.

'Where are you all meeting?'

'Her flat, well, their flat,' Annie said. 'For tea, apparently.' She made it sound like the most unusual and bizarre thing to offer in the afternoon.

Part of Ria was pleased to see the resentment against the woman who had taken their father away. Yet another part of her knew that the only hope of peace ahead was if the children were cooperative.

She scooped up the contents of Marilyn's envelope.

'Are you putting those away?' Annie asked.

'Yes, Brian's seen them and you're not coming with us, so I'll just keep them with my things. OK?'

'What will I do while you're there?'

'I don't know, Annie. Stay with Dad and Bernadette, I suppose. You'll work it out.' She knew it was unfair, but she just wasn't going to go down the road of pleading and begging.

Annie would go to Westville when the time came, they all knew that.

Bantry Court, the apartment block that Bernadette lived in, had been developed by Barney about five years ago. Danny had sold many of the flats. Perhaps this was how he had met Bernadette. Ria had never asked. There were so many questions that she had not asked. Like what she looked like. What they talked about. What she cooked for him. But today her daughter and son were going to this woman's apartment for tea. Somehow it was important that she had to see Bernadette before Annie and Brian did.

As soon as they left for school Ria got into her car and drove to Bantry Court. She noticed that it took fifteen minutes. On the many nights when he came home so late, Danny must have driven this route. If this girl had not become pregnant would it have just gone along like that for ever? Bantry Court, Tara Road, two different compartments of his life?

She parked in the forecourt and looked up at the windows. Her name was Bernadette Dunne. That much Ria knew. The children had told her.

Ria went to the list of bells. There it was. Dunne, Number 12, top floor. Would she press it? What would she say? She hadn't thought it out. She moved back a little and while she did a woman came along and went up to the row of bells. She pressed Number 12.

A voice answered. 'Helloo!' A thin young voice.

'Ber, it's Mummy,' the woman said.

Bernadette must have pressed a buzzer because the door snapped open. Ria shrank back.

'Are you coming in?' The woman was pleasant and a little puzzled by Ria hovering there.

'What? Oh, no, no. I've changed my mind. Thank you.' She looked hard at Danny's future mother-in-law. Small and quite smart, wearing a beige suit and a white blouse, she had short, well-cut brown hair and copper-coloured high-heeled shoes. She looked somewhere between forty and forty-five. Not much older than Ria and Danny.

Ria went back to the car. It had been very foolish to come here and upset herself. She would have to sit in this car park until she felt calm enough to move.

Minutes later she saw the woman coming out of the front door of Bantry Court accompanied by a girl with long straight hair, shiny and soft like an advertisement for shampoo. Ria felt her own hand go automatically to her frizzy curls.

She had a pale, heart-shaped face and dark eyes. She wore a long black velvet sweater, a short pink skirt and childish black shoes with pink laces. Ria knew that Bernadette Dunne was twenty-two going on twenty-three and that she was a music teacher. She looked about seventeen and being marched to school by her mother who had found her playing truant. They got into a smart new Toyota Starlet.

Ria found her strength and her car key, started the engine and followed them as they drove out of Bantry Court.

Marilyn looked around her house with an objective eye. How would it appear to someone who lived in a house that was over a hundred years old? The items of furniture pictured in Ria's home looked as if they were all antiques. That Danny Lynch must have done very well at his business. This house had been built in the early 1970s. Tudor Drive was an affluent neighbourhood. The homes all stood in their own grounds; the lawns and frontage were communally looked after.

There would be plenty of room for them all. Ria would sleep in the main bedroom, and there were three other bedrooms. Marilyn paused with her hand on the door of one room. Should she lock it? She didn't want strangers in there among these things. They would respect her for keeping her private memories behind a locked door. But then wasn't it *odd* somehow to lock a room in the house which was meant to be home to these people? Marilyn thought she might lock the room but leave the key somewhere for Ria so that it didn't look so like an act of exclusion. She wouldn't decide now, she'd see how she felt the morning she left.

And the time raced by. Summer came to Tara Road and Tudor Drive. Ria marshalled her troops well in advance and encouraged them to welcome Marilyn and to invite her into their homes. That's what Americans liked, visiting someone's home.

'Even mine?' Hilary was unsure.

'Particularly yours. I want her to meet my sister and get to know her. You will keep an eye out for Marilyn, won't you?'

'Ah, don't you know I will.'

And all the others had promised too. Her mother was going to take Marilyn to visit St Rita's; she might enjoy meeting elderly Irish people with lots of memories. Rosemary was having a summer party and said she would include Marilyn. Even Polly Callaghan called on Ria unexpectedly. 'I hear there's an American woman coming to stay here; if she wants any chauffeuring around at weekends tell her to get in touch.'

'How did you know she was coming?' Ria asked.

'Danny told me.'

'Danny doesn't approve.'

Polly shrugged. 'He can't have it every way.'

'He mainly has, I think.'

'Bernadette's not going to stay the distance, Ria,' Polly said.

Ria's heart leapt. This was what she so desperately wanted to hear. Someone who knew them all and could make a judgment on who would win in the end. But she pulled herself together sharply. Polly was Barney McCarthy's woman, she was in their camp when all was said and done. Ria must not give in to the need she felt to confide. 'Who knows whether it will last or not? Anyway, it's not important. He wants her, we're not enough for him, so be it.'

'All men want more than they can have. Who knows that better than I do?'

'Well, you went the distance, Polly. You and Barney lasted, didn't you?' It was the first time Ria had ever mentioned the relationship and she felt a little nervous at having done so.

'Yes, true, but only unofficially. I mean, I'm still the woman in the background; that's all I'll ever be. Mona is the wife, the person of status.'

'I don't think so, actually. I think Mona is a fool,' Ria said. 'If he loved you then she should have let him go to you.'

Polly pealed with laughter. 'Come on, you know better than that, he didn't *want* to leave her, he wanted us both. Just like Danny possibly wanted you both, you and the girl as well.'

Ria played that conversation over in her mind many times. She didn't think that Polly was correct. Danny had been anxious to leave, to start again. And of course times were so different now to what they were when Barney McCarthy and Polly Callaghan had fallen in love.

She was surprised to get a telephone call from Mona wishing her luck in the States and offering her a loan of suitcases. 'You have great courage, Ria. I admire you more than I can say. I didn't know one thing about this other woman, you know, I wasn't part of any cover-up.'

'I'm sure that's true, Mona.' Ria felt guilty then. For years she herself had been part of a cover-up.

'And, Ria, I think you are quite right to take a strong stand. I wish I had done that years ago, I really do.'

Ria could hardly believe this conversation was taking place. All the taboos with Polly and Mona suddenly broken after all the years. 'You did what was right then,' she said.

'I only did what made less waves, it wasn't necessarily what was right,' Mona said. 'But great good luck to you out there and if I can take your American friend anywhere just ask her to call me.'

Yes, they were all going to rally round when Marilyn arrived. Gertie was going to come and clean for her and Colm had phoned to say he would invite her to the restaurant, introduce her to a few people.

Now Ria waited at home to face the evening when she would say goodbye to her children.

They had told her little about their meeting with Bernadette. She had learned only practical things like that the holiday on the Shannon cruiser was on course, that the new house had been hurried on—Barney

McCarthy's men were there night and day finishing the renovations and it was now finally ready. Smelling of paint but ready; they would sleep there tomorrow night.

And they had met Bernadette's mother who was all right really and would drive them to a swimming pool for a course of six lessons. It was so that they could get themselves ready for the one in America. Ria felt she knew everything and yet nothing about the life that her children would live without her.

They had supper in the garden, kebabs, with sausages for Brian and lots of little vegetables that Colm had left in a basket for Annie.

'This isn't our house any more, not after tomorrow morning when you go,' Annie said.

'No, that's true, but on the other hand it will be lived in by someone whose own house *you* are going to visit. It would be nice to introduce yourselves to her.'

'Do we have to?' Brian saw tedious conversations with adults ahead.

'No, of course not. It would be nice, that's all.'

Rosemary had offered to drive the children to Danny's new house the next morning so that Ria would have time to leave the house unfussed. Most of their things were there already. Ria had taped to the inside of their suitcases lists of clothes that they were to pack for the boat trip. They were to check these carefully before they left.

'Dad's coming round here later to say goodbye, isn't he?' Brian's face was still hoping for some reassurance that things were normal.

'That's right, when you've gone to bed, there are a few last-minute things we have to discuss.'

Danny arrived at ten o'clock. With a shock Ria realised how physically attractive he still was to her and would always be. She had to control herself before she stretched out a hand to touch him. She must behave calmly, he must not know how much power he had to move her.

'We'll go out to the garden in a minute, it's so peaceful. But first what would you like? Tea? A drink?'

'I'll have tea,' he said.

'The kids say the new house is very nice,' she said.

'Good, good.'

They brought their mugs of tea out to the garden and sat on a stone bench. There was a silence.

'About money,' he said.

'Well *I* bought *my* air ticket, you've bought theirs. The rest is just as if we were here, isn't it?'

'Yes.' His voice seemed a bit flat.

'And the electricity, gas and phone are paid by banker's order here?'

'Yes,' he said again.

'So that's money sorted out, is it?' Ria asked.

'I suppose so.'

'And I hope you all have a lovely time on the Shannon. Are you going south or north when you get on the boat?'

'South to Lough Derg. Lots of lovely little places to moor, it would be fabulous if we got the weather.'

They were talking like two strangers.

'I've left your telephone number for Marilyn.'

'Good, good.'

'And perhaps you might bring the children round here to meet her one day?'

'What? Oh yes, certainly.'

There was nothing left to say. They walked up the stairs and stood awkwardly in the hall which had been full of crates and bicycles on the day they had vowed to make it a great home for ever and ever.

Now the polished floor with its two good rugs glowed warmly in the evening light. The door to the front room was open. There on their table was a bowl of roses that Colm had picked to welcome the American guest. They reflected in the wood, the clock on the mantelpiece chimed and the wind moved the heavy velvet curtains.

Danny went in and looked around him. Surely he was full of regret not just for these pieces but for the time and energy and love that had gone into gathering them. He was very still.

Ria knew she would never forget him standing here like this, his hand on the back of one of the chairs. He looked as if he had just thought of the one final thing that this room needed. Maybe a grand-father clock? Possibly another mirror to reflect the window? He did *not* look like a man about to go away from all that he had built up here to stay with a pregnant girl called Bernadette.

Ria said nothing. She stood holding her breath as if waiting for him to begin to rebuild the dream. The room was working a magic of its own. He would speak, he would say it was madness, he was so sorry that he had hurt so many people. And she would forgive him, gently, and he would know that he had come back home where he belonged.

Why was he taking so long to find the words? Should she help him, give him a pointer in the right direction? And then he looked at her directly and she saw he was biting his lip, he really was struggling to say what was almost too huge to be said.

She moved very slightly towards him, just one step, and it seemed to have been enough. He came and put his arms round her, his head on her shoulder. He wasn't actually crying but he was trembling and shaking so heavily that she could feel it all through his body.

'Ria, Ria, what a mess, what a waste and a mess,' he said.

'It doesn't have to be.' She was very gentle into his ear.

'Oh God, I wish it had all been different. I wish that so much.' He wasn't looking at her, still talking to her hair.

'It can be. It can all be what we make it,' she said.

Slowly, Ria, she warned herself. Don't come out with a long list of promises and resolutions. Let him do the asking. Stroke his forehead and say that it will all be all right in the end; that's what he wants to hear. He moved his face from her neck and he was about to kiss her.

She raised her arms from his shaking shoulders and almost clenched him round the neck. Her lips sought his, searching and demanding. It was so good to hold him again. She felt herself carried away in what could only be called a flood of passion, and didn't realise that he was tugging at her hands behind his neck.

'Ria, what are you doing? Ria, stop!' He seemed shocked and appalled.

She pulled away, mystified. He had reached for her; he had laid his head on her shoulder and said it was a waste, a mess. He had said he wanted to undo it, hadn't he? Why was he looking at her like this?

'It will be all right,' she said, flustered now but sure that her role must still be one of making smooth his homecoming. 'I promise you, Danny, it will be all right. This is where you belong.'

'*Ria!*' He was horrified now.

'This is your room, you created this. It's yours, like we are your family, you know that.'

'I beg you, Ria . . .'

'And I beg *you* . . . come back. It will all be as it was. I'll understand you have responsibilities to Bernadette and even affection . . .'

'Stop this . . .'

'She'll get over it, Danny. She's a child, she has her whole life ahead of her, with someone of her own age. She'll look back on it as something foolish, wonderful but foolish . . .'

'This is not possible . . . that you should . . . I don't know, suddenly change like this.' He did look bewildered.

But this was madness. *He* was the one who had reached out for her. 'You held me. You told me it was all a mess and a mistake and a waste and you were sorry you did it.' The tears were pouring down her face now. 'Danny, I love you so much I'd forgive anything you did, you *know* that. I'd do anything on earth that it takes to have you back.'

He took her hands in both of his. 'No, Ria, that's not the way things are, and I'm going now but I want you to know how . . .'

'How what?' she asked.

'How generous it would have been of you to make that offer, if there had been any question of it. It would have been a very unselfish thing to do.'

She looked at him in amazement. He didn't see that there was no unselfishness or generosity involved. It was what she ached for. He would never realise that, and now she had made a total fool of herself.

The weeks of planning and driving herself and discipline had been thrown away. Why had they come into this room anyway? If she had not seen that look on his face she might not have seen a possible lifeline. But she had seen it; she had not imagined it.

'Yes, it's late, of course you must go,' she said. The tears had stopped. She was in control again, and she could sense his relief.

'Safe journey,' he said to her on the steps.

'Oh yes, thank you, I'm sure it will be fine.'

'And we did make a lovely house, Ria, we really did.' He looked past her back into the hall.

'Yes, yes indeed, and two marvellous children,' she said.

On the steps of the house they had spent so long creating, Danny and Ria kissed each other cautiously on the cheek. Then Danny got into his car and drove away and Ria went into her home in Tara Road and sat for a long time at her round table, staring sightless in front of her.

6

ROSEMARY ARRIVED EARLIER than expected. Ria handed her a cup of coffee.

'You look fine,' Rosemary said approvingly.

'Sure.'

'I came early to leave you less time for tearful farewells. Where are they anyway?'

'Finishing their packing.' Ria sounded very muted.

'They'll be OK.'

'I know.'

Rosemary looked at her friend sharply. 'Was it all right last night with Danny and everything?'

'What? Oh yes, very civilised.' Never in a million years would anyone know how it had been last night with Danny.

'Well, then, that's good.' There was a silence. 'You know, I did think this whole jaunt to America was mad, but now I think it's the cleverest thing you could have done. Hey, here come the kids. What do you want, lingering or brisk?'

'Brisk, and you're wonderful,' Ria said gratefully.

In minutes Ria was waving goodbye as Rosemary drove the children to stay in a strange house for the month of July.

She walked through the duty-free shop wondering what she should buy. She stopped by the perfumes.

'I want something very new, something I've never smelt before, which will have no memories,' she said.

The assistant seemed used to such requests. Together they examined the new scents and settled on one that was light and flowery.

She fell asleep on the plane and dreamed that Marilyn had not left Tudor Drive but was sitting waiting for her in the garden. Marilyn had brown hair and copper shoes and was wearing a beige suit just like Bernadette's mother had worn. She spoke with a cackle when Ria arrived. 'I'm not Marilyn, you stupid woman, I'm Danny's new mother-in-law. I've got you out here so that they can all move into Tara Road. It was all a trick, a trick, a trick.' Ria woke sweating. Her heart was racing.

The air hostess was concerned. 'Are you all right? You're as white as anything.'

'Yes . . . I had a bad dream, that's all.'

'Have you anyone meeting you at Kennedy?'

'No, but I'll be fine.'

She lay back and closed her eyes. How ridiculous of her subconscious to have made Marilyn look like Bernadette's mother when of course she looked totally different. Ria opened her eyes suddenly in shock. She knew that Marilyn would have her fortieth birthday while she was in Ireland but she did not know whether she was fair or dark, tall or small, thin or fat. She had no idea whatsoever what Marilyn looked like.

She just had the names and phone numbers of two women called Carlotta and Heidi and photographs of Marilyn Vine's garden, swimming pool, main bedroom and carport in Tudor Drive.

The flights to Dublin were at night and Marilyn accepted Heidi's offer to drive her there. She closed the door and left the keys and an envelope of instructions with her neighbour, Carlotta, who had offered to meet Ria when she arrived in the early evening. She had left her house in perfect order. Clean, freshly laundered linen and towels everywhere, food in the icebox, flowers on the table.

She decided about locking the room only when she heard Heidi's car pull up outside the house. She left the door closed but not locked. Ria would understand.

All the instructions had worked like a dream. The coach was where Marilyn had said it would be, the fare was exactly as she had described. Ria took a deep breath when she saw the sign for Westville coming up. As the coach pulled in, Ria took her two suitcases and climbed down the steps. Carlotta must be the tall, full-bosomed, Mexican-looking woman waiting beside a car at the stop.

'Ria, welcome to the United States, I hope you're going to love Westville. We are just delighted that you're here.' It was so warm, so genuine, that Ria felt a prickle of tears in her eyes.

Carlotta pointed out all the amenities as she drove Ria to Tudor Drive.

Ria marvelled as they passed all the houses with their communal lawns in front. 'No fences,' she noticed.

'Well, it's neighbourly, I guess,' Carlotta said.

'Is it like that in Tudor Drive?'

'Not our part, no, it's more closed in.'

Carlotta told her the names of streets and drives that would become familiar in the next days and weeks. She pointed out the two hotels, the club and the library, the two antique shops, the florist, the OK deli, the truly great gourmet shop run by John and Gerry.

They were nearly there.

'Look, I'd love you to come in and have something to eat and drink in my place, but you're here for the summer, you'll want to get into your own place, and see what it's like.' Carlotta took out the envelope with the keys in it and prepared to hand them over.

'But aren't you going to come in with me?' Ria was surprised. 'I'd love you to come in and show me around, won't you?'

Carlotta bit her lip in indecision. 'I don't really know where their things are . . .' she began.

'Oh, please do, Carlotta. And Marilyn said she was going to leave me a bottle of wine in her fridge. So it would be a lovely start for me.'

Further protest was useless. Ria was already out of the car and looking up at her new home. 'Do we go in this gate or round by the carport?'

'I'm not sure.' Carlotta looked flustered. 'I've never been in the house.'

The pause was minimal. Then Ria spoke. 'So, it will be a new experience for both of us,' she said.

And taking a suitcase each they went in to explore Number 1024 Tudor Drive, home of the Vines.

Marilyn told herself that Ria's instructions about what to do on arriving in Dublin had been excellent. Ria advised that she should get a bus to the city, leave her bags and walk up to have breakfast in a Grafton Street coffee shop. After breakfast she should take a cab, pick up her luggage and head for Tara Road. One of the people already mentioned would be there to welcome her in and show her round.

The taxi driver told her that Tara Road was the fastest-moving bit of property in Dublin. A regular gold mine.

'If your friends own that house, ma'am, they're sitting on half a million,' he said confidently as he drove in the gateway and drew up at the foot of the steps.

The door was opened by a good-looking man in his early forties. He came down the steps, hand stretched out. 'On Ria's behalf, you're very welcome to Tara Road,' he said. 'I'm Colm Barry, neighbour and friend. I also dig the back garden but I use a back gate so I'll be no intrusion in your time here.'

Marilyn looked at him gratefully. He was courteous but also he was cool in a way that she very much liked. 'Indeed, the man who runs the restaurant,' she said.

'The very one,' he agreed. He carried her cases up the granite steps.

Ria's photographs had not lied. The hall was glorious with its deep-glowing wooden floor and elegant hall table. The door to a front room was open. Colm pushed it slightly. 'If it were my house I would never leave this room,' he said simply. 'It runs the whole depth of the house, windows at each end. It's just lovely.' On the table was a huge bowl of roses. 'Ria asked me to leave those for you.'

Marilyn felt a gulp in her voice as she thanked him. The place was so beautiful and these rich pink and red roses on such a beautiful table were the final touch.

He carried her cases upstairs and showed her the main bedroom. 'I expect this is where you'll be, I'm sure all the details were written out for you. Ria's been getting ready for weeks. I know she's gone to huge trouble.'

Marilyn knew it too. Her eyes took in the immaculate white bedcover, the folded towels, the shiny paintwork and the empty closet.

They went down to the kitchen and Colm opened the fridge. 'Ah, she's left you some basics, I see, including a soup made from vegetables grown in the garden. Shall I take some out for you to heat up? You've had a long journey, you'll want to settle in.'

What a restful pleasant neighbour, Marilyn thought, when Colm had left. He was a fellow spirit, a soul mate. He somehow understood that she wanted to be alone. She was glad he had been there to welcome her.

She wandered slowly about the house that would be hers until September. The children's rooms had been tidied, pictures of soccer players on Brian's wall, pop stars on Annie's. Plastic models of wrestlers on Brian's windowsills, soft furry toys on Annie's. Two well-kept bathrooms, one with what looked like genuine Victorian bathroom fittings. And one empty, lifeless room, a lot of shelving on the wall but nothing on display. This must have been a study that belonged to Danny.

A warm, almost crowded kitchen, shelves of cookbooks, cupboards full of pans and baking dishes, a kitchen where people baked, ate and lived. A house full of beautiful objects but first and foremost a home. There was very little wall space that did not have pictures of the family, mainly of the children but some which included the handsome Danny Lynch as well. He had not been cut out of their lives because he had gone away. Marilyn looked at his face for some clues about this man. One thing she knew from being in his home: he must love this new woman very much or have been very unhappy in his marriage to Ria to enable him to leave all this without a backward glance.

Carlotta and Ria toured the house. They moved from the big open-plan living room with its coloured rugs on the floor, also three white leather sofas circling an open fireplace, into the huge kitchen with its breakfast bar and dining table, into Greg's study room lined with books from ceiling to floor on three walls and with a red leather desk and big black swivel chair under one window. Three tables stood around, all of them with little sculptures, ornaments, treasures of sorts.

'What a beautiful room,' Ria said. 'If you could see *my* husband's study now . . . it's like, well it's like a shell.'

'Why is that?' Carlotta asked reasonably.

Ria paused and looked at her. 'Sorry, he's my ex-husband, and he's just moved out so his study's empty. But it was never like this. Should we tour the garden, do you think?'

'The garden will be there tomorrow,' Carlotta said.

'Then let's hit Marilyn's bottle of Chardonnay,' Ria suggested.

Just at that moment there was a knock on the door. Carlotta and Ria looked at each other, and went together to answer it. A woman in her forties stood there carrying a gift-wrapped bottle.

'I'm Heidi Franks. I work with Marilyn and I wanted to welcome you . . . well, hello, Carlotta, I didn't know you'd be here . . .'

'Ria insisted that I came by.' Carlotta seemed to be apologising, as if she had been discovered intruding.

'Come on in, Heidi,' Ria said. 'You arrived at a great time, we were just about to have a drink.'

'Well, I don't really like to . . .'

Ria wondered what made them both apologise for coming into this home. Americans were legendary for their friendliness and their ease, yet both Carlotta and Heidi seemed to be looking over their shoulders in case the shadow of Marilyn Vine might fall on the place and they would have to run away.

She put away the fanciful thoughts and ushered them into the kitchen.

Marilyn unpacked everything and had her soup. And a glass of the expensive French wine that Ria had left her. Then she lay for a long time upstairs in the claw-foot bath and soaked away the hours of travel.

She thought she might sleep, but no, all during the long afternoon her eyes were open and her mind was racing. Two sunny children smiled out of photographs in every room in Tara Road. A boy with a grin as wide as a watermelon, and a girl who would be almost the same age as Dale. Marilyn lay under the white bedspread in the master bedroom of this house which had everything, and thought of her life which had nothing.

Heidi and Carlotta left at about ten o'clock, which was three o'clock in the morning at home. Ria walked slowly round Marilyn's house. Was Marilyn asleep? Maybe she was awake thinking about her. Ria went into the room that she had just glimpsed before she had instinctively shut the door against Carlotta. She turned on the light. The walls were covered with pictures of motorbikes, Electra Glides, Hondas.

A bed had some boys' clothes strewn on it, jackets, jeans, shoes . . . as if a fifteen-year-old had come in, rummaged for something to wear and then gone out. The closet had clothes hanging neatly on a rail and on the shelves were piles of shirts and shorts and socks. The desk at the window had school papers on it, magazines, books. There were photographs too, of a boy, a smiling, good-looking teenage boy with hair that stuck up in spikes, always with a group of friends. They were playing basketball in one, they were swimming in another, they were out in the snow, they were in costume for a school play. The pictures were laid out casually.

There must be something in this house which would give her an image of what Marilyn Vine looked like. And then she found it. A summer picture of a threesome; the boy in tennis clothes, all smiles, with his arm round the shoulders of a man with thinning hair and an open-necked shirt. The woman was tall and thin and she wore a yellow track suit. She had high cheekbones, short, reddish hair and she wore her sunglasses on her head. They were like an advertisement for healthy living, all three of them.

Rosemary left a note in the letterbox.

> Dear Marilyn,
>
> Welcome to Dublin. When you wake up I'm sure you may want to go straight back to sleep and not get involved with nosy neighbours, but this is just a word to say that whenever you would like to come round for a drink or even to have a lunch with me in Quentin's, which you might enjoy, all you have to do is telephone.
>
> I don't want to overpower you with invitations and demands, but as Ria's oldest and I hope dearest friend I wanted to welcome you and say I hope you have a good time here.
>
> Most sincerely
> Rosemary Ryan

Marilyn had the note in her hand before Rosemary had run back to her car outside the gate. Through the window Marilyn saw a tall blonde woman in a well-cut suit that was most definitely power-dressing. With a flash of elegant smoky tights and high heels she was getting into a black BMW and driving away. This was the woman that Ria had described in her letters as her great friend, who was a business tycoon and Ms Perfect, but absolutely delightful at the same time.

Marilyn read the letter with approval. No pressure, but generous. But she didn't want to meet this woman, make conversation with her. It didn't matter how important these people were in Ria's life, they weren't part of hers. Marilyn hadn't come to Ireland to make a whole set of superficial acquaintances.

'I dreamed about you, Colm,' Orla King said as he came into the restaurant.

'No, you didn't. You decided you wanted to ask me could you sing here on Friday and you needed an excuse to come and see me.' He smiled at her to take the harm out of his words.

Orla laughed good-naturedly. 'Of course I want to sing here on Friday and Saturday, and every night in August during Horse Show week when you'll be full. But I actually did dream about you.'

'Was I a successful restaurant owner, tell me that?'

'No, you were in jail for life for murdering your brother-in-law, Monto,' Orla said.

'Always very melodramatic, Orla,' Colm said, but his smile didn't quite go to his eyes.

'Yeah, but we don't choose what we dream, it just happens,' Orla said with a shrug. 'It must mean something.'

'I don't *think* I murdered my brother-in-law,' Colm said as if trying to remember. 'No, I'm sure I didn't. He was here last night with a big crowd from the races.'

'Monto told me that . . . well, he sort of said that . . .' Orla stopped.

'Yes?'

'He sort of hinted that he had problems with your sister Caroline.'

'Yes, I think he has a problem remembering he is married to her. Anyway, Orla, you'd like to sing on Friday? A couple of pointers. You sing as background not as foreground. They want to talk to each other as well as listen to you. Is that understood?'

'Right, boss.'

'You'll sing much more Ella and lots less Lloyd Webber. OK?'

'You're wrong, but yes, boss.'

'You keep your hands and eyes off Danny Lynch. He'll be here with his new wife and his two kids and his mother-in-law.'

'It's not a new wife, it's his pregnant girlfriend so don't be pompous, Colm.'

'Hands and eyes. A promise or no slot and you never work here again.'

'A promise, boss.'

Colm wondered why he had warned Orla off, after all it might be some small pleasure for Ria out in America to hear that the love nest was less secure than everyone imagined. But business was business and who wanted a scene in a restaurant on a Friday night?

'We're going to take Mrs Dunne out to dinner on Friday night,' Danny told his children.

'Mam's going to ring on Friday night,' Brian objected.

'She told us to call her Finola, not Mrs Dunne,' Annie objected.

'OK, so she's Finola. Fine, fine. Now I thought we might go to Quentin's, but it turns out that she . . . Finola . . . wants to go to Colm's so that's where we're going.'

'Dead right too,' Annie said. 'Colm has proper vegetarian food not some awful poncey thing that costs what would keep a poor family for a month like the token vegetarian dish in Quentin's costs.'

'But what if Mam rings?' Brian asked.

'There's an answering machine and if we miss her we'll call her back.' Danny was bright about it all.

'She might be looking forward to talking to us though,' Brian said.

'We could change the message and say we were all at Colm's maybe?' Annie suggested.

'No, I think we'll leave the message as it is.' Danny was firm.

'But it's so easy, Dad.'

'People ring Bernadette, too, and they wouldn't want to hear all about our fumblings and foosterings.'

'It's not fumbling just to let Mam know that we hadn't forgotten she was going to call,' Annie said.

'Well, call her! Say we're going out.'

Marilyn had taken a chair and a cup of coffee out to the front steps; she sat in the sun examining the garden.

There was so much that could be done with it. Such a pity they hadn't given it any real love and care, unlike the house itself.

Outside the gate she noticed a woman in her sixties with a very mis-shapen and unattractive dog. The woman was staring in with interest.

'Good morning,' Marilyn said politely.

'And good morning to you too. I expect you're the American visitor.'

'Yes, I'm Marilyn Vine. Are you a neighbour?'

'I'm Ria's mother, Nora, and this is Pliers. Ria said most definitely that we should not call in unannounced.' Nora had come up the step to continue the conversation but she looked doubtful. Pliers gave a wide and very unpleasant yawn.

'Has Lady Ryan been round yet?'

'I beg your pardon?'

'Ria's friend, Rosemary?'

'No, she left a note though. People have been so kind.'

After Ria's mother left, Marilyn took out the wallet of photographs that she had been given. She had to know who these people were when they all turned up as they would, so when Gertie arrived, slightly hesitantly, Marilyn recognised her at once.

'Let's not be awkward about this,' Gertie began. 'I know Ria told you I need a few extra pounds a week, but it seems unfair on you to have to dig into your holiday money . . .'

'No, that's perfectly fine and I'd love to know that this beautiful house is being kept the way it always is.'

Gertie looked around her. 'But you've got the place looking great, there's not a thing out of place. It's just putting out my hand and asking for charity.'

'No, that's not the way I see it.'

'I'm not sure if Ria explained . . .' Gertie began.

'Oh, sure she did. You are kind enough to come and help to keep her house in its fine condition twice a week.'

Gertie had big black circles under her eyes. Still, it was none of her business. 'And would you like me to make you a cup of coffee?' Gertie began.

'No, thank you.'

'Well, would you like me to do anything for you like ironing maybe?'

'That's very kind. I hate ironing. I'm going out now, so shall I see you next time?'

'That's fine, and you're very welcome here, Marilyn.'

'Thank you,' Marilyn said. She took her keys and walked up Tara Road. Lord, but this house was going to be full of people. Not exactly the rest she had been looking for.

'What does it say?' Brian asked.

'It's an American woman's voice saying she's not there and to leave a message for the people who are there,' Annie replied.

'There aren't any people . . . there's only Mam.'

'Shut up, Brian. Hello, Mam, it's Annie and Brian, and everything's fine and it's just that we'll be going out to a big dinner with Dad and . . . well, what I mean is that we'll be going out to dinner in Colm's restaurant on Friday so we won't be back until maybe eleven o'clock our time. We didn't want you to ring and find nobody at home. That's it, Mam. Brian's OK too.'

'Let me say I'm OK,' Brian cried.

'You're not to waste the call, Mam knows you're OK.'

Brian snatched the phone. 'I'm OK, Mam, and getting on at the swimming. Finola says the coach told her that I'm making fine progress. Oh, Finola's Bernadette's mother by the way. She's coming with us to the dinner.'

Annie snatched the phone back and hung up. 'Aren't you the greatest eejit in the whole wide world to mention Finola? Aren't you a fool of the first order?' she said to him, her eyes blazing.

'I'm sorry.' Brian was crestfallen. 'I'm so sorry. I just didn't think. I was so excited about leaving the message for Mam.'

He looked so upset that even Annie Lynch's hard heart relented. 'It's not the end of the world, I suppose,' she said gruffly.

Ria came in from the pool wearing one of Marilyn's towelling jackets. For the first few times she had just flopped around luxuriating in the cold water and the beautiful flowers and the lovingly kept garden all around her. But she had taken to reading Dale's sports books all laid out so neatly in his room. There had been a swimming notebook recording how many lengths he and his friends had done on different days. One entry said: 'Mom has decided to stop behaving like a dolphin and be a proper swimmer. So she's doing four lengths each time, it's nothing but she's going to build it up.'

She saw the little red light flickering on the phone and rushed to play back the message. She sat at the breakfast bar listening to her children speaking to her from thousands of miles away. The tears poured down her face. Why was she not at home with them instead of leaving them to become bosom pals with Bernadette's bloody mother?

Maybe this woman who was somehow Finola to Ria's children and yet was Mummy to Bernadette was now a huge influence in their lives. She was going out to dinner with them, for heaven's sake. That hurt more than anything.

It was too much to bear. Ria put her head down on the breakfast bar in the sunny kitchen and cried and cried. She didn't see a man come to the glass doors and pause before knocking. He, however, saw a woman doubled over in grief. This was not the time to call and say that he was Greg Vine's brother just passing through and that he had come to see Marilyn. He picked up his canvas bag, walked back to his rented car and drove to a motel.

It had been such a house of tragedy since the accident he had hardly been able to bear visiting it. And now he had come across a strange woman in a pool wrap, crying with a kind of intensity he had never known. Still, he had promised his brother that if work took him east he would look up Marilyn. He had thought, wrongly, that it would be better to come without warning, otherwise she would have certainly found some excuse not to meet him.

He had a shower, a cool beer at the motel and then he telephoned his brother's house. A recording of Marilyn's voice said Marilyn and Greg were both away but to leave a message for the people staying in the house. On a whim he spoke.

'My name is Andy Vine. I'm Greg's brother, passing through Westville staying at the . . . sorry . . .' he hunted for the name and number of the motel. 'I know Greg's in Hawaii obviously, but perhaps you might kindly call me and tell me where Marilyn is? I would much appreciate this. Many thanks in advance.'

Ria sat listening to the message. Marilyn had not mentioned a brother-in-law. Perhaps there was a coldness. If he was a brother of Greg Vine then surely he'd know that Greg's wife was in Dublin. If he was a brother-in-law of Marilyn and had thought she was at home, why had he not called round? She decided she would call Greg Vine in Hawaii.

She was put through to him with great ease. He sounded younger and more relaxed than his photograph had suggested.

'Yes, of course,' he said when she gave her name.

'First, I must assure you that there's no problem here. Everything in your beautiful house is in fine shape,' she said.

'That's a relief, I thought you were going to tell me the plumbing wasn't working.'

'No, nothing like that, and I suppose in a way because I'm living in your home . . . I wanted to introduce myself to you . . . but not at length on your phone bill.'

'That's most courteous of you. I hope you have everything you need.' His voice was polite but cold.

Ria told him about the call from the motel. Greg assured her that he did have a highly respectable brother called Andy who worked in Los Angeles but came to Boston and New York City on business from time to time.

'That's fine then, I'll call him, I thought it wiser to check it out because he didn't seem to know anything about Marilyn's movements.'

'I appreciate your caution very much. But Marilyn was, let us say, a trifle reserved in telling people anything about her movements.' He sounded bitter.

Ria decided to ignore the tone. 'Well, I've spoken to her and she's arrived safely and is as well installed as I am in Tudor Drive. It would be good if you had the chance to go over there yourself.'

'Oh, I don't think that's in the master plan.' His voice sounded icy.

'I asked would you be going, she said she didn't know.'

There was a pause.

'And your son?'

'Yes?'

'He likes Hawaii?'

'I beg your pardon?'

'I suppose it's a place that all young people would like.' Ria felt flustered, although she did not know why.

'Oh, yes. Certainly.'

'I expect he's missing his mother.'

'I'm sorry?'

'They never pretend, but they do in a way that they can't even define.' She knew she was gushing. 'Boys . . .' said Ria nervously.

'Well, yes.' He seemed anxious to end the conversation.

'I won't keep you any longer,' she said. 'I'm not clear about what's going on in anyone's lives these days, but just be sure that your house is in fine shape.'

'Of course, of course. And is it working for you being over here?'

'It was,' Ria said truthfully. 'It was working quite well, but I just got a message from my children on your answering machine.'

'Are they missing you? Is that the problem?'

'No, Greg. They're not missing me, *that's* the problem.'

'**M**arilyn? This is Rosemary Ryan.'

'Oh yes, thank you for your note.'

Rosemary was to the point. 'I wondered can I take you and Gertie to Colm's restaurant on Friday for dinner? He has a special seafood evening, and you might enjoy it.'

'I don't want to intrude.'

'This would be a casual easy girls' night out. Gertie doesn't go out socially. Do say yes.'

'Thank you so much, Rosemary, I'd love to join you.'

Ria called Andy Vine at the motel, told him who she was and where Marilyn had gone.

'We both needed a little space in our lives and thought it would be a good idea,' she said.

He seemed happy enough with the explanation.

'And in the normal turn of events would you be staying here in Tudor Drive, I mean if Marilyn had been at home and everything?'

'Well, I might,' he said.

'So you shouldn't be paying for a motel really, should you? If you expected to stay here in your brother's house?' She was eager to do the right thing.

'No, please, Ria. Please don't think like that. It's your house now just as the house in Ireland belongs to Marilyn.'

'I feel bad about it. How long are you going to be in Westville?'

'I had thought that maybe I'd spend tonight and Saturday night here, you know, if Marilyn were about . . . then drive up to Boston on Sunday. My conference starts on Monday morning.'

'I'm sorry she didn't think of telling you. It was all arranged in a bit of a hurry,' Ria apologised.

This couldn't be the woman he had seen crying like no one had ever cried before. 'I had been going to ask Marilyn out to dinner in a new Thai restaurant.'

'Maybe next time,' she said.

'Would *you* like a Thai dinner, Ria?' he asked.

She paused. It was the last thing on earth she thought would happen to her in America, a man who hadn't even seen her inviting her out to dinner within a week of her arrival. But it was a Friday night. Back in Ireland her children were being taken to Colm's restaurant with a lot of strangers. 'Thank you, Andy, I'd be delighted to accept,' Ria Lynch said.

'**M**onto wants to bring in a crowd tonight,' Colm said.

'What did you tell him?' Caroline was immediately anxious.

'I told him we were full. Then he said I was to have a word with you and that he'd call back later and see if we had an unexpected cancellation for six people.'

'Give it to him, Colm.'

'Why? It upsets you when they're here. We don't need the business those guys bring in, six overdone steaks and round after round of double gins.'

'Please, Colm . . .?'

'It's utterly terrifying for me to see you so afraid of him.' He looked at her big sad eyes with such compassion that he could see the tears form in the corners. 'Still, I'll do what you say. Which table will they be least noticeable at, do you think?'

She gave him a watery smile. 'Look, do you think I'd be like this about him if there was any other solution?'

'There *is* a solution.'

'We've had this conversation a thousand times.'

'I'm so sorry, Caroline.' He put his arms round his sister and she laid her head on his shoulder.

'What have you to be sorry for? You've done everything for me, you've saved my life.'

He patted her on the back as he held her and behind him he heard the cheery voice of Orla King.

'Well, hello, everybody. Did I come a little early?'

'I brought you martinis in honour of the visiting American,' Colm said. It proved to be a great success.

Marilyn told Rosemary and Gertie about her happy day digging in the front garden. She was never happier than when up to her elbows in earth. She had decided to attack the undergrowth at Number 16. If the other two thought that she might have checked with Ria before embarking on it they said nothing. And of course it was quite possible that she had.

Gertie told them about a man in the launderette who came there every Saturday and washed a bag of women's black lacy underwear. Quite unconcerned as people saw him taking them out and folding them neatly into a big carrier bag. Gertie said that she'd love to be able to tell these little things to Jack, but that sadly you never knew how he would take them.

And when a good-looking blonde began to sing 'Someone to Watch Over Me', Gertie told Marilyn that this was about the most troublesome woman in Dublin and that she had been known to cause spectacular scenes in her time.

'She's a good singer, though,' Marilyn said, struggling to be fair and looking at the girl who played and sang as if every word had a huge meaning for her.

At that moment Danny Lynch and his party came into the restaurant and they were settled at a table across the room. Marilyn recognised them immediately from the photographs Ria had sent her. 'Is that Ria's husband?' she asked. And Rosemary and Gertie nodded glumly.

Until this stage in the meal Ria had not been spoken of at all. Now her whole personal story was here in the restaurant and they couldn't skirt round it any more. A glamorous, well-made-up woman in a black sequinned jacket was being very much the centre of things, pointing at where people were to sit.

'She doesn't look like a twenty-two-year-old to me, she's my age if she's a day,' Marilyn whispered.

'You're not going to believe this, Marilyn, but that's the twenty-two-year-old's mother,' whispered Rosemary.

'Mother!' said Marilyn in disbelief.

Then she saw, beside the two animated children familiar from their pictures, the waif in a shapeless blue jumper and skirt. A pale child with long straight hair who could definitely be taken for Annie's not very much older sister. Marilyn felt a pain that was almost physical to think that Ria Lynch had to endure this. How could anyone bear the pain of losing a man to this, this strange unformed young girl?

Orla began to sing 'The Man I Love'. Colm frowned. He frowned even more deeply when she went straight into 'They're Singing Songs of Love but Not for Me'. 'Cool it, Orla,' he said as he passed with the steaks for Monto's table.

'Pure Gershwin, boss, as you suggested. Coming up with "Nice Work if You Can Get It". That should set a few hearts fluttering.'

'You have a reasonably nice voice but you don't have all that much of a career. And while you're at it, if you go on like you're going on tonight, forget the Horse Show next month.'

'Be fair, Colm. You said Cole Porter and Gershwin. Can I help it, boss, if the titles have a bit of innuendo? I don't write them, I'm only singing them at your request.'

'Don't be a fool, Orla, please. I warn you, you'll be so very, very sorry tomorrow. I'll still have a restaurant, you won't have a job or a chance of ever getting one in Dublin.'

'He left me, he could have had me and he went for an old trout in a sequinned jacket.' Her eyes were too bright.

'That's not who's with Danny.'

'He's holding her bloody arm, who else is he with? The others are children.'

'The one in the blue sweater; the black sequins is his future mother-in-law.'

She looked over again, astounded. 'You're making it up.'

'I'm not, but you're not going to have a chance to check it.'

'She's under the age of consent, it's not legal.' She was standing up now, prepared to go over to Danny Lynch's table.

'Orla, sit down, this minute. Play. Don't sing. Play "Smoke Gets In Your Eyes". Play it, Orla, or leave. Now.'

'You and whose army will make me?'

'Monto's army.' He looked over at their table. Six rough vulgar men whom he disliked intensely.

'They like me, why would they throw me out?'

'Where did you put it? The drink? I was onto you the moment you came in, I checked your grapefruit juice.'

She threw her head back and laughed. 'It's in the flower vase, you fool. First line of defence. Half-bottle of vodka in with the carnations.'

He picked up the vase and emptied the contents into an empty wine bucket and indicated to a waiter to take it away.

'Hey, Colm, are you going to stand there looking down the singer's tits all night, or serve us our steaks?' Monto called from his table.

A few people laughed nervously. Others looked away.

Orla got up, and taking her microphone with her began to wander round the room. 'I'd like to do requests for people,' she said. 'I think this is what makes a night out special. But so often people don't always quite know exactly what they want to hear. So I thought that possibly tonight I could *choose* songs for people, something that could be appropriate. And sing a few bars at each table.'

People were laughing and encouraging her. To the customers who didn't know her, Orla King was an attractive, professional singer. Now she was doing something a little more personal, that was all there was to it. But many people in the room froze and they watched her edgily.

First she came to Rosemary's table. 'We have three lovely ladies here,' she said. 'Feminists, oh definitely. Lesbians? Very possibly. Anyway, no men. My grandmother used to sing a song called "There Were Three Lovely Lassies From Bannion". But it's a little too old even for this group. Suppose I were to sing "Sisters" for them . . . ?'

'Did I do anything except help you all your life?' Rosemary asked, with the mask of a frozen smile on her face.

'You had your reasons,' Orla said. She judged that a few bars were enough and moved to Monto's table. 'Six men, powerful men, rich men.' She smiled radiantly round the room. 'Now what song should we choose for them? Oh I know, "Four and twenty virgins came down from Inverness and when the ball was over there were four and twenty less".' She smiled and moved to the Lynches' table. Colm Barry was at Monto's table, whispering feverishly.

'Well, well, what a wonderful family group. What would you like?'

Only Brian thought it was a real question. He chose a Spice Girls song. 'Do you know "Whaddya Want, Whaddya Really Want"?' he asked eagerly.

His innocent face halted her in her tracks. Just for one moment, but for long enough to throw her. 'What about "Love and Marriage"? No, that's not permanent enough. What about that nice song "She Was Only Sixteen"? No, she must be older than that, isn't she, Danny?' As she turned, Monto and one of his henchmen lifted her bodily and were carrying her to the door. 'Don't think people don't know, Danny. They know what you and I had . . .'

Her voice was no longer heard. The embarrassed silence that fell on the restaurant seemed to last for ever. Rosemary sat white-faced and furious at her table, with the new American woman from Ria's house confused and bewildered beside her. And with them was Gertie, terrified to see yet again at first hand the damage drink could do.

Colm saw his waiters looking at him as if waiting for a lead. It could only have been seconds, he realised, since Orla's struggling body had been carried out of his restaurant. It felt like a lifetime. He straightened his shoulders, indicated by a gesture that one table should be cleared, that a wine bucket should be placed nearer to another.

Then he approached Rosemary Ryan's table. 'Well, well,' he said, looking directly at Marilyn Vine. 'You can't say we don't show you life in the fast lane in Dublin.'

'No, indeed.' Her face was impassive.

'I'm embarrassed that this should have happened the first time you come to my place,' he said. Marilyn nodded her head as if accepting his apology.

'It was all a bit like a cabaret really,' said poor Gertie, trying to put some favourable gloss on it.

At the Lynch table they hadn't quite recovered either. 'Sorry about the cabaret.' Colm had decided to play it low key.

'Was it something she ate, do you think?' Brian asked with interest.

'I very much hope not, speaking as a restaurant owner.' Colm forced a smile.

'More like something you gave her to drink.' Danny's voice was cold.

'No, Danny, you know I wouldn't do that. Like myself, Orla can't drink like all you people can, but she was upset by something and she had hidden vodka in the flower vase.'

Bernadette clapped her hand over her mouth to stop the giggle. 'The flower vase? It must have tasted *awful*,' she said.

'I hope it did.' Colm smiled at the pale girl that he had thought he would never speak to. She really *was* only a child, more a friend for Annie than for Annie's father.

'We were wondering was that the American?' Brian said. 'You know, Mam's friend Mrs Vine, over there with Rosemary and Gertie?'

'Yes, that's Marilyn Vine,' Colm said.

'Some welcome to Tara Road for her,' Danny said.

'That's what I told her, she thought it was very funny,' Colm lied and moved on to the next table.

'Thank you, Monto, I owe you for tonight.'

'You owe me for a lot more than just tonight and you know that. So you'll never tell me again that your restaurant is full.'

'No, of course not, a mistake.'

'Exactly.'

At Danny's table they had paid the bill and were leaving. 'I took the price of the wine off to compensate for the unpleasantness involved,' Colm said.

'Thank you.' Danny was cold.

'It wasn't Colm's fault,' Annie said.

'Of course not.' Danny was still chilly.

'Nor was it your father's fault that Orla picked on him specifically,' Colm said in an even icier voice.

'No indeed, and thank you very much for your generous gesture about the wine,' said Danny, changing his tack so swiftly it knocked them all off course.

Andy Vine didn't look at all like the photograph of his brother when he came in and had a drink by the pool, so Ria was glad she had telephoned Hawaii about him. He was about her own age or younger, slight and red-haired and somewhat academic.

'Do you know Thai food at all?' he was asking.

'Well, there *are* Thai restaurants in Ireland now, we are very international. But I've only been twice so I don't remember it all and I'd love you to choose for me when we get there.'

They talked easily in the restaurant. He told her about the kind of publishing his company was involved in. He explained how it had all changed so radically because of technology and CD-roms. His grandfather had been a door-to-door salesman for encyclopedias. Andy lived in LA in an apartment. He had been married, and was now divorced. There were no children.

'Did you leave her or did she leave you?' Ria asked.

'It's never as simple as that,' he smiled.

'Oh, it is,' she insisted.

'OK, I had an affair, she found out and she threw me out.'

Ria nodded. 'So you left really, by ending the marriage.'

'So you say, so she said. I didn't want it to end.'

'If you had your time all over again . . .?' She was keen to know.

'You can't rewrite history, I have no idea what I'd do. Tell me, are you divorced also?'

'I think so,' Ria said. He looked at her, startled. 'That's not as mad as it sounds. The answer is yes, I am about to be.'

'Did you leave him or . . .?'

'Oh, he left me.'

'And you won't forgive him?'

'I'm not being given the chance.' There was a pause. 'Andy, can I ask you about Dale?'

'What do you want to know exactly?'

'It's just that when I talked to Greg, well, I think I may have somehow said the wrong thing. He seemed upset.'

'What did you say?'

'I don't know, ordinary things, you know, good wishes, and so on.'

Andy shook his head slowly. 'Well, everyone takes things differently. Marilyn's never really accepted it, that's the way she copes.'

'Surely all Greg has to do is to work it out with her, dates and times of visits?'

'He was trying to and then she disappeared to Ireland.'

'But when does she think he will come back?'

'In the fall.'

'That's a long time and she still leaves that room like that?' Ria was puzzled.

'What did she tell you about it all?' Andy asked.

'Nothing at all. She never mentioned she had a son.'

Andy looked upset and a little silence fell between them. And then they didn't speak about the matter again. There were plenty of other things to talk about. He told her about his childhood in Pennsylvania, she told him about her mother's obsession with the movies, he explained the passion for baseball and she told him about hurling. He told her how to make a great Caesar salad and she explained about potato cakes. She enjoyed the evening and knew he had too.

He drove her back to Tudor Drive and they sat awkwardly for a few moments in the car. Then they both spoke at once.

'If ever business takes you to Ireland . . .' Ria began.

'The conference ends on Wednesday at lunchtime . . .' Andy said.

'Please go on . . .' she said.

So he finished what he was going to say. 'And I was wondering if I drove back this way and made you a Caesar salad would you cook those potato cakes?'

'It's a deal,' Ria said with a big smile and got out of the car.

Years ago when they went out with fellows the big question always asked was 'Are you seeing him again?' And now she was back in that situation, a fellow had asked to see her again. With all that implied.

Ria stood in her bedroom and looked out on the beautiful garden that Marilyn Vine had created. She felt very out of place here. Despite the admiration in Andy Vine's eyes she felt no real sense of being pleased and flattered. He was just a strange man from a different world to hers. True, Westville was peaceful and beautiful, a place of trees and a river and a gracious, easygoing lifestyle, but it wasn't home. And at home her children had gone out to Colm's restaurant for a great evening with their new family. Tears came down her face. She must have been mad to think this was a good idea. Totally mad.

It was dawn in Tara Road. Marilyn had not slept well. What an ugly scene that had been at the restaurant. Rosemary and Gertie had filled her in on some of the background. Stories of Ria's broken marriage, the new relationship, the puzzlement of the children, the known unreliability of that offensive drunken singer, the possible criminal connection of the heavy men who had eventually taken her away. These people knew everything about everyone and were not slow in discussing it. There was no dignity or reserve.

Why had she not kept her dignity, and refused to allow all these people into her life? The only way to cope with tragedy and grief was to refuse to permit it to be articulated and acknowledged. Deny its existence and you had some hope of survival. Marilyn got out of bed and looked down on the messy garden and the other large houses of the neighbourhood. She felt very lost and alone in this place where garrulous people wanted to know everything about you and expected you to need the details of their lives too.

7

MARILYN BRACED HERSELF for endless discussions about the scenes in the restaurant when Gertie next arrived. But the woman looked frail and anxious and wasn't at all eager to speak. Possibly Jack had not appreciated the girls' night out and had showed it in the way he knew best. Gertie for once seemed relieved to be left alone to iron and kneel down and polish the legs of the beautiful table in the front room.

Marilyn worked on in the front garden. She always left Gertie's money in an envelope on the hall table with a card saying thank you. Colm worked in the back garden; there was no communication there either. Rosemary had driven by but hadn't felt it necessary to call. Ria's mother and the insane dog hadn't been in for two days.

Marilyn felt her shoulders getting tense. Perhaps she had managed to persuade them that she didn't want to be part of some big holiday camp with them all.

As Gertie was leaving, she paused and congratulated Marilyn on the work she had done. 'You have a fierce amount of energy, Marilyn.'

'Thank you.'

'I hope it gets better for you, whatever it is that's wrong,' Gertie said, and then she was gone.

Marilyn flushed a dark red. How *dare* these people assume there was something wrong? She had confided nothing to them.

Marilyn had intended to call Ria in Westville but held off. There was nothing to say. Deciding to come here had been the worst decision she had ever made.

The phone rang in the sunny kitchen where Ria was busy making a scrapbook of Things to Do for when the children arrived.

'Hi, Ria? It's Heidi! I've found a course for beginners on the Internet. Shall we sign on? It's only five lessons.'

'Is it very expensive, Heidi? I do have to hold on to my dollars for when the kids come out.'

'No it's not expensive at all, but anyway it's my treat. We get a reduction through the Faculty Office and anyway I want someone to go with. Wednesday and Friday this week and then three days the following week and hey we're on the World Wide Web.'

'Oh, I'm not sure about this Wednesday,' Ria began.

'Come on, Ria, you're not doing anything else, are you? It's only for an hour—twelve to one.'

'Oh, it's in the *daytime*,' Ria said with relief. 'Then of course I'll come, Heidi. You tell me where to go.'

Greg telephoned Marilyn from Hawaii.

'Thank you for your letter,' he said.

'It was still very stilted, I tried to say more,' she said.

'Still, we're talking, writing. That's good. Better anyway.'

She didn't want him to begin defining things too much. 'And are *you* all right, Greg?'

'I'm OK . . . summer courses, kids who know nothing, then graduate. Then there are graduate students, far too many bright kids who'll never get appointments. What else is new in university?' He sounded relaxed. This was as near as they had been to a real conversation for a long time.

'I wish they had email here,' Marilyn said.

'You could have taken your laptop, I suppose?' he said.

'I know. I didn't think of it at the time.'

'I spoke to Ria Lynch by the way. She called me here, she sounded very pleasant.'

'Nothing wrong?'

'No, just to check if Andy was who he said he was. He was passing through Westville and wanted to contact you.'

'That was good of Andy. And did Ria meet him?'

'No, no she just called him at the motel.'

'I hope she's getting on OK. I don't want to call her there too often; it sounds as if I'm checking up on her,' Marilyn said.

'I know what you mean,' Greg said. 'What's the place you're staying in like?'

'It's a beautiful house, everything's so old here. People are different, they keep dropping by but they don't stay long. I garden a lot, and I walk and . . . it's all OK, Greg.'

'I'm glad you're happy,' he said.

'Sure, Greg, I'm all right,' she said.

Marilyn went back into the garden and dug with renewed vigour.

A shadow fell over her and there was Colm standing beside her. She put up a hand to keep the sun out of her eyes.

'Hello,' he said.

'Hi,' Marilyn said.

'I'm not a great believer in words as apologies, so I brought you some flowers instead.'

'It wasn't your fault.'

'It was my place where it all happened. Anyway, it's over. In all my anxiety-dreams about running a restaurant, and they were pretty vivid let me tell you, I never thought up that particular scenario.'

In spite of herself Marilyn found that she was smiling. 'As you say, it's over. Thanks for the flowers. I'll also need your advice about where to get soil and fertiliser when I've cleared this undergrowth.'

'I'll take you.' Colm looked amazed at her achievement. She had done the work of three men uprooting and cutting back. Soon the earth would be ready to function.

'Will you come out to dinner tonight? I want to check out some of the opposition. I'd love your company.'

'Thank you so much,' said Marilyn.

She would not mention it, however, when Gertie next came in to clean the house and iron her clothes. Nor did she refer to it in the thank-you note she wrote and left at Rosemary's elegant apartment. No need to overburden people with information.

'I was wondering would you like me to call you Nora, Granny?'

'Have you gone off your head, Brian?' his grandmother answered.

'Told you,' Annie said triumphantly.

'What's all this about?' Nora Johnson looked from one to the other suspiciously.

'It's one more sign that he should be in a straitjacket,' said Annie.

'Well, I know you're pretty old, Granny, but you're not *that* old, are you? And I thought it would be more friendly, make us all the same somehow.'

Annie raised her eyes to heaven. 'And will you call Dad "Danny" when we go down to the boat tonight? And will you have a few more upsetting things to say to your friend "Ria" when she rings up from America next?'

Nora Johnson looked at her grandson. His face was troubled. 'You know what, Brian? I'd actually like to be called Nora, on reflection I would. That's what Pliers calls me.'

Annie looked at her in horror. 'The *dog* calls you Nora, Granny?'

'In his heart he does, he doesn't think of me as a Mrs Johnson figure. Yes, Brian, I'm Nora to you from now on.'

The entire family was going mad, Annie decided. And now they had to go to Tara Road and say hello to Mrs Vine before they left for the boat on the Shannon. Mam wanted it. Mam lived in a different world when all was said and done.

Mrs Vine had a plate of horrible gingersnap biscuits that would break your teeth and she had made some ham sandwiches.

'Nothing, thank you,' Annie said firmly.

'But please do, I got them ready for you.'

'I'm very sorry, Mrs Vine, I don't eat dead animals, and I find the biscuits a bit hard, so is it all right if I just drink the tea?'

'Of course.'

'I eat ham sandwiches,' Brian said. 'I'll eat them all so that they won't go to waste. Apart from the ones you'll be eating yourself, Mrs Vine.'

Annie didn't have to say 'Brian'—her face said it loudly.

Marilyn felt that she couldn't have made a worse start. 'I hope you'll both enjoy your visit to Westville,' she began.

'Do they have proper biscuits there?' Brian wondered.

'Yes, quite a range,' Marilyn assured him.

He nodded, pleased.

'I'm sure it will be great, Mrs Vine, Mam says she loves it.' Annie was trying hard to be polite and to make up for rejecting both kinds of hospitality.

The much-repeated address of Mrs Vine was beginning to grate on Marilyn's nerves. The girl resented her somehow for being in their mother's house. Or maybe she resented her mother for having gone away. 'I wonder if I could ask you both to call me Marilyn?' she asked them suddenly.

Brian accepted that eagerly. 'Yes, I think it's much better, if you ask me,' he said.

'Is that you digging up the garden or is it Colm? We saw an awful lot of stuff out there.'

'Well, it's mainly me, I just love it. Colm *is* going to help me get new soil and fertiliser. Maybe you'd like to choose some plants?' she asked without much hope.

The telephone rang just then. They heard the sound of their mother's voice on the machine. 'Hi, Marilyn, it's Ria. I was just calling to say . . .'

'It's Mam,' cried Brian, running for the phone.

'Brian, wait,' Annie called.

'No, please,' Marilyn insisted.

'Mam, Mam, it's Brian, we're here, how did you know?'

Marilyn and Annie's eyes met. Somehow in that moment Marilyn felt the hostility beginning to depart. It was as if they were both adults looking at the baby Brian who thought his mother had tracked him down.

'Yeah, she's fine, she's chopped down most of the front garden.'

Annie sighed. 'You get to expect a lot of that sort of thing with Brian,' she explained to Marilyn. 'He always manages to say the one thing you don't want him to say. I'll sort it out.'

And to give her great credit she did sort it out.

'Hi, Mam. It's Annie. Yes, we're here having tea. Yes, very nice indeed. No, that is not Brian being mad this time, but don't mind him about the garden, it's only a few weeds, and Colm's helping her so stop panicking. And we're off tonight but we'll ring you on Saturday.'

When Marilyn finally did get on the telephone Ria was apologetic.

'I'm so sorry, I didn't mean to make it a family conference.'

'It was just good timing, and it's all going well?'

'Oh, yes, brilliantly, and with you?'

'Couldn't be better.'

'Look, it's silly us talking now, why don't you call me back later tonight using my phone?'

'I'm going out tonight.'

'Oh, good, where are you off to?'

'I arranged to go out to the cinema, there's a movie I really want to see,' lied Marilyn who did not want to say she was going out to dinner with Colm Barry.

They agreed to talk later in the week.

'Is Bernadette up to there with packing and everything for the holiday?' Barney asked.

'No, not at all.' Danny was constantly surprised at how gently she moved through life. There would be no lists, no plans, checking through things, emptying fridges, cancelling people, phone calls. Twenty minutes before they left she would put a few items in a bag. He would pack his own case. The children had lists of what they should take taped to their cases by Ria. 'No, she's amazing, Barney. I don't know where she gets her serenity. It's infectious too, seriously, it's catching. Sometimes when I get fussed, I only have to be with her for ten minutes and it's all all right again.'

'What do you get fussed about, Danny?'

'Lots of things. Money, work, Ria being so unaccepting of everything that's happened.'

'Hey, is it that bad?' Barney asked.

'I don't usually give a long list of moans, but you did ask and today's not a good day. There's a long drive ahead, then a cramped cruiser for seven days that I can ill afford to be out of the office, Bernadette's mother thinking I'm made of money, and the kids seem to be on top of us all the time.'

'And there was a bit of trouble with Orla King on Friday night?'

'God, you know everything, Barney! How did you hear that?'

'A friend of Polly's was with Monto's party. He said the owner came over to them with barked instructions that Orla be got out before she got to your table. It wasn't quite in time.'

'No, but nearly.'

'You'd want to watch it, Danny.'

'Tell me about it. I'm watching it so feverishly I'd need a dozen eyes.'

The river was full of families getting onto their Shannon cruisers. Danny and the children and Bernadette and Finola got out of the car and began to settle into their boat.

Bernadette's mother had arranged a box of groceries from a local store. 'I telephoned ahead to order them,' she explained to Danny.

'Great, Finola.' He seemed relieved. It had been a long car journey. They had left Dublin in the late-afternoon traffic and he was tense.

'So will you then?' she said to him.

'Will I what?' Danny was genuinely puzzled.

'Will you pay this man for the groceries?'

'What? Yes, of course.' He took out his credit card; the man shook his head, so he took out a chequebook. He saw the last cheque stub. It was a payment for their mortgage to the building society. The grocery bill was enormous. The cost of the cruiser was on his credit card. He didn't even want to think about it.

But he knew he would *have* to think about it one day soon.

Colm took Marilyn to Quentin's. He said he wanted to show off Dublin's finest. Also he knew the Brennans who ran the place and introduced Marilyn to Brenda Brennan.

'Very full for a Monday, that's the booming economy for you,' he said approvingly, looking round the many tables that were occupied.

'Nonsense, Colm. You should explain to Mrs Vine that they come because the food is so brilliant,' said Brenda Brennan.

'This I can believe,' Marilyn murmured politely.

'I see you've got Barney McCarthy in with a crowd,' Colm observed.

A shadow crossed Brenda's face. 'Yes, indeed we have,' she said. Colm raised his eyebrow as if to ask what was the problem. 'I'll let you study the menu,' Brenda Brennan said, and moved away.

'Does she not like those people?' Marilyn had picked up a vibe.

'No, it's not that. I think she may have had the same problem as I've had.'

'Which is?'

'A very big cheque returned from the bank.'

'Really!' Marilyn put on her glasses and studied the party by the window. 'They look very substantial people, not the kind that would bounce a cheque.'

'No, they never did before. And the problem is they're important people. They know everyone; you wouldn't want to insult them, *and* also to be fair they have brought in big business in the past. So it's all a bit tricky.' He looked over at the large man who was being expansive as a host to nine other people. A smart, much younger woman was laughing.

'Is that his wife?'

'No, that's Polly. His wife's at home in a mansion.'

'Will you sue him?'

'No. I'll be full next time he books. No point in going to court over one dinner.'

Marilyn looked at him admiringly. 'You're so right. In the States we are much too litigation-conscious. You're sensible not to worry too much about it.'

'But I do worry about it. Barney McCarthy more or less owns Danny Lynch. If he goes down so will Danny, and what will happen to Ria?'

They all took turns at steering the boat. It was simple while you were still in the river, but when it broadened into a lake there were real rules. You had to keep the black buoys on one side and the red on the other. They bought ice creams when they drew in and tied up at the small villages, or went to pubs where they played darts.

'Wouldn't Mam love this!' Brian said once as a flight of birds came out of the reeds and soared above them. The silence was worse than any number of people telling him to shut up.

'Sorry,' he said.

Bernadette spoke dreamily. 'Brian, of course you must mention your mother, she's not dead or anything. And maybe one day you'll take her on a trip like this.'

Annie and Brian saw Danny reach out and stroke Bernadette's face in gratitude. He sort of traced it with his fingers and pushed her hair back. There was such love and tenderness in the gesture it was almost embarrassing to watch.

Rosemary was legendary for the speed of her weekly business meetings. They were held early in the morning, a large dish of fresh fruit, a lot of strong coffee and a rapid agenda. Accountant, office manager, marketing manager, and her own personal assistant, all trained to present speedily their reports.

'A really big cheque returned from the bank, I'm afraid,' the accountant said.

'How much? Who?'

'Eleven thousand, Barney McCarthy.'

'That's an error, that's a bank oversight,' Rosemary said, about to go on to the next item.

'I see Polly's Dress Hire is for sale in this morning's paper.' The accountant was laconic.

'Thanks. Then it's not an oversight. I'll call the bank.'

When the meeting was over she dialled Danny Lynch's mobile phone. It was not picking up. 'You're not doing this to me, Danny, you little bastard. You've done enough to everyone, and I can tell you straight out you're not doing this to me, not after all we've been through.' But she was speaking to herself not to Danny, since he was on the Shannon without a care in the world.

The boy Hubie who taught the course 'Don't Fear the Internet' looked about sixteen. In fact he was not much older. Ria found to her surprise that she seemed to understand it. She saw how easy it would be to get sucked in and to spend all day browsing, looking up amazing facts and talking to strangers on the screen.

She had lunch with Heidi afterwards and they went over what they had learned. Hubie had asked them to send him messages which he would answer. It was easy for Heidi, she had computers in the Alumni Office. But where would Ria go?

'Marilyn has a laptop that she didn't take away with her. Tell her on the phone you want to use it. But, Ria . . . I don't think you should mention that Hubie is our teacher.'

'Why ever not?'

'Well, he was a friend of Dale's, you see.'

'What's so bad about that?'

'You know . . .'

'I don't know. All I know is that Dale's in Hawaii . . .'

'What?'

'Well, with his father. Isn't he?'

Heidi was silent.

'Heidi, where else is he? He's not here, he's not in Ireland—'

'Dale's dead,' Heidi said.

'No, he can't be dead. You should see his room, that's not the room of someone dead.'

'Dale's dead, that's what it's all about. Marilyn won't accept it.'

Ria was more shocked than she had been for a very long time. 'Why didn't she tell me?'

'She won't speak about it. Not to anyone. Not even to Greg. That's why he's in Hawaii.'

'He left her?'

'No, he thought she'd go with him.'

'How old was Dale?'

'Not quite sixteen.'

Oh God, thought Ria, Annie's age. 'How did he die?'

'A motorcycle accident.'

'But surely he was too young to ride a . . . ?'

'Exactly.'

'Why on earth didn't she tell me?' Ria shook her head. 'She'd know I'd see his room.'

Heidi was gentle. 'She doesn't have the words to tell people.'

'When did it happen?'

'March of last year. They turned off the life-support machine in August.'

'Poor Marilyn. What a decision to have to make.'

'She thinks they made the wrong one, that's why she has no peace.'

'Well, if she has no peace, I sure as hell wonder whether she'll find it in Tara Road,' said Ria.

Andy arrived with a cold-bag full of food. He had also brought a bottle of wine. 'You look very nice,' he said appreciatively. 'Very nice indeed.'

'Thank you.' It was so long since anyone had paid her a compliment. *You look fine, sweetheart*, was the most Danny had said to her for ages.

Then the cooking began by rubbing the garlic round the bowl for the Caesar salad. There was a lot of gesture, flourish and fuss but it tasted very good. And then they began on the potato cakes.

Ria had made a strawberry shortcake which they had with coffee. Andy was very impressed. Ria told him about the Internet lessons and that she had spoken to Marilyn, who had said of course she could use the laptop.

'Right, I'll set it up for you. Where does she keep it?'

'It's in the study.'

They went into the book-lined room and Andy opened the machine. 'I'll show you how to boot it up, then you'll be able to do it for yourself.'

'Let me get my notes.' She went for the sheet of paper that Hubie had given them all at the class.

Andy looked at it. 'My God, Hubie Green, he was one of the kids with Dale on the night of the accident.'

Ria looked at him levelly. 'Why didn't you tell me Dale was dead?'

He was shocked. 'But you knew, surely?'

'No, I didn't. I had to wait until Heidi told me.'

'But you mentioned his room, the way it was all laid out.'

'I thought he was in Hawaii. I asked you when was he coming back, you said in the fall.'

'I thought you meant Greg.'

There was a silence while they each realised how the misunderstanding had happened.

'Tell me about it, Andy. I know almost nothing about what happened. There's like a conspiracy of silence about it all. The fact that nobody mentions the accident. That room is like a shrine to him.'

'But you see—' Andy began.

'No, to be honest I don't see. Do you know what I said to your brother Greg when I was talking to him in Hawaii? I asked him how Dale was enjoying it out there.'

'He'd realise that Marilyn couldn't have told you,' Andy soothed her.

'Look, I'm as sorry as hell that it happened. I went into that room again and I cried over the child that I thought was out surfing in Honolulu. I cried to think he's dead and buried, but still we should be able to talk about it. She left his room like that and didn't tell me. That's not natural, Andy. Even you freeze up at the mention of Hubie's name. Maybe if nobody else tells me what happened I'll talk to Hubie about it.'

'Don't do that. Listen, in this world there was only one marriage that any of us could think was truly happy and that was Greg and Marilyn's. And yet from the night of the accident they were never able to relate to each other as human beings again.'

'Did they blame each other or something?'

'Well, there's no way they could have. Hubie and two other kids and Dale were all crazy about motorbikes, but they were too young and they all had parents who would have as soon let heroin into the house as let a motorbike into their back yards. So on Hubie's birthday the kids went out somewhere. It was meant to be a picnic. I know because I was here at the time.' He got up and started to walk round the study. 'And they drank some beer and found two bikes and they decided that this was a gift from the gods.'

'They *found* them?'

'Yes, found as in stole them outside a restaurant. Hubie and the other kid who died, Johnny, were a little bit on the wild side. Older too, but not much. But at that age a few months counts. And they went for what was described at the inquest as a kind of test drive and one of the bikes was hit by a truck. Which wasn't surprising really because the bike where Dale was hanging on to Johnny was on the wrong side of the road. Johnny was killed instantly. Dale was on a life-support machine for six months and then they agreed to let him go.'

They sat in silence at the tragedy that had come to this house.

'And Marilyn said that she would never forgive any of them as long as she lived, and Greg said that they would have no peace until they learned to forgive.'

Ria had tears in her eyes. 'And is that what drove them apart?'

'I imagine so. Greg doesn't say much about it. And you can see why it wouldn't be good to ask Hubie. That kid has had a lot to live with: his birthday, he got them drunk, his friend Johnny driving a stolen bike, and he and another kid walk away alive. I'm kind of impressed with him that he's setting up something like this to make his college tuition.'

'I know, but of course you feel bitter about him,' Ria said.

'It wasn't his fault; he didn't set out to kill Dale or anything,' Andy soothed her. He picked up Hubie's notes. 'Come on, Ria, homework time; let's get your assignments done.'

142

They sent Hubie an email message and he sent back *Congratulations, Mrs Lynch! You're a natural.*

'I wish we knew someone else with email,' Ria said.

'Well, we could send one to my laptop back in the motel,' he said.

'And you could ring me tonight to say that it had arrived,' she said.

'Or tomorrow?' he suggested gently. 'Wouldn't it be nice if we spent the rest of the evening together?' He had a hand under her chin, lifting her face up towards his.

She swallowed and tried to speak. He took the opportunity to kiss her. Gently but firmly.

She pulled away, startled. Ria Lynch would be thirty-eight this year. Nobody had kissed her since she was twenty-two except the man who had tired of her and told her that there was nothing left in what she thought was a fine happy marriage.

'I must explain,' she began.

'Must you?'

'Yes. I've had a lovely, lovely evening, but you see I don't . . .'

'I know, I know.' He was kissing her ear now, gently nuzzling in fact, and it was rather nice.

'Andy, you have to forgive me if I have been giving the wrong signals. I couldn't have had a happier evening. I mean that truly, truly I do, but I don't want it to go any further.'

He pulled away gently. 'I agree it was a delightful evening. It doesn't *have* to end in bed, it would be much much nicer if it did, but if it's not going to let's remember the good bits.'

'They were all good bits.' She smiled at him, grateful that he hadn't turned on her, outraged that he had been misled.

'Look in your machine tonight, there may well be a Message Pending,' he said, and left.

She cleared up everything and went into the study to see if there were any emails for her. There were two. One from Hubie. *Just a test, Mrs Lynch, to see can you retrieve as well as send! Hubie Green.* And then there was one from Andy. *Thank you so much for the most enjoyable dinner I have had in years. I will definitely be back at the alumni weekend as will Greg, but if there's a chance we could meet again before that I would so much enjoy it. Your new friend, Andy Vine.*

Imagine! Boring old Ria Lynch, poor deserted Ria, dreary mumsy tiresome Ria had a new friend called Andy Vine. And had she not said a persuasive no, then she could have had a lover of the same name as well. She looked at herself in the hall mirror and wondered what it would have been like.

'It's Danny.'

'Didn't *you* get the weather! I bet it's beautiful down there.' Barney sounded pleased for him.

'Barney, what's happening?'

'You're worse than I am about not being able to cut off and take a holiday.'

'Were you looking for me? My mobile's not charged up, I'm ringing from a bar.'

'No, I wasn't looking for you, I was letting you have your holiday in peace.' He sounded very unruffled.

'I saw the newspaper,' Danny said.

'The newspaper?'

'I saw Polly's is on the market.'

'That's right. Yes.'

'What does it mean, Barney?'

'It means that Polly wants a break from it, she got a good offer and we're just testing the market in case there's an even better one out there.'

'That's rubbish. Polly doesn't want a break, she's hardly ever in there anyway.'

'Well, that's what she says. You know women . . . unpredictable.'

Danny had heard Barney so often talking to clients like this. Or when speaking to accountants, lawyers, politicians, bank managers. Anyone who had to be kept at bay.

'Are we OK, Barney? Have we our heads above water? Are we in the black?'

Barney laughed. 'Come *on*, Danny, has the sun softened your head? When were we ever in the black? The red is where we live.'

'I mean will we be able to climb out this time?'

'We always did before.'

'You've never had to sell Polly's before.'

'I don't *have* to sell it now.' There was a slightly steely sound to Barney's voice.

'I could come back if you needed me. I'd just drive straight up, leave the others here.'

'See you Monday,' said Barney McCarthy, and hung up.

Danny bought himself a small brandy to stop the slight tremor in his hand. The barman looked at him sympathetically. 'Family life all cooped up in a small boat can get a bit ropy,' he said.

'Yes.' Danny spoke absently. His mind was far away in Barney McCarthy's office. He had been dismissed on the phone. He had seen Barney do it so often to other people. Now he was at the receiving end.

There was a letter from Ria's mother in the mailbox on Tudor Drive.

Dear Ria,

I should have been better about writing letters but somehow God does not put enough hours in the day.

Marilyn was a bit stiff in the beginning but I think she's getting used to our ways all right. A mother should not criticise her daughter's friends, and I don't intend to, but you know I don't like Lady Ryan and never will, and I regard Gertie as a weak slob who deserves what she gets by putting up with it. Marilyn is different, she's very interesting to talk to about everything, and very knowledgeable about the cinema. She drives your car like a maniac and has burned two saucepans which she has replaced. She's going to be forty on August 1st. I think she's sleeping with Colm Barry but I'm not certain. The children get back from the boat holiday tomorrow. I'm going to take Annie out for a pizza and hear all the gory details. Annie's anxious to bring her friend Kitty as well, so we may include her in the party and then let them go home together.

Lots of love from your Mam

Ria looked at the postmark wildly. Five days since her mother had written all this. Five whole days. And she hadn't known anything that had been going on. What kind of friends' support system was there that nobody had told her all of this vital information? It was eight o'clock in the morning. She rang Marilyn. The answering machine was on but she had changed the message. 'This is Ria Lynch's house but she is not here at present. Messages will be taken and relayed to her. Marilyn Vine speaking. I will return your call.' How *dare* she do that? Ria felt a huge surge of rage. She could hardly contain her hatred of Marilyn.

This woman had gone into her house, driven her car into the ground, chopped down the garden, burned Ria's saucepans, slept with Colm Barry. What else was there to discover about her?

Ria rang Rosemary. She was at a meeting, her secretary said. She rang Gertie in the launderette.

'What's Marilyn up to, Gertie?'

'She's great, isn't she?'

'I don't know, I never met her. Is she sleeping with Colm?'

'Is she *what*?' Gertie's laugh from the busy lunchtime launderette was like an explosion.

'My mother says she is.'

'Ria, your mother! You've never listened to a word your mother said.'

'I know, did she burn my saucepans?'

'Yes, and replaced them with much better ones. You'll be delighted. She got herself a couple of cheap ones in case she burned them again.'

'What is she . . . accident prone?'

'No, just not any good as a cook. But you should see what she's done with the garden!'

'Is there any of it left? Like are there any trees or bushes? Anything I'd recognise? Brian told me she'd cut it all down.'

'What is all this, Ria? She's a lovely person, she's *your* friend.'

'No, she's not. I never laid eyes on her.'

'Are you upset about something?'

'She changed the message on the phone.'

'You told her to when she was ready.'

'She's ready all right.'

'Annie helped her decide what to say.'

'Annie?'

'Yes, she comes round to the house a lot.'

'To Tara Road?' Ria asked through gritted teeth.

'Well, I think she misses you, Ria, that's why she comes round.' Gertie sounded desperate to reassure her.

'Yeah, I'm sure she does,' Ria said.

'She does, Ria, she said that the holiday on the Shannon was bizarre, that was the word she used. She said that Brian said every day "Mam would like this" and she agreed.'

'Did she?' Ria brightened a little.

'Honestly she did. I was talking to her this morning when I went up to the house. She's actually gone out with Marilyn today. The two of them have gone shopping.'

'What?'

'Yes. Apparently Annie has some voucher or something for clothes which your mother gave her. She wanted to use it so they went off to Grafton Street.'

'I suppose she's there now, ploughing up and down the pedestrian precinct in my car.'

'No, she went on the bus. I honestly don't know why you've turned against her, Ria, I really don't.'

'Neither do I,' said Ria.

And she hung up and burst into tears.

Ria changed the recorded message. 'This is the home of Greg Vine who is in Hawaii, and Marilyn Vine who is in Ireland. Ria Lynch is living here at the moment and will be happy to forward your messages to the Vines or return your calls.' She played it back several times and nodded. Two could play at that game. That would sort Ms Marilyn out.

She called Heidi. 'I'm having a little supper party here, won't you and Henry come? Carlotta's coming and that nice couple we met at the Internet class, and those two men who run the gourmet shop you told me about. I've got friendly with them but I have to show off to them seriously with my home-cooked food. I'm hoping they may give me a job.'

Danny Lynch was standing on the steps ringing the doorbell of what used to be his own house.

Marilyn, kneeling under the tree inside the gate, was invisible to him as he stood fidgeting and looking at his watch. He *was* a handsome man with all that nervous energy that she remembered from years back, but now there was something else, something she had seen in the restaurant that night. Something anxious, almost hunted. He took out some door keys and let himself in. Marilyn had been about to get up and approach him, but now she moved very sharply from her planting and ran lightly up to the house and followed him inside.

He was standing with his back to the door in the front room. He called out: 'It's only me, Danny Lynch.'

'You startled me,' she said with her hand on her chest, pretending a great sense of alarm and shock.

At the sound of her voice, he turned. 'I'm sorry, I did ring the bell but there was no answer. And you're Marilyn. You're very welcome to Ireland.' Despite his restlessness he had great charm. He looked at her as he welcomed her. He was a man who would look at every woman he talked to and make them feel special. That's why she had remembered him, after all.

'Thank you,' she said.

'And you're happy here?' He looked round the room, taking it all in as if he were going to do an examination on its contents.

'Very. Who wouldn't be?' She wished she hadn't said that. Danny Lynch had obviously not been happy enough to stay here. Why, out of courtesy, had she made that stupid remark?

He didn't seem to have noticed it. 'My daughter says you've been very kind to her.'

'She's a delightful girl. I hope she and Brian will enjoy visiting my home as much as I like being in theirs.'

'It's a great opportunity for them. When I was Brian's age I had only been ten miles down the road.' He was very engaging.

And yet she didn't like the fact that he had let himself in. 'I didn't actually know that there was another key to the house out. I thought Gertie and I had the only two.'

'Well, it's not exactly having a key *out*,' he said. 'Not *my* having one, surely?'

'No, it's just I misunderstood, that's all. I didn't realise that you come and go here, Danny. I'll tell Ria that she forgot to tell me about you and how I thought you were an intruder.' She laughed at the silly mistake but she watched him carefully at the same time.

He understood what she was saying. Slowly he took the key to Tara Road off his keyring and laid it on the table beside the bowl of roses. 'I don't come and go actually. It was just today I needed something and since you weren't in I thought . . . well, you know, old habits die hard. It was my front door for a long time.' His smile and apology were practised but nonetheless genuine.

'Of course.' She was gracious, she could afford to be. She had won in this little battle, she had got Ria's door key back too. 'And what was it you wanted?'

'The car keys actually. Mine has packed up so I need to take the second car.'

'Ria's car?'

'The second car, yes.'

'For how long? I'd need it back in an hour.'

'No, I mean take it, for the duration.'

'Oh, that's impossible,' she said pleasantly.

'What do you mean?'

'I mean I paid the insurance company an extra premium to cover my driving that car for eight weeks. Ria will be driving your children around Connecticut in my car. My husband can't suddenly appear and claim the car from *her* . . .' She paused. The rest of the sentence hung there unspoken.

'I'm sorry, Marilyn, very sorry if you'll be inconvenienced, but I have to have it. I have to go out and make calls on people, earn a living.'

'I'm sure your company will provide you with another car.'

'It suits me to have this one, and since you don't need—'

'Excuse me, you don't know what I need a car for. There isn't a question of my giving you Ria's car.'

'Danny?'

'Jesus, Barney, where are you?'

Barney laughed. 'I told you, a business trip.'

'No, that's what we tell the bank, the suppliers, other people, it's not what you tell me.'

'That's exactly what I'm doing, on the business of raising money.'

'And tell me you've managed to raise some, Barney, because otherwise we're going to lose two contracts this afternoon.'

'Easy, easy. It's raised. Ring the bank and check. The money's there.'

'It wasn't there an hour ago.'

'It's there now.'

'Where are you, Barney?'

'I'm in Málaga,' Barney McCarthy said and hung up.

Danny was shaking. He hadn't the courage to ring the bank. Suppose they knew nothing of any money? Suppose Barney was in the south of Spain with Polly and wasn't coming back? It was preposterous of course, but then people did that sort of thing. They left their wives and children without a backward glance. Hadn't he done it himself?

'Ms Ryan on the line for you, *again*,' the secretary said to him, rolling her eyes to heaven, pleading with him to take the call this time.

'Put her through. Sweetheart, how are you?' he said.

'Five calls, Danny, what's this?' Her voice was clipped.

'It's been hell in here.'

'So I read in the papers and hear everywhere,' she said.

'It's OK now, we're out of the fire.'

'Says who?'

'Says Barney. He's saying it from Spain, rather alarmingly.'

Rosemary laughed and Danny relaxed.

'We have to meet. There are a few things we must talk about.'

'Very difficult, sweetheart.'

'Tonight I'm going to one of Mona's dreary charity things with the woman who's living in your house.'

'Marilyn?'

'Yes. Have you met her?'

'I don't like her, she's a real ball-breaker.'

'Come round after ten,' Rosemary said and hung up.

Greg called Marilyn. 'No reason. Just to chat. I miss the emails.'

'So do I, but I gather Ria's making great progress on my laptop. She sent an email to Rosemary Ryan, a woman here—I'm going out to a fashion show with her shortly—and one to her ex-husband's office.'

'Oh, I know, she sends them to me too.'

'She does? What about?'

'Oh, this and that . . . arrangements for the alumni weekend . . . Andy will be coming up, her children will be there, so it will be a full house.'

'Yes.' Marilyn couldn't quite explain why this irritated her, but it did.

'Anyway, she seems to be getting on very well, she's cooking in John and Gerry's a couple of hours a day.'

'She's *not!*'

'Yes. Isn't she amazing? And Henry told me that he and Heidi were at a dinner party in the house. In Tudor Drive. There were eight of them apparently and—'

'In our house? She had eight people in our house? To dinner?'

'Well, she knows them all pretty well now. Carlotta comes in for a swim every morning, Heidi's round there for coffee after work. It didn't take her long . . .'

'It did *not*,' said Marilyn grimly.

As they drove home from Mona's fashion show, Marilyn talked easily to Rosemary. She spoke about Greg out in Hawaii. At no stage did she give any explanation why he was on one side of the world and she was on the other.

When Marilyn stopped the car outside Number 32, Rosemary thanked her for the lift. 'It was wonderful, it meant I could have four glasses of champagne. And I loved them. I would ask you in for coffee but I have such an early start . . . I think I'll give the plants in the garden a drink of water and then go to bed.'

'Heavens, no, and I want to get an early night too.'

Marilyn drove on and parked the car outside Number 16.

Just then she remembered that she had left the signed programmes she had got for Annie in Rosemary's bag. Annie and her friend Kitty were mad about two of the models. She had only left Rosemary two minutes ago, she would be watering the garden. Marilyn would just run up the back lane, it would be quicker. They didn't lock their back gate at Number 32.

It was such a pleasant neighbourhood, this, in ways; she had been very lucky to find it. She looked up at the sky, slightly rosy from the lights of the city, a big moon hidden from time to time by racing black clouds.

She was at the back gate of Number 32 now and she pushed it open. She expected to see Rosemary in her bare feet, having taken off her expensive shoes, directing the hose towards the beautifully planted herbaceous border.

But there was nobody there. She was about to walk into the garden when she heard two people talking in the summerhouse close by the gate. Not so much talking, she realised as she got nearer and peeped in through the window, more kissing. Rosemary had indeed taken off her expensive shoes and also her expensive rose silk dress. She lay in a silk slip across Danny Lynch and she had his face in her hands.

She was speaking to him urgently. 'Never, never again as long as you live, leave me with five phone calls unreturned.'

'Sweetheart, I told you . . .' he was stroking her thigh and raising the lacy edge of her slip.

Marilyn stood there frozen.

Rosemary was angry. 'Don't play with me, Danny. There's too much history here. I've put up with too much, saved you, warned you too often.'

'You and I are special, we've always agreed that what we have is something that's outside everything else,' he said.

'Yes, I put up with your housey-housey marriage, with your affairs, I even put up with you getting that child pregnant and moving away from this road. God knows why.'

'You know why, Rosemary,' Danny said.

And Marilyn fled. Back to the safety of her garden where she watered Colm's vegetables and everything else in sight with a ferocity that they had never known. She was astounded at how shocked and revolted she felt. Poor, poor Ria, so unlucky in her man, which could happen to anyone. But so doubly unlucky to be betrayed by her best friend as well.

In a fit of generosity, Marilyn decided she didn't care if Ria was entertaining coachloads of people in Tudor Drive, serving them platefuls of homemade delicacies. She deserved whatever pleasure she could get.

Ria was in fact on her own in Tudor Drive, bent over Marilyn's laptop. Hubie Green had given Ria a computer game and it was defeating her.

She sent Hubie an email. 'Hubie, it would only take you thirty minutes to explain this game to me. It's worth ten dollars of my time to learn it. Do you think you could come by at some stage? A seriously confused Ria Lynch.'

The kid must live beside his screen: he answered immediately. 'It's a done deal. Can you call me on the telephone at this number and tell me where you live?'

She called him and gave the address.

There was a silence. 'But that's Dale's house. Dale Vine.'

'That's right.' She had somehow thought he would have known.

'Oh, I couldn't go there, Mrs Lynch.'

'But why not?'

'Mr and Mrs Vine wouldn't like it.'

'They're not here, Hubie, I'm living in the house. Marilyn's in my house in Ireland, Greg's in Hawaii. But of course I understand, Hubie, if you don't want to come round here, if it has bad memories for you.'

She heard him take a breath. 'Hey, it's only a house, they're not there to get upset. Sure I'll come, Mrs Lynch.'

It was so simple once he explained it, and also quite exciting. They played on and on.

'That was much more than half an hour, I'd better give you twenty.'

'No, we agreed ten. I stayed because I enjoyed it.'

'Would you like some supper?' She brought him into the kitchen and opened the fridge.

'Hey, you've got one of those lovely Irish flag quiches they sell at John and Gerry's.'

'I make them,' she said, pleased.

'You *make* them? Fantastic,' he said. 'My mother bought two of them for a party.'

'Good, well I'll give you some Irish soda bread with currants in it to take home to her when you leave, then I won't feel too bad keeping you out for so long.'

He walked round the kitchen, restless, uneasy maybe to be in this home again. Ria said nothing about the past. Instead she busied herself talking about the visit of Annie and Brian. Hubie picked up a picture of the children. Ria kept it out where she could see it.

'Is this her? Your daughter? She's real cute,' he said.

'Yes, she's lovely, but then I would think so, and that's Brian.' She looked proudly at the son who would be here soon. Hubie showed no interest at all. They sat and talked companionably over the meal. Hubie used to come here a lot, he said. Great swimming pool and always a welcome. Not food like this, mind you, but cookies from the store and this was the house where the kids came. In fact his parents were quite friendly with Mr and Mrs Vine before everything.

'And now?' Ria was gentle.

'Well you see how she is, Mrs Lynch. You know what she's like now.'

'No, the funny thing is I don't know what she's like, I've never met her and I've only seen one photograph of her.'

'You don't know her? You're not a friend?'

'No, it was a home exchange, that's all. She's in my house you see.'

'She hates me.'

'Why should she hate you?'

'Because I'm alive, I guess.' He looked very young and sad as he sat there trying to make sense of what had happened.

'But surely if she were to hate anyone it would be the boy who died?'

'Johnny?'

'Yes, Johnny. I mean he was the one driving.'

He said nothing, just looked out at the garden lights and the sprinklers beginning to play on the lawn.

'She can't hate Johnny. Johnny is dead, there's no point in hating him. We're alive, David and I. She can hate us, it gives her life some purpose.'

'You sound very, very bitter about her.'

'I do, yes.'

'But it must have been so terrible for her, Hubie. So hard to forgive. If Johnny hadn't been drunk . . .'

'Johnny wasn't driving. Dale was driving.' She looked at him in horror. 'Dale stole the bikes, Dale set it up. It was Dale who killed Johnny.'

Ria felt her heart turn over. 'But why didn't you . . . ?'

'Everyone assumed it was Johnny driving and at that time we thought Dale was going to get better. They said he might survive; they had him on this machine. I went in once to see him before she had orders issued that I wasn't to be let near. I told him in case he could hear me that we'd let people go on thinking it was Johnny. Dale was underage, you see, and also he had these parents that worshipped him. Johnny had nobody.'

'Oh God,' said Ria.

'Yes, I know, and now I don't think what we did was right but we did it for the best. We did it to help Mrs Vine and then she wouldn't even let me go to Dale's funeral.'

'Oh God Almighty,' Ria said.

'You won't tell her, will you?' he asked.

Ria thought of the room along the corridor, the shrine to the dead son. 'No, Hubie, I won't tell her,' Ria said.

8

'MARILYN, THIS IS RIA. Sorry to miss you. Nothing really. Just to say that the Dublin Horse Show will be on next month, you might enjoy it. And Rosemary can get you tickets for the showjumping which is very spectacular. She'd do anything to help. I hear that you've done wonders in the garden, thank you so much. OK. Bye for now.'

Marilyn listened to the message. She felt such a surge of rage against Rosemary Ryan that she was glad she wasn't holding her coffee mug in her hand. She would surely have crushed it into her palm.

'Ria, this is Marilyn, sorry I missed you. Our machines are playing tag. No, I won't ask Rosemary for any tickets to the showjumping but I may go to the Horse Show when it's on. I see a lot of advertisements for it already. Glad to hear that you are getting to know people in Westville. Annie and Brian are coming to supper here tomorrow. I was terrified of cooking for them but Colm said he'd leave something suitable. The children are really looking forward to seeing you again. Bye for now.'

Ria listened to the message. For the first time she didn't feel excluded and annoyed that the children were going to supper with Marilyn. That woman needed any bit of consolation she could get.

Greg Vine telephoned to say that he would like to stay in Tudor Drive for the alumni weekend in August. 'Normally I would leave you the house to yourself and stay in a motel, but there won't be a bed for miles around. Even Heidi and Henry won't have any room.'

'Heavens, no, you must stay here. And Andy too.'

'We can't all descend on you surely?'

'Why not? Annie and I can sleep in one room. You have two guest rooms, you and Andy have one each. And there's a canvas bed that we can put anywhere for Brian.'

'That's very good of you, it will only be for two nights.'

'No, please, it's your house, stay as long as you like.'

'And when do your children arrive?'

'Tomorrow. I can hardly wait.'

When he had replaced the receiver Greg realised that she hadn't suggested that Brian sleep in Dale's room. It would have been perfectly acceptable. To him anyway. But not to Marilyn. Ria Lynch must have worked that out. She seemed highly practical and down-to-earth.

Marilyn went to Colm's restaurant to collect the food.

'I'd have brought it down for you,' he said.

'Nonsense, I'm grateful enough to you already. What have I got here?'

'A light vegetable korma for Annie, with some brown rice. Just sausage, peas and chips for Brian, I'm afraid. I did nothing special for you. I presumed you'd eat from both not to show favouritism.'

Marilyn said that seemed an excellent scheme. 'Thank you so much, Colm, truly.'

'Let me get you a basket to carry them.' He called out to Caroline, and his pale, dark-haired sister, whom Marilyn had only seen in the distance before, came in carrying the ideal container, with a couple of check dinner napkins. 'You have met Caroline, haven't you?'

'I don't think so, not properly. How do you do, I'm Marilyn Vine.'

Caroline put out her hand hesitantly. Marilyn glanced at her face and realised that she was looking straight into the eyes of someone with a problem. She didn't consider herself an expert, but as a young graduate she had worked for three years on a rehab project. She had not a shadow of doubt that she was being introduced to a heroin addict.

It was all quite clear now to Marilyn why Colm seemed so protective of his sister. The woman was hooked on drugs. Her husband, a coarse and flashily dressed man who had been present on the night of the restaurant debacle, did not look as if he would be any great help in such a situation. In fact he might well be part of it.

Hubie Green phoned Ria. 'There's going to be a party in my house next weekend, Mrs Lynch, if your daughter would like to come along.'

Ria bit her lip. Hubie had been so helpful and straight with her. Yet she didn't want to let Annie go to a party with a whole lot of young people that she didn't know. Apart from which she'd invited Sheila Maine and the two children to stay that weekend.

Hubie heard her reluctance. 'Hey, it's not going to be anything wild,' he said.

'No, of course not.' Suppose Annie got to know that her mother had refused a party for her before she even arrived, the summer would be off to a very poor start. Ria forced a cheerful smile to her face. 'Hubie, that would be great, but we will have friends staying here that weekend and the boy Sean is about Annie's age . . . can he be included too?'

'Why not?' Hubie was easy.

Annie's social life was hotting up already.

When we go in to Granny, if you ask for money I'll kill you there and then and let Pliers drag your body up and down the street before he devours it,' Annie said.

'I never ask anyone for money, they keep giving it to me,' Brian said. 'Howarya, Nora,' he said cheerfully as his grandmother opened the door.

'I'm fine,' Nora Johnson said. 'Imagine, this time tomorrow night you'll be in America.'

'I wish Marilyn had children,' Brian grumbled.

'If she had she'd have brought them with her, you wouldn't have them to play with out there,' Nora said.

'Mam didn't take us with *her*,' Brian said unanswerably.

'She does have a child but he's with his father in Hawaii, Mam told us ages ago, you just didn't listen,' Annie put in.

'Well, he's no use to us in Hawaii,' Brian said. 'Were you about to make tea, Nora?'

'I thought the pair of you were going down home for your supper?'

'Yes, well . . .'

Nora got out orange squash and biscuits.

'Why did you never go to America, Granny?' Annie asked.

'In my day working-class people only went to America to emigrate, they didn't go on holidays.'

'Are we working class?' Brian asked with interest.

Nora Johnson looked at her two confident, bright grandchildren and wondered what class they might consider themselves at the end of the summer when, according to informed opinion, their beautiful home would be sold. But she said nothing of that.

'You're to have a great holiday and you're to send me four postcards, one a week, do you hear?'

'I think postcards are dear out there,' Brian said.

'I was going to give you a fiver anyway for spending money.'

At that time by chance Pliers gave a great wail.

'I didn't ask for the money,' Brian cried out, remembering that Annie had threatened to feed his body to the dog.

'No, Brian, of course you didn't,' Annie said menacingly.

'I've got a wonderful supper for us from Colm,' Marilyn said. 'I checked what you'd both like.'

Annie and Brian helped her set the table as the food was warming in the oven. It was so different to the time when they had come first and she had found them hard going.

'Have you packed everything?'

'I think so,' Annie said. 'Mam emailed a list of the clothes we'd need to Dad's office. Imagine her being able to use machines.'

'She uses all these machines here.' Marilyn waved around at the food processors and high-tech kitchen equipment.

'Oh that's just kitchen stuff,' Annie said loftily. 'Mam would learn any-thing if it had to do with the house.'

'Maybe she's broadening out.'

'Are you broadening out here?' Brian was interested.

'In a way yes, I'm doing things that I wouldn't normally do at home.'

'What do you do that's so different?' Annie asked. 'I mean you liked gardening and walking and reading at home, you said, and you're doing all that here.'

'That's true,' Marilyn said thoughtfully. 'But I feel different inside somehow. Maybe it's the same with your mother.'

'I hope she feels more cheerful about Dad and everything,' Brian said.

'Well, being away from the problem is a help certainly.'

'Did it help you feel better about your husband?' Brian wanted to know. He looked nervously at Annie, waiting for her to tell him to shut up, but she obviously wanted to know too, so for once she said nothing.

Marilyn shifted a little uncomfortably at the direct question. 'It's a bit complicated. You see I'm not separated from my husband. Well, I am of course, since he's in Hawaii and I'm here, but we didn't have an argument, a fight or anything.'

'Did you just go off him?' Brian was trying to be helpful.

'No, it wasn't that, and before you ask I don't think he went off me. It's just we needed some time to be alone and then perhaps it will be all right, maybe at the end of the summer.'

As she served Colm's food, Marilyn told them more about Westville. She explained the alumni weekend and how everyone would come back and tell each other how young they looked. 'My husband will be coming back from Hawaii so you'll meet him then.'

'Will he be staying in the house, your house?' Annie asked.

'Yes, apparently your mother very kindly said he could.'

'Will your son be coming back too?'

'I beg your pardon?'

'Your son? Isn't he in Hawaii with Mr Vine?'

'My son?'

Annie didn't like the look on Marilyn's face. 'Um, yes.'

'Who told you that?'

'Mam did.'

'Your mother said that Dale was in Hawaii?'

'She didn't say his name but she said his room was all there ready for him to come back.'

Marilyn had gone very white.

Brian didn't notice. 'Will he be there when we're there? Maybe we could have competitions with the basketball?'

'Did your mother say anything more?' Marilyn's voice was scarcely above a whisper now.

Annie was very alarmed. 'I think she said she'd asked Mr Vine about him but she didn't get any details so she doesn't know if he's going to be coming back or not.'

'Oh, my God,' Marilyn said.

'I'm very sorry . . . should I not have asked? Is anything . . . wrong?' Annie began.

'What is it?' Brian asked. 'Is he not in Hawaii? Did he run away?'

'No.'

'Where is he then?' Brian was getting tired of this.

'He's dead,' Marilyn Vine said. 'My son Dale is dead.'

Danny came home late. Bernadette sat curled in her armchair, the table was set for two. 'Where are the children?' he asked.

Bernadette raised her eyes slowly to him. 'I beg your pardon?' she said.

'Where are Annie and Brian?'

'Oh. *I* see. Not . . . hello, Bernadette, or I love you, sweetheart, or it's good to be home. Well, since you ask where the children are, try to remember back as far as breakfast when they said they were going to make a series of visits saying goodbye to people like your mother-in-law, Marilyn, whoever, and you said they were to be home by ten.'

He was instantly contrite. 'Bernadette, I'm so sorry, I'm so crass and stupid and selfish. I had a day—boy, did I have a day, but that's not your fault. Forgive me.'

'Nothing to forgive,' she shrugged.

'But there is,' he cried. 'You've given up everything for me and I come in and behave like a boor.'

'I gave up nothing for you, it was you who gave up a lot for me.' Her voice was calm and matter-of-fact as if she were explaining something to a child. 'Let me get you a drink, Danny.'

'It might make me worse.'

'Not a long, cool, very weak whiskey sour, it's mainly lemonade.'

'I'm no company for you, a grumpy old man harassed by work.'

'Shush.' She handed him the drink and raised the level on the record player a little. 'Brahms, he works magic all the time.'

Danny was restless, he wanted to talk. But Brahms and the whiskey sour did their work. He felt his shoulders relaxing, the frown-lines going from between his eyes. In many ways there was nothing to talk about. What was the point of giving Bernadette a blow-by-blow account of the unpleasantness in the office today? How a big businessman had pulled out of a consortium that was going to do a major development in Wicklow because he said Barney and Danny were unreliable. How Polly had called to warn them that the word was out they were on the skids.

How Barney had proved elusive and distant over all these matters as if it didn't really concern him.

And, worst of all, Danny's niggling fear that the personal guarantee he had given to Barney on Number 16 Tara Road would be called in and that he would lose the house. And not only would there be no home for Ria and the children but there would be nothing to sell. Some things were too huge to talk about, Bernadette was quite right not even to attempt it.

Danny felt a lot calmer after an hour. Perhaps he was just exaggerating the situation. Bernadette drifted into the kitchen to prepare the smoked chicken salad. There was never any hiss of pots boiling, soufflés rising, pastry-making covering the whole place with flour. He had never known how gentle and undemanding life could be, how free from frenzied activity. And there was more than enough of that in the office.

In the kitchen of Number 16 Tara Road a silence had fallen.

Eventually it was broken by Brian. 'Did he have an awful disease or something?' he asked.

'No, he was killed. A motorcycle wreck.'

'What did he look like? Did he have red hair like you?' Annie asked.

'Yes, both Greg and I have reddish hair. We're both tall, so he was tall too. And lean. And sporty.'

'Have you a picture of him, a photograph?' Annie asked.

'No, none at all.'

'Why not?'

'I don't know. It would make me too sad, I suppose.'

'But you have pictures of him at home; Mam said he was very good-looking and he had a lovely smile. That's why I was sort of hoping he'd be there,' Annie said.

'Yes.'

'I'm sorry.'

'No, it's all right, he was good-looking.'

'Did he have any girlfriends?'

'No, Annie, I don't think so.'

'Bet he did, you can see it in all the movies. They start very young over in America,' Brian said wisely.

And they sat and talked on about the dead Dale until Annie realised that it was nearly ten o'clock and they'd better go.

'I'll drive you,' Marilyn offered.

They saw Rosemary on the street. Marilyn looked at Annie as if asking whether she wanted to stop and say goodbye to her mother's friend. Imperceptibly Annie shook her head. Marilyn accelerated so they wouldn't be noticed. She was very relieved. She found it increasingly hard to give the barely civil greetings that were required between neighbours. Interesting that Annie seemed to feel the same way.

Marilyn left the children at the end of their road. She had no wish to engage in any kind of conversation with Danny Lynch or his new love. She drove back to Tara Road, her mind churning.

When she arrived at Number 16 she realised with a sense of shock that she didn't really remember the journey. She was shaking as she parked Ria's car and let herself into the house. Ria had left three cut-crystal decanters on the sideboard. There was a little brandy in one, something that looked like port in another and sherry in the third. With a shaking hand Marilyn poured herself a brandy.

What had happened today? What had changed so that she could talk about Dale? Admit that she couldn't carry a picture of him in case she would convulse with grief just by looking at it? Why had the direct questions of two children whom she hardly knew released these responses?

It was an emotional occasion, that was all. These two living children were going to 1024 Tudor Drive where Dale had played and slept and studied in his short life. They would make friends as he had done, and swim in the swimming pool where he had swum.

She sipped her brandy and noticed that there were tears on her hand. She hadn't even realised she was crying. Now she sat weeping in this darkening room with the sounds of a foreign city around her. She had said his name aloud, and the world had not ended. Annie and Brian had asked questions about him. What would he have done as a career? Did he eat meat, which were his favourite film stars, what books did he read? They had even asked what kind of a motorbike he was riding when he was killed. She had answered all these questions and volunteered more information, told them stories about funny things that had happened at Thanksgiving, or Dale's school play, or the time of the great snowstorms.

Dale. She tried again, fearfully, but no, it hadn't disappeared. She could say his name now. It was extraordinary. It must have been there the whole time and she hadn't known. And now that she knew, there was nobody she could tell. It would be cruel and unfair to telephone her husband, poor baffled hurt Greg wondering what he had done wrong and how he had failed her.

She always knew that Dale had loved her own spirit of adventure. She had followed his lead in everything, only at motorbikes had she turned away from him. For month after weary month she had agonised in case it had all been her fault. Suppose she had promised him a bike when he was the age to drive one, then he might not have gone along with those wild boys and their dangerous drunken plans. But tonight somehow she felt a little differently.

Annie had said in a matter-of-fact way that of course you couldn't let him mess around with motorbikes, it would have been like letting him play with a gun. And Brian had said, 'I expect he's up in heaven and he's very sorry he caused you all this trouble.'

And nothing anyone had said before, since the moment she had been told the news about the accident, had made any sense at all until this. She put her head down on the table and cried all the tears that she knew she should have cried in the past year and a half.

Ria drove to Kennedy Airport. In another thirty days she would be going home. She closed her eyes and wished hard that this would be a wonderful, unforgettable month for the children.

She would *not* lose her patience with Annie and boss her and tell her what to do. She would *not* let Brian's gaffes irritate her. He would say the most insensitive things to everyone. He would ask Heidi why she didn't have children, Carlotta why she spoke funny English. At no stage would she be ashamed of him or urge him to be more thoughtful.

She ached to put her arms round him and for him not to pull away in embarrassment. She yearned for Annie to say, 'Mam, you look terrific you've got a suntan, I really missed you.' All the way to the airport Ria forced herself not to live in a world of dreams. It wasn't going to be perfect just because they hadn't seen her for thirty days.

Danny rang the bell of Rosemary's flat. It was ten o'clock at night. Rosemary was working at her desk, she put away her papers. She looked at herself in the mirror, fluffed up her hair, sprayed on some expensive perfume and pressed the buzzer to let him come in.

'Why won't you take a key, Danny? I've asked you often enough.'

'You know why, it would be too much temptation, I'd be here all the time.' He gave her the lopsided smile that always turned her heart over.

'I wish.' Rosemary smiled at him.

'No, the truth is I'd be afraid I'd come in and find you *in flagrante* with someone else.'

'Unlikely.' She was crisp.

'Well, you have been known to indulge,' he accused.

'Unlike yourself,' Rosemary said. 'Drink?'

'Yes, and you'll need one too.'

Rosemary stood calm and elegant in her navy dress by the drinks trolley. She poured them two large Irish whiskeys then sat down on her white sofa, her back straight and ankles crossed like a model.

'You were born graceful,' he said.

'You should have married me,' she said.

'Our timing was wrong. You're a businesswoman—you know that the secret of the universe is timing.'

'All this philosophy didn't stop you leaving Ria for someone else, and not for me, but we've been through all that. What are we drinking to? A success or a disaster?'

'You never lose control, do you?' He seemed both admiring and annoyed at the same time.

'You know I do, Danny.'

'I'm finished . . .'

'You can't be. You've a lot of fire insurance.'

'We've called it all in.'

'What about the Lara development?' This was their flagship, the forty-unit apartment block with a leisure club. The publicity had been enormous, every unit had been sold and resold long before completion. It was what was going to make them turn the corner.

'We lost it today.'

'What in God's name is Barney at? He's meant to have these hotshot advisers.'

'Yes, but apparently they need collateral . . . that we're not so strong on.' He looked tired.

'What are you going to do? she asked.

'What *can* I do, Rosemary?'

'Well, you can stop being so defeatist, you can go out there and ask somebody for the support. It's only money when all's said and done.'

'All right, I will,' he said suddenly. His voice was stronger than before.

'That's better,' she said.

'Lend me the money, Rosemary. I'll double it as I did with everything.' She looked at him open-mouthed in shock. He went on, 'I won't let Barney near it, he's past it and I owe him nothing. This will be my investment, our investment. I have a business plan . . .' He took out two sheets of paper covered with columns of handwritten figures.

She looked at him aghast. 'You're serious,' Rosemary said.

He appeared not to notice her shock. 'Nothing's typed up, I didn't want to use the machines in the office, but it's all here . . .' He moved to sit beside her on the sofa to show her what he had written.

Rosemary leapt to her feet. 'Don't be ridiculous, Danny, you're embarrassing us both.'

'I don't understand . . .' He was bewildered.

'You're demeaning us, what we have, what we were to each other. I beg you don't ask again.'

'But you have money, Rosemary, property, a business . . .'

'Yes.' Her voice was cold.

'You have all that, I have nothing. You have no dependants, I have people hanging out of me at every turn.'

'That's your choice.'

'If you were in trouble, Rosemary, I'd be in there helping you.'

'No, you wouldn't. Don't give me that line, it's sentimental and it's not worthy of you. You will be a loser, Danny, if you go round asking your lovers for support to help you keep your wife and your pregnant mistress.'

'I don't *have* any lovers except you, I never did.'

'Of course. Perhaps Orla King has hit the big time now as an international singer and *she* might bankroll you. Grow up, Danny.'

'I love you, Rosemary. I always have loved you. Don't throw everything back in my face. I just made a mistake, that's all.'

'You made two mistakes, one called Ria and one called Bernadette.'

He smiled slowly. 'Yet you didn't leave me over either of them, now did you?'

'If that's your trump card, Danny, it's a poor one. I stayed with you for sex, from desire not love. We both know that.'

'Well, even then, can't you see that this would work . . . ?' He indicated the papers again, thinking even at this late stage that she might read them and reconsider. She put her glass down firmly, showing that it was time for him to go.

'Rosemary, don't be like this. Listen, we're friends as well as . . . as well as the passion and desire bit. Won't that make you think that you might be able . . . ?' His voice trailed away as he looked at her cold face. He made one last try. 'If I had my own business, sweetheart, and you were involved in it, we'd be able to see each other much more often.'

'I've never had to pay for sex in my life and I don't intend to start now.' She opened the door of the apartment.

'You know how to kick someone so that it hurts.'

'You did that twice to me. You didn't know you were doing it when you married Ria, but you sure as hell knew it when you couldn't even tell me about Bernadette and I had to hear it from your wife.'

'I'm sorry,' he said. 'There are some things which are so difficult . . .'

'I know.' Her voice was momentarily softer. 'I do know. It's not that easy for me to let you go to the wall. But, Danny, I will not even contemplate financing two different homes for you, while I sit here alone. If you can't understand that then you understand nothing and you deserve to go under.'

When he was gone she went out onto her roof garden terrace. She needed the air to clear her head. There was almost too much to take in. The only man she had ever fancied in her whole life had really begged her to help him. It gave her no pleasure to remember how she had refused him. There was no sense of power in withholding money from him. But there would have been terrible weakness in giving it to him, in paying him for his mistakes.

It gave her no satisfaction to let him go under. What she wanted was for things to be different. For Danny to desire her so strongly and permanently that he would give up everything else for that alone. This, she realised, was what she must have wanted him to do all the time. Rosemary had always thought that she was so strong, she was a woman like Polly who could live her life and keep love in its place.

In so many ways Barney and Danny were alike, urgent and ambitious, men for whom one woman would never be enough. They loved two kinds of women, the ones they married and those they kept on the side. They married Madonnas—the quiet, worthy Mona and the earnest, optimistic Ria. But to her great annoyance, Rosemary realised that Bernadette had been cast in the Madonna role, too. She hadn't realised how angry that made her feel. How had Bernadette sneaked in there somehow?

Was it possible that after all Rosemary did love Danny Lynch? Love was never meant to be any part of it. Surely it couldn't be developing at this entirely inappropriate stage?

At times like these Ria wished she were taller. It was infuriating to have to jump up and down but unless she did she couldn't see the passengers coming through. And then she saw them. They wheeled a luggage trolley with their two suitcases on it, their eyes raking the crowds.

She forced herself not to shout out their names, neither of them would want the attention called to them. Instead she ran to a corner where she could reach out when they passed by. Don't hold them too long or too tight, she told herself. She waved with all the Irish-Americans who waved for their families and friends. And they saw her. With a lump in her throat Ria saw their faces light up.

'*Mam!*' Brian cried, and ran towards her. It was he who hugged the longest.

Ria had to release him to reach for Annie. She seemed taller, slimmer. 'You're beautiful, Annie,' Ria said.

'We missed you, Mam,' Annie said into her mother's hair.

'We're going straight back to Westville,' she said, an arm lightly round each of their shoulders. 'I want to show you your summer home.'

They seemed pleased, and with her heart light and happy Ria marched her little family to the car.

Polly Callaghan heard Barney's key in the lock. He looked tired, but not as tired as he deserved to look with all that was happening to him.

'Come in, you poor divil,' she said with a big warm smile.

'It's not good news, Poll.'

'I know it's not,' she said. 'Look, I've got the evening paper, I've been looking through Accommodation to Let for places to stay.'

He put his hand on hers. 'I'm so ashamed. First your business, now your apartment.'

'They were never mine, Barney, they were yours.'

'They were ours,' he said.

'So what's the bottom line? What date do I leave?'

'By September the 1st.'

'And your own house?'

'Is in Mona's name.'

'As this flat is in mine.'

'I know.' He looked wretched.

'And is she being as good a sport as I am? Giving it up without a murmur?'

'She's not in possession of all the facts, if you understand.'

'Well, she will be this week, you'll be declared a bankrupt.'

'Yes. Yes. We'll get back, Poll.'

'And you do have some money outside the country?'

'No, Poll, hardly anything. I was vain you know, I believed my own publicity. I brought it all back for schemes like Number 32 Tara Road, like the Lara development. And look where it got me.'

'Talking about Tara Road . . .' Polly Callaghan began.

'Don't remind me, Poll, telling them is as bad as telling Mona.'

They loved the house. 'My God, that's like a film star's swimming pool,' Annie said.

'Will we have a swim now?' Brian wanted to know.

'Why not? I'll show you your rooms and we'll all change.'

'You're going to swim too?' Annie was surprised.

'Oh, I swim twice a day,' Ria said. With her first earnings from the delicatessen she had bought a smart new swimsuit. She was anxious to show it off to the children. 'Annie, this is your room, I put flowers in it, there's lots of closet space . . . And, Brian, you're over here.'

They flung their suitcases on their beds and began to throw the clothes out. Ria was touched to see the email that she had sent to Danny's office telling them what to pack taped inside the lid of Annie's suitcase. 'Did Dad do that for you, help you pack?' she asked.

'No, Bernadette did. Mam, you wouldn't believe Dad these days . . . he honestly hardly noticed we were leaving.'

'And how's your dad?' She kept the question light.

'Fussed,' Annie said.

'Broke,' Brian said.

'I'm sorry to hear both of those things.' Ria knew this was a slippery slope. 'Is he broke, do you think, Annie?'

'I don't know, Mam, there's a lot of chat about it certainly but if he were he'd tell you, wouldn't he?' Ria was silent. 'He'd have to, Mam.'

'Yes, of course he would. Let's all get changed and go swim.'

Brian, already in his bathing trunks, was investigating the house. He opened the door to Dale's room that Ria had meant to lock until she could explain. 'Hey, look at all this!' he said in amazement, looking at the posters on the walls, the books, the music centre, the clothes and the brightly coloured cushions and rug on the bed. 'This is a room.'

'Well, I must explain . . .' Ria began.

Annie was in there, too. She was running her hand across the framed photographs on the wall. 'He is good-looking, isn't he?'

'Look at all the pictures of wrestlers! Aren't they enormous!' Brian was examining pictures of giant Sumos.

'And this must have been his school play,' Annie said. 'Let me see, oh, there he is.'

'I must tell you about this room,' Ria began.

'I know, it's Dale's room.' Annie was lofty, she knew everything.

'But what you don't understand is that he won't be coming back.'

'No, he's dead, he was killed on a motorbike,' Brian said.

'How do you know?'

'Marilyn told us all about it.' Annie was examining a picture of Dale shovelling snow. 'That must have been when they had the snowstorm and Dale dug out a path for them in the middle of the night as a surprise.'

'She told you all this?' Ria was astounded.

'Yes, why did *you* tell us he was in Hawaii?' Annie wanted to know.

'Not to upset us, maybe?' Brian suggested.

'I got it wrong,' Ria said humbly.

'Typical Mam,' said Annie, as if this was no surprise to her but no big deal either. 'Come on, Mam, let's swim. Hey, that's a nice swimming cozzy. And you're much browner than we are, but we'll catch up, won't we, Brian?'

'Sure we will.'

Hubie telephoned to know if he could call by the house and welcome Annie to Westville. Brian too, of course, he added as an afterthought.

'Please do, Hubie. They both love it here and they've been playing that game you set up.'

'Great.'

When Hubie arrived, the admiration in his eyes for shapely blonde Annie was obvious. 'You're even cuter than your picture,' he said.

'Thank you,' Annie said. 'That's very nice of you.'

Where had Annie, who was not quite fifteen, learned such composure? Ria wondered over and over. Certainly not from her mother, who was still unable to accept a compliment. Possibly from Danny, who had managed to appear calm no matter what was happening. She was very worried to hear the children say that he was broke and fussed.

As Hubie, Brian and Annie went up to the pool she decided she would call Rosemary about it. It would be nine o'clock at night at home. Rosemary would be in the cool elegant penthouse. At her desk maybe with papers. Entertaining people to one of her brilliant and apparently effortless meals? In bed with a lover?

There was nobody at home. Rosemary might be out at Quentin's, or in Colm's? Possibly she was with Marilyn, they had become friendly and gone to a fashion show organised by Mona.

'Rosemary, it's Ria. Nothing really. Only a chat. The children have arrived and everything's just wonderful. I wanted to talk to you about whether Danny and Barney's business is in any trouble. I can't call Danny obviously, and I thought you might know. Don't call me back about it because the kids will be here and if there is anything to tell I don't want them to hear. But you can see how I'm a bit out on a limb here and you're the only one I can ask.'

Barney had asked Danny to meet him in Quentin's.

'We can't go there, Barney, we owe them, remember?'

'I remember. That's been settled, and I told Brenda it would be cash.'

167

'With Bernadette or without?'

'Without. Nine o'clock OK?' He was gone.

Perhaps at the very last moment he had pulled something out of the fire. Barney was an old-time wheeler and dealer. It was inconceivable that he would declare himself and the company bankrupt next week.

Danny wore his best jacket and his brightest tie. Whoever he was being brought to meet would need to see a buoyant Danny Lynch, nothing hangdog. He had been putting on an act for years, that's how you bought and sold houses for heaven's sake. Tonight would be the biggest act because so much depended on it.

'I might be late, sweetheart,' he said to Bernadette. 'Big Chiefs' meeting called by Barney, sounds like light at the end of the tunnel.'

'I knew there would be,' she said.

Brenda Brennan directed him towards the booth. Danny knew that this was where they would be. Whoever he was going to meet might not want to be seen supping publicly with McCarthy and Lynch. Their names were not so good at the moment. He was surprised to see only Barney there, the other person or people hadn't turned up yet. He was even more surprised to see that the table was set for only two.

'Sit down, Danny,' Barney said to him. 'This is the day we hoped never to have to see.'

'Everything?' Danny said.

'Everything, including Number 16 Tara Road.'

Rosemary was also having dinner in Quentin's. With her accountant, her manager and two men from a multinational printing company who wanted to buy her out. They had approached her, she had not gone to them. They were suggesting very attractive terms but were finding it difficult to persuade her how lucky she was to have been approached in this way.

One man was American, one was English, but they knew that their nationality had nothing to do with their incomprehension about this beautiful blonde Irishwoman with her flawless make-up, shining hair and designer outfit.

'I don't think you'll ever be able to realise capital in this way again,' the Englishman said.

'No, that's true, nobody wants to take me over as much as you do,' she smiled.

'And there's nobody apart from us with the money to do so, as well as the will, so it's not as though you can play us off against anyone else,' said the American.

'Quite true,' she agreed.

Rosemary had seen Danny go into the booth with Barney McCarthy. Nobody had joined them. That was a bad sign. She knew that if she agreed to this deal, if she sold her business, she could save them. It was almost dizzying to think that she had that much power. She lost track of what the two men were saying.

'I beg your pardon?' She went back to the conversation.

'We were just saying that time is moving on and as you approach forty you may want to get a life for yourself, rest after all this hard work. Put your feet up, take a cruise, live a little.'

It had been the wrong thing to suggest to Rosemary Ryan. She didn't see herself as a person putting her feet up. She didn't like strangers telling her that she was approaching forty. She looked pleasantly from one to the other. 'Come back to me in about six years. You will of course have worked out that by then I'll be half of ninety. Ask me again then, won't you? Because it really has been such a pleasure talking to you.'

Her mind wasn't fully on what she was saying, she had just seen Barney McCarthy, white-faced, storming out of the restaurant. Danny was not with him. He must be still sitting in that booth. Rosemary Ryan would not rescue him from bankruptcy, but neither would she leave him on his own after a body blow.

'Gentlemen, I'll let you finish your coffees and brandies on your own. I'm so grateful for your interest, but, as you said, for me time is moving on and I can't afford to waste any of it. So I'll say good night.'

The men were only struggling to get to their feet when she was gone.

'Rosemary?'

'Brandy?'

'Why are you here?'

'Have you eaten?'

'No, no there wasn't time to eat.'

She ordered a large brandy for him and a bowl of soup and some olive bread. A mineral water for herself.

'Stop playing nursemaid, I don't want to eat, I asked you what are you doing here?'

'You need to eat. You're in shock. I was at another table and saw Barney leaving . . . that's why I'm here.'

'My house is gone.'

'I'm so sorry.'

'You're not sorry, Rosemary, you're glad.'

'Shut the hell up . . . pitying yourself and attacking me. What did I ever do bad to you except to betray your wife, my friend, by sleeping with you?'

'It's a bit late to be getting all remorseful about that, you knew what you were doing at the time.'

'Yes, I did, and you knew what you were doing playing with Barney McCarthy.'

'Why are you here?'

'To get you home.'

'To your home or my home?'

'To your home. My car is outside, I'll drive you.'

'I don't want your pity or this soup,' he shouted as the waiter laid down a bowl.

'Eat it, Danny. You're not functioning properly.'

'What do you care?'

'I care because you are a friend, more than a friend.'

'I told Barney McCarthy I never wanted to lay eyes on him again. You're right, that wasn't functioning properly.'

'That's panicky business talk, that's all. It will sort itself out.'

'No, some things can never be forgotten.'

'Come on, you and I were bawling at each other the other night and here we are sitting talking as friends. It will happen with Barney, too.'

'No, it won't, he's very shabby, he told me he'd settled up the bill here and it turns out he hasn't.'

'How much is the bill?'

'Over six hundred.'

'I'll pay that now on my card.'

'I don't want your charity. What I want is your investment, I told you.'

'I can't do it, Danny, it's not there. Everything's tied up.'

She caught Brenda Brennan's eye. They had known each other a long time. 'Brenda, there was a misunderstanding. An old bill. It was never settled. Here, can we do it now on my card?'

'Drive along Tara Road,' Danny asked her.

'Stop punishing yourself.'

'No, please, it's not taking us out of the way.'

They approached Tara Road from the top end, the corner near Gertie's launderette. They passed the old people's home. 'They're all asleep in St Rita's, and it's not even ten o'clock,' Rosemary said.

They passed Nora Johnson's little house at Number 48A. 'It must be about time for Pliers to go out and foul the footpath,' Danny said. 'Pliers always likes to go where it will cause maximum discomfort to everyone.'

The little laugh they managed over that got them past Number 32, the elegant renovation with its beautiful penthouse where Danny and Rosemary had spent so many hours together.

'Can you turn the car?'

'Why? This is the way.'

'I want to come home with you. Please.'

'No, Danny, it would be pointless.'

'Nothing between us was ever pointless. Please, Rosemary, I need you tonight. Don't make me beg.'

She looked at him. It had always been impossible to resist him. Rosemary had already been congratulating herself that her infatuation had not let her sell her company for this man. And he wanted her. As he had always wanted her more than his prattling little wife and the strange wan girl he lived with. She turned her car in the entrance of Colm's restaurant and drove back to Number 32.

Danny started to caress Rosemary before she had even put the key into the front door.

'Don't be idiotic,' she hissed. 'We've been so careful for so long, don't blow it now.'

'You understand me, Rosemary, you're the only one who does.'

They went upstairs in the lift and as soon as they were in the door he reached for her.

'Danny, stop.'

'You don't usually say that.' He was kissing her throat.

'I don't usually refuse to save your business either.'

'But you told me you couldn't, that your funds were all tied up.' He was trying to hold her and stop her slipping away.

'No, Danny, we have to talk.'

'We never had to talk before.'

She saw her message light winking on the answering machine but she would not press the button. It might be one of the men she had had dinner with increasing the offer, raising the stakes. Danny must never know what had been turned down only feet away from him in the restaurant.

'What about Bernadette?'

'It's early, she won't expect me for a long time.'

'It's foolish.'

'It was always foolish,' he said. 'Foolish, dangerous *and* wonderful.'

Afterwards they had a shower together.

'Won't Bernadette think it odd that you smell of sandalwood?' Rosemary asked.

'Whatever soap you get I get the same for our bathroom.' He wasn't being smug or proud of his cunning, just practical.

'I remember Ria always had the same soap as I did,' she said. 'I used to think that she was copying me, but it was you all the time. My, my.'

Rosemary wore a white towelling robe. She glanced at herself in the bathroom mirror. She did *not* look like someone for whom time was marching on, nor a woman approaching forty. Those men would never get their hands on her company.

'I'll call you a taxi,' she said.

'I needed you tonight,' he said.

'I suppose I need you too, in ways, otherwise you wouldn't have stayed. I don't do anything out of kindness.'

'So I notice,' he said drily.

She called a cab company, giving her own account number. 'Remember to get out at the end of your road, not your house, the less these drivers know the better.'

'Yes, boss.'

'Talk to Barney tomorrow, Danny. You're both up the same creek, there's nothing to be gained by fighting each other in it.'

'You're right, as usual. I'll go down and wait for the cab.' He held her very close to him. Over her shoulder he saw the light on her machine. 'You have a message,' he said.

'I'll listen to it later, probably my mother demanding that I find a suitable man and get married.'

He grinned at her, head on one side. 'I know I should hope you will, but I really hope you don't.'

'Don't worry, even if I did I expect we'd cheat on him as we have on everyone else.'

The honeymoon period was still on in Tudor Drive. Ria could hardly believe it, though she walked on eggshells. Sean and Kelly Maine proved to be perfectly satisfactory friends for Annie and Brian.

'I wish Sean was younger,' Brian complained. 'It's the wrong way round. Kelly's OK, but she *is* a girl.'

'I'm glad Sean's not your age. I think he's fine the age he is,' Annie said with a little laugh.

Ria opened her mouth to say that Annie wouldn't want to do anything silly with both Hubie and Sean fighting for her attention, but she closed it again. The weeks of having to think before she spoke were paying dividends. Ria felt she had grown up a lot in a way she had never had to at home. After all she had never lived alone, she had gone straight from her mother's house to Danny's. No years in between like girls who lived in flats might have known. Girls like Rosemary.

She had got an email from Rosemary saying that Dublin was Rumour City and that it was impossible to separate the truth from the fiction but it had always been that way. Still if there was anything to tell, she *would* tell it, and of course Danny wouldn't keep her in the dark if there was anything serious. Rosemary wrote that the children had disappeared without saying goodbye which was a pity because she had intended to send out a couple of dresses for Ria.

'You didn't say goodbye to Rosemary?' Ria asked them before she headed out to the gourmet shop.

Annie shrugged.

Brian said, 'We forgot her, we called on everyone else.' He seemed to hint that it was a source of income they had overlooked.

'Brian, she wouldn't have given you a penny,' Annie said.

'You don't like Rosemary, Annie, do you?' Ria was surprised.

'You don't like Kitty,' Annie countered.

'Ah, but that's different. Kitty's a bad influence.'

'So is Lady Ryan on you, Mam, giving you things, patting you on the head. You can earn money to buy your own dresses, you don't need her castoffs.'

'Thanks, Annie, that's true. Now, will you two be all right? I'll only be gone three hours.'

'It's so funny to see you going out to work, Mam, you're like a normal person,' said Brian.

Ria drove Marilyn's car to John and Gerry's, her knuckles white with rage. This was the thanks she got for staying in Tara Road to make the place into a home for them all. Danny had left her saying she was as dull as ditchwater and they had nothing to talk about. Annie thought she was pathetic and Brian thought she was abnormal. Well, she was going to make a success of business anyway.

She parked with a screech of brakes and marched into the kitchen.

'What thought have we given to making special alumni cakes?' she barked. The two men looked up, startled. 'None, I see,' she said. 'Well, I suggest we have two kinds, one with a mortarboard and scroll of parchment, and one with hands of friendship entwined.'

'Special cakes for the weekend?' Gerry said slowly.

'Everyone will be entertaining, won't they need something festive? Something with a theme?'

'Yes, but—?'

'So we'd better get started on them at once, hadn't we? Then I can get the graphics up and running and get young people at home to do work on the advertisements, posters for the window and leaflets.' They looked at her open-mouthed.

'Don't you think?' Ria said, wondering had she gone too far.

'We think,' said John and Gerry.

'I'm finding it real hard to see you alone,' Hubie said to Annie. 'Last weekend there was the party with all the other guys around, and then Sean Maine was everywhere like a shadow. Next weekend is the alumni weekend and then you're going off to stay with the Maines.'

'There's plenty of time left.' They were lying by the pool sailing a paper boat from one side to the other by flapping the water with their hands. Brian was practising his basketball at the net.

'Perhaps I could take you to New York City?' Hubie asked.

'I'd better not. Mam wants to show it to us herself, it's a big deal for her.'

'Do you never say no to her, Annie, and do what you want to do?' Hubie wanted to know.

'Yes, I do, quite a lot. But not at the moment. Things are hard for her. My dad went off, you see, with someone not much older than me. It must make her feel a hundred.'

'Sure, I know. But somewhere else then?' He was very eager that they should have a date.

'Look, Hubie, I'd love to, but not at the moment. We've just got here, OK?'

'OK.'

'And another thing. I was writing to Marilyn and Mam said I wasn't to say you come here.'

'Marilyn?'

'Mrs Vine. This is her house, you *know* that.'

'You call her Marilyn?'

'That's what she wanted.'

'You like her?'

'Yes, she's terrific.'

'You're so wrong. You have no idea how wrong you are. She's horrible and she's mad.' Hubie got up and gathered his things. 'I have to go now.'

'I'm sorry you're going. I like you being here, but I have no idea what all this is about.'

'Think yourself lucky.'

'I know you were with Dale when the accident happened, my mother told me, but that's all. And I'm not going to say that Marilyn is horrible and mad just to please you, that would be weak and stupid.' Annie had stood up too, eyes flashing.

Hubie looked at her in admiration. 'You're really something,' he said. 'Do you know what I'd really like?'

Annie never discovered what Hubie would really have liked, because at that moment Brian arrived on the scene. 'You were very quiet. I came to see were you necking,' he said.

'What?' Hubie looked at him, startled.

'Necking, snogging, you know, soul kissing. What do you call it here in America exactly?' He stood there, his shoulders and face red, his spiky hair sticking up.

'Hubie,' said Annie in a dangerously level voice, 'is just leaving. And the way things are, he may never come back.'

'Oh, I most definitely will be back,' said Hubie. 'As a matter of interest I would like you to know that the way things are is just fine with me.'

'Hubie fancies Annie,' Brian said at lunch.

'Of course he does. He fancied her before he met her, he was always looking at that photograph.'

'That's nonsense, Mam. Stop encouraging Brian.' Annie was pink with pleasure from it all.

'Well, we need Hubie here tonight, so you'll have to use all your powers of persuasion to get him to come over.'

'Sorry, Mam, impossible.'

'I need him, Annie. I want him to design a poster for my cakes on the computer.'

'No way, Mam, he'll think I put you up to it.'

'No, he won't. It will be a professional job, I'll pay him.'

'*Mam*, he'll think you're paying him to come and visit me. It would be terrible. It's not going to happen.'

'But it's my job, Annie, I need him here.' She stopped suddenly. 'I'll tell you . . . suppose you go out somewhere? Then he can't think that you're after him, can he?'

Annie thought about it. 'No, that's true.'

'In fact it might be playing hard to get. He would wonder where you might be.'

'And where *would* I be, Mam?'

Ria paused to think up a solution to this problem and then suddenly it came to her. 'You could go to work in Carlotta's beauty salon for two or three hours, folding towels, sterilising hairbrushes, sweeping up, making coffee . . . you know the kind of thing?'

'Would she let me?'

'She might if I asked her nicely, as a favour for tonight, since I know you want to be out of the house.'

'Please, Mam, would you? Please?'

Ria went to the telephone. Carlotta had suggested it days back, but Ria knew better than to tell her daughter straight out. She came back from the phone. 'Carlotta says yes.'

'Mam, I *love* you,' Annie cried.

Barney McCarthy said he would meet Danny any place and any time. How could there be hard feelings about what was said last night? By either of them. They had both been in shock, they knew each other far too well for mere words to create a barrier.

They met in Stephen's Green and walked round the park where children were playing and lovers were dawdling. Two men walking, hands clasped behind their backs, talking about their futures and their past.

On the surface they were friends. Danny said that he would never have had the start in business without Barney McCarthy. Barney said *he* owed Danny a great deal for his insights and hard work, not to mention his quick thinking the night of the heart attack in Polly's flat.

'How's Polly taking it?' Danny asked.

'On the chin, you know Poll.' They both thought for a few moments about the elegant woman who had let any chance of marriage pass her by just waiting in the background for Barney. 'Of course she's still young, Poll,' Barney said.

'And with no dependants,' Danny agreed. There was another silence. 'Have you told Mona?' Danny asked.

Barney shook his head. 'Not yet.'

He looked at Danny. 'And Ria?'

'Not yet.'

And then they walked in silence because there was nothing left to say.

'**I** think Sean is greatly taken with your Annie,' Sheila Maine said on the telephone.

'I know, isn't it amazing?' Ria said. 'It only seems such a short time since they were both in prams, now they're talking romance.'

'I guess we'll have to keep an eye on them.'

'Much good it did anyone keeping an eye on us,' Ria laughed.

'But we weren't as young as they are,' Sheila said. 'I don't expect Annie's on the pill?'

Ria was shocked. 'Lord no, Sheila. For heaven's sake, she's not sixteen

176

yet. I was only talking about kissing at the cinema and all that.'

'Let's hope that's all they're talking about, too. Anyway you're coming to stay with us the weekend after next.'

'Indeed we are.'

Ria was troubled by this conversation, but she hadn't much time to think too deeply about it. The orders for her alumni cakes were unprecedented, they had had to take on extra help in the shop, *and* she had to organise the house for her guests *and* prepare a buffet lunch for the friends of Greg and Andy Vine at alumni weekend.

Annie and Brian were the least of her worries. Brian had found a new friend called Zach four houses away, and had taken to wearing a baseball cap backwards and using phrases he didn't understand at all. Hubie was always calling for Annie and taking her out to see cultural things, and since it was always in broad daylight Ria could not object. Every afternoon at four o'clock Annie went to Carlotta's salon, and came home with amazing stories about the clientele. Ria had rented a chest freezer for a week and she cooked, labelled and stored way into the night.

Marilyn brought a cup of coffee out to Colm in the garden. 'What are you on today?' she asked.

'Sweet fennel,' he said. 'It's only to please myself, prove I can grow it. Nobody asks for it much in the restaurant.' He grinned ruefully.

Marilyn thought again what an attractive man he was and wondered why he hadn't married. She knew about his love affair with alcohol, but that never stopped people marrying. 'How long does it take?'

'About four months, or thereabouts. The books say fifteen weeks from sowing.'

'The books? You learned your gardening from books?'

'Where else?'

'I thought you came from a long line of committed gardeners, that you grew up with your hands in the soil.'

'Nothing as nice and normal as that, I'm afraid.'

Marilyn sighed. 'Well, which of us ever had the childhood we deserved?'

'It's true, sorry for the self-pity.'

'Hey, you don't have any of that.'

'Have you heard how they're all getting on, Annie and Brian?'

'Well, just great, they seem to know half the neighbourhood, dozens of kids in our pool.'

'That doesn't bother you?'

'Why should it? It's their house for the summer.'

'But you're a very private person.'

'I have been since my son died last year.'

'That's a terrible tragedy for you. I'm very sorry. You didn't speak of it before, I didn't know.'

'No, I didn't speak of it at all.'

'Some things can be almost too hard to talk about, let's leave the subject if you prefer.' He was very easy-going, Marilyn knew that he would have left it.

'No, strangely. I find recently when I *do* talk about it now it becomes a little easier to bear.'

'Some people say that, they say let some light in on it, like plants your problems need light and air.'

'But you don't agree?'

'I'm not sure.'

'Which is why you don't talk about Caroline?'

'Caroline?'

'This country has unhinged me, Colm. In a million years I would never have interfered or intruded in anyone's life like this. But I'll be away from here in less than three weeks; I'll never see you again. I think you should let a little light and air into what you're doing for your sister.'

'What am I doing for her?' His face was hard and cold.

'You're running a restaurant to feed her drug habit.'

There was a silence. 'No, Marilyn, you've got it wrong. She works in my restaurant so that I can keep an eye on her. Her habit is paid for by somebody else entirely.' Marilyn stared at him. 'She is very well supplied by her husband Monto, a businessman. One of his most thriving businesses is heroin.'

Greg Vine was tall, slightly stooped and gentle. He was courteous and formal to the children. He seemed overcome by the hospitality that Ria was providing for him, Andy and their friends. 'You must have been slaving for weeks,' he said, when she showed him the replies to the guest list he had sent out.

'Yes, well, I'll leave you to settle in,' she said. 'I didn't put anyone to sleep in Dale's room . . . and on that subject I must apologise.'

He cut straight across her. 'No, it is we who must apologise, it was unpardonable for you to come here without being told the whole story. I'm very, very sorry. All I can say in explanation is that she doesn't talk about it to anyone, anyone at all.' His face was full of grief as he spoke.

'Everyone's different,' Ria said.

'But this has gone beyond reason, to let you into this house, to see that room without knowing what happened. It probably doesn't matter now what she and I have left to say to each other, but for Marilyn's own health she will *have* to acknowledge what has happened and talk about it. To someone.'

'She's talking about it now,' Ria said. 'She told my children all about him, everything.'

Greg's eyes were full of tears. 'Maybe, maybe I should go to Ireland.'

Ria felt a pang of jealousy like she had never known before. Marilyn was going to be all right. Her husband still loved her and he was going to go over to Tara Road. Lucky, lucky Marilyn Vine.

The alumni picnic party in Tudor Drive was long talked of as one of *the* events of Westville. Ria had asked Greg if Hubie Green could come to the house as a waiter.

'Hubie?'

'Yes, he taught us the Internet and has been most helpful.'

'He's a wild and irresponsible young man,' Greg said.

'I know that he was with Dale that day. He says it was the worst day of his life.'

'I have no objections to his being here, I never had. Those were all Marilyn's . . . I suppose in a way I'm advising you to keep him away from your daughter.' Ria felt a shiver of anxiety, but she couldn't allow it to develop, there was too much to do.

When Hubie arrived he went straight to Greg. 'Mr Vine, if my presence here is unwelcome I quite understand.'

'No, son, I'm glad to see you in our home again,' said Greg.

Ria let out a slow sigh of relief.

'I think Greg's brother fancies you, Mam,' Annie said after the party.

Annie and Hubie had been a delightful double-act filling the wine-glasses and serving huge slices of the mouth-watering cake that had been such a success.

'Nonsense, we're geriatric people. There's no fancying at our age.' Ria laughed, admiring the sharp young eyes of her daughter.

'Dad was able to find someone else—why wouldn't you?'

'What a matchmaker you are. Now don't go encouraging me or I might stay over here cooking and fancying old men. What would you do then?'

'Well, I suppose I could stay here studying and fancying young men,' Annie said.

There was no time for Andy to meet Ria properly on her own. 'I could come back another weekend?' he said.

'It wouldn't be fair to ask you, Andy. I'll be up to my elbows in cooking and children and I couldn't concentrate on you.'

'You didn't, even when you could.' He was reproachful. 'I'm not giving up, I'll think of something.'

'Thank you, Andy.' She looked round to make sure there was nobody in sight and kissed him playfully on the nose.

'What did Mona say?' Danny asked.

'Nothing at all.'

'Nothing?'

'Total silence,' Barney said. 'It was much worse than any words. And Ria?'

'I haven't told her yet.'

'But, Danny, you'll have to tell her. She'll hear.'

'I must tell her face to face, I owe her that much.'

'You're going to bring her home?'

'No, *I'm* going out there.'

'On whose money, might I ask?'

'On your money, Barney. You've got my house, for heaven's sake. You can give me a lousy air ticket.'

They were sitting by the pool planning what to pack to go to the Maines'.

'Are you still into lists, Mam?'

'I think so,' Ria said. 'It makes life easier.' The telephone rang, Ria went to get it.

'Sweetheart, it's Danny.'

'I did ask you not to call me that.'

'Sorry. Force of habit.'

'I'll get the children.'

'No, it's you I want to talk to. I'm coming out there tomorrow.'

'You're what?'

'I'm coming out to see you all for the weekend.'

'Why?'

'Why not?'

'And is Bernadette coming too?'

'Of course not.' He sounded irritated. 'I'm coming to talk to you.'

He sounded very edgy. Something in her throat began to constrict. Was it over with Bernadette? Was he coming to ask her forgiveness?

'When do you arrive? Do you know how to get here?'

'I have all the details you gave the children and I'll get a taxi from the airport. I'll arrive at about five o'clock.'

'Yes, but, Danny, we were going away for the weekend . . . up to Gertie's sister.'

'Gertie's sister? That can be changed, surely?' He was very impatient.

'Yes,' she said.

'See you tomorrow,' he said.

Ria went slowly back to the pool. This was too big to blurt out. The new Ria nowadays thought before she spoke. She wouldn't cancel Sheila Maine. Perhaps the children could go for one night. And leave her alone with Danny.

It was her that he was coming to see. That's what he had said on the phone. 'I'm coming to talk to you.' He was coming back to her.

THE DOORBELL RANG in Number 16 Tara Road. It was Danny Lynch. The smile was very warm. 'I hope I'm not disturbing you, Marilyn?'

'Not at all, won't you come in?'

'Thank you.'

They went into the front room where Marilyn had been sitting reading. Her book and glasses were on the table.

'You like this room,' he said.

'Very much, it's so peaceful.'

'I liked it too. We didn't live in here enough, it was always down in the kitchen. I'd like to have sat here of an evening reading, too.'

'Yes, well, of course it's easy for me, I'm on my own. When there's a family it's different.'

'True,' he said. She looked at him enquiringly. 'I'm flying to New York tomorrow, I'll be staying at Tudor Drive. I thought I'd pay you the courtesy of telling you.'

'That's very kind of you, but not at all necessary. Ria's free to have whoever she likes, but thank you anyway.'

'And I need some documents to take with me.'

'Documents?'

'Yes, they're upstairs. I wonder if I might go and collect them?'

'Ria didn't say anything about—'

'Look, I appreciate your caution, but pick up the phone now and call her. This is kosher, Marilyn, she knows I'm coming.'

'I don't doubt it for a moment.'

'You do. Call her.'

'Please, Danny, please don't speak like that. Why shouldn't I believe you? You've given me no reason to think you might be deceiving Ria in any way.' Her voice was cold and her eyes were hard.

He seemed to flinch a little. 'You can come with me, I know where they are.'

'Thank you.'

They walked up the stairs in silence to the bedroom. Danny went to the chest of drawers and opened the bottom drawer. There was a plastic envelope labelled House Documents. He picked out four sheets of paper and returned the rest.

Marilyn watched him wordlessly. 'And if I'm talking to Ria tonight, what shall I say you took?'

'Some correspondence about the ownership of this house . . . she and I need to discuss it.'

'She'll be home in under three weeks.'

'We need to discuss it now,' he said. He looked around the big airy bedroom with its high ceiling and long window. Marilyn wondered what he was thinking about. Did he remember the years spent here with Ria or was he in fact working out what price the house would go for?

Marilyn hoped that in this complicated network of friends Ria had a good lawyer. She was going to need one. It was only too clear why Danny was going out to Westville to ruin the rest of Ria's visit. He was going to tell her that they had to sell Tara Road.

Ria was singing as she made breakfast.

'You never sing, Mam,' Brian said.

'She is now.' Annie defended her mother's right to croon tunelessly.

'Bernadette sings a lot,' Brian said.

'That's so interesting, Brian, thank you for sharing it with us,' Annie said.

'What kind of things does she sing?'

'I don't know. Foreign things.' Brian was vague.

'She only hums, Mam,' Annie said. 'Not real singing.'

Ria poured a cup of coffee and sat down at the table. 'Well, I have something marvellous to tell you,' she said. 'Something you'll be very pleased to hear.'

'What is it?' Brian asked.

'Your dad is coming to stay for the weekend,' she said.

Their mouths were open with shock.

'*Here*, here in Westville?' Annie said.

'But he said goodbye to us and he didn't say,' Brian said. 'Isn't that fantastic? When does he get here?'

'He'll be here about five o'clock.'

'But we're going to the Maines' this weekend,' Annie remembered in horror.

'I've spoken to Sheila. You're going up on the bus tomorrow just for one night then coming back on Sunday when we'll all have a big goodbye dinner for your dad.'

'I can't believe it. Dad coming here. He'll even meet Zach.'

'Well worth flying thousands of miles for,' Annie said.

'Dad could well put a stop to you and Hubie and your goings-on when he comes,' cried Brian, stung by the attack on his friend.

'Mam, there are *no* goings-on,' Annie appealed.

But Ria didn't seem interested in whether there were or there weren't. 'Let's think what we'll do tonight when your dad comes. Will we drive him round Westville and show him the sights? Would he like a barbecue here by the pool? What do you think?'

'Dad's got much quieter, you know,' Annie said thoughtfully. 'He sits and does nothing a lot nowadays.'

For some reason that made Ria feel uneasy. But she gave no hint of her anxiety. 'Well, if your dad would like to be quiet, then hasn't he picked a great place for it? Now, I have a job to go to. See you lunchtime.'

When she had gone the children looked at each other across the table.

'Why do you think he's coming?' Brian asked.

'I have no idea. But I don't think it could be anything bad,' Annie said reflectively.

'No, like he's given all the bad news already. It might be something good though, mightn't it?'

'Like what?' Annie wondered.

Danny was packing his things in the office when the phone rang.

'Rosemary Ryan?' The girl raised her eyebrows questioningly.

'Put her through,' Danny said.

'I hear that you're going out to America,' she said.

'You could hear the grass grow, sweetheart.'

'I didn't hear it from you,' she said crisply, 'when we were last talking. In bed.'

'I gather you're not in the office,' he said.

'You gather right, I'm on my mobile in my car very near your office. I'll drive you to the airport.'

'There's no need, honestly.'

'Every need,' she said. 'Ten minutes' time I'll be parked outside.'

He came out of the building where he would probably never work again. The offices would be repossessed on Monday. Danny carried the grip bag he was taking to Westville, and two large carrier bags, the contents of his desk. 'Do you know what would be wonderful? If you could keep these for me until I come back, save me going out to Bernadette and dropping them at home. And I can't leave them in Tara Road; that woman will hardly let me past the door.'

'It was actually Marilyn who told me you were going to America,' Rosemary said as she negotiated the traffic.

'Did she now?' He wasn't pleased.

'Yes, I met her this morning in Tara Road and she asked me whether I had heard anything of your plans. I told her she could call Ria to check. She said she didn't want to make waves. That was her expression.'

'Was it?' he grunted.

'You don't think she could *know* about us do you, Danny?'

'I certainly didn't tell her.'

'No, it's just that she looks at me coldly and says things like "your good friend Ria" . . . with what sounds like heavy sarcasm. Did she say anything to you?'

'She said something about . . . you've never done anything that would make me think you weren't trustworthy, have you? It seemed a bit odd at the time, I'm trying to remember the words. But . . . no, I think we're only imagining things.'

'Why are you going, Danny?'

'You know why I'm going. I have to tell Ria face to face.'

'It won't make it any better for either of you, it's a wasted journey.'

'Why do you say that?'

'Even if you do tell her she still won't believe that it's going to happen. Ria doesn't believe unpleasant things. She's going to say "Never mind, it will all turn out fine".' Rosemary put on a childish voice to imitate the way Ria might speak.

Danny looked at her. 'What did Ria ever do to you to make you despise her so much? She never says anything except good things about you.'

'I suppose she let me walk off with her husband under her nose and didn't notice. That's not a clever way to be.'

'Most people don't have to be so watchful of people that they think are their friends.' Rosemary said nothing. 'I'm sorry, that was smug and hypocritical.'

'I never loved you for your fine spirit, Danny.'

'It's not easy, what I'm going to do, but fine spirit or no fine spirit, I think she deserves to hear it from me straight out.'

'Did you tell her what you were coming out for?'

'No.'

'She probably thinks you're going back to her,' Rosemary said.

'Why on earth would she think that? She knows it's over.'

'Ria doesn't know it's over. In twenty years she still won't believe it's over,' said Rosemary.

The taxi drew up outside the carport. Danny stared up at the house where his family was spending the summer. It was much more splendid than he had imagined.

He could hear Brian shouting: 'He's here!' and his son hurtled down the slope to meet him and hug him.

A boy with a ball and a baseball cap on backwards stood watching closely. Brian's new friend no doubt. Annie, slim and tanned in pink jeans, was right behind him. The hug was as warm as when she was four years of age. At least he hadn't lost them.

Danny had tears in his eyes when he saw Ria. She had come out too to meet him but she didn't run to him as she would have done in times gone by. She stood there serene, pleased to see him, a big smile all over her face.

'Ria,' he said and stretched out his arms to her. He knew the children were watching.

She hugged him as she would have hugged a woman friend, and her cheek was against his. 'Welcome to Westville,' she said.

Danny let his breath out slowly. Thank God Rosemary had been wrong. All during the flight he had been wondering had he given the wrong message to Ria on the phone. But no, he knew that she saw him coming just as a friend. What a tragedy that he would have to change this mood entirely when he told her about Tara Road.

There was no opportunity to tell her the first night. Too much, far too much happening. There was a swim in the pool, a couple of neighbours or friends dropping in. He wasn't being presented in some cosy way as a current husband, Danny noted with relief. A glass of wine and club sodas in the garden and a platter of smoked salmon, then they were gone and there was a family barbecue beside the pool.

Danny learned that the children were going to stay with the Maines the following night. Ria must have realised that they needed to talk alone and she was packing them off there on a bus. He looked at her with admiration. She was handling it all so much better than he could ever have hoped. All he had to do now was to give her some realistic options about the bleak financial future that lay ahead of them, something that wouldn't make her believe that her whole world was ending.

'Thank you for making it so easy, Ria,' he said as she showed him into the guest room.

'It *is* easy,' she smiled. 'I've always been delighted to see you, so why not now and in this lovely place?'

'It's worked well for you then?'

'Oh, very much so.' She kissed his cheek. 'See you in the morning,' she said and left. He was asleep in under a minute.

Ria spent much of the night in her chair staring out into the garden. Several times during the evening she had had to shake herself to remember the events of the past few months. They still seemed such a normal happy family, the four of them. It was almost impossible to believe that he had left them.

Surely he realised that it had all been a terrible mistake. That was the only reason he could be here. Ria wondered why he hadn't said it straight out. Asked her to forgive him and take him home. He had already thanked her for making things easy for him. She must continue in the same manner, rather than throw herself into his arms and tell him that nothing mattered any more. It was like some kind of game, you had to play it by the rules. Danny was coming back to her and this time she was going to keep him.

Mona McCarthy listened to the story without interrupting. Her face was impassive as she heard the events unfolding.

'Say something, Mona,' he said eventually.

She shrugged her shoulders slightly. 'What is there to say, Barney? I'm sorry, that's all. You put so much into it, I'm sorry that in the end you won't be able to sit back and enjoy it.'

'I was never one for sitting back,' he said. 'You haven't asked how bad it is.'

'You'll tell me.'

'This house is in your name, that's one thing anyway.'

'But we can't keep it, surely?'

'It's all we have, Mona.'

'You're going to let all those people lose their jobs, all those suppliers go without payment and Ria Lynch lose her home, and expect me to live in this mansion?'

'That's not the way it is.'

'What way is it, then?' she asked.

He couldn't answer. 'I'm sorry, Mona,' he said.

'I don't mind being poor, but I won't be dishonest.'

'It's business. You don't understand, you're not a businesswoman.'

'You'd be surprised,' said Mona. 'Very surprised.'

Early next morning Ria took Danny a cup of coffee to his room.

'We usually have a swim before breakfast, will you join us?'

'I didn't bring any swimming trunks.'

'Now that was bad, if you'd only made one of my lists . . .' she mocked herself. 'I'll get you something from Dale's room.'

'Dale?'

'Their son.'

'Will he mind?'

'No, he's dead.' Ria went off and found him a pair of swimming shorts.

'Dead?' Danny said.

'Killed. That's why Marilyn wanted to get away from here.'

'I thought her marriage broke up,' Danny said.

'No, I think her marriage is fine actually.'

'But isn't her husband in Hawaii? That doesn't look very fine to me.'

'I think he's on the way to Ireland this weekend,' Ria said.

They took Danny on a tour, pointing out all the sights of Westville and ending up at the burger bar beside the bus station where Annie and Brian were catching the bus to the Maines'.

Zach and Hubie turned up to say goodbye. 'It's going to be real dull with you gone,' Zach said.

'It's going to be fairly dull with Kelly, she's a girl, you know,' Brian said. Zach nodded sympathetically.

'If that guy Sean Maine puts a hand on you, Annie, I'll know and I'll be up there so quick . . .' Hubie said.

'Will you stop talking about people putting hands on me? My parents are listening to you,' hissed Annie.

Danny and Ria got into the car and drove back to Tudor Drive.

'What's that place over there?' Danny pointed to a cluster of trees in the distance.

'That's Memorial Park, they keep it beautifully.'

'Could we go and walk there, sit there for a bit?'

'Sure, but would you not prefer to go home? The garden in Tudor Drive is as good as it gets.'

'I'd prefer somewhere . . . I don't know . . . somewhere a bit separate from things.'

'Right, Memorial Park it is. There's car parking round this way.'

They walked together and looked at the names of the men from Westville who had died in the World Wars, in Korea and Vietnam.

'What a waste war is. Look, that boy was only four years older than Annie,' Ria said.

They sat down on a wooden seat and he reached out to hold her hand in his.

'You probably know what I have to say,' he said.

She worried slightly, just a little. Surely he should say what he *wanted* to say not what he *had* to say. Still, it was only words. 'Say it, Danny.'

'I admire you so much, I really do . . . and I hate to have to tell you bad news. I can't tell you how much I hate it. The only one thing you'll have to give me some credit for is that I came out here to tell you.'

She felt a big heavy stone suddenly develop below her throat, under the jaunty scarf that she had tied so cheerfully that morning.

'So?' she said, not trusting herself to say anything more.

'It's very bad, Ria.'

'No, it can't be all that bad.' Ria realised that he was not coming back to her. This was not what this was all about.

She heard herself speaking. 'Danny, I've already *had* the worst news, nothing will ever be as bad as that. There can't be anything else you have to tell me.'

'There is,' he said.

And on a wooden seat in Memorial Park, Westville, he told Ria that her home was gone. Part of the assets in the estate of Barney McCarthy, which would be put into the hands of the receiver very shortly.

I've never had a real girlfriend before,' said Sean Maine to Annie. They sat on a window seat at a party in the Maines' house. There was dancing in the room and they were cooking the barbecue in the garden. Sean had his arm round her shoulder proudly, protectively almost. Annie smiled at him, remembering that she must not encourage him to think she was going to go any great distance. 'It's just my luck that the girl I like is going back to Ireland in a short time.'

'We can write to each other,' she said.

'Or maybe I could come over to Ireland, stay with my Aunt Gertie and Uncle Jack, go to school and be near you.'

'Yes, I suppose.' Annie sounded doubtful.

'Would you not like that?'

'Oh, I would, it's just . . . it's just . . .' She wasn't sure how to finish. Mam had told her not to go into details about Gertie's life, it wasn't necessarily known over here. She knew that somehow it was important. 'It's just that I think Gertie's pretty busy,' she said lamely.

'She'd find room for family.' He was confident.

'Sure.'

'It was a big surprise your dad coming back?' Sean knew the story.

'I'm not sure he is actually back.'

'But, Brian said—'

'Oh, Sean, what does Brian know? It's just that Dad looked a bit sad. And he *was* very taken with Bernadette. I can't see he's given her up already, with the baby and everything.'

'Still, he's at home there in Westville with your mom, that can't be bad.'

'No,' Annie agreed. 'That can't be bad at all.'

The shadows of the trees in Memorial Park grew longer as Danny and Ria sat on the wooden bench. They held hands, not like they used to do when they were young. Not even like friends, but like people in a shipwreck, holding on for fear of letting go and being totally alone. Sometimes they sat and said nothing at all. Other times Ria asked questions in a flat voice and Danny answered. At no stage did he call her sweetheart, and he offered no false hopes and glib reassurances that they would be all right.

'Why did you come over to America to tell me?' she asked. 'Couldn't it have waited until we came home?'

'I didn't want you to hear from anyone else.'

They were still holding hands, and she squeezed his as thanks. There were no recriminations. They had both known that the personal guarantee was there. It was just something that neither of them ever thought would be called in.

'Was Barney very sorry about us and Tara Road?' Ria asked.

Danny struggled to be truthful. 'He's so shell-shocked about himself, to be honest, that it's only one part of it.'

'Still, he sent you out here to tell me, he must care a bit?'

'No, I insisted on coming out.'

This was a very different Danny. No longer certain of anything. Even the great Barney McCarthy was no longer a fixed point in his life.

They spoke idly of what Danny would do now. There were other estate agencies where he might get a job. But he would go in on a very low rung of the ladder.

'What about Polly?'

'She's giving up her flat, getting a job, Barney says she's a brick or a sport, I can't remember which.'

Ria nodded. 'Yes, it would be one or the other.'

'And the staff, that's another very hard bit,' he said.

'Who told them?'

'I did as it happens.'

'You've had a lot of the telling to do.'

'Yes, well, I rode high and had a lot of the good times when they were there too.'

'I know you did, we both did.'

The silences that fell were not anxious or uneasy. It was as if they were both trying to take it all in.

'And what does Bernadette say about it all?'

'She doesn't know.'

'Danny?'

'No, she doesn't, truly, I'll tell her when I get back. She'll be calm. Her mother won't, but she will.'

A wind blew, lifting some of the leaves and blossoms up from their feet.

'Let's go back to the house, Danny.'

'Thank you so much.'

'For what?'

'For not screaming at me. I've had to give you the worst news anyone could ever give anyone.'

'Oh no,' she said.

'What do you mean?'

'You gave me much worse news than that before.'

He said nothing. They walked together across Memorial Park back to Marilyn Vine's car.

When they got back to Tudor Drive, Ria suggested they have tea.

'No, Ria, sit down, talk to me . . . try to talk, don't bustle about doing things like you used to do at home.'

'Is that what I did at home?' She felt very hurt, annoyed.

'Well, you know whenever I came in and wanted to talk there was this in the oven and that on the burner and something else coming out of the deepfreeze and people coming and going.'

'Is that what a lot of this was about?'

'I suppose it was to cover what wasn't there,' he said sadly.

'Well, of course, I won't get tea, I'll sit down and talk to you now.'

That didn't please him either. 'Now I do feel a heel,' he said. 'Come on, let's have tea.'

'You make it,' she said. 'I'll sit here.'

He put on the kettle and took out two mugs and the tea bags.

'You have a message on the machine,' he said.

'Take it for us, Danny, will you?' The old Ria would have leapt up with a pencil and paper.

'It's Hubie Green, Mrs Lynch. I didn't catch Annie's telephone number and I thought it would be good to give her a call during her weekend away. I did leave you an email about it, but I guess you don't have time to look at your messages now with all the action going on. Say hi to Mr Lynch for me.'

'Do you want to call him with her number?' Danny asked.

'No. If Annie had wanted him to have it then she'd have given it to him,' Ria said.

Danny looked at her admiringly. 'You're right. Shall we check your email in case there are any more messages?'

'I thought you wanted to talk, now who is putting it off?'

'We have the evening, the night to ourselves.'

Ria shrugged. 'Right, come into Greg's study and see how good I am at it.'

Expertly she went for her Mailbox and saw three messages. One from Hubie, one from Danny's office, and one from Rosemary Ryan.

'Do you want the office?' she asked.

'No, who needs any more grief?'

'Well, will I see what Rosemary says?'

'More bad news, surely,' he said.

'She knows? Rosemary knows?' Ria was startled.

'She had heard already from her own sources, then I met her yesterday just as I was leaving. She drove me to the airport.'

Ria brought Rosemary's message up on the screen. *Ria, Danny, you should access the* Irish Times *this morning. There's an item about Barney that would interest you. All may not be lost after all. Enjoy New England.*

'She says we should look up the *Irish Times*, the business gossip column,' she said.

'Can you do that?' he asked, impressed.

'Yes, hold on a minute.'

Very shortly they had the website and got the item. The paragraph said that there had been a rescue package from sources outside Barney McCarthy's company. Things didn't look as dire as had been thought. Ria read it aloud, her voice getting lighter all the time.

'Danny, isn't that magic?'

'Yes.'

'Why aren't you more pleased?'

'If there *was* anything, Barney would have phoned me here; he has the number. This is just him doing the PR job.'

'Well, let's see what your office says on this. He might have sent you an email.'

'I doubt it, but let's call it up anyway.'

'Message for Danny Lynch: could he please phone Mrs Finola Dunne at her home number urgently.'

'I *told* you it would be grief,' Danny said.

'Do you want to call her?'

'No, I can get the earful about how irresponsible I am when I get back,' he said.

They walked back into the kitchen and picked up their mugs of tea. The garden lights went on automatically, lighting up the place. Ria sat down and waited. She ached to speak, to reassure him about that paragraph in the newspaper, to encourage him to ring Barney and Mona at home. But she would do none of these things, she would wait. As, apparently, she should have waited in the past.

Eventually he spoke. 'What are you saddest about?' he asked.

She would *not* say that she was most sad because she thought he had been coming back to her. That would be the end of any meaningful conversation between them again. She tried to think what was the next most awful thing on the list.

'I suppose I'm sad that your dreams and hopes are ended. You wanted so much for the children and indeed for us all. It will be different now.'

'Will we tell them together tomorrow, do you think?' he asked.

'Yes, I suppose so. I was wondering if we should let them have their holiday in peace, but that would be lying to them.'

'And I don't want you to have to do it on your own, make excuses for me as I know you would,' he said.

'There are no excuses to make. Everything you did, you did for us all,' she said. Why did she not know what to do to help him or make things better? Almost everything that her instinct told her would be right would only annoy him.

Tears fell down her face and splashed off the table. She didn't lift her hand to wipe them away, half hoping that in the fading light he would not see. But he came up to her and gently took her tea mug out of her hand and placed it on the table, then he pulled her up from the chair, held her close to him and stroked her hair.

'Poor Ria, dear, dear Ria,' he said. She could feel his heart beating as she lay against him. 'Ria, don't cry.' He kissed the tears from her cheeks. But more came in their place.

'I'm sorry,' she said into his chest. 'I think I am a bit shocked, Danny. Maybe I should lie down for a bit.'

They went to the bedroom where she had been hoping he might join her tonight. He sat down and gently he took off her blouse, which he hung carefully on the back of the chair. Then she stepped out of her silk skirt and he folded that too. She stood in a white slip like a child being put to bed with a fever, and he turned back the sheet and counterpane for her.

'I don't want to miss your visit. I want to get value out of your being here,' she said.

'Shush, shush, I'll stay here beside you until you get a little sleep,' he said.

He brought a face flannel from the bathroom and wiped her face. Then he stroked her hand as he sat beside her in a chair.

He looked so tired as he sat there minding her, his face half in the light that came in from the garden. She sat up on her elbow and said, 'It will be sort of all right, won't it?'

He put his arms round her and held her again. 'Yes, Ria, it will be sort of all right.' His voice was weary.

'Danny, lie down on the bed and sleep too, just close your eyes. It's been worse for you.' She didn't mean any more than that, lie down in his clothes on top of the bedspread and sleep beside her for a couple of hours.

But he clung to her and she realised that he wasn't going to leave her go. Ria didn't allow herself to think about what might be happening. She lay back and closed her eyes while the only man she had ever loved gently removed the rest of her clothes and made love to her again.

Greg decided to tell Ria that he was going to Ireland, but the answering machine was on. He debated whether to leave a message and decided against it. He stood in the phone booth at Kennedy Airport and considered calling Marilyn. But suppose she told him not to come? Then they would be worse than they had ever been. His only hope was to call her and say he was in Dublin. Which he would be very soon.

He heard his flight being called. It was now too late to call his wife even if it were a good idea.

There had been no reply from Danny. Rosemary was very annoyed. She had driven him to the airport, he was in a house with an email facility, a telephone. He would have known what to make of that cryptic piece in the paper. Why didn't he call her?

What she felt for Danny Lynch was neither sensible nor in any game plan. It was in fact the most basic urge imaginable. No other man would do. She had put up with sharing him with Ria for years, and with others like that disgusting Orla King. She had even put up with the infatuation for the wraith-like Bernadette. But he had always been civil and courteous before. He wasn't even that these days.

She was glad that she had not rescued him; she was just quivering with curiosity to know who had. The woman who wrote this column in the *Irish Times* was very informed. It would not be a flier, something deliberately planted. Rosemary believed that Danny Lynch and Barney McCarthy were genuinely going to be pulled out of the fire. All she needed to know was by whom.

Marilyn was in the front garden in jeans and T-shirt. She looked very young and fit for her years, Gertie thought.

'I hate having to burden you with my problems, Marilyn.'

'Sure, what is it, Gertie?'

'Well, I never told Jack I did a bit of cleaning for you.' Gertie said. 'But things have changed. Now I do need him to know I come here. You see he thinks I get the money somewhere else.'

'Yes, but surely he won't come and ask me?'

'No, but suppose he does, it's all right now, I'd prefer him to think that this is where I get the money.'

Marilyn could easily have urged Gertie not to be so foolish, such a hapless victim encouraging more senseless violence and even neglecting her own children in the process. But one look at that haunted face made Marilyn retreat from any such action. 'Right,' she sighed. 'It's OK this week to tell him, let me know if it changes next week.'

'You're lucky and strong, Marilyn, I'm neither, but thank you.' Gertie left to go to the bus stop across the road. Polly Callaghan was the next person she must warn.

Rosemary drew up her car. 'Can I drive you anywhere, Gertie?'

'I was going over to Polly, I wanted to give her a message.'

'She's in London, back after the weekend.'

'Well I am glad I met you. Thanks, Rosemary, you saved me a trip, I'll just walk up home then.'

They slept wrapped up together as they had done for years in Tara Road. When Ria woke she knew she must not stir. So she lay there going back over all the events of the day and evening. She could see the time; it was eleven o'clock at night. She would like to get up, have a shower, and make them both an omelette. But she would take no initiative, she would lie there until he moved.

She pretended to be asleep when he got out of bed, picked up his clothes and went to the bathroom. When she heard the shower being turned on she joined him there with a towel wrapped round her. She sat down on one of the bathroom chairs. She would let him speak first.

'Where do we go now, Ria?' he asked.

'A shower, a little supper?'

He seemed relieved. 'Sandalwood?' he said of the soap.

'You like it, don't you?'

'Yes, I do.' He seemed sad about something, she didn't know what. He went to his own room to get clothes. She followed him into the shower, then put on yellow trousers and a black sweater.

'Very smart,' he said as they met in the kitchen.

'Annie says I look like a wasp in this outfit.'

'Annie! What does she know?'

There was not a mention of what had happened. Or of what might happen next. Nor did they talk of Barney McCarthy or Bernadette, or the future or the past. But somehow they filled the time quite easily. Together they made a herb omelette and a salad; they each drank a glass of wine from the fridge. They ignored the message light winking on the answering machine.

And when it was half past midnight, they went back to bed in the big double bed.

The phone kept ringing, as if someone was refusing to accept that there was nobody going to take the call.

'Technology,' yawned Danny.

'Hubie Green, desperate for our daughter's telephone number,' giggled Ria.

'I'll get coffee for us. Will I put whoever it is out of their misery?' Danny suggested.

'Do, of course.' Ria was chirpy and cheerful as she heard the message tape winding backwards. Anything at all he did was all right with her today. She was just pulling on her swimsuit, ready to go to the pool, when she heard the urgent voice on the answering machine. 'Danny, I don't care what time it is, or Ria or whoever is there, you've got to pick up, you have to. This is an emergency. It's Finola here. Bernadette's been taken to hospital, Danny, she's had a haemorrhage. She's calling out for you. You've got to talk to me, you've got to come home.'

Ria put a dress on over her swimsuit and went quietly out to the kitchen. She filled the percolator and switched it on. Then she took out a directory with the numbers of airlines in it and passed it to Danny without comment. He would go home today, and she must do absolutely nothing to stop him.

She caught sight of her reflection in the mirror. She had a half-smile on her face. She must lose this immediately. She must not let a hint of what she was feeling escape. If Bernadette was losing the baby then their problems might be over.

Danny looked at her with anguished eyes.

'Get dressed,' she said. 'We'll get you on a plane.'

He came over to her and held her very tight. 'There never was and never will be anyone like you, Ria,' he said in a broken voice.

'I'll always be here for you, you know that,' she said into his hair.

Marilyn was working in the garden, wondering whether in this Catholic country they would think she was breaking the Sabbath by doing so. But Colm Barry had reassured her, it would be regarded as purely recreational, and weren't all the shops open on Sundays now, football games played.

She heard a car draw up outside. Surely not a caller, she didn't want to talk to anyone now. She wanted to lose herself in this work. There were so many things she did not want to think about. Strange that. Once there had only been one topic that had to be forced away.

She heard voices outside the gate of Number 16. And as she knelt, trowel in hand, Marilyn Vine saw the slightly stooped figure of her husband come into the drive and look up at the house. She dropped the trowel and ran to him, crying out, 'Greg . . . Greg!'

He pulled back from her first. Months of rejection had taken their toll. 'I hope it's all right . . .' he began apologetically.

'Greg?'

'I did plan to call you from the airport. I sat there until it was a civilised time,' he explained.

'It's all right.'

'I didn't want to disturb you, or invade your space. It's just . . . well it's only for two or three days.'

She looked at him in wonder. He was apologising for being there, how terrible must have been the coldness she had shown to him. 'Greg, I'm delighted you're here,' she said.

'You are?'

'Of course I am. I don't suppose you'd think of giving me a hug?'

Hardly able to believe it, Greg Vine embraced his wife.

There were bus timetables there too, so Ria looked up an earlier bus back for the children, then she called Sheila. 'Could you be very tactful and get them on it for me? I'll explain everything tomorrow.'

Sheila knew an emergency when she heard one. 'No bad news?' she asked.

'Not really, very complicated. But Danny has to leave tonight and I want him to be able to say goodbye to the children himself.'

'How much will I tell them?'

'Just that plans have changed.'

'I'll do it, of course, but I want you to know the courage it will take to tell that to Sean Maine and Annie Lynch.'

On the bus Annie and Brian tried to work it out.

'He's coming back to live at home?' Brian was hopeful.

'They wouldn't bring us back early to tell us that,' Annie grumbled.

'We'll know soon.' Brian was philosophical. 'We're on the edge of Westville now.'

When they got off the bus Hubie Green was waiting. 'Your mom asked me to pick you up and drive you back to Tudor Drive,' he said.

'Are you sure, you're not just kidnapping us?' Annie asked.

'No. I was glad of the chance to see you again, but truly she did ask me.' They climbed into Hubie's car. 'Did you have a good time?'

'It was all right . . .' Annie said with a careless shrug.

Bernadette's face was very white. 'Tell me again, Mum, what did he say?'

'He said I was to listen carefully and repeat these words: "I am flying home tonight, I'll be there tomorrow and nothing has changed".'

'Did he say he loved me?' Her voice was very weak.

'He said "Nothing has changed". He said it three times.'

'Why do you think he said that instead of that he loved me?'

'Because his ex-wife may have been there, and because he wanted to tell you that if you *did* lose the baby, which you won't, Ber, it would still be the same.'

'Do you believe that, Mum?'

'Yes. I listened to him say it three times and I believe him,' said Finola.

'Sit down, Barney, we have to talk,' Mona McCarthy said. 'A lot of things have changed.'

'Like what?'

'Like that paragraph in the newspaper.'

'Well, you *said* that you had something put by over the years and you were prepared to rescue things.'

'We haven't yet discussed in what way. And I certainly didn't expect you to start telling the newspapers.' She was calm and confident as always, but this time with a steely hint that he didn't like.

'Mona, you know just as well as I do the need to build up confidence at a time like this,' he began.

'You'd be most unwise to build up anyone's confidence until we have discussed the terms.'

'Look, love, stop talking in mysteries. What do you mean "terms"? You told me you'd put something away, something that would rescue us.'

'No, that's not what I said. I said I had something, a way which *could* rescue you, that's a very different thing.'

'Don't play word games, this isn't the time.' There was a tic in his forehead. She couldn't have been leading him along. It wasn't her style.

'No games, I assure you.' She was very cold.

'I'm listening, Mona.'

'I hope you are,' she said. Then in very level tones she told him that she had enough money saved over the years in reputable pension funds and insurance policies which, when cashed in, would bale him out. But they were all in her name and they would only be cashed if Barney agreed to pay his debtors. *And* to sell this mansion they lived in and buy a much smaller and less pretentious house. *And* to return the personal guarantee on Number 16 Tara Road to the Lynches. *And* that Miss Callaghan be assured that any relationship with her, financial, sexual or social, was at an end.

Barney listened open-mouthed. 'You can't make these demands,' he said eventually.

'You don't *have* to accept them,' she countered.

He looked at her for a long time. 'You hold all the cards,' he said.

'People can always get up and leave the card table, they don't have to play.'

'Why are you doing this, you don't need me, Mona? You don't have to have me hanging around the place as some kind of an accessory.'

'You have no idea what I need and what I don't need, Barney.'

'Have some dignity, woman, for God's sake. At this stage everyone knows about me and Polly, we're not hushing anything up that isn't widely known already.'

'And they'll know when it's over too,' she said.

'This will give you pleasure?'

'These are my terms.'

'Do we have lawyers to fix it up?' He was scathing.

'No, but we do have the newspapers. You've used them already, I can do the same.'

If anyone had ever suggested to Barney McCarthy that his quiet compliant wife would have spoken like this to him Barney would have laughed aloud.

'What's brought this on, the thought of being poor?' His lip was twisted as he spoke.

'I pity you if you really think that. I never wanted to be rich. Never. It always sat uneasily on me. But anyway as it happens I *am* rich, and I'll be richer if I don't help you out of the hole that you are in.'

'So why then?'

'Partly from a sense of fairness. You worked hard for what you got, and I have enjoyed a comfortable life as a result. But mainly because I would like us to move with some grace into this period of our lives.'

He looked at her with tears in his eyes. 'It will be done,' he said.

'As you choose, Barney.'

Hubie left them at the carport and they ran inside. They saw Danny's bag packed.

'You really are going, then?' Annie said.

'Did you think I was making it up?'

'I thought you might just want to get us back from the Maines',' Annie said.

'No, we wouldn't,' Ria said. 'But let's not waste time, we only have an hour before I take your dad to the airport. There are a lot of things to be said so we must all talk now.'

Danny took control. 'I came over here to tell you that there are going to be a lot of changes, not all for the better.'

'Are any of them for the better?' Brian asked.

'No, as a matter of fact,' his father said. 'They're not.'

They sat silent, waiting. Danny's voice seemed to have failed him. He cleared his throat and found the words. He told them the story. The debts, the gambles that hadn't worked, the lack of confidence, the end result. Number 16 Tara Road would have to be sold.

'Will you and Bernadette sell the new house too?' Brian asked.

'Yes, yes, of course.'

'But Barney doesn't own that one?' Annie asked.

'No.'

'Well, maybe we could *all* live there?' Brian enclosed the whole room in his expansive gesture. 'Or maybe not,' he said, remembering.

'And I would have told you all this tonight, with more time for us to discuss what was best and to tell you how sorry I am, but I have to go home.'

'Is Mr McCarthy in jail?' Brian asked.

'No, no, it's not that at all, it's something else.' There was a silence. 'Bernadette isn't well. We've had a message from Finola. She's had a lot of bleeding and she may be losing the baby, she's in hospital. So that's why I'm going home early.'

'Like it's not going to be born after all, is that it?' Brian wanted to make sure he had it straight.

'It's not totally formed yet so it would be very weak and might not live if it were born now,' Danny explained.

Annie looked at her mother as she listened to this explanation, and bit her lip. Never had things been so raw and honest before.

Brian let out a great sigh. 'Well, wouldn't that solve everything if Bernadette's baby wasn't born at all?' he said. 'Then we could all go back to being like we were.'

Danny gave the taxi driver the address of the maternity hospital. 'As quick as you can, and I have to pay you in US dollars, I don't have any real money.'

'Dollars are real enough for me,' said the taxi driver, pulling out in the early-morning sunshine and putting his foot down.

'Is this the first baby?'

'No.' Danny was curt.

'Still, it's always the same excitement, isn't it? And every one of them different. We have five ourselves, but that's it. Tie a knot in it, they told me.' He laughed happily at the pleasantry and caught Danny's eye in the mirror. 'Maybe you're a bit tired and want to have a rest after the flight.'

'Something like that,' Danny said with relief, and closed his eyes.

'Well, make the most of it, you'll have plenty of broken sleep for the next bit, there's a promise,' said the driver, a man of experience.

Across the corridor was a men's toilet. When Danny was inside he just leaned over the hand-basin and looked at his haggard face, sunken eyes from a sleepless night on the plane, crumpled shirt.

He had been told she was still in intensive care, and he could see her in an hour or two. Her mother would be back shortly, she had been there most of the night. Oh yes, she had lost the baby; there had been no possibility of anything else. Bernadette would tell him everything herself, it wasn't hospital policy to tell him whether it had been a boy or a girl. In time. Go and have a coffee, they had urged him.

His shoulders began to heave and the tears wouldn't stop. Another man, a big burly young fellow, came in and saw him.

'Were you there for it?' he asked. Danny couldn't speak and the proud young father thought he had nodded agreement. 'I was too. It blew my mind. I couldn't believe it. I had to come in here to get over it. My son, and I saw him coming into the world.' He put an awkward arm round Danny's shoulder and gave him a squeeze of solidarity. 'And they say it's the women who go through it all,' he said.

Polly Callaghan came back from London early on Monday morning. Barney was waiting in his car outside her flat.

Polly was thrilled to see him. 'I didn't call you or anything, I wanted to leave you a bit of space. Aren't you good to come and meet me?'

'No, no, not at all.' He seemed very down.

Polly wasn't going to allow that. 'Hey, I bought the *Irish Times* at Victoria Station in London and I saw that piece about you, it's wonderful.'

'Yes,' he said.

'Well, isn't it?'

'In a way.'

'Well, get out of that car, come in and I'll make us coffee.'

'No, Poll, we must talk here.'

'In your car? Don't be ridiculous.'

'Please. Humour me this once.'

'Haven't I spent a lifetime humouring you? Tell me before I burst. Is it true, are you being rescued?'

'Yes, Poll, I am.'

'So why haven't we the champagne out?'

'But at a price. A terrible price.'

Marilyn Vine said to Greg that they were going to drive out to Wicklow for the day on Monday. It was less than an hour's journey, and very beautiful. She was going to make a picnic.

'Here, I'll show you a map, you love maps,' she said as she got out Ria's picnic basket. 'Now, you can see where we're going and navigate.'

He looked at her in amazement. The old enthusiasms were back. 'We can go to the country in one hour?' he said, surprised.

'This is an extraordinary city, it's got sea and mountains right on the doorstep,' she said. 'And I want to take you to this place I found. You can park the car and walk over the hills for miles and meet no one.'

'Why are we going there?' he asked gently.

'So that nobody can interrupt us. If we stay here in Number 16 Tara Road we might as well be in Grand Central Station,' said Marilyn, with the easy laugh that Greg Vine had thought he would never hear again.

Bernadette looked very white. His stomach nearly turned over when he saw her. 'Go on, talk to her. She's been counting the moments till you got here,' the nurse said.

'She's asleep,' he said, almost afraid to approach the bed.

'Is that you, Danny?'

'I'm here beside you, darling, don't speak. You're tired and weak. You've lost a lot of blood, but you're going to be fine.'

'Kiss me,' she said. He kissed her thin white face. 'Properly.' He kissed her on the lips. 'Do you still love me, Danny?'

'Darling Bernadette, of course I do.'

'You know about the baby?'

'I'm sad we've lost our baby, very sad,' he said, eyes full of tears. 'And, God, I'm sad I wasn't here to be with you when it happened. But *you* are all right and *I'm* here for you and that's what's going to make us strong for ever and ever.'

'You're not glad or anything, you don't think it sort of solves things just now?'

'Jesus, Bernadette, how could you even *think* that?' His face was anguished.

'Well . . . you know . . .'

'No, I don't know. Our baby is dead, the baby we were building a home for, and you're so weak and hurt. How could I be glad about anything like that?'

'It's just that I was afraid, you being out in America . . .' her voice trailed away.

'You know I had to go out to America to tell them face to face about the business. And that's done and I'm home now, home with you.'

'And did it go all right?' Bernadette asked.

'Yes, it went all right,' said Danny Lynch.

Finola Dunne drove Danny to his office.

'I have to talk to Barney about what this rescue business is all about. It may be nothing, only puff, but it just might be something we can cling on to. I'll be back to Bernadette before lunch.'

'You'll need some sleep, you look terrible,' Finola said.

'I can't sleep, not at a time like this.'

'Ber losing the baby . . . at this time . . . ?' Finola was tentative.

'Makes me love her still more and want to look after her even more desperately than I did before . . .' Danny finished the sentence for her.

'But there must be ways . . . ?'

'Surely you know, Finola, that I adore her, that I wouldn't have left my wife and children for her if I didn't love her more than anything else in the whole world. You *must* know that.'

In the office a full-scale meeting was taking place. The receptionist was surprised to see him. 'They didn't think you were coming back until tomorrow,' she said, startled at his dishevelled appearance.

'Yes, well, I'm here now, who's in there?'

'The accountant, the lawyers, the bank manager, and Mrs McCarthy.'

'Mona?'

'Yes.'

'And was anyone going to tell me about this summit or was I to hear about it when it was all over?'

'Don't ask me, Mr Lynch. I don't get told what's happening either.'

'Right, I'm going in there.'

'Mr Lynch?'

'Yes?'

'If I could suggest you sort of . . . well . . . cleaned yourself up a bit.'

'Thank you, sweetheart,' he said. The girl was right. Five minutes in the men's room would take the worst edges off.

The sun shone through the trees as Greg and Marilyn sat at a wooden table and unpacked their picnic.

'Why did you come here?' Marilyn asked.

'Because Ria said you had talked to her children about Dale. I thought you might be able to talk to me about him too.'

'Yes, of course I can. I'm sorry it took so long.'

'It takes what time it takes,' Greg said. He laid his hand on hers. Last night he had slept in the big white bed beside Marilyn. They really hadn't touched each other, not reached out towards the other, but they had held hands for a little. He knew he must be very gentle in asking questions. He wouldn't ask what had changed her. She would tell him.

And then she did. 'There's always some stupid unimportant thing, isn't there?' Marilyn said with the tears that he had never seen her shed in her eyes. 'I mean it's so idiotic that I can hardly bear to tell you. But it was all to do with those children. Annie said that of course we couldn't have let him play with motorbikes any more than you'd let someone play with guns. And Brian said that he imagined Dale was up in heaven looking down, sorry for all the trouble he had caused.' The tears fell down onto their joined hands. 'Then it all made sense somehow, Greg,' she said through her sobs. 'I mean, I don't think there's a real heaven or anything, but his spirit is somewhere, sorry for all the trouble. And I must listen to him and tell him it's all right.'

'The wanderer returns,' Danny said, coming in with a false smile and confident stance to the boardroom where the meeting was going on. The stolid figure of Mona McCarthy sat beside the bank manager, and the two lawyers.

'I'm sorry, we didn't know you were going to be in the country, Danny, there was no attempt to exclude you,' Mona said. Mona was speaking at a meeting like this?

In the space of fifteen minutes Danny learned that Mrs McCarthy had, entirely without any legal or moral need to do so, decided to rescue the firm from bankruptcy. Everything would be wound up, the assets sold, the debtors paid. There would be no more work for Danny Lynch since the company no longer existed.

The good news was that the personal guarantee on Number 16 Tara Road was now rescinded. The house would not be sold to pay Barney McCarthy's debts. Danny could feel his breath beginning to return to normal. But the bank manager added that on the Tara Road front there was also, on a practical level, bad news. Danny had no assets, no job and a considerable personal overdraft. The house would have to be sold anyway.

Greg had gone back to America. Marilyn had longed to get the plane with him. 'I can't leave her house, I can't abandon ship now, leave a house she's going to lose anyway, it would be too cruel.'

'Of course not,' he had said.

'I'll be back on September the 1st, back in Tudor Drive,' she promised.

'So will I, in that week anyway,' he said.

'Hawaii?'

'They'll understand.' Greg was confident. 'It was a compassionate posting anyway. They'll be glad that we got better.'

'What's Ria like?' Marilyn asked suddenly. 'As a person?'

'I forgot you don't know her. She's very warm, innocent in ways. She isn't short of a word. There was a time I didn't think you'd like her, but now I think you would. I think my brother Andy did too.'

'There!' Marilyn cried. 'We might end up being sisters-in-law.'

'Don't hold your breath,' said Greg.

'Ria, it's Danny.'

'Oh, thank God, I was hoping to hear from you. How are you?'

'Well, we lost the baby.'

'I am sorry.'

'Yes, I know you are, Ria.'

'But in a way . . .'

'I know you're not going to be like these people who wrongly say it's all for the best,' he interrupted her.

'No, of course I wasn't going to say that,' Ria lied.

'I know, but people do and it's very upsetting for us both.'

'I'm sure.' She was confused but she must never show it. 'Anyway the children are fine, they're winding down to go home now, and then we'll all meet and make plans about the future.'

'Yes, it's not quite as bleak as it looked on that scene,' he said.

'What do you mean?'

'Mona had some savings, Barney doesn't get our house after all.'

'Danny!' She was overjoyed.

'We'll still have to sell it, but at least this way you and I get the money, we'll find somewhere for you to live.'

'Sure.'

'So that's what I rang to tell you.'

'Yes . . .'

'Are you OK?' He sounded concerned. 'I thought you'd be so pleased.'

'Yes, of course I'm pleased,' she said. 'Sorry, Danny, I have to go, someone's ringing at the door.' She hung up. There was nobody at the door but she needed to go without him hearing the tears in her voice. And the total wretched realisation that it had all meant nothing to him and that there were no plans for them for the future.

'Monto will have a table for six tonight and he'd like the one near the door,' said one of the nameless friends who accompanied Colm's brother-in-law.

'We have no reservations,' Colm said carefully.

'I think you have.'

'Ask Monto to talk to me himself if he's in any doubt,' Colm said.

His friend Fergal, a detective whom Colm had met at AA meetings, had warned him that the word was that Monto was drug-dealing in the restaurant and there could be a raid. With Marilyn's help, Colm had persuaded Caroline to book into a rehabilitation programme where she could no longer be reached by Monto, offering her more supplies.

'Monto doesn't like people playing games.'

'Of course he doesn't.' Colm was pleasant.

'You'll be hearing from him.'

Colm knew he would. Fergal said he'd make sure there were a couple of guys in the vicinity, in an unmarked car.

'Can we have the Maines to stay? Our last visit *was* cut a bit short.'

'I know, Annie, but there was a reason.'

'Still. Please?'

'I don't know . . .'

'But, Mam, this is the last good holiday we might ever have, you know, if we're going to be broke, and Dad gone and everything. It would be nice to have something to remember.'

'It would,' Ria said.

'Are you all right, Mam?'

'Yes. I don't want you getting too fond of a boy that you're going to have to say goodbye to in ten days' time.'

'No, Mam, you'd much prefer that than one I might see every day and night for the rest of my life,' Annie said, her eyes dancing.

'Ask them,' Ria said. It didn't really matter now. Nothing did.

Rosemary called at Number 16. 'Just passing by, I heard from Gertie that your husband came over.'

'That's right.'

'Good visit?'

'Very nice, thank you.'

'And is there any news of Ria?' If Rosemary thought it odd that she was being left on the doorstep to ask these questions she showed nothing of it.

Suddenly Marilyn opened the door wider. 'Yes, there is as it happens. Come in and I'll tell you about her news.'

Marilyn led Rosemary into the beautiful drawing room. 'Would you care for a glass of sherry?' she asked in a very formal and courteous tone. She picked up a decanter and filled two of the small cut-crystal glasses that stood on a tray. They both sat down opposite each other. 'Ria is thinking of going into business when she comes back.'

'So she told me.'

'She won't need premises or kitchens or anything, but she's a very talented cook, as I suppose you know.'

'She's good, yes.'

'What she really needs, Rosemary, is someone to help her professionally, someone like you to write and print a brochure for her, business cards, menu suggestions.'

'Well, of course . . . if there's anything I can do to help . . .'

'And to give her a series of introductions, small receptions in your office, in places you visit.'

'Come on, Marilyn, you're making it sound like a full-time job.'

'I think you should invest a fair amount of time in it, yes, certainly.' Marilyn's voice was steely now. 'And even some money, Rosemary.'

'I don't invest in friends' schemes, Marilyn,' Rosemary said. 'I never have. If you don't lose money in their businesses then you've a better chance of keeping them *as* friends, if you see what I mean.'

There was a silence.

'Of course I'll be happy to mention her name,' Rosemary said. Still silence. 'And if ever I hear of anything . . .'

'I think we should get a list ready now of exactly what you'll do. We could write down what a good kind friend like you has done for Ria while she was away.' It sounded like a threat. Rosemary looked at her wildly. It couldn't be a threat, could it? 'Because she needs to know that friends can do things as well as say them. What good would a friend be, who betrayed her?'

'I beg your pardon?'

'Well it would be a betrayal, wouldn't it, if a friend took the things she most wanted in the world, while still pretending to be a friend?'

Rosemary's voice was almost a whisper now. 'What do you mean?'

'What do *you* think she wants most in the world, Rosemary?'

'I don't know. This house? Her children? Danny?'

'Yes. And of course you can't restore the house to her, her children she has already. So?' Marilyn paused.

'So?' Rosemary said shakily. The woman knew, she bloody knew.

'So, what you can help with is her dignity and self-respect,' Marilyn said brightly.

Danny's name had been left out of the list.

They both began to write down what Rosemary would do to help Ria's career.

Gertie had been ironing a dress for Marilyn. 'That's a beautiful shade. Fuchsia, is it?'

'I think so. It doesn't fit me properly, I rarely wear it.'

'That's a shame, it's a gorgeous colour. Years ago when I worked in Polly's dress-hire place we had an outfit that colour; people were always renting it for weddings.'

'Would you like it?' Marilyn asked suddenly. 'I don't wear it, I'd love you to have it.'

'Well, if you're sure.'

'Wear it tonight, the colour would suit you.' Gertie's face seemed to have a shadow. 'It's still on, tonight, isn't it?' Marilyn had booked a table for the two of them at Colm's restaurant.

'But of course it's on, Jack's pleased for me. I don't think he'd like to see me wearing such a classy dress though. One he didn't buy for me himself.'

'Change here on our way to the restaurant then.'

'Why not? Won't it do me good to dress up?' said Gertie with that heartbreaking smile which made Marilyn glad she hadn't said anything terrible about Jack.

At seven o'clock Monto and two friends arrived at the restaurant and headed for the table that they thought they had booked. The restaurant was still empty. This was better than Colm had believed possible.

'Colm, you didn't get the message that we have an important meeting and this is where we are having it.'

'Not tonight, Monto.'

'Tell me a little more.' Monto smiled a slow smile. He had very short hair and a fat neck. His expensive suit did nothing to hide his shape. Colm looked at him levelly.

'You have a short memory. Not long ago you told me you owed me.'

'And I paid you. You've done enough deals in this place.'

'Deals?' Monto looked at his two associates. 'Isn't the word "meals", Colm? That's what you serve, it's a restaurant, isn't it?'

'Goodbye, Monto.'

'Don't think you can talk to me like that.'

'I just have, and if you know what's good and wise you'll go.'

'And what makes you think I will?'

'The Guards in the car just outside.'

'You set me up?'

'No, I didn't as it happens. I told them that there would be no meeting, no deal here tonight or ever again. Good night, Monto.'

Jack was sitting up waiting when Gertie came home from the restaurant. 'Nice evening, was it, Gertie?'

'Yes, Jack, it was a nice girls' night out.'

'And who gave you the whore's purple dress?'

'Marilyn did, it doesn't suit her.'

'It wouldn't suit anyone except a whore,' he said.

'Ah, Jack, don't say that.'

'All my life I loved you and all you did was betray me and let me down.' He had never spoken like this before.

'That's not so, Jack. I never looked at another man, never.'

'Prove that to me.'

'Well, would I have stayed with you all these times you've been under the weather?' she asked.

'No, that's true,' he said. 'That's very true.'

They went to bed. She lay there hardly daring to move in case she might feel his fist. Out of the corner of her eye she saw him. Jack was awake and looking at the ceiling. He was dangerously calm.

The next morning Jack Brennan got very drunk very early. He went first to Nora Johnson's house at Number 48A. 'Does my wife clear up after your daughter and all her friends?' he shouted.

'I have nothing to say to you, drunk or sober,' Ria's mother said with some spirit. 'I have never met your wife without telling her that she should leave you. I'll bid you good day.'

He moved on to Rosemary's house. 'Swear to me on a stack of Bibles that Gertie never cleaned for you or anyone.'

'Oh, get the hell out of here before I call the Guards,' Rosemary said, and pushed past him.

Then he went and knocked loudly on Marilyn's door. 'Did you give Gertie a whore's dress?'

'Did she say I did?'

'Stop being Mrs Clever with me.'

'I think you should go, Jack.' She slammed the door and looked out of the window to see where he went. She saw him run across the road to the bus stop.

Polly Callaghan had everything ready. Today she was moving to rented accommodation. An unfurnished flat so she could take her own things with her. She dreaded to think of a lifetime without Barney. She wished she could hate him, but she couldn't. She just hated herself for having taken the wrong decision so long ago.

The furniture vans had arrived. Polly sighed and began to give the directions that would dismantle a large part of her life. The phone was disconnected but her mobile was still in operation. It rang just at that moment.

'Poll, I love you.'

'No, you don't, Barney, but it doesn't matter.'

'What do you mean it doesn't matter?'

'It doesn't,' she said, and clicked off.

She was going to drive ahead of the van to direct them to the new address. One final look and she was ready to close the door. Polly sighed. It was hard to say to Barney that it didn't matter, but she must be practical. She had always known Barney for what he was. Polly did not think she had been fooled or betrayed. She had always known the score. And there was plenty of life ahead.

She gave one last glance out of the window at the removal van. There were sounds of shouting, some drunk was yelling abusively. Polly couldn't quite see what was happening. Then there was a thump, an impact followed by a screech of brakes. There were screams from everywhere. The boy who was driving was being helped from his seat.

'I couldn't help it, he threw himself, I swear,' he was stammering.

It was Jack Brennan. And he was dead.

 # 10

THE LAUNDERETTE WAS BUSY when they arrived. Gertie looked up when she saw Polly Callaghan coming in and her hand flew to her throat when she saw that Polly was followed by two Guards.

'Jack?' she cried in a strangled voice. 'Has Jack done something? He was grand last night, very quiet, not a word out of him. What in heaven did he do?'

'Sit down, Gertie,' Polly said. 'There's been an accident. It was very quick, he didn't feel a thing. The ambulancemen said it would have been over in a second.'

'What are you saying?' Gertie was white-faced.

'We would all be lucky to go so quickly and painlessly, Gertie, honestly, when you think of the length it takes some people to die.'

'But Jack can't be dead,' Gertie cried. 'Jack's not even forty, he has years of good living ahead of him, ahead of both of us.'

Mrs Vine, Marilyn, we met briefly. I'm Polly Callaghan. I'm with Gertie Brennan now.'

'Yes?'

'There's been a most awful accident. Gertie's husband Jack was killed and of course she's devastated. I'm here with her now, and they're getting her mother and everything . . .'

'Would you like me to come to the launderette?' Marilyn asked.

'If you can, please.'

Marilyn heard the urgency, almost desperation, in the voice. 'I'll come right away.' She called out to Colm in the garden, 'I'm going out to Gertie, Jack had an accident.'

'Nothing trivial, I hope?' Colm said.

'Fatal, I believe,' Marilyn said tersely.

To her surprise Colm threw down his fork and rushed into the house. 'Jesus, what a stupid remark to make, I'll come with you,' he said.

Ria was having coffee with Sheila Maine when the call came from Sheila and Gertie's mother with the news of Jack's death. She said it was hard to speak because there were so many people there. Ria realised that it was also hard to speak since she too had been sworn to support the story of the fairy-tale marriage.

Sheila was appalled. 'What on earth will she do without him, she'll be devastated,' she cried.

We're going home two days early,' Ria said to Annie and Brian. 'I was able to get cancellations.'

'Oh, *no*, Mam, no. Not for awful Jack Brennan's funeral. You never liked him, it's so hypocritical.'

'Gertie's my friend, though. I like her,' Ria said.

'You *promised* we could stay here until September.'

'Well, I'd have thought you would like to be going on the same plane as Sean Maine, but what do I know?' Ria said.

'What?'

'Sheila's taking Kelly and Sean over to the funeral, we'll all travel together. But of course if you're violently opposed to that I suppose . . .'

'Oh, Mam, shut up. You'd never win a prize for acting,' Annie said, overjoyed.

Andy had a business meeting nearby. Or so he said. 'Can I take your mother out to the Thai restaurant on her own?' he asked Annie and Brian when he came to the house.

'On a date like?' Brian asked.

'No, just for boring grown-up conversation.'

'Oh, sure, I'll go to Zach's house. Will it be overnight?' Brian asked.

'No, Brian, it will *not* be overnight,' Ria said.

'I can go to the movies with Hubie,' Annie said. 'And before you ask, Brian, that's not a date and neither is it overnight.'

'You have a delightful family,' Andy said.

Ria sighed. 'I must remind myself not to cling to them too much, not to be the mother from hell.'

'You couldn't be that,' he laughed.

'Oh, easily. I don't know what we're going back to; it's real uncharted territory. I must not use them as my pair of crutches through it.'

'You don't need any crutches, Ria,' he said. 'Will you keep in touch with me, do you think?'

'I'd love to.'

'But just as a friend . . . that's all, isn't it?' He was disappointed but realistic.

'I need friends, Andy. I'd love to think you were one.'

'That's what it will be then. *And* I'll send you recipes, I'll actively seek them out for you to make you a legend in Irish cuisine.'

'You know, I really do think it might get off the ground. My friend Rosemary emailed me to say she is putting herself right behind it and she's a real dynamo.'

'I don't doubt it for one minute,' said Andy Vine.

Sheila Maine slept on the plane. Kelly and Brian played cards and watched the movie. Annie and Sean whispered plans for the future to each other.

Ria could not sleep. Her mind was full of pictures. The funeral, the meeting with Danny to discuss their future. Arranging to sell Number 16 Tara Road. Finding a new place to live. The whole business of starting to cook for a living. Meeting Marilyn face to face after all this time.

Marilyn had promised to have breakfast ready for them when they arrived at Tara Road. They would have time for that, to get changed, and then they would all go to the church together. Ria smiled as she remembered their conversation. 'The one good thing about this dreadful accident is that you and I get a chance to meet. Otherwise we would have passed in midair again,' she had said to Marilyn.

'I think there's a lot more than one good thing about this dreadful accident,' Marilyn had said. 'Not of course that any of us will ever admit it.' Marilyn had been in Ireland for two months. She was learning.

Just then the captain announced that due to weather conditions they were being diverted to Shannon Airport. He apologised for the delay which would not be more than a couple of hours. They would certainly be in Dublin by 11.00am.

'My God,' said Ria. 'We'll miss the funeral.'

The delay at Shannon Airport seemed interminable. Sheila Maine telephoned her sister. 'If we're not in time for the church, we'll go straight to the graveyard,' she said.

Gertie wept her gratitude on the phone. 'Oh, Sheila, if only poor Jack knew how much it turned out that people loved him.'

'Well, of course he did. Didn't everyone know you had a great marriage?' Sheila said.

Ria rang Marilyn. 'It seems we won't have that breakfast after all.'

'Then you'll never know what a bad cook I am,' Marilyn said.

'I wish you didn't have to leave tomorrow, that you could spend a couple more days,' Ria pleaded.

'I might easily do that. We'll talk later . . . Oh, and another thing . . . Welcome home!'

The church was crowded when Gertie, her mother and her children arrived. Gertie, pale and wearing a black dress, walked up the aisle looking proudly at all the people who had come to say goodbye to Jack. Surely now he was somewhere where he could see that he had worth in people's eyes?

The Mass had only just begun when Sheila Maine and her two children came up and joined the family. A little ripple of approval went through the church. The relatives had flown in from America, a further sign that Gertie was being honoured and made much of.

Ria, Annie and Brian slipped into a bench a little further back. Danny Lynch saw his wife and children. He bit his lip. Colm Barry saw them too. Ria looked magnificent, he thought, tanned, slimmer, holding herself taller. He had known she would try to be here even though she wasn't meant to be back today. She and Gertie went back a long way.

Polly Callaghan sat by herself. She averted her eyes from the pew where Barney McCarthy sat with his wife. If Mona saw Polly in the church she gave no sign or acknowledgment.

Rosemary had dressed carefully for the occasion. A grey silk dress and jacket, high heels and dark stockings. She was most surprised to see Ria and the children, nobody had told her they were coming back. But then she realised with a start there were few people to tell her anything. Apart from Ria herself, she didn't seem to have any friends any more.

Ria looked around the church to see could she identify Marilyn. She wasn't beside Rosemary, or Colm, or near Ria's mother. But surely one of them would have taken her under a wing. Ria couldn't concentrate on the prayers, she looked at the bouquets and wreaths all sent by people who had had nothing but scorn for the deceased.

Where was Marilyn Vine?

It was when the congregation was singing 'The Lord's My Shepherd' that Ria saw her. Taller than she would have thought, auburn-haired and wearing a simple navy dress. She was holding up the hymn sheet and singing along with the rest. Just at that moment she looked up and saw Ria looking at her. They gave each other a great smile across the crowded church. Two old friends meeting each other at last.

The sun was shining, the unexpected gales and rainstorms of the night before had blown away. The people stood and talked outside the church, a Dublin funeral where there weren't enough minutes in the hour for people to say what they wanted to say.

Ria was being embraced and welcomed home by everyone. She broke free to hug Gertie.

'You're such a true friend to come back early,' Gertie said.

'We travelled with Sheila and the children. And they'll be staying with you?'

'Yes, yes, we have the rooms ready. It's such a pity that they had to come for this reason. Jack would have loved to welcome them again.'

Ria looked at Gertie with shock. She realised that history was being rewritten here. There was no longer any need to pretend to Sheila that everything had been wonderful with Jack. Gertie had bought the story herself, she really thought it had been a great marriage.

Danny looked curiously like someone on the outside. Not the man who used to dart from group to group, shaking this hand, slapping that shoulder. Ria told herself that she must not think about him and care what became of him. He was not part of her life. She stood looking at him across the crowds. Soon the children would spot him and run over. But she would make no move.

'I'll give you twenty-four hours to get over your jet lag and then you start working for me,' Colm said. 'You look beautiful, by the way.'

'Thank you, Colm.' She thought she saw something of the admiring look that had been in Andy Vine's eye, but she shook off the notion.

Rosemary didn't come over, which was odd. She stood, a little like Danny stood, on the outside of a crowd. Ria went up to her, arms wide open.

'God, it's good to be back,' she said as she hugged her friend. She slipped an arm through Rosemary's. 'You're so good to put so much effort into getting me started up. I really do appreciate it.'

'Least I could do,' Rosemary said gruffly, looking over at Marilyn.

'It's a really beautiful house, Marilyn,' Annie said.

'I'm so pleased you had a good time.'

'You have no idea, it was like a house in the movies, honestly. And we swam before breakfast and even at night.'

'I'm so very happy it went well,' Marilyn said.

She knew that she and Ria were almost putting off the moment when they would speak to each other. And yet every time they took a step in each other's direction someone came to claim one of them.

Then they finally met. They put their arms round each other. And said each other's names.

'I'll drive us to the graveyard,' Marilyn said.

'No, no.'

'I have your car, all shiny and clean from a car wash. I want to show it off to you.'

'We cleaned your car too, Marilyn,' Brian said. 'And we got all the pizza off the seat at the back.'

There was a pause and then Annie, Ria and Marilyn broke into near-hysterical laughter.

Brian was startled. 'What on earth did I say now?' he asked, looking from one to the other and getting no answer.

When they did get back to Tara Road there wasn't nearly enough time for all they had to say to each other. The children eventually went to bed. Marilyn and Ria sat on at the table. It was unexpectedly easy to talk. They asked each other about the visits of their husbands. And each spoke thoughtfully and honestly.

'I thought Greg looked tired and old, and that I had taken away a year of his life.'

'But will it be all right from now on?' Ria asked.

'I guess he'll be cautious, even a little mistrustful of me from time to time. If I closed myself off so terribly before, I could do it again. It will all take time to get back to where we were.'

'But at least you will.' Ria sounded wistful.

'And nothing happened when Danny was over there to make you think that *you* might get back together again?' Marilyn asked.

'Something happened that made me certain that we *were* back together already. But I wasn't right. He told me all about the financial disaster, and losing the house and everything, in Memorial Park under a big tree. Then we went back to Tudor Drive and . . . I suppose if I were being realistic I would say he consoled me in the way he knows best. But I took more from it than there was.'

'That's only reasonable, and he probably meant it all at the time,' Marilyn said.

'Timing is everything, isn't it?' Ria was rueful. 'Just after that came the news that Bernadette was losing the baby and he was off like a flash. Even if we had had another twenty-four hours . . .'

'Do you think that would have made a difference?'

'No, to be honest,' Ria admitted. 'It might only have made me feel worse. Maybe it was for the best. The stupid bit was I kept thinking that it was all tied up with the baby. Once that no longer existed, perhaps the whole infatuation would go. But again I was wrong.'

Marilyn had been able to change her ticket. Now she was going to stay for an extra three days. This way she could arrive back at Tudor Drive at the same time as Greg. It was to be symbolic of their starting a new life together. And Marilyn said that by staying on she could help Ria settle in and start to face the whole business of selling the house.

They didn't shy away from personal questions. When they spoke of Colm Barry, Ria asked whether Marilyn had been having a thing with him. 'That was what I heard,' Ria apologised.

'Totally wrong. I think he was much more interested in waiting until *you* came home,' Marilyn said. 'And on the subject, can I ask whether you had anything going with my brother-in-law?'

'No, if Greg talked about that he was quite wrong,' Ria giggled.

'But Andy wanted to pursue the relationship?' Marilyn wondered.

'I don't know, because I didn't allow the situation to develop,' Ria replied.

And into the night they spoke of Gertie and how she was going to build a legend based on the dead Jack. They sat in the beautiful front room of Number 16 Tara Road as the moonlight came in at the window, and they each thought about the need to have some kind of legend in your life. Ria knew that for good or evil Marilyn must go on for ever without knowing it was her drunken son who had killed Johnny and himself that day. And Marilyn thought that for better or worse Ria should not learn how the husband she still loved and the friend she still trusted had conspired to betray her for so long.

'I'm taking on more private pupils this year, Mum, can I do it in your house?' Bernadette asked.

'Of course, Ber. If you're well enough.'

'I'm fine. It's just that I don't want to start them off in one place and then have to transfer them when we move from here.'

'Does he know when he's going to sell?'

'No, Mum, and I don't ask him, he has enough pressures.'

'Does he have great pressures about Tara Road? Is she on at him all the time?' Finola Dunne was always protective of her daughter.

Bernadette thought about it. 'I don't think so, I don't think she's even been in touch since she came back.'

'I wouldn't mind seeing those children again,' Finola said.

'Yes, I'd like to see them, too, but Danny says they're all tied up with this Marilyn until she leaves. They're mad about her apparently,' Bernadette reported gloomily.

'It's just because they stayed in her house, which had a swimming pool. That's the only reason,' Finola tried to reassure her daughter.

'I know, Mum.'

Ria had invited Gertie and Sheila round for lunch, but Gertie was so used to cleaning in Number 16 Tara Road that it was hard to get her to sit down. Once or twice she rose as if to clear the table, but Ria's hand gently pressed her back.

'Sean is so anxious to come back to study in Ireland after Christmas and find his roots,' Sheila said. The other three women hid their smiles. 'He has been round to all the various schools and colleges and of course I'd just *love* him to come back here,' Sheila said.

Gertie was excited about the proposition. 'There will be a small room in our flat, it's not elegant but it's convenient for schools and libraries.'

'Stop saying it's not elegant,' Sheila cried. 'Your property is in such a good area. It's a wonderful place for him to stay, it's a happy home. I'm only sorry his Uncle Jack won't be there to see him grow up.'

'Jack would have made him very welcome, that's one sure thing,' Gertie said, without any tinge of irony. 'But we'll paint up his room for when he comes back. He can tell us what colour he'd like. And maybe he'd get a bicycle. You know,' Gertie confided, 'a lot of people have asked me would I be financially able to manage without Jack?'

Ria wondered who had asked that and why. Surely they must have known that poor Gertie's finances would take an upturn now that she didn't have to find him an extra thirty or forty pounds' drinking money a week by cleaning houses. And now that she could concentrate on her business. But then perhaps other people didn't know the circumstances.

'And of course I am fine,' Gertie continued. 'My mother's looked through all the papers and there was a grand insurance policy there, and the business is going from strength to strength. There will be fine times ahead, that's what I have to think.'

'Will I make myself scarce while you meet Danny?' Marilyn asked as they cleared the dishes after lunch.

'No need, there'll be plenty of time after you've gone home. Let's not waste what we have.'

'You should talk to him soon, listen to what he has to say and add what *you* have to say. The more you put it off the harder it is.'

'You're right,' sighed Ria. 'I suppose I should ask him to come over.'

'I have to meet Ria this morning,' Danny said.

'Well, it's better that you get it over with,' Bernadette said. 'Are you very sad?'

'Not so much sad as anxious. I used to laugh at middle-aged men who had ulcers and said their stomachs were in a knot. I don't know why I laughed, that's the way I am all the time now.'

She was full of concern. 'But you *can't* be, Danny. None of this is *your* fault, and you are going to be able to give her half the proceeds of that house, which is very big nowadays.'

'Yes, true.'

'And she knows all this; she doesn't have any expectations of anything else.'

'No,' said Danny Lynch. 'No, I don't suppose that she can have any expectations of anything else.'

He came at ten o'clock, and rang on the front door.

'Haven't you got your keys?' she asked.

'I turned them in to Mrs Vine,' he said.

'What would she have done with them, do you think?'

'Search me, Ria. Cemented them to a stone maybe?'

'No, here they are, on the keyholder at the back of the hall. Shall I give them back to you?'

'What for?'

'For you to show people round, Danny.'

He saw the sense in that. 'Sure,' he said.

'Right, I have some coffee in a percolator up here in the front room. Will we sit in there and, if you'll forgive the expression, make a list?'

She had two lined pads ready on the round table and two pens. She brought the coffee over to them and waited expectantly.

'Look, I don't think that this is going to work,' he began.

'But it *has* to work. I mean, you said we'd have to be well out of here by Christmas. I made sure that the children and Marilyn were out this morning so that we could get started.'

'She hasn't gone home yet?'

'Tomorrow.'

'Oh.'

'So who will we sell it through, Danny? There will be a line of people waiting to sell it so that they can get two per cent of the price. Which one will we choose?'

'You've been out of the business for a long time. It's cutthroat nowadays, all of them trying to shave off a bit here and there.'

'So who, then?'

'Ria, I'm going to suggest something to you. These guys hate me, a lot of them. I've cut right across their deals, stolen their clients. You must sell it on your own, and give me half.'

'I can't do that.'

'I've thought about it, it's the only way, and we must pretend to be fighting as if I'm giving you nothing, and your only hope is to screw as much out of this as possible.'

'No, Danny.'

'It's for us, for the children. Do it, Ria. Get someone to help you.'

'Well, I suppose Rosemary could come in, she's a businesswoman.'

'Not Rosemary.' He was firm.

'Why not, Danny? You like her, she really does have a head for figures; look at her own company.'

'No, they'd walk over two women.'

'Come on. What do you think it is? People don't walk over women in business any more.'

'Get a man to help you, Ria, it's good advice.'

'Who, what man? I don't know any man.'

'You've got friends.

'Colm?' she suggested.

He thought about it. 'Yes, why not? He's got valuable property himself. They'd respect him.'

'So when should I start?'

'I suppose as soon as possible. And tell these guys that you'll be in the market to *buy* a house too. They'll be even more helpful if they think there are going to be two bites of the cherry.'

'The furniture and everything?'

He shrugged. 'Well, what will we do with it?'

She didn't really trust herself to speak. She touched one of the chairs. Everything here had been searched for and found with such love.

'So, it's not easy but we'll do it.'

'*I'll* do it apparently.' She hoped it didn't sound bitter. 'And will you say I could have got more, or I shouldn't have chosen this or that one?'

'No, believe me, I won't say anything like that.'

She believed him. 'Well, I'll ask Colm today. I'm anxious to get it done and start trying to work for a living. Will you be able to get work?'

'Not as easily as I thought. Not too many estate agencies opening their doors to me, I'm afraid. Still there's always something.' He was talking more cheerfully than he felt.

They went to a last dinner in Colm's. Sean and Annie held hands and ate an aubergine and red bean casserole. 'Sean doesn't eat dead animals now,' Annie said proudly.

'Sound man, Sean,' Colm said admiringly.

Barney and Mona McCarthy came up to the table. 'I just wanted to welcome you home, Ria, and to wish you *bon voyage*, Marilyn.' Mona spoke with confidence these days.

'Mam's going to be cooking things for money now, if you still know any rich people who'd buy them,' Brian said helpfully.

'We know a few,' Mona said. 'And we'll certainly be able to put the word around.'

Barney McCarthy was anxious to end the conversation. Colm ushered them to their table. You would never think from his manner that Barney had ever been at this restaurant with another woman. Or that his bills had remained unpaid until a solicitor had asked for any outstanding invoices to be presented.

The solicitor had been engaged by Mrs and not Mr McCarthy.

'Do you want us to call so that you can say goodbye to Rosemary tonight?' Ria asked Marilyn.

Annie looked up.

'I think I'll just leave her a note,' Marilyn said.

'Sure.' Ria was easy.

At that moment Colm asked Ria would she come into the kitchen. He wanted her to see the desserts that he had prepared for tonight so that they could discuss what she might dream up.

'Can I come into the kitchen?' Brian's eyes were excited.

'Only if you don't talk, Brian,' his mother said.

'Sean, would you ever go with them and clap your hand over his mouth if he says anything at all?' Annie begged.

Sean Maine was pleased to be seen as a hero and went willingly.

Annie and Marilyn looked at each other across the table. 'You don't like Rosemary,' Annie said.

'No, I don't.'

'Why don't you like her?' Annie asked.

'I'm not sure. But it's not something I need to say to your mother, they've been friends over many years. And you, Annie? Obviously you don't like her either. Why is that?'

'I couldn't explain.'

'I know. These things happen.'

It was time to go. 'I could get a taxi, Ria,' Marilyn began to protest.

'I'm driving you to the airport. Don't argue.' The telephone rang. 'Who now?' Ria groaned.

But it wasn't for her. It was Greg Vine from California. He was changing planes and about to check in for New York. He would wait for Marilyn at Kennedy Airport. They would go back to Tudor Drive together.

'Yes, you too.' Marilyn ended the conversation.

'Did he say "I love you"?' Ria asked.

'Yes, as it happens,' Marilyn said.

'Lucky Marilyn.'

'You have the children,' Marilyn said.

And they held each other tight in a way they wouldn't be able to do at the airport.

Annie was coming to say goodbye, accompanied by Sean Maine and Brian. As they got into the car, Colm came to wave them off. He had a gardening book for Marilyn, a very old one they had talked about; he had tracked it down in an antiquarian bookseller's.

'I hate to go,' Marilyn said.

'When you come back we'll welcome you somewhere new.'

'We can't go beyond here,' Ria said at the passenger check-in.

'Aren't we magnificent?' Marilyn said.

'Yes, we really took a chance, didn't we,' Ria said.

'And how very well it worked out,' said Marilyn.

They were still unable to say the goodbye.

Annie flung herself into Marilyn's arms. 'I hate you going, I just hate it, you're quite different to anyone else, you *know* that. Will you come back so that I'll have someone to talk to?'

'You live in a place where there are plenty of people to talk to.'

Ria Lynch wondered were people speaking about her over her head, but she must be imagining it.

'And you'll keep an eye on things from over there,' Annie said.

'Yes, and you from here?' Marilyn begged.

'Sure.'

Sean shook her hand gravely and Brian gave her an embarrassed hug. Marilyn Vine looked at Annie Lynch. The blonde, beautiful, nearly fifteen-year-old Annie walked up to her mother and put an arm around Ria's waist. 'We'll keep the world ticking over until you get back,' she said. 'Won't we, Mam?'

'Of course we will,' said Ria, realising it might be possible after all.

MAEVE BINCHY

'Someone once gave me a great piece of advice. They said, "Write about what you know and write as you speak."' For Maeve Binchy this became the platform on which she built her success as a writer. 'I know about love and disappointment—even betrayal—from my own life, and that's what I write about.' This, combined with her unique ability to gather together snatches of conversation and pertinent observations and weave them into fascinating, intricate plots, has brought her fame and made her one of Britain's richest women.

'The idea for *Tara Road* came when I was waiting in an airport and eavesdropping on a conversation between two women,' she recalls. 'One asked the other whether she was married, and she replied that she was divorced. The first woman said something very English and noncommittal and then the other one said, "Yes, I thought it was a happy marriage until he said he was going to leave."' Immediately, Maeve Binchy's brain clicked into gear and the story began to take shape.

The novel hinges on two women swapping houses, something that Maeve Binchy has experienced herself. She openly admits to having looked inside other people's cupboards. 'Yes, I did poke around, definitely, and they poked around in my house, I'm sure. It isn't human not to look in the medicine cabinet. But swapping homes builds a great bond and involves terrific trust.'

Home for Maeve Binchy and her husband of twenty-two years, Gordon Snell, broadcaster turned children's writer, is split between a modest house in London, which Gordon bought thirty years ago, and a small, but pretty house in Dalkey, the suburb of Dublin where Maeve grew up. For Maeve Binchy these two properties more than adequately suit her lifestyle. 'I have never been tempted to live in a mansion. I think it's something to do with the age at which money comes to you.'

Maeve Binchy was forty-three when her first novel, *Light A Penny Candle,* became an instant best seller. Although the money was very welcome, she knows from painful experience that health is more important than wealth. For years she has suffered from osteoarthritis, a crippling bone disease which made her a virtual prisoner in her own home. 'I live in a house like the ones in Coronation Street—you walk directly through the front door into the road. It's no distance at all, but until recently I would literally have to drag myself from the house to the car. It was impossible going to anything like an art exhibition because I could hardly stand.' Not long ago, she accepted that she desperately needed a hip-replacement operation, but before she was fit enough for surgery she had to shed five stone in six months. 'It was a night-mare, but the operation changed my life.'

Her stay in hospital led to the publication of her first nonfiction book, *Aches and Pains*, written as a tribute to all nurses and to cheer up people in hospital, as well as to raise money for the Arthritis Research Campaign.

Maeve Binchy has said that she plans to retire after her next book. 'My husband and close friends don't believe a word of it,' she says. Fans will all hope that they are right.

℘℧

When American professor Allan Kepinski
asks eighteen-year-old Milly to marry
him, so that he can remain in England
with his lover, Rupert, Milly happily
agrees. After all, it's only a signature on
a piece of paper, no harm can come of
it, and she will have fun dressing up in
a white dress with a flowing veil.
Soon after the ceremony, Milly and Allan
go their separate ways, and it will be
ten years before Milly has to face the
consequences of her youthful naiveté.

℘℧

Prologue

A GROUP OF TOURISTS had stopped to gawp at Milly as she stood in her wedding dress on the registry office steps. They clogged up the pavement opposite while Oxford shoppers, accustomed to the yearly influx, stepped round them into the road. A few glanced over to the registry office to see what all the fuss was about, and tacitly acknowledged that the young couple on the steps did make a very striking pair.

One or two of the tourists had even brought out cameras, and Milly beamed joyously at them, revelling in their attention; trying to imagine the picture she and Allan made together. Her spiky, white-blonde hair was growing hot in the afternoon sun; the veil was scratchy against her neck, the nylon lace of her hired wedding dress felt uncomfortably damp wherever it touched her body. But she still felt light-hearted and full of euphoric energy. And whenever she glanced up at Allan—at her husband—a new, hot thrill of excitement coursed through her body.

She had only arrived in Oxford three weeks ago. School had finished in July—and while all her friends had planned trips to Ibiza and Spain and Amsterdam, Milly had been packed off to a secretarial college in Oxford. 'Much more useful than some silly holiday,' her mother had announced firmly. 'And just think what an advantage you'll have over the others when it comes to job-hunting.' But Milly didn't want an advantage over the others. She wanted a suntan and a boyfriend, and beyond that, she didn't really care.

So on the second day of the typing course, she'd slipped off after lunch. She'd found a cheap hairdresser and, with a surge of exhilaration, told him to chop her hair short and bleach it. Then she'd wandered around the sun-drenched streets of Oxford, wondering where she might sunbathe. It was pure coincidence that she'd eventually chosen a patch of lawn in Corpus Christi College; that Rupert's rooms should have been directly opposite; that he and Allan should have decided to spend that afternoon lying on the grass, drinking Pimm's.

She'd watched, surreptitiously, as they sauntered onto the lawn, clinked glasses and lit up cigarettes. She'd listened to the snatches of their conversation, which wafted through the air towards her, and found herself longing to know these debonair, good-looking men. When, suddenly, the older one addressed her, she felt her heart leap with excitement.

'Have you got a light?' His voice was dry, American, amused.

'Yes,' she stuttered, feeling in her pocket. 'Yes, I have.'

'We're terribly lazy, I'm afraid.' The younger man's eyes met hers: shyer, more diffident. 'I've got a lighter; just inside that window.' He pointed to a stone mullioned arch. 'But it's too hot to move.'

'We'll repay you with a glass of Pimm's,' said the American. He'd held out his hand. 'Allan.'

'Rupert.'

She'd lolled on the grass with them for the rest of the afternoon, soaking up the sun and alcohol; flirting and giggling; making them laugh. At the pit of her stomach was a feeling of anticipation that increased as the afternoon wore on: a sexual *frisson* heightened by the fact that there were two of them and they were both beautiful. Rupert was lithe and golden like a young lion, his hair a shining blond halo. Allan's face was crinkled and his hair was greying at the temples, but his grey-green eyes made her heart jump when they met hers.

When Rupert rolled over onto his back and said to the sky, 'Shall we go for something to eat tonight?' she'd thought he must be asking her out. An immediate, unbelieving joy had coursed through her.

But then Allan rolled over too, and said 'Sure thing.' And then he leaned over and casually kissed Rupert on the mouth.

The strange thing was, after the initial, heart-stopping shock, Milly hadn't really minded. In fact, this way was almost better: this way, she had the pair of them to herself. She'd gone to San Antonio's with them that night; then the next night they'd played jazz on an old wind-up gramophone and drunk mint juleps and taught her how to roll joints. Within a week, they'd become a regular threesome.

And then Allan had asked her to marry him.

When she'd said yes, he'd laughed, assuming she was joking, and started on a lengthy explanation of his plight. He'd spoken of visas, of Home Office officials, of discrimination against gays. All the while, he'd gazed at her entreatingly, as though she still needed to be won over. But Milly was already won over, was already pulsing with excitement at the thought of dressing up in a wedding dress, holding a bouquet; doing something more exciting than she'd ever done in her life. It was only when Allan said, half frowning, 'I can't believe I'm actually asking someone to break the law for me!' that she realised quite what was going on. But the tiny qualms which began to prick her mind were no match for the exhilaration pounding through her as Allan put his arm round her and said quietly into her ear, 'You're an angel.' Milly had smiled breathlessly back, and said, 'It's nothing,' and truly meant it.

And now, almost to Milly's surprise, they were married. After they'd signed the register, Allan had given Milly a tiny grin and kissed her. Her mouth still tingled slightly from the touch of him; her wedding finger still felt self-conscious in its gold-plated ring.

'That's enough pictures,' said Allan suddenly. 'We don't want to be too conspicuous.'

'Wait!' said Milly desperately. 'What about the confetti?'

'OK,' said Allan indulgently. 'I guess we can't forget the confetti.'

He reached into his pocket and tossed a multicoloured handful into the air. At the same time, a gust of wind caught Milly's veil, ripping it away from the tiny plastic tiara in her hair and sending it up into the air like a gauzy plume of smoke. It landed on the pavement, at the feet of a dark-haired boy, who bent and picked it up.

'Hi!' called Milly at once. 'That's mine!' And she began running down the steps towards him, leaving a trail of confetti as she went. 'That's mine,' she repeated clearly as she neared the boy, thinking he might be a foreign student; that he might not understand English.

'Yes,' said the boy, in a dry, well-bred voice. 'I gathered that.'

He held out the veil to her and Milly smiled self-consciously at him, prepared to flirt a little. But the boy's expression didn't change; behind the glint of his round spectacles, she detected a slight teenage scorn. She felt suddenly a little foolish, standing bareheaded, in her ill-fitting wedding dress. 'Thanks,' she said, taking the veil from him.

The boy shrugged. 'Any time.' He watched as she fixed the layers of netting back in place. 'Congratulations,' he added.

'What for?' said Milly, without thinking. Then she looked up and blushed. 'Oh yes, of course. Thank you.'

'Have a happy marriage,' said the boy in deadpan tones. He nodded at her and before Milly could say anything, he'd walked off.

'Who was that?' said Allan, appearing at her side. Rupert was clutching his hand. His face was glowing; he seemed more beautiful than ever.

'I don't know,' said Milly. 'He wished us a happy marriage.'

'Milly, I'm very grateful to you,' said Allan. 'We both are.'

'There's no need to be,' said Milly. 'Honestly, it was fun!'

'We've bought you a little something.' Allan glanced at Rupert, then reached in his pocket and gave Milly a little box. 'Freshwater pearls,' he explained as she opened it. 'We hope you like them.'

'I love them!' Milly looked from one to the other, eyes shining. 'You shouldn't have!'

'We wanted to,' said Allan seriously. 'To say thank you for being a great friend—and a perfect bride.' He fastened the necklace round Milly's neck, and she flushed with pleasure. 'You look beautiful,' he said.

'And now,' said Rupert, 'how about some champagne?'

They spent the rest of that day punting down the Cherwell, drinking vintage champagne and making extravagant toasts to each other. In the following days, Milly spent every spare moment with Rupert and Allan. When, three weeks later, her time at secretarial college was up, Allan and Rupert reserved a farewell table at the Randolph, made her order three courses and wouldn't let her see the prices.

The next day, Allan took her to the station. He kissed her goodbye, dried her tears with a silk handkerchief, and promised to write.

Milly never saw him again.

Chapter One / Ten Years later

THE ROOM WAS LARGE and airy and overlooked the biscuity streets of Bath, coated in a January icing of snow. It had been refurbished some years back in a traditional manner, with striped wallpaper and a few good Georgian pieces. These, however, were currently lost under the welter of bright clothes, CDs, magazines and make-up piled high on every available surface. In the corner, a handsome mahogany wardrobe was almost entirely masked by a huge white cotton dress carrier; on the floor was a suitcase half full of clothes for a warm-weather honeymoon.

Milly, who had come up some time earlier to finish packing, leaned back comfortably in her bedroom chair. In her lap was a glossy magazine, open at the problem pages. 'Dear Anne,' the first began. 'I have been keeping a secret from my husband.' Milly rolled her eyes. She didn't even have to look at the advice. It was always the same. Tell the truth. Be honest. Like some sort of secular catechism, to be learned by rote and repeated without thought. She turned over the page to the homestyle section, and peered at an array of expensive wastepaper baskets. She hadn't put a wastepaper basket on her wedding list. Maybe it wasn't too late.

Downstairs, there was a ring at the doorbell, but she didn't move. It couldn't be Simon, not yet; it would be one of the bed-and-breakfast guests. Idly, Milly raised her eyes from her magazine and looked round her bedroom. It had been hers for twenty-two years, ever since she was six and the Havill family had first moved into One Bertram Street. Since then, she'd gone away to school, gone away to college, even moved briefly to London—and each time she'd come back again; back to this room. But on Saturday she would be leaving to set up her own home. As a grown-up, bona fide, married woman.

'Milly?' Her mother's head appeared round the door. 'Simon's here!'

'What?' Milly glanced in the mirror and winced at her dishevelled appearance. 'Don't let him come up,' she said. 'Tell him I'm trying my dress on. Say I'll be down in a minute.'

Her mother disappeared and Milly quickly closed her magazine and put it on the floor, then, on second thoughts, kicked it under the bed. Hurriedly she peeled off the denim-blue leggings she'd been wearing and opened her wardrobe. A pair of well-cut black trousers hung to one side, along with a charcoal-grey tailored skirt, a chocolate trouser suit and an array of crisp white shirts. On the other side of the wardrobe were all the clothes she wore when she wasn't going to be seeing Simon: tattered jeans, ancient jerseys, tight bright miniskirts. All the clothes she would have to throw out before Saturday.

She put on the black trousers and one of the white shirts, and reached for the cashmere sweater Simon had given her as a Christmas present. She looked at herself severely in the mirror, brushed her hair—now buttery blonde and shoulder-length—till it shone, and stepped into a pair of expensive black loafers. She and Simon had often agreed that buying cheap shoes was a false economy; as far as Simon was aware, her entire collection of shoes consisted of the black loafers, a pair of brown boots, and a pair of navy Gucci snaffles which he'd bought for her himself.

She closed her wardrobe door, stepped over a pile of underwear on the floor, and picked up her bag. She sprayed herself with scent, closed the bedroom door firmly behind her and began to walk down the stairs.

'Milly!' As she passed her mother's bedroom door, a hissed voice drew her attention. 'Come in here.'

Obediently, Milly went into her mother's room. Olivia Havill was standing by the chest of drawers, her jewellery box open.

'Darling,' she said brightly, 'why don't you borrow my pearls for this afternoon?' She held up a double pearl choker with a diamond clasp.

'Mummy, we're only meeting the vicar,' said Milly. 'It's not that important. I don't need to wear pearls.'

'Of course it's important!' retorted Olivia. 'You must take this seriously, Milly. You only make your marriage vows once!' She paused. 'And besides, all upper-class brides wear pearls.' She held the necklace up to Milly's throat. 'Proper pearls. Not those silly little things.'

'I like my freshwater pearls,' said Milly defensively. 'And I'm not upper class.'

'Darling, you're about to become Mrs Simon Pinnacle. His father's a multimillionaire.'

Milly rolled her eyes. 'I've got to go,' she said.

'All right. Have it your own way. And, darling, do remember to ask Canon Lytton about the rose petals, won't you?'

'I will,' said Milly. 'See you later.'

She hurried down the stairs and into the hall, grabbing her coat from the hall stand by the door.

'Hi!' she called into the drawing room, and as Simon came out into the hall, glanced hastily at the front page of that day's *Daily Telegraph*, trying to commit as many headlines as possible to memory.

'Milly,' said Simon, grinning at her. 'You look gorgeous.' Milly looked up and smiled.

'So do you.' Simon was dressed for the office, in a dark suit which sat impeccably on his firm, stocky frame. His dark hair sprang up energetically from his wide forehead and he smelt discreetly of aftershave.

'So,' he said, ushering her out into the crisp afternoon air. 'Off we go to learn how to be married.'

'I know,' said Milly. 'Isn't it weird?'

'Complete waste of time,' said Simon. 'I know what I want from marriage,' he said. 'We both do. We don't need interference from a crumbling old vicar who isn't even married himself.'

'We'll just listen and nod,' said Milly. She felt in her pocket for her gloves. 'Anyway, I already know what he's going to say.'

'What?'

'Be kind to one another and don't sleep around.'

Simon thought for a moment. 'I expect I could manage the first part.'

Milly gave him a thump and he laughed, drawing her near and planting a kiss on her shiny hair. As they neared his car he bleeped it open.

'I could hardly find a parking space,' he said, as he started the engine. 'The streets are so bloody congested.' He frowned. 'Whether this new bill will achieve anything . . .'

'The environment bill,' said Milly, casting her mind quickly back to the *Daily Telegraph*. 'Do you think they've got the emphasis quite right?'

And as Simon began to talk, she looked out of the window and nodded occasionally, and wondered idly whether she should buy a third bikini for her honeymoon.

Canon Lytton's drawing room was large, draughty and full of books. Books lined the walls, books covered every surface, and teetered in dusty piles on the floor. In addition, nearly everything in the room that wasn't a book, looked like a book. The firescreen was decorated with books, even the slabs of gingerbread sitting on the tea tray resembled a set of encyclopedia volumes.

Canon Lytton himself resembled a sheet of old paper. His thin, powdery skin seemed in danger of tearing at any moment; whenever he laughed or frowned his face creased into a thousand lines. At the moment—as he had been during most of the session—he was frowning. His bushy white eyebrows were knitted together in concentration and he was waving an undrunk cup of tea dangerously in the air.

'The secret of a successful marriage,' he was declaiming, 'is trust. Trust is the key. Trust is the rock.'

'Absolutely,' said Milly, as she had at intervals of three minutes for the past hour. She glanced at Simon, who was leaning forward, as though ready to interrupt. But Canon Lytton was not the sort of speaker to brook interruptions. Each time Simon had taken a breath to say something, the clergyman had raised the volume of his voice and turned away, leaving Simon stranded in frustrated but deferential silence. As for herself, she hadn't listened to a word.

Her gaze slid idly over to the glass-fronted bookcases to her left. There she was, reflected in the glass. Smart and shiny; grown-up and groomed. She felt pleased with her appearance. Not that Canon Lytton appreciated it. He probably thought it was sinful to spend money on clothes. He would tell her she should have given it to the poor instead.

She shifted her position slightly on the sofa, stifled a yawn, and looked up. To her horror, Canon Lytton was watching her. His eyes narrowed, and he broke off mid-sentence.

'I'm sorry if I'm boring you, my dear,' he said sarcastically. 'Perhaps you are familiar with this quotation already.'

Milly felt her cheeks turn pink.

'No,' she said, 'I'm not. I was just . . . um . . .' She glanced at Simon, who gave her a tiny wink. 'I'm just a little tired,' she ended feebly.

'Poor Milly's been frantic over the wedding arrangements,' put in Simon. 'There's a lot to organise. The champagne, the cake . . .'

'Indeed,' said Canon Lytton severely. 'But might I remind you that the point of a wedding is not the champagne, nor the cake; the sacrament of marriage is not simply the preamble to a good party.'

'No,' said Milly.

'As the words of the service remind us, marriage must not be undertaken carelessly, lightly or selfishly, but—'

'And it won't be!' Simon's voice broke in impatiently. 'Canon Lytton, I know you probably come across people every day who are getting married for the wrong reasons. But that's not us, OK? We love each other and we want to spend the rest of our lives together. The cake and the champagne have got nothing to do with it.'

He broke off and for a moment there was silence. Milly took Simon's hand and squeezed it.

'I see,' said Canon Lytton eventually. 'Well, I'm glad to hear it.' He took a sip of cold tea and winced. 'You've no idea how many unsuitable couples I see coming before me to get married.'

'I'm sure you do,' said Simon. 'But Milly and I are going to take it seriously. We're going to get it right. We know each other and we love each other and we're going to be very happy.' He leaned over and kissed Milly gently, then looked at Canon Lytton, as though daring him to reply.

'Yes,' said Canon Lytton. 'Well. Perhaps I've said enough. You do seem to be on the right track.' He picked up his folder and began to riffle through it. 'There are just a couple of other matters . . .'

'That was beautiful,' whispered Milly to Simon.

'It was true,' he whispered back.

By the time they emerged from the vicarage, the air was cold and dusky. Snowflakes were falling again; the street lamps were already on; fairy lights from Christmas twinkled in a window opposite. Milly took a deep breath, shook out her legs, stiff from sitting still for so long, and looked at Simon. But before she could speak, a triumphant voice came ringing from the other side of the street.

'Aha! I just caught you!'

'Mummy!' exclaimed Milly.

'Olivia,' said Simon. 'What a lovely surprise.'

Olivia Havill crossed the street and beamed at them both. Snowflakes were resting lightly on her smartly cut blonde hair and on the shoulders of her green cashmere coat. She fixed her eyes affectionately on Milly. 'I don't suppose you asked Canon Lytton about the rose petals, did you?' she said.

'Oh!' said Milly. 'No, I forgot.'

'I knew you would!' exclaimed Olivia. 'So I thought I'd better pop round myself.' She smiled at Simon. 'Isn't my little girl a scatterhead?'

'I wouldn't say so,' said Simon in a tight voice.

'Of course you wouldn't! You're in love with her!' Olivia smiled gaily at him and ruffled his hair.

'I'd better be going,' he said. 'I've got to get back to the office. We're frantic at the moment.'

'Aren't we all!' exclaimed Olivia. 'There are only four days to go, you know! And I've a thousand things to do!' She looked at Milly. 'How about walking back into town with me? I won't be long here. Perhaps we could have . . .'

'Hot chocolate at Mario's,' finished Milly.

'Exactly.' Olivia smiled. 'See you this evening, Simon.' She opened Canon Lytton's gate and began to walk quickly up the path.

Simon glanced at his watch. 'Look, I've really got to go.'

He pulled her towards him. His mouth was soft and warm on hers. Milly closed her eyes. Then, suddenly he let go of her, and a blast of cold snowy air hit her in the face. 'I must run. See you later,' he said.

'Yes,' said Milly. 'See you then.'

She watched, smiling to herself, as he bleeped open the door of his car, got in and, without pausing, zoomed off down the street. Simon was always in a hurry. He couldn't bear wasting time; didn't understand how Milly could spend a day happily doing nothing.

The first time she'd ever seen him, in someone else's kitchen, he'd been simultaneously conducting a conversation on his mobile phone, shovelling crisps into his mouth, and clicking through the news headlines on Teletext. As Milly had poured herself a glass of wine, he'd held his glass out too and, in a gap in his conversation, had grinned at her and said, 'Thanks.'

'The party's happening in the other room,' Milly had pointed out.

'I know,' Simon had said, his eyes back on the Teletext. 'I'll be along in a minute.' And Milly had rolled her eyes and left him to it. But later on that evening, he'd come up to her, introduced himself charmingly, and apologised for having been so distracted.

'It was just a bit of business news I was interested in,' he'd said.

'Good news or bad news?' Milly had enquired, taking a gulp of wine and realising that she was rather drunk.

'That depends,' said Simon, 'on who you are.'

'But doesn't everything? Every piece of good news is someone else's bad news. Even . . .' She'd waved her glass vaguely in the air. 'Even world peace. Bad news for arms manufacturers.'

'I suppose so,' Simon had said. 'I'd never thought of it like that.'

'Well, we can't all be great thinkers,' Milly had said, and had suppressed a desire to giggle.

'Can I get you a drink?' he'd asked.

'Not a drink,' she'd replied. 'But you can light me a cigarette.'

He'd leaned towards her, cradling the flame carefully, and as she'd inhaled on the cigarette, his dark brown eyes had locked into hers, and to her surprise a tingle had run down her back.

Later on, when the party had turned from bright, stand-up chatter into groups of people sitting on the floor and smoking joints, the discussion had turned to vivisection. Milly, who had happened to see a *Blue Peter* special on vivisection the week before while at home with a cold, had produced more hard facts and informed reasoning than anyone else, and Simon had gazed at her in admiration.

He'd asked her out to dinner a few days later and talked a lot about business and politics. Milly, who knew nothing about either subject, had smiled and nodded and agreed with him; at the end of the evening, just before he kissed her for the first time, Simon had told her she was extraordinarily perceptive. 'I saw you at that party,' he'd said, 'destroying that guy's puerile arguments. You knew exactly what you were talking about. In fact,' he'd added, with darkening eyes, 'it was quite a turnon.' And Milly, who'd been about to admit to her source of information, had instead moved closer so that he could kiss her again.

Simon's initial impression of her had never been corrected. He still thought she liked the same highbrow art exhibitions he did; he still asked her opinion on topics such as the American presidential campaign. He thought she liked sushi; he thought she had read Sartre. Without wanting to mislead him, or to disappoint him either, she'd allowed him to build up a picture of her which—if she were honest with herself—wasn't quite true. Perhaps she wasn't quite the sophisticated woman he thought she was, but she could be. She would be. It was simply a matter of discarding all her old scruffy clothes and cheap shoes and wearing only the smart, expensive new ones, making the odd intelligent comment—and staying discreetly quiet the rest of the time.

Once, as they lay together in Simon's huge double bed at Pinnacle Hall, Simon had told her that he'd known she was someone special when she didn't start asking him questions about his father. 'Most girls,' he'd said bitterly, 'just want to know what it's like, being the son of Harry Pinnacle. Or they want me to get them a job interview or some-thing. But you . . . you've never even mentioned him.'

Milly had smiled sweetly and murmured an indistinct, sleepy response. She could hardly admit that the reason she'd never mentioned Harry Pinnacle was that she'd never heard of him.

'So—dinner with Harry Pinnacle tonight! That should be fun.' Her mother's voice interrupted Milly's thoughts, and she looked up.

'Yes,' she said. 'I suppose so.'

'The really lovely thing about Harry,' mused Olivia, 'is that he's so normal.' She tucked Milly's arm cosily under her own and they began to walk down the snowy street together. 'That's what I say to everybody. If you met him, you wouldn't think, here's a multimillionaire tycoon. You'd think, what a charming man. And Simon's just the same.'

'Simon isn't a multimillionaire tycoon,' said Milly. 'He's an advertising salesman.'

'I know you don't like me saying it, but the fact is that Simon's going to be very wealthy one day. And so are you.'

Milly shrugged. 'Maybe.'

'And when it happens, your life will change. The rich live differently, you know.'

'A minute ago,' pointed out Milly, 'you were saying how normal Harry is. He doesn't live differently, does he?'

'It's all relative, darling.'

An hour later they emerged from Mario's Coffee House, and headed for home. By the time they got back, the kitchen would be filling up with bed-and-breakfast guests, footsore from sightseeing. The Havills' house was one of the most popular bed-and-breakfast houses in Bath: tourists loved the beautifully furnished Georgian townhouse; its proximity to the city centre; Olivia's charm and ability to turn every gathering into a party.

'I forgot to say,' said Olivia, as they turned into Bertram Street. 'The photographer arrived while you were out.'

'I thought he was coming tomorrow.'

'So did I!' said Olivia. 'Luckily those nice Australians have had a death in the family, otherwise we wouldn't have had room for him to stay. And speaking of Australians . . . look at this!' She put her key in the front door and swung it open.

'Flowers!' exclaimed Milly. On the hall stand was a huge bouquet of creamy white flowers, tied with a dark green silk ribbon bow. 'For me? Who are they from?'

'Read the card,' said Olivia.

Milly picked up the bouquet, and reached inside the crackling plastic. '"To dear little Milly,"' she read slowly. '"We're so proud of you and only wish we could be there at your wedding. With all our love from Beth, Scott and Adrian."' Milly looked at Olivia in amazement.

'Isn't that sweet of them! All the way from Sydney.'

Still holding her flowers, Milly pushed open the door to the kitchen, then stopped in surprise. Sitting at the table was a dark-haired young man wearing round metal spectacles and reading the *Guardian*.

'Hello,' she said politely. 'You must be the photographer.'

'Hi,' said the young man, closing his paper. 'Are you Milly?'

He looked up, and Milly felt a jolt of recognition.

'I'm Alexander Gilbert,' he said in a dry voice, and held out his hand. Milly advanced politely and shook it.

'Nice flowers,' he said, nodding to her bouquet.

'Yes,' replied Milly, staring curiously at him. Where on earth had she seen him before? 'They were sent by some Australian friends. It's really thoughtful of them, considering—'

Suddenly she broke off, and her heart began to beat faster.

'Considering what?' said Alexander.

'Nothing,' said Milly, backing away. 'I mean—I'll just go and put them in some water.'

She moved towards the door, her palms sweaty against the crackling plastic. She knew exactly where she'd seen him before. At the thought of it, her heart gave a terrified lurch and she gritted her teeth, forcing herself to stay calm. Everything's OK, she told herself as she reached for the door handle. As long as he doesn't recognise me . . .

'Wait.' His voice cut across her thoughts as though he could read her mind. Feeling suddenly sick, she turned to see him staring at her with a slight frown. 'Wait a minute,' he said. 'Don't I know you?'

Sitting in a traffic jam on his way home that night, Simon reached for his phone to dial Milly's number. He pressed the first two digits, then changed his mind and switched the phone off. He had only wanted to hear her voice; make her laugh; picture her face as she spoke. But she might be busy, or she might think him ridiculous, phoning on a whim with nothing to say. And if she was out, he might find himself talking to Mrs Havill, instead.

Olivia Havill was a pleasant enough woman, still attractive, charming and amusing; he could see why she was a popular figure at social events. But the way she treated Milly irritated him. She seemed to think Milly was still a six-year-old—helping her choose her clothes, wanting to know exactly what she was doing, every minute of every day. And the worst thing was, Simon thought, that Milly didn't seem to mind. Unlike her older sister Isobel, who had long ago bought her own flat and moved out, Milly seemed to have no natural desire for independence.

The result was that her mother continued to treat her like a child, instead of the mature adult she really was. And Milly's father and sister Isobel were nearly as bad. They laughed when Milly expressed views on current issues, they joked about her career. They refused to see the intelligent, passionate woman he saw; refused to take her seriously.

Simon had tried to talk to Milly about her family, but she had simply shrugged and said they weren't so bad. She was too good-natured and affectionate a creature to see any faults in them, thought Simon, turning off the main road out of Bath, towards Pinnacle Hall. And he loved her for it. But when they were married, her focus would have to change, and her family would have to respect that. She would be a wife; maybe some day a mother. And the Havills would just have to realise that she was no longer their little girl.

He parked his car and crunched over the gravel towards Pinnacle Hall. It was a large, eighteenth-century house which had been a luxury hotel during the eighties, complete with a leisure complex and a tastefully added wing of extra bedrooms. Harry Pinnacle had bought it when the owners had gone bust and turned it back into a private home, with his company headquarters housed in the extra wing.

The panelled hall was empty and smelt of beeswax. From his father's study came a light; Simon could hear his voice, muffled behind the door, then a burst of low laughter. Resentment, never far from the surface, began to prickle at Simon's skin.

For as long as he could remember, Simon had hated his father. Harry Pinnacle had disappeared from the family home when Simon was three, leaving his mother to bring up Simon alone. His mother had never elaborated on exactly why the marriage had broken down, but Simon knew it had to be the fault of his father. His overbearing, arrogant, obnoxious father. His driven, creative, successful father.

The story was well known. In the year that Simon had turned seven,

Harry Pinnacle had opened a small juice bar called Fruit 'n Smooth. It served healthy drinks at chrome counters and was an instant hit. The next year, he opened another, and then another. Then he began selling franchises. By the mid-eighties, there was a Fruit 'n Smooth in every town and Harry Pinnacle was a multimillionaire.

As his father had grown in wealth and stature, the young Simon had watched his progress with fury. Cheques arrived every month, and his mother always exclaimed over Harry's generosity. But Harry never appeared in person, and Simon hated him for it. Then, when Simon was nineteen, his mother had died and Harry had come back into his life.

Simon frowned as he remembered the moment, ten years ago, when he'd met his father for the first time. Simon had been pacing the corridor outside his mother's hospital room, desperate with grief. Suddenly he'd heard a voice calling his name, and he'd looked up to see a face which was familiar from a thousand newspaper photographs. Familiar—and yet strange to him. As he'd stared at his father in silent shock, he'd realised for the first time that he could see his own features in the older man's face. And in spite of himself he'd felt emotional tentacles reaching out; instinctive feelers like a baby's. It would have been so easy to fall on his father's neck, to accept his overtures and make him a friend. But even as he'd felt himself beginning to soften, Simon had stamped on his feelings and ground them back into himself. Harry Pinnacle didn't deserve his love, and he would never have it.

After the funeral, Harry had welcomed Simon into his house. Simon had accepted everything—the home, the car, the holidays—politely. But expensive gifts could not buy his affections. Although his adolescent fury had soon simmered down, there had arisen in its place a determination to outdo his father on every front. He would run a successful business and make money—but, unlike his father, he would also marry happily, become the figurehead of a contented, loving family.

And so he'd begun, by launching his own little publishing company. He'd started with three specialist newsletters, a reasonable profit and high expectations. Those expectations had never been realised. After three years of struggle, he went into liquidation.

Humiliation still burned through Simon as he remembered the day he'd had to admit to his father that his business had gone bust. His father had poured him a deep glass of whisky, had uttered clichés about the rough and the smooth, had offered him a job with Pinnacle Enterprises. Simon had turned it down with a few muttered words of thanks. At that low point he'd despised himself almost as much as he despised his father.

Then he'd found himself a job selling advertising on a business magazine. 'It's not much of a job,' he'd told Harry defensively. 'But at least I'm in work.' And at least he could begin to pay off his debts.

Three months after starting on the magazine, he'd met Milly. A year later he'd asked her to marry him. His father had congratulated him; had offered to help out with the engagement ring. But Simon had refused his offer. 'I'll do this my way,' he'd said, and looked his father straight in the eye with a new confidence, almost a challenge. If he couldn't beat his father at business, then he would beat him at family life. He and Milly would have a perfect marriage.

Suddenly his thoughts were interrupted by another burst of laughter from inside his father's room, a mumble of conversation, and then the sharp ping which meant his father had replaced the old-fashioned receiver of his private-line telephone. Simon took a deep breath, approached his father's door and knocked.

As Harry Pinnacle heard the knock at his door he gave an uncharacteristic start. Quickly he put the tiny photograph he was holding into the desk drawer in front of him and closed it. For a few moments he sat, staring at the drawer, lost in thoughts.

There was another knock, and he looked up. He swivelled his chair away from the desk and ran his hand through his silvering hair.

'Yes?' he said and watched the door open.

Simon came in, took a few paces forward and looked angrily at his father. It was always the same. He would knock on his father's door and would be kept waiting outside, like a servant. Never once had Harry exhorted him not to knock; never once had he even looked pleased to see Simon. He always looked impatient, as though Simon were interrupting crucial business.

'Hi,' Simon said in a tense voice. 'I came to remind you about dinner tonight. The Havills are coming.'

'I remember,' said Harry. 'Feel like a whisky?'

'No. Thanks.'

'Well, I do.' As he got up to pour himself a drink, Harry caught a glimpse of his son's unguarded face: tense, miserable, angry. 'Not long now till the big day,' he said. 'Are you nervous?'

'No, not at all,' said Simon at once.

Harry shrugged. 'It's a big commitment,' he said.

Simon could feel a string of words forming at his lips; pent-up words which he'd carried around for years. 'Well,' he found himself saying, 'you wouldn't know much about commitment, would you?'

A flash of anger passed across his father's face. But as suddenly as it had appeared, the animation vanished and he walked away, towards the huge sash windows.

Simon felt himself tense up with frustration. 'What's wrong with commitment?' he shouted.

'Nothing,' said Harry, without turning.

'Then why . . .' began Simon, and stopped. There was a long silence, punctuated only by the crackles of the fire. Simon gazed at his father's back. Say something, he thought desperately. Say something.

'I'll see you at eight,' said Harry at last.

'Fine,' said Simon, in a voice scored with hurt. 'See you then.' And without pausing, he left the room.

Harry gazed at the glass in his hand. He hadn't meant to upset the boy. Or maybe he had. He couldn't trust his own motives any more. Sympathy so quickly turned into irritation; guilt so quickly transformed into anger. Good intentions towards his son disappeared the minute the boy opened his mouth. Simon was so full of anger, the anger he'd been carrying around ever since he'd first seen him outside his mother's hospital room. Part of him couldn't wait for the moment when Simon married; left his house; finally gave him some peace. And part of him dreaded it; didn't even want to think about it.

Frowning, Harry went back to his desk. He reached for the phone, dialled a number and listened impatiently to the ringing tone. Then, with a scowl, crashed the receiver down again.

Milly sat at the kitchen table with a thumping heart, wishing she could run away and escape. It was him. It was the boy from Oxford. The boy who had seen her marrying Allan; who had picked up her wedding veil. He was older now, his face was harder. But his round metal spectacles were just the same, and so was his arrogant, almost scornful expression. Now he was leaning back in his chair, staring at her curiously. Just don't remember, thought Milly, not daring to meet his gaze. For God's sake don't remember who I am.

'Here we are,' said Olivia, coming over to the table. 'I've arranged your flowers for you, darling!'

'Thanks,' muttered Milly.

'Now, would you like some more tea, Alexander?'

'Yup,' said the boy, holding out his cup. 'Thanks very much.' Olivia poured the tea, then sat down.

'Milly, have you shown Alexander your engagement ring?'

Slowly, feeling her insides clenching, Milly held out her left hand to

Alexander. His gaze passed inscrutably over the antique diamond cluster, then he raised his eyes to hers. 'Very nice,' he said. 'You're engaged to Harry Pinnacle's son. The heir to Fruit 'n Smooth. Is that right?'

'Yes,' said Milly reluctantly.

'Quite a catch,' said Alexander.

'He's a sweet boy,' said Olivia at once, as she always did when anyone referred to Simon's family background. 'Quite one of us, now.'

Alexander took a sip of tea and frowned at Milly. 'I'm still sure I recognise you from somewhere.'

'Well, I'm afraid I don't recognise you,' said Milly, trying to sound light-hearted.

'Have you always had your hair like that?' he asked, as his eyes ran over Milly's face. Milly's heart lurched in fright.

'Not always,' she said. 'I . . . I once dyed it red.'

'Not a success,' said Olivia emphatically. 'I told her to go to my salon, but she wouldn't listen. And then of course—'

'That's not it,' said Alexander, cutting Olivia off. He frowned again at Milly. 'You weren't at Cambridge, were you?'

'No,' said Milly.

'But Isobel was,' Olivia said triumphantly. 'She read modern languages. And now she's doing *terribly* well, interpreting at conferences all over the world.'

'What does she look like?' said Alexander.

'That's a picture of her there,' said Olivia, pointing to a photograph on the mantelpiece. 'And there are lots more in the album.'

'It wasn't her.' He shrugged, and stood up. 'I've got to go. I'm meeting a friend in town.'

'How nice.' said Olivia. 'Have fun!'

'Thanks,' said Alexander. He paused by the door. 'I'll see you tomorrow, Milly. I'll take a few informal shots and we can have a little chat about what you want.' He nodded at her, then disappeared.

'What an interesting man,' exclaimed Olivia, when he had gone.

Milly didn't move. She stared straight at the table, hands still clenched round her cup, her heart beating furiously.

'He and Isobel really should meet each other,' Olivia was saying. 'As soon as she gets back from Paris.'

'What?' Milly's attention was momentarily drawn. 'Mummy, no! Stop trying to marry Isobel off.'

'It's just a thought,' said Olivia defensively. 'What chance has poor Isobel got to meet men, stuck in dreary conference rooms all day, interpreting for dreary businessmen?'

'She doesn't want to meet men. Not your men!' Milly gave a tiny shudder. 'And especially not him!'

'What's wrong with him?' said Olivia.

'Nothing,' said Milly quickly. 'He's just . . . not Isobel.'

An image of her sister came into Milly's mind—clever, sensible Isobel. Suddenly she felt a surge of relief. She would talk to Isobel. Isobel always knew what to do. Milly looked at her watch.

'What time is it in Paris?'

'Why? Are you going to make a call?'

'Yes,' said Milly. 'I want to speak to Isobel.' Suddenly she felt desperate. 'I need to speak to Isobel.'

Isobel Havill arrived back at her hotel room at eight o'clock to find the message light on her telephone furiously blinking. She frowned, rubbed a weary hand over her brow, and opened the minibar. The day had been even more draining than usual. She had spent all day listening, translating and speaking into her microphone in the low, measured tones that made her so highly sought after. And now she felt like a dried-out, empty shell.

Holding a glass of vodka, she went slowly into the bathroom and swtiched on the light. All day, she'd managed to put this moment from her mind. But now she was alone and her work was finished, and there was no longer any excuse. With a trembling hand she reached into her handbag and pulled out a pharmacist's bag; took out a little oblong box. Inside was a leaflet bearing instructions printed in French, German, Spanish and English. Her eyes flicked impatiently over each of them; all seemed agreed on the short time span of the test. Only one minute.

She carried out the test, then left the little phial on the edge of the bath and went back into the bedroom. The telephone was still furiously blinking. She pressed the button for messages. Thirty seconds to go.

'Hi, Isobel. It's me.' A man's low voice filled the room, and Isobel flinched. 'Call me if you have time. Bye.'

Isobel looked at her watch. Fifteen seconds to go.

'Isobel, it's Milly. I need to speak to you. Please can you call me back as soon as you get this? It's really urgent.'

'Isn't it always urgent?' said Isobel aloud.

She took a deep breath and strode towards the bathroom. The little blue stripe was visible even before she reached the door.

'No,' she whispered. 'I can't be.' She backed away from the pregnancy test, as though from something contaminated, and took a deep, shuddering breath. A lonely dismay crept over her.

'Isobel?' the machine was saying brightly. 'It's Milly again. I'll be at Simon's tonight, so could you call me there?'

'No,' shouted Isobel. 'I couldn't, all right?' Like a wounded animal, she crawled into bed, buried her head in her hotel pillow. And as the telephone rang again, she silently began to cry.

Chapter Two

AT EIGHT THIRTY, Olivia and Milly arrived at Pinnacle Hall. They were met at the door by Simon and shown into the drawing room.

'Well,' said Olivia, wandering over to the fire. 'Isn't this nice!'

'I'll get some champagne,' said Simon. 'Dad's still on the phone.'

'Actually,' said Milly faintly, 'I think I'll try Isobel again. I'll use the phone in the games room.'

'Can't it wait?' said Olivia. 'What do you want to speak to her about?'

'Nothing,' said Milly at once. 'Nothing. I just . . . need to talk to her.' She swallowed. 'I won't be long.'

When they'd gone, Olivia settled herself into a chair by the fireplace. The door opened, and a pretty blonde girl in a smart trouser-suit entered, holding a tray of champagne glasses.

'Simon's just coming,' she said. 'He's just sending a fax.'

'Thank you,' said Olivia, taking a glass and giving a small, regal smile.

The girl left the room, and Olivia took a sip of champagne. The fire was warm on her face; her chair was comfortable; classical music was playing pleasantly through concealed speakers. This, she thought, was the life. A pang went through her—part delight, part envy—at the knowledge that soon her daughter would be entering this kind of existence. In fact, Milly was already as much at home at Pinnacle Hall as she was at One Bertram Street.

Olivia clenched her hand more tightly round her glass. When the engagement had first been announced, she'd been overcome by an astonished, almost giddy delight. Then, as the wedding plans had progressed, she'd prided herself on keeping her triumph concealed; on treating Simon as casually as any other young beau; on playing down—to herself as much as anyone else—the significance of the match.

245

But now, with only a few days to go, her heart was beginning to beat quickly again with jubilation. In only a few days the whole world would see her daughter marrying one of the most eligible bachelors in the country. It would be a beautiful, romantic wedding day, a day they would carry in their thoughts for ever.

Olivia's pleasant dream world was interrupted as the door suddenly opened. She quickly smoothed down her skirt and looked up with a smile, expecting to see Harry. But it was the pretty blonde girl again.

'Your husband's here, Mrs Havill,' she said.

Into the room walked James. He'd come straight from the office; his suit was crumpled and he looked tired. 'Been here long?' he said.

'No,' said Olivia with a forced cheerfulness. 'Not very.'

She rose from her seat and walked towards James, intending to greet him with a kiss. Just before she reached him, the girl tactfully withdrew and closed the door.

Olivia stopped in her tracks, suddenly feeling self-conscious. Physical contact between herself and James had, over the last few years, become something which only happened in front of other people. Now she felt awkward, standing this close to him without an audience. She leaned forward, flushing slightly, and gave him a peck on the cheek.

'Where's Milly?' said James in an expressionless voice.

'She's popped off to make a telephone call.'

Olivia watched as James helped himself to a glass of champagne and took a deep swig. He sat down on a sofa and stretched his legs out comfortably in front of him.

'So,' she began—then stopped and took a sip of champagne. Topics of conversation passed through her mind like shrink-wrapped food on a conveyor belt, each as unappealing and difficult to get into as the next.

Once, long ago, their conversation had flowed like a seamless length of ribbon. James had listened to her stories in genuine amusement; she'd laughed at his dry wit. But these days all his jokes seemed tinged with a bitterness she didn't understand, and a tense boredom crept over his face as soon as she began to speak.

So they remained in silence, until finally the door opened and Milly came in. She gave James a brief, strained smile. 'Hello, Daddy,' she said. 'You made it.'

'Did you get through to Isobel?' asked Olivia.

'No,' said Milly shortly. 'I had to leave another message.' Her eye fell on the tray. 'Oh good. I could do with a drink.'

She took a glass of champagne and raised it. 'Cheers.'

'Cheers!' echoed Olivia.

'Your good health, my darling,' said James. All three drank; there was a little silence.

'Did I interrupt something?' said Milly.

'No,' said Olivia. 'You didn't interrupt anything.'

'Good,' said Milly without really listening, and walked over to the fire, hoping no one would talk to her.

For the third time, she'd got through to Isobel's message machine. She'd felt a spurt of anger, an irrational conviction that Isobel was there and just wasn't answering. She'd left a brief message, then remained staring at the phone for a few minutes, hoping desperately that Isobel would call back. Isobel was the only one she could talk to—the only one who would think of a solution rather than lecturing.

But the phone had remained silent. Milly couldn't stand this niggling, secret panic. Alexander would never remember, she'd told herself again and again. It had been a two-minute encounter, ten years ago. He couldn't possibly remember that. And even if he did, he wouldn't say anything about it. Civilised people didn't deliberately cause trouble.

'Milly?' Simon's voice interrupted her thoughts.

'Hi,' she said. 'Did you send your fax all right?'

'Yes.' He took a sip of champagne and looked more closely at her. 'Are you OK? You're looking tense.'

'Am I?' She smiled at him. 'I don't feel it.'

'You're tense,' persisted Simon, and he began to massage her shoulders gently. 'Worrying about the wedding. Am I right?'

'Yes,' said Milly.

'I knew it.'

Simon liked to think that he was in tune with her emotions; that he could predict her moods. And she'd got into the habit of agreeing with him, even when his assertions were wildly inaccurate. After all, it was sweet of him to have a go. Most men wouldn't have bothered.

'Let me guess what you're thinking,' he murmured. 'You're wishing it was just the two of us tonight.'

'No,' said Milly honestly. She turned round and looked at him, breathing in his musky, familiar scent. 'I was thinking how much I love you.'

It was nine thirty before Harry Pinnacle strode into the room. 'My apologies,' he said. 'This is unforgivable of me.'

'Harry, it's utterly forgivable!' exclaimed Olivia, now on her fifth glass of champagne. 'We know what it's like!'

'I don't,' muttered Simon.

'Well, let's not hang about,' said Harry. He turned politely to Olivia. 'After you.'

They slowly made their way into the dining room.

'All right, sweetheart?' said James to Milly as they sat down round the magnificent mahogany dining table.

'Fine,' she said, and gave him a taut smile.

But she wasn't, thought James. He'd watched her knocking back glasses of champagne as though she were desperate; watched her jump every time the phone rang. Was she having second thoughts? He leaned towards her. 'Just remember, darling,' he said in an undertone. 'If you change your mind about Simon—now, or even on the day itself—don't worry. We can call the whole thing off. No one will mind.'

'I don't want to call the whole thing off!' hissed Milly, looking close to tears. 'I want to get married! I love Simon.'

'Good,' said James. 'Well, that's fine then.'

He sat back in his chair, glanced across the table at Simon and felt unreasonably irritated. The boy had everything. Good looks, a wealthy background, an annoyingly calm and balanced personality, and he obviously adored Milly. There was nothing to complain about. But tonight, James admitted to himself, he was in a mood for complaint.

He'd had a grisly day at work. The engineering firm in whose finance department he worked had undergone restructuring in recent months. Endless rumours had that day culminated in the announcement that there would have to be four junior redundancies in his department. When he'd left the office, all the younger members of the team had still been hunched dutifully over their desks. Some had kept their heads down; others had looked up with scared eyes as he passed. Every one of them had a family and a mortgage. None of them could afford to lose their job. None of them deserved to. By the time he'd arrived at Pinnacle Hall he'd felt unspeakably depressed.

'I'd like to propose a toast.'

Harry's voice interrupted James's thoughts and he looked up, frowning slightly. There he was. Harry Pinnacle, his daughter's prospective father-in-law. James was aware that this alliance made him the envy of his peers and knew that he should be pleased at Milly's future financial security. But he refused to rejoice, as his wife did, in the fact of his daughter becoming a Pinnacle. He'd heard Olivia on the phone, dropping Harry's name into the conversation, assuming an intimacy with the great man that she did not have, and it made him curl up with shame.

'To Milly and Simon,' declaimed Harry, in the gravelly voice which made all his utterances sound more significant than everyone else's.

'To Milly and Simon,' echoed James, raising the heavy Venetian glass in front of him.

'Simply delicious wine,' said Olivia. 'Are you a wine expert as well as everything else, Harry?'

'Christ, no,' replied Harry. 'I rely on people with taste to tell me what to buy. It's all the same to me.'

'You're too modest,' exclaimed Olivia. James watched in disbelief as she reached over and patted Harry intimately on the hand. He turned away, slightly sickened, and caught Simon's eye.

'Cheers, James,' he said, raising his glass. 'Here's to the wedding.'

'Yes,' said James, and took a huge gulp of wine. 'To the wedding.'

There was a choice of puddings.

'Oh!' said Olivia, looking from lemon mousse to chocolate torte and back again. 'Oh dear, I can't decide.'

'Then have both,' said Harry.

'Really? Is anyone else going to have both?' Olivia asked.

'I'm not going to have any,' said Milly, pleating her napkin nervously between her fingers. 'I'm not very hungry.'

'You're as bad as Isobel!' said Olivia. 'She eats like a bird.'

'How is she?' asked Harry politely.

'She's great!' said James with sudden animation. 'Forging ahead with her career, travelling the world . . .'

'Does she have a boyfriend?'

'Oh no,' James laughed. 'She's too busy doing her own thing. Isobel's not going to get tied down in a hurry.'

'She might,' objected Olivia. 'She might meet someone tomorrow! Some nice businessman.'

'God help us,' said James. 'Can you really see Isobel settling down with some dreary businessman? Anyway, she's far too young still.'

'She's older than me,' said Milly.

'Yes,' said James, 'but the two of you are very different.'

'How?' said Milly. She looked at her father. The tensions of the day were throbbing unbearably inside her head. 'Are you saying I'm too stupid to do anything but get married?'

'No!' said James. He looked shocked. 'Of course not! All I mean is that Isobel's a bit more adventurous than you. She likes taking risks.'

'I've taken risks in my time!' cried Milly. 'I've taken risks you know nothing about!' She broke off and stared at her father, breathing hard.

'Milly, don't get upset,' said James. 'All I'm saying is that you and Isobel are different.'

'And I prefer you,' whispered Simon to Milly, who smiled gratefully.

'Anyway, what's wrong with businessmen?' said Olivia. 'You're a businessman, aren't you, and I married you.'

'I know, my love,' said James tonelessly. 'But I'm hoping Isobel might do a little better than someone like me.'

Later on, after pudding, Harry cleared his throat for attention. 'I don't want to make a big thing of this,' he said. 'But I've got a bit of a present for the happy couple.'

Simon looked up defensively. He'd bought a present of his own to give Milly this evening and had planned to spring it on her while they were all drinking coffee. He felt in his pocket for the small leather box containing the earrings he'd chosen, and wondered whether to leave it for another day—a day without competition from his father. But then a small wave of indignation rose through him. Why should he?

'I've got a present too,' he said, trying to sound casual. 'For Milly.'

'For me?' said Milly confusedly. 'But I haven't got anything for you. At least, not anything to give you tonight.'

'This is something extra,' said Simon.

He leaned over and gently pushed Milly's blonde hair back behind her shoulders, exposing her little pink ears. As he did so, the gesture seemed suddenly erotic; and as he stared at her flawless skin, breathing in her sweet, musky scent, a proud desire surged through him. Sod the rest of them, he thought. He had Milly's divine body all to himself, and that was all that counted.

'What is it?' said Milly.

'Dad first,' said Simon, magnanimously. 'What have you got us, Dad?'

Harry felt in his pocket, and dropped a key on the table.

'A key?' said Milly. 'What's it for?'

'A car?' said Olivia in incredulous tones.

'Not a car,' said Harry. 'A flat.'

There was a unanimous gasp.

'You're joking,' said Simon. 'You've bought us a flat?'

Harry pushed the key across the table. 'All yours.'

Simon stared at his father, feeling all the wrong emotions rise to the surface. He tried to locate a feeling of gratitude, but all he could feel was the beginnings of a defensive, smarting anger. He glanced at Milly. She was gazing at Harry with shining eyes. Simon felt a sudden despair.

'How . . .' he began, trying to summon the correct, grateful tones, but only managing to sound peevish. 'How do you know we'll like it?'

'It's the one you wanted to rent. The one you couldn't afford.'

'The flat in Parham Place?' whispered Milly. 'You *bought* it for us?'

Simon stared at his father, and felt like punching him. Fuck him for being so thoughtful.

'This is very good of you, Harry,' said James. 'Incredibly generous.'

Harry shrugged. 'One less thing for them to worry about.'

'Oh, darling!' said Olivia, clasping Milly's hand. 'Won't it be lovely? And you'll be so near us.'

'Well now, there's a plus,' said Simon, before he could stop himself.

James glanced at him, and said tactfully, 'Now, what about Simon's present?'

'Yes,' said Milly. She turned to Simon and touched his hand gently. 'What is it?'

Simon presented her with the little box. Everyone watched as she opened it to reveal two tiny, twinkling diamond studs.

'Oh, Simon,' said Milly. She looked at him, her eyes suddenly glittering with unshed tears. 'They're beautiful.'

'Pretty,' said Olivia dismissively. 'Oh, Milly! Parham Place!'

'They're nothing very special,' said Simon, his heart pounding with a raw, hurt anger. It seemed to him that everyone was laughing at him.

'Of course they are,' said Harry gravely.

'No they're not!' Simon found himself shouting. 'Not compared with a piece of fucking real estate!'

'Simon,' said Harry calmly, 'no one is making that comparison.'

'They're lovely!' said Milly, putting them on. 'Look.' She smoothed her hair back and the little diamonds sparkled in the candlelight.

'Great,' said Simon, without looking up.

Harry caught James's eye, then rose to his feet. 'Let's have coffee,' he said. 'Nicki will have put it in the drawing room.'

'Absolutely,' said James, taking his cue. 'Come on, Olivia.'

The three parents moved out of the dining room, leaving Milly and Simon in silence. After a few moments Simon looked up, to see Milly gazing at him. She wasn't laughing, she wasn't pitying. Suddenly he felt ashamed. 'I'm sorry,' he muttered. 'I'm being a complete prick.'

'I haven't said thank you for my present yet,' said Milly.

She leaned forward and kissed him with warm, soft lips. Simon cupped her face, feeling nothing but sweet sensation. The soreness began to lessen. Milly was all his—and nothing else mattered.

'Let's elope,' he said suddenly. 'Sod the wedding. Let's just go and do it on our own in a registry office.'

Milly pulled away. 'Do you really want to?' she said, staring at him intently. 'Shall we, Simon?' she said with an edge to her voice. 'Tomorrow?'

'Well,' he said, feeling a little taken aback. 'We could do. But wouldn't everyone get a bit pissed off?'

Milly stared at him for a moment, then bit her lip. 'You're right,' she said. 'It's a stupid idea.' She stood up. 'Come on. Are you ready to be grateful to your father yet? He's very kind, you know.'

'Wait,' said Simon. He reached out and grasped her hand tightly. 'Would you really elope with me?'

'Yes,' said Milly simply. 'I would.'

'I thought you were looking forward to the wedding. The dress, and the reception, and all your friends . . .'

'I was,' said Milly. 'But . . .' She shrugged slightly.

Simon gazed at Milly and thought he'd never known such love, such generosity of spirit. 'God, I love you. I don't know what I've done to deserve you. Come here.'

He pulled her down onto his knee and began kissing her neck, tugging urgently at the zip of her skirt.

'Simon . . .' began Milly. 'Your father . . .'

'He made us wait for him,' said Simon, against Milly's warm, scented skin. 'Now he's going to wait for us.'

Chapter Three

THE NEXT MORNING, Milly woke feeling refreshed. The rich food, wine and conversation from the night before seemed to have disappeared from her system; she felt light and energetic.

As she went into the kitchen for breakfast, a couple of guests from Yorkshire, Mr and Mrs Able nodded pleasantly.

'Morning, Milly!' said her mother, looking up from the phone. 'There's another special delivery for you.' She pointed to a large cardboard box on the floor.

'What's this?' Milly said, smiling. She poured herself a cup of coffee, sat down on the floor and began to rip open the cardboard.

'It looks exciting,' said Mrs Able encouragingly.

'And Alexander says he'll meet you at ten thirty,' said Olivia. 'To take some shots and have a little chat.'

'Oh,' said Milly, suddenly feeling sick. 'Good.'

Milly tugged at the plastic wrapping with shaky hands, feeling bubbles of panic rise inside her. Silently, she pulled out a pair of Louis Vuitton travel bags. Another sumptuous gift. She tried to look pleased, but all she could think of was the thudding fear growing inside her.

'Geoffrey! Just look at that for a wedding gift. Who are they from, dear?' said Mrs Able.

Milly looked at the card. 'Someone I've never even heard of.'

'One of Harry's friends, I expect,' said Olivia.

'I've never known a wedding like this,' said Mrs Able, shaking her head. 'The stories I'm going to tell when I get back home!'

'I told you about the procession, didn't I?' said Olivia. 'We're having an organist specially flown in from Geneva. And three trumpeters are going to play a fanfare as Milly arrives at the church.'

'A fanfare!' said Mrs Able to Milly. 'You'll feel like a princess.'

'Darling, have an egg,' said Olivia.

'No, thanks,' said Milly. 'I'll just have coffee.'

'Still a little fragile after last night,' said Olivia airily, cracking eggs into a pan. 'It was a wonderful dinner, wasn't it, Milly?' She smiled at Mrs Able. 'Harry's a wonderful host. And soon he'll be family.'

'I've got to go,' said Milly, unable to bear any more. She stood up, leaving her coffee undrunk.

'That's right,' said Olivia. 'Go and put some make-up on. You want to look your best for Alexander.'

'Yes,' said Milly faintly. She paused by the door. 'Isobel hasn't called this morning, has she?' she asked casually.

'No,' said Olivia. 'I expect she'll ring you later.'

At ten forty, Alexander appeared at the door of the drawing room.

'Hi, Milly,' he said. 'Sorry I'm a bit late.'

Milly felt a sickening thud of nerves, as though she were being called for an exam. She put down the copy of *Country Life* she had been pretending to read.

'By the window, do you think, Alexander, or by the piano?' said Olivia, following in behind Alexander.

'Just where you are, I think,' said Alexander, looking critically at Milly's position on the sofa. 'I'll need to put up a couple of lights . . .'

Within minutes he had transformed the room into a photographer's studio. A white cloth was draped on the floor and white umbrellas and light stands surrounded the sofa on which Milly sat. She looked up at Alexander with all the calmness she could muster.

'That's right,' he said. 'Now relax. Sit back a bit.' He stared critically at her for a while. 'Could you sweep your hair back, off your face?'

'That reminds me!' exclaimed Olivia. 'Those photographs I was telling you about. I'll fetch them.'

'OK,' said Alexander absently. 'Now, Milly, I want you to lean back a little and smile.'

Without intending to, Milly found herself obeying his commands. As she smiled, she felt her body relax; felt herself sink into the cushions of the sofa. Alexander seemed utterly preoccupied with his camera. Any suggestion that they'd met before seemed to have been forgotten. She'd been worrying over nothing, she told herself comfortably.

'Here we are!' said Olivia, bustling up beside Alexander with a photograph album. 'These are of Isobel, just before she graduated. Now, we thought they were marvellous shots. What do you think?'

'Nice,' said Alexander, glancing briefly down.

'Do you really think so?' said Olivia, pleased. She flipped the page backwards. 'And this is one of Milly at around the same time. It must be ten years ago, now. Just look at her hair!'

'Nice,' said Alexander automatically. He turned his head to look, then, as his eyes fell on the picture, stopped still. 'Wait,' he said. 'Let me see that.' He took the album from Olivia and stared at the photograph.

'She cut all her hair off and bleached it without telling us!' Olivia was saying. 'She was quite wild back then!'

Alexander gazed down, mesmerised, at the album. 'The wedding girl,' he said softly, as though to himself.

Milly felt her insides turn to ice. He remembered. He remembered who she was. But if he would just keep his mouth shut, everything could still be all right.

'Well,' said Alexander, finally looking up. 'What a difference.' He gave Milly a small, amused smile and she stared back, her stomach churning.

'It's the hair,' said Olivia eagerly. 'That's all it is.'

'I don't think it's just the hair,' said Alexander. 'What do you think, Milly? Is it just the hair? Or is it something else completely?'

He met her eyes and she gazed at him in terror.

'I don't know,' she managed eventually.

He paused, loading film into his camera. 'By the way, Milly,' he said conversationally. 'Is this your first marriage?'

'Of course it's her first marriage!' exclaimed Olivia. 'Does Milly look old enough to be on her second marriage?'

'You'd be surprised,' said Alexander, adjusting something on the camera. 'These days.' A sudden white flash went off, and Milly flinched as though she were being attacked. Alexander looked up at her.

'Relax,' he said, and a smile passed across his face. 'If you can.'

'You look lovely, darling,' said Olivia, clasping her hands together. As she caught Milly's eye she backed deferentially away. 'I'll see you later, shall I?' she whispered.

'That's good,' said Alexander. 'Now turn your head to the left. Lovely.' The room flashed again. In the corner the door closed softly. 'So, Milly,' said Alexander. 'What have you done with your first husband?'

The room swam around Milly's head; every muscle in her body tightened. 'I don't know what you're talking about,' she said.

Alexander laughed. 'You know exactly what I'm talking about. And it's obvious no one knows about it except me. I'm intrigued. Try crossing your legs,' he added, looking at her through the lens. 'Left hand on your knee so we can see the ring.'

The white flash went off again. Milly stared desperately ahead, trying to frame a reply, a put-down, a witty riposte. But her thoughts were inarticulate and feeble, as though her brain-power had been sapped by panic. She felt unable to do anything but follow his commands.

'A first marriage isn't against the law, you know,' observed Alexander. 'So what's the problem? Would your bridegroom disapprove? Or his father?' He took another few shots, then eyed her thoughtfully. 'Or maybe there's a bit more to the story.' He lowered his eye to the lens. 'Can you come slightly forward?'

Milly edged forward. Her stomach was tense, her skin felt prickly.

'I've still got an old photograph of you, by the way,' said Alexander. 'In your wedding dress, on the steps. It made a good shot.'

The room flashed again. Milly felt giddy with fright. Her mind scurried back to that day in Oxford; to the crowd of tourists who had taken photographs of her and Allan on the steps, as she smiled and encouraged them. How could she have been so stupid? How could she have . . .

'Of course, you look very different now,' said Alexander. 'I nearly didn't recognise you.'

Milly forced herself to meet his eye. 'You didn't recognise me,' she said. A note of pleading entered her voice. 'You didn't recognise me.'

'Well, I don't know,' said Alexander, shaking his head. 'Keeping secrets from your future husband, Milly. Not a good sign.' He peeled off his jersey and threw it down. 'Shouldn't someone tell the poor guy?'

Milly moved her lips to speak but no sound came out. She had never felt so scared in all her life.

'That's great,' said Alexander, looking into the camera again. 'But try not to frown.' He looked up at her and grinned. 'Think happy thoughts.'

After what seemed like hours, he came to an end.

'OK,' he said. 'You can go now.' Milly stared at him speechlessly. If she appealed to him—told him everything—he might relent. Or he might not. A tremor ran through her. She couldn't risk it.

'Thank you,' she said, getting up from the sofa. She walked to the door as quickly as she could without looking rushed, forced herself to turn the doorknob calmly and slipped out into the hall. As the door closed behind her, she felt almost tearful with relief. She reached for the phone. By now she knew the number off by heart.

'Hello,' came a voice. 'If you would like to leave a message for Isobel Havill, please speak after the tone.'

Milly crashed the receiver back down in frustration. She had to talk to someone. She couldn't stand this any more. Then a sudden note of inspiration hit her, and she picked up the phone again.

'Hello?' she said, as it was answered. 'Esme? It's Milly. Can I come and see you?'

A fire was crackling in Esme Ormerod's drawing room and a jug of mulled wine was sending fragrant steam into the air. As Milly sank gratefully into the sofa, she found herself marvelling that such an urbane, sophisticated woman could be related to her own dull father.

Esme Ormerod was the second half-cousin of James Havill. She had been brought up in London by a different, wealthier side of the family, and James had never known her well. But then, at around the time Milly was born, she had moved to Bath, and had made courteous contact with James. Olivia, impressed by this new, rather exotic relation of James's, had immediately asked her to be Milly's godmother, thinking that this might promote some intimacy between the two women. It had not done so. But then few could boast that they knew Esme well. Even Milly, who was closest to her of all the Havills, was often at a loss to know what she was thinking or what she might say next.

'So, how are the wedding preparations going?' said Esme, sitting by the fire and pushing back the sleeves of her grey cashmere sweater.

'Fine,' said Milly. 'You know what it's like.' Esme shrugged noncommittally, and it occurred to Milly that she hadn't seen her godmother for weeks, if not months. But that was not unusual. Their relationship had always gone in phases, ever since Milly was a teenager. Whenever things had gone badly at home, Milly would head straight for Esme's house. They would sit in Esme's drawing room drinking pale, chilled wine, listening to chamber music. Esme always understood her; Esme always treated her like an adult.

'So, darling,' Esme was saying. 'If it's not the wedding, then what is it?'

'It is the wedding,' said Milly. 'But it's a bit complicated.'

'Simon? Have you argued?'

'No,' said Milly at once. 'No. I just . . .' She exhaled sharply. 'I just need some advice. Some . . . hypothetical advice.'

There was a little pause, then Esme said, 'I understand.' She gave Milly a cat-like smile. 'Continue.'

Milly hunched her shoulders up and stared into the flickering fire. 'Suppose there was a person. And suppose that person had a secret she'd never told anyone about. Not even the man she loved.'

'Why not?'

'Because it was just some stupid, irrelevant thing which happened ten years ago. And if it came out, it would ruin everything.'

'Ah,' said Esme. 'That kind of secret.'

'Yes,' said Milly. 'That kind of secret.' She took a deep breath. 'And suppose someone came along who knew about the secret. And he started threatening to say something.'

Esme exhaled softly. 'I see.'

'But she didn't know if he was serious or not.'

Esme nodded.

'The thing is,' said Milly, 'what should she do?' She looked up. 'Should she tell the . . . the partner? Or should she just keep quiet and hope that she'd get away with it?'

Esme reached for her cigarette case. 'Is it really a secret worth keeping?' she said. 'Or is it just some silly little indiscretion that no one would really mind about?'

'No,' said Milly. 'It's a very big secret. Like a . . .' She paused. 'Like a previous marriage. Or something.'

Esme raised her eyebrows. 'That is a big secret.'

'Or something,' repeated Milly. 'It doesn't matter what it is.' She met Esme's eyes steadily. 'The point is, she's kept it secret for ten years. No one's ever known about it. No one needs to know.'

'I see,' said Esme. She lit a cigarette and inhaled deeply.

'What would you do, if you were that person?' said Milly.

Esme blew out a cloud of smoke thoughtfully.

'What is the risk of this other character giving her away?'

'I don't know,' said Milly. 'Quite small at the moment, I think.'

'Then I would say nothing,' said Esme. 'And I would try to think of a way of keeping the other one quiet.' She shrugged. 'Perhaps the whole thing will quietly fade away.'

'Do you think so?' Milly looked up. 'Do you really think so?'

Esme smiled. 'Darling, how many times have you tossed and turned at night, worried about something, only to find in the morning that there was nothing to fear?' She took a deep drag on her cigarette. 'Nine times out of ten, it's better to say nothing and hope that everything will proceed smoothly. And no one need ever know.' She paused. 'Hypothetically speaking, of course.'

'Yes, of course.'

There was silence, broken only by the crackle and spitting of the fire. Outside, it had begun to snow again, in thick, blurry flakes.

'You don't think I . . . the person should be honest with her partner.'

'Why should she?'

'Because . . . because she's going to marry him!'

Esme smiled. 'Darling, it's a nice idea. But a woman should never try to be honest with a man. Women and men speak different languages. And the truth is, you can't be completely honest with someone you don't properly understand.'

Milly thought for a few moments. 'People who've been happily married for years understand each other,' she said at last.

'They muddle through,' said Esme, 'with a mixture of sign language and goodwill and the odd phrase picked up over the years. But they don't have access to the rich depths of each other's spirits. The common language simply isn't there.'

'So you're saying there's no such thing as a happy marriage.'

'I'm saying there's no such thing as an honest marriage,' said Esme. 'Happiness is something else.'

'I suppose you're right,' said Milly doubtfully, and glanced at her watch. 'Esme, I've got to go.'

'Well, I hope I've been some help.'

'Not really,' said Milly bluntly. 'If anything, I'm more confused than before.'

Esme smiled amusedly. 'Oh dear. I'm sorry.' She surveyed Milly's face. 'So—what do you think your . . . hypothetical person will do?'

'I don't know,' said Milly. 'I really don't know.'

James Havill had left the office at lunchtime that day and headed for home. As he let himself in, the house was silent apart from the odd creak. At this time of day the guests would be out, sightseeing.

He climbed the stairs as soundlessly as possible. As he rounded the corner to the second floor his heart began to beat in anticipation. He had planned this encounter all morning; had thought of nothing else.

The door to her room was closed. James stared for a moment at the little porcelain plaque bearing the word PRIVATE, before knocking.

'Yes?' Her voice sounded startled.

'It's only me,' he said and pushed the door open. Olivia was sitting in her faded chintz armchair. A cup of tea was at her elbow and her hands were full of pale pink silk.

'Hello,' said James. 'I didn't mean to disturb you.'

'Don't worry,' said Olivia. 'What do you think?'

'What do you mean?' said James, taken aback.

'Isobel's dress!' said Olivia, holding up the pink silk. 'I thought it looked a little plain, so I'm trimming it with some roses.'

'Lovely,' said James. 'Um . . . I wanted to talk to you.'

'And I wanted to talk to you,' said Olivia. She picked up a red exercise book lying near her chair and consulted it. 'First, have you checked the route to the church with the council?'

'I know the route,' said James.

Olivia sighed exasperatedly. 'Of course you do. But do you know if any roadworks or demonstrations are going to spring up on Saturday? No! That's why we have to ring the council. Don't worry. I'll do it myself.' She began to write in the exercise book.

James said nothing. He looked around for somewhere to sit, but there were no other chairs. After a pause he sat down on the edge of the bed. Olivia's duvet was soft and smelt faintly of her perfume. It was anchored down with lacy cushions, neat and sexless as though she never slept in it. For all he knew, she didn't. James had not seen the underside of Olivia's duvet for six years.

'Olivia, listen for a moment,' he said. 'I wanted to talk about—' He broke off. 'About what's going to happen. After the wedding.'

'For goodness' sake, James! Let's just get the wedding safely over before we start talking about what happens next.'

'Just hear me out.' James took a deep breath. 'I think we both realise that things will be different when Milly's gone, don't we? When it's just the two of us in this house.'

'Fees for the choir . . .' murmured Olivia, ticking off on her fingers. 'Buttonholes . . .'

'There's no point pretending things are the same as they were. We've been drifting apart for years, now. You've got your life, I've got mine . . .'

'Speech!' said Olivia, looking up. 'Have you composed your speech?'

'Yes,' said James, staring at her. 'But no one seems to be listening.'

'Good.' She smiled brightly at him. 'Well, that's it.' She stood up. 'Now I must pop along to see the choirmaster. Was there anything else?'

'Well—'

'Because I am running a little late. Excuse me.' She gestured to James to stand up, and laid the pink silk carefully on the bed. 'See you later!'

'Yes,' said James. 'See you later.'

The door closed behind him and he found himself staring again at Olivia's little plaque. 'So what I'm saying,' he said to the door, 'is that after the wedding, I want to move out. I want a new life. Do you understand?'

There was silence. James shrugged and walked away.

When Milly arrived home, she heard voices in the kitchen, and winced as it occurred to her that Aunt Jean might have arrived early. But when she pushed open the door, it was Isobel she saw, standing on a kitchen chair, wearing a pink bridesmaid's dress.

'Isobel!' she exclaimed, feeling sudden, almost tearful relief. 'When did you get back?'

Isobel grinned. 'This afternoon. I got back home, and what do I find? My bloody water pipes have gone.'

'Isobel's going to stay here until the wedding,' said Olivia, with a mouthful of pins. She shoved one into Isobel's hem. 'There. That's better.'

'If you say so,' said Isobel. She grinned at Milly. 'What do you think?'

Milly looked up and for the first time registered what Isobel was wearing. 'What happened to your dress?' she asked, trying not to sound appalled.

'I added some silk roses,' said Olivia. 'Aren't they pretty?'

Milly met Isobel's eye. 'Beautiful,' she said.

Isobel grinned. 'Be honest. Do I look like an idiot?'

'No,' said Milly. She looked at Isobel and frowned. 'You look tired.'

'That's what I said!' exclaimed Olivia. 'She looks peaky.'

'I don't look peaky,' said Isobel impatiently.

Milly gazed at her sister. Isobel's skin was almost grey; her fair, straight hair was lank. The garland of dried flowers in her hair only emphasised the lack of bloom in her cheeks. 'You'll look fine on the day,' she said uncertainly. 'Once you're wearing some make-up.'

'She's lost weight too,' said Olivia disapprovingly. 'We could do with taking this dress in.'

'I haven't lost that much,' said Isobel. 'Anyway, it doesn't matter what I look like. It's Milly's day, not mine.' She looked at Milly. 'How are you doing?'

'I'm OK,' said Milly. She met her sister's eyes. 'You know.'

'Yup,' said Isobel. She began to slip the pink dress off. 'Well, I might go upstairs and get sorted out.'

'I'll come and help you,' said Milly at once.

Isobel's room was next door to Milly's, at the top of the house. Now that she had left home it was occasionally used by bed-and-breakfast guests, but more often than not remained empty, waiting for her return.

'Jesus!' said Isobel, as she opened the door. 'What's all this?'

'Wedding presents,' said Milly. 'And this is just a few of them.'

They both looked silently around the room. Every spare piece of floor was piled high with boxes. A few had been opened. 'What's this?' said Isobel, prodding one of them.

'I don't know,' said Milly. 'I think it's a soup tureen.'

'A soup tureen,' echoed Isobel disbelievingly. 'Are you planning to cook soup when you're married?'

'I suppose so,' said Milly.

'You'll have to, now you've got a special tureen to put it in.' Isobel caught Milly's eye and she began to giggle, in spite of herself. 'You'll have to sit in every night, and ladle soup out of your soup tureen.'

'Shut up!' said Milly.

'And drink sherry out of your eight sherry glasses,' said Isobel, reading the label on another parcel. 'Married life is going to be a riot.'

'Don't!' said Milly. She was shaking with giggles.

'Electric breadmaker. Now, I wouldn't mind one of those.' Isobel looked up. 'Milly, are you OK?'

'I'm fine,' said Milly. But her giggles were turning into sobs; suddenly a pair of tears landed on her cheeks.

'Milly!' Isobel came over and put her hands on Milly's shoulders. 'What's wrong? What did you want to talk to me about in Paris?'

'Oh God, Isobel! Why didn't you call me back?' More tears landed on Milly's face. 'It's all gone wrong!'

'What do you mean?' Isobel's voice rose in alarm. 'What's happened?'

Milly looked at her for a long time.

'Come here,' she said at last. She went back into her own room, waited until Isobel had followed her inside, and closed the door. Then, as Isobel watched, she reached up inside the chimney and pulled down an old school shoe-bag, drawn tightly at the neck.

'What—'

'Wait,' said Milly, groping inside. She produced a box tied tightly with string. She tugged at the string and wrenched it off, taking the lid off with it. For a few moments she stared at the open box. Then she held it out to Isobel. 'OK,' she said. 'This is what's happened.'

'Blimey,' said Isobel. Staring up at them from inside the box was a photograph of Milly in a wedding dress, beaming through a cloud of confetti. Isobel picked it up and stared at it more closely. Glancing at

Milly, she put it down and picked up the photograph underneath. It was a picture of a dark-haired man kissing Milly's hand. Milly was simpering at the camera; she looked wildly happy.

Isobel looked up. 'Who the hell is he?'

'Who do you think he is, Isobel?' said Milly in a ragged voice. 'He's my husband.'

As Milly came to the end of her faltering story, Isobel exhaled sharply. She got up, strode to the fireplace and stood for a moment, saying nothing. Milly watched her apprehensively.

'I can't quite get my head round this,' said Isobel eventually. 'You really married a guy to keep him in the country?'

'Yes,' said Milly. She glanced at the wedding pictures; at herself, young, vibrant and happy. As she had told the story, all the romance and adventure of what she'd done had flooded back into her, and for the first time in years she'd felt a nostalgia for those heady Oxford days.

'Those bastards!' Isobel was shaking her head. 'They must have seen you coming!'

Milly stared at her sister. 'It wasn't like that,' she said. 'I helped them because I wanted to. They were my friends.'

'Friends,' echoed Isobel scathingly. 'Well, if they were such great friends, how come I never even heard about them?'

'We lost touch.'

'Oh, Milly,' said Isobel. She sighed. 'Did they pay you?'

'No,' said Milly. 'They gave me a necklace.' Her hands reached for the little pearls.

'Well, that's a lot of compensation,' said Isobel sarcastically. 'Bearing in mind you broke the law for them. You could have been prosecuted. The Home Office investigates phoney marriages, you know!'

'Don't go on about it, Isobel,' said Milly in a trembling voice. 'It's done, OK? There's nothing I can do about it.'

'OK,' said Isobel. 'Look, I'm sorry. This must be awful for you.' She picked up one of the pictures and stared at it for a few moments. 'And you've never told Simon about it.'

Milly shook her head, lips clamped together tightly.

'Well, you've got to,' said Isobel. 'Before this Alexander character decides to say something to him.'

'He might not say anything,' said Milly in a small voice.

Isobel sighed. 'Look, just tell him. He won't mind! There's no shame in it! Plenty of people are divorced these days.'

'I know they are, said Milly tightly. 'But I'm not.'

'What?' Isobel stared at her.

'I'm not divorced,' said Milly. 'I'm still married.'

There was a silence. 'You're still married?' said Isobel in a whisper. 'You're still *married*? But, Milly, your wedding's on Saturday!'

'I know!' cried Milly. And as Isobel gazed at her in horror, she buried her head in a cushion and sank into blinding tears.

'Why didn't you get a divorce?'

'We were always going to,' said Milly, biting her lip. 'Allan was going to sort it out. I even got some papers from his lawyers. But then it all fizzled out and I didn't hear any more. I never went to court, nothing.'

'And you never chased it up?'

Milly was silent.

'Not even when Simon asked you to marry him?' Isobel's voice sharpened. 'Not even when you started planning the wedding?'

'I didn't know how to! Allan left Oxford, I didn't know where he was, I lost all the papers . . . And the more time went on, the more it was as though the whole thing had never happened. A few years went by, and still nobody knew about it, and gradually it just . . . stopped existing.'

'What do you mean, it stopped existing?' said Isobel impatiently. 'Milly, you married the man! You can't change that.'

'It was three minutes in a registry office,' said Milly. 'One tiny signature, ten years ago. It wasn't a proper marriage. It wouldn't have counted.'

'What do you mean?' exclaimed Isobel. 'Of course it would have counted! Jesus, Milly, how can you be such a moron? I don't believe you sometimes!'

'Oh, shut up, Isobel!' cried Milly furiously.

'Fine. I'll shut up.'

'Fine.'

There was silence for a while. Milly glanced at her sister, momentarily distracted. 'Are you OK?' she said. 'Mummy's right, you look awful.'

'I'm fine,' said Isobel shortly.

'You're not anorexic, are you?'

'No!' Isobel laughed. 'Of course I'm not.'

'Well, you've been losing weight . . .'

'So have you.'

'Have I?' said Milly, plucking at her clothes. 'It's all this stress.'

'Well, don't stress,' said Isobel firmly. 'OK? Stressing is useless.' She sat down on the windowsill, pulled her knees up and hugged them. 'If only we knew how far your divorce had actually got.'

'It didn't get anywhere,' said Milly hopelessly. 'I told you, I never went to court.'

'So what? You don't have to go to court to get a divorce.'

There was a little pause, then Milly said, 'Oh.'

'Your lawyer goes for you.'

'What lawyer? I didn't have a lawyer.'

Isobel was silent, her brow wrinkled perplexedly. Then suddenly she looked up. 'Well, maybe you didn't need one. Maybe Allan did all the divorcing for you.'

Milly stared at her. 'Are you serious?'

'I don't know. It's possible.'

Milly swallowed. 'So I might be divorced after all?'

'I don't see why not. In theory.'

'Well, how can I find out?' said Milly agitatedly. 'Is there some official list of divorces somewhere?'

'I'm sure there is,' said Isobel. 'But there's a quicker way.'

'What?'

'Do what you should have done years ago. Phone your husband.'

'I can't,' said Milly. 'I don't know where he is. And anyway—' Milly broke off and looked away.

'What?'

'I don't want to speak to him, OK?' Suddenly tears were springing to her eyes. 'You're right, Isobel! Those two were never my friends, were they? They just used me. All these years, I've thought of them as my friends. They loved each other so much, and I wanted to help them . . .'

'Milly . . .'

'You know, I wrote to them when I got back,' said Milly. 'Allan used to write back, then gradually we lost touch. But I still thought of them as friends.' She broke off. 'And they were probably just laughing at me the whole time, weren't they?'

'No,' said Isobel. 'I'm sure they weren't.'

'They saw me coming,' said Milly bitterly. 'A naive, gullible little fool who would do anything they asked.'

'Look, don't think about it,' said Isobel, putting her arm round Milly's shoulders. 'That was ten years ago. It's over. Finished with. You have to look ahead. You have to find out about your divorce.' She took out a pen from her pocket and tore a piece of card off one of the wedding present boxes. 'Now come on,' she said briskly. 'Tell me where he used to live. And his parents. And Rupert, and Rupert's parents. And anyone else they used to know.'

An hour later, Milly looked up from the phone with triumph on her face. 'This could be it!' she exclaimed. 'They're giving me a number!'

'Hallelujah!' said Isobel. She gazed down at the road map in her lap. It had taken Milly a while to remember that Rupert's father had been a headmaster in Cornwall, and another while to narrow the village name down to something beginning with T. Since then they had been working down the index, asking Directory Enquiries each time for a Dr Carr.

'Here it is,' said Milly, putting down the receiver and staring at the row of digits.

'Great,' said Isobel. 'Well, get dialling!'

'OK,' said Milly. 'Let's see if we've got the right number.'

I should have done this before, she thought guiltily, as she picked up the phone.

'Hello?' Suddenly a man's voice was speaking in her ear and Milly gave a jump of fright.

'Hello,' she said cautiously. 'Is that Dr Carr?'

'Yes, speaking.' He sounded agreeably surprised that she should know his name.

'Oh good,' said Milly. 'May I . . . may I talk to Rupert, please?'

'He's not here, I'm afraid,' said the man. 'Have you tried his London number?'

'No, I haven't got it,' said Milly, glancing over at Isobel, who nodded approvingly. 'I'm an old friend from Oxford. Just catching up.'

'Ah, well he's in London now. Working as a barrister, you know, in Lincoln's Inn. But let me give you his home number.'

As Milly wrote down the number, she felt a bubble of astonishment expanding inside her. It was that simple.

'Have I met you?' Rupert's father was saying. 'Were you at Corpus?'

'No, I wasn't,' said Milly hurriedly. 'Sorry, I must go. Thank you so much.'

She put the receiver down and stared at it for a few seconds. Then she lifted it again and, before she could change her mind, tapped in Rupert's telephone number.

'Hello?' A girl's voice answered pleasantly.

'Hello,' said Milly. 'May I talk to Rupert, please?'

'Of course. Can I say who's calling?'

'It's Milly. Milly from Oxford.'

While the girl was gone, Milly twirled the telephone cord round her fingers and tried to keep her breathing steady.

Suddenly the girl was speaking again.

'I'm sorry,' she said, 'but Rupert's a bit tied up at the moment. Can I take a message?'

'Not really,' said Milly. 'Maybe he could call me back?'

'Of course,' said the girl.

Milly gave her the number, feeling a sudden relief. She should have done all this years ago. 'Are you Rupert's flatmate?' she asked.

'No,' said the girl. She sounded surprised. 'I'm Rupert's wife.'

Chapter Four

RUPERT CARR SAT by the fire of his Fulham house, shaking with fear. As Francesca put down the phone she gave him a curious look, and Rupert felt his insides turn to liquid. What had Milly said to his wife?

'Who's Milly?' said Francesca, picking up her glass of wine and taking a sip. 'Why don't you want to talk to her?'

'Just a weird girl I once knew,' said Rupert. He tried to shrug casually, but his face was hot with panic. 'I've no idea what she wants. I'll call her tomorrow at the office.' He forced himself to meet his wife's eyes steadily. 'But now I want to go over my reading.'

'OK,' she said, and smiled. She came over and sat down beside him on the sofa—a smart Colefax and Fowler sofa that had been a wedding present from one of her rich uncles. Opposite, on a matching sofa, sat Charlie and Sue Smith-Halliwell, their closest friends. The four of them were enjoying a quick glass of wine before leaving for the evening service at St Catherine's, at which Rupert would be reading. Now he avoided their eyes and stared down at his Bible. But the words swam before his eyes.

'Sorry, Charlie,' said Francesca. 'What were you saying?'

'Nothing very profound,' said Charlie, and laughed. 'I simply feel that it's up to people like us'—he gestured to the four of them—'to encourage young families into the church.'

'Instead of spending their Sunday mornings at Homestore,' said Francesca, then frowned. 'Do I mean Homestore?'

'After all,' said Charlie, 'families are the core structure of society.'

'Yes, but Charlie, the whole point is, they're not!' exclaimed Sue. 'It's all single parents and lesbians these days . . .'

'Did you read,' put in Francesca, 'about that new gay version of the New Testament? I was quite shocked.'

'The whole thing makes me feel physically sick,' said Charlie.

'Yes, but you can't ignore them,' said Sue. 'You can't just discount a whole section of society, can you? However misguided they are. What do you think, Rupert?'

Rupert looked up. His throat felt tight. 'Sorry,' he managed. 'I wasn't really listening.'

'Oh sorry,' said Sue. 'You want to concentrate, don't you?' She grinned at him. 'You'll be fine. What's the reading?'

'Matthew 26,' said Rupert. 'Peter's denial.'

'Peter,' echoed Charlie. 'What can it have been like, to be Peter?'

'Don't,' said Francesca, and shuddered. 'When I think how close I came to losing my faith altogether . . .'

'Yes, but you never denied Jesus, did you?' said Sue. She reached over and took Francesca's hand. 'Even the day after it happened, when I visited you in hospital.'

'I was so angry,' said Francesca. 'And ashamed. I felt as though I somehow didn't deserve a child.' She bit her lip.

'Yes, but you do,' said Charlie. 'You both do. And you'll have one. Remember, God's on your side.'

'I know,' said Francesca. She looked at Rupert. 'He's on our side, isn't he, darling?'

'Yes,' said Rupert. He felt as though the word had been forced off his tongue with a razor. 'God's on our side.'

But God wasn't on his side. He knew God wasn't on his side. As they left the house and headed towards St Catherine's Church—ten minutes away in a little Chelsea square—Rupert found himself lagging behind the others. He felt like lagging so slowly that he would be left behind altogether, to be forgotten about. But that was impossible. No one at St Catherine's was ever forgotten. Anyone who ventured through its portals immediately became part of the family. Even the most casual visitors were welcomed in with smiling enthusiasm, were made to feel important and loved, were exhorted to come again. Sceptics were welcomed almost more keenly than believers. They were encouraged to stand up and express their reservations; the more convincing their arguments, the broader the smiles. The members of St Catherine's wore their happiness visibly; they walked around in a shiny halo of certainty.

It had been that certainty which had attracted Rupert to St Catherine's. During his first year in chambers, miserably riddled with self-doubt, he had met Tom Innes, another barrister. Tom was friendly and outgoing. He had a secure social life built around St Catherine's, and was the happiest man Rupert had ever met. And Rupert had fallen with an almost desperate eagerness into Tom's life; into Christianity; into marriage. Now his life had a regular pattern, a meaning to it which he relished. He'd been married to Francesca for three contented years, his house was comfortable, his career was going well.

No one knew about his past life. No one knew about Allan. He had told nobody. Not Francesca, not Tom. He hadn't even told God.

Tom was waiting for them at the door as they arrived. He was dressed in a well-cut suit, Thomas Pink shirt, silk tie.

'Rupert! Good to see you. All set to read?'

'Absolutely!' said Rupert.

'Good man.' Tom smiled and Rupert felt a tingle go up his spine. 'I'm hoping you'll read at the next chambers Bible study group, if that's OK?'

'Of course,' said Rupert. 'What do you want me to do?'

'We'll talk about it later,' said Tom. He smiled again and moved away—and ridiculously, Rupert felt a small dart of disappointment.

In front of him, Francesca and Sue were greeting friends with warm hugs; Charlie was vigorously shaking the hand of an old schoolfriend. Everywhere he looked, well-dressed professionals were thronging.

Gradually the crowd dispersed, filing into pews. Some knelt, some sat looking expectantly ahead, some were still chatting. Many were holding crisp notes, ready for the collection. This congregation could afford to give extravagantly without their lifestyles being affected; they still drove expensive cars, ate good food, travelled abroad. They were an advertisers' dream audience, thought Rupert; if the church would only sell space on its walls, it would make a fortune. A grin passed over his face. That was the sort of remark Allan would have made.

'Rupert!' Tom's voice interrupted his thoughts. 'Come and sit at the front.'

'Right you are,' said Rupert. He sat down and looked at the congregation facing him. Familiar faces looked back at him; there were a few friendly smiles. Rupert tried to smile back. But suddenly he felt conspicuous under the scrutiny of five hundred Christian eyes. They all think I'm like them, he thought. But I'm not. I'm different.

He had always been different. As a child in Cornwall he'd been the headmaster's son; had been set apart before he even had a chance. While other boys' fathers drove tractors and drank beer, his father read Greek poetry and gave Rupert's friends detention. Dr Carr had been a popular headmaster, but that hadn't helped Rupert, who was by nature academic, poor at games and shy. The boys had scoffed at him, the girls had ignored him. Gradually he had developed a taste for being on his own.

Then, at around the age of thirteen, his childish features had matured into golden good looks, and things had become even worse. Suddenly the girls were following him around, giggling and propositioning him; suddenly the other boys were gazing at him in envy. It was assumed, because he was so good-looking, that he could sleep with any girl he wanted to; that indeed he had already done so. But the truth was that by the time he was eighteen, although he had taken out all the girls in the school, he was still a virgin.

He'd thought that at Oxford it would be different. That he would fit in. He'd arrived tanned and fit after a summer on the beach, and immediately attracted attention. Girls had flocked round him; intelligent, charming girls. The sort of girls he'd always longed for.

Except that now he'd got them, he didn't want them. He couldn't desire the girls he met, with their high foreheads and flicking hair and intellectual gravitas. It was the men in Oxford who had fascinated him. Foppish law students in waistcoats; crop-haired French students in Doc Martens. Members of the dramatic society piling into the pub after a show, wearing make-up and kissing each other playfully on the lips.

Occasionally one of these men would look up, notice Rupert staring, and invite him to join the group. A few times he'd been openly propositioned. But each time he'd backed away in terror. He couldn't be attracted to these men. He couldn't be gay. He simply couldn't.

By the end of his first year at Oxford he was still a virgin and lonelier than ever before. Because he was so good-looking, others in his college read his shyness as aloofness. They assumed his social life was catered for out of college and left him alone. By the end of Trinity term, he was spending most nights drinking whisky alone in his rooms.

And then he'd been sent for an extra tutorial to Allan Kepinski, an American junior research fellow at Keble. They'd discussed *Paradise Lost*; had grown more and more intense as the afternoon wore on. By the end of the tutorial Rupert was utterly caught up in the debate and the charged atmosphere between them. Allan was leaning forward in his chair, close to Rupert; their faces were almost touching.

Then, silently, Allan had leaned a little further and brushed his lips against Rupert's. Excitement had seared Rupert's body. He'd closed his eyes and willed Allan to kiss him again, to come even closer. And slowly, gently, Allan had put his arms round Rupert and pulled him down, off his armchair, onto the rug, into a new life.

That summer remained etched in Rupert's memory as a perfect bubble of intoxication. He'd subsumed himself entirely to Allan, had spent the entire summer vacation with him. He'd eaten with him, slept with him, loved him. No one else had seemed to exist.

The girl Milly had not interested him in the slightest. Allan had been quite taken with her—he'd been amused by her innocent babble, her charming naiveté. But to Rupert, she had been just another shallow girl. A waste of time, a waste of space, a rival for Allan's attention.

'Rupert?' The woman next to him nudged him and Rupert realised everybody had got to their feet for a hymn. Quickly he stood and tried to compose his thoughts.

But the thought of Milly had unsettled him; now he couldn't think of anything else. 'Milly from Oxford', she'd called herself tonight. A spasm of angry fear went through Rupert. What was she doing, ringing him after ten years? How had she got his number? Didn't she realise that it had all been a terrible mistake?

'Rupert! You're reading!' The woman was hissing at him, and abruptly Rupert came to. He carefully picked up his Bible and walked to the lectern, placed his Bible on it and faced his audience.

'I am going to read from St Matthew's Gospel,' he said. 'The theme is denial. How can we live with ourselves if we deny the one we love?'

He opened the Bible with trembling hands and took a deep breath. I'm reading this for God, he told himself—as all the readers at St Catherine's did. I'm reading this for Jesus. The picture of a grave, betrayed face filled his mind, and he felt a familiar stab of guilt. But it wasn't the face of Jesus he saw. It was the face of Allan.

The next morning, Milly and Isobel waited until a foursome of guests descended on the kitchen, then slipped out of the house before Olivia could ask them where they were going.

'OK,' said Isobel, as they reached the car. 'I think there's an eight thirty fast to London. You should catch that.'

'I didn't sleep all night,' said Milly, as Isobel began to drive off. 'I was so tense.' She wound a strand of hair round her finger. 'For ten years I've thought I was married. And now . . . maybe I'm not!'

Isobel glanced at her sister. 'I wouldn't celebrate yet.'

'I'm not celebrating,' said Milly. 'I'm just . . . hopeful. After all, why would Allan begin divorce proceedings and not see them through?'

'Of course,' said Isobel, 'if your charming friend Rupert had bothered to call back, you might know, one way or the other.'

'I know,' said Milly. 'Bastard. *Ignoring* me like that. He must know I'm in some kind of trouble. Why else would I ring him?' Her voice rose incredulously. 'And how come he's suddenly got a wife?'

Isobel shrugged. 'There's your answer. That's why he didn't call back.'

Milly drew a circle on the fogged-up passenger window and looked out of it at the passing streets, at the commuters hurrying along the pavements, scuffing the new morning snow into slush.

'So, what are you going to do?' said Isobel suddenly. 'If you find out you are divorced? Will you tell Simon?'

There was silence. 'I don't know,' said Milly slowly.

'But, Milly—'

'I know I should have told him in the first place,' interrupted Milly. 'But everything's different now! Our wedding is in two days' time. Everything's perfect. Why ruin it all with . . . this?'

Isobel was silent and Milly looked round defensively. 'I suppose you think I should tell him anyway. I suppose you think you can't have secrets from someone you love.'

'No,' said Isobel. 'Actually, I don't.' Milly looked at her in surprise. Isobel's gaze was averted; her hands gripped the steering wheel tightly. 'You can love someone and still keep a secret from them,' she said.

'But—'

'If it's something that would trouble them needlessly.' Isobel's voice grew slightly harsher. 'Some secrets are best left unsaid.'

'Like what?' Milly gazed at Isobel. 'What are you talking about?'

'Nothing.'

'Have you got a secret?'

Isobel was silent. For a few minutes Milly stared at her sister, scanning her face, trying to read her expression. Then suddenly it came to her. A thunderbolt of horrific realisation.

'You're ill, aren't you?' she said shakily. 'That's why you're so pale. You've got something terrible wrong with you—and you're not telling us! You think it's best left unsaid! What, until you *die*?'

'Milly!' Isobel snapped. 'I'm not going to die. I'm not ill.'

'Well, what's your secret, then?'

'I never said I had one. I was talking theoretically.' Isobel pulled into the station car park. 'Here we are.' She opened the car door and, without looking at Milly, got out.

Reluctantly, Milly followed. 'Oh God,' she said, catching up with Isobel, who was striding towards the station concourse. 'I don't want to go. I don't want to find out.'

'You've got to go. You haven't got any choice.' Suddenly Isobel's face changed colour. 'Get your ticket,' she said in a gasp. 'I'll be back in a moment.' And to Milly's astonishment, Isobel began running towards the Ladies. Milly gazed after her for a moment, then turned round.

'A day return to London, please,' she said to the girl behind the glass. What on earth was wrong with Isobel? She wasn't ill, but she wasn't normal, either. She couldn't be pregnant—she didn't have a boyfriend.

'Right,' said Isobel, reappearing by her side. 'Got everything?'

'You're pregnant!' hissed Milly. 'Aren't you?'

Isobel took a step back. She looked as though she'd been slapped in the face. 'No,' she said.

'Yes you are. It's obvious! You're pregnant. Bloody hell, Isobel, you should have told me. I'm going to be an aunt!'

'No,' said Isobel tightly. 'You're not.'

Milly stared at her uncomprehendingly. Then suddenly she realised what Isobel was saying. 'No! You can't do that! You can't! Isobel.'

'I don't know. I don't know, OK?' Isobel's voice rose savagely. She took a couple of paces towards Milly, clenched her hands, then took a couple of paces back, like a caged animal.

'Isobel—'

'You've got a train to catch,' said Isobel. 'Go on.' She looked up at Milly with glittering eyes. 'Go on!'

'I'll catch a later train,' said Milly.

'No! You haven't got time for that. Go on!'

Milly stared at her sister for a few silent seconds. She had never seen Isobel looking vulnerable before; it made her feel uneasy. 'OK,' she said. 'I'll go. But we'll talk about . . . about it—when I get back.'

'Maybe,' said Isobel. When Milly looked back from the ticket barrier to wave goodbye, she had already gone.

Isobel arrived back home to find Olivia waiting for her in the kitchen.

'Where's Milly?' she demanded.

'She's gone to London to get a present for Simon,' said Isobel, reaching for the biscuit tin.

Olivia stared at her. 'Are you serious? All the way to London? She can get a perfectly good present for him in Bath!'

'She just felt like going to London,' said Isobel, ripping open a packet of digestives. 'Does it matter?'

'Yes,' said Olivia crossly. 'Of course it matters! Do you know what day it is today?'

'Yes, I do,' said Isobel, biting into a biscuit with relish. 'It's Thursday.'

'Exactly! Only two days to go! I've a thousand things to do and Milly was supposed to be helping me. She's such a thoughtless girl.'

'Give her a break,' said Isobel. 'She's got a lot on her mind.'

'So have I, darling! I've got to check all the place settings—and to top it all, the marquee's arrived. Who's going to come with me to see it?'

There was silence.

'Oh God,' said Isobel, stuffing a biscuit into her mouth. 'All right.'

Simon and Harry were walking along Parham Place. It was a wide road, civilised and expensive and, at this time in the morning, busy—as its residents left for their jobs in the professions and the law and the higher echelons of industry.

'Here we are,' said Harry as he stopped by a flight of stone steps leading to a glossy blue door. 'Have you got the keys?'

Silently, Simon walked up the steps and put the key in the lock. He stepped into a spacious hall and opened another door, to the left.

'Go on then,' said Harry. 'In you go.'

As he stepped inside, Simon immediately remembered why he and Milly had fallen in love with the flat. He was surrounded by space; by white walls and high, distant ceilings and acres of wooden floor.

'Like it?' said Harry.

'It's great,' Simon said, wandering over to a mantelpiece. 'It's great,' he repeated. He didn't trust himself to say any more. The flat was more than great. It was beautiful, perfect. But as he stood, looking around, all he could feel was resentful misery.

'Nice high ceilings,' said Harry. He wandered over to a window, his steps echoing on the bare floor. 'Nice wooden shutters,' he said, tapping one appraisingly.

'It's a beautiful flat,' said Simon stiffly. 'Milly will love it.'

'Good,' said Harry.

They wandered out of the main room into a light, wide corridor. The bigger bedroom overlooked the garden: long windows opened onto a tiny wrought-iron balcony. 'You don't need more than two bedrooms,' said Harry. There was a slight question mark in his voice. 'Not thinking of having children straight away.'

'Oh no. Plenty of time for that. Milly's only twenty-eight.'

'Still . . .' Harry turned a switch by the door and the bare bulb swinging from the ceiling suddenly came alight. 'You'll need lampshades.'

'Yes,' said Simon. He looked at his father. 'Why?' he said. 'Do you think we should have children straight away?'

'No,' said Harry emphatically. 'Definitely not.'

'Really? But you did.'

'I know. That was our mistake.'

Simon stiffened. 'I was a mistake, was I?' he said.

'You know that's not what I meant,' said Harry irritably. 'Stop being so bloody touchy.'

'What do you expect? You're telling me I wasn't wanted. Well, I'm sorry for gate-crashing the party,' said Simon furiously.

'Listen, Simon. All I meant was—'

'I know what you meant!' said Simon, striding to the window. He stared out at the snowy garden, trying to keep his voice under control. 'I was an inconvenience, wasn't I? I still am.'

'Simon—'

'Well, look, Dad. I won't inconvenience you any more, OK?' Simon wheeled round, his face trembling. 'Thanks very much, but you can keep your flat. Milly and I will make our own arrangements.' He tossed the keys onto the polished floor and walked quickly to the door.

'Simon!' said Harry angrily. 'Don't be so fucking stupid!'

'I'm sorry I've been in your way all these years,' said Simon at the door. 'But after Saturday, I'll be gone. You'll never have to see me again. Maybe that'll be a relief for both of us.'

And he slammed the door, leaving Harry alone, staring at the keys winking in the winter sunlight.

It was the biggest marquee Isobel had ever seen. It billowed magnificently in the wind, a huge white mushroom, dwarfing the cars and vans parked next to it. 'Bloody hell!' she said. 'How much is this costing?'

Olivia winced. 'Quiet, darling!' she said. 'Someone might hear.'

'I'm sure they all know how much it costs,' said Isobel, staring at the stream of young men and women coming in and out of the marquee, carrying crates or lengths of flex or pieces of wooden boarding.

'Over there we'll have a tube linking the marquee to the back of Pinnacle Hall,' said Olivia, gesturing. 'And cloakrooms.'

'Bloody hell,' said Isobel again. 'It looks like a circus. Come on, let's look inside.'

The two of them picked their way over the snowy ground towards the marquee and lifted a flap.

'Blimey,' said Isobel slowly. 'It looks even more enormous on the inside.' They both gazed around the massive space. People were everywhere, carrying chairs, setting up heaters, fixing lights.

'It's not so big,' said Olivia uncertainly. 'Once the chairs and tables are all in, it'll be quite cosy.' She paused. 'Perhaps not cosy, exactly . . .'

'Well, I take my hat off to Harry!' said Isobel. 'This is something else.'

'We've contributed too!' exclaimed Olivia crossly. 'More than you might realise. And anyway, Harry can afford it.'

'I don't doubt that.'

'He's very fond of Milly, you know.'

'I know,' said Isobel. 'Gosh . . .' She looked around the marquee and bit her lip.

'What?' said Olivia suspiciously.

'Oh, I don't know,' said Isobel. 'All this preparation, all this money. All for one day.'

'What's wrong with that?'

'Nothing, I'm sure it'll all go swimmingly.'

'Isobel, what's wrong with you? You're not jealous of Milly, are you?'

'Probably,' said Isobel lightly.

'You could get married, you know! But you've chosen not to.'

'I've never been asked,' said Isobel.

'That's not the point!'

'I think it is,' said Isobel, 'very much the point.' And to her horror she suddenly felt tears pricking her eyes. She turned away from her mother and stalked off, towards the far end of the marquee.

Olivia hurried obliviously after her. 'This is where the food will be,' she called excitedly. 'And that's where the swans will be.'

'The swans?' said Isobel, turning round.

'We're going to have swans made out of ice,' said Olivia. 'And each one will be filled with oysters.'

'No!' Isobel's laugh pealed around the marquee. 'That's the tackiest thing I've ever heard of. Whose idea was that?'

'Harry's,' said Olivia defensively. 'He said he thought weddings were such tacky affairs anyway, there was no point trying to be tasteful. So we decided to go for broke!'

'He will be broke,' said Isobel, 'after he's fed all his guests oysters.'

'No, he won't!' snapped Olivia. 'Stop saying things like that, Isobel.'

'All right,' said Isobel in mollifying tones. 'Truthfully, I think it's going to be a lovely wedding.' She looked round the vast tent and, for the hundredth time that day, wondered how Milly was getting on. 'Milly will have the time of her life.'

'She doesn't deserve it,' said Olivia crossly. 'Rushing off to London like this. There are only two days to go, you know! Two days!'

'I know,' said Isobel. She bit her lip. 'And believe me, so does Milly.'

By the time Milly reached the building in High Holborn where the divorce register was held, a winter sun had begun to shine and she could feel an optimistic excitement rising through her. Within minutes she would know, one way or the other. And suddenly she felt sure she knew which way the answer would be. As she entered and found the department she needed, her spirits were lifted further. The man in charge of divorce decrees had twinkling eyes and a quick computer.

'You're in luck,' he said cheerfully, as he tapped in her details. 'All records since 1981 are on computer file.' He winked at her. 'But you would have been just a baby then! Now, just bear with me, my dear . . .'

Milly beamed back at him. Already she was planning what she would do when she'd received confirmation of her divorce. She would take a taxi to Harvey Nichols and go straight up to the fifth floor and buy herself a buck's fizz. And then she would call Isobel. And then she would—

Her thoughts were interrupted as the computer pinged. The man peered at the screen. 'No,' he said in surprise. 'Not found.'

A stone dropped through Milly's stomach.

'What?' she said. Her lips felt suddenly dry. 'What do you mean?'

'There's no decree absolute listed,' said the man, tapping again. The computer pinged again and he frowned. 'Not for those names.'

'But there has to be,' said Milly. 'There has to be.'

'I've tried twice,' said the man. He looked up. 'Are you sure the spellings are correct?'

Milly swallowed. 'Quite sure.'

'And you're sure the petitioner applied for a decree absolute?' Milly looked at him numbly. She didn't know what he was talking about.

'No,' she said. 'I'm not sure.'

The man nodded back at her, and explained. 'Six weeks after the decree nisi is issued, the petitioner has to apply for a decree absolute.'

'Yes,' said Milly, 'I see.'

'You *were* issued with a decree nisi, weren't you, dear?' he asked, a sudden curiosity in his eyes.

'Yes,' she said quickly, before he could ask anything else. 'Of course I was. I'll . . . I'll go back and check up on what happened.'

'If you require any legal advice—'

'No, thank you,' said Milly, backing away. 'You've been very kind. Thank you so much.' She shot him an over-bright smile as she walked out of the room, feeling sick and panicky. She'd been right all along. Allan was a selfish, unscrupulous bastard. And he'd left her well and truly in the lurch.

She reached the street and began to walk blindly, aware of nothing but the seeds of panic already sprouting rapaciously inside her mind. She was only back where she'd been before—but somehow her position now seemed infinitely worse; infinitely more precarious. An image came to her of Alexander's malicious, gleaming smile, like the grin of a vulture. What was she to do? What *could* she do?

It was lunchtime, and the pavement was crammed with people hurrying briskly along, hailing taxis, crowding into shops and pubs and sandwich bars. She gazed at the blurry crowds of people, wishing with all her heart to be one of them, and not herself. She would have liked to be that cheerful-looking girl eating a croissant, or that calm-looking lady getting onto a bus, or . . .

Suddenly Milly froze. She blinked a few times, and looked again. But the face she'd glimpsed was already gone, swallowed up by the surging crowds. Filled with panic, she hurried forward. For a few moments she could see nothing but strangers: girls in brightly coloured coats, men in dark suits, lawyers still in their courtroom wigs. Then her heart stopped. There he was again, walking along the other side of the street, talking to another man. He was older than she remembered, and fatter. But it was definitely him. It was Rupert.

A surge of white-hot hatred rose through Milly as she stared at him. How dared he saunter along the streets of London, so happy and at ease with himself? How dared he be so oblivious of all that she was going through? Because of him and Allan.

With a pounding heart, she began to run towards him.

'Rupert,' she cried, when she caught up with him. 'Rupert!' He turned round and looked at her with friendly eyes devoid of recognition.

'I'm sorry,' he said. 'Do I . . .'

'It's me,' said Milly, summoning up the coldest, bitterest voice she possessed. 'It's Milly. From Oxford.'

'What?' Rupert's face drained of colour. He took a step back.

'Yes, that's right,' said Milly. 'It's me. I don't suppose you thought you'd ever see me again, did you, Rupert?'

'Don't be silly!' said Rupert in jocular tones. He glanced uneasily at his friend. 'How are things going, anyway?'

'Things,' said Milly, 'could not be going more badly, thanks for asking. Oh, and thanks for calling back last night. I really appreciated it.'

'I didn't have time,' said Rupert. His blue eyes flashed a quick look of hatred at her and Milly glared back. 'And now, I'm afraid I'm a bit busy.' He looked at his friend. 'Shall we go, Tom?'

'Don't you dare!' exclaimed Milly furiously. 'My life is in ruins, and it's all your fault. You and bloody Allan Kepinski.'

'Rupert,' said Tom. 'Maybe you and Milly should have a little talk?'

'I don't know what she's going on about,' said Rupert. 'She's mad.'

'Even more reason,' said Tom quietly to Rupert. 'Here is a distressed soul. And perhaps you can help. Why don't I do your reading? And you can catch up with Milly.' He smiled at her. 'Good to meet you, Milly,' he said, grasping her hand. 'I'll give you a call, Rupert,' and he was off, across the road.

Milly and Rupert looked at each other.

'You bitch,' hissed Rupert. 'Are you trying to ruin my life?'

'Ruin your life?' exclaimed Milly in disbelief. 'Ruin *your* life? Do you realise what you did to me? You used me!'

'It was your choice,' said Rupert brusquely, starting to walk away. 'If you didn't want to do it, you should have said no.'

'I was eighteen years old!' shrieked Milly. 'I didn't know then that one day I'd want to marry someone else, someone I really loved . . .'

'So what?' said Rupert tersely. 'You got a divorce, didn't you?'

'No!' sobbed Milly, 'I didn't! And I don't know where Allan is! And my wedding's on Saturday!'

'Well, what am I supposed to do about it?'

'I need to find Allan! Where is he?'

'I don't know,' said Rupert, beginning to walk off again. 'I can't help you. Now, leave me alone.'

Milly gazed at him, anger rising through her like hot lava.

'You can't just walk away!' she shrieked. 'You've got to help me!' She began to run after him, grabbed his jacket and managed to force him to a standstill.

'Listen, I did you and Allan a favour. I did you a huge, huge, enormous favour. And now it's time for you to do me a tiny little one. You owe it to me.'

She stared hard at him, watching as thoughts ran through his head; watching as his expression gradually changed. Eventually he sighed, and rubbed his forehead. 'OK,' he said. 'We'd better talk.'

They went to an old pub on Fleet Street, full of dark wood, winding stairs and little, hidden nooks. Rupert bought a bottle of wine and two plates of bread and cheese and set them down on a tiny table in an alcove. He sat down heavily, took a deep slug of wine and leaned back. Milly looked at him. Her anger had subsided a little; she was able to study him calmly. He was still handsome, still striking—but his face was pinker and more fleshy than it had been at Oxford. Ten years ago, she thought, he had been a golden, glowing youth. Now he looked like an unhappy, middle-aged man.

'You look terrible, Rupert,' said Milly frankly. 'Are you happy?'

'I'm very happy. Thank you.' He took another deep slug of wine.

Milly raised her eyebrows. 'Are you sure?'

'Milly, we're here to talk about you,' said Rupert impatiently. 'Not me. What precisely is your problem?'

Milly looked at him for a silent moment, then sat back.

'What's my problem?' she said lightly, as though carefully considering the matter. 'My problem is that on Saturday I'm getting married to a man I love very much. My mother has organised the hugest wedding in the world. It's going to be beautiful and romantic and perfect in every detail.' She looked up with bright eyes like daggers. 'Oh, except one. I'm still married to your friend Allan Kepinski.'

Rupert winced. 'I don't understand. Why aren't you divorced?'

'Ask Allan! He was organising it. I got some papers through the post. I signed the slip and sent them back. But I never heard anything more.'

'And you never looked into it?'

'No one knew,' said Milly. 'It didn't seem to matter.'

'The fact that you were married didn't seem to matter?' said Rupert incredulously.

'No one knew!' she repeated. 'No one suspected anything!'

'So what happened?' said Rupert.

Milly picked up her wineglass and cradled it in both hands. 'Now someone knows,' she said. 'Someone who saw us in Oxford. And he's threatening to say something.'

'I see.'

'Don't look at me like that,' said Milly sharply. 'OK, I know I should have done something about it. But Allan said he would sort it all out and I trusted him! I trusted you both. I thought you were my friends.'

'We were,' said Rupert after a pause.

'Bullshit!' cried Milly. Her cheeks began to pinken. 'You just used me for what you wanted—and then as soon as I was gone, you forgot about me. You never wrote, never called . . .' She crashed her glass down on the table. 'Did you get all those letters I wrote to you?'

'Yes,' said Rupert, running a hand through his hair. 'I'm sorry. I should have replied. But . . . it was a difficult time.'

'At least Allan wrote. But you couldn't even be bothered to do that. And I still believed in you.' She shook her head. 'God, I was a little fool.'

'We were all fools,' said Rupert. 'Look, Milly, for what it's worth, I'm sorry. I honestly wish none of it had ever happened. None of it!'

Milly stared at him. His eyes were darting miserably about; fronds of golden hair were quivering above his brow. 'Rupert, what's going on?' she demanded. 'How come you're married?'

'I'm married,' said Rupert. He shrugged. 'That's all there is to it.'

She hesitated. 'When did you realise that you were straight?'

'Milly, I don't want to talk about it,' said Rupert. 'All right?' He reached for his glass with a trembling hand and took a gulp of wine.

Milly gave a shrug and leaned back in her chair. Idly she allowed her eyes to roam around the room.

'You've changed a lot since Oxford, you know,' said Rupert abruptly. 'You've grown up. I wouldn't have recognised you.'

Milly gave him a hard look. 'We're all allowed to change, Rupert.'

'I know,' said Rupert, flushing. 'And you look . . . great.' He leaned forward. 'Tell me about the guy you're marrying.'

'He's called Simon Pinnacle,' said Milly, and watched as Rupert's expression changed.

'No relation to—'

'His son,' said Milly. She gave a half-smile. 'I told you. This is the wedding of the century.'

Rupert stared at Milly for a moment, then sighed. 'OK. Tell me exactly how far your divorce got.'

'I don't know,' said Milly. 'I told you. I got some papers through the post and I signed something and sent it back.'

'And what precisely were these papers?'

'How should I know?' said Milly exasperatedly. 'Would you be able to tell one legal document from another?'

'I'm a lawyer,' said Rupert. 'But I get your point. You need to speak to Allan.'

'I know that!' said Milly. 'But I don't know where he is. Do you?'

A look of pain flashed briefly across Rupert's face. 'No, I don't.'

'But you can find out?'

Rupert was silent. Milly stared at him in disbelief.

'Rupert, you have to help me! You're my only link with him. Where did he go after Oxford?'

'Manchester,' said Rupert.

'Why did he leave Oxford?'

Rupert took a gulp of wine. 'Because we split up,' he said.

'Oh,' said Milly, taken aback. 'I'm sorry. When was that?'

'At the end of that summer,' said Rupert in a low voice. 'September.' Milly stared at him in disbelief. Her heart began to thump.

'You're telling me you were only together for two months?' cried Milly in anguish. 'I wrecked my life to keep you together for two *months*?'

'Yes!'

'Then fuck you!' With a sudden surge of fury, Milly threw her wine at Rupert. It hit him straight in the face, staining his skin like blood. 'Fuck you,' she said again, trembling. 'I broke the law for you! Now I'm stuck with a first husband I don't want! And all so you could change your mind after two months.'

For a long while, neither of them spoke. Rupert sat motionless.

'You're right,' he said finally. He sounded broken. 'I've fucked it all up. I've fucked up your life, I've fucked up my life. And Allan . . .'

Milly cleared her throat uncomfortably. 'Did he . . .'

'He loved me,' said Rupert, as though to himself. 'That's what I didn't get. He loved me.'

'Look, Rupert, I'm sorry,' said Milly awkwardly. 'About the wine. And—everything.'

'Don't apologise,' said Rupert fiercely. 'Don't apologise.' He looked up. 'Milly, I'll find Allan for you. And I'll clear up your divorce. But I can't do it in time for Saturday. It isn't physically possible.'

'I know.'

'What will you do?'

There was a long silence. 'I don't know,' said Milly eventually. She closed her eyes and massaged her brow. 'I can't cancel the wedding now,' she said slowly. 'I just can't do that to my mother.'

'So you'll just go ahead?' said Rupert incredulously. 'But what about whoever it is who's threatening to say something?'

Milly shrugged. 'I'll . . . I'll keep him quiet. Somehow.'

'You do realise,' said Rupert, lowering his voice, 'that what you're proposing is bigamy. You would be breaking the law.'

'Thanks for the warning,' said Milly sarcastically. 'But I've been there before, remember?' She looked at him silently for a moment. 'What do you think? Would I get away with it?'

'I expect so,' said Rupert. 'Are you serious?'

'I don't know,' said Milly. 'I really don't know.'

A while later, when the wine was finished, Rupert went and collected two cups of black coffee from the bar. As he returned, Milly looked up at him. His face was clean but his shirt and jacket were still spattered with red wine. 'You won't be able to go back to work this afternoon,' she said.

'It doesn't matter,' said Rupert. 'Nothing's happening.' He handed Milly a cup of coffee and sat down.

There was silence for a while, then Milly said, 'Does your wife know? About you and Allan?'

Rupert looked at her with bloodshot eyes. 'What do you think?'

'But why?' said Milly. 'Are you afraid she wouldn't understand?'

Rupert gave a short little laugh. 'That's underestimating it.'

'But why not? If she loves you . . .'

'Would you understand?' Rupert glared at her. 'If your Simon turned round and told you he'd once had an affair with another man?'

'Yes,' said Milly uncertainly. 'I think I would.'

'You wouldn't,' said Rupert scathingly. 'I can tell you that now. And neither would Francesca.'

'You're not giving her a chance, Rupert! Be honest with her.'

'Be honest? You're telling *me* to be honest?'

'That's my whole point!' said Milly, leaning forward earnestly. 'I should have been honest with Simon from the start. I should have told him everything. But as it is . . .' She spread her hands helplessly on the table. 'As it is, I'm in a mess.' She paused and took a sip of coffee. 'What I'm saying is, if I had the chance to go back and tell Simon the truth, I would grab it. And you've got that chance, Rupert! You've got the chance to be honest with Francesca before . . . before it all starts going wrong.'

'It's different,' said Rupert stiffly.

'No, it isn't. It's just another secret. All secrets come out in the end. If you don't tell her, she'll find out some other way. Do you want to risk that? Just tell her, Rupert! Tell her.'

'Tell me what?'

A girl's voice hit Milly's ears like a whiplash, and her head jerked round in shock. Standing at the entrance to the alcove was a pretty girl with pale red hair. Next to her was Rupert's friend Tom.

'Tell me what?' the girl repeated in high, sharp tones, glancing from Rupert to Milly and back again. 'Rupert, what's happened to you?'

'Francesca,' said Rupert shakily. 'Don't worry, it's just wine.'

'Hi, Rupe!' said Tom easily. 'We thought we'd find you here.'

'So this is Milly,' said the girl. She looked at Rupert with gimlet eyes. 'Tom told me you'd met up with your old friend. Milly from Oxford.' She gave a strange little laugh. 'The funny thing is, Rupert, you told me you didn't want to talk to her. You told me she was a nut.'

'A nut?' cried Milly indignantly.

'I didn't want to talk to her!' said Rupert. 'I don't.' He looked at Milly, blue eyes full of dismay.

'Look,' she said hurriedly. 'Maybe I'd better go.' She stood up. 'Nice to meet you,' she said to Francesca. 'Honestly, I am just an old friend.'

'Is that right?' said Francesca. Her pale eyes bored into Rupert's. 'So what is it that you've got to tell me?'

'Bye, Rupert,' said Milly hastily. 'Bye, Francesca. I'm afraid I've got a train to catch.'

Avoiding Rupert's eyes, she quickly made her way across the bar and bounded up the wooden steps to the street. As she stepped into the fresh air she realised that she'd left her cigarette lighter on the table. It seemed a small price to pay for her escape.

Isobel was sitting in the kitchen at One Bertram Street, stitching blue ribbon onto a lace garter. Olivia sat opposite her, folding bright pink silk into an elaborate bow. Every so often she looked up at Isobel with a dissatisfied expression, then looked down again. Eventually she put down the bow and stood up to fill the kettle.

'How's Paul?' she said brightly.

'Who?' said Isobel.

'Paul! Paul the doctor. Do you still see much of him?'

'Oh, him,' said Isobel. She screwed up her face. 'No, I haven't seen him for months. I only went out with him a few times.'

'What a shame,' said Olivia. 'He was so charming.'

'He was OK,' said Isobel. 'It just didn't work out.'

'Oh, darling. I'm so sorry.'

'I'm not,' said Isobel. 'If you must know, he was a bit weird.'

'Weird?' said Olivia suspiciously. 'What kind of weird?'

'Just weird,' said Isobel.

'Well, I thought he was very nice,' said Olivia, pouring boiling water into the teapot. Isobel said nothing, but her needle jerked savagely in and out of the fabric.

'I saw Brenda White the other day,' said Olivia, as though changing the subject. 'Her daughter's getting married in June.'

'Really?' Isobel looked up. 'Is she still working for Shell?'

'I've no idea,' said Olivia testily. Then she smiled at Isobel. 'What I was going to say was, she met her husband at an evening function organised for young professionals. In some smart London restaurant. Apparently the place was *packed* full of interesting men. Brenda said she could get the number if you're interested.'

'No, thanks.'

'Darling, you're not giving yourself a chance!'

'No!' snapped Isobel. She put down her needle and looked up. '*You're* not giving me a chance! You're treating me as though I don't have any function in life except to find a husband.'

'What about babies?' said Olivia sharply.

Colour flooded Isobel's face. 'Maybe I'll just have a baby without a husband,' she said after a pause. 'People do, you know.'

'Oh, now you're just being silly,' said Olivia crossly. 'A child needs a proper family.' She brought the teapot over to the table, sat down, and opened her red book. 'Right. What else needs doing?'

Isobel stared at the teapot without moving. It was large and decorated with painted ducks; they'd used it at family teas ever since she could remember. Ever since she and Milly had sat side by side in matching smocks, eating Marmite sandwiches. A child needs a proper family. What the hell was a proper family?

'Do you know?' said Olivia, looking up in surprise. 'I think I've done everything for today. I've ticked everything off my list.'

'Good,' said Isobel. 'So you should spend the evening doing something fun. Not hymn sheets. Not shoe trimmings. Fun!' She met Olivia's eyes sternly and, as the phone rang, they both began to giggle.

'I'll get that,' said Olivia.

'If it's Milly,' said Isobel quickly, 'I'll speak to her.'

'Hello, One Bertram Street,' said Olivia. She pulled a face at Isobel. 'Hello, Canon Lytton! How are you? Yes . . . Yes . . . No!'

Her voice suddenly changed, and Isobel looked up.

'No, I don't. I've no idea what you're talking about. Yes, perhaps you'd better. We'll see you then.'

Olivia put the phone down and looked perplexedly at Isobel.

'Is something wrong?' said Isobel.

'That was Canon Lytton,' she said. 'He said he'd received some information, and he'd like to come and discuss it with us.'

'What information?' said Isobel, her heart starting to thump.

'I don't know,' said Olivia. She raised puzzled blue eyes to meet Isobel's. 'Something to do with Milly. He wouldn't say what.'

Rupert and Francesca sat silently in their drawing room, looking at each other. On Tom's suggestion, they had both phoned their offices to take the rest of the afternoon off. Neither had spoken in the taxi back to Fulham. Francesca had shot Rupert the occasional hurt, bewildered glance; he had sat, staring at his hands, wondering what he was going to say. Wondering whether to concoct a story or to tell her the truth.

'Right,' said Francesca. 'Well, here we are.' She gazed at him expectantly and Rupert looked away. From outside he could hear birds singing, cars starting, the wailing of a toddler. Afternoon sounds that he wasn't used to hearing. He felt self-conscious, sitting at home in the winter daylight; self-conscious, facing his wife's taut, anxious gaze.

'Rupert, what's wrong?' cried Francesca. 'Why are you so strange? Are you in love with Milly?'

'No!' exclaimed Rupert.

'But you had an affair with her when you were at Oxford.'

'No,' said Rupert.

'No?' Francesca stared at him. 'You never went out with her?'

'No.' He would have laughed if he hadn't felt so nervous. 'Francesca, you're on the wrong track completely.' He tried a smile. 'Look, can't we just forget all this? Milly is an old friend. Full stop.'

'I wish I could believe you,' said Francesca. 'But it's obvious that something's going on.' Her voice rose. 'Rupert, I'm your wife! Your loyalty is to me. If you have a secret, then I deserve to know it.'

Rupert stared at his wife. Her pale eyes were shining slightly; her hands were clasped tightly in her lap. 'I don't want to lose you,' he found himself saying. 'I love you. I love our marriage. I'll love our children, when we have them.'

'But?' she said anxiously. 'What's the but?'

Rupert didn't know how to reply, where to start.

'Are you in trouble?' said Francesca suddenly. 'Are you hiding something from me?' Her voice rose in alarm. 'Rupert?'

'No!' said Rupert. 'I'm not in trouble.' He took a deep breath. 'When I was at Oxford,' he said, and stopped. 'There was a man.'

'A man?'

Rupert looked up and met Francesca's eyes. They were blank, unsuspecting, waiting for him to go on. 'I had a relationship with him,' he said, gazing at her. 'A close relationship.'

He paused, willing her brain to process what he had said and make a deduction. For what seemed like hours, her eyes remained empty.

And then suddenly it happened. Her eyes snapped open and shut like a cat's. She had understood. She had understood what he was saying. Rupert gazed at her fearfully, trying to gauge her reaction. 'I don't understand,' she said at last, her voice suddenly truculent with alarm. 'Rupert, you're not making any sense! This is just a waste of time.'

She got up from the sofa and began to brush imaginary crumbs off her lap, avoiding his eye.

'Darling, I was wrong to doubt you,' she said. 'I'm sorry. Of course you have the right to see anybody you like. Shall we just forget this ever happened?'

Rupert stared at her in disbelief. Was she serious? Was she really willing to ignore the questions that must be gnawing at her brain?

'I'll make some tea, shall I?' continued Francesca with a bright tautness. 'And get some scones out of the freezer. It'll be quite a treat!'

'Francesca,' said Rupert, 'stop it. You heard what I said. Don't you want to know any more?' He stood up and took her wrist. 'You heard what I said.'

'Rupert!' said Francesca, giving a little laugh. 'I've already apologised for mistrusting you. What else do you want?'

'I want . . .' began Rupert. His grip tightened on her wrist; he felt a sudden certainty anchoring him. 'I want to tell you everything.'

'You've told me everything,' said Francesca quickly. 'I understand completely. It was a silly mix-up.'

Leave her alone, Rupert told himself. Don't say any more; just leave her alone. But the urge to talk was unbearable; having begun, he could no longer contain himself.

'I had an affair with a man,' he said.

He paused, and waited for a reaction. A scream; a gasp. But Francesca's head remained bowed. She did not move.

'His name was Allan.' He swallowed. 'I loved him.'

He gazed at Francesca, hardly daring to breathe. Suddenly she looked up. 'You're making it up,' she said. 'You're feeling guilty about this girl Milly, so you've made up this silly story to distract me.'

'I haven't,' said Rupert. 'It's not a story. It's the truth.'

'No,' said Francesca, shaking her head. 'No.'

'Yes, Francesca!' shouted Rupert. 'Yes! It's true! I had an affair with a man. His name was Allan. Allan Kepinski.'

There was a long silence, then Francesca met his eyes. She looked ill.

'I don't want to hear any more,' she whispered. 'I don't feel well.' Rupert watched her making uncertainly for the door. Guilt poured over him like hot water.

'I'm sorry,' he said. 'Francesca, I'm sorry.'

'Don't say sorry to me,' said Francesca in a jerky, scratchy voice. 'Say sorry to Our Lord. You must pray for forgiveness. I'm going—' She broke off and took a deep breath. 'I'm going to pray too.'

'Can't we talk?' said Rupert desperately. 'Can't we at least talk about it?' He walked towards her. 'Francesca?'

'Don't!' she shrieked as his hand neared her sleeve. 'Don't touch me!' She looked at him with glittering eyes in a sheet-white face, then ran out of the room.

Rupert remained by the door, listening as she ran up the stairs and locked the bathroom door. He was trembling all over; his legs felt weak. The revulsion he'd seen in Francesca's face made him want to crawl away and hide. She'd backed away from him as though he were contaminated; as though he was an untouchable.

Suddenly he felt that he might break down and weep.

Pray, she had said. Pray for forgiveness. Rupert walked over to the drinks cabinet and took out a bottle of whisky. Lord, he tried. Lord God, forgive me. But the words weren't there; the will wasn't there. He didn't want to repent. He didn't want to be redeemed. He was a miserable sinner and he didn't care.

God hates me, thought Rupert, staring at his reflection in the mirror. God doesn't exist. Both seemed equally likely.

Rupert sank down into the sofa, holding his bottle of whisky. The birds were still twittering outside the window; cars were still roaring in the distance. Everything was the same. Nothing was the same.

Rupert stared down at his trembling hands. At the signet ring Francesca had given him for their wedding. With a sudden flash, he recalled the happiness he'd felt that day; the relief he'd experienced as, with a few simple words, he'd become part of the legitimate married masses. When he'd led Francesca out of the church, he'd felt as though he finally belonged; as though at last he was normal.

It had all happened just as Allan had predicted. Allan had understood; Allan had known exactly how Rupert felt. He'd watched as, over those late summer weeks, Rupert's feelings had gradually turned from ardour to embarrassment. He'd been sympathetic and supportive and understanding. And in return, Rupert had fled from him.

The seeds of his defection had been sown at the beginning of September. Rupert and Allan had been walking down Broad Street together, talking closely, smiling the smiles of lovers. And then someone had called Rupert's name.

'Rupert! Hi!'

His head had jerked up. Standing on the other side of the road, grinning at him, was Ben Fisher, a boy from the year below him at school. Suddenly Rupert had remembered his father's letter of a few weeks before. The wistful hope that Rupert might come home for some of the vacation; the triumphant news that another boy from the little Cornish school would soon be joining him at Oxford.

'Ben!' Rupert had exclaimed, hurrying across the street. 'Welcome! I heard you were coming.'

'I'm hoping you'll show me around the place,' Ben had replied, his dark eyes twinkling. 'And introduce me to some girls. You must have the whole place after you!' Then his eyes had swivelled curiously towards Allan, still standing on the other side of the road. 'Who's that?'

Rupert's heart had given a little jump, and with a flurry of panic, he saw himself in the eyes of his friends at home. His teachers. His father.

'Oh him?' he'd said after a pause. 'That's no one. Just one of the tutors.'

The next night he'd gone to a bar with Ben, drunk Tequila slammers and flirted furiously with a couple of pretty Italian girls. On his return, Allan had been waiting for him in his room.

'Good evening?' he'd said pleasantly.

'Yes,' Rupert had replied, unable to meet his gaze. 'Yes. I was with— with friends.' He'd stripped quickly, got into bed and closed his eyes as Allan came towards him; had emptied his mind of all thought or guilt as their physical delight had begun.

But the next night he'd gone out again with Ben, and this time had forced himself to kiss one of the pretty girls who hung around him like kids round a sweet counter. She'd responded eagerly, encouraging his hands to roam over her soft, unfamiliar body.

At the end of the evening she'd invited him back to the house she shared on the Cowley Road. He'd undressed her slowly and clumsily, hoping her obvious experience would see him through. Somehow he'd managed to acquit himself successfully; whether her cries were real or false he didn't know and didn't care. The next morning he'd woken up in her bed, curled up against her smooth female skin, breathing in her feminine smell. He'd kissed her shoulder as he always kissed Allan's shoulder, reached out experimentally to touch her breast—and then realised with a jolt of surprise that he felt aroused. The thought of making love to her again excited him. He was normal.

'Are you running away from me?' Allan had said a few days later, as they ate pasta together. 'Do you need some space?'

'No!' Rupert had replied, too heartily. 'Everything's fine.' But after that, things had deteriorated swiftly. They'd had one final conversation in a deserted Keble College bar, the week before the new term began. 'I just can't . . .' Rupert had muttered, stiff with self-consciousness, one eye on the incurious gaze of the barman. 'I'm not—' He'd broken off and taken a deep gulp of whisky. 'It was a mistake. I'm not gay.'

'You're not attracted to me?' Allan had said, and his eyes had fixed on Rupert's. 'Is that what you're saying? You're not attracted to me?'

Rupert had gazed back at him, feeling as though something inside him was being wrenched in two. Waiting in a pub were Ben and a pair of girls. Tonight he would almost certainly have sex with one of them. But he wanted Allan more than he wanted any girl. 'No,' he said at last. 'I'm not.'

'Fine,' Allan had said, his dry voice cracking with anger. 'Lie to me. Lie to yourself. Get married. Have a kid. Play at being straight. But you'll know you're not, and I'll know you're not.'

'I am,' Rupert had retorted feebly, then wished he hadn't as Allan's eyes flashed with contempt.

'Whatever.' He'd drained his glass and got to his feet.

'Will you be all right?' Rupert had said, watching him.

'Don't patronise me,' Allan had snapped back fiercely. 'No, I won't be all right. But I'll get over it.'

'I'm sorry,' Rupert said feebly.

As Allan made his way out of the bar, Rupert felt nothing but raw pain. He'd gone to meet Ben in the pub as arranged, and after a few pints and a good many whiskies he'd felt a little better. Later that night, after having had sex with the prettier of the two girls Ben had procured, he'd lain awake and told himself repeatedly that he was normal; he was happy. And for a while, he'd almost believed himself.

'Tom'll be here in a few minutes.' Francesca's voice interrupted his thoughts. Rupert looked up. She had changed into jeans and a jersey. 'He wants to help.' She was standing at the door, holding a tray. On it was the cream-coloured teapot they'd chosen for their wedding list, together with cups, saucers and a plate of chocolate biscuits.

'Francesca,' said Rupert wearily. 'I don't want to see Tom. I don't want him to know. This is private.'

She came slowly forward, towards him. 'He wants to help,' she repeated. 'And, darling . . .' Her tone changed and Rupert looked up in surprise. 'I want to apologise. I was wrong to react so badly. I just panicked. Tom said that's perfectly normal. He said—' Francesca broke off and bit her lip. 'Anyway. We can get through this. With a lot of support and prayer . . .'

Rupert shrugged. For a few moments neither spoke. Then Francesca bit her lip. 'I was wondering,' she said hesitantly, 'if you should maybe see a doctor, as well. We could ask Dr Askew to recommend someone. What do you think?'

Rupert stared at her speechlessly. He felt as though she'd hit him in the face with a hammer. 'A doctor?' he echoed eventually. 'You think there's something medically wrong with me?'

'No! I just meant . . .' Francesca flushed pink. 'Perhaps there's something they could give you.'

'An anti-gay pill?' He couldn't control his voice. Who was this girl he'd married? Who was she? 'Are you serious?'

'It's just an idea!'

For a few silent seconds, Rupert gazed at Francesca. Then, without speaking, he strode past her and snatched his jacket from the peg.

'Rupert!' she said. 'Where are you going?'

'I've got to get out of here.'

'But where!' cried Francesca. 'Where are you going?'

'I'm going,' he said slowly, 'to find Allan.'

Chapter Five

CANON LYTTON HAD ASKED for all the members of the family to be assembled in the drawing room, as though he were about to unmask a murderer in their midst.

'There are only the two of us,' Isobel had said scornfully. 'Would you like us to assemble? Or do you want to come back later?'

'Indeed, no,' Canon Lytton had replied solemnly. 'Let us adjourn.'

Now he sat on the sofa, his cassock falling in dusty folds around him, his face stern and forbidding. 'I come here on a matter of some gravity,' he began. 'To be brief, as parish priest and official at the intended marriage of Milly and Simon, I wish to ascertain whether Milly is, as she stated on the form she filled in, a spinster of this parish, or whether—in fact—she has been married before. I will ask her myself when she returns. In the meantime, I would be grateful if you, as her mother, could answer on her behalf.' He stopped and looked impressively at Olivia, who wrinkled her brow.

'Married before?' said Olivia. She gave a shocked little laugh. 'What are you talking about?'

'I have been given to believe—'

'What do you mean?' interrupted Olivia. 'Is someone saying Milly's been married before?' Canon Lytton inclined his head slightly. 'Well, they're lying! How on earth can you believe such a thing?'

'It is my duty to follow up all such accusations.'

'What,' said Isobel, 'even if they come from complete crackpots?'

'I use my discretion,' said Canon Lytton. 'The person who told me this claims to have a copy of a marriage certificate.'

'Who was it?' said Isobel.

'That, I am not at liberty to say,' said Canon Lytton.

You love this, thought Isobel, gazing at him. You just love it.

'Jealousy!' said Olivia suddenly. 'That's what this is. Somebody's jealous of Milly and they're trying to spoil her wedding. Who's she supposed to have married, anyway? The postman?'

There was a short silence. Isobel tried not to look too tense.

'A man named Kepinski,' said Canon Lytton, reading from a piece of paper. 'Allan Kepinski.'

Isobel's heart sank. Milly didn't have a hope.

'Allan Kepinski?' said Olivia incredulously. 'That's a made-up name, if ever I heard one! The whole thing's obviously a hoax. You read about this sort of thing all the time. Don't you, Isobel?'

'Yes,' said Isobel weakly. 'All the time.'

'And now,' said Olivia, standing up, 'if you'll excuse me, Canon Lytton, I've a thousand things to do. We do have a wedding on Saturday, you know!'

'I am aware of that fact,' said Canon Lytton. 'Nevertheless, I will need to speak to Milly about this. I will return later this evening,' he said portentously. 'Permit me to see myself out.'

As the front door slammed behind him, Olivia looked at Isobel. 'Do you know what he's talking about?'

'No, of course not!' said Isobel.

'Isobel,' Olivia said sharply, 'you may have fooled Canon Lytton, but you don't fool me! You know something about this, don't you?'

'Look, Mummy,' said Isobel, trying to sound calm. 'I think we should just wait until Milly gets back.'

'Wait for what?' Olivia stared at her in dismay. 'Isobel, what are you saying? There's no truth in what Canon Lytton said, is there?'

'I'm not saying anything,' said Isobel. 'Not until Milly gets back.'

Milly was trudging back from the station when a car pulled up alongside her. 'Hello, darling,' said James. 'Would you like a lift?'

'Oh,' said Milly. 'Thanks.'

Without meeting her father's eye, she got into the car and stared straight ahead, trying desperately to organise her thoughts. All the way back from London she had tried to think rationally, to form some sensible solution. But now she was back in Bath, minutes away from home, and she was still in a state of uncertainty.

'Did you have a good time in London?' said James. Milly jumped.

'Yes,' she said. 'Shopping. You know.' There was a pause, and she realised that she didn't have any shopping bags. 'I bought . . . cuff links for Simon.'

'Very nice. He said he would call for you later, by the way. After work.'

A spasm of nerves hit Milly in the stomach. 'Oh good,' she said, feeling sick. How could she even look him in the eye?

As they got out of the car she felt a sudden desire to run away. Instead, she followed her father up the steps to the front door.

'She's back!' she heard her mother's voice cry as the door opened. Olivia appeared in the hall. 'Milly,' she said in clipped, furious tones. 'What's all this nonsense about you being married?'

'What do you mean?' she said shakily.

'What's going on?' said James, following Milly into the hall. 'Olivia, are you all right?'

'No, I'm not all right,' said Olivia jerkily. 'Canon Lytton came to see us this afternoon with some ridiculous story about Milly. He said she'd been married before!'

Milly didn't move. Her eyes flickered to Isobel and back again, the fear rising inside her like choking gas.

'Only Isobel doesn't seem to think it is so ridiculous!' said Olivia.

'Mummy!' exclaimed Isobel, scandalised. 'That's not fair! Milly, honestly, I only said we should wait till you got back.'

'Yes,' said Olivia. 'And now she's back. So one of you had better tell us what this is all about.'

Milly looked from face to face. 'All right,' she said shakily. 'Maybe we should all have a drink.'

'I don't want a drink!' exclaimed Olivia. 'I want to know what's going on. Milly, is Canon Lytton right? Have you been married before? Yes or no, Milly? Yes or no?'

'Yes!' screamed Milly. 'I'm married! I've been married for ten years!'

Her words resonated round the silent hall. Olivia took a small pace back and clutched the stair banister.

'I got married when I was at Oxford,' Milly continued in a trembling voice. 'I was eighteen. It . . . it didn't mean anything. I thought no one would ever find out. I thought . . .' She broke off. 'What's the point?'

There was silence. Isobel glanced apprehensively at Olivia. Her face was an ugly scarlet; she seemed to be having trouble breathing.

'Are you serious, Milly?' she said eventually.

'Yes.' There was a pause.

'Then you're a stupid, stupid girl!' shrieked Olivia. Her voice lashed across the room like a whip and Milly turned pale. 'How could you have thought that no one would find out? You've ruined everything for all of us!'

'Stop it!' said James angrily. 'Stop it, Olivia.'

'I'm sorry,' whispered Milly. 'I really am.'

'It's no good being sorry!' screamed Olivia. 'It's too late for sorry! Who was he, anyway? A student?'

'A research fellow.'

'Swept you off your feet, did he? Promised you all sorts of things?'

'No!' shouted Milly, suddenly snapping. 'I married him to help him! He needed to stay in the country!'

Olivia stared at Milly, her expression gradually changing as she worked out what Milly was saying. 'You married an illegal immigrant?' she whispered. Her voice rose to a shriek. 'An illegal *immigrant*?'

'Olivia,' said James. 'Calm down. You're not helping.'

'Helping?' Olivia turned on James. 'Why should I want to help? Do you realise what this means? We'll have to call the wedding off!'

'Postpone it, maybe,' said Isobel. 'Until the divorce comes through.' She pulled a sympathetic face at Milly.

'We can't!' cried Olivia desperately. She thought for a moment, then whipped round to Milly. 'Does Simon know about this?'

Milly shook her head. Olivia's eyes began to glitter.

'Well, then we can still go through with it,' she said quickly. Her eyes darted urgently from face to face. 'We'll fob Canon Lytton off! If none of us says a word, if we all hold our heads high . . .'

'Mummy!' exclaimed Isobel. 'You're talking about bigamy!'

'Olivia, you're mad,' said James in disgust. 'Obviously the wedding must be cancelled. And if you ask me, it's no bad thing.'

'What do you mean?' said Olivia hysterically.

'Frankly, I think it would be good for us all to get back to normal!' exclaimed James angrily. 'This whole wedding has got out of hand. It's nothing but wedding, wedding, wedding! The whole family's obsessed! I think it would be a very good thing for you, Milly, if you just got your feet back on the ground for a while.'

'What do you mean?' said Milly shakily. 'My feet are on the ground.'

'Milly, your feet are up with the birds! You've gone rushing into this marriage without considering all the other options. I know Simon's a very attractive young man, I know his father's very rich . . .'

'That's got nothing to do with it!' Milly stared at James with an ashen face. 'I love Simon! I want to marry him because I love him.'

'You think you do,' said James. 'But perhaps this is a good chance for you to wait for a while. See if you can stand on your own two feet, for a change. Like Isobel.'

'Like Isobel,' echoed Milly, in a disbelieving voice. 'You always want me to be Isobel. Perfect bloody Isobel.'

'Of course I don't,' said James impatiently. 'That's not what I said.'

'You want me to do the things that Isobel does.'

'Maybe,' said James. 'Some of them.'

'Daddy—' began Isobel.

'Well, fine!' screamed Milly, feeling blood rush to her head. 'I'll be like Isobel! I won't get married! I'll get pregnant instead!'

There was a sharp silence.

'Pregnant?' said Olivia incredulously.

'Thanks a lot, Milly,' said Isobel shortly, stalking to the front door.

'Isobel—' began Milly. But Isobel slammed the door behind her without looking back.

'I didn't mean to say that,' muttered Milly, appalled at herself. 'Can you just forget I said it?'

'You're married,' said Olivia, groping for a chair. 'And Isobel's pregnant.' She sat down. 'Is she really pregnant?'

'That's her business,' said Milly, staring at the floor. 'I shouldn't have said anything.'

The doorbell rang, jolting them all. 'That'll be Isobel,' said James, getting up. He opened the door and took a step back.

'Ah,' he said. 'It's you, Simon.'

Isobel strode along the pavement, not stopping, not looking back, not knowing where she was going. The snow had turned to slush; a cold drizzle was coating her hair and dripping down her neck. But with every step she felt a little better. With every step she was further into anonymity; further away from the shocked faces of her family.

She felt angry, betrayed, too furious with Milly to speak . . . and yet too sorry for her to blame her. She'd never witnessed such an ugly family scene, with Milly defenceless in the middle of it. No wonder she'd lashed out with the first diversionary tactic she had to hand.

Isobel closed her eyes. She felt raw and vulnerable; unready for this. On her return, her parents would surely expect her to talk to them, to help them digest this piece of startling information. But she had barely digested it herself. She couldn't articulate what she thought about it; could no longer distinguish between emotional and physical sensation. Energy and optimism alternated with tearfulness, and the nausea made everything even worse.

She stopped at a corner and cautiously laid her hand over her stomach. She didn't want to think of herself as carrying a child. When she imagined whatever was inside her, it was as a small shellfish, or a snail. Something indeterminate, whose life had not begun. Whose life might, if she chose, progress no further.

The thought transfixed her. She felt almost overcome by her burden, overwhelmed by the decision she was going to have to make, and for a moment she thought she might collapse, sobbing with grief, on the pavement. But instead, with an impatient shake of the head, she thrust her hands deeper into her pockets and began once more to walk.

Simon and Milly sat, facing each other on armchairs in the drawing room, as though appearing on a television chat show.

'So,' said Simon finally. 'What is all this?'

Milly gazed at him silently. Her fingers shook as she pushed a frond of hair back from her face; her lips opened to speak, then closed again.

'You're making me nervous,' said Simon. 'Come on, sweetheart.' He grinned at her.

'You won't like it,' she said.

'I'll be brave,' said Simon. 'Come on, hit me with it.'

'OK,' said Milly. She took a deep breath. 'The thing is, we can't get married on Saturday. We're going to have to postpone the wedding.'

'Postpone?' said Simon slowly. 'Well, OK. But why?'

'There's something I haven't told you,' said Milly, meshing her hands together, twisting them round until her knuckles felt as though they might break. 'I did something very stupid when I was eighteen. I got married. It was a fake marriage. It didn't mean anything. But the divorce never went through. So I'm—I'm still married.'

She glanced at Simon. He looked bewildered but not angry, and she felt a sudden flood of reassurance. After her mother's hysterics, it was a relief to see Simon taking the news calmly.

'All it means is, I'll have to wait for the decree absolute before we can get married,' she said. She bit her lip. 'Simon, I'm really sorry.'

There was a long silence.

'I don't get it,' said Simon eventually. 'Is this a joke?'

'No,' said Milly. 'No! God, I wish it was! It's true.'

She gazed at him miserably. His dark eyes scanned her face; slowly a look of disbelief crept over his features.

'You're serious.'

'Yes. But it wasn't a proper marriage,' said Milly quickly. She stared down at the floor, trying to keep her voice steady. 'He was gay. The whole thing was fake. To keep him in the country. It honestly meant nothing. You do understand, don't you? You do understand?'

She looked up at his face. And as she saw his expression she realised, with a thud of dismay, that he didn't.

'It was a mistake,' she said, almost tripping over the words in her haste. 'A big mistake. I see that now. But I was a child. I know I should have told you about it before. I know I should. But I just—' She broke off and looked at him desperately. 'Simon, say something!'

'What am I supposed to say? Congratulations?'

Milly winced. 'No! Just—I don't know. Tell me what you're thinking.'

'I don't know what to think,' said Simon. 'I don't even know where to start.' His glance fell on her left hand; on the finger wearing his engagement ring, and she flushed.

Suddenly he leapt up and stalked away to the window. 'Christ, Milly!' he exclaimed, his voice shaking slightly. 'Why didn't you tell me?'

'I don't know. I thought it wouldn't matter! I thought—'

'You thought you wouldn't bother to tell me at all?' He turned round and gazed at her in sudden comprehension. 'Am I right?'

'No! I *was* intending to tell you!'

'When? On our wedding night? When our first child was born?'

Milly opened her mouth to speak, then closed it again. She felt a hot fear creeping over her.

'So, what other little secrets are you keeping from me? Any hidden children? Secret lovers?'

'No.'

'And how am I supposed to believe that?' His voice lashed across the room, and Milly flinched. 'How am I supposed to believe anything you say any more?'

'I know I should have told you,' she said desperately. 'But the fact that I didn't doesn't mean I'm keeping anything else from you. Simon—'

'It's not just that,' said Simon, cutting across her. He sank into a chair and rubbed his face.

'What is it, then?'

'Milly—you've already made the wedding vows to someone else. You've already promised to love someone else. Cherish someone else.'

'But I didn't mean a word of it! Not a word!'

'Exactly.' His voice chilled her. 'I thought you took those vows as seriously as I did.'

'I did,' said Milly in horror. 'I do.'

'How can you? You've spoiled them! You've tainted them.'

'Simon, don't look at me like that,' whispered Milly. 'I made a mistake, but I'm still me. Nothing's changed!'

'Everything's changed,' said Simon flatly. There was a heavy silence. 'To be honest, I feel as if I don't know you any more.'

'Well, I feel as if I don't know *you* any more!' cried Milly in a sudden anguished burst. 'I know I've messed the wedding up. I know I've fucked things up completely. But you don't have to be so sanctimonious.' She gulped. 'I made a mistake. I made one mistake! And if you really loved me, you'd forgive me!' She began to shake with sobs.

'And if you really loved me,' shouted Simon, suddenly looking distraught, 'you would have told me you were married!'

Milly stared at him, suddenly feeling unsure of herself.

'Not necessarily,' she faltered.

'Well, we must have different definitions of love,' said Simon. 'Perhaps we've been at cross-purposes all along.' He stood up and reached for his coat.

Milly stared at him, feeling a horrified disbelief creep over her. 'Are you saying'—she fought a desire to retch—'are you saying you don't want to marry me any more?'

'As I recall,' said Simon stiffly, 'you've already got a husband. So the question's academic really, isn't it?' He paused at the door. 'I hope the two of you will be very happy.'

'Bastard!' screamed Milly. Tears blurred her eyes as she tugged feverishly at her engagement ring. By the time she managed to throw it at him, the door was closed and he was gone.

Isobel arrived back to find the house quiet. She pushed open the kitchen door and saw Olivia sitting at the table in the half-light. A bottle of wine was in front of her, half full. As Olivia heard the sound of the door she looked up with a pale, puffy face. 'Well,' she said flatly. 'It's all over.'

'What do you mean?' said Isobel suspiciously.

'They had some sort of row—and Simon called the whole thing off.' Olivia took a slug of wine.

'What about? Her first marriage?'

'I imagine so,' said Olivia. 'She wouldn't say.'

'Where is she?'

'She's gone to Esme's for the night. She said she had to get away from this house. From all of us.'

'I don't blame her,' said Isobel. She sat heavily down on a chair, her coat still on. 'God, poor Milly. I can't believe it! What exactly did Simon say?'

'Milly didn't tell me. She doesn't tell me anything these days. For ten years she was married to that—that illegal immigrant! Ten years without telling me!'

'She couldn't tell you. How on earth could she tell you?'

'And then, when she was in trouble, she went to Esme Ormerod.' Olivia raised bloodshot eyes to Isobel. 'And then she went to you.'

Olivia's voice grew higher. 'Didn't it occur to her to come to me? Her own mother?'

'She couldn't!' exclaimed Isobel. 'She knew how you would react. And, frankly, she didn't need that. She needed calm, rational advice.'

'I'm incapable of being rational, am I?'

'When it comes to this wedding,' said Isobel, 'then yes. Yes, you are!'

'Well, there isn't going to be a wedding now,' said Olivia jerkily. 'So perhaps you'll all start to trust me again.'

'Oh, Mummy, stop feeling sorry for yourself!' said Isobel, suddenly exasperated. 'This wasn't your wedding. It was Milly's wedding!'

'I know that!' said Olivia indignantly.

'You don't,' said Isobel. 'You're not really thinking about Milly and Simon and how they must be feeling. All you're thinking about is the wedding. The flowers that will have to be cancelled, and your lovely smart outfit that no one will see, and how you won't get to dance with Harry Pinnacle! Beyond that, you couldn't give a damn!'

'How dare you!' exclaimed Olivia, and two bright spots appeared on her cheeks.

'It's true though, isn't it?'

There was a long silence. Isobel blinked a few times in the dim kitchen light. She suddenly felt drained, too tired for argument.

'Right,' she said with an effort. 'Well, I think I'll go to bed.'

'Wait,' said Olivia, looking up. 'You haven't eaten anything.'

'It's all right,' said Isobel. 'I'm not hungry.'

'That's not the point,' said Olivia. 'You need to eat.'

Isobel gave a noncommittal shrug. 'You need to eat,' repeated Olivia. She met Isobel's eyes. 'In your condition.'

'Mummy—not now,' said Isobel wearily.

'We don't have to talk about it,' said Olivia in a voice tinged with hurt. 'You can keep all the secrets you like.' Isobel looked away uncomfortably. 'Just let me make you some nice scrambled eggs.'

There was a pause.

'OK,' said Isobel at last. 'That would be nice.'

'And I'll pour you a nice glass of wine.'

'I can't,' said Isobel, taken unawares. Silently she tried to sort out the contrary strands of thought in her brain. She couldn't drink, just in case she decided to keep the baby. What kind of a twisted logic was that?

'All that phooey!' Olivia was saying. 'I was on three gins a day when I had you. And you turned out all right, didn't you? More or less?'

A reluctant smile spread over Isobel's face.

'OK,' she said. 'I could do with a drink.'

'So could I,' said Olivia. 'I've never known such a dreadful night.'

'Tell me about it.' Isobel sat down at the table. 'I hope Milly's OK.'

'I'm sure Esme will look after her,' said Olivia, and a touch of bitterness edged her voice.

Milly sat in Esme's drawing room, nestling a hot, creamy drink made from Belgian chocolate flakes and a splash of Cointreau. Esme had persuaded her to take a long, hot bath, then lent her a white waffle-weave bathrobe and some snug slippers. Now she was brushing Milly's hair with an old-fashioned bristle hairbrush. Milly stared ahead into the crackling fire, feeling the heat on her face. She'd arrived at Esme's an hour or so ago; had burst into tears as soon as the door was opened. But now she felt strangely calm. She took another sip of the hot, creamy chocolate and closed her eyes.

'Feeling better?' said Esme in a low voice.

'Yes. A lot better.'

'Good.'

There was a pause. 'You were right,' said Milly. 'I don't know Simon. He doesn't know me.' Her voice trembled slightly. 'It's hopeless.'

Esme said nothing, but continued brushing.

'I know I'm to blame for all of this,' said Milly. 'It's me that got married, it's me that messed up. But he behaved as though I'd done it all on purpose. He didn't even *try* to see it from my point of view.'

'Typical,' said Esme. 'Just another intractable man.'

'I feel so stupid,' said Milly. 'So bloody stupid.' A fresh stream of tears suddenly began to spill over onto her face. 'How could I have wanted to marry him? He said I'd tainted the wedding vows. He said he couldn't believe anything I said any more.'

'I know,' said Esme soothingly.

'We should never have got engaged. All along, it's just been—' She suddenly broke off, with a new thought. 'Do you remember when he asked me to marry him? He had it all planned, the way he wanted it. He led me to this bench in his father's garden, and he had a diamond ring all ready in his pocket, and he'd even put a bloody bottle of champagne in the tree stump! None of that was to do with me, was it? It was all to do with him.'

'Just like his father,' said Esme, with a sudden edge to her voice.

Milly turned slightly in surprise. 'Do you know Harry, then?'

'I used to,' said Esme, brushing more briskly. 'Not any more.'

'I always thought Harry was quite nice,' gulped Milly. 'But then, what the hell do I know? I was completely wrong about Simon, wasn't I?' Her shoulders began to shake with sobs, and Esme stopped brushing.

'Darling, why don't you go to bed,' she suggested. 'You're over-wrought, you're tired, you need a good night's sleep.'

'I won't be able to sleep.' Milly looked up at Esme with tear-stained cheeks, like a child.

'You will,' replied Esme calmly. 'I put a little something into your drink. It should kick in soon.'

'Oh,' said Milly, in surprise. She stared into her mug for a moment, then drained it. 'Do you give drugs to all your guests?'

'Only the very special ones,' said Esme, and gave Milly a serene smile.

Having persuaded Olivia to go to bed, Isobel finished the last of her scrambled eggs, sighed and got up to make a cup of tea. She was leaning against the sink, looking out into the dark, silent street, when suddenly there was the sound of a key in the lock.

'Milly?' she said. 'Is that you?'

A moment later, the kitchen door opened and a scruffy young man came in. He was wearing a denim jacket and carrying a large bag. Isobel stared at him curiously for an instant. Then, with a sudden start, she realised who he must be. A hot, molten fury began to rise inside her. So this was Alexander. The cause of it all.

'Well, hello,' he said, dumping his bag on the floor and grinning insouciantly. 'You must be multilingual, multitalented Isobel. They didn't tell me you were beautiful, too.'

'I don't know how you dare come back in here,' said Isobel softly, trying to control her voice.

'That's not very friendly.'

'Friendly! You expect me to be friendly? After everything you've done to my sister?' Alexander looked up and grinned.

'So you know her little secret, do you?'

'The whole world knows her little secret, thanks to you!'

'What do you mean?' said Alexander innocently. 'What's happened?'

'Let me think,' said Isobel sarcastically. 'Oh, yes. The wedding's been cancelled. But I expect you already knew that.'

Alexander stared at her. 'You're joking.'

'Of course I'm not bloody joking!' cried Isobel. 'The wedding's off. So congratulations, Alexander, you've achieved your aim. You've fucked up Milly's life completely. Not to mention the rest of us.'

'Christ!' He ran a shaking hand through his hair. 'I never meant—'

'No?' said Isobel furiously. 'No? Well, you should have thought of that before you opened your big mouth.'

'Why the hell did she call off the wedding?'

'She didn't,' said Isobel. 'Simon did.'

'What?' Alexander looked at her. 'Why?'

'I think that's their business, don't you?' said Isobel in a harsh voice. 'Let's just say that if no one had said anything about her first marriage, everything would still be OK.'

'Jesus! I never wanted anyone to cancel any wedding. I was just . . . stirring things a little.'

'God, you're pathetic!' said Isobel, staring at him. 'You're just a pathetic, inadequate bully!' She looked at his bag. 'You needn't think you're staying here tonight.'

'But my room's booked!'

'And now it's bloody well unbooked,' said Isobel, kicking his bag towards the door.

'Look, I'm sorry, OK!' said Alexander, picking up his bag. 'I'm sorry your sister's wedding's off. But you can't blame me.'

'We can and we do,' said Isobel, opening the front door.

'But I didn't do anything,' exclaimed Alexander angrily, stepping outside. 'I just made a few jokes!'

'You call telling the vicar a *joke*?' said Isobel furiously, and as Alexander opened his mouth to reply, she slammed the door.

Olivia walked up the stairs slowly, feeling a flat, dull sadness creep over her. The adrenaline of the early evening was gone; she felt weary and disappointed. It was all over. The goal to which she'd been working all this time had suddenly been lifted away, leaving nothing in its place.

She stopped at Milly's bedroom door, which was slightly ajar, and found herself walking in. Milly's wedding dress was still hanging up in its cotton cover on the wardrobe door. When she closed her eyes, Olivia could still see Milly's face as she tried it on for the first time; both of them had known immediately that this was the one.

Unable to stop herself, Olivia unzipped the wrapper, pulled out a little of the heavy satin and stared at it. From inside the cotton cover, a tiny iridescent pearl glinted at her. It was a truly beautiful dress. And now it would never be worn. Olivia sighed, and reached for the zip to close the wrapper again.

James, walking past the door, saw Olivia gazing at the dress and felt a stab of irritation. 'For God's sake, Olivia,' he said brutally. 'The wedding's off! Haven't you got that into your head yet?'

Olivia's head jerked up in shock and she stuffed the dress back into its cover. 'Of course I have,' she said. 'I was just—'

'Just wallowing in self-pity,' said James sarcastically.

Olivia zipped up the cover and turned round. 'James, why are you behaving as though all this is my fault?' she said shakily. 'I didn't push Milly into marriage. I didn't force her to have a wedding! She wanted one! All I did was to organise it for her as best I could.'

'Organise it for yourself, you mean!'

Olivia stared at him. 'I don't understand you, James,' she said. 'Weren't you ever happy that Milly was getting married?'

'I don't know,' said James. He walked stiffly over to the window. 'What the hell has marriage got to offer a young girl like Milly?'

'Happiness,' said Olivia after a pause. 'A happy life with Simon.'

James turned round and gave her a curious expression. 'You think marriage brings happiness, do you?'

'What do you mean?' said Olivia in a trembling voice. 'James, what are you talking about?'

'What do you think I'm talking about?' said James.

The room seemed to ring with a still silence.

'Just look at us, Olivia,' said James at last. 'Do we give each other happiness? We haven't grown together over the years. We've grown apart.'

'No, we haven't!' said Olivia in alarm. 'We've been very happy together!'

James shook his head. 'We've been happy separately. You have your life and I have mine. Admit it. You're more interested in your bed-and-breakfast guests than you are in me!'

'That's not fair!' cried Olivia at once. 'I run the bed and breakfast *for* our family! To give us holidays. Little luxuries. You know that!'

'Well, perhaps other things are more important,' said James.

Olivia looked at him uncertainly. 'What are you saying, James?'

There was a long pause. Eventually James sighed. 'I suppose,' he said slowly, 'I just want you to need me.'

'I do need you,' said Olivia in a small voice.

'Do you?' A half-smile came to James's lips. 'Olivia, when was the last time you confided in me? When was the last time you asked my advice?'

'You wouldn't be interested in anything I've got to say!' cried Olivia defensively. 'Whenever I tell you anything, you look bored. You behave as though nothing I've got to say is of any importance. And anyway, what about you? You never confide in me, either!'

'I try to!' said James angrily. 'But you never bloody listen! You're always rabbiting on about the wedding. And before the wedding there was always something else. Rabbit, rabbit, rabbit! It drives me mad.'

There was silence.

'I know I run on a bit,' said Olivia at last. 'But you've never said anything. You never seem to care one way or the other.'

James rubbed his face wearily. 'Perhaps I don't,' he said. 'Perhaps I've got beyond caring. All I know is . . .' He paused. 'I can't go on like this.'

The words resounded round the tiny room like gas from a canister. Olivia felt the colour drain from her cheeks and a slow, frightening thud begin like a death knell in her stomach.

'James,' she said, before he could continue. 'Please. Not tonight.'

James looked up and felt a jolt as he saw Olivia. Her cheeks were ashen, her eyes were full of a deep dread. 'Olivia—' he began.

'If you have something you want to say to me—' Olivia swallowed, 'then please don't say it tonight.' She began to back jerkily away, groping for the door handle. 'I just . . . I just couldn't bear anything more tonight.'

Rupert sat at his desk in chambers, staring out of the window at the dark, silent night. On the desk in front of him was a list of phone numbers, some now crossed out or amended. He'd spent the last two hours on the phone, talking to people he'd thought he would never speak to again. Half-remembered acquaintances, friends of friends, names he couldn't even put to faces. No one knew where Allan was.

But this last phone call had given him hope. He'd spoken to an English professor at Leeds, who had known Allan at Manchester.

'He left Manchester suddenly,' he'd said.

'So I gather,' said Rupert. 'Do you have any idea where he went?'

There was a pause. 'Exeter,' the professor said eventually. 'That's right. Exeter. I know, because about a year later, he wrote to me and asked me to send him a book. I may even have typed the address and telephone number into my electronic organiser.'

'Could you . . .' Rupert had said, hardly daring to hope.

'Here we are,' the professor had said. 'St David's House.'

'What's that?' said Rupert, staring at the address. 'A college?'

'I haven't heard of it,' the professor had replied. 'Perhaps it's a new hall of residence.'

Rupert had put the phone down and immediately tapped in the number. He felt almost sick with apprehension.

'Hello?' A young male voice answered. 'St David's House.'

'Hello,' said Rupert. 'I'd like to speak to Allan Kepinski, please.'

'Just a second, please.'

There was a long silence, then another young male voice came on the line. 'You wanted to speak to Allan.'

'Yes.'

'May I ask who's calling?'

'My name's Rupert.'

'Rupert Carr?'

'Yes,' said Rupert, gripping the receiver tightly. 'Is Allan there?'

'Allan left here five years ago. He went back to the States.'

'Oh,' said Rupert. 'Oh.' He gazed blankly at the phone. It had never even occurred to him that Allan would go back to the States.

'Rupert, are you in London?' the young man was saying. 'Could we meet up tomorrow by any chance? Allan left a letter for you.'

'Really?' said Rupert. 'For me?' His heart began to pound in sudden exhilaration. It wasn't too late. Allan still wanted him.

Suddenly his attention was distracted by a sound at the door. Standing in the doorway was Tom. Rupert's cheeks began to flush red.

'Mangetout on Drury Lane. At twelve,' the young man was saying. 'I'll be wearing black jeans. My name's Martin, by the way.'

'OK,' said Rupert hurriedly. 'Bye, Martin.'

He put the phone down and looked at Tom. Humiliation began to creep slowly through him.

'Who's Martin?' said Tom pleasantly. 'A friend of yours?'

'Go away,' said Rupert. 'Leave me alone.'

'I've been with Francesca,' said Tom. 'She's very upset. As you can imagine.' He sat down casually on Rupert's desk and picked up a brass paperweight. 'This little outburst of yours has quite thrown her. But she's willing to stand by you. We'll all help you.'

'Help me do what? Repent? Perhaps you'd like me to confess in public?'

'I understand your anger,' said Tom. 'It's a form of shame.'

'It's not! I'm not ashamed!'

'Whatever you've done in the past can be wiped clean,' said Tom. 'You can start again.'

'I can't,' he said. 'I just can't. I'm not who you all think I am. I was in love with a man. Not misguided, not led astray. In love.'

'Platonic love—'

'Not platonic love!' cried Rupert. 'Sexual love! Can't you understand that, Tom? I loved a man sexually.'

'You committed acts with him, acts which you know to be abhorrent to the Lord.'

'We didn't harm anybody!' cried Rupert. 'We did nothing wrong!'

'Rupert!' exclaimed Tom. 'Can you hear yourself? You committed perhaps the most odious sin known to mankind! You can wipe it clean—but only if you acknowledge the evil which you've done.'

'It wasn't evil,' said Rupert in a shaking voice. 'It was beautiful. Can't you understand that?'

'No,' snapped Tom. 'I'm afraid I can't. I can't understand how two men could possibly love each other.'

Rupert leaned forward. Fronds of his hair touched Tom's forehead. 'Are you really repulsed by the idea?' he whispered. 'Or just afraid of it?'

Like a cat, Tom leapt backwards. 'Get away from me!' he shouted, his face contorted with disgust. 'Get away!'

'Don't worry,' said Rupert. 'I'm going.'

With trembling hands, Rupert picked up his papers and thrust them into his briefcase. Tom watched without moving. 'You know you're damned,' he said, as Rupert picked up his coat. 'Damned to hell.'

'I know,' said Rupert. And without looking back he opened the door and walked out.

Isobel woke to a thumping headache and grey-green nausea. She lay perfectly still, trying to exercise mind over matter—until a sudden urge to throw up propelled her from her bed and into the bathroom. 'It's a hangover,' she told the bathroom mirror. But her reflection looked unconvinced. There were sounds coming from the kitchen and she decided to go down and make herself a cup of tea. James was standing by the Aga as she walked in, dressed in his work suit and reading the paper.

'Morning,' he said as she sat down at the table. 'Cup of tea?'

'I'd love one,' said Isobel. James put a mug of tea in front of her and she took a sip, then frowned. 'I think I'll have some sugar in this.'

'You don't normally take sugar,' said James in surprise.

'No,' said Isobel. 'Well. Maybe I do now.' She heaped two spoons of sugar into her mug, then sipped pleasurably, feeling the hot sweetness seep slowly through her body.

'So,' said James. 'Milly was right.'

'Yes.' Isobel stared down into her tea. 'Milly was right.'

'And the father?'

Isobel said nothing. 'I see.' James cleared his throat. 'Have you decided what you're going to do?'

'No, I haven't decided.' Isobel looked up. 'I suppose you think I should get rid of it, don't you? Forget it ever happened and resume my glittering career.'

'Not necessarily,' said James, after a pause. 'Not unless—'

'My exciting career,' said Isobel bitterly. 'My wonderful life of aeroplanes and hotel rooms and foreign businessmen trying to chat me up because I'm always on my own.' She took a sip of tea. 'Sometimes I wish I'd just got married and had three kids and lived in divorced bliss.'

James stared at her. 'I had no idea, darling,' he said, frowning. 'I thought you liked being a career girl.'

'I'm not a career girl,' said Isobel, putting down her mug loudly. 'I'm a person. With a career.'

'I didn't mean—'

'You did!' said Isobel exasperatedly. 'That's all you think I am, isn't it? My career and nothing else. You've forgotten all about the rest of me.'

'No!' said James. 'I wouldn't forget about the rest of you.'

'Yes, you would,' said Isobel. 'Because I do. Frequently.'

There was a pause. James took a final sip of tea then reached for his briefcase. 'I must go, I'm afraid.'

'You're really going to work today?'

'I don't have much choice. There's a lot going on at the moment. If I don't show my face, I may find my job gone tomorrow.'

'Really?' Isobel looked up, shocked. 'I had no idea.'

'No, well, I haven't exactly been forthcoming about it.'

Suddenly Isobel grinned at him. 'I bet you're glad to get away from it all, really.'

'I'm not getting away from anything,' said James. 'Harry Pinnacle's already been on the phone to me this morning, requesting a meeting at lunchtime.' He pulled a face. 'No doubt to talk about the costs of this whole fiasco.'

'Oh well,' said Isobel. 'Good luck.'

By the door, James paused. 'Who would you have married, anyway?' he said. 'And had your three kids with?'

'I dunno. Who was I going out with? Dan Williams, I suppose.'

James groaned. 'Darling, I think you made the right choice.' He suddenly stopped himself. 'I mean—the baby isn't . . .'

'No,' said Isobel, giggling in spite of herself. 'Don't worry. It's not his.'

Simon woke feeling shattered. His head ached, his eyes were sore, his chest felt heavy with misery. Why hadn't he seen this coming? Why had he ever let himself believe he could achieve a happy marriage? Why couldn't he just accept the fact that he was an all-round failure? He'd failed dismally at business and now he'd failed at marriage, too. At least, thought Simon bitterly, his father had actually made it to the altar.

An image came to him of Milly's face the night before: red, tear-stained, desperate with unhappiness. And for a moment he felt himself weakening. For a moment he felt like calling her up. Telling her he still loved her, that he still wanted to marry her. He would kiss her poor swollen lips; take her to bed; try to forget all that was past. The temptation was there. If he was honest with himself, the temptation was huge.

But he couldn't do it. How could he marry Milly now? This was no small rift that might be patched up and healed. This was a gaping, jagged chasm which changed the whole order of things; turned their relationship into something he no longer recognised.

An angry hurt began to throb inside him, and he sat up in bed, trying to clear his mind. He pulled open the curtains and, without seeing the beautiful view before him, quickly began to get dressed. He would throw himself into work, he told himself. He would start again and he would get over this, however long it took.

Briskly, he walked downstairs and into the breakfast room. Harry was sitting at the table, hidden behind a newspaper.

'Morning,' said his father.

'Morning,' said Simon. He looked up suspiciously, ready to detect a note of mocking or ridicule in his father's voice. But his father was looking up at him with what seemed genuine concern.

'So,' he said, as Simon sat down. 'What's this all about?'

'The wedding's off.'

'So I gather. But why? Or don't you want to tell me?'

Simon said nothing, but reached for the coffeepot. He had stormed in the night before, too angry and humiliated to talk to anyone. He was still humiliated; still angry; still inclined to keep Milly's betrayal to himself. On the other hand, misery was a lonely emotion.

'She's already married,' he said abruptly.

There was a crackling sound as Harry thrust down his paper. 'Already married? To whom, for God's sake?'

'Some gay American. She met him ten years ago. He wanted to stay in the country, so she married him as a favour. As a favour!'

'Thank God for that,' said Harry. 'I thought you meant really married.' He sipped his coffee. 'So what's the problem? Can't she get a divorce?'

'The problem?' said Simon incredulously. 'The problem is that she lied to me! The problem is that I can't trust anything else she says!'

Harry stared at him in silence.

'Is that it?' he said at last. 'Is that the only reason it's all off? The fact that Milly married some dodgy guy, ten years ago? I thought there must be something really wrong between you.'

'There is! She lied to me! We had a relationship built on trust. Now I can't trust her any more.' He closed his eyes. 'It's finished.'

'Simon, just who the fuck do you think you are?' exclaimed Harry.

'The Archbishop of Canterbury? Why does it matter if she lied to you? She's told you the truth now, hasn't she?'

'Only because she had to.'

'So what?'

'So it was perfect before this happened!' shouted Simon desperately. 'Everything was perfect! And now it's ruined!'

'Oh, grow up!' thundered Harry. 'And for once in your life stop behaving like a spoilt brat. So your perfect relationship isn't as perfect as you thought. So what? Does that mean you have to chuck it away?'

'You don't understand.'

'I understand perfectly. You want to bask in your perfect marriage, with your perfect wife and kids, and gloat at the rest of the world! Don't you? And now you've found a flaw, you can't stand it. Well, stand it, Simon! Stand it! Because the world is full of flaws. And frankly, what you had with Milly was about as good as it gets.'

'And what the hell would you know about successful relationships?' said Simon savagely. 'Why should I listen to a word you say?'

'Because I'm your fucking father!'

'Yes,' said Simon bitterly. 'And don't I know it.' He stood up, turned on his heel and stalked out of the room, leaving Harry staring after him.

Midmorning, there was a knock on Milly's door.

'Are you awake?' said Esme. 'Isobel's on the phone.'

'Oh,' said Milly dazedly, sitting up and pushing her hair back off her face. Her head felt heavy; her voice sounded like a stranger's. She looked at Esme and tried to smile. But her brain felt as though it was missing a cog. What was going on, anyway? Why was she at Esme's house?

'I'll get the cordless phone,' said Esme, and disappeared.

Milly sank back on her pillow and wondered why she felt so light-headed, so unreal. And then, with a dart of shock, she remembered.

The wedding was off. She ran the idea experimentally round her head, waiting for a stab of grief, a rush of tears. But this morning her eyes were dry, the sharp emotions of the night before had been rounded over by sleep. She could scarcely believe it. The wedding—her huge, immovable wedding—wasn't going to happen.

'Here you are,' said Esme, suddenly appearing by her bed. Milly took the phone and Esme walked softly out of the room.

'Hi,' came Isobel's voice down the line. 'Are you OK?'

'Yes,' said Milly. 'I suppose so.'

'You haven't heard from Simon?'

'No.' Milly's voice quickened. 'Why? Has he—'

'No,' said Isobel hurriedly. 'No, he hasn't. I just wondered. In case.'

'Oh,' said Milly. 'Isobel, I'm sorry. For landing you in it like that.'

'Oh, that,' said Isobel. 'Don't worry. It doesn't matter.'

'I just got rattled. I just—Well. You know what it was like.'

'Of course I do. I would have done exactly the same.'

'No, you wouldn't,' said Milly, grinning faintly. 'You've got a zillion times more self-control than me.'

'Well, anyway, don't worry,' said Isobel. 'It hasn't been a problem.'

'Really? Hasn't Mummy been lecturing you all day?'

'She hasn't had time,' said Isobel. 'We're all too busy.'

'Oh,' said Milly, wrinkling her brow. 'Doing what?'

There was silence.

'Cancelling the wedding,' said Isobel eventually.

'Oh,' said Milly again. Something heavy sank inside her stomach. 'Oh, I see. Of course.'

'Oh God, Milly, I'm sorry,' said Isobel. 'I thought you would realise.'

'I did,' said Milly. 'I do. Of course you have to cancel it.' She swallowed. 'Who have you told?'

'About half our guests,' said Isobel. 'Up to the Madisons. Harry's people are doing his lot.'

'Wow,' said Milly, feeling stupid, irrational tears coming to her eyes. 'You didn't hang about, did you? What are you telling them?'

'We've said you're ill,' said Isobel. 'We didn't know what else to say.'

There was silence.

'When are you coming back home?'

'I don't know,' said Milly. She thought of her room. Presents everywhere; her wedding dress hanging up, shrouded like a ghost. 'Not yet,' she said. 'Not until—'

'No,' said Isobel after a pause. 'Fair enough. Well, look. I'll come round and see you. When I've finished.'

'Isobel—thanks. For doing all this.'

'No problem,' said Isobel. 'I expect you'll do the same for me one day.'

'Yes.' Milly managed a wan smile. 'I expect so.'

She put the phone down. When she looked up, she saw Esme at the door. She was holding a tray and looking thoughtfully at Milly.

'Coffee,' she said, putting the tray down. 'To celebrate.'

'Celebrate?' said Milly disbelievingly.

'Your escape.' Esme came forward, holding two porcelain mugs. 'Your escape from matrimony.'

'It doesn't feel like an escape,' said Milly.

'Of course it doesn't,' exclaimed Esme. 'Not yet. But it will. Just think,

Milly—you're no longer tied down. You're an independent woman!'

'I suppose,' said Milly. She stared miserably into her coffee.

'Don't brood, darling!' said Esme. 'Drink your coffee and watch some nice television. And then we're going out for lunch.'

The restaurant was large and empty, save for a few single men reading newspapers over their coffee. Rupert gazed about awkwardly, wondering which one was Martin. Black jeans, he'd said. But most of them were wearing black jeans. He felt over-smart in his suit.

'Rupert?' a soft voice called, and he looked round. Standing up at a nearby table was a young man dressed in black jeans. He had close-cropped hair and a single earring and looked very obviously homosexual. In spite of himself, a shiver of dismay went through Rupert.

'Hello,' he said, aware that he sounded pompous. 'How do you do.'

'We spoke on the phone,' said the young man. 'I'm Martin.'

'Yes,' said Rupert, clutching his briefcase tight. He felt suddenly petrified. Here was homosexuality. Here was his own hidden, unspoken side, duplicated in front of him for all to see.

He sat down and shifted his chair slightly away from the table.

'It was good of you to come up to London,' Rupert said stiffly.

'Not at all,' said Martin. 'I'm up at least once a week. And if it's important . . .' He spread his hands.

'Yes,' said Rupert. He began to study the menu intently. He would take the letter and if possible a telephone number for Allan, then leave, as soon as possible.

'I've been waiting for your call,' Martin said. 'Allan told me a great deal about you. I hoped that one day you might start to look for him.'

'What did he tell you?' Rupert raised his head slowly.

Martin shrugged. 'Everything.'

A fiery red came to Rupert's cheeks and he put the menu down on the table. He looked at Martin, ready for a surge of humiliation. But Martin's eyes were kind; he looked as though he wanted to understand. Rupert cleared his throat. 'When did you meet him?'

'Six years ago,' said Martin.

'Did you . . . have a relationship with him?'

'Yes,' said Martin. 'We had a very close relationship.'

'I see.'

'I don't think you do.' Martin paused. 'I was his counsellor.'

'Oh,' said Rupert confusedly. 'Was he—'

'He was ill,' said Martin, and looked straight at Rupert.

A flash of deadly understanding passed through Rupert and he lowered his eyes. So here it was, without warning. His sentence; the end of the cycle. He had sinned, and now he was being punished.

'AIDS,' he said calmly.

'No,' said Martin, the tiniest note of scorn creeping into his voice. 'Not AIDS. Leukaemia. He had leukaemia.'

Rupert's eyes jerked up, to see Martin staring sadly at him. He felt suddenly sick, as though he'd entered a nightmare.

'I'm afraid so,' said Martin. 'Allan died, four years ago.'

For a while there was silence. A waiter came up and Martin discreetly ordered, while Rupert stared ahead with glassy eyes, trying to contain his pain. He felt as though his whole body was filling up with grief and guilt. Allan was dead. Allan was gone. He was too late.

'Are you OK?' said Martin in a low voice.

Rupert nodded, unable to speak.

'I can't tell you much about his death, I'm afraid. It happened in the States. His parents came over and took him home. I understand it was quite peaceful at the end.'

Rupert closed his eyes and a fresh pain swept over him and suddenly he felt as though he might break down.

'Don't think it,' said Martin.

'What?' Rupert opened his eyes.

'What you're thinking. What everybody thinks. If only you'd known he was going to die. Of course you would have done things differently.'

'What . . .' Rupert licked his lips. 'What did he say about me?'

'He said he loved you. He said he thought you loved him. But he wasn't angry any more.' Martin leaned forward and took Rupert's hand. 'It's important you understand that, Rupert. He wasn't angry with you.'

A waiter suddenly appeared at the table, carrying two cups of coffee.

'Thank you,' said Martin, without taking his hand from Rupert's. Rupert saw the waiter's gaze run over the pair of them, and, in spite of it all, he felt like running for cover. But instead he forced himself to leave his hand calmly in Martin's. As though it were normal.

'I know this is hard for you,' said Martin as the waiter left.

'I'm married,' said Rupert roughly. 'That's how hard it is.'

Martin nodded slowly. 'Allan thought you might be.'

'I suppose he despised me,' said Rupert, gazing into his cup of coffee.

'No,' said Martin. 'Allan *hoped* you were married. He agonised over whether to contact you. He didn't want to rock the boat if you were happy with a woman. But equally, he couldn't face discovering that you were with some other man. What he wanted to believe was that if you had ever changed your mind, you would have come back to him first.'

'Of course I would,' said Rupert, his voice trembling. 'He knew I would. He knew me like no other human being has ever known me.'

Rupert closed his eyes, and when he opened them again, Martin was pulling a letter out of his bag.

'Allan left you this,' he said. 'In case you ever came looking.'

'Thank you,' said Rupert. He took the envelope and looked at it silently for a few moments. There was his name, written beautifully in Allan's handwriting. He blinked a few times, then tucked the letter away, unopened, into his jacket. 'Do you have a mobile phone?' he said.

'Sure,' said Martin, reaching into his pocket.

'Milly needs to know about this,' said Rupert. 'The girl he married to stay in Britain.' He tapped in a number, listened for a moment, then switched the phone off. 'Busy,' he said.

Martin frowned. 'Allan told me about Milly,' he said. 'But she ought to know. He wrote to her.'

'Well, if he did, she never got the letter,' said Rupert. 'Because she doesn't know.' He tapped in the number again. 'And she needs to.'

Isobel put down the telephone and ran a hand through her hair. 'That was Aunt Jean,' she said. 'She wanted to know what we're going to do with the present she sent.'

She leaned back in her chair and surveyed the cluttered kitchen table. Lists of names, address books and telephone books were spread over the surface, each covered in brown coffee-cup rings and sandwich crumbs.

'I'm very sorry, Andrea,' Olivia was saying into her mobile phone. 'Yes, I do realise that Derek bought a morning suit especially. Please give him my apologies . . .' There was a pause and her hand tensed round the phone. 'No, they haven't set a new date as yet. Yes, I'll let you know . . . Yes, dear, goodbye.'

She turned the phone off with a trembling hand, ticked off a name and reached for the red book. 'Right,' she said. 'Now, who's next?'

'Why don't you take a break?' said Isobel. 'You look whacked.'

'No, darling,' said Olivia. 'I'd rather carry on. After all, it's got to be done, hasn't it?' She smiled brightly at Isobel. 'We can't just sit around feeling sorry for ourselves, can we?'

'No,' said Isobel. 'I suppose not.' She looked down at her list. 'I just had a call from the florist. She suggested that as Milly's bouquet is already made up, we might like it pressed and dried. As a memento.'

'A memento?'

'I know,' said Isobel, shaking with giggles in spite of herself.

'A memento! As if we'll ever forget! As if we'll ever forget today!'

Isobel glanced up sharply. Olivia's eyes were glittering with tears.

'Mummy!'

'I'm sorry, darling,' said Olivia. A tear landed on her nose and she smiled brightly. 'I don't mean to be silly.'

'I know how much you wanted this wedding,' said Isobel. She reached over and took her mother's hand. 'But there'll be another one. Honestly, there will.'

'It's not the wedding,' whispered Olivia. 'If it were just . . .' She broke off and reached for the phone.

Isobel looked at her mother, whose face was now streaked with tears.

'I really think you should have a break, Mummy,' Isobel said. 'Watch the telly. Or go to bed for a bit.'

'I can't,' said Olivia. 'We need to keep telephoning.'

'Rubbish,' said Isobel. 'Everyone I've spoken to has already heard. Gossip travels fast, you know. We've called the most important people. All the others will keep.'

'Well,' said Olivia after a pause. 'I do feel a little bit weary. Maybe I'll lie down for a bit. Are you going to have a rest, too?'

'No,' said Isobel. She reached for her coat. 'I'm going to see Milly.'

Esme's drawing room was warm and tranquil. As Isobel sat down on a pale, elegant sofa she looked about her pleasurably, admiring the collection of silver boxes heaped casually on a side table.

'So,' said Milly, sitting down opposite her. 'Is Mummy still furious?'

'Not really,' said Isobel, screwing up her face. 'She's weird.'

'That probably means she's furious.'

'She isn't, honestly. She said to give you her love.'

'Really?' said Milly. She curled her feet underneath her and sipped at her coffee.

'Here you are,' said Esme, handing a mug of coffee to Isobel. 'But I'm afraid I'll have to steal Milly in a little while. We're going out to lunch.'

'Good idea,' said Isobel. 'Where are you going?'

'A little place I know,' said Esme, smiling at them both. 'About ten minutes, Milly?'

'Fine,' said Milly. They both waited for Esme to close the door.

'So,' said Isobel, when she'd gone. 'How are you really?'

'I don't know,' said Milly slowly. 'Sometimes I feel fine—and sometimes I just want to burst into tears.' She closed her eyes. 'I don't know how I'm going to get through tomorrow.'

'Get drunk.'

'I'm doing that tonight.' A flicker of a smile passed over Milly's face. 'Care to join me?'

'Maybe,' said Isobel. She sipped at her coffee. 'And Simon hasn't been in touch?'

'No.' Milly's face closed up.

'I can't believe it's really all over between you two.' Isobel shook her head. 'Oh, Milly,' she said. 'It's such a shame.'

'It doesn't matter,' said Milly lightly. 'Come on. It's not as if I was pregnant. Now, that really would be a disaster.' She grinned.

Isobel met her eyes and gave an unwilling smile. For a while there was silence.

'Do you know what you're going to do?' said Milly at last.

'No.'

'What about the father?'

'He doesn't want a baby. He's made that very plain.'

'Isobel, you wouldn't really get rid of it, would you?'

'I don't know!' Isobel's voice rose in distress. 'I'm only thirty, Milly! I could meet some fantastic guy tomorrow. I could be swept off my feet. But if I've already got a kid . . .'

'It wouldn't make any difference,' said Milly stoutly.

'It would! And having a baby is no picnic. I've seen friends do it. They turn into zombies. And they're not even doing it on their own.'

'Well, I don't know,' said Milly, after a pause. 'It's your decision.'

'I know it is,' said Isobel. 'That's the problem.'

The door opened and they looked up. Esme smiled at them from under a huge fur hat.

'Ready to go, Milly? Isobel, sweetheart, do you want to come too?'

'No, thanks,' said Isobel, getting up. 'I'd better get back home.'

She watched as Milly got into Esme's red Daimler and they roared off round the corner. She couldn't quite face returning to the claustrophobic, sad atmosphere of the kitchen and making yet more awkward phone calls to curious strangers. Now that she was out in the fresh air, she wanted to stay out and stretch her legs.

She began to walk briskly back towards town, but then, as a sudden thought struck her, she paused and, propelled by a curiosity she recognised as ghoulish, she turned towards St Edward's Church.

As she stepped into the porch, she almost expected to hear bridal music playing on the organ. The church was filled with flowers; the pews were empty and waiting; the altar was shining brightly. Slowly she walked up the aisle, imagining the church filled with happy, expectant faces; imagining what it would have been like to watch her sister make the ancient vows that everyone knew and loved.

As she reached the front she stopped, and noticed a pile of white, redundant orders of service stacked at the end of a pew. With a stab of sadness, she reached for one—then, as she saw the two names printed in silver on the cover, blinked in surprise. *Eleanor and Giles*. 'Who the hell are Eleanor and Giles?' she said aloud.

'I beg your pardon?' A man's voice came from behind her, and she whipped round. Walking towards her was a young man in a cassock.

'Hello,' said Isobel. 'I'm Milly Havill's sister.'

'Ah, yes,' said the priest embarrassedly. 'What a shame. We were all very sorry to hear about that.'

'Were you?' said Isobel. 'So how come Eleanor and Giles have been given Milly's wedding day?'

'They haven't,' said the curate nervously. 'They're getting married in the afternoon. They booked it a year ago.'

'Oh,' said Isobel. She looked at the order of service, then put it down again. 'Well, all right then. I hope they have a happy day.'

'I'm really very sorry,' said the curate awkwardly. 'Maybe your sister will be able to get married at some time in the future. When she's straightened everything out.'

'It would be nice,' said Isobel. 'But I doubt it.'

With one last glance round the church, she strode out and walked straight into someone.

'Sorry,' she said, looked up, then stiffened. Harry Pinnacle was standing in front of her, wearing a navy-blue cashmere overcoat.

'Hello, Isobel,' he said. He glanced over her shoulder at the curate, who had followed her out. 'Terrible business, all this.'

'Yes,' said Isobel. 'Terrible.'

'I'm on my way to meet your father for lunch.'

'Yes,' said Isobel. 'He mentioned it.'

There was a clanking sound as the curate pulled the church door closed; suddenly they were alone.

'Well, I must be off,' muttered Isobel. 'Nice to see you.'

'Wait a minute,' said Harry.

'I'm in a bit of a hurry,' said Isobel, and she began to walk away.

'I don't care.' Harry grabbed her arm and pulled her round to face him. 'Isobel, why have you been ignoring all my messages?'

'Leave me alone,' said Isobel, twisting her head away.

'Isobel! I want to talk to you!'

'I can't,' said Isobel, her face closing up. 'Harry, I just . . . can't.'

There was a long silence. Then Harry dropped her arm.

'Fine,' he said. 'If that's what you want.'

'Whatever,' said Isobel in a dead voice. And without meeting his gaze, she thrust her hands in her pockets and strode off down the street.

Chapter Six

HARRY WAS SITTING BY THE BAR, beer in hand, when James arrived at the Pear and Goose in the centre of Bath.

'Good to see you, James,' he said, standing up to shake hands. 'Let me get you one of these.'

'Thanks,' said James. They both watched silently as the barman filled a pint glass with beer, and it occurred to James that this was the first time they had ever met alone.

'Cheers,' said Harry, raising his glass.

'Cheers.'

'Let's sit down,' said Harry, gesturing to a table in the corner. 'It's more private over there.'

'Yes,' said James. He cleared his throat. 'I imagine you want to talk about the financial practicalities of the wedding. Milly's little revelation must have cost you a small fortune.'

Harry waved a hand. 'That's not important.'

'It is important,' said James. 'I'm afraid it's not within my means to pay you back fully. But if we can come to some arrangement—'

'James,' interrupted Harry. 'I didn't ask you here so we could talk about money. I just thought you might like a drink. OK?'

'Oh,' said James, taken aback. 'Yes. Of course.'

'So let's sit down and have a fucking drink.'

They sat down at the corner table. Harry opened a packet of crisps. 'How is Milly?' he said. 'Is she OK?'

'I'm not sure, to be honest. She's with her godmother. How's Simon?'

'Stupid kid,' said Harry, crunching on crisps. 'I told him he was a spoilt brat this morning.'

'Oh,' said James, unsure what to say.

'The first sign of trouble, he runs away. The first hitch, he gives up. No wonder his business failed.'

'Aren't you being a little harsh?' protested James. 'He's had a huge shock. We all have . . .' He shook his head.

'So you really had no idea she was married,' said Harry.

'None whatsoever,' said James soberly. He looked up, to see Harry half grinning. 'What? You think it's funny?'

'Oh, come on,' said Harry. 'You've got to admire the girl's chutzpah! It takes a lot of guts to walk up the aisle knowing you've got a husband out there just waiting to trip you up.'

'That's not the way I see it,' said James, shaking his head. 'Milly's thoughtlessness has caused a lot of trouble and distress to a lot of people. Frankly, I'm ashamed to think she's my daughter.'

'Give the girl a break!'

'Then give Simon a break!' retorted James. 'He's the innocent one, remember. He's the wronged one.'

'He's a highhanded, moralistic little dictator.' Harry took a slug of beer. 'He's had it far too easy for far too long, that's his trouble.'

'You know, I'd say just the opposite,' said James. 'It can't be easy, walking in your shadow. I'm not sure I'd be able to do it myself.'

Harry shrugged silently. For a while neither of them spoke. Harry finished his beer, paused for a second, then looked up.

'How about Isobel?' he said casually. 'How's she reacted to all of this?'

'As usual,' said James. 'Gave very little away.' He drained his glass. 'Poor old Isobel's got enough on her plate as it is.'

'Work problems?' Harry leaned forward.

'Not just work.'

'Something else, then? Is she in some kind of trouble?'

James stared into his empty beer glass.

'I don't suppose it's any great secret,' he said after a pause, and looked at Harry's frowning face. 'She's pregnant.'

A look of utter shock came over Harry's face. 'Isobel's pregnant?'

'I know,' said James. 'I can't quite believe it myself. We don't even know who the father is.'

'Ah,' said Harry, and took a large gulp of beer.

'All we can do is support her in whatever decision she makes.'

'Decision?' Harry looked up.

'Whether to keep the baby or . . . not.' James shrugged awkwardly and looked away.

A strange expression passed over Harry's face. 'Oh, I see,' he said slowly. 'I see.' He closed his eyes. 'Stupid of me.'

317

'What?'

'Nothing,' said Harry, opening his eyes again. 'Nothing.'

'Anyway,' said James. 'It isn't your problem.' He looked at Harry's empty glass. 'Let me get you another.'

'No,' said Harry. 'Let me get you one.'

'But you've already—'

'Please, James,' said Harry. He sounded suddenly dejected, James thought. Almost sad. 'Please, James. Let me.'

Isobel had walked as far as the Garden for the Blind. Now she sat on an iron bench, watching the fountain trickle endlessly into the little pond and trying to think calmly. In her mind, she saw Harry's expression as she'd left him; heard his voice. She felt physically torn apart.

They had met for the first time only a few months before, at the party to celebrate Simon and Milly's engagement. As they'd shaken hands, a startled recognition had passed between them; and, like mirror images, they had each turned away quickly to talk to other people. But Harry's eyes had been on her every time she turned, and she had felt her entire body responding to his attention. The next week, they had met for dinner. He had smuggled her back into the house; the next morning, from his bedroom window, she had seen Milly in the drive waving goodbye to Simon. The month after that they had travelled to Paris on separate planes. Each encounter had been exquisite; a fleeting, hidden gem of experience. They had decided to tell no one; to keep things casual. Two adults enjoying themselves, nothing more.

But now nothing could be casual. Whichever way she turned, she would be taking an action with huge consequences. One tiny, unwitnessed biological event meant that, whatever she chose to do, neither of their lives would be the same again.

Harry didn't want a baby. If she went ahead, she would be on her own. She would lose Harry. She would lose her freedom.

If, on the other hand, she got rid of the baby . . .

A slow pain rose through Isobel's chest. Who was she kidding? What was this so-called choice? Yes, she had a choice. Every modern woman had a choice. But the truth was, she had no choice. She was enslaved to maternal emotions she'd never known she possessed; to the tiny self growing within her; to the primal, overpowering desire for life.

Rupert sat on a bench in the National Portrait Gallery, staring at a picture of Philip II of Spain. For the two hours since Martin had said goodbye, clasping Rupert's hand and exhorting him to call whenever he felt like it, Rupert had wandered mindlessly, not noticing where he was going, unaware of anything except his own thoughts.

The letter was still in his jacket pocket, unopened. He hadn't yet dared to read it. He had been too afraid—both that it wouldn't live up to his expectations and that it would. But now, under Philip's stern, uncompromising stare, he brought the envelope out. With shaking hands, he ripped at the paper and pulled out the thick, creamy sheets, each covered on one side only with a black, even script.

Dear Rupert,

Fear not. Fear not, said the angel. I'm not writing to you just so that you'll feel bad. At least not consciously. Not much.

I'm not sure why I'm writing at all. Will you ever read this letter? Probably not. Probably you've forgotten who I am; probably you're happily married with triplets.

And yet I keep writing—as though I'm sure that one day you'll trace a path back towards me and read these words. Perhaps you will, perhaps you won't. But the truth is, Rupert, I cannot leave this country, let alone this world, without somewhere recording a farewell to you.

When I close my eyes and think of you, it's as you were at Oxford. Five years on, who and what is Rupert? What I hope is that you're happy. What I fear is that if you're reading this letter you're probably not. Happy people don't trawl through the past looking for answers. What is the answer? I don't know. Perhaps we would have been happy if we'd stayed together. But you can't count on it.

As it turns out, what we had might have been as good as it was ever going to get. So we broke up. But at least one of us had a choice about that, even if it wasn't me. If we'd left it until now, neither of us would have had a choice. Breaking up is one thing; dying is something else. Frankly, I'm not sure I could cope with both at once. It'll take me long enough to get over my death as it is.

But I promised myself I wouldn't talk about dying. This isn't a guilt letter. It's a love letter. I still love you, Rupert. I still miss you. That's really all I wanted to say. If I don't see you again then . . . I guess that's just life.

Yours always,
Allan

Some time later, a teacher arrived at the door of the gallery with a class of cheerful children. They had intended to spend the afternoon sketching the portrait of Elizabeth I. But as she saw the young man sitting in the middle of the room, she swiftly turned the children round and shepherded them towards another painting.

Rupert, lost in silent tears, didn't even see them.

Harry arrived back that afternoon to find Simon's car parked in its usual place. He went straight up to Simon's room and knocked. When there was no answer, he paused for a moment, then retraced his steps down the stairs and along the corridor to the leisure complex.

The swimming pool was gleaming with underwater lighting, but no one was swimming. In the far corner, the steam-room door was misted up. Without pausing, Harry strode to the steam room and opened the door. Simon looked up, his face vulnerable with surprise.

'Dad?' he said, peering through the thick steam. 'What are you—'

'I need to talk to you,' said Harry, sitting down on the moulded plastic bench opposite Simon. 'I need to apologise.'

'Apologise?' said Simon in disbelief.

'I'm sorry. I shouldn't have yelled at you this morning. You've had a big shock. And I should have understood that. I'm your father.'

'Oh,' said Simon, looking away. 'Well. It doesn't matter.'

'Some fucking father I've been.'

Simon shifted awkwardly on his seat. 'You—'

'Don't feel you have to be polite,' interrupted Harry. 'I know I screwed up with you. For sixteen years you never see me, then suddenly bam! I'm in your face all the time. No wonder things have been a bit tricky. If we were a married couple, we'd be divorced by now. Sorry,' he added after a pause. 'Sensitive subject.'

'It's OK.' Simon turned his head and gave him an unwilling grin, then, for the first time, registered his father's appearance. 'Dad, you know you're meant to take your clothes off?'

'That's for a steam bath,' said Harry. 'I came in here for a conversation.' He frowned. 'OK, so I've said my piece. Now you're supposed to tell me I've been a wonderful father, and I can rest easy.'

There was a pause. 'I just wish . . .' began Simon at last, then stopped.

'What?'

'I just wish I didn't always feel like a failure,' said Simon in a rush. 'Everything I do goes wrong. And you . . . By the time you were my age, you were a millionaire!'

'No, I wasn't.'

'It said in your biography . . .'

'That piece of shit. Simon, by the time I was your age, I *owed* a million. Fortunately, I found a way of paying it back.'

'And I didn't,' said Simon bitterly. 'I went bust.'

'OK,' said Harry, 'so you went bust. But at least you never came crying to me to bail you out. I'm proud of you for that.' He paused. 'I'm even proud you gave me back the keys to that flat. Pissed off—but proud.'

There was a long pause, punctuated only by the two of them breathing in the steamy air.

'And if you have a go at working things out with Milly,' continued Harry slowly, 'instead of walking away—then I'll be even prouder. Because that's something I never did. And I should have done.'

There was silence for a while. Harry looked at his son through the steam. 'So, are you going to give Milly another chance?'

Simon exhaled sharply. 'Of course I am. If she'll give me another chance.' He shook his head. 'I don't know what I was thinking of last night. I was just a . . .' He broke off. 'I tried calling her this afternoon.'

'And?'

'She must have gone out with Esme. Esme Ormerod, her godmother.'

Harry looked up. 'That's Milly's godmother? Esme Ormerod?'

'Yes,' said Simon. 'Why?'

Harry pulled a face. 'Strange woman. I took her out to dinner a few times. Big mistake.'

'Why?'

Harry shook his head. 'It doesn't matter. It was a long time ago.' He leaned back and closed his eyes. 'So, she's Milly's godmother? That surprises me.'

'She's some cousin or something.'

'And they seemed such a nice family,' said Harry in half-jesting tones. Then he frowned. 'I'm serious, you know. They are a nice family. Milly's a lovely girl. James seems a very decent guy. I'd like to get to know him better. And Olivia . . .' He opened his eyes. 'Well, what can I say? She's a fine woman.'

'You said it.' Simon grinned at his father.

'I just wouldn't like to meet her on a dark night.'

'Or any night.'

There was a short silence.

'The only one I'm not sure about,' said Simon thoughtfully, 'is Isobel. She's a bit of an enigma. I never know what she's thinking.'

'No,' said Harry after a pause. 'Neither do I.'

'She's nothing like Milly. But I still like her.'

'So do I,' said Harry in a low voice. 'I like her a lot.' He stared silently at the floor for a few moments, then abruptly stood up. 'I've had enough of this hell. I'm going to take a shower.'

'Try taking your clothes off this time,' said Simon.

'Yes,' said Harry. 'Clever.' And he gave Simon a friendly nod before closing the door.

Simon stood on Esme's doorstep and rang the bell, a large bunch of flowers in his hands. Esme answered the door in a white bathrobe.

'Oh,' said Simon awkwardly. 'Sorry to disturb you. I wanted to speak to Milly.' Esme scanned his face, then said, 'She's asleep, I'm afraid.'

'Oh,' said Simon. He shifted from one foot to the other. 'Well . . . just tell her I called round, would you? And give her these.' He handed the flowers to Esme and she looked at them with faint horror.

'I'll tell her,' she said. 'Goodbye.'

'Perhaps she could give me a ring. When she's up.'

'Perhaps,' said Esme. 'It's up to her.'

'Of course,' said Simon, flushing slightly. 'Well, thanks.'

'Goodbye,' said Esme, and closed the door. She looked at the flowers for a moment, then went into the kitchen and put them into the rubbish bin. She went upstairs and tapped on Milly's door.

'Who was that?' said Milly, looking up. She was lying on a massage table and Esme's beautician was rubbing a facial oil into her cheeks.

'A salesman,' said Esme smoothly. 'He tried to sell me some dusters.'

'Oh,' said Milly, relaxing back onto the table.

Esme wandered over to the window, tapped her teeth for a few moments, then turned round. 'You know, I think we should go away,' she said. 'I should have thought of it before. You don't want to be in Bath tomorrow, do you?'

'Not really,' said Milly. 'But then . . . I don't really want to be any- where.' Her face suddenly crumpled and tears began to ooze out of the sides of her eyes. 'I'm sorry,' she said huskily to the beautician.

'We'll drive into Wales,' said Esme. 'I know a place in the mountains. Fabulous views and Welsh lamb every night. How does that sound?'

Milly was silent.

'Tomorrow will be difficult,' said Esme gently. 'But we'll get through it. And after that . . .' She came forward and took Milly's hand. 'Just think, Milly. You can remould your life into whatever you want.'

'You're right,' said Milly, staring up at the ceiling. 'Anything I want.'

'And to think you were about to settle for becoming a Mrs Pinnacle!' A note of scorn entered Esme's voice. 'Darling, when you look back on all of this, you'll be grateful to me. You really will!'

'I already am grateful,' said Milly, turning her head to look at Esme. 'I don't know what I would have done without you.'

When James arrived home that evening the lights were low and the house silent. He hung up his coat and pushed open the door to the kitchen. The table was covered in forlorn wedding debris, and Olivia was sitting in the dim stillness, her shoulders hunched and defeated.

After a few moments she raised her head. Her eyes met his and flickered quickly away. James stepped forward awkwardly. 'So,' he said, putting his briefcase down. 'It's all done. You must have had a hell of a day.'

'Not so bad,' said Olivia huskily. 'Isobel was a great help. We both . . .' She broke off. 'What about *your* day? Isobel told me you've been having trouble at work. I . . . I didn't realise. I'm sorry.'

'You couldn't have realised,' said James. 'I didn't tell you.'

'Tell me now.'

'Not now,' said James wearily. 'Maybe later.'

'Yes, later,' said Olivia, her voice unsteady. 'Let me make you some tea,' she said.

'Thank you,' said James. 'Olivia—'

'I won't be a moment!' She stood up hurriedly and turned towards the sink. James sat down at the table and picked up the red book in front of him. He began to leaf idly through it. Page after page of lists, of ideas, self-reminders, even small sketches. The blueprint, he realised, for something quite spectacular.

'Swans,' he said, stopping at a starred item. 'You weren't really going to hire live swans for the occasion?'

'Swans made of ice,' said Olivia, brightening a little. 'They were going to be full of . . .' She halted. 'It doesn't matter.'

'Full of what?' said James. There was a pause.

'Oysters,' said Olivia.

'I like oysters,' said James.

'I know,' said Olivia. She picked up the teapot with fumbling hands, turned to put it on the table and slipped. The teapot crashed loudly onto the quarry tiles and Olivia gave a small cry of distress.

'Olivia!' exclaimed James, leaping to his feet. 'Are you all right?' Pieces of broken china lay on the floor amid a puddle of hot tea. The yellow-rimmed eye of a duck stared up at him reproachfully.

'It's broken!' said Olivia in anguish. 'We've had that teapot for thirty-two years!' She picked up a piece and stared at it disbelievingly.

'We'll get another one,' said James.

'I don't want another one,' said Olivia shakily. 'I want the old one. I want . . .' She suddenly broke off and turned round to face James. 'You're going to leave me, aren't you, James?'

'What?' James stared at her in shock.

'You're going to leave me,' repeated Olivia calmly. She looked down at the jagged piece of teapot in her hand. 'For a new, exciting life.'

There was a pause, then James exhaled in sudden comprehension.

'You *heard* me,' he said, gathering his thoughts. 'I hadn't realised . . .'

'Yes, I heard you,' said Olivia, not looking up.

'Olivia, I didn't mean—'

'I assume you've been waiting until the wedding was over,' broke in Olivia. 'You didn't want to ruin the happy event. Well, the happy event's been ruined anyway. So you don't have to wait any longer. You can go.'

James looked at her. 'You want me to go?'

'That's not what I said.' Olivia's head remained bowed.

'The trouble at work,' said James suddenly, walking to the window. 'The trouble that Isobel was talking about. It's a restructuring of the company. They're relocating three departments to Edinburgh. They asked me if I'd like to move. And I said . . .' He turned round. 'I said I'd think about it.'

Olivia looked up. 'You didn't mention it to me.'

'No,' said James defensively. 'I didn't. I knew you wouldn't want to leave your business and your friends. But I just felt as though I needed something new!' Pain flashed across James's face. 'Can you understand that? I felt trapped and guilty. I thought maybe a new city would be the answer to my malaise.'

The kitchen was silent.

'I see,' said Olivia eventually, her voice clipped and brittle. 'Well, then, off you go. Don't let me hold you up. I'll help you pack, shall I?'

'Olivia, don't be like this!'

'What do you expect? You've been planning to leave me!'

'Well, what was I supposed to do?' said James furiously. 'Just say no on the spot? Settle down to another twenty years in Bath?'

'No!' cried Olivia, her eyes suddenly glittering with tears. 'You were supposed to ask me to come with you. I'm your wife, James. You were supposed to ask me.'

'What was the point? You would have said—'

'You don't know what I would have said!' Olivia's voice trembled and she lifted her chin high. 'You don't know what I would have said, James.'

There was a long silence.

'What would you have said?' asked James finally. He tried to meet Olivia's eye, but she was staring at the piece of teapot in her hands.

The doorbell rang. Neither of them moved.

'What would you have said, Olivia?' said James.

'I don't know,' said Olivia at last. She put the piece of teapot down on the table and looked up. 'I probably would have asked you if you were really so unhappy with your life here. I would have asked if you really thought a new city would solve all your problems. And if you'd said yes—' The doorbell rang again, and she broke off. 'You'd better get that,' she said. James gazed at her for a few seconds, then got to his feet.

He strode into the hall, opened the door and took a step back in surprise. Alexander was standing on the doorstep. His face was unshaven, he was surrounded by bags and his eyes were wary.

'Look,' he said, as soon as he saw James. 'I'm sorry. I really am. You've got to believe me. I didn't mean to set all this off.'

'It hardly matters any more, does it?' said James wearily. 'The damage is done. If I were you, I'd just turn round and go.'

'It matters to me,' said Alexander. He paused. 'Plus, I've still got some stuff here. Your daughter chucked me out before I could get it.'

'I see,' said James. 'Well, you'd better come in, then.'

Cautiously, Alexander entered the house. 'Is Milly all right?' he asked.

'What do you think?' said James.

Alexander flinched. 'Look, it wasn't my fault!' he said.

'What do you mean, it wasn't your fault?' Olivia appeared at the kitchen door, her face indignant. 'Perhaps you thought you were doing your duty. But you could have come to us first, or Simon, before informing the vicar.'

'I didn't want to expose her, for God's sake,' said Alexander impatiently. 'I just wanted to tease her a bit. And that's all I did. I didn't tell the vicar! Why should I want to wreck Milly's wedding? You were paying me to photograph it!'

There was silence. James glanced at Olivia.

'Listen, I didn't tell anyone about Milly. I really didn't.' Alexander sighed. 'Jesus, she could have six husbands for all I care!'

'All right,' said James, exhaling sharply. 'All right. But if you didn't say anything, who did?'

'God knows! Who else knew about it?'

'No one,' said Olivia. 'She hadn't told anyone.'

There was silence.

'She told Esme,' said James eventually. 'She told Esme.'

Isobel sat in a remote corner of the drive to Pinnacle Hall, looking through her car windscreen at Milly's marquee, just visible behind the house. She had been sitting there for half an hour, quietly composing her thoughts, honing her concentration as though for an exam. She would say what she had to say to Harry, brook as little objection as possible, then leave. She would be friendly, but businesslike. If he refused her proposal, she would . . . Isobel's thoughts faltered. He couldn't refuse such a reasonable plan. He simply couldn't.

Her heart aching a little, she reached inside her bag and gave her hair one final comb, then opened the car door and got out. Calmly she walked across the gravel towards the big front door, for once unafraid of being observed. Today she had every reason to be at Pinnacle Hall.

She rang at the door and smiled at the girl who answered.

'I'd like to see Harry Pinnacle, please. It's Isobel Havill. Milly's sister.'

'I'm not sure he's available,' said the girl in less than friendly tones.

'Perhaps you could ask,' said Isobel politely.

After a few minutes the girl returned, and showed her into Harry's study.

'Isobel Havill,' the girl announced.

'Yes,' said Harry, meeting Isobel's eyes. 'I know.'

As the door closed behind the girl he put his pen down and looked at Isobel without saying anything. Isobel didn't move. She stood, trembling slightly, feeling his gaze on her skin like sunshine, then closed her eyes, trying to gather her thoughts. She heard him come towards her. His hand had grasped hers; his lips were pressed against the tender skin of her inner wrist, before she opened her eyes and said 'No.'

He looked up, her hand still in his, and she gazed desperately into his face, trying to convey all that she had to say in a single look. But there were too many conflicting desires and thoughts for him to read. A flash of something like disappointment passed over his face and he dropped her hand abruptly. 'A drink,' he said.

'I've got something to say to you,' said Isobel.

'I see,' said Harry. 'Then say it!'

'Fine!' said Isobel. 'Here it is.' She paused, steeling herself to utter the words. 'I'm pregnant,' she said, and the guilty word seemed to echo round the room. 'With your baby,' she added. Harry made a slight start. 'What?' said Isobel defensively. 'Don't you *believe* me?'

'Of course I fucking believe you,' said Harry. 'I was going to say . . .' He broke off. 'It doesn't matter. Carry on.'

She took a deep breath and fixed her eyes on the corner of the mantelpiece. 'I've thought about it very hard and I've decided to keep it.' She paused. 'I've taken this decision knowing you don't want a child. So she'll have my name and I'll be responsible for her.'

'You know it's a girl?' interrupted Harry.

'No,' said Isobel shakily, put off her stride. 'I just tend to use the feminine pronoun if the gender is unspecific.'

'I see,' said Harry. 'Carry on.'

'I'll be responsible for her,' said Isobel, speaking more quickly. 'Financially, as well as everything else. But I think every child needs a father if at all possible. I know you didn't choose for things to be this way—but neither did I, and neither did the baby.' She paused and clenched her fists tightly by her sides. 'And so I'd like to ask that you carry some parental responsibility and involvement. What I propose is a regular meeting, perhaps once a month, so that this child grows up knowing who her father is. I'm not asking any more than that.'

'Once a month,' said Harry, frowning.

'Yes!' said Isobel angrily. 'You can't expect a child to bond on twice-yearly meetings.'

'I suppose not.' Harry stalked to the window. Suddenly he turned round. 'What about once a week? Would that do?'

Isobel stared at him. 'Yes,' she said. 'Of course—'

'Or once a day?'

'Yes. But . . .' Harry began to walk slowly towards her, his warm eyes locked onto hers.

'How about every morning and every afternoon and all through the night?' He gently took hold of her hands; she made no effort to resist. 'How about I love you? How about I want to be with you all the time? And be a better father to our child than I ever was with Simon.'

Isobel gazed up at him. Emotions were pushing up to the surface in an uncontrollable surge. 'But you said you didn't want a baby!' The words rushed out of her in a hurt, accusatory roar. 'You said—'

'When did I say that?' interrupted Harry. 'I never said that.'

'You didn't exactly say it,' said Isobel after a pause. 'But when I said a friend of mine was pregnant you pulled this . . . this face.' Isobel swallowed. 'And I said, Oh, don't you like babies? And you changed the subject.' She looked up, to see Harry staring at her incredulously.

'You might have got rid of our baby because of that?'

'I didn't know what to do!' cried Isobel defensively. 'I thought—'

Harry shook his head. 'Are you this good at interpreting your foreign diplomats? No wonder the world's at war—Isobel Havill's been conducting the negotiations. She thought you didn't want peace because you pulled a nasty face.'

Isobel gave a shaky half-giggle half-sob, and nestled into his chest.

'You really want to have this baby?' she said. 'Seriously?'

'I seriously do,' said Harry. They stood for a while saying nothing, then Isobel pulled reluctantly away. 'Someone might see me.'

Harry began to laugh. 'Isobel, haven't you got it into your head yet?' he said. 'I *want* everyone to see you! I love you! I want to—' He broke off and looked at her with a different expression. 'Try this for size. What would you think about . . . about giving the baby my name?'

'You don't mean . . .' Isobel felt her skin begin to tingle.

'I don't know,' said Harry. 'It depends. Do you already have a husband I should know about?'

'Bastard!' said Isobel, kicking his shins.

'Is that a yes?' said Harry, starting to laugh. 'Or a no?'

Simon was sitting by the window of his bedroom, trying to read a book, as the doorbell rang. A spasm of nerves went through him and he quickly got to his feet. It was Milly. It had to be Milly.

He had driven back to Pinnacle Hall from Esme's house with a hopeful happiness bubbling through him like spring water. He'd made the first move towards a reconciliation with Milly; as soon as she responded, he would renew his apologies and try to heal the wound between them as best he could. They would wait for her divorce to come through; organise another wedding; start life again.

And now here she was. He descended the wide stairs, a foolish grin on his face, and briskly crossed the hall. But before he was halfway across, his father's study door opened and Harry appeared. 'Oh, hello,' he said. 'Are you expecting someone?'

'I don't know,' said Simon awkwardly. 'Milly, maybe.'

'Ah,' said Harry. 'I'll get out of your way, then.'

Simon grinned at his father and, without thinking, allowed his eyes to roam inside the open study door. To his surprise he caught a glimpse of female leg by the fire. A mild curiosity began to rise through him and he glanced questioningly at his father. Harry seemed to think for a couple of seconds, then he flung the study door open.

Isobel Havill was sitting by the fire. Her head shot up, a shocked expression on her face, and Simon stared back at her in surprise.

'Hi, Isobel,' said Simon. 'What are you doing here?'

'I'm here to talk about the wedding,' she said after a pause.

'No, you're not,' said Harry. 'Don't lie to him.'

'Oh,' said Simon confusedly. 'Well, it doesn't—'

'We have something to tell you, Simon,' said Harry. 'Although this may not be quite the best time . . .'

'No, it's not,' interrupted Isobel firmly. 'Why doesn't one of you answer the door?'

'What have you got to tell me?' said Simon. His heart began to thud. He looked from one to the other. Isobel was giving his father a private little frown; Harry was grinning back at her teasingly. Simon stared at the two of them, communicating in a silent, intimate language, and suddenly, with a lurch, he understood.

'Get the door,' said Isobel. 'Somebody.'

'I'll go,' said Simon in a strangled voice.

He strode up to the front door and yanked it open. On the doorstep was a stranger. A tall, well-built man, with blond hair that shone under the lantern like a halo, and wary, bloodshot blue eyes.

Simon stared back at the stranger in disappointment, too nonplussed by events to speak.

'I'm looking for Simon Pinnacle,' said the stranger at last. 'Are you him, by any chance?'

'Yes,' said Simon, pulling himself together. 'How can I help you?'

'You won't know who I am,' said the man.

'I think I do,' interrupted Isobel, from behind Simon. An incredulous note entered her voice as she said, 'You're Rupert, aren't you?'

Giles Claybrook and Eleanor Smith were standing at the altar of St Edward's, gazing silently at one another.

'Now,' said Canon Lytton, smiling benevolently at the pair of them. 'Is it to be one ring or two?'

'One,' said Giles, looking up.

'Ellie, love,' said Eleanor's uncle, filming behind on a video camera. 'Could you move slightly to the right? Lovely.'

'One ring,' said Canon Lytton, making a note on his service sheet.

There was a rattle at the doors at the back of the church, and he looked up in surprise. The door swung open, to reveal James and Olivia.

'Forgive us,' said James, walking briskly up the aisle. 'We just need a moment with Canon Lytton.'

'I am busy!' thundered Canon Lytton. 'Kindly wait at the back!'

'It won't take a second,' said James. 'We just need to know—who told you about Milly's first wedding?'

'If you are trying to convince me, at this late stage, that the information is false . . .' began Canon Lytton.

'We're not!' said Olivia impatiently. 'We just need to know.'

'Was it my cousin, Esme Ormerod?' asked James.

There was silence.

'I was told in confidence,' said Canon Lytton at last, a slight stiffness entering his voice. 'And I'm afraid that—'

'I'll take that as confirmation that it was,' said James. He sank down onto a pew. 'I just don't believe it. She's supposed to be Milly's god-mother! She's supposed to help and protect her!'

'Indeed,' said Canon Lytton sternly. 'And would it be helping your daughter to stand back as she entered a marriage based on falseness?'

'She was acting out of spite and you know it!' said Olivia. 'She's a malicious troublemaker! I never liked her from the start.'

Canon Lytton had turned to Giles and Eleanor.

'My apologies for this unseemly interruption,' he said. 'Now, let us resume. The giving and receiving of the ring.'

'Hold on,' said Eleanor's uncle. 'I'll rewind the video, shall I? Or do you want me to keep all this?' He gestured to James and Olivia. 'We could send it in to a TV show.'

'No, we bloody couldn't,' snapped Eleanor. 'Carry on, Canon Lytton.' She shot a malevolent look at Olivia. 'We'll ignore these rude people.'

'Very well,' said Canon Lytton. 'Now, Giles, you will place the ring on Eleanor's finger, and repeat after me: With this ring, I thee wed.'

Giles said self-consciously, 'With this ring, I thee wed.'

'With my body, I thee worship.'

'With my body I thee worship.'

As the ancient words rose into the empty space of the church, every-one seemed to relax. Olivia looked at James and a wistful expression came over her face. She sat down next to him. 'Do you remember our wedding?' she said quietly.

'Yes,' said James. He met her eyes cautiously. 'What about it?'

'Nothing,' she said. 'I was just remembering how nervous I was.'

'You, nervous?' said James, half smiling.

'Yes,' said Olivia. 'Nervous.' There was a long pause, then she said, without meeting his eye, 'Perhaps next week—if you felt like it—we could go up to Edinburgh. Just for a break. We could have a look around. Stay in a hotel. And . . . and talk about things.'

There was silence.

'I'd like that,' said James eventually. 'I'd like that very much.' He paused. 'What about the bed and breakfast?'

'I could close it for a bit,' said Olivia. She flushed slightly. 'It's not the most important thing in my life, you know.'

James stared at her silently. Cautiously, he moved his hand across towards hers. Olivia remained motionless. Then there was a sudden rat-tling at the door, and they jumped apart like scalded cats. The young curate of the church was striding up the aisle, cordless phone in hand.

'Canon Lytton,' he said, a note of excitement in his voice. 'You have a very urgent telephone call from Miss Havill. I wouldn't interrupt, normally, but—' He handed the phone to Canon Lytton, his eyes gleaming. 'Apparently there's been a rather startling development.'

Isobel put down the telephone and looked at the others.

'I just spoke to Mummy at the church,' she said. 'It wasn't Alexander who told the vicar about Milly.' She paused for effect. 'It was Esme.'

'That doesn't surprise me,' said Harry.

'Do you know her?' said Isobel, staring at him in surprise.

'I used to,' said Harry. 'Not any more. Not for a long time,' he added hastily. Isobel gave him a briefly suspicious look, then frowned.

'And Milly doesn't even realise! I must call her.'

'No wonder she wouldn't let me in the house,' said Simon, as Isobel picked up the phone again. 'The woman's a bloody weirdo!'

There was a tense silence as Isobel waited to be connected. Suddenly her face changed expression, and she motioned the others to be quiet.

'Hi, Esme,' she said, her voice casual. 'Is Milly there? Oh, right. Could you maybe wake her up?' She pulled a face at Simon, who grimaced back. 'Oh, I see. OK, well, not to worry. Just give her my love!'

She put down the phone and looked at the others.

'I don't trust that woman,' she said. 'I'm going round there.'

Chapter Seven

As SHE REACHED the bottom of the stairs, Milly stopped and put her case down on the floor.

'I'm not sure about going away,' said Milly. 'Maybe it would be better to stay and be brave and face it out.'

Esme shook her head. 'Darling, the best place for you at the moment is somewhere far away, tranquil and discreet, where you can take some time out, rebalance yourself, work out your priorities.'

Milly stared at the floor for a while. 'It's true,' she said at last. 'I do need a chance to think.'

'You won't regret it,' said Esme, smiling. 'Come on. Let's go.'

Esme's Daimler was parked on the street outside. As they got in, Milly turned round in her seat and peered curiously through the back window. 'That looks like Isobel's car,' she said.

'There are lots of these little Peugeots around the place,' murmured Esme. She turned on the ignition and a blast of Mozart filled the car.

'It *is* Isobel's car!' said Milly, peering harder. 'What's she doing here?'

'Well, I'm afraid we can't hang around,' said Esme, swiftly putting the car into gear. 'You can give her a ring when we get there.'

'No, wait!' protested Milly. 'She's getting out. She's coming towards us. Esme, stop!' Esme began to drive off, and Milly stared at her in astonishment. 'Esme, stop!' she said. 'Stop the car!'

Hurrying along the street, Isobel saw Esme's car pulling away from the kerb and felt a thrust of panic. She began to run after the car, and as she ran, she saw Milly turn and see her, then say something to Esme. But the car didn't stop. A surge of fury went through Isobel and she upped her pace to a sprint, unsure what she would do when Esme turned the corner and zipped off down the main road.

But the traffic lights at the end of the road were red, and Esme's car was forced to slow down. Feeling like a triumphant Olympic athlete, Isobel caught up with the car and began to bang on Milly's window. Inside, she could see Milly shouting animatedly at Esme, then struggling with the handbrake. Suddenly the door opened and Milly spilled out. 'What is it?' she gasped. 'I thought it must be important.'

'Too right it's important!' managed Isobel, panting hard, almost unable to speak for anger. 'For a start, you might like to know it was this bitch who shopped you to the vicar.' She gestured scornfully at Esme, who stared back with furious, glinting eyes.

'What do you mean?' said Milly. 'It was Alexander.'

'It wasn't Alexander, it was Esme! Wasn't it?' snapped Isobel at Esme.

'Really?' said Milly, looking at Esme with wide eyes. '*Really?*'

'Of course not!' said Esme tartly. 'Why would I do such a thing?'

'To get back at Harry, perhaps,' said Isobel, a new, scathing note entering her voice. 'He's told me all about you. Everything.'

There was silence. Esme's glinting eyes ranged sharply over Isobel's face, then suddenly flickered in comprehension. 'I see,' she said slowly. 'So that's how it is.' She gave Isobel a tiny, contemptuous smile. 'You Havill girls do have a penchant for money, don't you?'

'You're a bitch, Esme,' said Isobel.

'I don't understand,' said Milly, looking from Isobel to Esme. 'Did you really tell Canon Lytton about me being married, Esme?'

'Yes, I did,' said Esme. 'For your own good. I saved you from a life of mediocrity with that immature, sanctimonious little prig!'

'You betrayed me!' cried Milly. 'You're supposed to be on my side!'

Behind them, a line of cars was beginning to mount up. One of them sounded its horn. Towards the back of the queue, a driver got out of his car and began to walk along the pavement.

'Darling, I know you well,' began Esme. 'And I know that—'

'You don't!' interrupted Milly. 'You don't know me well. You don't bloody know me at all! All of you think you know me—and none of you do! You haven't got any idea what I'm really like, underneath . . .'

'Excuse me.' A truculent male voice interrupted them. 'Have you seen the light?'

'Yes,' said Milly dazedly. 'I think I probably have.'

'The lady was just leaving,' said Isobel, and slammed the passenger door of Esme's car viciously. 'Come on, Milly,' she said, taking her sister's arm. 'Let's go.'

As they sped away in Isobel's car, Milly sank back into her seat and massaged her brow with her fingertips. Isobel drove quickly and efficiently, glancing at Milly every so often but saying nothing. After a while, Milly sat up and smoothed back her hair.

'Thanks, Isobel,' she said.

'Any time.'

'How did you guess it was Esme?'

'It had to be,' said Isobel. 'No one else knew. If Alexander hadn't told anyone, it had to be her. And . . .' She paused. 'There were other things.'

'What things?' Milly swivelled her head towards Isobel. 'What was all that about getting back at Harry?'

'They had a liaison,' said Isobel shortly. 'Let's just say it didn't work.'

'How do you know?'

'He told Simon. And me. I was over there just now.' A tinge of pink came to Isobel's cheeks and she put her foot down rather hard on the accelerator. Milly stared at her sister. 'Isobel, what's going on?'

Isobel said nothing, but changed gear with a crunch. She signalled to turn left and turned the windscreen wipers on by mistake.

'There's something you're not telling me, Isobel,' said Milly. 'You're hiding something. What were you doing at Pinnacle Hall?' Milly's voice suddenly sharpened. 'Who were you seeing?'

'No one.'

'Don't play games with me! Have you and Simon been seeing each other behind my back?'

'No!' said Isobel, laughing. 'Don't be ridiculous.'

'Well, what is it, then?' Milly's voice rose higher. 'What's going on!'

'OK!' Isobel said. 'OK. I'll tell you. I was going to break it to you gently but since you're so bloody suspicious . . .' She glanced at Milly and took a deep breath. 'Harry is the father.' She glanced at Milly's face, still blank and uncomprehending. 'Of my child, Milly! He's . . . he's the one I've been seeing.'

'What?' Milly's voice ripped through the car like the cry of a bird. 'You've been having an affair with Simon's *dad*?'

'Yes!' said Isobel defensively. 'But—' She stopped at the sound of Milly bursting into sobs, her face in her hands. 'Milly, I'm really sorry,' she said. 'I know this is a terrible time to tell you. Oh, Milly, don't cry!'

'I'm not crying,' managed Milly, gasping for breath. 'I'm laughing.' She looked at Isobel, then erupted into hysterical giggles again. 'You and Harry! But he's so old!'

'He's not old!' said Isobel. 'Anyway, I don't care. I love him. And I'm going to have his baby!'

Milly raised her head and looked at Isobel. She was staring ahead defiantly but her lips were trembling and tears had spilled onto her cheeks. 'Oh, Isobel, I'm sorry!' Milly said in distress. 'I didn't mean it! He's not old really.' She paused. 'I'm sure you'll make a lovely couple.'

'Of fogeys,' said Isobel, signalling to turn right.

'Don't!' said Milly. A tiny giggle erupted from her and she clamped her mouth shut. 'I can't believe it. My sister, having a secret affair with Harry Pinnacle. I knew you were up to something. But I never would have guessed in a million years.' She glanced at Isobel's profile. 'You're very good at keeping secrets, you know.'

'Speak for yourself!'

As they approached Pinnacle Hall, Milly's eyes suddenly focused on her surroundings, and she stiffened.

'Isobel, I don't want to see Simon,' she said. 'If you've set up some meeting, you can forget it. I'm not going to see him.'

'You know, he came to apologise to you this afternoon,' said Isobel. 'He brought you flowers. But Esme wouldn't let him in.' She turned towards Milly. 'Now do you want to see him?'

'No,' said Milly, after a pause. 'He can't undo the things he said.'

'I think he's genuinely sorry,' said Isobel, as they approached Pinnacle Hall, 'for what that's worth.'

'I don't care,' said Milly. As the car crackled on the gravel drive, she shrank down in her seat. 'I don't want to see him.'

'Fine,' said Isobel calmly. 'It's not him I've brought you to see, anyway.

There's someone else who's come to see you.' She switched off the engine and looked at Milly. 'Brace yourself for a shock,' she added.

'What?' But Isobel was already out of the car and walking towards the house. Hesitantly, Milly got out and began to follow her sister. Automatically her eyes rose to Simon's bedroom window. The curtains were drawn, but she could see a chink of light. Perhaps he was behind the curtains, watching her. She began to walk more quickly, wondering what Isobel had been talking about. As she neared the front door, it suddenly opened and a tall figure appeared in the shadows.

'Rupert!' said Milly. She stopped in astonishment. 'What are you doing here? You were in London.'

'I came down by train,' said Rupert. 'I had to see you. There was no one at your house, so I came here.'

'I suppose you've heard, then,' said Milly. 'The wedding's off.'

'I know. That's why I'm here.' He rubbed his face, then looked up. 'Milly, I tracked down Allan for you.'

'You've found him? Already?' Milly's voice rose in excitement.

Rupert walked slowly towards her and took her hands. 'Milly, I've got some bad news. Allan's dead. He died four years ago.'

Milly stared at him in stunned silence. Allan couldn't be dead. People his age didn't die. It must surely be a joke. But Rupert wasn't smiling or laughing. He was gazing at her with a strange desperation, as though waiting for a reaction. Milly blinked a few times, and swallowed, her throat suddenly dry like sandpaper.

'What . . . how?' she managed. Visions of car crashes ran through her mind. Aeroplane disasters; mangled wreckage on the television.

'Leukaemia,' said Rupert.

Milly gazed at him for a few silent seconds, and a thousand shared memories seemed to pass between them. 'It's all wrong,' she said eventually. 'He didn't . . .' Something was constricting her throat. 'He didn't deserve to die.'

'No,' said Rupert in a trembling voice. 'He didn't.'

Then, in a moment of pure instinct, Milly reached out her arms. Rupert half fell against her and buried his head in her shoulder. Milly held on tightly to him and looked up at the inky sky, tears blurring her view of the stars. And it occurred to her that she was a widow.

As Isobel entered the kitchen, Simon looked up warily from his seat at the huge refectory table. He was cradling a glass of wine and in front of him was the *Financial Times*, open but—Isobel suspected—unread.

'Hi,' he said.

'Hi,' said Isobel. She sat down opposite him and reached for the wine bottle. For a while there was silence.

'So,' he said at last. 'I gather you're pregnant. Congratulations.'

'Thanks,' said Isobel. She gave him a little smile. 'Are you finding this difficult to deal with?'

'Well, to be honest, just a tad!' said Simon, taking a deep swig of wine. 'One minute you're going to be my sister-in-law. The next minute you're not going to be my sister-in-law. Then all of a sudden, you're going to be my stepmother, and you're having a baby!'

'I know,' said Isobel. 'It's all a bit sudden. I'm sorry. Truly.' She took a thoughtful sip of wine. 'What do you want to call me, by the way? "Stepmother" seems a bit of a mouthful? How about "Mum"?'

'Very funny,' said Simon irritably. 'Where the hell's Milly? They're taking a long time, aren't they?'

'Give the girl a chance,' said Isobel. 'She's just found out that her husband's dead.'

'I know,' said Simon. 'I know.' He stood up and walked to the window, then turned round. 'So, what do you think of this Rupert, then?'

'I don't know,' said Isobel. 'I have to say I was expecting a complete bastard. But this guy just seems . . .' She thought for a moment. 'Very sad. He just seems very sad.'

'The truth is,' said Rupert, 'I should never have married her.' He was leaning forward, his head resting wearily on his knuckles. Next to him, Milly wrapped her arms more tightly round her knees. They were sitting on a low wall behind the office wing, above them was the old stable clock. 'I knew what I was. I knew I was living a lie. But, you know, I thought I could do it.' He looked up miserably.

'Do what?' said Milly.

'Be a good husband! Be a normal, decent husband. Do all the things everybody else does. Have dinner parties and go to church and watch our children in a nativity play . . .' He broke off, staring into the darkness. 'We were trying for a baby, you know. Francesca was pregnant last year. It would have been due in March. Maybe I'm being selfish. But I wanted that baby. I would have been a good father to it.'

'It would have been lucky to have you,' said Milly. 'But a baby isn't glue, is it? A baby doesn't keep a marriage together.'

'No,' said Rupert. 'It doesn't.' He thought for a moment. 'The odd thing is, I don't think we ever had a marriage. We were like two trains, running side by side, barely aware of each other's existence. We never argued, we never clashed. To be honest, we hardly knew each other.'

'Were you happy?'

'I don't know,' said Rupert. 'I pretended to be. Some of the time I even fooled myself.'

There was silence. Somewhere in the distance a fox barked. Rupert sighed. 'How about you?' he asked.

'What about me?'

'You know Allan's death changes everything.'

'I know,' said Milly.

At the sound of the front door opening, Simon stood up, as abruptly as though a small electric current had been passed through his body. He began to make awkwardly for the kitchen door, checking his appearance as he passed the uncurtained window. Isobel looked at him with raised eyebrows.

'She probably won't want to talk to you,' she said, as she heard Milly step back into the hall. 'You really hurt her, you know.'

'I know,' said Simon, halting at the door. 'I know. But . . .' He reached for the doorknob, hesitated, then pushed the door open.

'Good luck,' called Isobel after him.

Milly was standing just inside the front door, her hands deep in her pockets. At the sound of Simon's tread, she looked up.

'Milly,' Simon said shakily. She gave a faint acknowledgment. 'Milly, I'm sorry. I'm so sorry. I had no right to speak to you like that. I had no right to say those things.'

'No,' said Milly in a low voice. 'You didn't.'

'I was hurt and shocked. And I lashed out without thinking. But I'll make it up to you.' Simon's eyes suddenly shone with tears. 'Milly, I don't care if you've been married before. I don't care if you've got six children. I just want to be with you.' He took a step towards her. 'And so I'm asking you to forgive me and give me another chance.'

There was a long pause.

'I forgive you,' said Milly at last, staring at the floor. 'It was understandable, the way you reacted. I should have told you about Allan in the first place.'

There was an uncertain silence. Simon tried to take Milly's hands but she flinched. He dropped his hands and cleared his throat.

'I heard what happened to him,' he said. 'I'm really sorry.'

'Yes,' said Milly.

'You must be—'

'Yes.'

'But . . .' He hesitated. 'You know what it means for us?'

'What?' she said, as though he were speaking a foreign language.

'Well,' said Simon. 'It means we can get married.'

'No, Simon,' said Milly.

Simon paled slightly. 'What do you mean?' he said, keeping his voice light.

Milly met his eyes briefly, then looked away. 'I mean, we can't get married.' And as he watched her in disbelief, she turned on her heel and walked out of the front door.

Milly didn't stop walking until she reached Isobel's car. Then she leaned against the passenger door and scrabbled in her pocket for a cigarette. She had done the right thing, she told herself. She had been honest. Finally, she had been honest.

With shaky hands she put the cigarette in her mouth and flicked repeatedly at her lighter, but the evening breeze blew the flame out every time. Eventually, with a little cry of frustration, she threw the cigarette on the ground and stamped on it.

There was a sudden crunching on the gravel and she looked up and saw Simon striding towards her, a look of serious intent on his face.

'Look, Simon, don't even bother,' she said. 'It's over, OK?'

'No, it's not OK!' exclaimed Simon. He reached the car, panting slightly. 'What do you mean, we can't get married? Is it because of the things I said? Milly, I'm just so sorry. I'll do anything I can to make it up.'

'It's not about that!' said Milly. 'Yes, you hurt me. But it's more basic than that. It's . . . us. You and me as a couple, full stop.' She gave a small shrug and began to walk off.

'What's wrong with you and me as a couple?' said Simon, starting to follow her. 'Milly, I'm not going to just let you walk out of my life like that! Milly, I love you. I want to marry you. Don't you love me? Have you stopped loving me? If you have, just tell me!'

'It's not that!' said Milly.

'Then what's wrong!' His voice jabbed at the back of her head.

'OK!' said Milly, suddenly stopping. 'OK!' She closed her eyes, then opened them and looked straight at him. 'What's wrong is that . . . I haven't been honest with you. Ever. I'm not talking about Allan,' she said desperately. 'I'm talking about all the other lies I've told you.' Her words rose into the evening air like birds escaping. 'Lies, lies, lies!'

Simon stared at her in discomposure. He swallowed, and pushed his hair back. 'What lies? What are you talking about?'

'I can't be what you think I am! I can't be your perfect Barbie doll.'

'I don't treat you like a fucking Barbie doll!' said Simon in outrage. 'I treat you like an intelligent, mature woman!'

'Yes!' cried Milly. 'And that's the trouble! You treat me like some thinking man's version of a Barbie doll. I can't live up to your expectations any more. You want an attractive intelligent woman who wears expensive shoes and thinks soap operas are trivial and knows all about the effect of the exchange rate on European imports. Well, I can't be her! I can't be something I'm not. Rupert tried to do that in *his* marriage, and look where it got him!'

'I don't want you to be something you're not. I want you to be you.'

'You can't want that. You don't even know me,' said Milly despairingly. 'You don't know the real Milly Havill. I keep trying to tell you. I've been lying to you ever since we first met. About everything!'

'You've been lying to me about *everything*?'

'Yes.'

'Like what, for Christ's sake?'

Milly paused, and ran a hand through her hair. 'I don't like sushi.'

There was a stupefied silence. 'Is that it?' said Simon eventually.

'Of course that's not it,' said Milly quickly. 'Bad example. I . . . I never read the newspapers. I only pretend to.'

'So what?' said Simon.

'And I don't understand modern art. And I . . . I buy cheap shoes and don't show you them.'

'So what?' said Simon, laughing. He began to walk towards her.

'What do you mean, so what?' Angry tears started to Milly's eyes. 'All this time, I've been pretending to be something that I'm not. At that party, where we first met, I didn't really know about vivisection! I saw it on *Blue Peter*!'

There was a long silence. 'You saw it on *Blue Peter*,' he said at last.

'Yes,' said Milly tearfully. 'A *Blue Peter* special.'

With a sudden roar, Simon threw back his head, and began to laugh.

'It's not funny!' said Milly indignantly.

'Yes, it is!' said Simon through his laughter. 'It's very funny!'

'No, it's not!' cried Milly. 'All this time, I've been feeling guilty about it. Don't you understand? I've been pretending to be mature and intelligent. And I fooled you. But I'm not intelligent. I'm just not!'

Simon abruptly stopped laughing. 'Milly, are you serious?'

'Of course I am,' said Milly, in tears. 'I'm not clever! Not like Isobel.'

'Like *Isobel*?' echoed Simon incredulously. 'You think Isobel's clever? How clever is it to get knocked up by your boyfriend?' He raised his eyebrows at Milly and suddenly she gave a little giggle.

'Isobel may be intellectual,' said Simon. 'But you're the brightest star of your family.'

'Really?' said Milly in a little voice.

'Really. And even if you weren't—even if you had only one brain cell to call your own—I'd still love you. I love *you*, Milly. Not your IQ.'

'You can't possibly love me,' said Milly jerkily. 'You don't . . .'

'Know you?' said Simon. 'Of course I know you.' He sighed. 'Milly, knowing a person isn't like knowing a string of facts. It's more like . . . a feeling.' He lifted his hand and gently pushed back a strand of her hair. 'I can feel when you're going to laugh and when you're going to cry. I can feel your kindness and your warmth and your sense of humour. I feel all that inside me. And that's what matters.'

There was silence. In the distance a clock chimed. Milly exhaled shakily and said, almost to herself, 'I could do with—'

'A cigarette?' interrupted Simon. Milly raised her head to look at him, then gave a tiny shrug.

'Maybe,' she said.

'Come on,' said Simon, grinning. 'Did I get that right? Doesn't that prove I know you?'

There was a pause, then Milly said again, 'Maybe.' She reached in her pocket for her cigarette packet and allowed Simon to cradle the flame of her lighter from the wind.

There was a still, tense silence. Milly inhaled her first drag, not meeting Simon's eyes.

'I was thinking,' said Simon.

'What?'

'If you'd like to, we could go and get some pizza. And maybe . . .' He paused. 'You could tell me a little bit about yourself.'

'OK,' said Milly. She blew out a cloud of smoke and gave him half a smile. 'That would be nice.'

'You do like pizza?' added Simon.

'Yes,' said Milly. 'I do.'

'You're not just pretending, to impress me?'

'Simon,' said Milly. 'Shut up.'

'I'll go and get the car,' he said, feeling in his pocket for his keys.

'No, wait,' said Milly, waving her cigarette at him. 'Let's walk. I feel like walking. And . . . talking.' Simon stared at her.

'All the way into Bath? It's bloody freezing!'

'We'll warm up as we walk. Come on, Simon.' She put her hand on his arm. 'I really want to.'

'OK,' said Simon, putting away his car keys. 'Fine. Let's walk.'

'They're going into the garden,' said Isobel. 'Together.' She turned back from the window. 'But they haven't kissed yet.'

'Relax,' said Harry from his seat by the fire. 'Everything will be fine.' Isobel looked at him. He had a piece of paper in his hand and a pen.

'What are you doing?' she asked.

Harry glanced up and quickly folded the paper in two. 'Nothing,' he said.

'Show me!' said Isobel, crossing the room in a moment. She whipped it out of his grasp.

'It's just a few names that sprang to mind,' said Harry stiffly, as she uncrumpled it. 'I thought I'd jot them down.'

Isobel stared down at the page and started to laugh.

'Harry, you're mad!' she said. 'We've got seven months to think about it!' She looked down the list, smiling at some of the names and pulling faces at others. Then she turned over the paper. 'And what's all this?'

'Oh . . . that,' said Harry. A slightly shamefaced look came to his face. 'That was just in case we have twins.'

Milly and Simon were walking slowly through the gardens of Pinnacle Hall, towards a wrought-iron gate which opened onto the main road.

'This isn't at all what I was supposed to be doing tonight,' said Milly, gazing up into the starry sky. 'Tonight, I was supposed to be having a quiet supper at home and packing my honeymoon case.'

'I was supposed to be smoking a cigar with Dad and having second thoughts,' said Simon.

'And are you?' said Milly. 'Having second thoughts?'

'Are you?' rejoined Simon.

Milly said nothing, but continued to stare at the sky. They carried on walking silently, past the rose garden, past the frozen fountain and into the orchard, where Simon had proposed to her.

'Are you quite sure you want to walk?' Simon said.

'Yes,' said Milly. 'Walking always clears my head.'

Half an hour later, in the middle of the dark road, Milly stopped, and said, in a little voice, 'I'm cold, Simon.'

'Well, let's walk more quickly then.'

'And my feet hurt. My shoes are giving me blisters.'

Simon stopped, and looked at her. She had wrapped her hands in the ends of her jersey sleeves and buried them under her armpits; her lips were trembling and her teeth were chattering.

'Is your head clear?' he asked.

'No,' said Milly miserably. 'All I can think about is a nice hot bath. I can't go on any more. Are there any taxis?'

'I don't think so,' said Simon. 'But you can have my jacket.' He took it off and Milly grabbed it, snuggling into the warm lining. She began to hobble forward again.

After a few yards Simon stopped, and looked at her. 'Is that the best you can do?'

'My feet are *bleeding*,' wailed Milly. Simon's eyes fell on her feet.

'Are those new shoes?'

'Yes,' said Milly dolefully. 'And they were very cheap. And now I hate them.' She took another step forward and winced. Simon sighed.

'Come here,' he said. 'Put your feet on my feet. I'll walk you for a bit.' He grasped Milly firmly round the waist and began to stride awkwardly forward into the night, carrying her feet on his own.

'This is nice,' said Milly after a while.

'Yes,' grunted Simon. 'It's great.'

'You walk very quickly, don't you?'

'I do when I'm hungry.'

'I'm sorry about this,' said Milly in a subdued voice. 'It was a nice idea though, wasn't it?'

Simon began to laugh, his voice hoarse from the evening air.

'Yes, Milly,' he said at last, almost gasping with the effort of speaking. 'One of your best.'

When they opened the door of the pizza restaurant, the warmth of the air and the garlic-laden smell of food hit them in the face in an intoxicating blast. The place was full, buzzing with people and music; the cold dark road suddenly seemed a million miles away.

'A table for two, please,' said Simon, depositing Milly on the floor. 'And two large brandies.'

Milly smiled at him as they were shown to a booth by a red-dressed waiter, who immediately returned with the two brandies.

'Cheers,' said Milly. She met Simon's eyes hesitantly. 'I don't quite know what we're toasting. Here's to . . . the wedding we never had?'

'Let's toast us,' said Simon, looking at her suddenly seriously. 'Let's toast us. Milly—'

'What?'

There was silence. Milly's heart began to thump.

'I haven't planned this,' said Simon. 'God knows I haven't planned this. But I can't wait any longer.'

He put down his menu and sank to one knee on the floor beside the booth. There was a slight flurry around the restaurant as people looked over and began to nudge each other.

'Milly, please,' said Simon. 'I'm asking you again. And I . . . I hope beyond hope that you'll say yes. Will you marry me?'

There was a long silence. At last Milly looked up. Her cheeks were tinged a rosy pink.

'Simon, I don't know,' she said. 'I . . . I need to think about it.'

As they came to the end of their pizzas, Milly cleared her throat and looked nervously at Simon. 'How was your pizza?' she said.

'Fine,' said Simon. 'Yours?'

'Fine.' Their eyes met very briefly; then Simon looked away.

'Do you . . .' he began. 'Have you . . .'

'Yes,' said Milly, biting her lip. 'I've finished thinking.'

Her gaze ran over him—still kneeling on the floor beside the table, as he had been throughout the meal. A tiny smile came to her face.

'Would you like to get up now?' she said.

'Whatever for?' said Simon, taking a swig from his glass of wine. 'I'm very comfortable down here.'

'I thought . . .' Milly's lips were trembling, 'you might want to kiss me.'

There was a tense silence.

'Might I?' said Simon eventually. Slowly he put down his wineglass and raised his eyes to hers. For a few moments they just gazed at each other, oblivious of anything but themselves. 'Might I really?'

'Yes,' said Milly, trying to control her shaking voice. 'You might.' She put down her napkin, slid down off her seat beside him onto the marble floor and wrapped her arms round his neck. As her lips met his, there was a small ripple of applause from around the restaurant. Tears began to stream down Milly's cheeks, onto Simon's neck and into their mingled mouths. She closed her eyes and leaned against his broad chest, inhaling the scent of his skin, suddenly too weak to move a muscle.

'Just one question,' said Simon into her ear. 'Who's going to tell your mother?'

At nine o'clock the next morning the air was bright and crisp. As Milly pulled up outside One Bertram Street in her little car, her heart was beating in a mixture of anticipation and dread.

'Mummy?' she called as she entered the house, her voice high with nerves. 'Mummy?' She took off her coat, trying to stay calm. But suddenly excitement was bubbling through her like soda and she could feel a wide grin licking across her face. 'Mummy, guess what?'

She threw open the door of the kitchen joyfully and saw her mother and father sitting companionably together at the kitchen table, still in their dressing gowns, as though they were on holiday.

'Milly!' exclaimed Olivia, putting down her paper. 'Are you all right?'

'We assumed you stayed the night at Harry's,' said James.

'Have you had breakfast?' said Olivia. 'Let me get you some coffee—how about some toast?'

'Yes,' said Milly. 'I mean, no. Look, listen!' She pushed a hand through her hair, and smiled. 'I need to tell you some good news. Simon and I are going to get married!'

'Oh, darling!' cried Olivia. 'That's wonderful!'

'I'm glad you made up with him,' said James. 'He's a good chap.'

'I know he is,' said Milly. A smile spread across her face. 'And I love him. And he loves me. And it's all lovely again.'

'This is simply marvellous!' said Olivia. She picked up her mug and took a sip of coffee. 'When were you thinking of having the wedding?'

'In two hours' time,' said Milly happily. 'It's all arranged. We told Canon Lytton last night. So come on!' She gestured to the pair of them. 'Get dressed! Get ready!'

'Wait!' called Olivia, as Milly disappeared out of the kitchen door. 'What about Simon? He hasn't got a best man!' The door opened and Milly's face appeared again.

'Yes he has,' she said. 'He's got a jolly fine best man.'

'It's all very easy,' said Simon, taking a gulp of coffee. 'Here are the rings. When the vicar asks you for them, you just hand them over!'

'Right,' said Harry heavily. He took the two gold bands from Simon and stared at them for a couple of seconds. 'Do I hold them out on the palm of my hand, or in my fingers, or what?'

'I don't know,' said Simon. 'Does it matter?'

'I don't know!' said Harry. 'You tell me! Jesus!'

'Dad, you're not nervous, are you?' said Simon.

'Of course I'm not!' said Harry. 'Now go and shine your shoes.'

'See you later,' said Simon at the kitchen door, grinning.

'*Are* you nervous?' said Isobel, from the window seat, when Simon had gone.

'No,' said Harry, then looked up. 'Maybe a bit.' He pushed back his chair abruptly and strode over to the window. 'It's ridiculous. I shouldn't be Simon's best man, for Christ's sake!'

'Yes you should,' said Isobel. 'He could easily have phoned up a friend. You know he could. But he wants you.' She reached for his hand

and after a moment he squeezed hers. Then she glanced at her watch and pulled a face. 'I must go. Mummy will be having kittens.'

'I'll see you there, then,' said Harry.

'See you there,' said Isobel. At the door, she turned back.

'Of course, you know what the perk of being the best man is.'

'What's that?'

'You get to sleep with the chief bridesmaid.'

'Is that so?' said Harry, brightening.

'It's in all the rule books,' said Isobel. 'Ask the vicar. He'll tell you.'

As Isobel went into the hall, she saw Rupert coming down the stairs. Unaware that he was being watched, his face was full of an unformed grief; a raw misery that made Isobel's spine prickle. For a few moments she stood silently, then walked forward, giving him a chance to gather his thoughts before he saw her.

'Hello,' she said. 'We were wondering if you were all right. Did you sleep well?'

'Great, thanks,' said Rupert nodding. 'Very kind of Harry to put me up.'

'That was nothing,' said Isobel. 'It was very kind of you to come all this way to tell Milly about . . . ' She tailed off awkwardly. 'You know the wedding is back on?'

'No,' said Rupert. He gave her a strained smile. 'That's great news. Really great.' Isobel stared at him in compassion, wanting somehow to make everything right for him.

'You know, I'm sure Milly would want you to come,' she said. 'It isn't going to be a big, smart wedding any more. Just the six of us, in fact. But if you'd like to, we'd all be delighted if you could come.'

'That's very kind,' said Rupert after a pause. 'Very kind indeed. But . . . I think I might go home instead. If you don't mind.'

'Of course not,' said Isobel. 'Whatever you want. I'll find someone to drive you to the station. There's a fast London train every hour.'

'I'm not going to London,' said Rupert. A distant, almost peaceful expression came to his face. 'I'm going home. To Cornwall.'

By ten thirty, Olivia was fully dressed and made up. She peered at her reflection in the mirror and gave a satisfied smile. Her bright pink suit fitted perfectly and the matching wide-brimmed hat cast a rosy glow over her face and shiny blonde hair.

'You look stupendous!' said James, coming in.

'And you look very handsome,' said Olivia, running her eyes over his morning coat. 'Very distinguished. Father of the bride.'

'Mother of the bride,' rejoined James, grinning at her. 'Speaking of which, where is she?'

'Still getting ready,' said Olivia. 'Isobel's helping her.'

'Well, then,' said James, 'I suggest we go and partake of a little pre-wedding champagne. Shall we?' He held out his arm and, after a moment's hesitation, Olivia took it. As they descended the stairs into the hall, a voice stopped them.

'Hold it. Just for a second. Don't look at me.'

They paused, smiling at each other while Alexander snapped away.

'OK,' he said. 'You can carry on now.' As Olivia passed him, he winked at her. 'Great hat, Olivia. Very sexy.'

'Thank you, Alexander,' said Olivia, a slight blush coming to her cheeks. James squeezed her arm and her blush deepened.

'Come on,' she said quickly. 'Let's have that champagne.'

They went into the drawing room, where a fire was crackling and James had laid out a champagne bottle and glasses. He handed her a glass and raised his own. 'Here's to the wedding,' he said.

'The wedding,' said Olivia. She sipped at her champagne, then sat down gingerly on a chair, being careful not to crease her skirt.

James met her eyes compassionately. 'Do you mind that we aren't having the big lavish wedding that you planned?' he said.

'No,' said Olivia after a pause. 'I don't mind.' She smiled brightly at James. 'They're getting married. That's the important thing, isn't it?'

'Yes,' said James. 'That's the important thing.'

There was a pause. Olivia stared into the fire, cradling her drink.

'And you know,' she said suddenly, 'in many ways, it's more *original* to have a tiny, private wedding. Big weddings can become rather vulgar if one isn't careful. Don't you think?'

'Absolutely,' said James, smiling.

There was a sound at the door and he looked up. Isobel was standing in the doorway, dressed in a long flowing column of pale pink silk. Her hair was wreathed in flowers and her cheeks were flushed.

'I've come to announce the bride,' she said. 'She's ready. Come and watch her walking down the stairs. Alexander is taking pictures.'

'Darling, you look wonderful,' said Olivia as Isobel turned to go. 'What happened to the roses?' she added sharply.

'What roses?'

'The silk roses that were on your dress!'

'Oh, those,' said Isobel after a pause. 'They . . . fell off.'

'Fell off?'

'Yes,' said Isobel. She looked at Olivia's perplexed face and grinned.

'Come on, Mummy. The roses don't matter. Come and see Milly.'

They all filed into the hall and looked up the stairs. Coming slowly down, smiling shyly through her veil, was Milly, wearing a starkly cut dress of ivory satin. The stiff, embroidered bodice was laced tightly round her figure; the long sleeves were edged at the wrist with fur; in her hair sparkled a diamond tiara.

'Milly!' said Olivia shakily. 'You look perfect. A perfect bride.' Tears suddenly filled her eyes and she turned away.

'What do you think?' said Milly tremulously. 'Will I do?'

'Darling, you look exquisite,' said James. 'Simon Pinnacle can count himself a very lucky young man.'

'I can't believe it's really happening,' said Olivia, holding a tiny hanky to her eyes. 'Little Milly. Getting married.'

'How are we going to get there?' said Alexander, taking a final picture.

'Milly?' said James, looking up at her. 'It's your show.'

'I don't know,' said Milly, a perturbed expression coming over her face. She descended a few steps. 'I hadn't thought about it.'

'If we take both cars,' said James, looking at Olivia, 'you could drive Alexander and Isobel, and I could come on with Milly . . .'

He was interrupted by a ring at the front door and they all looked up.

'Who on earth—' said James. He looked around, then silently went to open it. A man holding a peaked cap under his arm was standing on the steps. He bowed stiffly.

'Wedding cars for Havill,' he said.

'What?' James peered past him onto the street. 'They were cancelled!'

'Not according to my information,' said the man.

'Not according to your information,' echoed Olivia, shaking her head in exasperation. 'Does it ever occur to you people that your information might be wrong? I spoke to a young woman at your company—'

'Mummy!' interrupted Milly in agonised tones. 'Mummy!' She pulled a meaningful face at Olivia, who suddenly realised what she was saying.

'However,' she said, pulling herself up straight. 'By very good fortune, the situation has changed once again.'

'So you do want the cars,' said the man.

'We do,' said Olivia haughtily.

'Very good, madam,' said the man, and as he disappeared down the steps the word 'nutter' travelled audibly back towards them.

'Right,' said James. 'Well, you lot go off . . . Milly and I will follow.'

'See you there,' said Isobel, grinning at Milly. 'Good luck!'

As they descended the steps to the waiting cars, Alexander drew Isobel back slightly. 'You know, I'd really like to take some shots of you on your own some time,' he said. 'You've got fantastic cheekbones.'

'Oh, really?' said Isobel, raising her eyebrows. 'Is that what you say to all the girls?'

'Only the stunning ones.' He looked at her. 'I'm serious. And maybe, when all this is over . . . you and I could go for a drink?'

Isobel stared at him. 'You've got a nerve!' she said.

'I know,' said Alexander. 'Do you want to?'

She began to laugh. 'I'm very flattered,' she said. 'I'm also pregnant.'

'Oh.' He shrugged. 'That doesn't matter.'

'And . . .' she added, a faint tinge coming to her cheeks, '. . . I'm going to get married.'

'What?' Ten yards ahead of them, Olivia wheeled round on the pavement, her eyes bright. 'Isobel! Who is he, darling? Have I met him?'

Isobel gazed dumbly at Olivia. She opened her mouth to speak, closed it again, looked away and shifted on the ground. 'He's . . . he's someone I'll introduce you to later,' she said at last. 'Let's just get the wedding over first. All right?'

'Whatever you say, darling,' said Olivia. 'Oh, I'm so thrilled!'

'Good!' said Isobel, smiling weakly. 'That's good.'

Harry and Simon arrived at the church at ten to eleven. They pushed open the door and looked silently around the huge, empty space.

'Aha!' said Canon Lytton, appearing out of a side door. 'The bridegroom and his best man! Welcome!' He hurried down the aisle towards them, past rows of empty pews, each adorned with flowers.

'Where do we sit?' said Harry, looking round. 'All the best seats are taken.'

'Very droll,' said Canon Lytton, beaming. 'The places for the groom and his best man are at the front, on the right. Ah, here's Mrs Blenkins, our organist. Fortunately she was free this morning!'

An elderly woman in a brown anorak was walking up the aisle towards them. 'I haven't practised anything up,' she said as soon as she reached them. 'Will "Here Comes the Bride" do you?' ·

'Absolutely,' said Simon, glancing at Harry. 'Whatever. Thanks very much. We're very grateful.' The woman nodded and marched off, and Canon Lytton disappeared in a rustle of linen.

Simon sat down on the front pew and stretched his legs out in front of him. 'I'm terrified,' he said.

'So am I,' said Harry, giving a little shudder.

'Will I be a good husband?' Simon threw back his head and looked up into the cavernous space of the church. 'Will I make Milly happy?'

'You already make her happy,' said Harry. 'Just don't change anything.' He met Simon's eye. 'You love her. That's enough for anyone.'

There was a noise at the back of the church and Olivia appeared, a vision in bright pink. She walked up the aisle, her heels clacking lightly on the floor. 'They'll be here in a minute,' she whispered.

She sat down in the front pew on the bride's side and there was a few minutes' silence. Then, from out of nowhere the organ began to play.

Suddenly there was a rattling at the back of the church and they all jumped. Simon took a deep breath, trying to steady his nerves. But his heart was pounding and his palms felt damp.

Olivia turned and peered towards the back of the church.

'I can see her!' she whispered. 'She's here!'

The organ music slowed down, then stopped altogether. Looking hesitantly at each other, the three of them stood up. There was an agonised silence; no one seemed to be breathing.

Then the familiar chords of Wagner's *Wedding March* swelled into the air. Simon felt a lump coming to his throat. Not daring to look round, he stared ahead, blinking furiously, until he felt Harry tugging his sleeve. Very slowly he swivelled his head round until he was looking down the aisle, then felt his heart stop. There was Milly on her father's arm, looking more beautiful than he'd ever seen her. Her lips were parted in a tremulous smile, her eyes were sparkling behind her veil, her skin glowed against the pale creaminess of her dress.

As she reached his side she stopped. She hesitated, then, with trembling hands, slowly lifted the gauzy veil from her face. As she did so, her fingers brushed the necklace of freshwater pearls she was wearing. She paused, holding one of the tiny pearls, and for a few moments her eyes dimmed. Then she let go of it, took a deep breath and looked up.

'Ready?' said Simon.

'Yes,' said Milly, and smiled at him. 'I'm ready.'

When Rupert arrived at the little Cornish cottage, it was nearly midday. He glanced at his watch as he walked up the path, and thought to himself that Milly would be married by now. She and Simon would be drinking champagne, as happy as two people could ever be.

The door opened before he reached it, and his father looked out.

'Hello, my boy,' he said kindly. 'I've been expecting you.'

'Hello, Father,' said Rupert, and gave his father a hug. As he met the older man's mild, unquestioning gaze, he felt his defences crumble completely, as though he might suddenly burst into unstoppable sobs. But his emotions were run dry; he was beyond tears now.

'Come and have a nice cup of tea,' said his father, leading the way into the tiny sitting room, overlooking the sea. He paused. 'Your wife called today, wondered if you were here. She said to tell you she was sorry. And she sends you her love and prayers.'

Rupert said nothing. He sat down by the window and looked out at the empty blue sea. It occurred to him that he'd almost completely forgotten about Francesca.

'You also had a call from another young woman a few days ago,' called his father from the tiny kitchen. There was a clatter of crockery. 'Milly, I think her name was. Did she manage to track you down?'

The flicker of something like a smile passed across Rupert's face.

'Yes,' he said. 'She tracked me down.'

'I hadn't heard of her before,' said his father, coming in with a teapot. 'Is she an old friend of yours?'

'Not really,' said Rupert, pausing. 'Just the wife of a friend of mine.'

And he leaned back in his chair and stared out of the window at the waves breaking on the rocks below.

MADELEINE WICKHAM

It is hardly surprising that Madeleine Wickham chose to write a novel set around a wedding because she has strong views on marriage. 'I got married at twenty-one and, looking back, I'm amazed I had the courage—for, in its own way, marrying early these days flouts convention as much as remaining single did in Jane Austen's time. Yet marrying young does not have to be limiting. Marital vows do not include any references to vacuuming, dusting or bypassing ambition. They are founded on a promise to love and cherish. If your idea of this is receiving a housekeeping allowance every month, fine. If it's being encouraged to pursue your ambition as energetically as you can, then that's good, too. My own ambition was to write a book. For nearly four months, I spent every spare moment working on it. I didn't have time to cook, see films or dust. So my husband made supper, went to the cinema with friends, read chapters as they were printed out, and never complained. The thing about marriage is that it's for ever. You can take out four months without feeling that the relationship is going to crumble. You can think long term; you have the freedom to gamble. For me, the gamble paid off.'

It certainly did. Madeleine Wickham sent her first novel, *The Tennis Party*, to just two agents and it was immediately accepted. Since then she has written a book a year and had two children, Freddy and Hugo, the latter arriving while she was writing *The Wedding Girl*. 'I am very disciplined when I'm writing. If I am on a roll I will write all day and all night and hopefully finish the book in a few months. I work in my study, which is along the corridor from the kitchen. The children are happy knowing that I am there and, when inspiration is running thin, I know that all I have to do is to head down the corridor and spend time with them.'

As well as writing novels, Madeleine Wickham also writes short stories and articles for magazines, most recently for *Resident Abroad*, the *Financial Times*'s expatriate magazine, and *What House*. She has recently finished her sixth book, *Cocktails for Three*, about three friends who get caught up in trying to right a wrong. 'But what I would really like to get into now is screenwriting.' She has just finished a course at Carlton TV.

When asked about her own wedding day, Madeleine Wickham smiles enigmatically. 'It was great fun. We were married in New College Chapel, Oxford, and had the full works: a big white wedding with over two hundred guests—well, I think it was two hundred, we are not sure who actually came as we lost the guest list! It was certainly a day I will treasure for ever.' Their marriage has given both Madeleine and her husband, an opera singer, the springboard to achieve their ambitions. It has also given them their two wonderful sons, Freddy (pictured above left) and Hugo.

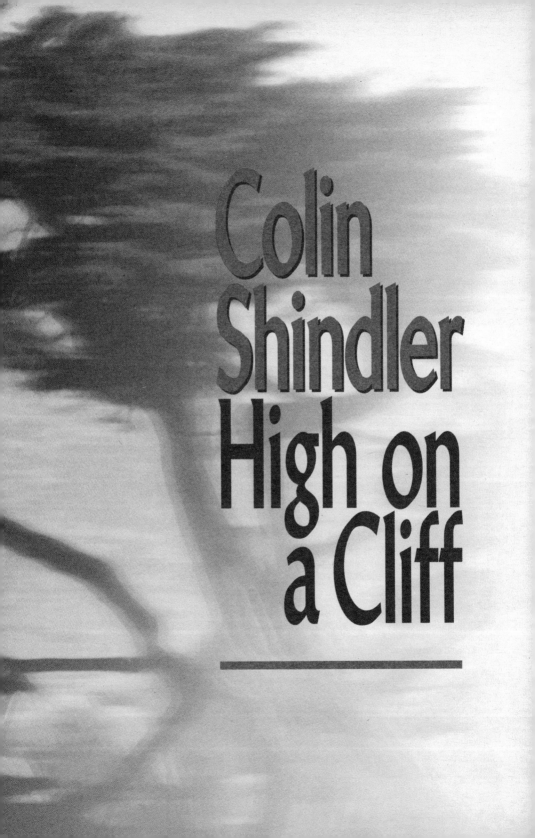

Colin Shindler
High on a Cliff

ßa

When his mother is killed
in a car crash, Danny is raised
single-handedly by his father. The
relationship between them is a deep
and very special one, as together
they keep alive the memory of the
woman both have lost. But Danny
knows his father needs a new
woman in his life—he just does
not want it to be Helen.

ßa

 Danny

I CAN'T REMEMBER A TIME when I didn't know her and yet I can't remember a time when I did. She died, my mum, when I was eleven months old, so there's no way I can remember much. Sometimes when I can't get to sleep at night, I imagine her coming into my bedroom and kissing me good night. She bends over me and I can smell her perfume, which makes me want to bury myself in her. She is dressed up ready for a big posh party. I tell her I can't sleep and she sits on the bed and tells me of all the things we're going to do together. Only I suppose it never could have happened like that. Sometimes, though, on nights like those, she seems so real.

I know what she looked like of course. Dad has lots of photos of her round the house and three big albums of them when they were students and after they were married. I've got the videos she made too. She was an actress and she made a few television programmes. It says ANGELA FROST on the front of the video box. Dad calls that her maiden name. He says all actresses keep their maiden names when they act because if they get divorced they won't have to change them. But I can't imagine my dad and mum getting divorced. You've only got to look at the pictures to see how happy they were.

Sometimes the other mothers at school look at me with this strange expression. I know they're thinking how sad it must be for me to be growing up without a mother. But I don't see it that way. Mothers spend a lot of time saying 'Don't do this' and 'Don't do that'. When there are mothers about there are always rules. Stupid rules most of the time. So when I see those mothers I'm glad I don't have one. In any case, I have Dad.

My dad is really cool. He's a freelance sports writer. He writes about lots of different sports and he goes to lots of games. He brings me back souvenirs—like a Barcelona replica shirt when he flew to Spain to write about a big match with Real Madrid. It made quite a change in the playground from all the Arsenal, Chelsea and Man United shirts that the kids mostly have. I even wore it rather than my Spurs one for a while—but only till we signed Klinsmann.

The other kids really envy me my dad and his cool job. In many ways my dad is my mum and my dad all rolled up into one person. I mean, he used to dress me when I was small, he'd walk me to school when I was at primary school and he's nearly always waiting outside the school gates at the end of the day.

My favourite picture of Mum is of her asleep in the garden. She is on a sun lounger. We've still got that sun lounger but it's all rusty now. In the picture Mum is wearing a red T-shirt and a pair of white tennis shorts. Dad says they played a lot of tennis that summer. I wasn't born yet and he says it was a golden time. I know he doesn't mean they didn't want me—but he is trying to tell me those years by themselves were special.

My dad is a good tennis player so when he says that Mum was really good, he must mean it. She hit the ball hard but her backhand was weak. Dad is very keen to make sure that my backhand is as strong as my forehand. We spend hours on the tennis court and he stands at the net and volleys ball after ball into my backhand court. If I get back six in a row I get a Crunchie on the way home. I like Crunchies, particularly the way the yellow bit in the middle is all hard when you bite on it but if you let it stay on your tongue it just dissolves. Wicked.

My mum was dead sexy. I know boys don't usually think of their mothers as sexy and in the case of all my friends they're usually right. Something must happen to women when they become mothers. You can't think of mothers as sexy and the ones who think they are—like Darren Foxton's mum who wears low-cut dresses in the summer—are just embarrassing to their children. I wouldn't like to be best mates with Darren. Will Stevens is and he gets fearful stick from the rest of us when he gets into the Foxton Range Rover after school.

But my mum was different from all the rest, just like my dad is different. She was an actress, and not just an actress, as Dad keeps saying, but a star. So being sexy was, in a way, what she did for a living. And the reason I like that photo of Mum so much is that I think she looks supercool there. She isn't trying to look sexy, which is what those blonde bimbos in the tabloids are always doing. She looks so peaceful there, so happy. My friends see it and though they're sort of respectful because Mum's dead, I can see they think she's dead beautiful too.

I think of her as still around, kind of frozen in time. She died when she was only twenty-three and I suppose she might have started to age a bit if she'd lived, like Neville Thornton's mum who has great gobs of grey streaked through her hair. My mum will never grow old. There's a bit in the Founder's Day service about 'they shall not grow old—at the going down of the sun and in the morning, we will remember them'. Something like that. I like that bit. It reminds me of my mum. But I don't need a church service or the sun to set, or one special day of the year. She's with me always. That's what I mean when I say I remember her even though I can't actually remember her.

Ralph

WHEN I CAME BACK TO ENGLAND after the funeral, my first instinct was to bury Angela metaphorically all over again. I thought if the baby didn't know anything about his mother he wouldn't have a loss to adjust to. I'd probably marry again within a couple of years, and to all intents and purposes that woman would become Danny's mother.

It didn't work out that way, because I just didn't have the strength to cut Angela out of my life. Maybe it would have been better for Danny as I had first planned it, but whatever the baby's needs I also had my own. I needed to grieve. If they had sackcloth and ashes at Sainsbury's I'd have loaded the car up with them twice a week.

I went to see a psychiatrist, who recommended that I talk about her to Danny and show him pictures so it wasn't a shameful secret but a joyous celebration of her life. That was the turning point really. As soon as I grasped the fact that I was allowed to hang on to Angela's memory, I started on the long road to recovery. So I talked to Danny a lot about his mummy when he was growing up. I would tell him stories about how we met and the great times we had together, and he would treat it as a kind of favourite story. Even her death became something glorious.

She was cremated close to where she was killed and I took the ashes to Big Sur on the coast of California. It was a place where she and I had been particularly happy. I stopped the car just off the main highway and scrambled through the redwoods and the sequoias until I rediscovered that plateau of grassland stretching towards the ocean. The plateau finished at a headland that fell precipitously to meet the pounding surf. Behind me was the wilderness of the Los Padres National Forest. In front the Pacific Ocean spread itself like a giant sapphire-blue tablecloth flecked with white.

I had no interest in the wishes of Angela's parents. They had never liked me, they never came to our wedding, never approved of our marriage. This was where she belonged. I unscrewed the lid of the urn and deposited the remains of the only woman I had ever loved where the sky meets the sea. I know, in reality, that's not possible, but Danny has always loved that description, so, as far as I am concerned, that's the official version.

'High on a cliff,' I would always end the story, 'Mummy's soul sits, watching over us both always.' In black and white that looks a bit ghoulish, not to say New Ageish. I'm not like that at all. I support Tottenham Hotspur and the American baseball team the California Angels—now, disappointingly, known as the Anaheim Angels. I find that in supporting the Angels who, unlike Spurs, don't even have a history of success to sustain them in their current mediocrity, it is necessary to keep both feet firmly planted on the ground. The story of Angela's end is one of the few poetic touches I allow myself. It was Danny who called the story 'High on a Cliff'. It had the same magic as 'Once upon a time', except that the words came at the end so really it was closer to 'and they all lived happily ever after'.

I always thought it was comforting that he loved this story so much. It proved that he and I were living happily ever after. When he was three or so he had a number of favourite stories: one about an owl who was afraid of the dark, one about a hungry caterpillar who ate so much he turned into a butterfly, and one about a family who lived in a lighthouse. I had to read them to him every night for years and years. Maybe it was only two or three years, but it certainly seemed like about five or six. But however much he loved them, I always had to finish with 'High on a Cliff' before I tucked him up in bed and kissed him good night; it was part of a never-changing ritual. The most important part, I always felt, was saying to him 'high on a cliff, Mummy's soul sits, watching over us both always'.

Of course, living where we do, Cambridge, I'm surrounded by memories of Angela. Not just where we met as students and where we kissed for the first time, where we made love and where we fought and where we made up, but every year it seems to renew itself. Over the course of the academic year I can see relationships start to blossom.

Glances over lectures or during dinner in Hall, sizing up in the pub, the first date, the first kiss, the first sense of rapture. Then it all hibernates for the winter as the wind whips in across the Fenlands straight from the Urals and right into the vitals as you struggle your way round the coldest spot in the British Isles, North Sea oil rigs notwithstanding. When the crocuses appear along the Backs, it all starts again.

I got over the envy long ago. If I had felt envious, I couldn't have stuck it. Instead I welcome the sight of young couples holding hands or snogging on the banks of the river when they are supposed to be revising. It symbolises the triumph of life over death. I can deal with it all now because, despite the occasional bout of deep depression, I'm sorted.

All right, I'm not perfect. Much as I love Danny, there are times when I'm tired and frustrated and Danny's still a kid and he knows how to get up my nose. I don't smack him but I do shout, perhaps quite a lot, but it's only under provocation. I keep the black moods well away from him. So, in general, I think it's true, I *am* sorted.

Danny

MY DAD THINKS he's sorted. I'm twelve and I know he's not. He thinks he hides it, but he doesn't. I've seen it. I can't tell him though. I don't think anyone can. There's no point, anyway, because he needs to think he's sorted.

On the surface it certainly looks like he is sorted. He's got this great job and we live in a nice house, though the mother of one of my friends said it was a stranger to Domestos. It's an old Victorian terraced house off the Chesterton Road. It's got high ceilings, which I like because I can play badminton in the living room with my friends.

My room's up at the top. It's got all my favourite things in it—my stereo, my tapes and CDs, my games and my computer. Dad's got a computer, too, which he keeps downstairs in his study. I remember the day he got it. Dad sort of tried to be a comedy writer when he first started out after university. Anyway, he was commissioned to write a sitcom pilot by Channel Four with a friend of his called Andy, who lives in London. It was about two girls and two blokes who live in a flat in Fulham. They wrote it by email, transferring each scene as they finished it. Dad seemed to think this was some kind of major technological breakthrough, but to me it just looked like common sense. I mean, that's what email is for.

I think Dad thought it was going to earn us a fortune.

One day he came into my bedroom saying Channel Four had bought the outline and we were all going to be rich and we could go and live in the West Indies. About six weeks later the move to the West Indies was off. It turned out that Channel Four had rejected his script because they'd bought a new American sitcom that was a bit like it instead.

It was called *Friends*. I know my dad's cool and brilliant and everything, but I don't see how he and Andy could ever have come up with anything as wicked as *Friends*. My favourite is Chandler because he's really funny. I don't think the writers have to write anything for Chandler. He just makes up those funny lines as he goes along.

One of the big things about our house is the garden. It's not that big, like my friend Jamie Kirk's garden on Millington Road, but it's nearly all grass, which is great for diving on, and it has very few flowers which are the bane of a boy's life. I go to my friends' houses and when we ask if we can play in the garden they have mothers who always say, 'Watch out for the flowers . . .' I hate that.

The Brazilian star Ronaldo, the best player in the world, can't always judge where the ball is going to land, so how can we at the age of twelve? And yet these mothers, who have never trapped, kicked or headed a ball in the whole of their pathetic lives, think we can control the ball so it doesn't touch their precious lupins or tulips. That's what I mean about not missing a mother.

The reason I think Dad's not sorted is that he has this sad look that comes over him on certain occasions. During the summer we wander through Cambridge and we see those disgusting students snogging on the banks of the river or lazing around punting. I think Dad takes that route deliberately. Not that he's a dirty old man or anything, but he seems to need to remind himself of what it was like when he and Mum were young and in love.

He's always looking for her. Still. I can feel his eyes searching the back of a young woman with long blonde hair (like Mum had) and his pace of walking quickens just a bit and then we overtake and he shoots a sideways or backwards glance at her and of course it's not Mum, I mean how could it be? But Dad is always being disappointed like that and I can sense the expectancy escaping from him like the air from a punctured bicycle tyre. Believe me, I've had enough of those to know what that's like.

I want him to find someone. I do. Honest. He doesn't see it that way, of course. He thinks I'm dreading it and nobody can take the place of his precious Angela. Well, he's right about that. No one can. But what really annoys me is that he thinks he's doing it for me and I know he's not. He's doing it for himself. That's another reason why he's not sorted.

I've seen him crying. Quite a few times. And I know it's about Mum. There's something hollow inside Dad, something he can't shake.

He's been telling me these stories since I was very small, about him and Mum and how happy they were. I used to like them a lot, particularly one we called 'High on a Cliff'. It was a story about how he'd been really happy with her in one place—I think it was by a lighthouse or something—and so he scattered her ashes on the grass in front of the lighthouse. I liked the last line of the story which was how Mummy's soul watches over both of us at all times. I was always happy when Dad said that.

All this, though, was when I was a kid, and I don't need to listen to 'High on a Cliff' before I can go to sleep any more. It's been twelve years since Mum died. Surely he should have got over her by now. I don't mean that he should stop treasuring her memory. I just mean I think he should move on with his life. There's a hole in Dad's heart. I want someone to fill it and I'm sure he must. Yet he constantly fights it. Whenever there's a chance that someone might, he blows it.

Occasionally there's a woman having breakfast with us on Sunday morning. It's embarrassing, but usually more for them than for me. Dad always starts off by introducing us formally and then there's always a reason, like they're working together on an article or whatever and it got too late for her to take the train home. I mean quite pathetic stuff, but it seems to be important to Dad that he should convince me that the woman only stayed because there was a reason other than that they wanted to have sex together.

Then Dad's like monitoring me for the slightest sign of emotional trauma. I think, Why shouldn't he have sex? He's thirty-five years old and a widower. Jesus! I hope I'm a little more mature about all this when I get to his age.

These encounters—you couldn't call them affairs—never last and they've never stopped Dad from crying. He doesn't talk to me about them, but I think he breaks them off and uses me as an excuse.

I feel so sorry for Dad. There's something inside him that makes him reject these women before anything can really start. And I think he came back to Cambridge not just to keep Mum's memory alive but to leave the competition behind. It's easier for him to do all his work by email. He doesn't go into an office.

When Mum died he closed up his feelings and ran away. There's something about the world that frightens him now. And it didn't when Mum was alive. Now do you see what I mean when I say he's not sorted? Not sorted at all.

Ralph

I USED TO HAVE such grand dreams. I always felt I would be famous, not in the television-presenter way, and hopefully not in the serial killer way either, but in a thoroughly laudable way that would produce sycophantic interviews in the women's magazines and grudgingly respectful ones in the broadsheets.

Like all the rest of the intake in my freshman year at Cambridge, I scrambled to find my place on the starting line in the fame race. I tried almost everything—journalism, acting, Footlights, speaking at the Union, and it was all pretty successful. But then I met Angela and my world altered for ever.

It was the most unfortunate of opening acts. The only copy of the book I needed for my weekly essay was overdue at the faculty library. Despite repeated requests, the student concerned had failed to return it. With only twenty-four hours to go before I was supposed to hand in the as yet unwritten essay, I smiled winningly at the librarian and was handed a piece of paper on which was written 'A. Frost, Jesus'.

I cycled slowly down Jesus Lane, rehearsing in my mind the withering epithets I would shower on this selfish bastard Frost. I rapped on the door of Frost's room before hearing a girl's melodious voice sing out, 'Come in!' . . . and was confronted by the sight of A. Frost in her underwear, smiling sweetly before pulling a rollneck sweater over her head.

I'm a little embarrassed to admit that I hadn't seen a real live girl in her underwear before, but she was completely unfazed. She immediately got the sweater caught in a hair clip and was soon shouting for help. By the time I had untangled the sweater I had fallen hopelessly in love with her. By the time she had slipped into a pair of ripped jeans and put the kettle on I had entirely forgotten about reclaiming the library book.

The following night we went to the cinema together—*Gandhi*, which, despite its worthiness, was long enough for us both to become a little restless before the end. This necessitated a whispered apology which itself necessitated hot breath on ear hole. The erotic effect was precisely what each of the participants had planned, so when poor Ben Kingsley was assassinated, neither of us was looking at the screen.

I wanted to get married in the middle of our second term. We had already started sleeping together, so in addition to wanting to erect warning signs to every other male, I felt I was morally obliged to make the offer which Angela laughingly dismissed as charmingly old-fashioned. She didn't see herself as getting married until she had won at least one Academy Award.

I took the decision with bad grace, I'm afraid. I was so utterly in love that, every second Angela wasn't in my sight, I feared some bounder would sweep her away from me. I don't think I ever felt completely sure that this wouldn't happen until after she was dead.

Clearing out her things after I came back to London, I found her diary which I knew she jotted in but had no idea it was quite so detailed.

I soon discovered that she knew all about my jealousy and posses-siveness. Other women might have found all this emotional baggage distinctly off-putting, but Angela was so laid-back about everything that she found it endearing.

Angela was quite used to men laying themselves at her feet. Had she lived in the Middle Ages, knights would have been charging at each other with lowered lances to seek her favour twenty-four hours a day. They would have invented Kleenex 700 years early because of the number of her handkerchiefs that would have fluttered down to the jousting arena.

She had her own fantasy about me too. I was the man who was going to write something for her that was going to rocket her to stardom. We started with the Footlights.

Until Angela came along, I was the one who seemed destined for Footlights stardom. I had hoped to attract some attention myself in the May Week revue sketch I had written, in which I played a demented Japanese visitor to Cambridge. It seemed to go down pretty well, but there was no question that Angela was the star turn. After that there was no stopping her. I found myself writing more for her and appearing less and less myself. And, when I did appear on stage, I was acutely con-scious that there was only one real star and it wasn't me.

It took me a little while to come to terms with how much everyone loved her. When I got jealous I used to think it was pure sexism. They liked her because she had a great figure. She could sense how much she was desired and she used her sex appeal and that intensity of interest like a matador uses his cloak. Most men in my position would have enjoyed the salivating of other men, but I was too possessive. I wanted to lock her up in a tower like a storybook princess. I would have the only key. But I knew it was a hopeless fantasy. So I concentrated on becoming a writer, her writer.

I adapted *Antony and Cleopatra* as it might have been played by J.R. Ewing and Su Ellen from *Dallas*. I played J.R., with the traditional ten-gallon Stetson; Angela looked quite stunning as Su Ellen. I was OK, I guess, but Angela was quite brilliant, somehow portraying the essence of the Queen of Egypt crossed with a dipsomaniac Texan oil baron's wife. At least I had the consolation of being the one to bring her talent to the notice of the public. On the first night we performed that sketch, I effectively decided I would retire from appearing in public. I couldn't stand the competition.

After that I knew what Destiny really wanted me to do—to tailor Angela's talents for the adoring masses. I was convinced that stardom would envelop my beloved in her embrace as soon as she graduated from university. There was one small problem. On graduation day Angela was eight months pregnant.

 Angela

November 2, 1983. Finished essay, gave Ralph library book back at cinema. He's cute. I really like him. He seems pretty keen on me too, which helps, but I wish he'd learn to disguise it. I mean, it's sometimes fun to make them run after you, but if they come on strong right at the beginning it's just too easy.

Having said that, I think this one might be different. He's not conventionally handsome, but he has kind eyes and a lovely smile. He's also funny and he told me a very good joke about a girl who was stranded on a desert island with a one-legged jockey.

February 3, 1984. Well! My first proposal of marriage! It's been getting a bit hot with Ralph lately, but even I never suspected this was what he was building up to.

Because we've been sleeping together he feels he's in love with me and wants to marry me. I told him we were both only nineteen and in our first year and weren't we a bit young? But he's been reading lots of romantic novels this term and I know that he's written a good essay on nineteenth-century women novelists.

I let him down gently. I told him there was nobody else because I think he's the jealous type. Then I told him that I loved him as much as he loved me, though I think that might be a slight exaggeration. Then I said if we still felt this way about each other in our final term we should get married on graduation. Then I took him back to college and gave him a royal command performance.

In the morning, when I woke up, I found him looking at me with his big soulful eyes. When I asked what was the matter he told me he wanted to do this every day for the rest of his life. Wow! Fortunately he meant waking up next to me rather than me going through the royal command performance every night. I told him that could still happen whether we were married or not. At that he looked a bit brighter, thank God. A lot can happen between now and graduation.

June 15, 1984. We opened the Footlights May Week revue last night after less than two weeks of frantic rehearsal. The *Dallas* parody which Ralph wrote was a smash hit. As soon as I read it, I felt a natural affinity for its comic rhythm. Ralph is a truly gifted writer. One day he's going to write me a fabulous play and I'll star in it in the West End and it'll make both our names.

I do wish he wouldn't be so damn jealous. It's starting to grate on me.

October 31, 1984. I've made a terrible mistake. I'd had enough of Ralph's jealousies and after that miserable summer inter-railing round Eastern Europe I was fed up of him. I didn't want to sleep with Ralph and nobody else for the rest of my life. There had to be something else out there.

There was. There was this young director I met who's come up with a bit of a reputation from the National Youth Theatre. They gave him the main show to do—*Cabaret*. I've always longed to play Sally Bowles. His name's Oliver and I loved his passion. Also he was a bloody good director.

The problem isn't the ten-day affair, it's what I've done to Ralph. He just crumbled. At first I lost my respect for him. If he wanted me so much why didn't he fight for me? Then, after ten days, when the first flush of sexual excitement wore off, I realised that I missed Ralph dreadfully. For all his possessiveness, he did genuinely love me, and for all Oliver's flashing brilliance, he never would. I doubt whether this man will ever love anyone but himself.

Last night was the first night of *Cabaret*. After I'd taken my make-up off, I went to the bar where I saw Oliver deep in discussion with one of the London critics. He looked up, saw me and quickly lowered his eyes, clearly anxious not to introduce me for fear I should somehow spoil the impression he was creating. I stood there shocked for a moment.

A moment later I felt a tap on my shoulder. It was Ralph. There were tears in his eyes. 'You were brilliant,' he said. And he meant it. In that split second I saw Ralph afresh. He just loved me for what I was, not for what I might do for his career. He was still hurting from our breakup, but he dragged himself in to see me in this new show, knowing that the guy I had dumped him for was directing me. And he stayed to tell me to my face how good he thought I was. He waited for me in the bar, knowing Oliver would be around and flaunting his triumph. How humiliating must that have been for Ralph. What a guy! He was so reliable, dependable, trustworthy. I loved him so much. I suppose I always have. I just needed that shit Oliver to come along and make me realise it.

Christmas Eve 1985. I'm pregnant.

It's just the most ironic thing ever! Mummy won't let Ralph and me share a bedroom and yet we've come here to tell my parents that I'm pregnant. We're planning to tell them after everyone's opened all the presents tomorrow, but we haven't decided whether or not to do it before lunch. Will lunch be the saving grace or the Last Supper?

Will Mummy be shocked because a) I'm with child without benefit of wedlock, or shocked because b) my pregnancy means I'm no longer the virgin she still fondly believes me to be, or shocked because c) Ralph has literally screwed me out of a degree and/or career? Or I suppose there's always d)—Go, and never darken my towels again, as Groucho said—but that's surely the least likely option.

December 27, 1985. Well! Who would have believed it? It was option d)! We told them just before we sat down to Christmas dinner. Mummy burst into tears and ran out of the room.

'Now look what you've done,' said Daddy, and went after her.

Ralph and I set out the dinner in almost total silence—apart from the sound of James Bond destroying the underground cave of the megalomaniac who wants to blow up the rest of the world, which came from the television in the living room playing to a non-existent audience.

I went upstairs to tell them everything was ready. Mummy was sitting on the bed dabbing at her nose with a Kleenex. Daddy was sitting next to her with his arm round her shoulder. He looked at me with such pain in his eyes. We left that night straight after supper.

July 23, 1986. The happiest day of my life. Daniel Glenn Warren born today at 3.53pm, 3.8 kilos. Glenn, after Ralph's great hero Glenn Hoddle. Blue eyes (Ralph), bald (my dad), sweet disposition (modesty forbids). Baby doing fine.

When the pain eventually stopped after about twenty-four hours (three, I was told later), I was too exhausted to care about anything, but Ralph was still in raptures that he had fathered a new England footballer. Then they washed off the blood and mucus and stuff and laid him, wrapped in a white sheet, in my arms.

I have never known a moment like it. I felt whole in a way I have never felt before—as if there was a physical, spiritual, emotional hole at the centre of me which I never knew about until they slotted that missing piece into it.

Ralph

I LOVE CALIFORNIA. I grew up in the sixties, so my earliest television-induced images were of big American cars cruising down sun-drenched, palm-tree-lined boulevards with the Pacific Ocean rolling away into the distance and the Beach Boys' 'California Girls' on the soundtrack. To me California is the very definition of life, liberty and the pursuit of happiness.

I think that's why I took to the California Angels so readily. They were owned by the cowboy star Gene Autry and seemed to regard themselves as a branch of show business first and serious professional ball players second. But they had the name 'California' attached and I was hooked.

I always wanted to go there because it seemed like Paradise on Earth. For Angela it was different: she wanted something slightly more—fame. Not money, not the Hollywood razzmatazz, but celebrity. She had talent and she wanted the chance to display it. She didn't want to give a series of magnificent performances of Ibsen above a pub in Stoke Newington.

We used to joke about 'the' phone call—the one from Hollywood promising untold fame and riches. And then one day it came. We couldn't believe our luck.

Perhaps it wasn't as entirely unexpected as I'm suggesting. After all, she had left university as the golden girl, despite not acting after January when she was two months pregnant. Her previous efforts had created a small buzz among the London agents and they were there in force to see her play Nora in *A Doll's House*.

I thought, if I'm being honest, that it was some way below her Sally Bowles in *Cabaret*, but it was still mightily impressive. All the agents wanted to take her on immediately, but she told them about the baby and they melted away—with one exception.

Martyn Frank was quite shy, very soft spoken, but he had vision. He looked beyond the pregnancy and, when he revealed that he had seen *Cabaret*, I knew he was the right one for Angela.

She went up to London and had lunch with him. She came back bubbling with praise for Martyn, energised by the prospect of the world he painted for her. I must admit something tugged at me, some antediluvian jealousy. By this time she was in the middle of her pregnancy and I was quietly thankful that the pressure of exams might dull the enticing prospect of showbiz for a few brief months. I felt as if I was holding in my hands a rare and precious butterfly that was flapping its wings against my fingers, desperate for its freedom.

Just before we were due to go down for Easter, Martyn called. An American movie was shooting in London. It was a so-called crazy comedy with Chevy Chase. In one sequence, Chevy's wife is taken to hospital and is mixed up with a pregnant woman. Martyn thought Angela would be great as the pregnant woman and persuaded the casting director to meet her. Martyn was right. The casting director flipped, so did the director.

The scene was shot one day and forgotten about the following day. The movie died as we thought it would, but Angela's performance translated the Cambridge buzz into a London buzz. Three weeks after Danny was born, Angela was auditioning in Stratford at the Royal Shakespeare Company. Two weeks later she was invited to join the company, and six weeks after that she opened at the Barbican as Desdemona in *Othello*.

Yes, it was that fast. Her feet, our feet, barely touched the ground. She bubbled with life and I loved her for it.

I had by no means lost my corrosive streak of jealousy, but the sight of her with Danny eased my soul. She loved that baby as much as I did. She left him with me for long periods while she rehearsed, but she was always desperate to see him. She conveyed an aura of such earth-mother contentment, that not even the infamously randy male members of the world's second-oldest profession dared to approach with anything on his mind other than Shakespeare or baby talk.

It was tough going for us in those early days after graduation. Angela's success in the theatre took little of the financial pressure off us, because stage actresses get paid so badly. But we just about managed to pay the rent on our one-bedroom basement flat in Highgate. She fitted in a small but showy part in a successful sitcom and that paid relatively big money for work that was altogether less worthy.

It was fortunate, because I wasn't doing so well. I was getting bits and pieces—sports previews in *Time Out*, sketches on a late-night BBC Radio comedy programme called *Weekending*—but it was casual work. My career seemed to be going nowhere fast. I had always felt sure of my talent, but it was so competitive out there and progress was non-existent. I started to have real doubts about myself.

I couldn't even confide in Angela. She was surfing a gigantic wave of success that didn't seem to want to crash onto the shore. She kept encouraging me to write a play for her, but I didn't have an idea in my head. The more she mentioned it, the more I froze. I started to feel like an incubus, the lead weight round her neck. When the phone rang, it was always for her. I could hear the disappointment in the voices on the other end when she was out. Especially if they were male.

This of course only helped to fuel my spiralling jealousy. There were rows. Lots of them. I was a rotten husband at the time, I know I was, but at least I was a good father. Thank God I had Danny. Without that little baby to look after I think I would have committed the *crime passionnel* which would have kept me in prison for life.

Then Martyn rang and said a Hollywood studio wanted to see Angela because they were planning a remake of *Gone with the Wind*. So we're off to California, staying at the Beverly Wilshire Hotel, no less.

 Angela

July 4, 1987. I feel so incredibly blessed. They told me last night I'd got the part. I was in the bath in our hotel, or 'in the tub', as they say out here—when the phone rang. Ralph called out from the bedroom that it was Morgan, the agent from ICM Martyn had set me up with here.

I got out of the bath, grabbed one of those luxurious towels that make life worth living, and dripped my way into the bedroom. Morgan was incredibly excited. I behaved like a perfect English convent-educated schoolgirl and thanked him courteously, replaced the receiver and sprang into Ralph's arms. The towel fell off and he got my wet body all over his nice new Armani T-shirt.

There was something wrong with our lovemaking as Ralph and I rolled around on that American king-size bed last night. A sense of something missing. He wasn't there emotionally. Given the news we'd just had I thought it might be one of the great fucks of all time. He must have felt I was on my way to a Hollywood career full of glitz and glamour with the constant presence of other men. If the RSC had been difficult for him, what was the glare of the studio spotlight going to be like?

I made it my task to reassure him. There never would be anyone else for me but him. What we were facing was a test of my acting ability not a test of my marital fidelity. I could see he didn't believe me though.

I got my agent to ring the RSC and pinch another few days' holiday. It's really important for my marriage that Ralph and I go away somewhere, away from this crazy town, and spend some time together. If we go straight back to London I'll be into performances of *Othello* immediately and he'll be stewing about the prospect of moving out here and losing me permanently. He hasn't said anything, but I can tell.

July 8, 1987. Our last day in Hollywood. I rang my mother this morning, which was about 6.00pm in England. My parents have never forgiven us for the Christmas eighteen months ago, but my mother fell in love with Danny the moment she laid eyes on him. She loves looking after him and was just putting him to bed, but I insisted that she bring him to the phone. I know he recognises my voice and both Ralph and I thought it was important that he heard our voices as frequently as possible. That gurgle of his made us both smile for hours.

He's a sweet and lovely baby. I wonder so often how he will grow up. Will he be kind and intelligent and sensitive and handsome? I really hope he'll be all of these things, but how can we tell if we're doing the right thing as parents? Maybe in our attempt to be the best parents ever we've already unwittingly done something wrong. Maybe just the fact of leaving him now for a couple of weeks will be enough to turn him into some antisocial Neanderthal devoid of brains or feelings.

All I know is I want to spend the years to come watching him (and his sister and/or brother) growing up, taking delight in each stage of their lives. I'll never let my career stop me from doing that.

July 12, 1987. We're in Carmel. Clint Eastwood used to be the mayor here, or maybe he still is. I'd vote for him. For anything. We've just been on this fantastic seventeen-mile drive round the Monterey peninsula. It is absolutely gorgeous here in the central bit of California. So much nicer than Los Angeles, which is best seen, I found out, through the tinted windscreen of a studio limo. Once we left LA, and drove up on the coastal route, we both started smiling again. Ralph had brought with him his Beach Boys cassette and we started rocking in our seats to the sound of 'California Girls' and 'Surfin' USA'. All the worries that seemed to be wearing him down in LA just lifted from him like the heat that rose almost tangibly from the convertible when we took the top down.

I watched him as we drove north past Santa Barbara and on to San Luis Obispo, and my heart leapt to see him so happy. This afternoon we pulled the car over to a kind of picnic area laid out for travellers to use. It all seems very civilised, I must say, and a long way from those people in Vauxhall Cavaliers who spend the first sunny afternoon of the year in little canvas-backed folding chairs eating fish-paste sandwiches in a lay-by on the A34.

We walked for some time parallel to the ocean, until we glimpsed a gap in the trees. We had heard the sound of the crashing surf but had been unable to see it because the forest ran directly to the top of the rocky cliffs. After we had been walking for a mile or so we saw a patch of green land, a plateau, reaching out of the dark and slightly dank forest, isolated above the pounding waves as they gathered strength and dashed themselves against the rocks.

We said nothing as we walked hand in hand, but words weren't necessary. There was nobody on that grassy headland. Only the birds hovering overhead saw us as we stopped high on a cliff overlooking the ocean and looked into one another's eyes. It was a blissful, magical moment. Ralph's fingers slowly unbuttoned my blouse and gently cupped my breasts. A warm breeze (God's studio wind machine?) blew softly from the ocean and lifted the hair from my head. Eventually I stood there naked.

There have been other erotic moments in my life, but never anything as uplifting as this. Everything Ralph did was perfect. OK, I'm an actress, I'm probably dramatising this a little—but only a little. It was perfect, the highest form of lovemaking, a sexual experience that transcended the physical and reached for something quite eternal.

I know Ralph experienced the identical emotion. If ever either of us doubted our love for each other, that magical hour high on that cliff must surely have banished our fears. That place overlooking the Pacific Ocean is where I lived truly and fully for the first time in my life. I cannot believe that life has another experience of similar importance in store for me. I am complete.

Danny

SOMETIMES, WHEN I GET lonely or there's nothing on TV, I take out the scrapbook Dad made of Mum's short career and look through it.

The bit I like best is when they went to America. That's when Dad started supporting the California Angels and he's bought me lots of their stuff which I've got in my room.

They left me with my gran when they went to Hollywood. I don't see her much these days. She still sends me birthday cards with a cheque in the envelope for ten pounds, but she and my dad don't like each other much. He doesn't say much about her. Just that she wasn't very nice to him after Mum died. My dad's mum is dead, so my gran is actually the only grandparent I have because both grandpas died before I knew them. I don't care though. I've got my dad and he's all that counts.

They went to Hollywood because Mum was going to be in a remake of an old film called *Gone with the Wind*. The studio put them up in a big posh hotel which sounds wicked. They travelled around in limos, like a rock star, and they were only a year out of university. They didn't make the film after she died. Dad says it was out of respect for her. I think Dad says that to me so that I'll be impressed with how famous Mum was. Actually, I don't care how famous she was. I just care that she was my mum and I loved her.

She was badly hurt in a car crash and then the ambulance took her to a hospital where she died. The man who killed her, the car driver, went to prison but not for a very long time. I don't know why he wasn't hanged. He had been drinking because his wife had left him. Big deal! At least he could still see his wife. I hate that guy.

Can you love someone you don't know? At times, at night, I screw my eyes up and think and think so hard and try to make the picture of my mum come back to me. I can sometimes do it, but then I think I'm kidding myself. What I really know is that scrapbook and all the stories Dad has always told me about her.

That favourite bedtime story of mine, 'High on a Cliff', made me think that Mum watched over us from the lighthouse, that her soul was somehow trapped in the light that goes round and round. I suppose the lighthouse was my weird idea of Heaven when I was three or four years old.

The story wasn't as creepy as it sounds. It was more like a handsome prince and a beautiful princess sort of a story. There was this place, a magical kind of a place, where the sky meets the sea. Only my dad and my mum knew about it and they used to lie there together. Now I know all about sex. I realise Dad must have meant sex, but I don't like to think about it in that way. To me it's always meant that they lay down together looking at the clear blue sky like I do sometimes in the garden or at the stars at night when it's warm enough.

After she died they asked my dad if he wanted to take her body back to England to bury her but he said no. They had been really happy in California and Dad wanted her to be buried there. He wanted to take her body to lie in this magical place, but he couldn't bury her there so she had to be cremated. I think about it and I get so sad for my father. Fancy having to go through something as horrible as that by yourself. But I'm glad they had their private place next to the lighthouse, up on that cliff, overlooking the ocean. I know my mum's happy there because my dad's happy for her. His happiness means everything to me, but I know that really he's still sad inside and there's nothing I can do about it. I wish there was.

Ralph

I WAS STILL IN A DAZE when I came back from California. There were two of me. First was the writer (I was concentrating on sports by now) and father who had to earn a living, forge a career, raise a child. He was the practical one, the one who was forever being complimented by people on how 'organised' he was. He wasn't. He never knew when the Doppelgänger would take over. The other me was like the zombie in bad horror movies. A blank face with dead eyes, he staggered through life in a trance. You expected him to fill his pockets with stones like Virginia Woolf and walk into the river.

Had it not been for Danny I fear that is precisely what I would have done. I poured into that baby all the love I would have had for my first-born child anyway, as well as all the love I could no longer give his mother. And, in the popular phrase, we bonded. If anything positive came out of that terrible tragedy, it was the hoops of steel that bound me and that boy. Danny was my best friend as well as my son. We were sharing an adventure and that bound us as tightly as men roped together on a mountaineering expedition. Deprived of whatever input we would have had from Angela, we simply set off down the long road together, hand in hand—like that illustration of Christopher Robin and Winnie the Pooh.

I decided I wanted to go back to live in Cambridge for practical rather than morbid reasons. It was a town I knew, where I still had friends who might be persuaded to look after Danny for a few hours if necessary. London was only an hour away by train, and by virtue of new technology I could communicate with most sources of potential work from my living room.

Although I took so much joy in the developing Danny, I wouldn't wish to give the impression that it was unalloyed pleasure. Teething was a nightmare. Potty training wasn't much fun either. I was convinced we'd done it, so I left him with Linda Walling, whose husband was my squash partner Ian, because I had a commission to interview John McEnroe before the start of Wimbledon. When I returned, I found Danny in the garden up against the wall, with Linda wiping him off with a kitchen towel and a bucket of soapy water.

To all outward appearances Danny's life was completely normal. He went to playgroup at two and a half, started reception class at Grantchester Street Primary when he was rising five and passed the exam for the local grammar school when he was ten and a half. He had a hot breakfast before he went to school and a conventional tea when he came home. Fortunately, his gastronomic tastes, which ran the gamut from fish fingers to baked beans, precisely complemented my culinary skills. At school Danny did well, which I reckoned was a tribute to what we had achieved at home. He was reading and writing long before the rest of his classmates because he did so much at home.

He was a sporty kid, thank God. I don't know what would have happened had he turned into the class nerd. I knew from my own experience the sort of status kids accord the best sports players in their group, and though Danny was never the best he more than held his own. I fostered my love of Tottenham Hotspur on Danny from an impressionable age and took him to matches as soon as he was old enough to sit on my knee uncomplainingly for most of the game.

Despite the changing times in which we live—I mean the social changes like male unemployment, the increasing employment of women—I was invariably the lone man outside the school railings at half past three. The women had their own support groups and I soon found out I wasn't a member of any of them. Nobody ever invited me over for coffee. I can only assume that it was because the neighbours or the husbands would look askance at a single man coming round to the house in the middle of the day. They were perfectly friendly, those women, happy to have Danny over to play with their children after school or during the holidays, but the rules of behaviour dictated that I could never be admitted inside their circles.

I suppose I got used to the loneliness so that eventually it seemed like normality. Something inside me started to shrivel up. Maybe that's why I clung to Angela's memory so tenaciously. It wasn't that I was frightened by the prospect of love; it was more that the longer I went without a relationship, the more difficult it became to believe that I would ever meet anyone.

I mean where would I do it, for a start? I began each day getting Danny dressed, cooking him breakfast, walking him to school. Then there was the shopping and the launderette and the minor matter of making a living. This consisted of reading, writing and telephoning, all of which are largely solitary occupations.

I realised that I needed to be higher profile in my work than I had been till then. There was an explosion of sports magazines, and radio and television programmes about sport, which coincided with England's defeat in the World Cup in Italy in 1990 and the growth of the Premier League. But this trend was accompanied by the arrival of a new group of young and hungry journalists. What did I have that made me more employable than they were?

When sport on satellite and cable became big business, the companies found they had to fill the airwaves with something. They decided to import vast quantities of cheap American sport.

American football had already taken off on Channel Four and I was one of the few British writers who knew his linebacker from his wide receiver. I had already made a bit of a mark with a series of articles on baseball for the *Independent*, and I was the only British journalist to track down the late great Flo Jo after she won her gold medals in the Seoul Olympics.

The NBA, the NHL, the USPGA and Major League Baseball joined the National Football League as an important component of the satellite and cable television schedules. Inevitably, in their wake came the ancillary marketing: the endorsed sports equipment and the magazines. My dream came true when *US Sports Today* started. A British version of *Sports Illustrated*, it was designed to fill what the American publishers (owned by a New York-based conglomerate) perceived as a gap in the European market. Jack McGinty—an old pal from my first days sniffing for work—was appointed editor, and within days he had invited me to a slap-up lunch to offer me the coveted and probably slightly overpaid post of contributing editor. On the strength of this new contract, I moved Danny and me out of our flat near the station and into the house off Chesterton Road we now occupy.

The loneliness abated somewhat as the new work expanded to fill the emotional vacuum. I still didn't meet anyone—nobody special, that is. There was the occasional night when I wanted female company so badly I let my guard down. One was a student I met who expressed an interest in baby-sitting. I was always looking for someone who could be relied upon for a couple of hours so I could see a film or a play, and this girl, Melanie, seemed keen and reliable.

I got back after a showing of *The English Patient*, which I just loathed. I was bored after the first hour and a half and it turned out that Melanie had felt the same. A shared dislike of the film led to an offer of a glass of wine, which in turn led to other matters. I was so tired and so emptied by the experience that I fell into a deep sleep, which wasn't broken until the following morning when Danny woke us both up wanting breakfast.

Both Melanie and I were covered in embarrassment, the only covering available to us. Ironically, Danny appeared to be entirely unmoved. He seemed to take in his stride the explanation that I had been helping Melanie with an essay and it had got so late that we had fallen asleep on the bed, being much more interested in his breakfast and whether he would be late for school. It was probably unnecessary of me, but I felt I couldn't see Melanie again. So I kept on looking for a baby sitter and a possible partner for sex or life, but I abandoned the idea that they could be one and the same person. Years seemed to go by, and though the baby-sitter position was filled without further alarms, the partner bit remained permanently available.

 Helen

THE FIRST TIME I MET Ralph, I was determined to fire him. I had arranged to do things over a decent lunch. If I'd been a coward I could easily have told that old lush Jack McGinty to do it and not soiled my dainty hands, but I maintained a naive view that people who were being let go were owed a rational explanation by the person who was firing them.

Ralph had this regular column in *US Sports Today* in which he profiled a big US sports star of the month and for which he was being overpaid. I should point out, however, that I liked his writing. Unlike some of his colleagues he had a certain sense of style, and in other circumstances I would have been happy to have kept him on. Unfortunately it didn't really matter how great his pieces were; I'd been given the task of removing all the feature writers from their staff contracts. I'd see to it that *US Sports Today* commissioned a monthly piece, but his gravy-train staff job was being derailed.

The parent company, Waverley Bros Inc, figured I was the one to get *US Sports Today* out of the hole its managerial team had dug it into, because I had made my name in the States doing something similar in San Francisco. I turned around their business magazine *Profits*. I certainly rationalised the managerial structure, but the Clinton economic resurgence was the most decisive factor in the dramatic growth in sales volume. Still, there's nothing like being in the right place at the right time and I was happy to take all the corporate credit that was flying around.

I've been pretty lucky in life. I was born in London. My mother is American, though my dad was English. They split up when I was two years old and my mom took me and my older brother Michael back to the States to live. I grew up in Boston, Massachusetts, as an all-American kid. My dad, the stuck-up sonofabitch, never bothered to see us or help my mom in any way. Mom wasn't the kind of woman to feel sorry for herself. She set herself to manage fine as a single parent and always taught us the importance of being able to stand on your own two feet.

To put myself through the Columbia School of Journalism on which I had set my heart, I hit the books real hard and eventually got this special scholarship, the Levenshulme Bursary. On the panel were journalists and editors from the *New York Times*, *Washington Post*, *Chicago Tribune*, *Time*, etc, and winning the bursary put me on the fast track. While most of my fellow graduates went off to learn the business in Des Moines and Talahassie, I was offered a job on the *Wall Street Journal*.

I thought a year or two learning about the financial side of things was bound to be good experience—this was the eighties, remember, the time of junk bonds and 'greed is good for you'. In fact I became obsessed with this new kind of journalism. I was like a historian who discovers Marxism and suddenly realises that everything he thought about the way society operated is wrong. Money dominates society and in learning to look at the world through gold-tinted glasses, I found explanations where previously there had only been irrational behaviour.

I did a good job for the *Journal* so I was given a bonus—a year in Stanford Business School. That, too, was an eye-opener—a bunch of people as highly motivated as myself, and most of them far brighter, future CEOs. I learned a lot from those guys and when I came out, the prospect of going back to New York and earning $43,750 a year when they were set to make hundreds of thousands suddenly became unappealing.

So when a job offer came from Waverley Bros Inc, it found me well prepared. The *Journal* pointed out that it had paid for me to go to Stanford so that I would return to the paper a better journalist. But Waverley were offering me the chance to move from journalism into executive management while still retaining my contact with journalists.

At the same time I was genuinely impressed by the CEO, Charles Schmidt, who was dressed in an impeccable Savile Row suit and hand-made Italian shoes.

Over dinner, I discovered that Charles was married, but I was aware that here was a man who was pressing all the right buttons with me.

He dropped me off at the Sherry Netherland, my hotel, with the chastest kiss on the cheek. I promised I would give him my answer first thing in the morning. He scribbled down the number of his mobile phone. Was this some sort of coded invitation or the action of a go-getting chief executive? That night I wondered whether I should walk away from this chance of a lifetime. I should go back to the *Wall Street Journal* and get on with a career that was progressing quite satisfactorily. I didn't need the dangerous excitement that Charles Schmidt and his millions were offering.

At seven thirty I was awake, already showered and wrapped in a voluminous Sherry Netherland bath towel. I dialled Charles Schmidt's number. His tone was civilised and warm. He said how much he had enjoyed our dinner and was looking forward to working with me.

The sound of his voice destroyed all my good intentions. The fact was that I liked this man, I liked his mind and I liked the job he was offering. I would probably enjoy turning around the leisure magazines, which were based in Los Angeles. Plus I liked California. I would be a fool to turn him down. I told him that after much careful thought I would be very happy to join his organisation. As far as I could tell from his reaction he was delighted to have another good person on his team. There wasn't the slightest hint that he saw me as a potential notch on his belt. Six weeks later we were lovers.

Charles, who was based at head office in New York, decided that the California operation needed more of his time than ever before. He moved out to the coast on a semi-permanent basis. Although he stayed at the exclusive Bel Air Hotel, he encouraged me to buy a house outside LA, just south of Santa Barbara.

The affair lasted about two and a half years. There were plenty of times when I wanted to call a halt, when I simply couldn't take the pretence a moment longer. But I just loved being with him. He had such an air of command, an irresistible charisma, that being deprived of it was heartbreaking. It wasn't so much I resented his returning to Gwen, his wife, or the New York office when problems back East prevented his return to the Coast. I was somehow diminished as a person when I was deprived of his physical presence. I had fallen in love with Charles Schmidt and the wise woman inside me knew that the only way now was down.

We finished not because I finally heeded my own sensible advice but because Mr Schmidt found a new bright shiny object with a low-cut dress. I didn't mind. No, really, I didn't. I did not become hysterical when I found I was being replaced in his affections. I was maturing. We maintained a civilised courtesy towards one another and continued to work productively together.

I am quite sure, however, I never wore anything quite as low cut as that simpering bitch flounced round the building in. I'm not being catty. I was just slightly surprised that the man whose taste in all things from mistresses to interior decoration I had previously found impeccable should have been so easily seduced by a pair of bouncing boobs. I was never tempted to call Gwen and spill the beans or any one of a half-dozen friends on different gossip columns and let them have the story. I did, however, demand a raise. I suppose I was taking a risk in that Charles could simply have fired me, but I knew that even with his Calvin Klein boxer shorts on, he needed me. It would have been an odd decision to have fired me having spent the previous two years singing my praises at every opportunity.

He knew exactly the price he could extract from me. I got everything I asked for in salary and pension provisions. In return I signed a contract which exiled me to Europe.

It was only when I got off the plane in London and heard the strangulated sounds of English as spoken by the British that I fully realised what had happened. Charles Schmidt was the big love of my life and I knew I would never see him again. Not the way I wanted to see him. In immigration I broke down and wept.

So it was with red eyes and a coat pocket full of wet Kleenex that Waverley Bros Inc's ice-cold asset stripper arrived in London to fire Ralph Warren.

 **Ralph**

BEFORE HELEN ARRIVED IN LONDON I had felt my life was as good as it was likely to get. Danny was growing up into such a great kid. I was always so proud of him. Although he 'only' went to a state primary school, he won a scholarship to the grammar school, beating off competition from prep school kids. I had what I thought was a cast-iron three-year contract with *US Sports Today*, which guaranteed me a decent income for almost the first time in my professional life. All right, there was no regular woman around, but the memory of Angela was so strong I didn't feel too badly about it. I didn't feel I was some kind of widower whose life was at an end, more like a husband whose actress-wife had been away on location for a long time—a very long time.

I didn't expect to like Helen Cooper at all when I met her, though that's partially because before I met her my telephone had started ringing with advance warnings. OK, so the magazine hadn't exactly been *People* or *Hello!* but then it wasn't designed to be, it was targeted at a specialised audience. Jack McGinty told me the proprietors had been sanguine at the planning stages about the possibility of sustaining heavy losses for the first few years until people learned to appreciate the quality of the writing. Now, eighteen months after the launch, she had breezed into town and set about her with an axe because we weren't making a profit. Jerks!

One Thursday morning, I was sitting at home typing up my notes on an interview with Tiger Woods, who I thought was a nervous breakdown waiting to happen, when the phone rang. It was the temporary secretary of Helen Cooper, yes, the very woman the mention of whose name caused grown journalists to tear their own heads off, rather than upset her. The secretary told me I was expected at the office in London at ten thirty the following morning. I told her that wasn't possible. I had to take Danny to school so I couldn't leave until after nine, which meant I wouldn't be able to get a train until after nine thirty, which would take me to Liverpool Street rather than King's Cross, so the best I could do was eleven o'clock. Even then Friday was inconvenient because the deadline on the Tiger Woods piece was close of play tomorrow. Besides, Danny had cricket practice after school and I was one of the coaches. Monday would be far more convenient.

I might as well have asked for the moon. The girl made it quite clear that I was expected in the office tomorrow at ten thirty. I wasn't being asked whether this was convenient for me, I was being told to be there or else. I was going to give this American bitch a piece of homespun English common sense.

I realise that this sounds like what Hollywood screenwriters call a 'meet cute': a contrived situation in which the boy meets the girl when the girl has her skirt caught in a suitcase or they have each been booked into the other's hotel room by mistake. They start by hating each other and ninety minutes later they're living happily ever after. Maybe this sort of thing became a screen convention because it can happen in real life. I mean, people do meet through strange circumstances. One of my best friends met his wife only because she was too dense to understand perfectly comprehensible directions, got lost, and he rescued her.

I arrived at reception at the skyscraper in Marylebone Road at ten thirty-seven. I wasn't going to give the bitch the satisfaction of seeing me there bang on time, though usually I'm so anal that's invariably when I do show up. In the end the gesture was entirely pointless, because Helen was running late and I didn't get in to see her until after eleven. I could have got that Liverpool Street train after all and saved the money I spent on the taxi to catch the nine ten King's Cross express.

She was not exactly what I expected. I found a thirtyish woman with good legs, thick curly black hair and minimal make-up and jewellery. A dark blue business suit, of course, but no starched white blouse, shoulder pads or other standard issue female executive attire. The overall effect was pleasingly feminine, although her dress still proclaimed that she was one of those women whose main ambition is to be taken 'seriously', like a man.

Angela used to spend considerable time fretting about what to wear. Whatever she wore she never looked anything other than gorgeous. She also had thick, lustrous blonde hair, which she could do anything with. I always preferred it spilling down her back. It gave her a look of sexual abandon that I found constantly arousing.

Angela had instilled in me a sense that for a woman to look sexually attractive she had to dress in a particular way. It had been more than twelve years since I had found any other appearance to create that effect. The Laura Ashley look was now *passé*, but so, I guess, was I. Until I laid eyes on Helen Cooper. This was a most unexpected turn of events.

I had to admit that Helen was pretty much on top of her brief. The meeting had been called so that she could meet all the contributing editors, not just me. Now it made a bit more sense as to why it was so important that I came at that time. Helen had all the tools of the trade—flip charts and all that presentation stuff—and her performance was both eloquent and perceptive.

When she left her analysis of the business and launched into the quality of the journalism, I felt the hackles rising. As far as I was aware, she knew little about sports and less about Britain. Now she was going to fall flat on her cute little face. Oh yes, I forgot to mention that she had a soft round face with very kissable lips. I know I shouldn't really have been thinking this way, but when she talked passionately she was very cute indeed.

As it turned out she didn't know too much about sports, but she knew a hell of a lot about good writing. I hadn't realised she'd been a journalist herself. I thought she was a kind of management figure who simply increased profit margins, but she really knew her stuff. She had a built-in shit detector that told her which articles were sloppy, poorly researched and badly written. She got after two guys in the room in particular—Mike Staunton had done a very ordinary piece on the French clay court championships at Roland Garros and Jim Fullerton had turned in a scissors-and-paste analysis on the decline of Nick Faldo on the US PGA tour. She was right on both counts.

The meeting broke up with all of us sweating. I believed we were all going to lunch afterwards, so I was surprised when Jack McGinty shook my hand and wished me good luck. Apparently it was going to be lunch à deux. A shiver ran down my spine.

I had come up prepared to take some kind of bollocking. We'd be made aware that we were on Easy Street and the company had shown faith in us by giving us these staff jobs and the least we could do in return was to write and fight for the good old parent company conglomerate.

Instead, I was completely wrong-footed. I now made the inevitable assumption based on Jack's apologetic handshake that I was about to be fired. Well, I thought grimly, it will be fun finding out precisely what excuse she was going to dredge up for giving me the boot.

She was civil in the taxi on the way to the restaurant, apologising for dragging me up from Cambridge at ten thirty when she knew I was a single parent. I was wrong-footed again. What was this woman up to? I said it was fine, and I could see that if everyone else was coming in at ten thirty there was no point in my showing up half an hour late, but the secretary hadn't told me that. She looked at me sharply.

'She didn't tell you there was a meeting?'

'Not a general meeting. I thought it was just the two of us.'

'I'm so sorry. That's inexcusable. You think I should fire her?'

'Good God, no. People don't lose their jobs in England over something as petty as that.'

'Maybe they should. That would keep people on their toes.'

'Is that a coded warning?'

'I thought you knew Americans have no sense of irony.'

I was flummoxed. I had no idea how to talk to this woman. Was I being softened up for the fatal bullet or was I being hung out to dry here? We both fell silent and stared out of the window.

In the bright but noisy restaurant we were shown to a corner table. Should I fall on my sword, I wondered, resign in high dudgeon so at least I could stage a magnificent exit with my head held high?

'I'm sorry about the noise. We could go someplace else if you prefer.'

She left my two-footed tackle sprawling on the ground as she headed for goal with the ball at her feet. Why this sudden humility?

'No. This is fine. Really.'

'I asked for the closest decent restaurant. Everyone I talked to recommended this place. Have you been here?'

I shook my head. Couldn't write, lived in the wrong place, didn't know which London restaurants to go to for lunch. I was dead meat, surely. Silence fell as we studied the menu.

'It always strikes me,' I declared ingratiatingly, 'that the national dish of America is menus.'

I expected her to cut me dead with a blistering broadside on how advanced American cooking is, so it was another surprise when she laughed.

'That's great! Yours?'

I shook my head. 'Saw it on some travel programme on TV ages ago.'

'I like it.' Maybe I wasn't dead meat yet.

The appetisers arrived.

'You're a good journo, Ralph.' Here it comes. The pause at the end of the sentence was like that moment in cartoons when a character sprints over the edge of the cliff and appears to hover in midair for two seconds, with his feet still kicking away, before gravity snaps into action.

'I sense a reservation.'

'I've got to make some changes. The guys back home are looking at the bottom line. We invested heavily in the Asian economy. We got badly burned so we have to make cuts to get back on track. There are too many journos on high-paying staff contracts. They're going to have to go back onto freelance work.'

I had been so relieved when I got that sense of financial security that came with the staff contract. Now this Yank was going to yank it away from under my nose.

'Does that mean me?' I affected an indifference to my fate I did not feel.

She nodded, rather sadly. I liked that.

'I'm sorry. I think you're an excellent writer. Truly I do. You'd be the last person I'd fire if it was a question of talent.'

'That's a comfort.'

'I can see you don't believe me, but I assure you it's true. I think the magazine will be lucky to get you on a freelance basis. I'm sure you'll be swamped with offers of work.'

Another awkward pause. At this critical moment the waiter arrived to clear away the plates. Helen reached across and poured the sparkling water into both our glasses. Into my mind now came the image of a judge reaching for the black cap. 'Ralph Michael Warren, you have been found guilty of signing a lucrative staff contract. You shall be taken from hence to a place of execution where you shall be hanged by the laptop recharger extension cord until you are dead. And may the Inland Revenue have mercy on your soul.'

What she said was, 'Tell me about your son. I see you don't wear a wedding band.'

My mind crashed its gears as it changed down abruptly.

'I'm sorry?'

'No. I'm the one who's sorry. I shouldn't be sticking my big fat nose in. This is a business lunch. And it's none of my business.'

'I'm not divorced. My wife died.'

'Oh, that's so sad. When?'

And so I told her the story. *Gone with the Wind II* and all the rest of it. She didn't cluck with empty sympathy the way most women did, nor turn monosyllabic with embarrassment as most men did. She asked searching questions but I felt they were genuine attempts to understand rather than prurient prying. The main course arrived and disappeared. Dessert was fashionably dispensed with and I smiled as she countered my decaffeinated cappuccino with a double espresso.

I looked at my watch instinctively.

'That's the twelfth time you've done that since we sat down.'

'You're keeping score?'

'I was wondering if you had some place more important to be.'

I explained. I needed to get the two forty-five train from King's Cross so I could coach Danny's cricket team. Besides, I was fed up of being dangled on the end of the rope like this. 'If you're going to make a change, why don't you make it? Put us both out of our misery.'

She drank her double espresso like a cowboy downing a double shot of whisky. I slurped at the cappuccino, conscious of the danger of leaving traces of the milky foam on the tip of my nose. How is it that a cup of coffee could be filled with such dangers?

'I want to talk to you some more.'

'Can we do it on the phone? Or on Monday? I have to email that piece on Tiger Woods this afternoon.'

'How you gonna do that if you're out coaching?'

I gestured to the laptop. 'On the train.'

I could see her mind flicking through a number of possibilities. I knew she wasn't likely to rescind her decision to fire me, but then again I'm a Spurs and Angels supporter and I believe that hope springs eternal.

'That train of yours . . . Did you have to book a ticket? I mean, is it like a bus or an airplane?'

'More like a bus.'

'OK. Let's go.'

I must have looked shocked at the impulsive decision.

She smiled. 'I'm in therapy. He wants me to work on my spontaneity.'

'You're in therapy? Really?'

'All Americans with incomes over a hundred thousand dollars have a therapist. You must know that.'

I could see that she regretted the sentence as soon as it was out of her mouth. She hadn't meant to rub my face in the spectacular difference between her guaranteed income and my own situation.

'I've got no appointments this afternoon. I'm really interested in you as a writer. I'd like to be able to work something out, and seeing you in your natural habitat might help. Make sense?'

What did I have to lose? 'Sure.'

Danny

THE FIRST TIME I SAW HER, I was cross with her because I was cross with my dad for showing up late. He'd told my teacher Mrs Hargreaves that he could help with coaching the school team and at ten past four we were all on the playing field in our cricket clothes. By twenty past four there was still no sign of Dad. Mr Banks, who ran the school first eleven, came by and made some barbed comment about Dad, and I cringed. He split us up into four groups and we'd just started catching practice when there was a loud blast from a car horn.

We all looked up to see Dad waving furiously from a taxi. If that wasn't embarrassing enough, he was with some woman. The other lads didn't waste any time, calling her a tart and lots of other names which I didn't understand, but which I knew were rude. I hated him for embarrassing me like this. How could he do it? He'd never done anything like this before. And this woman! I know I said I thought it was about time he found someone, but not here! I meant at home one Saturday night or something. I just wanted the ground to open up and swallow me.

Turned out it wasn't Dad's fault. The train was half an hour late leaving King's Cross. He said there were leaves on the line. I didn't understand because it was nearly May and all the trees were in bloom. But Mr Banks laughed and said we must have started practising with the wrong kind of balls because none of us could catch them. Dad laughed and suddenly it looked like Dad and Mr Banks were best friends. Grown-ups are really peculiar sometimes.

Anyway, it wasn't half as bad as I had feared. Dad had spent two days with the England cricket team at the start of the one-day international series, watching their pre-season training in the Canary Islands. He was able to tell everyone the special exercises they do for strengthening what he called 'hand–eye coordination'.

By the time we got to play a short game, we had forgotten all about the bird. She was called 'Helen from work' and I thought at first, oh God, no, she's one of his 'research assistants' or whatever he calls his short-term girlfriends. But she kicked off her shoes, sat on the grass watching us for a few minutes, obviously got bored, lay back in the sunshine and went to sleep. She forgot about us and we forgot about her.

Afterwards Dad said we could go to Pizza Express, but Helen said why didn't we buy something at Sainsbury's and she'd cook it? She never got the chance to usually, which I thought was weird. If she never cooked, how did she eat? Anyway, we went to Sainsbury's, which I hated because you can't just go in and buy something and come out again. You have to get a trolley and all that fuss and I was really thirsty.

I made Dad stop at a newsagent's and buy me a Coke first, but he was in a funny old mood. He and Helen kept staring at each other and laughing a lot. They bought chicken and baked potatoes which I like, and salad stuff which I absolutely hate. I mean, if you're really hungry, and I was because I'd had nothing to eat since lunch, the one thing you don't want is a salad.

This Helen was American and apparently chicken and baked potato and salad is what people have for dinner in America. I thought they just ate hamburgers. When we got home I was sent upstairs to do my homework although I wanted to watch *The Simpsons* first. Usually Dad lets me while he's cooking dinner, but this time he got all stern and said I had to start my homework because it would be too late after dinner blah blah blah. I think he was showing off in front of the American woman.

And she was American, this woman, American in her looks and in her way of behaving. Not like my mum. Mum was beautiful. She was tall and she had long golden hair like a fairy princess and she wore long flowing dresses. This Helen person is only average in height and her hair is dark and curly, whereas I know for a fact that Dad likes women who have long fair hair. He's always going on and on about how beautiful Mum's hair was.

In the end Dad did the cooking anyway because Helen's mobile kept ringing. She went into the study and then she came back in saying she had to get online to talk to head office in America and she asked me if I could help because 'kids know so much more about the Internet than we wrinklies'. It made me want to puke.

I was starting to explain that Dad had told me to start my homework when Dad interrupted and said he'd show her how to do it. When he came back he gave me this long lecture about how we always have to be polite to guests and he'd taught me all these manners and why didn't I use some of them occasionally.

This made me mad because a) I hadn't been rude to Helen and b) how come this system of Dad's about being extra polite to guests only works the one way? Whenever we go to other people's houses I can't do anything except what other people tell me to do. But when people come to our house I can't do anything and the guest can do whatever she pleases. Now is this unfair or what?

Anyway, Dad then decided that I could do my homework after dinner and that I now had to set the table with the best crockery, and I thought that was stupid too. We don't normally eat with the best plates. She was getting a false impression of how we normally lived and ate. Particularly since there was live football on the telly. It was Celtic v. Juventus and normally we'd sit in the front room with the plate on our knees and watch the game on TV. Dad always said it was his work, it wasn't that he wanted to watch it but he had to. (That's a joke of course.) But now we were stuck in the dining room eating off the posh dinner plates.

I could see it wasn't worth having a go at Dad about it. I wasn't going to win so what was the point? I decided to be dead cool about everything, so when she came back I was smiling and chirpy. Inside I was still sending her up, but she didn't know. I did suggest, just casually, that she might be interested in watching the Celtic v. Juventus game but Dad chipped in smartly, 'Oh, I think Helen would much prefer to talk to you.' And his eyes were flashing warning signs. She said, 'Oh yes, Danny, your dad's been telling me all about you on the train.' Which I hate because I hate him talking about me to other people.

Dad and me, we have a great relationship but it's ours. When he talks about us to other people I sometimes feel it's not special any more. The Red Indians thought that if they had their photo taken their souls would be taken with it. I do sort of see their point. It's like you've got something dead private, then it becomes public and everyone has a piece of it and suddenly it's not your private thing any more.

Helen

I'VE NEVER BEEN WHAT YOU might call a maternal person. I have never had that urge to procreate, never wanted to hold a baby in my arms, mine or anybody else's, never heard that mythical baby clock ticking anywhere near me.

So when I met Danny for the first time I felt nothing special. In fact, if anything, I was kind of disappointed. On the train Ralph had talked endlessly about what a great kid he was, how if it hadn't been for Danny he couldn't have gone on after Angela's death and all that kind of crap, so by the time the train rolled into the station I was expecting to see a mixture of the juvenile Sigmund Freud and baby Jesus.

What I found, of course, was a normal kid, good-looking in a freckly pubescent way, in cricket clothes which made him look like all the other kids. On the way back to the house he set up this whine about being thirsty and I could tell Ralph was getting increasingly impatient with him. I thought, Uh-oh, I'm not getting involved in playing Happy Families with these two.

But as soon as we got to the house the cellphone went and I left the room. When I got back, the grumpy adolescent had turned into this really nice kid. Danny was cheerful and Ralph was relaxed and dinner went with a swing. I felt a bit guilty because I'd promised to cook, but then the phone rang and I got online with California and by the time I'd finished Ralph had done all the cooking.

He's a good cook, better than me, if only because he's had more practice. For me, cooking is something I only do when there is no alternative. Because of my job I'm frequently being taken out to eat, or else I'm so exhausted I'm crashed out in front of the TV and I wind up with a bowl of gourmet soup heated up in the microwave. When Charles came for the weekend, even when I offered to cook, he would invariably want to demonstrate his largesse and self-importance by sweeping me off to the best restaurant in town. Charles has never been a homebody.

Frequently when I go to people's houses for dinner there is something about family life which gives me a pain in the ass. It's so damn smug, you know, so 'I bet you wish you could sit down every night with your own family like we do'. I thought I might feel similarly about Ralph and Danny but my fears were soon calmed. For a start, I liked the way they talked to each other. It was gentle teasing on both sides and it was clear that Ralph was keen to allow Danny to develop his own ideas. Lots of parents take great delight in ridiculing their kids. Not Ralph. So many kids of that age either parrot their parents' attitudes or are just plain contrary. Danny's ideas were thought out and well articulated. Over dinner it became clear to me that Danny and Ralph did have a special relationship, one I'd never seen before between a father and a son.

When he found out I lived in California, Danny's eyes lit up. He wanted to know if I'd been to Disneyland and when I said 'No' I felt like a freak. He knew everything about Disneyland and he couldn't believe that someone who lived only a hundred miles away had never been. I promised I would take him there. His eyes glowed with pleasure at the prospect. I was getting to like this kid.

Danny and Ralph washed the dishes. I offered to help but they wouldn't hear of it. This was a routine they did every day. Danny cleared the table, Ralph washed the dishes. I was surprised they didn't have a dishwasher, but then I could see with just the two of them there probably wasn't the need.

One thing I couldn't help noticing of course were the photographs of Ralph's dead wife, Angela. They were all over the house. I wouldn't say it was creepy, like a shrine or anything. It's just that there were lots of them. It was like her presence hung over the house.

It was when Danny went to bed that the evening started. I had no real idea why I had got on that train other than I knew I wanted to be with Ralph a while longer. Was this going to be a relationship? I wondered. Did I dare contemplate the prospect of something as meaningful as a 'relationship'? My last experience had been with a man so different from Ralph that it seemed incredible that the same species could have produced two such contrasting individuals.

But as the evening progressed I found myself becoming increasingly attracted to this new kind of male animal. I had always dismissed 'the sensitive lover' syndrome as a limp-wristed waste of time and space. I always thought that what I wanted was a man who exuded power, who was strong enough to withstand my withering sarcasm and all-round cynicism. I liked men who were strong and hard in attitude as well as muscle. Charles Schmidt was just such a man. Ralph assuredly was not. So how was it possible that Ralph Warren was now exercising this creeping fascination for me? Something deep and uncontrollable was happening to me.

It was the smell of Ralph which changed all these feelings: his own body smell, a warm, enveloping smell that made me want to curl up inside it. It seemed very safe and the more I smelt it as we sat on the couch after dinner, the more I wanted him. I made the first move because of it, unbuttoning his shirt and running my fingers up and down his chest, putting my face close to it.

He pulled my hands away gently, whispering about Danny not being in bed yet upstairs. But he did it beautifully. It wasn't a wimpish petulant act, it wasn't brutal or unfeeling. He managed to soothe my injured pride and still retain a measure of masculine control.

In that very act of rejection, although as it turned out it was less rejection than delayed gratification, he showed me the true measure of the man. If I'd been hypersensitive I would no doubt have risen grandly to my feet and called for a taxi. But I did no such thing. Instead, I just sat and waited for him to return.

Ralph

I NEED TO REMEMBER the rows and the jealousies that came between us, because otherwise I would romanticise Angela into sainthood and she was never that ethereal. But it's certainly true that she was my first and best and in many ways my only. The women who have come since have been unable to live up to Angela, I suppose because I never let them. It's not that I didn't want these other women—at the time anyway. There is a limit to the fevered imagination of even a sports writer's brain and it was certainly great to experience the feeling that I was still normal on those infrequent occasions when I spent the night with a woman. But there was always Danny.

I loved Danny and I thought he was too young to deal with my re-marrying. There would be all the problems that stem from step-families. Either the woman I married would bring her own children from a former marriage, and I didn't think it would ever be possible to treat her children identically to the way in which I responded to Danny or, worse, she would be a bad mother to Danny. Then there was the problem of our having children together. I could not see how this could benefit Danny. It was bound to get in the way of the tight relationship that had developed between us. How could I possibly give myself to children from a new marriage knowing that Danny would inevitably feel displaced in my affections no matter how hard I tried to reassure him?

After being married and revelling in the security of sex in such protected circumstances, it was a rude shock to discover that sex with women after Angela involved all these ancillary questions. No wonder the relationships rarely lasted beyond the first serious encounter.

But that first night with Helen, I knew I was attracted to her and that this wasn't like the other abortive sexual encounters of recent years.

She took the initiative, which was perhaps as well considering this was the woman who had been trying to fire me a few hours ago. It was I who blinked first of course. It was instinctive, accentuated by the knowledge that Danny was still awake upstairs. I excused myself on that basis, calculating that by the time I returned she would either have recovered her professional poise or stripped down to bra and panties.

Upstairs the conversation took a predictable turn.

'Is she staying the night?'

'That's none of your business. Have you brushed your teeth?'

'Yes. She's after you, Dad.'

'She's just friendly. Americans usually are.'

'Why?'

'I don't know. They're less uptight.'

'Can you record the highlights of the Celtic v. Juventus game?'

'They'll be on *Football Focus* at lunchtime.'

'Please.'

'All right. But only if you go straight to sleep.'

'Can you turn on the tape?' He had a tape recorder on which he played audio cassettes. It was an excellent way to get him to go to sleep while absorbing a little culture. I switched on *The Thirty-Nine Steps* and turned off the light.

I made a detour into the bathroom. A quick brush of the teeth and a squirt of aftershave behind the ear made me feel better prepared for what might happen downstairs. Now that Danny was 98 per cent secure, I was starting to get quite excited.

I wanted her, there was no doubt. If she was all buttoned up when I got downstairs I was going to be disappointed. It did occur to me as I flicked off the bathroom light that the traditional manner of seduction— predatory male, reluctant yet interested female with child to worry about making a quick dash to the bathroom to effect emergency repairs before the big moment—had been reversed. Did I care? Not by the time I was halfway down the stairs and could see into the living room.

Danny

I KNEW SOMETHING was wrong as soon as I woke up. Even the way he made breakfast was different. He had this soppy look on his face and he didn't listen to anything I said. And he'd forgotten to record the Celtic v. Juventus game. On the other hand, I was going to be allowed to watch television all morning and usually I'm only allowed an hour on Saturday mornings.

'Is that woman still here?' I shook a large stream of Crunchy Nut Corn Flakes into my bowl.

'That woman's name is Helen. And yes, she's in the spare bedroom.'

I smirked but Dad didn't see it. Did he think I was five years old or something? Honestly!

She came down a few minutes later, dressed in the same clothes as the night before. At least she hadn't nicked Dad's dressing gown or something that would have made it seem like she belonged in our house. One of the others had tried that once so I gave her marks for that. But not too many.

After breakfast they decided to go for a walk. Dad wanted to show her the sights of Cambridge. This wasn't unusual. He does this for all the people who come and stay with us. He shows them where he first met Mum and then takes them on a guided tour of their romance. Actually it's not quite as sick as it sounds because it's also a tour of the university. I can't get very excited about looking at King's College Chapel or any building, but lots of people seem to like it.

Cambridge in summer is full of tourists and tour buses. I hate them. If you go into town you can hardly move. Plus they don't seem to understand that I can go dead quick on my bike and they casually saunter across your path even if you've rung your bell at them. That's one reason why I didn't much like Helen at first. She was just another American tourist. And I didn't like the way Dad was looking at her. It wasn't like the others. He seemed to ignore me entirely.

As soon as they left, though, it was OK. I had the house to myself so I lay on the couch and watched the cartoons on Junk TV and played with my Gameboy. I sometimes like to get my weekend homework out of the way on Saturday mornings, but then sometimes I just don't want to do it and I leave it as late as bathtime on Sunday nights and Dad screams at me, but then he helps me with it so it's dead easy.

This time, though, Dad forgot about it altogether, because she stayed the whole weekend and we did things together as if we were a family, which we weren't. When they came back from their walk I was watching a match on TV, but Dad didn't seem to mind because he was chatting to Helen and she was smiling at him and they seemed to be having a jolly good time.

After lunch they decided we were going to play tennis. Dad said that Helen could borrow a spare pair of his tennis shorts, but since she was so slim she'd better come upstairs and try them on first. They took ages upstairs, which I couldn't understand. I mean either a pair of shorts fits you or it doesn't. When they did come down I wasn't too pleased that they'd borrowed a pair of my white shorts for her because all Dad's were too large. It looked weird seeing her in my shorts.

She was an OK tennis player. She hit the ball hard enough but she couldn't run and she had a crap backhand. Dad was full of encouragement. Lots of 'well played's and 'great shot's, but that's what he usually says to me and I'm miles better than she is. I won the set I played against her 6–3. I kept looking at Dad for approval because some of my backhand returns were really good, particularly off her serve, because I was finally understanding what Dad had always told me about using the power of your opponent's shot to return the ball with interest, but he couldn't keep his eyes off Helen. He said afterwards that of course he was looking at me, but I know he wasn't, not like he usually does.

They sent me off to buy three cans of Coke, a diet one for her, she said. I didn't think they sold that kind at the newsagent's so I said I'd ask but I wouldn't really. I'd give her the same Coke as Dad and I usually had and hope the sugar would make her explode or something.

When I got back he was teaching her to serve. Only not like he does it with me, which is to stand to one side and let me copy his throw up and the way he moves his body. Instead he was standing directly behind her and his body was leaning right into hers. I don't think he was teaching her to serve at all. I think he was trying to feel her up in public.

I decided I'd get his attention once and for all so I shook up one of the cans of Coke and handed it to her. She put it on the ground as Dad did with his until he was finished with the exercise. When they picked up the cans, I saw to my horror that Dad had picked up the one I'd shaken. So of course, as soon as he snaps it open, it shoots all over his face.

Helen burst out laughing and I would have done too, only I could see that Dad knew instantly what had happened. So I felt a bit guilty.

'When do you have to be back in London?' I asked Helen, hoping for the answer 'In an hour'.

She said, 'Oh, not till Monday morning. Tell me, Dan, are there lots of fun things to do round here?'

I wanted to scream at her that my name was Danny not Dan, but I didn't. Dad interrupted instead, grinning all over his face.

'Sure. Cambridge is the funnest city on the globe, isn't it, Dan?' He'd never called me 'Dan' before. Ever.

'Yeah? Like what? What's like a typical fun day for you?'

'Piano lessons, swimming lessons, tennis lessons, judo lessons, home-work, TV and Pizza Express,' I said, running all the words together so she'd get the idea that there was no fun anywhere in Cambridge and go home immediately.

Instead she seemed delighted. 'You know they never put anything like that in the tourist brochures. It's full of punting on the river and even-song at King's College Chapel. I never knew Cambridge had a Pizza Express.'

'Actually it's rather a good one. It's in a sort of mock classical building on Jesus Lane.'

'This I gotta see. Would it be OK if I bought Danny a large pepperoni pizza with extra toppings and a giant Coke to go with it?'

I was salivating. Maybe this woman wasn't so bad after all. She was doing her best to be nice.

Dad looked dubious. 'Well, I don't know. I mean he's got an awfully busy schedule. He's got piano lessons, tennis lessons, swimming lessons, judo lessons, homework . . .'

I fell for it. 'Please, Dad, we never go out to eat, *please*.'

'OK. You sure about this?' He looked at Helen.

'Never been surer of anything.'

We went to Pizza Express. We had to wait for ever for the food to arrive. But it was worth it.

I suppose I could see it that first day that Helen and Dad were falling for each other. I've never seen anyone fall in love so I didn't know that's how it would be. The boys at my school, sometimes they talk about their girlfriends, but it doesn't really mean anything. Maybe they've seen someone in a shopping centre on Saturdays and they've gone to the cinema that evening, but nobody ever talks about falling in love. A girl-friend is a kind of a status symbol, but only kind of because most of us haven't got one. And if I'm being honest, most of the twelve- or thirteen-year-old girls you see aren't like Claudia Schiffer or Kate Moss who really are beautiful. All the twelve-year-old girls I've ever seen are dead ugly or they've got braces on their teeth which make them look dead ugly. So you can't blame me for being sort of unprepared when Dad fell in love with Helen.

Helen

IT WAS NEVER on my itinerary, never in my scheme of things. It wasn't that I didn't expect to fall in love ever again, or that Ralph was not my type. It's just that the whole thing took me by surprise. I left the office that Friday lunchtime prepared to fire the bullet. I came back in on Monday morning bewitched, bothered and bewildered—by myself as much as by him.

Most of my colleagues returned very much the same people who had left on the Friday afternoon. But not me.

When I first 'did it' all those years ago, I used to look in the mirror for days afterwards for some kind of telltale sign. I was changed inside, so surely there had to be some kind of physical change. Were my cheeks red, was my graceless walk a little more poised? Or did I just have an enormous V with a line through it, to indicate that my cherry had been officially consumed? Sadly, none of the above appeared to apply and I was left to whisper of my new-found status in the locker room.

I had a small rerun of those feelings when I walked back into the office on that Monday morning. I wanted so much to shout from the rooftops that I had fallen in love. I contented myself with sending a long email to Los Angeles explaining why I thought the company should retain the services of Ralph Warren, guaranteeing his current salary while switching his status from staff to freelance.

I tried very hard to keep my business with Ralph separate from our relationship, but it proved difficult. For a start, that old lush Jack McGinty was clearly deeply sceptical when he discovered that I had kept Ralph's guaranteed income at its former level. I expect he made an immediate cause-and-effect link in his mind.

Every time his name came up in discussion, a little tremor went through me and my mind was filled with the memory of his touch and his smell, and a slow warmth permeated my body, which made my toes curl in pleasure.

We talked a lot on the cellphone in order to avoid the main office switchboard, but in the end it emerged like the election of the Pope, but without the white smoke. One day I was having a wonderful secretive private affair and the next I was the clear target of smirks and whispered giggles. Two secretaries stopped gossiping and turned bright red when I came into the women's room. In the excruciating silence that followed, it was plainly obvious that I had been the subject of their conversation.

I knew I was in love because I didn't care. I didn't care that these snooty secretaries looked down on me from their lofty perches behind the Tampax dispenser. I didn't care that Jack McGinty was now bringing his Jack Daniel's into the office and hiding it in the filing cabinet as if I would never know or if I found out he had 'something' on me.

Previously I would have bawled him out in front of the whole office. Now I just asked him for a shot at the end of the working day and suggested that in future if he wanted one he came to my office after six thirty when most of the workers had left. I knew he'd never do it and he'd go back to the pub as he had always done in the past, but I achieved what I wanted without bad feelings or public executions. And it felt good. Falling in love with Ralph Warren made me better at my job while making me care less deeply about it.

I had been in love before, with Charles certainly, but it was a hard, almost competitive kind of love and remorseless consumption of each other. It was different with Ralph. He was, in many ways, a more rounded individual than Charles; you could argue that he was more of a man. His talents were just as impressive. He could write anything and he could lead the life of a domestic housewife without losing a jot of his mental sharpness. Plus he was an amazing father.

I knew how difficult life as a single parent could be because I had watched my mom struggle so hard for so long. But when it came down to the grim reality of single parenting, I never even made it to first base, as Ralph would say. There was just so much to *do*. Danny was in many ways more responsible than many kids of his age, simply because he had been used to helping his dad around the house. But still the sheer volume of stuff necessary to raise a kid blew my mind. It wasn't just getting him up in the morning, because he was quite capable of sleeping through the sound of his alarm clock, and making sure he had brushed his teeth before turning the bedroom light off at night. Spending time with Ralph and Danny made me realise that you could pass the whole day doing almost nothing but either plan for his future welfare or just keep going now.

I soon discovered that though the best time for Ralph to work was when Danny was at school, he still had things to do for Danny in those hours. By the time Ralph got back from dropping Danny off, it was nearly nine thirty, and to pick Danny up at four Ralph had to set off just after three thirty. The day, such as it was, didn't shape up remotely like any day I've ever worked. No wonder Ralph had kept looking at his watch during that first lunch.

Most weekends I went down to Cambridge. Danny (I thought) accepted me pretty quickly. I didn't think it was going to be that difficult. I just bought him stuff—video games I got from the US and CDs from new bands he hadn't heard of but had already made it big in LA and were on their way to Europe. Ralph said his affections couldn't be bought, but I soon found out different—it just depended how much you were prepared to spend.

He was a sweet kid, I soon saw that. I knew what Ralph was talking about that first time, not so much because he was unlike every other twelve-year-old kid I've ever known, but because he *was* like them yet still retained this special bond with his dad. It wasn't that he came out of school and flung himself into his dad's arms, but that they immediately slipped into a way of relating to each other that was easy and familiar, not just father and son, but also two old friends. It wasn't true all the time but I could see evidence of it often enough to be aware that it existed.

That summer was idyllic. Ralph and Danny liked to go to the Lake District region of northwest England. Since every time I look out of the window it is either raining or just about to rain or just stopped raining, I couldn't believe anyone would want to vacation in England voluntarily, but apparently people do. I arranged to take my last week of vacation with them in Keswick.

Discreetly I booked a single room in the same hotel, some way away from them so as not to embarrass Danny. This was Danny's special time with his dad and I wanted to make no waves. I wasn't sure they really wanted me to come, but Ralph was insistent and Danny seemed to want me.

Considering the hours I work and my diet, I keep myself pretty fit. I belong to a gym, but I don't go every morning from 6.00am to 7.00am or anything stupid like that. Maybe on a Friday night after work I'll go and spend forty minutes or so on the Stairmaster. I'm not too crazy about red meat and I haven't got a sweet tooth so I manage to keep my shape. So when Danny was telling me all about the mountains they climb I wasn't too worried. Of course when I called them mountains he was quick to correct me. Apparently the appropriate term is 'fells'. They decided they'd take me up something called Bowfell, which didn't sound too bad. It was less than 3,000 feet and Danny had climbed it when he was nine.

Jesus! That was some climb. I kept looking nervously at the mountain, sorry, fell, looming in front of us, but I consoled myself with the prospect of little nine-year-old Danny leaping to the top.

The whole way up the two of them never stopped jabbering. Then the path gave out completely.

'This is Esk Hause,' said Ralph. 'Over there's the Scafell range and beyond is Pillar and Great Gable. They're my two favourites.'

I said nothing, being incapable of speech. My calves and the backs of my thighs were singing ('Climb ev'ry mountain' it sure wasn't) and my lungs were bursting. Sweat was pouring from my head down my face. My whole body felt like it had been heated up in a sauna. I longed for a swimming pool under the warm Californian sun and an iced drink and a sun lounger. That was my idea of a holiday.

'It gets a bit harder till we get to the summit,' Ralph said apologetically.

'You mean this isn't the goddamn summit?' I gasped.

'This is Esk Hause,' piped up the infuriating Danny. 'That's the summit up there.' He pointed towards Mount Everest.

'I thought that was the next mountain.'

'Fell. Nope. That's the top of Bowfell.'

'You don't have to come to the top,' Ralph interjected quickly. 'You can wait here if you like. We'll leave your sandwiches and a drink and pick you up on the descent.'

'Oh, Dad, I thought we were going down the other side into Eskdale.'

'This is Helen's first time on the fells. We'll come back the same way and pick her up.'

'Oh, no.' I breathed deeply. 'I'm coming up there with you. If you can do it so can I.' I set off in the lead, not looking back.

'Helen?'

'What?' I marched grimly on.

'I can help you.' Danny ran after me till he caught me up—a matter of some five or six yards. He looked at me earnestly, although I had the niggling suspicion that he was making fun of me. 'I can put your earrings in my pocket.'

I stopped.

'They're long and dangly and they look heavy.'

Ralph was smiling broadly. I pretended to consider Danny's suggestion, then extracted the earrings and solemnly handed them over.

'What about your watch?'

My watch was a very expensive Rolex bought for me by my brother Michael in Japan. I must have looked hesitant.

'I'll make sure he doesn't sell it before we get to the top,' said Ralph.

I unstrapped the watch and Danny put it into his pocket.

'Feel lighter now?'

'Thanks! I feel like Flo Jo!' I shouted and sprinted ahead.

'Careful!' yelled Ralph. 'The next bit's the most difficult.'

Ralph was right. The climb to the summit was much tougher than anything so far. Soon I was faced with a huge rock buttress we had to scramble up. Frankly I was terrified.

'Shouldn't we have ropes or something?' I panted.

'No, no. That's for rock climbing.'

'Well, what the hell is all this?'

'This? This is just fell-walking.'

Even when we had climbed the sheer north face of Mt McKinley, the top we could see wasn't the top of Bowfell, as Danny took great delight in telling me. The real summit of Bowfell was two big climbs away.

I couldn't look around because it was too damn dangerous and, frankly, I was angry. Not at them, but at myself. I knew how much it meant to them and here I was acting like a Grade A grouch. In my defence, all I could enter as evidence was the fact that I was exhausted and frightened and wished I'd never come. Somehow with Ralph guiding me over a particularly tricky series of loose rocks and even larger boulders and the sight of Danny steaming ahead, I managed to keep going.

'There it is. That's the top, over there by that pile of stones.'

I've heard some memorable phrases in my life—'We'd like you to join the company at a starting salary of one hundred and twenty-five thousand dollars' was certainly one—but no arrangement of words in the English language could possibly have been more gratifying at that moment. With a groan of release I flung myself onto the grass.

For a full ten minutes I lay on my back on the top of Bowfell gasping for breath. Then I felt the warmth of the afternoon sun caress my cheeks and a gentle breeze dried my forehead. I sat up and looked around. Ralph and Danny were standing a few feet away looking at a map and pointing towards the horizon.

'Is that Scafell?' I asked.

'No, that's Mickledore. That's Scafell, the one behind,' answered Ralph.

Danny slurped his carton of drink through a straw and nodded in agreement.

I dragged myself across to join them, grasping Ralph's discreetly proffered hand. The squeeze that followed, I felt sure, meant more than congratulation on my herculean efforts. It seemed an acknowledgment that this climb wasn't just to the summit of Bowfell, but to a peak in our developing relationship. I returned the squeeze then looked around me.

Only then did I fully comprehend the vista they were examining. Wherever you looked it was simply breathtaking. Mountains of different shapes and sizes surrounded us. The sunlight illuminated a valley with its myriad green fields enclosed by dry-stone walls as if in a children's picture book. I felt as if we had climbed onto the roof of the world. It was like no other feeling I had ever known.

It wasn't just the range of mountain peaks which so overwhelmed me, but the lakes which floated in the distance like huge white flags laid out on the ground for display. Ralph and Danny showed me the map and pointed to lakes, though I didn't want to know their names and I didn't want to talk. I felt like I had been escorted to the most wonderful meal on earth, seated formally at a table for one, had a napkin unfolded onto my lap and a dish of great beauty and heavenly aroma placed in front of me. Before picking up my spoon I just wanted to absorb everything.

For the first time, I truly connected with both Ralph and Danny. Admittedly I had connected in a very basic way with Ralph some weeks before, but there on the top of Bowfell, I felt a genuine intimacy which no amount of sexual gymnastics could match. They had introduced me to a world I had never known, never thought about. I hugged Danny, who didn't object as many twelve-year-olds might have done. He solemnly presented me with my watch and earrings as if they were Olympic gold medals. I laughed and hugged him tighter. Then I did feel him tensing so I let him escape.

I turned to Ralph. I was a little hesitant because I didn't want to embarrass Danny. But I had entered his world and my whole being cried out for him to recognise the fact. He didn't fail me. The kiss he imparted was not the kiss of a friend congratulating someone on a task successfully completed. It was not the kiss of a horny male who was turned on by the erotic possibilities of alfresco sex. It was the kiss of a man who had found his soul mate.

As Danny drifted away, drawn magnetically to the very edge of the summit, a party of noisy teenagers arrived and the spell was broken.

California has so many places of outstanding natural beauty that we kind of take them for granted. Instead Californians spend all their lives and all their money searching for inner peace. I don't know if any of them find it but I know I found it for those few minutes on the top of Bowfell.

Ralph

I THOUGHT THERE WAS only one way to be in love and that was the way it was between Angela and me. That dominated my whole life, even twelve years after her death. I did not know whether it would ever be possible to fall in love again. On top of Bowfell I knew that it was.

I thought I remembered all those emotions—the joy that her presence could bring, the physical ecstasy that her touch could provoke—but I was wrong. It was all new again, nothing like what I had remembered. I was thirty-five years old, but I felt nineteen again. Not in the 'What the hell are all these spots doing here?' nineteen, but in the 'I have never been so happy in my life and this feeling will last for ever' nineteen.

I hadn't forgotten Angela, but I was in love again and I wanted to shout it from the top of Bowfell. Instead, because I believe absolutely in the Right of Man to enjoy felltops without litter, I restricted myself to asking the kids politely to pick up their empty cans. Not even that prosaic conversation could puncture the euphoria that took possession of me.

On the descent, Danny and I sang our way through our regular song-book (Beach Boys for me, Oasis for him), but the discovery that my darling new love had the worst voice on God's earth (as opposed to Angela, who, as you might suppose, sang divinely) perversely only increased my love for her. I couldn't stop smiling. By the time we reached the car, I felt that the man who had locked it up had metamorphosed into an entirely new human being—a happy one.

Did I deserve such happiness? Was God playing a particularly cruel trick on me, I wondered, showing me the mirage of happiness only to snatch it away from under my nose? Were those signs which I interpreted as her having fallen in love with me also credible or was I just misreading the whole situation? Such doubts consumed me as I lay in the bath. The hot water, however, coaxed the ache from my weary limbs and the doubts were sucked down the drain with the dirty bath water.

The food at dinner was excellent, and to my great satisfaction Danny raced off after dessert with a boy who had just arrived from Manchester. They disappeared into the table-tennis room, which left Helen and me the chance for a last walk under the stars as night closed in.

Each night the hotel left on the doorknob of each room an order form for breakfast. You just had to fill in the blanks for fruit juice, cereal, cooked breakfast, etc. If Mother Nature had left something similar for me to request the evening climate of my dreams, I couldn't have arrived at a more perfect combination than the one provided that night.

It was a still night in late summer, the first nip of autumn wouldn't be felt for a week or two yet and I doubted that a stroll on a Caribbean beach could produce a more congenial temperature. Helen's hand was clasped within mine, and her perfume, fresh and delicate, intoxicated my senses.

In the long grass beyond Keswick railway station, we joined our bodies in warmth and security, to say nothing of pleasure. We had made love before of course, but nothing had prepared me for the amazing experience which now overwhelmed me.

I have always been a visual person and loved women's bodies, and making love with the lights out always struck me as being almost entirely pointless. Now I found something to compensate for the inability to see Helen's body in the almost total darkness.

This wasn't just physical union, but the emotional confluence of two beings in love. Helen wasn't taking from me or giving herself to me, she was joining me. Our bodies remained firmly interlocked on the ground, but our spirits rose as one and wandered away together. It was such a perfect moment I doubted that it could ever be repeated.

I felt the hot pricking of tears forming in my eyes. By some miracle Helen must have felt the identical emotion, for she held my face between her hands and slowly licked the salty tears from my eyes. There could be no more intimate moment ever.

The weeks which followed that sublime experience confirmed that I was starting to live again. Not live as in earning a living and picking up the dry-cleaning. I mean live as in opening up again to a range of emotions I had not known for twelve years.

It wasn't as if the pattern of my life underwent a major change. I still had my job, I still had Danny and the routine of my life was still built around him. But everything to do with that routine was changed by the way I felt. I was more patient with Danny, more resilient when interviews fell down or the car didn't start, more tolerant of all of life's many imperfections. It's a shame you can't bottle the buzz you get from falling in love and sell it.

Every time the phone rang, a tremor of excitement passed through me. I tried hard to keep the note of disappointment out of my voice whenever it wasn't her. Occasionally, I would spring out of my chair when I heard the sound of a diesel engine and a car idling loudly. To me that always meant a taxi and a taxi might mean Helen had impulsively leapt onto the train again, grabbed a cab at the station and come to see me because she could stay away no longer. Constant frustrations never lessened the thrill of anticipation the next time round.

Even if she hadn't arrived like a genie out of a bottle, I was certain that when the phone went at 11.15pm it had to be her. In addition, I had the freedom to call her last thing at night, so if I couldn't have her physical presence in my bed, I had the means of communicating desire in words.

Just the thought of her and our future life together now made me happy. Such thoughts were idly running round my head as I sat at my desk one morning when the fax machine started to spew out the details of Mike Tyson's arrival in Britain. A press conference was being arranged for noon the following day.

Noon is my favourite time for a press conference, because I can usually get back home by four o'clock to meet Danny after school. And thank God it was tomorrow and not today, because today was Danny's big school game and I had promised him faithfully I'd be there as always. Just as I was looking up the train timetable, the doorbell rang.

I had imagined the moment so many times, yet I was completely flummoxed when it happened. There at the front door stood Helen, a smile creasing her face for a second before she threw herself into my arms. I kissed her and held her before enquiring the reason for her visit. She pointed to the shiny new BMW parked illegally in a Residents Only bay. I looked askance.

'One of our lifestyle magazines,' she explained. 'We get to test drive the car and stay overnight at a country house hotel. All expenses paid.'

'I thought you were a high-flying executive, not a journalist.'

'What's wrong?'

'I'm just not a big fan of BMWs. Why couldn't you find a Mercedes?'

She laughed and nudged me inside, pushing me, not exactly unwillingly, into the lounge until I fell backwards onto the couch. She proceeded to disrobe in a mesmerising performance that convinced me she had missed her calling and that Soho was a lesser place for her absence.

'Well,' she said afterwards, 'I hope the BMW gives a ride of similar style and comfort.'

'I doubt,' I said, fondling her breasts, 'that the upholstery will provide such agreeable support.'

I must have been out of my mind. Well, I *was* out of my mind. We were halfway to our country house hotel before I realised that I had forgotten about Danny and the school match. Though Danny wasn't in the team he wanted me to come as usual and watch so we could work out how he could win his place back in the starting line-up.

I picked up the mobile phone and made a couple of calls. Elaine Kirk kindly agreed to pick Danny up after the match and take him home to stay the night. I had never been away from Danny without telling him exactly where I was going to be.

But Helen pointed out he was twelve years old and as he'd been staying with the Kirks on and off for most of that time he'd be fine. I wasn't so sure. Danny liked the security of our routine together. I had always tried so hard to keep things on an even keel for him. I played down Helen's significance, rarely mentioned her name, redoubled my efforts to help him distinguish between the French verbs which take *être* and those which take *avoir*. My first priority was always to create a stable home environment for him.

Elaine is the mother of Jamie, Danny's best friend, and usually he's quite keen to go there because the Kirks have a big house in Millington Road with a big garden the two boys can play football in. Jamie also has, I am reliably informed, an enviably cool collection of computer games.

Since we had returned from the Lake District I had made a point of spending one night a week, if possible, in London with Helen. I tried to settle on the same night each week so that again Danny would feel secure. When I first started to stay in town, Danny seemed rather quiet on my return. I asked Elaine if he'd been all right and she always seemed to think he had, but after the fourth time I was surprised to discover that Danny wanted to stay at home by himself in the future. Of course I said he couldn't and sent him back to the Kirks the following week, but it started to bug me. Why, I wondered, did he suddenly want to stop at home by himself?

Answer came there none except an anxiety that either he knew what was going on and wanted somehow to punish me or he was up to something. Drink, drugs, sex went racing through my head, but despite intense scrutiny I could find no evidence to support any one of those theories.

Maybe, though, I thought, the whole thing was a product of my imagination. Danny was twelve going on thirteen, the dreaded puberty.

There was no point in worrying about him. He'd come out the other side OK and surely the best thing I could do was to show him the wonders of being in love. If I was sublimely happy, surely that happiness would transmit itself to him.

The journey to the south coast was wonderful. It was one of those bright autumn days when the English countryside can be at its most captivating, a last poetic reminder of the eternal promise it always held before the onset of winter frosts and rain. As we neared our destination and the light faded rapidly, a soft mist bathed the rolling vista in a paler shade of grey. The Mozart Clarinet Concerto gave out its sublime slow movement from the CD player, and Helen's left hand strayed from the steering wheel to squeeze my own with such love and tenderness it sent a shiver of prickly heat up my spine. I didn't deserve such happiness. Something must surely go badly wrong soon.

'I love you, Helen.'

She turned to look at me. 'I know. I love you, too.'

My heart was pounding. I meant it and she meant it. I wanted to say something that would seal the moment. My head pulsated as I sought in vain for the right words. I looked at Helen. She smiled. No words were necessary.

The hotel itself was luxurious in both appointments and tariff. The meal in the Michelin one-star restaurant was delicious, although in my heightened state of existence I might have said the same about a tin of baked beans.

'I think I'm too full to make love,' said Helen when we got back to our room.

'I hope that is a deliberately provocative remark.'

'Good heavens, Mr Warren,' she said, batting her eyelashes at me furiously, 'do I understand that you have designs on my virtue?'

'Your virtue went out the window when you were seventeen years old, you shameless hussy,' I growled. 'Now come over here.'

The following morning, I woke with a start at a quarter to eight, suddenly conscious that I hadn't thought about Danny for about fifteen hours, the longest stretch of time since he was born. There was something nagging at the back of my mind, something I had forgotten to do, but my brain was still dozy and I couldn't remember what.

Besides, I thought, if there were an emergency he has my mobile number. So I might as well just lie back and think of California. There was no point trying to pretend anything other than that I was in love with this woman. My body was giving both of us the clearest possible sign.

California Girl next to me turned over to face me. She smiled.

'Oh, you must love me a lot.'

I grinned. 'And unless you help me do something about it, the top of my head will explode and shoot off into space, orbiting the earth every sixty-three minutes.'

She laughed, lay back and like the best patient in the world opened wide and said, 'Aaah.'

Danny

He MISSED IT. He'd never missed a game of football the whole term. Now that sodding woman comes along and he's not there. Suddenly he's too busy with her, he's got no time for me. Well, no, I know that's not entirely fair, but it's the way I was feeling.

I had been bitterly disappointed that I hadn't been picked for the school team. Last year I was top scorer, but this year some new kids had joined, and though I didn't think they were any better than I was, they were bigger, with the strength of fourteen-year-olds. So I was dropped.

I said to Dad I should do some weight training but he thought I was too young. Then I said perhaps I should have lots of steak, because I'd heard that it helps to develop the body, but Dad doesn't like us to eat red meat since the BSE thing came out. He pointed out that, in any case, the fashion in sports teams today is for things like pasta, which don't increase your body weight but allow you to run harder for longer. I didn't fancy eating nothing but spaghetti seven nights a week so I knocked that one on the head too and I remained out of the school team.

The night before a game, I would always pray to God to give our two strikers, Mark Leonard or Ollie Church, some terrible disease, but nothing ever happened. Until that day. I got to school and we had registration and Ollie Church wasn't there. My heart leapt. It wasn't till we were back in our form rooms for afternoon registration that our form master made the stunning announcement. I was to report to the main changing room at three o'clock because I was playing for the school that afternoon. Yes!!! I was back in the team for the big one, the big local derby match against our hated rivals, St Bede's School.

I had no time to tell Dad, nor any need to really, because he had promised to come and watch. But as we ran onto the pitch he wasn't among the group of parents on the line. During the warm-up I kept looking to the main road, searching for a man racing towards us, but there was nothing. I was gutted. It wasn't the same if Dad wasn't there to share it with me. Still, he'd come in the end. I knew Dad.

We kicked off and I was soon struggling. It was so different from the crappy standard I had become used to playing in regular house matches. The defenders I was up against were big strong lads and I was getting kicked on the back of my legs before I even received the ball. After twenty minutes I was tired and the big lads marking me reckoned they had kicked me out of the game and spent all their time on Mark Leonard.

Then it happened. From a corner on the right Mark jumped for the ball. The two big lads went with him and the ball cannoned off one of them against the post and before the goalkeeper could drop on it I managed to stab it into the net. I felt like the greatest player in the history of the world. I ran all over the field until my teammates caught up with me and jumped on me in celebration. I picked myself up and looked round for Dad again, but all I could see was Jamie's mum jumping up and down and smiling at me. I ran over to her.

'Where's Dad?'

'He can't come. You're coming home with me.'

I was stunned. He can't come? What the hell could ever have made him miss it? Then I knew. He was with that woman.

Well, it was obvious now that I was less important to him than that bloody woman. I hated her. And I hated that horrible defender. After ten minutes of the second half, when I'd got bruises all up the back of both legs and I'd been pushed and shoved every time the ball came anywhere near me, I lost it.

One of our centre backs got the ball and he whacked it over the top of their defence for me to run on to. This hulking brute of a defender was pulling my shirt and tapping my ankles as we raced for the ball. He also called me 'a fucking Mummy's boy', which I thought was a bit rich in the circumstances. The red mist came down and I just let him have it. Only it was dead pathetic. I tried to elbow him off. I made the slightest contact with his body, somewhere round his shoulder, I think, but suddenly he went down like he'd been shot by a bullet, rolling over and holding his face though I never touched him anywhere near his face. Our sports teacher Mr Banks, who was the referee, came tearing over.

'I saw that, Warren. There was no provocation. Off you go. Foul play.'

I couldn't believe my ears. 'I never touched him.'

'Then what's he doing down there?'

'He's play-acting. Just like on *Match of the Day*!'

The opposing team's sports teacher was helping the bully to his feet. Amazingly, the bully found he was able to continue.

'I am very disappointed in you, Warren. Get changed and go home.'

The walk back to the changing room was the longest, most miserable walk in history. I knew now what David Beckham must have felt like when he got sent off playing for England in the World Cup. I was ashamed but also angry, because I didn't deserve it, not the way I looked at it. I felt like killing Helen. It was because she made Dad walk out on me that I lost my temper like that. It was all Helen's fault, the bitch.

I knew I wouldn't play for the school team again. Mr Banks wouldn't pick me again, not this term anyway, maybe not ever. That would be my punishment. And I had to go home with Jamie's mum, and Jamie would spend the whole night teasing me.

I hadn't told Dad, but I hadn't been getting on with Jamie Kirk for quite a few months now. In fact I really hadn't told Dad much of anything since we got back from the Lakes.

Jamie came with me from Grantchester Street Primary, but, even though we'd been really close friends there, the friendship didn't mean as much as it did before. I hated staying the night with him, because he wanted to talk about bums and girls' things and stupid stuff like that, and it made me feel uncomfortable.

Dad thought he was doing me this big favour letting me stay with Jamie, but I thought if I told him the truth he wouldn't understand, so I just said I'd like to stay in the house by myself instead. I couldn't see why not. I would be thirteen on my next birthday and Dad had always trusted me to do things round the house like putting the dishes away. I'd just lock the door and not answer if the bell rang. I could put the telephone answering machine on and just pick it up if it was someone I knew. What could be safer? But Dad insisted that I had to stay with Jamie.

I started to blame Helen for things even before that disastrous school game, because I knew that's why he wasn't paying attention to me any more. At first I was sorry in a way that I was starting to feel like this because a) Dad liked her and I think she made him happy and b) she was always OK with me.

I wasn't too sure about Helen till she struggled her way up Bowfell. Plus I liked the way she spoke. It was dead American. She talked with a funny upward twist of her voice at the end, a bit like Monica in *Friends*. She never talked down to me and she didn't do what lots of grown-ups do—be dead nice while you're alone with them in the room then when Dad comes in just blank you. I always thought Helen enjoyed talking to me. And in a way it was exciting when she was there. Her mobile was always ringing. She could talk a lot on her phone, very fast and serious and sort of threatening sometimes, then she'd switch it off and we'd pick up the conversation exactly where she'd left it.

I didn't think she was drop-dead gorgeous or anything, like Rachel or Phoebe, but I could see why Dad liked her. I looked at the girls our age and I thought they'd never grow into women like Helen. Sometimes she kissed me good night and then I could smell her perfume, but instead of being comforted as I was by the memory of Mum, I was confused and sort of excited by Helen in a way that made me feel very mixed up.

Once when she bent over me to kiss me good night a couple of buttons on her shirt were undone and I saw all the way down to the start of her titties. When she left the room I couldn't get to sleep for ages. I wanted to touch them to see what they felt like, but I knew I shouldn't and I could hardly ask permission.

I was having problems adjusting to Helen's presence, but I couldn't talk to Dad about it. That was an odd feeling, too, because we had always talked about everything till then. Dad once tried explaining how he felt about Helen and how she wasn't supposed to be a mum to me and wouldn't want to be, but he liked her a lot and did I mind? Well, what could I say? The moment he started I knew what he was going to say and it made me squirm with embarrassment. What I wanted to say was, 'OK, Dad, but could you ask her if I could see her naked as well?'

If I said that everything was OK, he'd take that as meaning he had my approval to do anything he wanted with her. I couldn't talk to Helen about these feelings, because although I supposed I fancied her, I didn't really feel I knew her and, besides, she belonged to Dad. But I wanted to. I thought she might be sympathetic and tell me things that Dad couldn't—because she was a woman. But I didn't have the courage.

It was so difficult, so confusing. I just didn't know how to behave to Helen or to Dad, so I sort of resented them both. I was angry that Helen had stirred up something inside me, but I couldn't tell anybody about it; and all these feelings about other girls and the whisperings and jokes of the older boys, which I pretended to understand but didn't really, it all just left me frustrated.

That was how it was when they both buggered off and left me to face the worst crisis of my life alone. I stopped having those lustful thoughts about Helen then all right. She was just as much to blame as I was for me being sent off. So I decided I was going to make her suffer just like I was suffering.

Helen

OH GOD, OH GOD! It was just what I didn't mean to happen. Here I was doing something fun with the guy I had fallen in love with and the net result was complete disaster.

It had been the best time. The look on Ralph's face, the warmth coursing through my body, the hotel, waking up next day and still wanting him. It all convinced me that here was the man I had been waiting for all my life. I looked back at myself as a rising executive at Waverley Bros Inc, and in the throes of a passionate affair with one of the great moguls of the American press, and I thought it was utterly bizarre that I should find true happiness with an anonymous journalist, a single parent with a twelve-year-old kid.

I hadn't lost my ambition, I didn't suddenly want to give it all up and become a mommy and housewife. I just knew for sure that Ralph Warren and I were destined to be together in a way I had never felt about Charles Schmidt and me. I guess I was just acting out a part with Charles: female, smart, savvy, sexy exec. type, slim, thirty, into Mozart, books, movies and *Seinfeld*, wants to meet male, fiftyish, distinguished, powerful, wealthy, sexually experienced—married, not a problem. I posted the personal ad. Charles was the first to reply.

Ralph's love made me complete in a way that the key to the executive washroom could never do. I didn't even mind taking on Danny, because he was twelve, nearly a teenager. He seemed well adjusted, and I took great comfort in the fact that he had such a good relationship with his dad. In fact they had such a great domestic routine it didn't need me to do anything except stay out of the way.

That's what I thought I was doing when I drove up to Cambridge in that BMW. It was a school day, so if Danny was looked after overnight as I knew he was occasionally, we could get back the following afternoon and nothing would have happened to shake their precious routine.

I dropped Ralph off at King's Cross at lunchtime, and then sped across town for a meeting. When I got back to the office around four, I didn't bother to call Ralph because I knew that he'd be busy doing stuff with Danny. Then the phone calls from the East Coast started, so I didn't get the chance to make contact with Ralph till around eleven o'clock. I was looking forward to one of our bedtime chats.

When he picked up the phone his 'hello' was enough to warn me that something had happened. Apparently Danny was almost monosyllabic after school and wouldn't talk to him about the game, so he rang the woman who usually picks Danny up after school when Ralph can't be there, and got the full story. I guess he was expelled from the game for something, Ralph wasn't exactly clear.

What I soon gathered was that something had gone disastrously wrong for the kid and he was mad at Ralph for not being there, and Ralph was beating up on himself because he wasn't there. I was torn. On the one hand I was sympathetic. The man I was in love with was suffering, and his kid was really important to him, so of course I wanted them both to be happy again immediately. Yet I couldn't help thinking Danny was twelve years old, not two. Ralph had sacrificed himself for eleven years for the kid; wasn't he entitled to a little happiness too? Stand your ground, Ralph, I wanted to say. I couldn't because I quickly figured that at the root of it all was me. I was the reason that Danny was mad at Ralph and I sure didn't intend getting in the middle. Much as I wanted to knock Danny's head against the wall and tell him not to be so goddamn selfish, I knew that wasn't possible. Ralph wanted sympathy and love and no judgment calls. That's what I gave him and I felt he put the phone down happier than when he had picked it up. Unlike me.

I couldn't sleep that night. My body temperature fluctuated from the very cold to the scalding hot. I kicked the bedcovers off, then hauled them back again. I flipped on the light, read for a while, but I couldn't concentrate, so I got out of bed, grabbed my robe and sat at the desk in the living room trying to work on some financial projections. It was hopeless. Was this what true love did to you? Even when I was at the height of passion with Charles, I never had any problems concentrating on work. But now the figures just swam before my eyes. I couldn't get Ralph out of my head.

The next morning I called him. I decided that I had to remain calm and add a sense of perspective. This was easier said than done, because I found him very down, almost despairing of the possibility of reconciling his love for Danny with his love for me. This made me mad.

This was a side of Ralph I hadn't really seen before and I wasn't too crazy about it. I don't mind sensitive men, but I don't much care for weak men, and what Ralph was demonstrating right now was a weakness I couldn't stand.

'Ralph, you can't give in to Danny every time he sulks.'

'He's not a great sulker. He's hurting.'

'You want us to break up then?'

'How can you say that? You know how much I love you.'

'Then tell him you have a life too.'

'It's not that easy.'

'It sure is. You just say that, in those exact words. If he runs upstairs and slams the bedroom door, he's going through adolescence. If there's a real problem he can talk it out with you.'

There was a deathly pause. I knew I had pushed him between a rock and a hard place, making him choose between his son and his new lover. Well, if he ran away from me now I'd walk out of his life and castigate him for being too weak to fight for me. A split second later, I realised that I loved him and I did not want Ralph Warren out of my life. *Please say the right thing, Ralph, please!*

'You know what?'

'What?' The world stopped spinning on its axis. I wondered if this was how OJ felt when the verdict was being read out.

Ralph took two seconds to say, 'You're absolutely right.'

Ralph

I HANDLED IT BADLY, NO QUESTION. It was a mistake not ringing Danny that night—it wouldn't have taken long. Then I shouldn't have spilled everything out to Helen. It wasn't her fault. She had behaved really well with Danny, and I knew Danny liked her.

I was trying my best to have it all, I suppose—the love of this new woman and the love of my son. They were both important to me. Other men in my position must surely have achieved something similar. Why was it so bloody difficult for me?

It was Helen who brought me to my senses. I was entitled to my own life. I was being too soft on Danny, who probably was behaving like a spoilt teenager. My only defence is that he wasn't technically a teenager yet and he had never done anything like this before. The reason we had such a special relationship was that though we were father and son, we were also best friends; there was nothing he couldn't talk to me about. But in the last few months, since I'd met Helen, I suppose, he had stopped confiding in me. Well, three or four years ago he'd also stopped wanting me to give him his bath, which was fine. It meant he was growing up. Maybe this manifestation of teenage behaviour was just another indication that he was maturing. When I confronted Danny as Helen had suggested, he didn't exactly apologise for his behaviour, though he did start to calm down. It was an awkward forty-eight hours, that was for sure. I tried to reassure him about the sending off. I told him I'd be happy to go and see Mr Banks and plead for leniency. After all, it was entirely out of character for Danny to go around elbowing defenders; I can hardly remember him ever conceding a foul before. But I accepted Danny's plea for me to stay out of it. He said he had to look after himself. It wouldn't help the perception of him at school if his daddy were seen to be protecting him. I took that as the evidence I needed that he was maturing.

Helen was wonderful. She counselled me through this difficult period and I appreciated her ability to look at the position objectively. Thank God, too, she didn't shy away from a fraught family situation. I couldn't have blamed her had she decided to stay in London, but she didn't, and I took that as evidence that we had a future together. It wasn't just sex, though that was totally fulfilling. It was love, and for that I thanked God.

The next weekend the three of us all went to watch Tottenham Hotspur. Helen and I had decided that it was best if we carried on as we meant to continue. All right, I hadn't told Danny I was going away, but I was in love with Helen and she was going to be a feature of our lives for a long time to come, so he had better get used to it.

There were two important debutants at the Spurs v. Arsenal derby match that day. It was Helen's first visit to my spiritual home and it was George Graham's first match as the new Spurs manager in a match against his old team. I was supposed to observe the game from the press box, but I decided to buy tickets and watch with the other two from seats high up in the main stand. There were problems from the start.

The first was the quality of the football, or rather the lack of it. It was a typically attritional encounter between bitter local rivals. Fouls stifled the flow and, despite a lot of frenetic activity, neither side created a worthwhile chance.

Before the kickoff, Helen had donated her American enthusiasm to the cause.

'OK, guys, which is our team?'

'The ones in white.'

She leapt to her feet with everyone else as the two teams emerged from the tunnel together, shouting raucously. Danny and I smiled at each other. This was going to be fun, we thought, but I had misjudged the American desire for everything to be clear-cut. There were no goals and no real chances. Although Danny and I revelled in the tension of the closely fought encounter, it soon became obvious that Helen was bored. And cold.

I sat between her and Danny, wretchedly torn between empathising with Helen's discomfort and being totally wrapped up in the importance of securing a win. Every time I stood up to shout the traditional abuse at the Arsenal players and fans, I became conscious that I was widening the gap between Helen and myself. American sport doesn't really operate on the same hate-filled lines that powers British football, and I could see she was disenchanted by the genuine loathing for Arsenal that the crowd was demonstrating.

She couldn't wait for the half-time whistle, and I ushered her quickly into the queue for the hot drinks. Not quickly enough, though. By the time we had manoeuvred our way into the refreshment area, there must have been fifty people in front of us. By the time the teams reappeared for the second half, there were still twenty or thirty people between us and the hot chocolate.

Helen sent us back to our seats. She was quite happy to continue waiting out of that vicious easterly wind and the negative football.

'She's not enjoying it, is she?' Danny was clearly taking some pleasure in her discomfort. I wanted to hit him.

'Well, unless you're an Arsenal or Spurs fan, nobody would.'

'I don't know why she came.'

I wanted to tell him that she came because she was doing something nice to make him feel part of a family, but at that very moment Armstrong burst free with the Arsenal goal at his mercy, but pulled his shot tamely wide. After that burst of adrenalin, I couldn't find the anger to get into a row with Danny even though I could sense he was pushing me that way.

Twenty minutes into the second half Helen reappeared with the drinks.

'Hi! I'm sorry it took so long.'

'I was beginning to get worried about you.'

'I went for a walk.'

'Where?'

'As far as I could until I got to a locked gate.'

'Good idea. You've missed nothing here.'

'What time does the game finish?'

'About ten to five,' I replied.

'Plus injury time,' added Danny sadistically.

'Shut up, Danny. Look, if you want to go, they will let you out.'

'No, that's OK. I'll wait with you.'

'It's just that I have to file my report.'

'Offside!'

'What's offside?' asked Helen innocently.

Danny grinned. He knew how difficult the offside laws were to explain so he volunteered to do it. I let him, because it seemed the easiest alternative. Of course he then gabbled them out in such a deliberately obtuse way that even I didn't understand them. He was trying to make Helen feel like a mental incompetent.

I felt frustrated. I decided I'd give Danny some of his own medicine, so, as we finally left the ground after a stultifying 0–0 draw, I insisted that Helen come and stay with us the following weekend and I didn't care what Danny said or thought.

On the following Saturday afternoon I took Helen along the towpath. Offered the chance to join us, Danny looked as if he would prefer to throw himself into the river. He was in some deep way still annoyed with Helen for existing. Instead he scuttled off into town to join his mates at the video-game store. Helen and I smiled at each other. We would just have to go on our own.

We had intended to walk along the river bank only as far as Magdalene Bridge, but it was such a beautiful bright autumnal afternoon that we decided we would walk a little further. In the end we walked all the way into Grantchester.

To our delight the village pub was open and we managed a very satisfactory pint of Special for me and a cup of hot chocolate for her while we sat and watched the classified football results on a TV screen above the bar. Tottenham had managed a most unexpected 2–0 win against Manchester United at Old Trafford.

It was dark when we emerged, so we took a taxi back into town. It was only then that I realised with a start I had walked all the way to Grantchester and not once thought of Angela. So many times I had taken that walk in the past twelve years in the company of some woman or other, and all that had flashed through my mind constantly was, 'This was where Angela and I came, this was where we made love, this was where she told me she was pregnant, this was where I begged her to marry me.' Helen had succeeded in blotting out those fifteen-year-old memories. She just made me happy.

To formalise our rapture I asked the taxi driver to drop us off at the fish-and-chip shop, where I impetuously bought three haddock and chips with pickled onions and mushy peas. When I got home I found that Danny had raided the housekeeping jar (where I always keep two ten-pound notes for him to use in an emergency) in order to buy three cod and chips with three pickled onions but no mushy peas.

'Isn't there a book called *The Cambridge Diet* or something?' I asked as I sprinkled salt and vinegar over Helen's chips.

'Yeah. Big seller in the States a few years back.'

'This is it,' I said.

'I think that was Cambridge, Massachusetts, not Cambridge, England, and it involved eating only one sprout for ten days.'

'Fish and chips contain most of the protein and carbohydrates a body needs for healthy living.'

'Not in this quantity, surely?'

'This is the minimum quantity,' I said, swallowing heavily.

'And don't call him Shirley,' said Danny, attempting to join in the banter.

'Oh, I just love those *Naked Gun* movies,' said Helen, acquiring instant street cred.

'It's from *Airplane*,' said Danny, ever the pedant I had unwittingly raised him to be.

We were getting on together so well. Danny had obviously had a good afternoon with his mates and I knew how exhilarated he would have been by the Spurs victory. Helen belonged here now, and Danny had thankfully, if only temporarily, abandoned his scorched earth campaign against her. I know she felt the same way. I could feel the warmth emanating from her like heatwaves from an open fire. That's when she came up with the idea that we should all go away for Christmas.

 **Danny**

WHEN HELEN ASKED if we wanted to go away for Christmas, I thought she meant only one place.

'America?' I said immediately, because that's always been my dream to go there.

'Danny!' said Dad, annoyed, I don't know why. Helen looked let down. As usual, I'd only said one word and everyone was cross with me.

'I figured the Lake District. I really loved my time up there with you guys and I'd like to take you back there for two or three days over the holidays. My treat.'

I love the Lakes. So does Dad, but neither of us said anything for a moment. I said in a sort of small voice, 'But we always spend Christmas here. We've never stayed in a hotel before.'

'Doesn't mean you can't do it this year.'

'It would be great,' said Dad. 'Can you imagine climbing Skiddaw when it's covered in snow?'

'Is it tougher than Bowfell?'

Dad was looking at me, so I had to tell the truth.

'No. It's not. It looks difficult from below, but it's actually quite easy. I did it when I was seven.'

'I think I carried you the last five hundred feet.'

'So what do you say, guys?'

'Are you sure, Helen? This is very generous.'

'But what about Christmas here, Dad? The Boxing Day matches and the Christmas pudding and everything.'

'Well, we can go and see Carlisle United and I'm sure the hotel will serve turkey and Christmas pudding and all the things you like.'

'It won't be the same, though.'

'Might be better.'

'Doesn't Helen have to visit her mother at Christmas?'

'Well, usually I do but this year I'm spending New Year's with my mom and I thought it'd be kinda cool to have a real English Christmas with fog and carols and snow.'

'So what do we say to Helen, Danny?'

'Great.' There was a marked lack of enthusiasm in my voice, but I don't think anyone noticed or, if they did, they didn't care. I was beginning to get the feeling that Dad was sticking this woman down my throat whether I cared or not.

We left the day before Christmas Eve after we had loaded all our Christmas presents into the car, but that was the last good thing that happened. The traffic was terrible and then the engine overheated. We had to stop and call the AA, and they took over two hours to come. While we were waiting I discovered that I'd left my favourite Oasis tape at home.

We usually take the M1 to Leeds and travel through the Yorkshire Dales to get to the Lake District, which is a really nice way in the summer when you can see the sheep in the fields and we can sit and have lunch in a pub garden. This time we were late and we had to stay on the motorway the whole way there to make up time. So we decided just to buy sandwiches and drinks and eat them in the car, which would have been OK but I put my can of Coke down for a second on the seat to change tapes in my Walkman and I accidentally knocked it over. It went everywhere, into the gearbox and onto Helen's seat so she was sitting in it. Dad shouted at me for being careless, as if I had meant to do it in the first place.

The journey from Windermere to Keswick is my favourite journey in the whole world, because the scenery is both spectacular and dead familiar so I feel like I'm coming home. Dad and I get really excited just talking about what we can see and what's round the next bend. But now it was about four thirty in the afternoon so it was dark and I couldn't see anything. Driving to Keswick with the car headlights on felt really strange and very disappointing.

It picked up a bit when we got to the hotel, because there was a big Christmas tree in the lobby and the entrance was covered in lights. Our room was on the top floor and I knew it would have a good view of Cat Bells and Maiden Moor in the morning. Helen was booked into a single room next to our twin-bedded one, which I thought was somehow significant. Four months previously she had been on the far side of the hotel. I didn't mind, but it was like something had happened between Helen and Dad but nobody had told me about it because I was only a kid.

It wasn't snowing when we woke up and for a moment I thought it was just a bit overcast. Then I saw the rain. It was more like a fine wet mist than a drizzle and we went down for breakfast believing that it might stop. In the summer, sometimes if it was raining in the morning it could all change at lunchtime and you'd have blue skies and bright sunshine for a climb in the afternoon.

After breakfast we walked into Keswick and bought the sandwiches and drinks as usual, which we packed in Dad's rucksack. He complained that it was really heavy and he suggested I took it up the mountain and he took it down. I was keen to show I could do it, but he said he was only joking. Since it wasn't funny I don't know why he bothered, but then I thought I'll bet he was just showing off to Helen how strong he was and then I thought that she'd be a lot more impressed if I did it, so I asked again and he said I couldn't, then I got cross and jealous all at the same time. I didn't want Dad to turn into a sort of rival but he was making it like that.

The misty rain had eased off when we were walking into town, but by the time we got in the car to drive to Honister Pass, the rain had started again and this time it was much worse. We parked the car near the old slate mine at the foot of Green Gable. This was a much easier way to the top of Great Gable than walking from Seathwaite Farm up Sty Head Pass, but Dad thought it was only fair to Helen and I didn't mind because it would be getting dark by four o'clock and I could see it was sensible for us not to get caught on a difficult descent by going up the long way.

When we got out of the car it was horrible. The wind whipped up into a gale and drove the rain into our faces. We could none of us talk because we were concentrating on putting one foot in front of the other. I knew there was no way we were going to go up Gable like this. You couldn't see anything and the walk would be slippery and dangerous.

Dad was the first one to say it. 'This is pointless. I think we should go back.'

I said nothing. I wasn't going to be the one to wimp out.

'I'm up for it,' said Helen brightly, 'if you guys are.'

'Me too,' I said as the wind-driven rain lashed into our faces.

'Who would prefer a cup of hot chocolate and a Danish pastry?' said Dad.

'I think I vote for coffee and Danish, but it's up to Danny.'

Oh, yeah, like it's really going to make any difference what I say. I decided to be long-suffering and noble.

'I don't care.' I think it probably came out just petulant.

'OK. Danny's vote wins it.'

So much for Christmas Eve.

I like Christmas Eve at home because there are always lots of good films on the telly and Dad and I would spend hours unpacking a big cardboard box stuffed full of special Christmas things that we decorated the house with. There was even a video of a *Pink Panther* Christmas special, which I had loved when I was three and which I played on Christmas Eve to get me into the Christmas mood. I know it sounds silly but I really missed it.

After dinner I went off to my bedroom. There was nothing else to do really. There was going to be a quiz in the bar, which Dad wanted to go to with Helen, so he suggested if I didn't want to join them I should go off to the games room with 'the other kids'. Well, the other kids were like eight and nine years old; there was no one of my age. I didn't want to play with them so I went back to find Dad. But when I got to the bar the quiz hadn't started yet and Dad and Helen weren't there. Instead I went back to our bedroom and watched *Escape to Victory* on telly.

When it got to the game itself, when Michael Caine and Stallone and the other prisoners of war have to play against a crack Nazi team who are supposed to be like the German World Cup side, I went downstairs to get Dad. He loves this film.

But they still weren't in the bar even though the quiz was now going on. I just wanted Dad to come to the room and watch it with me and I

wouldn't have minded Helen being with us. I would have started explaining the offside laws again and if she laughed that would be OK, but if she didn't it wouldn't have mattered because it was all about me and Dad sharing the same outlook on the world.

My stomach gave a lurch when I saw they weren't there, because I knew where they were instantly. They were in Helen's room and I knew what they were doing too. I didn't mind it so much at home. I felt secure in my home. But the hotel seemed strange to me at Christmas, and Dad going into Helen's room and having sex with her made me really mad. Hot tears welled up in my eyes, though I didn't understand why.

It shouldn't have been as bad as it had been when he missed the game against St Bede's, but it felt even worse. It was like when you scrape the skin off your knee and it bleeds, then it starts to heal and form a scab, but if the scab gets torn off again before it's properly healed, it hurts worse than it did the first time.

If Helen was there on a Sunday morning at home I knew they must have had sex the previous night, but it was over with and we could do things together on Sunday. Now they were at it in her bedroom, and my mind was filled with horrible crude images of the two of them that made me want to puke. I went back to the bedroom and when Dad came in later I pretended to be asleep. He kissed me on the cheek and I turned over to wipe the kiss off onto the pillow. He didn't see, though I wouldn't have cared if he had.

Helen

GOD, THAT WAS such a dumb thing to do. Take them both to the Lake District, I mean. But I meant so well and they both said yes. If only I'd gone back to see my mom over Christmas, which had been my first thought. But I was too much in love with Ralph.

I suppose I should have learned from my mistake when I went to that soccer game with them both. No matter how hard Ralph tried to include me, it was only too easy for Danny to remind me that I was an outsider. Still, I remembered what a great time we'd all had in the summer, how I felt my relationship with Ralph had deepened because I'd been initiated into one of the family's most hallowed traditions. Maybe the Lake District magic would work again.

I hadn't thought about the weather other than to imagine it might be like hiking up near Big Bear above Lake Arrowhead, which can be spectacular over Christmas. I suppose I should have guessed it rains in that part of the country. The British are great at some things—don't push me too hard, nothing comes to mind right now except the theatre—but they've a lot to learn about consumer welfare. In the USA, if you went to a hotel over Christmas, there'd be costume parties, dances, that kind of stuff. In Keswick we got a pub quiz and an inedible Christmas lunch with massacred vegetables, turkey cooked to remove all the juice and a traditional fruit-cake dessert smothered in brandy that I could feel shoot straight to my hips.

That wasn't why I felt so bad about the holiday though. It was the day after Christmas when it all turned really sour, though Danny was kinda weird on Christmas Day itself. He just got out of bed the wrong side, his dad said, when I asked him why he looked so miserable when he had half a dozen presents to open.

A fleeting anxiety passed through me. I knew Ralph had been reluctant to go to bed with me on Christmas Eve in my room, even though there was no way Danny could come in.

However, if it started going off the rails on Christmas Eve, Boxing Day, as they engagingly call it in Britain, for reasons no one has explained to my satisfaction, was the day it plunged over the bridge and down into the ravine.

I heard the sound of doom before I threw back the curtains. The rain was pelting against the window and I couldn't see more than a hundred feet in the direction of the big mountain out there, whose name I kept forgetting but which sounded like 'skidding'.

Over breakfast we turned on the TV for the weather forecast and saw nothing but little black clouds all over the country. Ralph felt it was important to take Danny out. I'd have been happy watching TV or reading a book, but I guess when you're twelve you want to do things, so Ralph decided to drive round the area looking for historic houses to visit.

I could have told him before we left that nothing would be open on December 26, but Ralph was convinced that, because it was a holiday and lots of people like us had arrived in the area, all the tourist attractions would be open. So I put on my warmest coat and my thickest gloves and hoped for the best, while fearing the worst.

We tried all sorts of places—ruined castles and abbeys, half a dozen historic manor houses—but all were closed. The performance was always the same: a desperate examination of the tourist book, a frantic hopeful drive, a sinking feeling when there were only two cars in the car park, the frenzied scramble out of the car to put up the umbrella, the inevitable sign saying CLOSED.

Just before lunch we actually managed to find something that was open. It was some kind of a museum of local history. I was surprised to discover that I found it real interesting and on another day I'd have been fascinated by its re-creation of local houses with their bedrooms and living rooms and kitchens down the centuries. Today, however, was not a good day for any of us.

Danny was restless, unhappy, dragging behind Ralph and me. He had wanted to have lunch as soon as we had arrived, but Ralph told him we'd only just had breakfast and he'd have to wait till we'd finished in the museum. Danny's response was to ask for the car keys, and when he came back he had his Walkman with him. He obviously planned to visit the museum plugged into his music. It wasn't a smart move. Ralph was trying, as ever, to keep both Danny and me happy. I was doing OK myself, but I knew I had to stay clear of it.

We raced through the museum, which was quite crowded as other families, too, had discovered this was the only open attraction in the whole of the Lake District. Ralph was constantly whispering loudly to Danny to turn the wretched Walkman off, which Danny eventually did with obvious irritation. Thankfully, we eventually reached the litttle coffee shop attached to the museum shop, where Danny asked for the chocolate cake that was on the menu. Unfortunately it was Boxing Day, the woman behind the till told him, and as they always baked fresh they hadn't got it today. He had to settle for a wrapped chocolate bar, but you could tell that he was seething with this latest insult.

Danny rarely acted up in public, and I was as surprised as Ralph as his performance continued to deteriorate. It burst into open warfare in the car on the way back to the hotel.

As the rain hammered into the windshield, Ralph began to talk to Danny. I could hear him fighting for control.

'Danny, I'd like you to apologise for your behaviour in there.'

There was no reply. Danny was in thrall to Blur.

'Danny!' Ralph's voice rose sharply.

Danny reluctantly removed the headphones again. 'What?'

'I said I want you to apologise for the way you behaved this morning.'

'What's wrong with the way I behaved?'

'You were rude and discourteous.'

'Who to?'

'To Helen. And to me.'

'No I wasn't. How?'

'By wearing that stupid thing on your head when I was talking to you, by your attitude when that lady said there was no chocolate cake—'

'Well, it shouldn't have been on the menu.'

'You've been a pain in the neck for two days. Helen's given you this lovely treat—'

'Not me!'

'What?'

'She wants to be with you. She doesn't want to be with me.'

Oh Christ! Here it comes.

Ralph slammed on the brakes and the car screeched to a halt.

'Excuse us for a moment,' he said to me shortly, got out of the car, opened the back door and dragged Danny out. I watched them disappear into the mist and rain and prayed to be able to close my eyes and wake up in my mom's living room.

When they came back a few minutes later, wet and bedraggled, I was not surprised to hear Danny's first words.

'I'm sorry if I was rude to you, Helen.'

It was spoken with all the conviction of President Clinton's first public apology for his 'improper' relationship with Monica Lewinsky.

'That's OK, Danny. It's just this miserable rain that's making everyone upset. How about we stop at one of your famous English pubs and we have a nice hot toddy?'

'The pubs are all shut, I'm afraid, like everything else,' said Ralph. 'At least till tonight.'

We drove back to the hotel in silence. Danny, suitably chastened, fiddled with the Walkman for a long time before immersing himself in it, waiting for his dad to tell him he couldn't listen to it. But reprimand came there none and he retreated with gratitude into the comforting isolation.

By one of those strokes of irony with which the meteorological world is governed, we left the hotel the following morning in dazzling sunshine. The air was still bracing but the light was astonishing. The fells seemed to change colour as the sun's rays played on them, shifting their contours from soft to sharp. The blue skies didn't do much to lift the depression that had settled over us. If anything, the contemplation of what might have been made it all worse.

I cared about both Ralph and Danny. I knew they were upset, that something fundamental now seemed to divide them, and I knew it was in a way my fault, but I was darned if I could see what I had done wrong. I wanted to get the relationship between them back the way it had been before, but I didn't know how to do it, other than by leaving. As the sun disappeared behind the grey clouds that loomed over us again, I was thinking seriously that this was the only solution. Leave now, before I was sucked in irretrievably and all three lives went down the pan.

I had left my car in Cambridge and though Ralph wanted me to stay the night and Danny raised no objections, I figured it would be a mistake. They needed the time and space to talk to each other, and my presence would only prolong their differences. Danny was on the phone to his friends two minutes after we walked in the door. It gave Ralph and me the chance to be alone in the bedroom.

We sat on the bed, finding words difficult.

'Do you think,' I ventured after a while, 'that he's got a crush on me?'

'What?' Ralph was genuinely surprised.

'He's twelve.'

'It's possible.'

'Exactly. He's not got a girlfriend of his own. I'm here, he's got all these thoughts going through his head.'

'But we're not in competition for you.'

'Wouldn't that explain some of his behaviour?'

'He's mad because he thinks I'm spending more time with you than I am with him. I think you were right before. He's behaving badly and I've got to discipline him. It worked last time. It'll work again.'

'Sure?'

'Absolutely.'

'Ralph, I think I ought to go home now.'

'Back to London?' He grabbed my hand, but I withdrew it, though with a smile.

'I'll feel easier. He'll feel easier. I'll call you tonight.' I got off the bed and headed for the door.

'Wait.'

I stopped. He turned me round, his hands on my shoulders.

'I think you're wonderful. I don't have the words to tell you how wonderful.'

'I love you, Ralph. I just think a few days away from each other will give Danny and you time to work things out.'

'You *are* coming back?'

I blushed. Did he know what I had been thinking? He looked so anxious. My heart was bursting for love of him.

'I love you so much, Helen. I'd die if I lost you.'

'Ralph, I'll always love you, even if . . .' I couldn't finish the sentence because I didn't want to express the anxieties that had been troubling me.

'If what? What do you mean if? Where's the if come from?' Now he looked frightened.

'Ralph, our love is a wonderful thing, the best thing that has ever happened to me.'

'So why do I have this sinking feeling in the pit of my stomach?'

'Because you haven't eaten since lunch and it's nearly eight thirty and I have to go.'

'Helen! There's something bothering you.'

'It's nothing. Nothing that I haven't already said.'

'Please don't leave me. Stay here tonight. You can get up at six in the morning and drive back.'

He was getting needy. I always hated that in a man, because I had trained myself so hard not to need anyone else. And then I thought that it was just another manifestation of love. He needed me because he loved me and I felt protected and cherished by it. I kissed him lightly but with as much feeling as I could impart. I pulled back and noticed his eyes filling with tears. This man meant so much to me, but I wasn't going to be the one to come between him and Danny. I had to be strong for both of us.

'I'll call you later. I love you.'

Two days later Ralph insisted on coming to London to drive me the twenty-five miles to Heathrow Airport where I was catching a flight to Boston. I told him I could easily call a cab, it made no sense for him to drive two hours out of his way to take me on a half-hour journey. But I knew he needed to see me again, extract from me a promise which I wasn't sure I could give him.

I insisted that he drop me off outside Terminal 3 and not come in with me. It was partly because I didn't trust myself to say the right thing in the departure terminal. But if the truth were known, I didn't want him to see me change my ticket from round trip to one way. I wasn't coming back. My mind had been in a turmoil since we'd left the Lake District. One minute I was sure we could work it out together, the next I was terrified I was going to end up ruining all our lives. Waverley was pleased with the way I'd handled the problems in the UK so I knew they'd offer me something in California or New York. The night before I flew out I made the decision to separate—and then changed it twice more before morning.

Maybe it wasn't them, I kept thinking. Maybe it was me. I'd spent so long scrambling for my place in the sun it was hard for me to understand that love also means pain and sacrifice. I'd seen what happened to my mother. I grew up knowing I must never allow myself to be reliant on anyone except myself. Maybe I had to sacrifice the possibility of happiness with Ralph for his relationship with Danny. He loved Danny and Danny loved him. Who was I to come between them? But what could I say to Ralph? How could I ever make him understand that I loved him so much I was prepared to give him up? How could I possibly explain this convoluted piece of reasoning to him? I couldn't even try. Ralph would be devastated. I knew how sensitive he was, how Angela's death had numbed his feelings for years. Now I was going to break his heart a second time. The drop-off zone outside Terminal 3 was not the place to start explaining.

I knew I loved him, but sometimes love isn't enough. We'd like to think it is because it seems to have an irresistible logic behind it. Ralph was a widower who had been waiting to find love again. I was a single woman who had magically found love where I least expected it. We made each other happy. Surely that was enough to make the relationship work? But I knew in my heart it wasn't. It hurt me desperately to kiss Ralph goodbye and tell him blithely that I would see him in a week or so.

My head was telling me I was making the sensible grown-up decision for both of us, but as the wheels of the Boeing 767 left the tarmac and the plane rose into the sky and headed for the Atlantic Ocean, I burst into tears.

Ralph

WHEN IT CAME it was a bolt out of the blue. I suppose I should have seen it coming because there was all that trouble over Christmas, but that was just Danny behaving like a twelve-year-old and I didn't take it too seriously because that's what kids are like. Then there was the funny mood Helen was in before she left. But she kissed me as I loaded her case onto the trolley and told me she loved me. I remember her exact words. So when the call came I was shocked.

It was almost exactly a week since she'd left and I was somewhat hurt that she hadn't bothered phoning, but then I reckoned she was with her mother and maybe her mother wouldn't approve of the transatlantic phone call—it wasn't difficult to find reasons to rationalise the silence.

Sometimes when you pick up the phone, you can tell merely by the way someone says hello that there's trouble brewing. Such was my immediate sensation when I lifted the receiver that Thursday night to hear Helen's faltering voice.

I had never heard her so hesitant, so indecisive. One of the things that had always appealed to me about her was her clarity of thinking, which allowed her to make fast decisions and stick to them. The voice was completely unlike her normal self. She claimed she was getting between Danny and myself and making everyone miserable. In vain I argued that she wasn't, that if there was a problem between Danny and me it was none of her making, but she didn't want to listen.

I tried to calm her down, telling her there was no need to get upset, that when she came back at the weekend we could talk it through.

'I'm not coming back.'

'What do you mean?' My heart sank. I knew exactly what she meant.

'Just that. I'm staying here in the States.'

I was too stunned to speak for a moment.

'Ralph? Are you still there?'

'Yes, I'm here. I don't understand. I mean, why?'

'I told you. I'm making things worse between Danny and you.'

'No, you're not. And I love you.'

'I love you.'

'So what the hell's going on?'

'Ralph, it will never work out. If I go now you'll be able to repair the damage quickly, get you and Danny back to the life you had before.'

'I don't want the life I had before. You're the best thing that's happened to my life in twelve years.'

'Ralph, it's better this way. For all of us.'

'Not for me.'

'Well, then, for Danny.'

'Danny likes you.'

'But he doesn't like me when I'm with you.'

'That's nonsense. I love you, Helen. I want to spend the rest of my life with you.'

'Ralph, please don't make it any harder for me.'

'This thing with Danny. We just have to give him time to adjust.'

'I saw how it was going to be when we went off to that hotel and then again over Christmas. He wants you to be the dad he's grown up with. Go back and make him happy, Ralph. It'll make you happy as well. I can't.'

'But what about us?'

There was a pause while she searched for the right phrase. It came from *Casablanca*.

'We'll always have Bowfell.'

So that was it. She'd resigned the European job and was going back to work in Waverley's office in California. It meant she could commute from her house in Santa Barbara. She explained that it had all worked out perfectly for her because the lease had run out on December 31 and the agent hadn't yet rented it out for this year. Not perfect for me, for sure. And was it really perfect for her?

I put the phone down, numb with shock. She was exactly what I had always liked in a woman—bright, sharp, funny, independent, sexy. If we'd married, which I'd started to allow myself to think was the obvious culmination to the affair, I thought she would be the one woman I had ever met who would know how to deal with the Danny and the Angela situations. I could see a wonderful family life opening up for all of us, maybe one day with a new baby. Danny'd be fourteen or fifteen years older, so there wouldn't be any sibling rivalry. I know Danny, he's such a lovely kid, he'd be so pleased to be a big brother. And now it was all gone, with a single phone call.

In one respect Helen was certainly right. The best thing I could do to repair the damage was to carry on as normal, which I did. Danny did ask when she was coming back, so I told him the truth, but not the reason why. I didn't want him to blame himself.

Besides, I wasn't sure I agreed with Helen's diagnosis. Maybe she was frightened of commitment. Maybe I didn't earn enough for her; maybe she thought marrying me might set back her career. She had never said this, never even implied it, but I was tortured with the reasons for her shocking decision and I wasn't prepared to accept the one she gave me.

Over the next few weeks I tormented myself with such thoughts. On the face of it I was doing exactly the same things—telephoning, interviewing, writing, shopping, running the house, looking after Danny—but now I did them with a heavy heart.

The only time I came alive during those days was when I played squash with Ian Walling. I had known Ian a long time, but though I counted him one of my closest friends, we never talked about anything that could be mistaken for emotional honesty. Our conversation ranged across the full spectrum of male obsessions—careers, sport, money, our children—but I knew no more of the reality of his marriage than he knew of the state of my affairs.

One Wednesday afternoon, we were having a drink after a hectic game of squash when Ian startled me by asking the sort of direct question we had assiduously avoided over the years.

'Is it over with Helen?'

'Why do you say that?'

'Because for the last four months you've never missed a chance to drone on about her.'

'Really? I don't know. She says it is.'

'Well, I thought there was a reason you played like shit today. Other than spectacular incompetence on your part.'

I smiled. 'She says she can't make a go of it because of Danny.'

'What's wrong with Danny? He's great.'

'He's been a bit weird when Helen and I have been together.'

'Jealous of her?'

'I don't know.'

Ian looked surprised. 'You must know. Danny tells you everything.'

'We haven't talked. Not properly.'

'Since when?'

'Since the summer, I guess.'

'Since Helen moved into your life.'

'I thought that was coincidence.'

'Jesus, Ralph, I know you're a sports writer but you're quite a bright one. Surely even you—'

'All right, yes. I know what you're saying. I've just been unwilling to confront it. Besides, he is going through puberty, kids change. Their emotions are all screwed up.'

'Tell me about it.' Ian drained his drink. 'Do you love her?'

'Yes!'

'You sound amazingly sure for a man who has dithered in this area for twelve years.'

'But I love Danny too. Why the hell can't I reconcile these two great emotions?'

Ian sat back in his chair and thought for a while. I felt sure he was going to come up with some pithy piece of advice. At length he stood up.

'How should I know? I can't even figure out how the video recorder works. Same time next week?'

I tried hard to make sure Danny never noticed my depression. I thought I succeeded quite easily, but then the complexity of adult relationships were not something he was likely to spend much time thinking about. In fact, while he was around was the easiest time for me—the panics in the morning and the after-school scenario tended to occupy me fully. It was only when he was at school or in bed that I found the time dragged and my mind was filled with images of Helen.

One thing I did notice, though. Although Helen had not yet driven the memory of Angela out of my head, she had certainly caused a certain amount of displacement. I suppose, if I'm being honest now, the obsession with Angela had been unhealthy, but I never saw that until after Helen had arrived in my life. Helen had been totally phlegmatic about Angela, quite unfazed by the possible challenge the ubiquitous framed photographs posed to her. I felt with Helen that I could hold on to Angela in my heart without betraying her memory.

I never saw Helen as another Angela and I certainly never saw her as Danny's mother. Helen was so utterly different from Angela, I didn't have any difficulty reconciling the previous position with the recognition of the fact that I had fallen in love with another woman.

When I got over the shock of that initial telephone call I started to think that maybe I was somehow unlovable. For years I had believed that the reason I hadn't found the right woman was that there was something wrong with the women I met. But there was nothing wrong with Helen and still she had run away. So maybe it wasn't those other women who were at fault. And it wasn't Danny either. It was me. I knew I hadn't been unlovable twelve years ago, but maybe my reaction to Angela's death had made me so.

When I woke up now in the mornings, a heavy weight lay across my heart. I felt as wretched as the day the doctor looked at me with such sadness in his eyes as he drew the sheet over Angela's face. For the second time in my life, a bleak and empty future stretched in front of me.

Danny

THE MOMENT DAD told me Helen wasn't coming back I felt really, really bad. I didn't say anything, because I didn't know what to say. I felt sick in the pit of my stomach. It was my fault, I knew it was, but I couldn't see how I could make things right.

Though I felt wretched, I thought Dad would be able to cope. There had been women before who had come and gone, so I told myself that Helen was only the latest in the line, but I knew deep down inside this wasn't so. Helen was special to Dad.

Life went back to what it had been before, but every time I looked at Dad's face when he didn't know I was looking at him, I could see that he was miserable. The way he sat down in the armchair with a sort of whoosh, as if he had lost control of his body, or just the way he walked, which was sort of heavy, like he had suddenly put on ten kilos. But what made the whole thing clear to me was what happened after a football game about a month later.

At the end of January, Spurs were drawn away at Ipswich in the fourth round of the FA Cup. Ipswich were a useful First Division side and we were in the Premiership but hardly setting the world alight, so all the experts said it was going to be an awkward game for us. Still, the great thing about the new season in any sport is that we can all dream again.

Dad got the commission to cover the game for one of the Sunday papers so he would have to stay at the ground after the game was over to file his report. I didn't mind that, because I usually got to eat all the left-over sandwiches in the press room and poke about in the dressing rooms, maybe get an autograph or speak to the players.

We won, with a goal scored from a controversial penalty kick five minutes from the end of the game. Dad says that when we play away from home we never get given decisions that favour us like that, so it was really wicked. Everyone was happy so it was cool. In the car on the way home we listened to the radio to catch the final reports, which always cheer us up even more.

But all the way home he didn't say a word. This is so unlike Dad, it really worried me. It was weird him not speaking after we'd won this really difficult match. I made the odd comment about the penalty and so on, but he just grunted. About ten miles from Cambridge it hit me.

When I realised what was wrong, I got the same horrid feeling in my tummy back again. It wasn't that I thought he was over Helen. The way he looked in those unguarded moments told me he wasn't. But I didn't, till that moment, realise how bad it was for him. If he wasn't dead chuffed that Spurs had won this really difficult and important game, there was something very wrong with him.

I grew up by about five years in those five minutes. It made me scream inside, because it was my fault he was hurting so badly. I loved my dad so much, I had to do something about it. Since Mum died he had looked after me, loved me, and helped me. Now it was time for me to do something for him.

I knew what it was I had to do to make things come out right, but I couldn't think of how I could do it. I could probably pass myself off as fifteen under a baseball cap, but no way would anyone think I was older than that. I lay awake at night thinking desperately; by day I stared out of the window during lessons, willing myself to find a solution.

Then one school night we didn't get any French homework, so after tea I watched a film on TV with Tom Hanks and that pretty blonde actress whose name I forget but who looks a bit like Mum. The film was called *Sleepless in Seattle*. By the time the film was over I knew how I could do it.

Ralph

I KNEW SOMETHING was wrong almost as soon as he went back to school after the Christmas holidays. He was never a loud or particularly boisterous kid, though he always made his presence felt at home. During January, however, his demeanour subtly changed. He no longer wanted me to test him on his homework, which was unusual. But I was so wrapped up in my own misery that I never bothered to enquire further. I had no spare strength for Danny.

One Monday lunchtime I got a call from Mrs Hargreaves, his form mistress. Danny's work was giving cause for concern and could I go into school to have a chat about it. I went in on the Wednesday.

I listened to her expressions of concern over Danny's recent waywardness, but I wasn't exactly overwhelmed. For a start, significant exams were still three and a half years away, but the real reason was that it only came as a confirmation of Danny's domestic behaviour. She tried to press me on what might be wrong at home, but I wasn't keen to pursue the conversation down this track and, besides, in teacher-speak, there wasn't anything 'wrong' at home. My problems were my concern and I couldn't see how a discussion of the vacuum in my love life was going to help Danny's schoolwork.

I promised to talk to Danny and find out what the problem might be. I volunteered the fact that Danny had always struggled with his French irregular verbs, but that still didn't explain his dip in his maths and English. I did mention that Danny had been growing that year, as boys rushing headlong into puberty are wont to do. We decided to part on the understanding that it was hormonal and nothing else. I don't think she believed it either, but it was a face-saving compromise.

I didn't even mention the meeting to Danny. I didn't want to start alarm bells ringing and I was anyway just too depressed by the loss of Helen. For the first time since Angela had been killed, I didn't put him first. His adolescent moods were making me cross and I just wanted to be back in Helen's arms; I didn't want a row about French verbs or algebraic equations. So I provoked one about a can of Coca-Cola instead.

The image of Helen was so strong in my head that it interfered with my concentration. I frequently found myself in the middle of a phone call with someone, aware that I hadn't heard a word they had said because I was remembering Helen. One night I walked into the kitchen in just such a mood, when I stepped straight into a puddle of Coke.

Danny had hurled the can across the kitchen towards the recycling bag, missed and just left it on the floor, unaware, presumably, that the can wasn't empty and that a puddle of brown liquid was forming on the lino. My sock was completely soaked by the sticky stuff. I yelled for Danny.

'What?'

'Look at that!'

'Look at what?'

'You left a trail of Coke all over the bloody floor.'

'No, I didn't.'

I was infuriated. 'Yes, you did. That's your bloody can. Clean it up.'

Sisyphus couldn't have exhibited a greater reluctance.

'Clean what?'

I wanted to hit him. 'The bloody floor. I've got sticky goo all over my socks.'

'Well, hadn't you better clean it?'

'Danny!' I was really yelling now. Life was so unfair. First Helen breaks my heart, now Danny spills Coke on the floor.

By this time he got the message that I was angry. He went to the sink and picked up a sponge, then held it under the tap until it was full of water. He made a pathetic attempt to wipe up the Coke, but only succeeded in spreading the puddle wider.

'Danny!'

'What?'

God I hate the way adolescent kids whine at you. That 'What?' sent me into orbit. 'Put the fucking chairs on the table, then use the mop and the detergent and wash it properly.'

I rarely swore, so the shock value worked. He did what I asked but very slowly and with evident loathing for me and the operation. I didn't care. It was that sort of attitude that had sent my darling back to America.

I left the room because I couldn't stand to watch him. When I returned ten minutes later the whole kitchen floor was almost under water and he was grinning. I wasn't going to let him get away with this.

'Right, that's it. Go to bed.'

'Don't you want me to finish the job?'

'Not like that. I'm stopping your pocket money for a month and you won't be allowed to watch television at all except at weekends.'

'Why?' Now he was losing his cool.

'You know why.'

'That's fucking unfair.'

'And don't you swear at me.'

'Why not? You swore at me!'

I grabbed the mop off him. 'Go to bed now!' I yelled. 'Just go!'

He did. We didn't speak to each other again that night.

I had to leave for London early the following morning, so I was out of the house before his alarm went off. I thought of waking him up and instigating a reconciliation, but I thought Helen had been right when she'd encouraged me to discipline Danny and I felt he could sweat out my displeasure for another day.

I got back around two thirty in the afternoon. A white envelope with the word 'Dad' written on it was propped up on the mantelpiece in the living room. I thought that this was strange. He'd never done this before. I tore it open, hoping that it was an apology.

Dear Dad,

I love you and I'm going to fix it. It was my fault to begin with. I'm sorry if I upset you. Don't worry. I've got money and everything so I'll be fine.

Love, Danny

My first reaction was puzzlement. What the hell was he talking about? Then anxiety. Certainly not panic. Not at that point. I looked at my watch. I had just enough time to get to school when they came out. I raced out.

Danny tended to be one of the first to sprint out of the school gates so after ten minutes my anxiety started to grow. It was possible I had missed him, of course. Then I saw Jamie Kirk coming towards me.

'Where's Danny, Jamie?' I asked.

'He didn't come to school today.'

A cold hand clutched at my heart. I ran into school, looking desperately for the staff room. I hammered on the door and Mrs Hargreaves came to open it.

'Have you seen Danny?' I demanded.

'Isn't he at home?' she asked evenly. 'He didn't come to school today. I thought he might have the flu.'

'No. If he was at home I wouldn't be here, would I?'

'No. Of course not. Do you think he's playing truant?'

'He left me this letter.'

She took it and read it slowly, absorbing every word.

'I don't understand. What does this mean?'

'I was hoping you might know.'

She shook her head.

I groaned in despair. 'Oh God, it's all my fault!'

'There's probably a perfectly logical explanation.'

'There is. We had this terrible row last night.'

'Oh.'

She invited me into the staff room to call the police, while she made me a cup of tea. After I'd made the call I slumped into one of the coffee-stained armchairs all staff rooms seem to specialise in. She waited for me to speak.

'I've been . . . a bit moody recently. When you mentioned to me that Danny's work had got worse, I knew it was my fault. It's been a bit awkward at home recently, one or two domestic upheavals. It's too complicated to explain. I've had some problems and I thought I was hiding them from him, but obviously I wasn't. The point is, I suppose, that Danny and I have not been getting along in the last few weeks.' I paused. How much of this was relevant, I wondered. 'I made him clean the kitchen floor.'

She said nothing. Nobody runs away from home because they have to clean the floor, do they? I thought I'd better elaborate.

'He'd spilt some Coke and I pointed it out and he said it wasn't him, which it was, and I'm afraid I lost my temper.'

'Did you hit him?'

'Good God, no! I made him clean it up so he ran a sponge under the tap and just left a pool of water on the floor. I got even angrier and made him do the whole room properly.'

'Well, good for you.'

'So now he's run away from home.'

'Mr Warren, believe me, whatever that letter means, if Danny has run away it won't be because he had to clean the kitchen floor. You mustn't blame yourself.'

'Then it got worse. There was a bigger row and I stopped his pocket money for a month and banned him from watching television at all except at weekends.'

'Life imprisonment without the possibility of parole.'

'You can joke, but we never have rows like that.'

'I'm sorry, I had no intention of trivialising what's happened. I was just trying to make you see it wasn't your fault.'

'How can you possibly know?'

'You're right. Of course I can't. Let's just concentrate on what the note means and where he might be now.'

As the minutes passed while we waited for the police, all likely locations were explored and dismissed. My concern grew rapidly. The newspapers carry articles about missing children all the time. I had no cause to be anything but desperate. We all know the routine by now: the police issue a statement of facts asking for help in their enquiries; then the hysterical parents go on television to appeal to the public; a few days or a few weeks later a body is discovered. Was I really facing this?

Mrs Hargreaves knew quite a few of Danny's friends, so before the police arrived she took the official school list and telephoned them at their homes. They could only say they hadn't the faintest idea where Danny might have gone. He never said anything significant to them and they didn't even realise he'd acted any differently since the beginning of term. Really, adolescent boys can be quite breathtakingly unobservant. With each dead end my spirits slipped further.

Mrs Hargreaves went with me to the police station, where I signed my statement, and then back to the house, where she cooked me dinner. I didn't want much, so she opened a tin of soup and made some toast. I was almost paralysed with anxiety. I was so grateful to her.

She insisted gently that we should look around Danny's bedroom, to see if there was something that might give us a clue as to where he had gone. We opened drawers and rummaged through his wardrobe. After a while I straightened up.

'All I can see is his cricket bag's not here.'

'He's gone to play cricket?'

'I don't think so. His bat and his pads are still in the wardrobe.'

'Has his toothbrush gone or his toilet bag?'

'No.'

'I think the disappearance of the cricket bag is a very good sign, because it looks like he's made a conscious decision to go somewhere.'

For a moment I felt really quite hopeful. I could see the logic in what she said. Then I shook my head. 'That note could mean anything. I don't even know what money he's talking about. How much does he need to get to wherever he's going?'

'You had that argument last night. He's probably too embarrassed to explain more.'

'I don't know why I shouted at him. He's such a good kid.' My eyes began to well with tears.

She put her hand on my arm. 'We'll find him, Mr Warren. We will.'

Then the doorbell rang. I went to the door and opened it. I could see the outline of the peaked cap through the frosted glass, so I knew what to expect. Except it wasn't a policeman, it was a policewoman. My heart missed a beat. They always send women to deliver the bad news.

'Mr Warren?'

I nodded, wondering if the next five seconds would destroy my life.

'There's no news, Mr Warren. I'm sorry.'

Was this good or bad? If he wasn't in hospital or in a police station somewhere, was this a good thing? Or did it just increase the likelihood of his body lying at the bottom of the river? As if to confirm this terrible image, the policewoman told me they would send a frogman into the River Cam at dawn. Meanwhile, her superior, Detective Chief Inspector Chamberlain, had sent a message to the Child Protection Services at Scotland Yard, who would in turn inform all ports and airports. If he was still in the country, they would find him, she assured me.

'And if he's already left the country?'

'Well, obviously it would take longer to find him, but if an airport immigration authority had a record of him entering their country today or tomorrow, say, then at least we'd know where to start looking.'

Silence fell. Nobody dared to voice what we were all feeling. That she was assuming that Danny was still alive.

Danny

I COULDN'T BELIEVE how easy it was. I'd always kept my own passport and Dad had had this travel agent for ages and the last couple of times he had needed to fly he had let me do the booking on the phone. It was his way of teaching me to be independent. When I was watching *Sleepless in Seattle* and I saw Tom Hanks's kid get a ticket to fly to New York, I knew that I could do it too.

I gave the man who answered the telephone the account number Dad always uses and they had the credit card number attached to it on the computer. After we had sorted out which flight I was going to take, he asked, as I knew he would from my previous times when I was booking for Dad, if I wanted to use Dad's credit card even though it was my name on the airline ticket. I said of course I did. I mean is he stupid or what? Where was I going to get £384 including airport tax from? He never even asked me why I was travelling by myself to the USA, though I had my story all worked out if he had.

A part of me wanted to tell Dad about what I was planning to do, because I didn't want him to worry, but the other bit of me said I shouldn't. He wouldn't let me go and I'd be in terrible trouble for using his credit card. He was totally out of order, though, making me wash the kitchen floor just because there was a bit of sticky stuff on it. He said it came from my Coke can, but in fact it could have come from anything. He was so unreasonable about it I had to do it, but I was seething inside. I went to bed without saying good night to him, which was unusual, but in fact it meant that I didn't feel quite so guilty about leaving home.

I put my spare clothes in my big cricket bag and I simply took the bus to the station, changed into my Saturday clothes in the toilet and bought a bus ticket to London. At Victoria I got a tube to Heathrow Airport. I was a bit worried about checking in but I told the woman I was on half term and I was being met by my mother in Los Angeles. I don't think she cared much. She just asked me if I had a valid US immigration visa.

My heart stopped. I never thought about an immigration visa. My eyes began to fill with tears. I felt like such a fool. Why hadn't they asked me at the travel agency? That was their job, surely? I told the woman that I hadn't got one and waited for the sentence of death. But all she did was reach under the counter and give me a US visa waiver form to fill in. I could have kissed her.

I thought the letter I wrote was just right. I left out the reason I was going to see Helen, because that was all to do with my feelings and those are very difficult things to write about. Mostly, though, I didn't want to give too much away in case he came chasing after me and told me not to be so stupid, that it was all over between him and Helen, and anyway it was nothing to do with me. But I knew that it wasn't over and that the only way I could make Dad happy again was to go to Santa Barbara and find Helen and tell her it was all my fault that Dad and she had broken up and that if she came back I wouldn't be this really annoying creep any more. Then Dad would be happy and she would be happy and I would be happy because the two of them would be happy.

Yes, I know I could have telephoned Helen, but it wouldn't have been the same. Telephoning Helen would have been the same as telling Dad exactly what I was doing. She wouldn't have taken me seriously or she'd think Dad had put me up to it and then she'd really have hated Dad. Besides, when I got to the airport I found that I didn't have Helen's phone number with me, only her address, which I'd taken off Dad's computer. But that was cool, because I didn't need the phone number. After all, I was going straight to her house from the airport.

I reckoned that if I went to her, went to California, made everything right, then rang up Dad and told him to come over or flew back with her to England, then I would be the hero. Then I would have made everything come out right. I was really looking forward to being a hero. Maybe I'd be on telly, perhaps on the evening news or *The Big Breakfast* or even *TFI Friday* with Chris Evans. They like kids who tell stories like that.

I first started thinking seriously about it when I found $200 in an envelope in Dad's desk drawer. Sometimes he leaves an opened packet of Liquorice Allsorts there and that's what I was looking for the day after the Spurs match at Ipswich. I then figured if I could get the airline ticket on Dad's credit card, I could get a bus to Santa Barbara. Even if Helen was away for a day or two I'd have enough money to stay in a motel, and I know you can get hamburgers for ninety-nine cents at McDonald's. It was a perfect plan.

It was only after the plane had taken off that I got a bit worried. The stewardess was very nice, asking if someone was meeting me at the other end. I guessed she was used to seeing kids of divorced parents flying between London and Los Angeles. She seemed so sympathetic and had such a nice warm smile that I did think about telling her everything, but I thought she might stop the plane or tell the pilot to return to Heathrow, so I said nothing. She was really pretty, that stewardess, and she was wearing lots of perfume that I liked. I fell asleep thinking about that, because now that I was past the dangerous bit I sort of relaxed. When I woke up, I looked at my watch and I discovered, after doing a lot of really difficult maths to account for the time difference, that we wouldn't be landing for another six and a half hours.

What was even worse was that the man in the seat next to me said that he hadn't woken me for dinner because I looked like I was really enjoying my sleep. I smiled and said thank you, although what I wanted to say was, 'You stupid idiot, I was really hungry.'

I wanted to go and ask that nice stewardess if she had kept my dinner on one side for me, but I didn't dare. I wanted something to eat really badly but now I was worried that because I'd missed the proper dinner, if I asked for something special they'd make me pay a lot of money for it. I didn't think I should spend that $200 on the plane, otherwise I wouldn't have enough to get to Helen's.

I got through another hour or so by wondering whether the next meal, when it came (as come it better had or I would die of starvation and that would be terrible publicity for the airline), would be chicken and potatoes and a nice piece of cake for dessert, or perhaps we'd already flown through the night so the next meal would be orange juice and a huge pile of waffles with maple syrup (yes!).

Eventually I saw the trolley coming and I almost cried with relief.

Chicken and rice or egg and bacon, I didn't care what was on it. Then I saw people reaching into their bags for money, which made me go 'Oh no!' to myself. This was the duty-free trolley.

When the nice stewardess smiled and asked what we wanted, I wanted to tell her 'Food! Food! Any kind of food!' but I just said nothing. Well, my dad would be proud of me, I thought grimly. I was being the perfect guest and he was paying about £400 for it. That started to bother me a bit. I told myself I'd pay it back out of my pocket money, but at that rate it would take me four years. Then I thought maybe I could sell my story to a tabloid newspaper for £400. Dad would know who to get in touch with. I felt a bit better.

We still had another five hours in the air. I watched the movie for a while, but I couldn't see the screen very well because I was so far back, and I dozed off. Eventually they brought the landing cards and the customs forms round and I knew we must be getting close to Los Angeles. Now my heart started beating faster again. I screwed my eyes shut tight and thought hard about Helen's beautiful house near Santa Barbara and her opening the door and shrieking with delight, then getting on the phone to Dad and making everything all right. Then I would have a swim in her pool and she would feed me lots of American food and a cold drink and then I would go to sleep.

But all the time I was thinking these nice thoughts, a black vision of something else seemed to want to lie across it. In this vision I would be stopped at immigration and arrested. Then they would snap the cuffs on and I would be forced into a police car and driven away at high speed.

 **Ralph**

AT TWENTY TO TWO in the morning I woke up covered in sweat, but with the same euphoria of discovery as has been attributed to Archimedes. He, according to legend, shouted 'Eureka!' I shouted 'Shit!' which is a pretty accurate modern English equivalent. Of course! He'd gone to see Helen!

The practical difficulties were so enormous I had never considered it. But when I fell into my troubled sleep that night, the second person's face I saw was Helen's. She was standing on the edge of a cliff, and she had her arms wide open and Danny was running towards them.

HIGH ON A CLIFF

I raced downstairs stark naked to look for Helen's telephone number in California. My fingers had all the dexterity of my toes as I sought desperately to punch out the numbers. It took me three attempts, only to be greeted by the busy signal.

I made myself a cup of tea. Spilling the milk across the counter in my anxiety, I remembered in all its painful details the argument with Danny about his spilt Coke. What wouldn't I give now to take back those words. I returned to the study and jabbed at the redial button. The same infuriatingly even response awaited me. I turned on the computer and emailed Helen, sitting there in an incongruous state of total nudity like the mad organist in *Monty Python's Flying Circus*.

I went back upstairs and got into bed again. He was there, I knew he was there. But then why hadn't Helen called me?

I dialled very deliberately and heard to my inexpressible joy the sound of a telephone ringing. She picked it up on the second ring.

'Hello?'

'Hi. It's me. Is Danny there?'

'Danny?'

My heart slumped again. She's not a dense woman, so I had to assume that she knew nothing about Danny, but then it was only about six o'clock in the evening out there and maybe he hadn't got there yet. I told her the events as they had unfolded in the past twelve hours. Although she said nothing apart from the odd sympathetic 'Oh no!' I sensed she was with me. This was a great help. We were a team.

'How did he get a ticket?' she asked.

'I don't know yet. He must have done it through my travel agent. He's seen me do it. I guess he used my credit card.'

'The little rascal. How d'you know he's not gone to Hawaii on vacation?'

'This is Danny we're talking about, Helen.'

'Right. Sorry. You want me to call the cops out here?'

'If you wouldn't mind.'

'Don't be so goddamn British.'

'Hey! I've just remembered. I can ring the credit card company and find out the last transaction.'

'Call me back.'

The credit card company was quite happy to do business at two thirty in the morning. They confirmed that a charge of £384 in favour of my travel agency had been made the previous Saturday. That seemed to me the right sort of amount a return ticket to Los Angeles would cost. I pulled open the desk drawer. The envelope with the $200 was gone. I instantly realised the significance of this and I started to cry with happiness. He was alive! Jesus Christ! Just wait till I get my hands on that kid again. I'll kill him!

I called Helen back and told her. She was so happy. I wanted to reach out for her and touch her. In the circumstances she must surely be feeling something for me, for us.

'I've told the cops out here, but frankly a missing British kid isn't the kind of emergency they're going to take too seriously.'

I was outraged. 'Why the hell not?'

'Well, for a start, he's British, not American—'

'Xenophobes! What does a twelve-year-old kid wandering through the streets of Los Angeles need before the cops take him seriously?'

'A gun.'

'What? Helen, I just want my son back safe and sound.'

'OK, listen. You tell the cops your end in the morning what's going on. I'll keep a lookout for him here . . . Let me know if you get a confirmation from Immigration Control. I'll chase it up here, but really you're the parent and they might think me a bit suspicious.'

'I'll be out on the first plane.'

'What if he tries to call you?'

'Why would he? He's coming to see you. If he was going to phone me he'd already have done it.'

'Ralph . . .'

'Yes?'

'What's he want with me anyway?'

'I think,' I said slowly, 'he's rumbled me.'

'What?'

'I think he knows how much I love you. He's coming out to make it all better.'

'Some kid.'

'Helen, you know there hasn't been a single minute of a single day when I haven't stopped thinking about you, loving you.'

There was another of those desperate pauses.

'Yes, there was.'

'When?'

'When Tottenham defeated Ipswich.'

'How did—'

'I've been following the Spurs scores in the LA Times.'

'Really?' I was affecting a dangerous cool I was certainly not feeling. It paid off.

'How's Danny been these past few weeks? I've missed him.'

'Just him?'

'No. And you.'

'Just missed me?' I was really pushing it now.

'Not just missed you. I'm still in love with you, Ralph.'

Her words made my heart pound. She still loved me. I always knew she did. We'd find Danny and everything would be OK. For ten seconds I was on cloud nine. Damn that kid for the agony he's put me through these past few hours, but he's given me the chance to see Helen again. When I put the phone down, my head was still swimming with all the thoughts and emotions that were in there.

I tried to get back to sleep, but I managed nothing more than the occasional doze until the alarm went off at seven o'clock. At one minute past nine o'clock I found the idiot at the travel agency who had authorised Danny's ticket. The manager got on the line and was very apologetic, but pointed out that the transaction was not made illegally and that there was nothing he could do about it. I finished letting him grovel and scrape, then told him I wanted a ticket for Los Angeles for myself, leaving that day. He had ten minutes to get it sorted because the 'call waiting' noise was bleeping in my ear.

It was Detective Chief Inspector Chamberlain, telling me that a boy answering Danny's description had passed through Immigration Control in Los Angeles yesterday afternoon. He gave his address as Helen's house in Santa Barbara.

 **Danny**

I STOOD BEHIND the yellow line in the Tom Bradley International Terminal at Los Angeles Airport waiting to be interrogated by the secret immigration police. Eventually I was summoned over. I gave the man my passport and he flicked slowly through. He stared at me as if he had seen my face before, which he hadn't, and then he started tapping away at his computer. Sweat broke out on my neck and rolled in little drops down my back before coming to rest on the back of my underpants. This was it. This was the moment they came and snapped the cuffs on.

The man stared at the screen. The tension was unbearable. Finally, he spoke to me.

'Vacation?'

I wanted to tell him all about my dad and Helen and so on. I was doing nothing wrong. A little voice inside me made me say the magic word.

'Yes.'

The secret police had another flick through the passport, found a blank page and stamped it like it was a library book, stapled the appropriate bit of the landing form into it, handed it back to me and called 'Next'. My heart leapt. I was through. No more problems, except to tell them I wasn't bringing any citrus fruit or meat into the country. I wondered who would bring oranges or meat riddled with BSE from a British supermarket into California, which Dad always said had the best food in the world. The thought of food reminded me that I hadn't eaten for twelve hours. The tension had made me forget it for the last hour or so.

I was so pleased to see my cricket bag on the conveyor belt, it reminded me of home. A lot of people were jostling at the conveyor belt so I had to run after it till I could find a space so I could haul it off, put it on the trolley and wheel it through customs.

I had this dream that I would be coming through customs into the part where the relatives and friends are waiting and Helen would be there and she'd be so pleased to see me and she'd drive me to her home in a posh American sports car. But she wasn't there. And I know it sounds ridiculous because how could she be, she didn't know I was coming, but I still felt really disappointed.

Instead, I saw a brightly lit shop selling T-shirts and magazines and chocolate. I saw a huge, I mean a gi-normous, bar of Toblerone. I love Toblerone. It said $9.95 on the label so I handed over ten dollars at the till. The cash register rang up $10.75. I said in a small voice that I thought it was $9.95. 'Tax,' the girl at the register said briefly, holding out her hand. I gave her another of my precious ten-dollar bills.

I wheeled the trolley over to where I could sit down on a ledge and ate nearly the whole thing. Then I put the remaining bit into my cricket bag. I felt a bit sick.

I headed outside and decided I wouldn't get a bus because it was all so confusing. Hundreds of vehicles were trying to manoeuvre their way round in about six different lanes, all of them jammed. None of the buses said Santa Barbara on the front. I counted my money again. I had $189.25. I wasn't too sure where Santa Barbara was, so I thought the safest thing to do was to show the taxi driver the address and ask him how much it would be to drive me there.

I stood under a sign that said TAXI and when I got to be the first in the queue I showed the man Helen's address—2535 Santa Maria Street, Montecito, near Santa Barbara, California.

He thought for a while. 'How much you got?'

'One hundred and eighty-nine dollars and twenty-five cents.'

He smiled. He had big white teeth. 'OK. I take you there.'

'Thanks.'

'You show me the money, OK?'

I showed it to him and he got out and opened the boot, where he slung my cricket bag. I was a bit worried because the boot was really dirty with old cans of oil and a filthy towrope and Dad had given me that cricket bag brand new for my birthday. Then he opened the door for me to get in the back. It was just like he was my chauffeur. The seat was peculiar because it was so low—and really slippery leather. He drove too fast and screeched round corners and I kept sliding every-where. There were no seat belts.

Still, I was sure I had done the right thing. It didn't matter that I was giving this guy all the money I had because he was taking me straight to Helen's house. As soon as she saw me, everything would be all right. I could feel it in my bones. There was going to be a happy ending. It had all been worth it.

I enjoyed the ride. It was just like being in a movie or a TV series and I was glad I was in a taxi and not having to worry about getting on the right bus and having the right change and how to get to Helen's house from the bus station.

I tried to keep myself awake, but after about twenty minutes it was like a great tidal wave of tiredness washed over me and I just lay down on the seat and fell asleep. I was so zonked I could have slept for ever.

Instead I was shaken awake by the taxi driver, who was pulling me out of the car. He almost dumped me on the kerb, where I tripped over my cricket bag which he'd already taken out of the boot.

'Money,' he said and he wasn't half as nice as he had been before. I got my wallet out and gave him all the money except for the quarter which was still in my trouser pocket. He almost leapt into the driver's seat and roared away. Suddenly I got frightened. I knew Helen lived in a nice part of town and I thought I'd be on a nice tree-lined street full of detached houses like Millington Road in Cambridge, but I was standing on a little road with small run-down houses.

The sun was setting and there was a chill in the air now. I asked a man if this was Santa Barbara and he said no. The taxi driver had taken me to the wrong place and he'd driven off with all my money.

I felt very alone and very frightened. I wished I'd never left Cambridge.

I picked up my bag and followed the main road to a junction with another main road. A police car came cruising towards me. My first instinct was to run away and hide, but then I thought they couldn't possibly know who I was. So when the car stopped, because the traffic light was on red, I went over and asked where Santa Barbara was.

'A hundred miles north, you're in Hollywood, pal,' the one who wasn't driving said as the lights changed to green and the car roared away.

A hundred miles! I had twenty-five cents in my pocket. I would have to ring her. I could get the number from directory enquiries.

But I couldn't. Helen turned out to have an unlisted number, which is what we call ex-directory, and they wouldn't give it to me even though I said it was an emergency. In fact the woman was really rude and unhelpful. I wished I'd brought the number with me. I didn't think I'd need anything besides her address. I was a hundred miles away, it was getting to be night-time, I didn't know anyone and I had no money.

I'M A REAL ACTIVE TYPE of person. My philosophy has always been that the phone won't ring of its own free will. You have to do something that prompts the return call. But after informing the authorities that Danny was missing, there was nothing I could do but will the stupid thing to ring. I knew now that I should have stayed and fought for Ralph. Instead I ran away, and look what happened. This was all my fault. I just prayed to God it wouldn't turn into one of those tragedies you read about in the papers.

At first I was grateful enough to return to my old office in the Waverley Building on Wilshire Boulevard. I didn't even mind the commute as I tried to bathe my mind in the music from the CD player. But as soon as Ralph called to tell me about Danny, that all changed.

The phone rang often enough with work stuff, but that wasn't what I wanted to hear. I couldn't disguise the disappointment in my voice when the call turned out to be from an editor or executive at work. I don't suppose I won too many friends that day but I didn't care. I was totally wrapped up in the Danny saga. Until he was found I wouldn't know an untroubled moment.

I was on my way to pick up Ralph at LAX, when I realised I could put a name to the nature of the condition I now found myself in. I had diverted my phone at home onto the cellphone, in case the police called me. I had been out to buy some of the food Danny had told me he longed to eat when he came to the USA, and made up the guest bed for him. In fact, I realised with a shock, I was behaving like a mom.

He wasn't my kid, Ralph wasn't my husband, but in the last six weeks, ironically since that ill-fated expedition to the Lake District, I had turned into a wife and mother. I didn't leave Ralph because I wanted to run away. I left Ralph so he would run after me. I genuinely had no idea that this was the agenda of my subconscious, but I suddenly knew it was true. I loved Ralph and I loved Danny and what we were going through now was a family trauma. If there was anything to be gained from such a nightmare, it was the realisation that we were going through it together as a unit and not as individuals.

When a tuckered-out Ralph pushed his suitcase through the exit from the customs hall, I felt such a raging torrent of emotion that, most unlike me, I threw my arms round his neck. He was so exhausted after the flight and the anxiety that he barely had the strength to return my kiss, but we stood for a long moment with our arms round each other, each trying to draw strength from the other's body.

In the car on the way back to Santa Barbara he perked up, keeping one hand clenched in my free hand. I would have done anything to have taken away his pain, but his mind, like mine, was tormented with black thoughts. The cellphone shrilled.

'Hello?'

It was the cops. I could sense Ralph's desperation to listen in with me. I snapped off the phone and turned to him. 'No news. That's good.'

He was quiet for a moment, but I knew what he was thinking.

'You know he's a smart kid. He's going to be OK.'

'He's a smart kid in Cambridge. In Los Angeles he's a helpless English kid. With no gun.'

'He's got that cash. Two hundred dollars goes a long way when you're a kid.'

'If he's still got it. If he's still alive.'

'Ralph, don't. Don't torture yourself.'

'What else can I do?'

I didn't have an answer.

We turned into the driveway and I thought, sadly, how often I had wanted to come here with Ralph and show off my beautiful home. I said I'd fix him something light to eat, if he wanted to take a shower first.

I busied myself in the kitchen, breaking off to stare at the irritatingly silent phone. I called up to Ralph to tell him that dinner was fixed, but I got no answer. I walked up to the bathroom, but I couldn't hear the shower. I knocked on the door. No response. I went in. No sign of Ralph.

He was on my bed, fast asleep. He had made an attempt to get undressed, but hadn't managed it. His socks and boxer shorts were still on. Feeling like a nurse rather than a lover, I disrobed him completely and rolled him into my bed.

I don't remember doing this for any previous boyfriend. I don't remember feeling like this about any previous boyfriend. All the lyrics of all the love songs in the world suddenly seemed to make sense.

Danny

THAT FIRST NIGHT IN LOS ANGELES was the worst night I had spent since I was born. I sat on a bench that had an advert for a mortuary on the back. I knew mortuary was the American word for cemetery, because I remembered a Latin vocab test we'd done which went 'mors, mortis, feminine, death'. Then I thought about Mum and then about Dad. The tears were starting to prick at my eyes, because though I was twelve, which sounded old to me, it didn't feel very old on the streets of Hollywood.

Hollywood was a disappointing dump. I'd heard a lot about Universal Studios, but I couldn't take the tour with only twenty-five cents in my pocket. I wandered through Grauman's Chinese. I assumed it was a Chinese restaurant but then I saw lots of people behind a velvet rope looking at some footprints in cement. They belonged to some old movie stars, so I didn't find them very interesting. I hoped Disneyland was going to be better than Hollywood, but then I felt teary again because I had always planned to visit Disneyland with Dad and maybe Helen.

It was getting dark, so I started to worry about where I could spend the night. It wasn't too cold, even though it was February, but I put on my extra pullover. I walked towards where the houses started getting grander, because I thought that would make it a safer neighbourhood. I eventually settled down on another of those wooden benches. My mind was racing so I couldn't fall asleep, but I guess I managed to doze off because I didn't hear him come up to me.

I smelt a horrible, overpowering stink of BO and then I felt my shoes loosening. I struggled to sit up and found a filthy old tramp with a nasty stubbly beard trying to undo my trainers. I staggered to my feet and kicked him as hard as I could. He roared with pain like a wounded animal. I grabbed my cricket bag and didn't stop running for half an hour, when I came to a tall sign that said BEVERLY HILLS.

I felt strangely comforted, because I'd watched *Beverly Hills 90210* so it was familiar in a funny sort of way. It still didn't solve the problem of where I was going to sleep. I knew the British police weren't very nice, unless I was with Dad, so the American cops were going to be worse. I didn't want to spend any time in prison, even waiting for Dad to pick me up, because Darren Foxton told me once that you can get lost in the system and be in prison for twenty years, because nobody knows you're there.

I walked past the shops and restaurants and offices on Sunset Boulevard and turned right into a street that seemed to have some nice houses on it. By now I was really tired. I saw a long wall that looked as if it was protecting a big estate. I turned up a hill to see where the entrance was and found it was a park. It had tall iron gates but it didn't seem to be alarmed like the gates to people's houses round there.

I tossed the cricket bag over—it took me three goes to do it. Slowly I started to pull myself up. I slipped when I got to the very top and nearly impaled myself on a spike. I sort of fell down the other side, but I was inside and safe for the night. Or so I hoped.

I picked up my cricket bag and walked slowly into the park, navigating by the moon and the stars like Sir Francis Drake and the British sea dogs of the Elizabethan Age did. There was a big car park at the top of the hill, and from the edge of it I could see right across the city with its millions of lights winking back at me.

I walked down some steps and saw a rectangle of grass. I threw myself on it and stretched out. I looked in my bag and put on almost everything I'd brought. I didn't want to die in the night of that thing that old people die of in the winter when they can't afford to put the electric fire on. I had the last few triangles of the giant Toblerone bar and fell asleep under the stars. I told myself I was on a camping trip.

I woke in the morning a bit stiff but pleased to feel the warmth of the sun on my face. I had to keep reminding myself it was February and that all my friends had been off school last week with the flu. Last week! It seemed like five years ago. English homework, a physics test, football practice—it all belonged to another me.

I felt on top of the world. I had done it all myself. I had made it from Cambridge to Beverly Hills. Santa Barbara was still a hundred miles away, but somehow I'd make it there too. I was going to get to Helen's today and solve everyone's problems.

I was already delayed by a day, which meant Dad was probably starting to worry, even though I'd left that note telling him not to. I'd better
do something about that. I passed a public phone in the car park. I hit
the '0' button which said OPERATOR on it and asked if I could make a call
to England and my dad would pay for it.

'You wanna call collect?'

'I want my dad to pay on our phone bill.'

'Station to station or person to person?'

Why was this so complicated? 'I don't know.'

'You wanna talk to your dad or anyone who answers the telephone?'

'My dad.'

'That's person to person.'

'But only my dad lives there.'

'Station to station.'

Eventually I heard the lovely sound of our home phone ringing. But
Dad wasn't there. I put the phone down. I'd ring again later.

I was starving. I needed to get a bus to Santa Barbara, which probably
went from the town centre, and I needed something to eat. I walked
back to Sunset Boulevard and looked at the front of a bus to see where it
was going to. It didn't say bus station or railway station or something
useful like that. It just said 6th and Figueroa.

I watched as people got on and off. They got on at the front but they
got off in the middle of the bus where the doors opened with a whoosh.
I had no money, apart from that twenty-five cents, so I couldn't pay. But
I knew what I had to do. As soon as the next bus arrived and the doors
opened, I crawled onto it through the legs of the people who were getting off. I counted on the fact that nobody likes drawing attention to
themselves on public transport, and if the driver was busy taking fares
up front he wouldn't be able to see me crawling into the back of the bus.

It worked perfectly. I soon discovered that everyone who went on the
bus in Los Angeles wore the same dazed expression. Schoolkids got on
separate yellow school buses (I knew that from watching *The Simpsons*),
and most people in America seemed to have a car, so the buses were
occupied only by poor people and they obviously couldn't be arsed to
turn me over to the cops.

I got out when we got to what looked like the centre of town and
looked around for a newsagent's where I could spend my last twenty-
five cents on something and ask for directions to the bus station. I was
really annoyed to discover that America doesn't have newsagents. The
newspapers are all in a plastic-fronted bin that lifts up if you put the
right coins into a slot.

I walked slowly down the street until I saw a 7-11. I felt a little stab of recognition. We've got 7-11 shops in England. I wandered in and was quickly appalled at the prices. It was a dollar for a can of Coke, which I can get for thirty-seven pence in Cambridge. Twenty-five cents was going to get me nowhere.

I was going to have to continue my life of crime. I asked for directions to the bus station and got a torrent of Mexican or something back at me. I wandered to the back of the store and took a Pepsi Max out of the cold fridge thing and a cake called a Tootsie Roll, which I slipped into my pocket when I was pretty sure the man at the front couldn't see me.

I made certain I left the shop with a couple of other people so I wouldn't even be visible. I decided to walk on for a bit before I unwrapped the cake and drank the Pepsi Max, but I hadn't gone more than twenty yards when I heard a shout behind me and saw the guy from the 7-11 shop racing towards me.

I turned and ran across the road and down an alleyway. I might have dodged him for a bit longer, but I was weighed down by my cricket bag. The man flung himself on me and I fell to the ground. I felt cold steel pressed hard into my cheek. This maniac had taken the safety catch off his gun and he was going to kill me! For a Tootsie Roll and a Pepsi Max!

My right arm was forced up my back which was really painful. I cried out. I was so afraid I thought I was going to wet myself. The man took the drink and the cake and smacked me half a dozen times around the face really hard. Then he started kicking me. I pleaded with him to stop, but he didn't till I was fainting. Then he picked up the gun and left me in the gutter.

The odd thing was I didn't cry. I was so in shock it seemed to freeze all the tears inside me. It took me nearly an hour sitting there on the ground, cradling the cricket bag to me, before I felt I could get to my feet. I hobbled away, still looking for the bus station, but I had lost all that confidence I had had in the morning.

When I got to the bus station, I sat slumped on a seat watching people getting on the buses. It wasn't like the morning. They had all bought tickets at the ticket office and the side doors didn't open at all. The bus driver tore the ticket as passengers got on the bus. There was no way of getting onto the bus without a ticket. Maybe it was time I just gave up.

I found a public phone and asked for a collect call home. The phone rang and rang. I got very frightened again. It was the middle of the night in England. Dad's always in the house at night. Where was he? I was seized by panic. Something must have happened to Dad. In trying to find me, something had happened. My head was filled with sudden flashing thoughts of how wonderful Dad was and how the last night I was home we'd had that terrible row. Was that the last time I was ever going to see him? All I wanted to do in the whole world was to be with Dad again.

Ralph

I COULDN'T BELIEVE how uninterested the Santa Barbara police were in Danny's disappearance. The last sighting of him was in Los Angeles, therefore it was no use complaining to them—'Sorry, guv'nor, not my patch.'

Helen kept shooting me warning glances, but it was difficult for me to restrain my impatience. I was usually calm, pragmatic. Not today. Not with my son's safety at stake.

It was Helen who persuaded them to post Danny's description on the NCIS computer, which transmitted it to every law enforcement agency in the land. The fact that he was twelve years old was the only thing that motivated them. There was growing concern in California that paedophiles were an increasing threat to children. So what were they going to do about it?

'We'll check all the hospitals, mental hospitals and morgues.'

'That's it?'

'That's all we're permitted to do, sir.'

'What about us? Can't we do something?'

'You can contact the FBI. There are field offices in most major cities.'

'And how long is all this supposed to take?'

'That's impossible to tell. If he went missing in LA it's not good news. Kids disappear all the time. It's an awful big city.'

'Well, next time I'll tell him to disappear round the back of your police station. Or would that be an inconvenience too?'

All right, I said the wrong thing, but I was miserable, out of my mind with fear, and to make it worse I had slept badly. I woke up in the middle of the night, which was about ten o'clock in the morning in England, and couldn't stop worrying about Danny. This was his second night on American soil and no one had any idea where he was. I decided to have breakfast and let my body find its own way of adjusting to the time difference.

I crept downstairs, anxious not to wake Helen. I opened the fridge and took out milk and a packet of granola, and poured them into a bowl.

'I heard a noise. I thought it might be Danny.'

Helen was standing there.

I stood up and kissed her, feeling a swirl of confusing emotions—fear for Danny's plight, lust for Helen. The feel of her body was like opening the front door after a holiday. It was warm and comfortable and familiar and I belonged there. She took my hand and led me back to her bedroom.

As she pulled me down onto the bed with her I suddenly realised that I hadn't showered since I had arrived. I pulled away from her, and in the bathroom I let the jet of hot water wash away my tiredness and tried hard to gather my optimism for the ordeal of looking for Danny. Eventually, I stepped out of the shower, feeling at least a whole lot better prepared for whatever was now to ensue in her bedroom. The one thing I didn't expect, when I finally made my appearance, was that my intended paramour should herself be *hors de combat*.

My initial response was of a disappointed bride on her wedding night, but before we progressed too far down this sitcom road I realised that it was a quarter past three in the morning. I snuggled under the sheets and felt her wonderful naked body sliding over to wrap itself unconsciously around mine.

In the morning the Santa Barbara police called round and said they would tell their officers about Danny and make sure the California Highway Patrol was kept informed in case he was wandering along the Ventura Freeway. Then they replaced their sunglasses and drove off in the glare of the California sunshine.

'Thanks for nothing,' I said, as Helen closed her front door.

'You didn't help yourself or Danny just now.'

'Well, they were so bloody unhelpful.'

'So were you.'

'So what was I supposed to have said?'

She paused. 'I did tell you. If he had a gun . . .'

'I'm sorry, I failed as a father. He hasn't got his own Kalashnikov.'

'Too bad. What were you waiting for?'

'His thirteenth birthday.' I must have looked thoroughly miserable.

'Would you like some tea?'

I smiled. 'I'd love a cup of tea. Thank you.'

I watched in awe as she filled two mugs with cold water from a bottle which she kept in the fridge, then dropped a tea bag into each of the mugs. She opened the microwave door, slid the two mugs inside, slammed the door shut and set the controls for three minutes on full power.

'Listen, I've got a plan.'

'Does it involve the microwave? Or tea bags?' I asked carefully.

'No.'

'Great. What is it?'

She told me that whatever the cops did, LAPD or FBI, would take for ever unless we were incredibly lucky. By for ever she meant months, depending on what sort of a hole Danny had got himself into. We could shorten the process. She had an idea.

One of the news magazines the parent company owned was a new American version of a photo magazine. A year ago one of the best journalists she knew, Conor O'Neil, had done an award-winning feature on the lost kids of Los Angeles. Even though it was unlikely Danny was caught up in that underworld, it was worth checking out.

It sounded like a lead of sorts, and at least we'd be doing something practical, which was a whole lot better than sitting at home and waiting for the cops not to ring. At that exact moment the microwave bell sounded.

'Tea?'

'Thank you, Vicar,' I said, fishing the tea bag out of the cup with my fingers. 'Milk?'

'Only that non-fat stuff you hate.'

'Sugar?'

'Are you kidding? I got some Sweet and Low somewhere.'

I emptied the tea surreptitiously into the sink. She came back into the room waving a packet of sweetener.

'I was so thirsty,' I explained, rinsing the cup quickly.

'OK. You ready?'

Helen

DOING SOMETHING OURSELVES had to be the best way for us as well as Danny. Conor was an inspired idea, though I say it myself. She came into the corporate building in the Miracle Mile district of LA on Wilshire and caused Ralph's next major surprise. For some reason he had assumed that Conor was a man, so when she turned out to be a woman, nearly six feet tall with wild red hair, he found it difficult to articulate his thoughts for a few minutes.

Fortunately he didn't need to because Conor and I did most of the talking. I had shown Ralph the brilliant series of articles she had written about the seamy underside of Los Angeles and its disappearing kids, which was complemented by some of the most poignant, searing photographs you are ever likely to see. Conor thinks it's getting to be like Rio de Janeiro in Los Angeles, but the authorities won't do anything about it because the kids are invariably from poor ethnic minorities. There's no political capital to be made out of it, so the problem is allowed to get worse.

'You think Danny might be mixed up in this?'

Conor shook her head. 'White middle-class kid? Dangerous. Bound to be someone looking for him.'

'So where do you think he is?'

'Sleeping rough, begging . . . could be a lot of places.'

'He had two hundred dollars with him.'

'Not now.'

'How do you know?'

'If he's not gotten in touch with you guys, he's not got the two hundred bucks.'

She was right. It made total sense. I had work to do, so I waited in the office while Conor and Ralph drove into South Central. Two was company but three was a crowd of nosy white folks. I worked as best I could until late in the evening, when Ralph returned alone looking very depressed. They had spent six hours fruitlessly searching the streets, going into stores, following Conor's route round the homeless shelters of Los Angeles. Nobody had seen Danny. Nobody knew anything or cared at all.

I tried to explain to Ralph that he couldn't expect to succeed so quickly; that would have been quite unrealistic. He was in need of some tender loving care. He had arranged to meet Conor again at six thirty in the morning, to continue looking, so we had to stay in town overnight. I drove him to the Beverly Wilshire, which was the nearest luxury hotel, but as the valet parking guy came out to open my door, Ralph suddenly grabbed my arm.

'No. Not here!'

'What? Why not? It's a great hotel.'

'I can't. I stayed here with Angela.'

I understood instantly and jammed my foot down on the gas pedal, screaming away from the place like an armed robber. The valet parking guy leapt into the air in surprise. If Ralph still had demons about Angela, this sure as hell was not the time to confront them.

We checked into a room at a small hotel in West Hollywood. It was intimate and friendly, and about as far away from the anonymity of the big Beverly Hills hotels as you could get. It was the right choice. Ralph came out of the shower to find the bed turned down and a steak and salad waiting on the table, courtesy of room service.

'Thank you.'

'You haven't tasted it. It might be crap.'

'Thank you for loving me.'

I turned my face towards him and he kissed me. He held me and I could feel the pain of Danny's disappearance almost coursing through his body. He looked at the meal in front of him and stood there indecisively.

'What do you want? A written invitation?'

'I know it sounds crazy, but I can't eat. I can't eat when Danny might be in a gutter somewhere, starving.'

'This is like the conversation you have with kids when they won't finish what's on their plate and you tell them there's millions of kids starving in Africa. So they say, "Send it to them."'

'OK. I'll eat if you eat.'

'Sure I'll eat. I'm starving.'

He sat down opposite me in the white towelling robe the hotel provides. Maybe it was all due to the artificially charged nature of the situation but I couldn't take my eyes off him as he tentatively dragged the steak knife across the grain of the filet mignon.

'Ralph, I'm sorry I ran out on you like that. I know that's what started this whole mess.'

'It's not your fault. Why are you blaming yourself?'

'If I'd stayed, tried to make a go of it, Danny wouldn't be out here now.'

'It's nobody's fault, certainly not yours.'

'I don't think I realised how much I loved you till the plane left the ground.'

He laid the knife and fork down. 'I couldn't believe I could love someone again. I just thought you didn't love me back.'

I pushed back the chair and sat on his lap, kissing him passionately. He picked me up and carried me over to the bed.

'This is all very macho. What did you put on that salad?'

'I just want to introduce you to an old friend.'

We fell asleep in each other's arms as the filet mignon coagulated on the plate.

Danny

WHEN I PUT the phone down in the bus station I just didn't know what to do next. I looked back to where I'd been sitting near the Santa Barbara bus and I saw my place had been taken by another kid, a bit younger than me maybe, about nine or ten. He looked like he hadn't stopped crying for hours. I went and sat next to him. I tried to cheer him up the way they always start on those American talk shows.

'Hi! I'm Danny Warren from England.'

He just stared into the distance.

'Where are you from?'

He took a dirty, scrunched-up note out of his pocket and handed it to me. I can't remember the exact words but it was a letter 'to whom it may concern'. It was written by his stepmother, who said she couldn't cope with him any longer because the boy's father was dying of AIDS. They were heading to Mexico so he could die by the seaside. They couldn't look after themselves, let alone the boy, who had never been to school. His real mother had died soon after he was born and the family had lived all the time in shelters and eaten in soup kitchens. Stuck to the back of the note was his birth certificate. His name was Paul.

I handed it back to him. I didn't know what to say so I said the first thing that came into my head.

'Have you really never been to school?' I couldn't imagine what it would be like to never go to school. I've known boys who were ill or something and they missed a term, but I couldn't understand how a boy could just never go to school. I mean, I know there's lots of kids who live on those sink estates and everyone's unemployed and they spend their days mooching about town, but even they've been to school.

Paul was still staring dead ahead, but he was speaking. 'You eat today?'

I shook my head.

Now he turned and looked at me. 'I found a place last night.'

He got up and walked past me. I supposed he meant me to follow him, so I picked up my cricket bag and did.

I walked behind him a few paces; I wasn't sure where we were going so I wanted to be free to run away, but I was so knackered and hungry I didn't have the strength to run anywhere. We walked for about half an hour into an area where there were no white faces apart from ours. I guess this is what it must feel like to be black in Cambridge, but I'd never really thought about it till now. They weren't just black, they were mostly Mexican or Orientals. I was starting to feel that someone could jump on me any moment.

I was so relieved when we turned into a church. We went down into the basement where there was a trestle table and a big tureen, and a large black woman was ladling out some kind of soup into paper cups.

Nobody was talking in the room. There must have been thirty or forty people there. I think some of them must have slept there, because it was smelly the way a bedroom is when you get up in the morning. In the toilets off to one side I could see a mother giving her little girl a wash with a paper towel, but instead of throwing the towel away, she folded it up and put it into a plastic bag.

We took our soup outside. It was a kind of lukewarm minestrone. It was horrible, but I drank every drop. I could feel it settling in my tummy. Two other kids about ten years old came outside too. One of them had disgusting brown-looking teeth. Neither of them spoke either. Everyone looked tired, worn down by life. I suppose I must have looked like everyone else.

A young black man came up to us. He must have been about eighteen or nineteen. His hair was in dreadlocks. He was holding out a bottle of something.

'You guys want some toncho?'

Paul grabbed the bottle and swallowed like a cowboy in a saloon in the Wild West. He passed it to me. I wiped the top with my sleeve and did the same. My throat nearly burned off. A smell a bit like petrol fumes went up my nose and I began to choke and pant for air. At least it made me not feel hungry any more.

'You wanna go to the movies?' The black guy looked at both of us. I looked at my 'friend'.

'Sure,' I said. 'What's on?'

The black guy laughed. 'Say, that's good. Where you from?'

'I'm from England.'

'England, huh? Jolly good, old chap.' He spoke in a voice which I guessed was his idea of an English accent. 'You come to the movies?'

'I haven't got any money.'

'You get money at the movies.'

I stood up. This seemed like the best offer I'd had for quite a while. Paul had resumed his blank look, just staring off into space.

'Just call me Batman. Everyone does.'

'I'm Danny.'

'Hey, Danny, my man, you want something to eat first?'

'I'd love something to eat. All I've had for ages is that soup and a bar of Toblerone.'

Further down the street was a small café. There was a counter where you ordered and a ledge thing where you stood up and ate it. Batman said, 'Two hot dogs.'

It was a horrid greasy place, but I loved the smell of frying meat. The man picked out a hot dog from a boiling vat of them and stuck it into a pre-sliced bun and handed it over. I nearly choked I was so hungry. I wanted to ask for a Coke or a Fanta, but I didn't have the courage.

Batman was being really nice to me and I remembered how Dad always said that Americans were so hospitable. I wondered why Paul hadn't wanted to come to the movies but maybe it was a '15' and he was too young to get in.

'What film are we going to?'

'We're gonna see porno,' said Batman, as we resumed walking the streets of Los Angeles. My heart fluttered. This was cool, this was something to tell the guys about when I got back. I knew I shouldn't, but my street cred would climb about a thousand per cent.

It wasn't a multiplex like I expected. It was a sleazy little place with a poster of two men with moustaches and wearing nothing but thongs. I knew instantly what was going on now. I wasn't interested in this.

'Batman, I don't . . .'

And that was as far as I got. Batman put down fifteen dollars and pushed us through a turnstile like at White Hart Lane. I really, *really* wished I was back in England watching football now.

Batman pushed me up against a wall. 'Listen, kid, you go in there and you sit down. Someone will come and sit next to you. You just do whatever he asks and he'll give you money. Ask for twenty bucks first, OK? *Before* he does anything. You give me all the money and I'll give you twenty-five bucks. OK?' He snatched my bag. 'I'll be here when you come out.'

I felt like I was drowning, the water closing over my head and I couldn't breathe. Batman pushed me through the swing door and I went into the cinema. It wasn't a cinema. It was just a large room with a small screen and a fuzzy picture. I couldn't make out what was up there on the screen for a good five seconds. I looked around but I could hardly see anything because my eyes hadn't got used to the darkness. I groped my way to the first empty seat and almost fell into it. On the screen I finally realised what one man was doing to another. I felt sick again. I closed my eyes and tried to think about things that made me happy, Spurs beating Arsenal, eating pizza and watching TV with Dad at home . . .

A fat man sat down in the seat next to me. I kept my eyes screwed tightly shut. He was breathing heavily. His breath was smelly. In my mind I was trying to remember who Spurs were playing this Saturday. I had a vague memory that they were away to Middlesbrough. I felt the man's hand slide onto my thigh. I grabbed it and pushed it away. He silently put a piece of paper in between my fingers. It felt like money. He tried to unzip my fly.

'Don't!'

'C'mere, kid!' He grabbed my hand and tried to force it down into his lap. It brushed against something firm and warm. I didn't want to think what that might be.

I managed to slip my hand out of his grasp and stumble blindly towards the exit. The man made to come after me but then he must have found the money, which I'd left on the seat, and didn't bother.

I ran into the lobby and went out into the open air which felt pure and refreshing after the stinking atmosphere inside the porno house. I saw Batman standing by the traffic lights about fifty yards away. My bag was at his feet and he was talking on a mobile phone.

I started running as hard as I could. I had to leave my cricket bag behind and I was pretty angry about that. I felt weird. Glad to be out of that horrible porn cinema, out of Batman's clutches, but I still had no money, nowhere to stay, no way of finding Dad, no way of getting to Helen's, and I was starting to get hungry again. I realised I'd become a street kid, like the ones you see on the news. I remembered with a growing sense of panic a story that Dad read out to me from a newspaper about these kids who lived wild on the streets of somewhere in Brazil. They didn't grow up to be Ronaldo. They didn't grow up at all.

Ralph

AT THE END of the second day of searching, the third day since Danny went missing, a black cloud of despair descended on me. Despite Conor's help and Helen's hope, I felt utterly weary, ground down in spirit as much as energy.

I thought of all the times I'd had with Danny since the day he was born, when I parked the car in Hampstead and sauntered into the Royal Free Hospital to see his little head sticking out. I thought of his solemn little face when I lifted him out of his cot in his grandma's house and told him, with tears running down my face, that his mummy wasn't coming home and from that moment on it was just him and me against the world. I remembered rolling up my shirtsleeve and testing the temperature of his bath water with my elbow, seeing his face crack open into a wide smile as I flicked droplets of water onto him, lifting him up and wrapping him up in the bath towel like a big parcel. I could savour the talcum powder and the soft sweet odour of the top of his head, the feel of his silky thin hair. I could see him sitting up in bed at the end of his favourite stories, throwing out his arms wide for a good-night hug and kiss.

They were safe, these memories. But reality intruded all the time. I asked Conor for details and she gave them to me starkly. Street kids were twice as likely to be murdered, three times as likely to commit suicide. I couldn't get my head round this. Danny was only really allowed out in the daytime at weekends or during the school holidays. Otherwise I pretty much knew where he was every second of the day. The idea that a child might be murdered obviously, at some point, touches every parent, but my perception was that this sort of thing happened to other people's kids.

Those first two or three days, Conor must have driven me under every bridge and freeway overpass in Greater Los Angeles. Under most of them there was a village of homeless people, some with kids, some without. One place under the Harbor Freeway seemed as if it was only for kids. They were all visibly malnourished. I couldn't bear to think of Danny in that condition.

It was around six o'clock, it was dark and the occasional BMW or Porsche would pull off the road and flash its headlights. Two or three kids would rush over, the driver's window would glide down electronically and one of the kids would scramble into the car with the driver. A few minutes later the kid would get out again and the others would crowd round to see how much money he'd made. Was this what Danny had been reduced to?

Conor answered all my questions with predictable honesty, but frankly I only had to spend a couple of hours with these people to feel the hopelessness and the sense of despair.

'How much do they make, these kids?'

'Twenty bucks for a hand job, anything up to forty for oral.'

'What do they spend the money on?'

'High top basketball shoes.'

'You're kidding!'

'The ones with families go home and give it to their mothers.'

'Their mothers know?'

She didn't answer. She didn't need to.

'If they haven't got families?'

'Burger King. Toncho.'

'Toncho? What's that?'

'A kind of high-octane booster. Rot gut. Like a combination of nail varnish and gasoline. It staves off hunger and gets them good and crazy.'

'Jesus! Anything else?'

'The usual.'

'Drugs?'

She nodded. 'If their parents ever were together, the chances are the father's inside and the mother's on heroin or crack cocaine.'

We walked downstairs into a church basement which served as a soup kitchen. It was strangely quiet. The faces were worn, tired, blank, reflecting the turmoil they must have been feeling inside.

There were kids here as young as three or four. One kid, he was maybe five or six, he'd been given a pair of battered old Barney the Dinosaur slippers. His mother lay in a stupor on the floor. The boy was proudly putting on the slippers, which had presumably come out of some charity sack. He went over to his mother and said, 'Mom, are these new?'

It was ridiculous. They were scarcely wearable, but to the little boy, who had probably never had anything new in his whole life, it was very important. His mother didn't answer, so he said out loud to himself, 'They are. These are new.'

I couldn't bear it. I strolled towards him.

'Hey! Neat slippers. Are they new?'

The look the kid gave me nearly broke my heart. I hurried back to Conor. 'I want to do something.'

She shrugged her shoulders. What was I going to do? Solve the whole homeless kids issue with a twenty-dollar bill? I saw what she meant. If I gave the kid twenty bucks then I'd have to do something for everyone else.

I got back in the car and asked Conor to drive to the nearest Winchell's Donuts, where I spent fifty dollars on five big boxes of donuts. Conor drove back to the church, where I left the donuts on the trestle table next to the soup tureen. Maybe Danny would wander in there and there'd be one or two left for him.

Danny

AFTER I'D RUN about a mile I thought I was safe from Batman. I was utterly knackered. I saw a little park across the road and ran into it. I threw myself down on the ground and tried to think as calmly as my racing heart would let me.

I had to find some sort of job to earn the money that I needed for the bus ticket to Santa Barbara. I needed it quickly, but not quick enough to risk my life going with strange men in porn cinemas. I thought of all the Saturday jobs kids did in England—a lot of my friends had older brothers and sisters who did jobs on Saturdays in shops.

I couldn't do a girlie sort of a job like being an assistant in a clothes shop, but I could work in a restaurant. That put it into my head that I could maybe work in a café sort of a place near the bus station, and get tips and a wage.

If there was a sort of café that had tables and waiters, a café that served things like bacon, egg and chips, that would be say four or five dollars a meal so I might get a tip of fifty cents. So if I carried a hundred plates in a day I could earn nearly the full amount in tips and then there would be the day's wage.

I found a café. It didn't serve egg, bacon, sausage and chips, but horrible hamburgers. I mean really horrible smelly things. The whole place smelt. They served hash browns and pancakes, but they were all cooked on the same hot plate in the same grease and it stank.

So did the man who owned it. He had a Chinese name and I didn't understand what he said half the time. I had to clear the plates away and take them into the kitchen, where it was a hundred degrees. The tips weren't fifty cents or a dollar, but a quarter and often nothing at all.

When they did leave a tip, I scooped up the quarter or the dimes and stuck them down my sock. It made walking hard, but I thought it would be safe. At the end of the day I'd only made about twelve dollars and the man wouldn't give me my wages till the end of the week. I couldn't stay a whole week there. I'd die first. The man shouted at me because I didn't know how to do things. And he also hit people.

It wasn't a clip round the back of the head like you sometimes get from the bigger kids at school. It was a punch in the shoulder as you were carrying a hot plate or a smack across the side of the face. I wasn't going to give him the satisfaction of watching me cry, but I wasn't staying there a minute longer than I had to. At least he allowed me to eat there and I wolfed down a hamburger, which smelt bad but tasted good.

I had to spend the night somewhere. I managed to find some old cardboard boxes at the end of the alleyway that ran behind the café. When the man went home and locked up, I started to construct a little tent out of them. I fell asleep almost as soon as I lay down on the bed that I'd made out of flattened boxes. I'd stolen some towels from the café, which I used as a blanket.

It was the middle of the night when I heard the sound of a police siren getting nearer. I heard shouting and running feet, then the car headlights shone on me and I got up in a blind panic. I knew that the cops were no friends of the homeless and I was terrified.

I scuttled over to where the alleyway was still in darkness, and jammed myself against the wall. When the cops went screaming past me, I started walking quickly the other way. I hung around the streets for an hour or so until I thought it might be safe to go back. When I got to the alleyway again I found my tent had been demolished.

It was starting to rain. I tramped the streets again looking for a doorway to shelter in. Eventually I found one and slumped to the ground. I stretched out on the cold tiles and was in a world that wasn't quite asleep and wasn't quite awake, when I felt a violent pain in my side. I was being given a good kicking by an old tramp.

'This is mine, you fucking thief!' he kept shouting. I staggered to my feet and ran off. I didn't care which doorway I slept in. I just wanted to sleep.

I was woken at eight in the morning when the shopkeeper came to open up. I scooted off. It took me another half an hour to find the café. Kicked from pillar to post I'd totally lost my sense of direction.

The owner shouted at me that I was late. I tried to say it was illegal to work kids so hard for so many hours, but as soon as he heard the word illegal he clouted me across the face, so I stopped. I could have walked out but I was so near to the money I needed I thought it was better to stick with the devil I knew. And he was a devil.

By the second day I was almost getting used to it. The worst sort of day I'd had at school—waiting for punishment, getting sent off in the school match—did not come even close to what I was going through now. It all seemed so petty compared with trying to find something to eat, somewhere to sleep. Just staying alive took all my concentration. Who could learn Latin vocabulary if his whole mind was taken up by just surviving?

Just before we closed at the end of my third day there, I'd collected $27.30 in tips. Then the man saw me scoop three dollars from a table. He screamed at me that the money was his. I shouted back and said it wasn't, it was mine, but he wouldn't listen and he hit me again and dragged me over to the cash register. I went mental. If he stole my tips from me I'd never get to Santa Barbara. I'd be a prisoner here for the rest of my life.

As he snatched the three dollars from my left hand, I thrust my right hand into the open cash drawer and grabbed whatever I could and fled. He bellowed at me. And I went all round the block with him racing after me screaming in Mexican or Japanese or whatever it was he spoke, but he wasn't as nimble as I was. It was a great feeling and I had all that money in my pocket. I counted it. Eighty-seven dollars. It was enough to get me onto the Santa Barbara bus!

Helen

ALTHOUGH RALPH and I started off by becoming real intimate, as time slipped by and we got no closer to discovering anything about Danny, I began to feel Danny was destroying us by his absence as surely as he had with his presence. I was coming to the sickening realisation that I would not be able to get Ralph through this tragedy, if that's what it turned out to be. I had no intention of abandoning Ralph, but the Danny trauma was starting to weigh down our relationship. He couldn't give himself to me, he didn't want anything from me, he was just totally obsessed by what had happened to Danny.

I didn't blame him. I fully supported him. How could I not? I loved him. But, as the days went by, I was dreading the call that I knew must surely come.

On the third day it happened. A body had been discovered. Could Ralph come down to the morgue and identify it? I called Conor in the car. Ralph was buying lunch in a McDonald's. Conor said she'd break it to Ralph and they'd meet me down at the city morgue.

I squeezed Ralph's hand tightly as they pulled the drawer out and zipped open the body bag. Ralph stepped forward. He stared for the longest time as if he couldn't recognise his own son any longer. I moved forward too. It wasn't Danny. We went back outside.

It was a bleak LA February afternoon and I shivered. Ralph put his arm round my shoulder and pressed his face to mine.

'What were you thinking of back there?' I asked him.

'I was thinking of his parents. How long had they been looking for him?'

'You know, Ralph, this could go on for quite a while.'

'I don't care how long it takes. I'm going to find him.'

Our lives were full of such conversations. I felt so helpless.

The following afternoon the phone on my desk rang. I heard a strange excited voice down the phone. I wasn't at all sure who it was. Eventually it became clear it was Ralph. He was yelling,. 'We've found him!'

'You have! Oh my God, that's amazing! I mean, like how——?'

'Well, we haven't got him with us exactly.'

'What have you got exactly?'

'You know that picture of the two of us you took at the top of Bowfell? We've been showing it around and some Chinese bloke went ballistic when he saw it. He said Danny robbed him. He's alive, for Christ's sake.'

'Thank God! It's just great. And pretty amazing considering the way you trained that kid to be so polite in other people's houses . . .'

'Yeah, well, I don't think I was anticipating him having to survive on the streets of South Central Los Angeles. Helen, can't you see, he's alive, I'm so happy!'.

'And I'm just so happy for you. For both of us. Now, what do you want to do?'

'I want to hang around here for a bit. Keep showing the photograph. Find out where he's gone.'

He handed the cellphone back to Conor, who said it was best if they waited now till night because a whole new bunch of weirdos come out when the neon lights come on. She would take Ralph back to crash out at her place. We agreed I should go back to Santa Barbara and see if Danny showed up there. In any case, my brother Michael was coming to stay the night before taking a flight to Nairobi the next day.

Meanwhile, of course, there had been no word from the uniformed upholders of the law. Now that Danny was more of a reality, I decided to take matters into my own hands and I summoned every available resource. Every radio and television station was told and every researcher and runner, however minimally connected to Waverley Bros Inc on the West Coast, was conscripted to aid in the search. This was going to be a hell of a story. This way I squared my appropriation of other people's resources with the greater good of Waverley Bros Inc.

I drove back to Santa Barbara. When I got home the message light was flashing on the machine. None of the six calls was the one I wanted. I wondered whether Danny had copied down both my address and phone number—he could always have placed a collect call. Unfortunately my number was unlisted, so calling Information wasn't going to help.

The pasta was boiling away on the stove when the phone did ring. I grabbed it, my heart pounding, only to hear the familiar voice of my brother, Michael. I drove over to the airport in Goleta to pick him up.

I was delighted that he was here. We don't get to see each other too often these days and we had much to catch up on. Michael works for the United Nations and is always on a plane or just getting off a plane or just boarding a plane. Growing up he was a royal pain in the ass, hogging the TV, taking Mom's car to football practice when I wanted it to go to the movies, but we have always been close, could always rely on each other for support since we left home. He's separated from his wife but married to his job, being capable of giving of himself to the underprivileged peoples of East Africa but not to his wife.

Michael polished off two helpings of pasta and arrabiata sauce, while I poured a glass of white wine and told him all about Ralph and Danny. He regarded the saga with amused tolerance. I don't think it is biologically possible for brothers and sisters to take their siblings' love affairs too seriously. On the other hand his face went all grave when I told him Danny was missing. Funnily enough, his attitude to Ralph changed as well. Ralph as a boyfriend was an object of gentle fun; Ralph as the father of a twelve-year-old, middle-class British kid missing on the streets of Los Angeles was another guy completely.

By the time I had poured out my heart to Michael, I knew that the emotion I had been feeling about Danny was true. I had become that little boy's mom. I hadn't asked to be. I had flown 6,000 miles back home to avoid it, but somehow what had happened this week only confirmed that I was being drawn ever deeper into a situation in which I appeared to have lost my own free will. Michael was moved by my confession, and came and put his arms round me, holding me, not saying anything. I felt his strength, hoping it might somehow pass into me by osmosis and fortify me for the terrifying things which I suspected were still lying ahead.

The phone rang and I raced for it. It wasn't Danny, of course, it was Ralph, a bit depressed. After the wonderful, miraculous discovery that Danny was alive and thieving, the trail had gone completely cold. I tried hard to lift his spirits, reassured him that at least Danny now had money to look after himself with, and reminded him that Conor was a supremely gifted investigative journalist. We kissed each other good night down the phone.

Michael was catching an early connecting flight to LA, so he had called the local cab company for a taxi to pick him up in the morning. I'm a pretty light sleeper at the best of times, but, weighed down by the current anxieties, there was no way I was going to sleep through Michael's attempts to get out of the house without waking me. For a start, he failed to get to the front door before the chimes rang.

I glanced out of the window and saw the cab driver sauntering back to the taxi, smoking a cigarette. I was shocked. I hadn't seen a cigarette in California since the late 1980s.

I flew out of the house, gathering my robe around me. The driver smiled as he saw this slightly demented female in a state of undress hurling herself on a man who was being driven to the airport. I knew he had got hold of the wrong end of the stick, but I had no desire to set him straight. I hugged and kissed Michael, unwilling to let him go.

Michael searched for the right note of sincerity. 'I'll stay if you'd like.'

'OK.'

'No, I mean it.'

'I know. That's why I said OK.'

'Well, you'll have to let go of me so I can call the government of Kenya and tell them to put the famine on hold for a while.'

'Go on. Get outta here. I was just playing my sisterly role to perfection.'

'That's what I thought.'

'Then why are you sweating like a stuck hog?'

'Am I?'

I laughed. I didn't want him to say anything else. The knowledge that he truly cared for me was all that I really needed from him.

Danny

WHEN I SAW HELEN kissing that man, my whole world collapsed. And now I felt like a total spas. Everything I had gone through had been a waste of time. She didn't love Dad. She loved this guy getting into a taxi. Why else would she be kissing him wearing a nightie and nothing else? Why would she kiss someone in public unless she loved him? Maybe he was her husband. Did Dad know all this and not tell me?

I thought and thought so hard, my head started to hurt. What had I done? I hated it when Dad interfered in my life, when he went to see my teacher when I was at primary school and complained about Luke Josephs bullying me. I told him about it because he was my dad. I didn't expect him to go and solve anything. He just made things worse. I swore to myself that I'd never do anything like that to my children. So I did it to Dad instead.

I felt so confused. I never wanted Helen to be my mum, not even when I was trying to get her back together with Dad. Nobody could ever replace my mum, and I didn't want Helen to try. But the reason I think I sort of liked her was that she didn't try. And I know I didn't behave too well before, when I thought she might have been moving in on Dad and me, but the weird thing is, over the past week or so, when I had become so uptight about getting to Helen's house, I was looking forward to her coming to live with us and making us into a real family.

Helen wouldn't be a mum like Darren Foxton's mum. She's got an important job and she'd be travelling a lot, which would be cool because she'd bring back lots of presents, and when she wasn't at home it would just be me and Dad as usual. So that's why I was telling myself, all the way over on the plane and then in Los Angeles and then on the bus to Santa Barbara, that if Helen and Dad got back together again, it would be so worth all the aggro. And I did think maybe she could explain to me why I felt so strange when she kissed me good night that time. She could be like a grown-up sister to me, but someone who would make Dad happy.

But now she was off with some other guy. I felt like she had stabbed me in the gut with a kitchen knife and then twisted it about. I was fifty yards or so away down the hill and behind a parked car. I ducked down as the taxi came past where I was. I didn't want her to see me. I didn't know if she'd pretend that there wasn't a man, but I did know she wouldn't be happy if she knew I'd seen her with that guy. And I knew she'd never come back to Dad now.

I sat on the pavement and cried. I cried more than I'd cried for days. There was no point in staying around to go and see Helen now. I started to wander back down the hill. At home I used to hate walking to school or back home after school when Dad wasn't there to collect me. I was used to walking long distances now. I would never have believed how far I had walked these last few days. It must have been miles and miles. I'd be dead fit for the rest of the football season. And then I started to think about playing football with my friends and the tears started to prick at my eyes. I was just crying all the time.

I had two banknotes worth twenty dollars each, three one-dollar notes and a handful of change left from the money I took, because I had got a child's fare bus ticket from Los Angeles to Santa Barbara. I didn't steal it. It was mine. The man lied to me, robbed me, hit me, cheated me, so I had no guilty feelings about taking the money. Besides, it was in a good cause—the best possible cause. If he hadn't been so horrible I'd have asked Dad to pay him back.

Where was my dad now? Going off his nut with worry, I guessed as I walked back towards the bus stop where I'd got off. When I reached the main road I found a payphone. I rang home, but there was no reply. I wanted to see him so badly, just to hug him and say, 'Oh, Daddy, I'm so sorry. I'll never do anything like this again.'

I caught the bus from Montecito to Santa Barbara. I kept trying to think about what I could do next, but I was now really, really tired. I hadn't slept properly for days and days. Dad might have already arrived and be looking for me somewhere. But where? Where would he go that he knew I would go too?

I got off the bus at the station and sat on a bench. It wasn't as bad as Los Angeles. Santa Barbara seemed safe and clean in comparison, and the sky was blue and the sun was warm. I thought this was what it must have been like for Dad and Mum when they were on their holiday in California. I thought about the pictures of Mum in our house back home, especially the one I liked so much, lying on the sun lounger. She'd have liked today's weather.

The tears were coming again. I couldn't stop them. I had never cried like this before. I felt so alone and I wanted my dad and my mum. My mum would know where Dad was because they loved each other so much, and she would help me, too, because though she was dead I knew her spirit watched over me, like Dad always said. I didn't have a hankie or anything, so I just wiped my nose on the back of my hand and rubbed my eyes furiously.

I got up and walked towards the exit, where there was a travel agency or ticket office or something. It had lots of posters in the window. I recognised the Golden Gate Bridge. There was a picture of a lake which said Lake Tahoe and a big Disneyland-type castle at San Simeon called Hearst's Castle. I wasn't thinking much about these places because my mind was filled up with thoughts of my mother. Then I saw it.

It was a picture of a lighthouse standing on a rocky island while the waves smashed all around it. And then it all came together in my mind like the missing piece of a gigantic jigsaw.

There was only one place in California that I knew about and that must be the place where Dad would go too. Almost from the time I was old enough to remember anything, I knew about this place. There had to be a reason why that story about scattering Mummy's ashes in front of the lighthouse high on a cliff was so special. Apart from the obvious one, that is. And now I knew. That's where I'd go. If my dad wasn't there, my mum was and she'd know where he was. Somehow she'd find a way of telling me. High on a cliff, Mum's soul watches over us both.

Ralph

I ARRIVED BACK AT HELEN'S house exhausted and frantic at the same time. I was disappointed at how quickly the trail had gone cold and felt on the verge of hysteria. I needed to watch some football just to calm me down, but there was none on television. In fact I got something far better: a totally focused Helen.

Galvanised into action by my earlier phone call, Helen seemed to have tipped off every journalist in southern California. She had a private army combing the streets down in South Central. She placed a number of telephone calls to the Los Angeles Police Department.

The LAPD changed their tune when they realised the scale and the nature of the search Helen had organised. They couldn't afford the bad publicity that would come their way if the journalists found Danny and they didn't. They were in bad odour anyway, with a couple of investigations for internal corruption constantly on the local television news, so finding Danny would be a major coup for them.

Helen was just wonderful—so calm, so organised, so supportive. She wouldn't hear any kind of defeatist talk. I was to stay with her that night, and the following morning we could leave at five thirty before the freeways clogged so we'd be in LA soon after seven. I kept having to remind myself that I shouldn't expect too much. After all, Danny wasn't her son. But I wanted so much for her to spend the rest of her life with us—unless tragedy struck, and I kept trying to suppress that fear. I also kept reminding myself that Angela, if she could see us now, would be cheering us on. She would want me to find Danny, she would want Danny to have Helen as a friend and a supporter.

Helen ran a bath for me with a handful of bath salts. After my bath, I climbed into bed and fell asleep with Helen's beautiful body wrapped around me.

I'm one of those people who rarely dream, or if I do I never remember the substance of it in the morning. This was different. This was a nightmare, the like of which I had never experienced.

When I saw him, it was as if he was asleep. He was thin, with dirty clothes and tousled hair, and he bore the marks not of violence, but neglect. It was just chance I found him as I walked along the street. There was a kid under a filthy blanket. I rolled him face upwards and saw that it was the dead body of my child. I screamed and screamed but nobody came. A policeman told me to move the kid away, he was causing an obstruction. I yelled at him that it was Danny, my son, but the cop just said something to the effect that the world couldn't stop just because my son was dead.

I awoke in a cold sweat. It was still dark outside. Helen was with me, but where I was in my head she couldn't follow. I needed Danny back or I wouldn't be able to live any longer. To lose my little boy would be insupportable. I went back to sleep as dawn broke.

I was so out of it in the morning, Helen almost had to push me into the shower, which she turned on cold at full blast. I woke up pretty damn quick then. She was waiting for me as I stepped out, holding the towel. I started to dry myself, looking for the right words.

'Helen . . .'

'Shhh!' She put her index finger to my lips and kept it there. I took it off and kissed it.

'I'm sorry if I haven't been much of anything . . .'

'Ralph, don't. Don't say anything.'

'I just want to tell you how much I love you.'

'You've done that. Now let me tell you something.' We sat together on the edge of the bath. She took my hand and kissed the palm tenderly. 'Ralph, when I met you, I thought I was still in love with Charles. I know now I was living a shallow, silly life really, full of the wrong people and the wrong values. You and Danny have made me feel like a whole person. I can't say I care about Danny like you do, but as far as I'm capable, I love him just as much in my own way because I love you so much. We're going on and we're going to find him. OK?'

My eyes filled with tears as she spoke. The words were so kind. All I could do was nod.

She made some coffee and we hit the freeway. I wasn't too talkative, because my mind was still dashing maniacally from one possible scenario to the next. Helen, concerned by my returning sombre mood, began to apologise for California's appearance in my life as nothing more than a background for my personal tragedies. I demurred.

'It's not like that. I love California.'

'I don't see how you can, seeing as how we've done nothing but screw your life up.'

'I love you. And you're in California.'

'You should never come back here. Keep the whole thing a fantasy.'

'I disagree. I should come here all the time. If Danny knew his way round the state . . .' My voice trailed away.

'You've never been back? In twelve years?'

'I come to the East Coast. I don't feel so far away from Danny then.'

'But you talk to Danny about California. He told me.'

'Sure. I talk to him about Angela, about what happened. I've always tried to make her death into a story.'

'Like a fairy story?'

'When he was little I used to tell him a bedtime story about how I scattered his mother's ashes high on a cliff overlooking the ocean. Danny loved it. It was his favourite bedtime story.'

'How did you finish it?'

'I used to say "High on a cliff, Mummy's soul sits, watching over us both always."'

'That's cute.'

'I wanted him to feel that Angela still had a presence in his life. If I wasn't there he could somehow turn to . . . Shiiiiiit!' I flung my arm out across Helen's chest.

She screamed in panic. 'Ralph!' She jammed on the brakes. Vehicles behind hooted and flashed their lights, but she managed to keep control of the car and bring it to a stop on the hard shoulder.

The cars continued to zoom past with the sound of their horns trailing behind them as I turned and looked at Helen. I stammered out the words like a stroke victim. 'I'm sorry! I'm sorry, I didn't mean to scare you. I just remembered. That's where he is! High on a cliff! I'm sure of it.'

Helen

HE TOLD ME the whole spiel as we headed north. About the bedtime stories he used to read, the one about an owl, the one about a hungry caterpillar, the family that lived in a lighthouse, and always ending with Angela and the special place high on a cliff. As he did so, his whole attitude changed. It was like he'd had some deep religious experience or he'd watched his beloved Tottenham Hotspur defeat some other team. His face shone with certainty.

'How can you be sure Danny knows?'

'He's always known. I told these stories almost every night for about five or six years from the age of two onwards. I can't tell you what a powerful effect they had on him.'

'And you think he's going to find his way in a strange country to the exact spot? Ralph, honey, be realistic.'

'I am, darling, I am. I used to say if he was ever in trouble and I wasn't there to help him he must always ask his mummy what to do. Her soul was with both of us always, watching over us.'

While I was delighted that Ralph now had a strength and an assurance that I had not seen since he had arrived at LAX, I couldn't help feeling concerned. The chances of Danny having found his way to the exact spot were on the far side of remote.

I let Ralph take over the driving because I wanted to stay in touch by cellphone with the continuing search for Danny. It was a struggle to get Ralph to keep to the speed limit.

'There are Highway Patrol cars all over the place.'

'I thought they were all out looking for Danny.'

'LAPD jurisdiction ends two hundred miles south of here.'

'You know just about everything.'

'I don't know where this place is you're taking me to. What's it called?'

'I don't remember. But I'll recognise it when I see it again.'

Just beyond the turnoff for Hearst's Castle at San Simeon he started to slow down.

'This is it?'

He looked round, puzzled. 'Looks sort of familiar but I'm not . . .'

'Why don't we stop?'

We were in Mill Creek, at the southern tip of the California Sea Otter State Game Refuge, and it was a truly beautiful sight. We were experiencing a glorious fresh February morning with the sun shining brightly out of a cloudless California sky. Ralph stopped the car in the official car park and almost ran towards the sound of the ocean.

'Is this the place?'

Ralph's face betrayed his anxiety. 'I sort of recognise the mountains behind us, but I just can't be sure . . .'

It was hopeless. We must have spent nearly an hour combing the place. Every time he thought he recognised a patch of ground, a clump of trees, he sprinted forward and then came to a stop, shaking his head in frustration. I tried to be positive. It just came out negative.

'You'd know it if this was the place.'

What neither of us said was that Danny wasn't here. This was just crazy. There was no way Danny had made his way this far upstate.

Eventually Ralph turned back towards the car. 'Let's drive on. It's been twelve years.'

We got back in the car and headed north again. I could read Ralph like a book just by looking at his eyes. Something was stirring. There was an intensity about him now that I hadn't seen before, like a dog sniffing some old familiar smell.

'What?'

A smile crept across his face. 'I can feel it. Sense it.'

'This is it?'

'I know it is. I know it.'

I looked at the map. 'We're coming up to Vista Point.'

'Makes sense, doesn't it? "High on a Cliff"? Vista Point.'

'Yes, but there's a hundred vista points on Route One.'

'This is it!'

We skidded to a halt. He leapt out of the car, leaving the engine running. I turned it off, locked the car and tried to catch up with him. He plunged on through the woods and out onto the open grassland. In the distance I could hear the roar of the ocean as it pounded the rocks.

Ralph was waving his arms about. 'This is the place. This is high on a cliff. That's where we made love. Come on!'

He grabbed my hand and pulled me towards the edge of the cliff.

'I stood here, Helen, right here. I opened the urn . . .'

He threw out his arm like a man scattering ashes. He turned to me. His eyes were burning bright. 'You do believe me, don't you?'

'Yes, Ralph, I do believe you. But, look, Danny isn't here.'

It took a minute for it to sink in.

'He's not here,' whispered Ralph. 'Danny! Danny!' He was now yelling and racing around as if he believed that Danny would magically appear from the forest. Eventually he stopped and slumped to the ground. I sat down next to him, cradling his head in my lap.

'I was so sure.'

'I know, darling.'

I stroked his hair and kissed his face, chapped by the winds that blew off the ocean.

'Shall we go back?'

'No!' Ralph scrambled to his feet. 'He's here. He's at high on a cliff.'

'But you just said—'

'Well, maybe *I'm* wrong. Maybe I'm wrong and this isn't high on a cliff.'

We drove on northwards through Big Sur towards Carmel and Monterey. The atmosphere in the car had changed. What had, at first, seemed such an overwhelming certainty became an increasingly forlorn hope. We stopped the car at every conceivable possibility—the Ventana Campground, Cooper Point, Riverside Park, the Andrew Molera State Park. At each juncture the routine was the same. Ralph was certain this was the place, a clump of trees, the sound of the waves and then nothing. No Danny. We would trudge back to the car.

We headed on towards Carmel and Monterey. Ralph had always been sure that he had driven south from Carmel with the ashes so the chances of our finding the place now were almost non-existent. Besides, I'd believed him when we stopped at Vista Point. That was high on a cliff all right, but Danny hadn't found it because he was still living on the streets of LA.

With every disappointment Ralph got crazier with anxiety. I was beginning to be seriously concerned for his mental health.

'Ralph, let's stop somewhere and talk this thing through.'

'I've got to find Danny. If I don't, my life will disintegrate.'

'You'll still have me. I'm not going to run away again.'

'But I will. I know myself too well, Helen. If I lose Danny, there'll be nothing left. You won't want to be with me. Believe me.'

Ralph swung the car off the highway and along a forested track. His eyes were fixed on something in the distance. I tried again.

'Ralph, I'll drive, if you like.'

'Look, Helen, can you see that lighthouse?'

'It's the Point Sur lighthouse. What about it?'

'Such a coincidence. Right next to high on a cliff, there's a lighthouse.'

'Hardly right next to it. It's been thirty miles since Vista Point.'

'I wonder. I wonder.'

Ralph got out of the car, his eyes almost magnetically attracted to the lighthouse. The grassland ran to the top of the cliff and I could hear the sound of the crashing surf below.

'He's here, Helen.'

'What? You're crazy.' I looked around. The place was deserted. 'Is this high on a cliff then?'

'No. We found high on a cliff. But Danny's here. Can't you feel it? Danny's here somewhere.'

But he wasn't. There was no Danny. There wasn't a soul. Just something that looked like a bunch of old clothes on the far side of the grassy headland. Ralph was staring at it.

'He's not here, Ralph.'

Ralph wasn't listening. He started to walk towards the pile of clothes. Then he broke into a run. Suddenly he was yelling.

'Danny! Danny!'

The pile of clothes sat up, animated. It stood up. 'Dad! Dad!'

'Oh, my God! It's him! It's Danny!'

It was. It was Danny. I ran after Ralph, screaming my head off. They both ran towards one another so fast that I thought for a moment they would knock each other out, such was the force of their impact. It wasn't a pile of old clothes. It was Danny. And he was there, I really believe, because Angela's spirit was watching over the two of them. It was she who found them and made them whole.

Ralph just held Danny in his arms for the longest time. Both of them were crying and I stood there watching. I was so relieved, so happy for both of them. I wanted to join in, but I knew my place so I hung back.

'I knew you'd be here, Dad. I knew it. This is the place, isn't it? This is high on a cliff, isn't it?'

'What? No . . . I mean yes, darling. It is. This is the place.'

'I knew it was here somewhere. I just had to find the lighthouse. I knew you'd find me if I could get to the lighthouse. Oh, Dad, I thought I'd never see you again.'

'Shhh, it's all right now. I'm here.'

'I'm sorry about spilling the Coke and I'm sorry I didn't clean the floor properly.'

'Oh, Danny, don't. I love you so much.'

'Mummy's soul is watching over us. Just like you always said.'

'That's right, I did, didn't I?'

I couldn't help the tears either. I didn't have their history, but I felt it almost as deeply as they did. They turned towards me. Danny broke away from his father and came over to me. He looked at me, the tears still streaming down his face.

'Helen, I'm sorry, I went to your house. I saw you with that man. I didn't know what to do. I thought it must be your husband. I'm sorry. I've just messed everything up.'

A cold stab of realisation pierced me. *Michael! He saw me with Michael! He'd got so close . . .*

'Oh, Danny! That was my brother you saw. My brother Michael.'

'The man who drove off in the taxi? He's your brother?'

'Just my brother. I haven't got a husband.' I held and kissed him. He looked up at me.

'I'm sorry I was horrible to you, Helen. I didn't mean it. Will you come and live with us?'

I couldn't speak. I could only nod.

'I tried to come to your house to tell you that Dad loved you, but I got robbed and I had to . . .'

I hugged him again, rocking back and forth, kissing and kissing him on his precious head. 'It's all right, Danny, it's OK. I do love your dad. And I love you and we're all going to be together now. For the rest of our lives.'

Ralph came over and kissed me, and the three of us stood in a group clinging on to each other for dear life, high on a cliff overlooking the Pacific Ocean, while the pounding waves, which somehow symbolised the forces that had tried to destroy us, dashed themselves unavailingly against the rocks below.

COLIN SHINDLER

Colin Shindler was born and raised in Manchester and educated at Bury Grammar School, before going on to read history at Caius College, Cambridge. After graduation he remained at Cambridge University to complete his PhD thesis about Hollywood and the Great Depression. He then went on to write the screenplay for the movie *Buster* and to work for ITV and the BBC, producing and writing scripts for series such as *Wish Me Luck*, *Lovejoy*, *Juliet Bravo* and *Heartbeat*. 'I always have enormous fun working in television, especially on the set of *Lovejoy*. I am an avid supporter of Manchester City Football Club, and Ian McShane, who played Lovejoy, decided that his character would be a fan of Manchester United, our greatest rivals. In some scenes he would drink out of a Manchester United mug just to wind me up, and when the scene was finished I would take the mug away. But in the next scene, there he would be again drinking from a Manchester United mug. He must have had a supply of them!'

After many years working in film and television and keeping his hand in as a book reviewer, sports journalist and radio writer, Colin Shindler decided to try a different medium: books. His autobiography, *Manchester United Ruined My Life*, was a runaway best seller. 'Interestingly,' says Colin Shindler, 'I discovered that women enjoyed this book as much as men because it was more than just another book about football. My women readers skipped the football bits and liked the realism in dealing with life. In fact, it gave me the idea for writing *High on a Cliff*.

'In the world of television, programmes such as *Lovejoy* and *Heartbeat* are termed "family dramas", but I soon discovered that in publishing a similar story is firmly placed "in the women's market". Well, women liked my auto-biography and so I thought I would give novel-writing a try. From the beginning I very much wanted to portray the four different voices, because through my work as a scriptwriter, I have always been interested in character and dialogue and how people relate to one another. People see things from their own perspectives to such a degree that they will all have different interpretations of the same event, and I thought it would be interesting for the reader to see this. The only character I found difficult to portray was Ralph, because it was harder to divorce him from me.' He is currently working on his second novel, which is about a married woman who meets up with her first love twenty years on. 'I am writing this one entirely from the female perspective though,' he says.

Colin Shindler has been married to his wife Lynn, who he met in a movie theatre in America, for twenty-seven years. They have two children: Amy, who is currently playing Brenda Tucker in the radio show *The Archers*, and David, who is a management consultant. 'When people ask me where I live, I say London. When they ask me where I come from, I say Manchester.' Colin Shindler is proud of his roots and whenever possible he heads northwards to support his beloved Manchester City and to watch Lancashire play cricket.

Originations by Rodney Howe Ltd
Printed and bound by Maury Imprimeur SA, Malesherbes, France

601-004-1